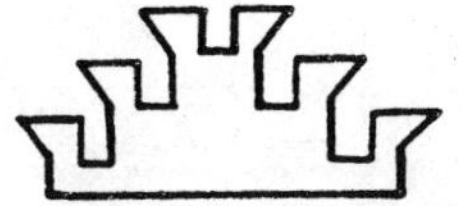

YUROK MYTHS

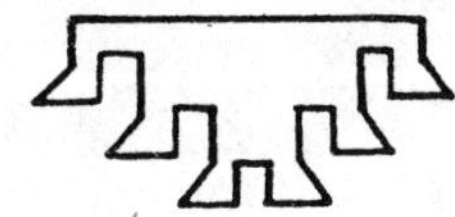

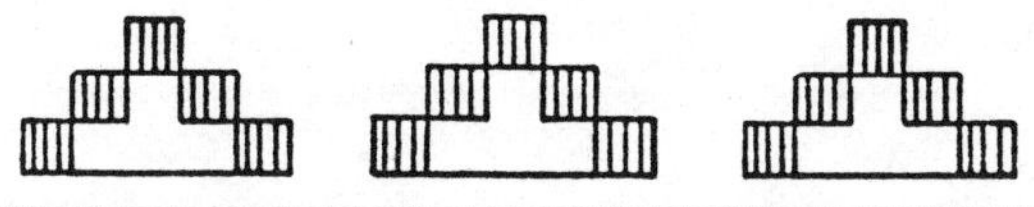

YUROK MYTHS

A. L. KROEBER

UNIVERSITY OF CALIFORNIA PRESS
BERKELEY • LOS ANGELES • LONDON

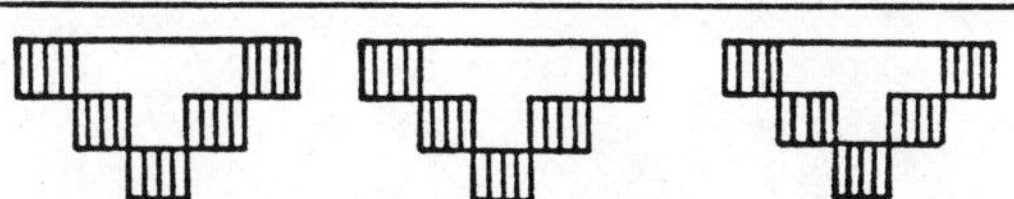

Decorations on the cover and in the front matter
are motifs from Yurok basketry.

University of California Press
Berkeley and Los Angeles, California

University of California Press, Ltd.
London, England

ISBN 0-520-02977-1
Library of Congress Catalog Card Number: 75-3772
Printed in the United States of America

Designed by William Snyder

CONTENTS

INFORMANT A.
LAME BILLY OF WEITSPUS

Informant B.
TSKERKR OF ESPEU

Informant C.
STONE OF WEITSPUS

Informant D.
BILLY WERK OF WEITSPUS

Informant E.
DOCTOR OF WEITSPUS

Informant F.
MACK OF WEITSPUS

INFORMANT G.
FRANK OF WEITSPUS

INFORMANT H.
DAVE DURBAN OF WEITSPUS

INFORMANT I.
DOMINGO OF WEITSPUS

INFORMANTS J.
JULIA WILSON AND KATE OF WAHSEK

INFORMANT K.
SAINTS' REST JACK OF LO'OLEGO

INFORMANT L.
LUCKY OF WAHSEK

Informant M.
SANDY OF KENEK

Informant N.
AMITS OF KEPEL

Informant O.
LONG CHARLIE OF MŪREK

Informant P.
JACK OF MŪREK

Informant Q.
OPN OF SREGON

Informant R.
BARNEY OF SREGON

Informant S.
DOCTOR OF PEKWON

Informant T.
JIM OF PEKWON

Informant U.
WETS'OWA OF PEKWON

Informant V.
PETSUSLO OF PEKWON

Informant W.
DICK OF WOHKERO

Informant X.
CAPTAIN SPOTT OF REKWOI

Informant Y.
WILLIAM JOHNSON OF REKWOI

Informant Z.
JOHNNY SHORTMAN OF WEŁKWÄU

Informant AA.
GEORGE MÄHÄTS OF REKWOI (AND MÄ'ÄTS)

Informant BB.
ANN OF ESPEU

Informant CC.
JIM OF TSURÄU (AND WEITSPUS)

DD1-13. Various Informants: Fragments and Outlines

MAPS

Abbreviations

UC-AR University of California Publications in Anthropological Records. (Those referred to in this monograph are currently out of print.)

UC-PAAE University of California Publications in American Archaeology. (Reprints of complete volumes only are available from Kraus Reprint Corporation, 16 East 46th Street, New York, N. Y. 10017.)

UC-PL University of California Publications in Linguistics, University of California Press, Berkeley and Los Angeles.

Phonetic Symbols

' glottal stop

ä as in cat or varying between cat and met

ǟ as in awl

ī as in see

kw as in quick

ɬ voiceless spirantal l, similar to sleep

ū as in boot

FOREWORD

Alfred Kroeber (1876-1960) left a legacy of some five hundred and fifty published works, books, monographs, and reviews—whose time span is 1898 to 1960 and whose intellectual range is from linguistics through the various faces of anthropology and archaeology, into psychology, history, and art, on into the science and theory and aesthetics of styles and civilizations.

He left as well a "literary testament" as guide to those of us responsible for disposition of his yet unpublished materials, both the whole and the fragmentary, the completed and the incomplete. Thus we come to the present work. Except for the single remaining manuscript of Karok myths, which will follow the Yurok collection as a related coda, it is my reading of the "testament" that these Yurok myths are the final work to be brought out under the signature, A. L. Kroeber.

There is, as I see it, an aesthetic rightness, a closing of the full circle of Kroeber's life's work in the presentation of the oral literature of the Yurok as his concluding statement. The Yurok were not the first Indians he knew and studied and wrote of, nor were they the last. But they were the first Californian Indians he would come to know, and they were the people and culture who most engaged his curiosity and imagination. Kroeber's opening sentence in his massive *Handbook of the Indians of California* (1925) reads: "This history begins with an account of the Yurok, a nation resident on the lower Klamath River, near and along the Pacific Ocean, in extreme northern California, surrounded by peoples speaking diverse languages but following the same remarkable civilization." Through four chapters and ninety-seven pages, he goes on to describe this remarkable civilization, its land and towns and material culture, its political and national sense, its law and custom, its religion, its radius and focus, its quality and essence. It is the most exhaustive of the descriptions within the book.

In the preface to *Yurok Narratives* by Robert Spott and A. L. Kroeber (1942), Kroeber writes,

> Our [his and Robert's] association goes back to the time when he was a boy of twelve and I, twice as old, at the threshold of my professional career. From 1900 to 1907 I visited the Yurok repeatedly, working with their old men but pivoting my activities around the personal connection with Robert's two fathers [one by way of adoption] at Weitchpec and Requa, the upriver and downriver foci of the Yurok stretch of the Klamath. Then followed a long break, only partly restored by occasional visits to a cabin at Sigonoi on the coast above Orick between 1923 and 1927; until, in 1933 and again in 1939 and 1940, visits by Robert to Berkeley and St. Helena [California] and by me to Requa, resulted in the present collection of stories, plus information on rituals and general ethnography.

The association, the visits, and the collaboration continued until Robert's death in 1953. "On the total system of Yurok mythology," the preface continues,

> I collected from a variety of older men and women years ago a body of tales ten times as numerous as those included here, and still hope before too much longer to make these available by publishing them. The present little group of myths, in comparison, is rather a sample, designed to evidence in its variety the range of ideas and sentiments with which the Yurok mind was preoccupied in dealing with the past of its world.

Between and beyond those years of collecting and recording and working with Robert, there were the times, short or longer, when Kroeber worked on the materials of the myths, alone or with one or another Yurok man or woman, the thrust linguistic or folkloristic or literary. He turned to this occupation with the sort of refreshment he brought to a game of chess with a congenial player. These were the times when he would be likely to discuss and ponder the history of the Yurok he meant to write once the myths were published, a history at once more personal, psychological, and biographical than any he had yet undertaken. But these were the times when he would say as well, "Perhaps I cannot write of the Yurok in this way. I feel myself too much a Yurok." He may indeed have hit upon the reason he wrote no such history, for he was without impulse to autobiography; the closest he came to it was his selection of his articles and his comments upon them, which compose his *Nature of Culture* (1952).

By his own statement Kroeber was accustomed to use an interpreter with an informant. Also, he often made phonograph recordings of songs, vocabularies, formulas, and texts, which he later had Englished, phrase by phrase, by Yurok translators. Except for his taking down of a long Mohave tale from a very old Mohave whose English was minimal, I myself never saw Kroeber with an interpreter, since the informants who were also our friends and frequent house guests happened also to be bilingual—Juan Dolores of the Papago of southern Arizona was trilingual (Papago, Spanish, English)—and the native languages of these informants were those in which Kroeber had done much work. I see

Robert Spott, nephew of Captain Spott, photographed about 1907. He was not an informant for this collection of tales, but he was co-author with A. L. Kroeber of *Yurok Narratives*, U.C. Publications in American Archaeology and Ethnology, vol. 35, no. 9 (1942), pp. 143-256. Photo courtesy the Bancroft Library, University of California, Berkeley.

him, sitting close to his informant, usually out-of-doors, his right ear turned to catch each syllable (he was deaf in the left ear), writing on his knee, filling page after page in a compact, bound notebook, the sort familiar to anyone who knew Kroeber or who has consulted his notes; a sharpened pencil, never a pen, in his right hand.

Robert Spott one day told me the story of "The Inland Whale," Kroeber being elsewhere during the telling. I took no notes, the story having come to Robert's mind apropos of his saying something about bastards. When Kroeber returned, I asked him if he knew the story. He did not, nor does it seem to have been recorded by another collector. The following morning Robert dictated the story to Kroeber in Yurok, and during succeeding days, Kroeber read the story back to Robert, a sentence, a phrase, a word at a time, correcting until both of them were satisfied. I report this occasion for its specialness.[1]

To my knowledge, Kroeber made no claim to control a speaking knowledge of Yurok. He was fluent in several non-Indian languages, and hence his standard of what constitutes "speaking" a language was realistic. I have, nonetheless, been present during longish exchanges between Kroeber and a Yurok, both speaking Yurok. This was likely to happen when we went to see

1. ["The Inland Whale" was included in Spott and Kroeber, *Yurok Narratives,* as tale no. 24. It was reinterpreted by Theodora Kroeber in *The Inland Whale: Nine Stories Retold from California Indian Legends* (Bloomington: University of Indiana Press, 1959).—Ed.]

Fanny Flounder at her house in Requa. Fanny was the last and one of the great Yurok doctors. So far as I know, she was never a direct informant to Kroeber; the materials he had from and about her came to him by way of Robert Spott, her nephew. Fanny was quite aware that she was excluding me when she addressed Kroeber in Yurok. We were friends and she talked to me in English of other matters Yurok, but not those having to do with doctoring; nor could she, with me, engage in the sly, often bawdy, double-entendre repartee she, along with most Yurok, delighted in. At Sigonoi, Orick Bob's house was just below Kroeber's cabin; the two of them passed the time of day more often in Yurok than in English. I remember also that when I went upriver with Kroeber, his old Yurok friends, recognizing him as our canoe came close, hurried to greet him, often to embrace him, the rush of words, his and theirs, coming first in Yurok.

To turn now to the present text, "The Geographic Setting" by Kroeber places the reader physically in the Yurok world. As the reader proceeds to the myths themselves, he is told who is the teller of each tale, his public name (never the private name), his village, something of his biography, frequently even to the ancestral houses from which his parents and grandparents came, and something of his personality. Kroeber organized his world, first, around Person, and second, around Place, as do the Yurok. The myths open with those told Kroeber by Lame Billy of Weitspus, Informant A. Weitspus, the village, is at the junction of the Klamath and Trinity rivers; it is as well at the Center of the World. Next come the tales from Tskerkr of Espeu on the coast, Informant B: Kroeber made the hard literary choice of keeping his two principal informants' collections contiguous. With Informant C, Stone of Weitspus, Kroeber is back at the Center. Reading on through Stone and beyond, Kroeber's orderly progress downriver may be followed on the maps. Village after village comes in sight around a bend, beyond a riffle, on the right bank, on the left, each village yielding its informants and their tales, until at last the journey ends at the mouth of the river, beside the ocean, at Rekwoi.

At this time-distance from 1900, the reader should perhaps be reminded that Kroeber's use of the historical present in describing Yurok life should be taken as the historical present of the first decade of the twentieth century, and earlier. (The writer of this Foreword learned to think in historical present time with Robert Spott, to whom all matters and persons Yurok, even back to the most ancient Woge times, were living, present reality.)

You who read, particularly you who work in depth with folklore material, will share in some measure my own immense gratitude and respect for the selfless task Alan Dundes, folklorist, and Grace Buzaljko, editor, together have brought to completion with the publication of *Yurok Myths*. There is, first, Dundes' analysis, without which most of us might well become lost in the complexities and assumptions of the literary-folkloristic world of the Yurok.

And there is, second, Buzaljko's river trip, Weitspus to Rekwoi, word by stony word. Beyond scholarship and workmanship, Dundes and Buzaljko comprehended Kroeber's intended goal and the very Kroeberian pattern and organization by which he meant to reach that goal. Comprehended it, and, despite time and age gaps, orthographic inconsistencies and changes, and the sheer mass of manuscript, some in longhand, they won through to that goal, closer, I am sure, than anyone other than Kroeber himself could have come. If only he could have seen in print this whole body of Yurok heart! I do hope in whatever cloud-universal consciousness may blow through the winds of heaven Kroeber knows the job has been done.

THEODORA KROEBER

KROEBER AND THE YUROK, 1900-1908

The bulk of Kroeber's field work among the Yurok was in two bursts of activity in 1900-1902 and in 1906-1907. What follows here is a brief sketch of some of the circumstances that conditioned that work.

In the spring of 1900, Kroeber was a graduate student in anthropology under Franz Boas at Columbia University. He was not quite 24 years old and had made two trips of a few months each among the Plains Indians under the auspices of the American Museum of Natural History in New York. In April of that year, David Starr Jordan, president of Stanford University, offered Kroeber the position of Curator of Anthropology at the California Academy of Sciences in San Francisco. Kroeber accepted the offer, but since he had not yet completed his doctoral program, he made preliminary arrangements with Boas to return to the east in the spring of 1901 to finish and defend his thesis.

Evidently Boas, Kroeber, and others of their eastern colleagues considered the California appointment at least semipermanent, for at the annual meeting of the American Folklore Society in December, 1900, Kroeber was appointed to a three-year term as a Councilor of the Society. William Wells Newell's letter of announcement to Kroeber indicated indirectly that the reason for Kroeber's election was his opportunity to develop folklore work along the west coast. Certainly Kroeber himself considered the appointment in long-range terms, for after arriving in San Francisco in August, 1900, he completed his basic work on the Academy's ethnological collections within about six weeks and then asked Jordan for permission to visit the California Indians living along the coast to the north. Jordan agreed, allowing Kroeber $100 for expenses. When this amount was exhausted, Kroeber returned to San Francisco, was given a second $100, and returned to the field until Christmas. In those two trips Kroeber visited the Yurok in northwestern California and the Mohave in the southeastern part of the state, and apparently spent a little time among the Yokuts and their neighbors in central California. Ostensibly the trips were for collecting artifacts; practically they were a survey of prospects for future work.

Kroeber's was a museum appointment which he treated as similar to ethnological research appointments in New York's American Museum or Chicago's Field Museum. That is, the task of the museum ethnologist was to collect not only material specimens but also linguistic and mythological information. The directors of the California Academy objected, however. Kroeber later explained to George A. Dorsey that there had been "lack of a definite understanding as to the future," but in any case the directors informed him during the Christmas holidays that it was not Academy policy to give a curator field funds beyond his salary. He was reminded that most of the Academy collections had been gifts, and he was told that his position would be terminated at the end of 1900. Boas arranged for Kroeber's return to New York by way of Montana, where he was to buy a canoe for the American Museum and see it safely transported east, and Kroeber took advantage of the occasion to supplement his information on the Arapaho. Once back in New York he completed his doctoral thesis, becoming Columbia's first Ph.D. in anthropology, and began looking for a new position. Significantly, his opportunities were almost entirely in museums, and in discussing one such possibility with George Dorsey of the Field Museum he indicated that his preferences for work assignments were the Arapaho and the Californians.

His preference was finally realized in the form of an appointment from Mrs. Phoebe Apperson Hearst to make ethnological and archaeological investigations in California. Kroeber's appointment was one of several similar personal contracts which Mrs. Hearst had been making since the mid-1890's, initially through the University of Pennsylvania and then in loose conjunction with the University of California. This particular appointment was part of a second stage in her expansion of the California arrangements, which within a month after Kroeber's return to the west coast led to the formation of a Department and Museum of Anthropology within the University. Mrs. Hearst had been encouraged in this by several ethnologists and archaeologists, but much of the impetus for the new organization seems to have come from Frederic Ward Putnam, Curator of the Peabody Museum of American Archaeology and Ethnology in Cambridge. Kroeber knew Putnam, probably through Boas, and during his first trip to California he had met University of California President Benjamin Ide Wheeler. Probably it was the combined recommendations of Putnam and Wheeler that brought Kroeber back to California in August, 1901.

The new Department was almost unique in the University for two features: it was to be wholly a research department, with regular teaching to begin only at some vague date in the future; and it was to be funded entirely by non-University sources, meaning the patronage of Mrs. Hearst, who was the widow of the mining magnate and U. S. Senator, George Hearst. Within less than a decade, modifications in both arrangements were to seriously restrict all of Kroeber's research activity, with the consequence, for example, that his mass of Yurok texts remained unpublished until today. In the beginning, however, no one except perhaps Boas anticipated that kind of problem. Like the other officers of the Department, Kroeber carried an academic title but his primary responsibilities were the collection and study of California ethnological material. Within the ethnological theory of the day, ethnology in practice meant anything and everything that could be *collected* as illustrative of the life and nature of the Indian—from baskets and mortars to measurements of crania to vocabulary lists to texts of mythological material. On any given trip, Kroeber or his linguist colleague in the University's Californian field, Pliny Earle Goddard, or the Department's first graduate student, Samuel A. Barrett, usually sought specific kinds of information to fill out their collections. But a trip that began with a search for baskets among the Yurok, for example, might well result also in notebooks full of lists of names for Yurok habitation sites with estimated population, information on house types, statements of both reported and observed dietary practices, and several myths with comments on the informants.

There were of course several large general questions animating the California collecting, and these can be illustrated with excerpts from Kroeber's report to the Department's Advisory Committee at the end of his first full year with the University. Kroeber stated that he had arrived in California in the last days of August, and had left San Francisco for the Klamath River region on September 16. His goals there were to find what were thought to be the only two surviving Chimariko, and to see the autumn ceremonials of the Yurok. The Chimariko turned out to be "nearly worthless" informants, so he went on to spend about a month among the Yurok, collecting specimens and recording customs and religious beliefs. He then spent a week each with the Karok and the Wishosk in the same general area, collecting similar materials.

Kroeber explained to the Advisory Committee that in the course of this trip he had become convinced of "the necessity of an immediate systematic survey, however rapid, of the entire state of California, more especially for language." He broached a plan of cooperation to Roland B. Dixon, a former Boas student who was working among the Maidu, and for the rest of 1901 and 1902 his linguistic and ethnological work consisted of gathering material to determine the structure of the Californian languages while following a similar but less rigorous plan in collecting ethnological information.

The importance of language study needs to be emphasized. In the only complete linguistic classification of North American languages by that date, the Bureau of Ethnology's *Indian Linguistic Families of America North of Mexico* (1891; this excepts Daniel G. Brinton's *The American Race* of the same year), fifty-five language stocks were outlined for the continent as a whole, and twenty-two of these were represented within the state of California. Such diversity within a relatively small area made California virtually a linguistic laboratory. Furthermore, since language was the principal basis for classifying native American peoples, language was quite simply an ethnological problem requiring that linguistic research had to be interrelated with the study of social organization, folklore, and ethnohistory. Typical practice was to collect a native text in both English and the relevant Indian language and to study this text for overt content about the life of the people, for patterns of what was called "ethnic psychology," and for distributional correlations of motifs among various peoples as an aid to inferring their history, as well as for analysis of grammatical structure.

All this was more or less explicit in Kroeber's survey work as he moved generally from northern to southern California, giving special attention to the coast regions. Leaving the Maidu to Dixon, and the Hupa and other Athabascans to Goddard, Kroeber spent the first three weeks of December among the Pomo and Yuki. Then, moving south of San Francisco, he visited Monterey, San Luis Obispo, and Santa Barbara counties, returning to Berkeley in January. In February a Yuki Indian stayed and worked with him in San Francisco, and in March he himself spent several weeks among the Mohave, with a shorter trip the next month among the Rumsien near Monterey.

By the close of the University session and the start of the regular season of field work, Kroeber's initial linguistic survey was nearly completed. The ethnological counterpart was less so, but on the rationale that what remained of the preliminary work could be accomplished in half a dozen short separate trips, Kroeber left the gap-filling to the following fall and winter and returned instead to a two-month unbroken period along the Klamath. That trip, which lasted from May 12 to July 24, was focused toward four objectives: one, to continue investigation among the Yurok; two, to try again to work with the surviving Chimariko; three, to study the Karok, neighbors of the Yurok and of special interest because these two peoples were distinct in language and yet nearly identical in culture; and four, to determine the "affiliations" of the Indians of the Salmon River. Tentatively settling this last question first, Kroeber spent two weeks among the Karok, then again unsuccessfully tried the Chimariko informants, and went on to the Yurok. He made a careful enumeration of Yurok settlements along the Klamath and collected material specimens along the way as part of a cooperative plan with R. B. Dixon whereby the University exchanged Yurok material with the American Museum in return for Shasta and Maidu material. Kroeber then went back to his home in San Francisco for a month, where he worked over his notes before going out into the field again, this time intending to work with the Yuki. But having erred in judging hop-picking time, when all the Yuki were occupied, he went back to the Klamath to fill in gaps in his Yurok information.

This second trip of 1902 was much shorter than the first and was followed by a rapid tour through "the long narrow strip of Athabascan territory in the state," complementing Goddard's similar trip through that area in order to determine the boundaries of various groups. The result, Kroeber reported to the Advisory Committee, was that these "investigations by Mr. Goddard and myself will materially alter the ethnological map of this part of the state." One theoretical point which he noted was that the Athabascans formed an almost complete chain of transitional forms of culture between the highly contrasting lifeways of the Indians of Humboldt County and the Pomo and Yuki of neighboring Mendocino County to the south. With this much determined, and with only a week remaining in his summer field season, Kroeber returned to the Yuki, verified the information given him the previous spring, and made arrangements for further work during the coming winter. Early in October he was back in San Francisco and within a few days was on his way east to attend the International Congress of Americanists.

In short, Kroeber spent most of his first year with the University in field research, and the bulk of that in linguistically oriented survey work. The effort was fundamentally a mapping exercise, verifying and correcting the published record and filling in blank spots on a very real ethnological map. From the long hindsight of Kroeber's overall career and especially of his lifelong interest in the Yurok, the period of work that ended in October, 1902, ended his most intensive field work in the state even though his affiliation with California had barely begun. Several reasons can be offered for this, including changes in his own personal interests as well as in the larger community of anthropologists, but two stand out: the addition of teaching and related University responsibilities, and a change in the financing of the Department.

Shortly after his arrival in California, Kroeber was asked by President Wheeler to offer some kind of regular course or series of lectures, this despite Putnam's public announcement that there would be no regular instruction. Wheeler and Putnam saw the Department from different perspectives, but since Putnam was back in Cambridge, the result was that Kroeber gave a course in North American ethnology during the spring term of 1902. Among the students the course attracted was one potential professional, Samuel A. Barrett, and the next year both Kroeber and Goddard were offering courses during the spring term. By the third year, the teaching was sufficiently institutionalized to prompt Kroeber and Goddard to alternate semesters as an aid to both themselves and potential students. The courses were fairly specialized, aimed at training investigators in ethnology and linguistics. Very few years' experience proved this arrangement impractical for lack of students, however, while other responsibilities within the University suggested the need for a more serviceable introduction to the discipline. To his usual load of two courses, therefore, Kroeber added a course entitled General Anthropology in the fall of 1906.

In itself the added teaching might not have affected research, for even during his teaching semesters Kroeber was usually able to bring Indian informants to campus. But, within about a year after the Department's founding, several changes in personnel and departmental administration gave Kroeber added work. When the initial assistant secretary of the Department resigned at the end of 1902, for example, Kroeber took over his duties as executive officer and attempted to consolidate what he could of Mrs. Hearst's disparate anthropological enterprises. Overall administration of the Department was further formalized when Putnam was made Professor and Chairman in 1903, and an ethnological survey of California was organized. The anthropological collections were moved from the Berkeley campus to San Francisco, and some semblance of a museum gradually took shape. Kroeber's involvement in these changes may be inferred from his cryptic comment in one of his quarterly reports that his time had been taken up chiefly with "executive work." Through the whole of 1903 he hardly left the Bay area, and not until January and February, 1904, did he get out for a few weeks of research in the central and southern counties. Repeatedly during this period he stated his intention to return to Humboldt County to continue his work with the Yurok and Karok, but most of his actual work was with the Yokuts and Yuki in the central region. He was able to write up some of his material, though, and by mid-1905 had completed his Arapaho monograph and had prepared several papers on California languages, plus one general paper on types of culture in California.

Some of Kroeber's writing was affected by pressures from the larger professional community. In the summer of 1902, for example, the American Anthropological Association was formed. Kroeber was not present at any of the constituting meetings, and he later declined when Boas arranged his election as secretary of the new society. Nevertheless, he took part as he could, and when the Association's council decided to hold a special summer meeting in Portland, Kroeber successfully lobbied to have the meeting moved to San Francisco, where he took care of arrangements and also presented a provocative paper on Indian language nomenclature. Simultaneously he kept his folklore ties active, and was instrumental in organizing a local branch of the American Folklore Society in 1905. The branch survived through three seasons of meetings. It finally died because of financial straits and criticism from eastern folklorists, yet this effort too was an important aspect of Kroeber's ethnology. Folklore, ethnology, linguistics, and to a slightly lesser degree archaeology shared concepts, research methods, and often personnel with only slightly different emphases in each professional setting.

This overlapping did not mean an absence of disagreement on fundamentals. One of Kroeber's problems was to be caught in a tension that showed most clearly in the loose administration of his Department. One dimension was in the respective claims of Museum and University and whether to emphasize pure investigations, publication, and perhaps incidentally the training of future investigators, or whether to expand teaching for a general nonprofessional audience. Another dimension involved funding and its consequences, a conflict of interests between the academically trained and academically oriented scholars dependent on formal institutions, and those equally dedicated but sometimes less formally trained investigators dependent on the wealthy patron. This conflict in turn was related to a long-standing question in archaeology, whether it was properly an esthetic or an ethnological discipline.

While the officers of the Department and the members of the Advisory Committee were divided in their sympathies, the Department's patron, Mrs. Hearst, seems to have been ambivalent about what kind of institution she wanted to support, and eventually she simply abdicated the responsibility of making a clear choice. She had initially agreed to support the Department for five years, until July, 1906. While she was traveling abroad late in 1903, however, her mother became dangerously ill and died in January, 1904, before Mrs. Hearst could reach her. Adding to this loss, she returned to California only to learn that because of necessary expansions in her mines, her income would be reduced for an indefinite period. On top of this she had been working so hard at her various charities that by 1904 she had reached a state of exhaustion which required brief hospitalization. A general reduction in the scope and number of her activities seemed essential.

For several weeks in the spring of 1904 the future of the Department was very uncertain. Then in May the immediate crisis passed when Mrs. Hearst agreed to extend her support on a reduced scale for another year. Salaries were to be continued and certain publications were guaranteed, but the survey of California was to be suspended. Later in the year Mrs. Hearst made the decision to fulfill her original five-year obligation, and in the spring of 1905 Kroeber made a frantic appeal to Putnam to begin enough new lines of work so that unfinished projects in 1906 would force at least some continuation beyond that date. Kroeber's strategy may have been partly responsible for Mrs. Hearst's decision to make an additional two-year extension. Some research money was allocated, the ethnological survey was resumed, and regular budgets for 1906-1907 and 1907-1908 were approved. That two-year extension of the California work became one of the most productive periods in the Department's history as Kroeber, Goddard, and Barrett made almost desperate salvage efforts before both the data and their money ran out.

Kroeber's own work during that time was concentrated on expanding and complementing the considerable information he had already gathered among the Yurok, the Mohave, and the Yokuts. How much both folklore and material culture were integral parts of his ethnological work among those peoples was evident in his budget request in the spring of 1906: "Such collections are as directly illustrative of general conclusions, and as necessary as material for research, as are the myths and texts and vocabularies that we obtain from the Indians for mythological and linguistic work." It happened that before this particular budget could be implemented, San Francisco suffered its famous earthquake and fire. The Department sustained remarkably little material loss, however, and Kroeber's planned summer trip to Humboldt County was only delayed for about two months. When he finally left early in July for what was a combined field trip and honeymoon following his marriage to Henriette Rothschild, he had one of his most successful trips.[1] Early in August, he enthusiastically reported to Dixon and to Putnam that he had collected over three hundred specimens of material culture and about one hundred and ten phonograph recordings, mostly of a religious nature—invaluable material that became the basis of his and Thomas T. Waterman's study of Yurok language and religion in the next several years.[2]

The successes of 1906 were matched the next year as Kroeber and his wife traveled in March to the southern counties to work among the Cahuilla, and then in mid-May went north for six weeks in the Klamath River region. This time, besides rechecking his earlier data on Yurok, Karok, and Hupa settlements, Kroeber tried to collect specimens from among the Wiyot, Wishosk, and other neighbors, and added a new dimension by taking physical measurements and photographs of two hundred Yurok and Hupa. Goddard too was collecting specimens as well as linguistic data, and when Kroeber returned to campus at the end of June, Barrett took his turn to collect artifacts and measurements among the Pomo, Miwok, Yuki, and Modoc before going east for a year of study with Boas at Columbia University. Meanwhile, T. T. Waterman had joined the Department as museum assistant, and Kroeber put him in the field to collect mythological and religious information among the Diegueño in southern California. About the same time, Nels C. Nelson was beginning his serious study of San Francisco Bay area shellmounds, and Edward Sapir was gathering what remained of the Yana language. The results of all this activity were that for the first time nearly every language stock and ethnic region of the state was documented, mapped, and represented in the University's museum by tangible artifacts. To President Wheeler, Kroeber now offered the assessment that the Department was "one of the six principal anthropological centers of the country."

Kroeber was specifically appealing for the continuation of Museum funds, but he was only partly successful. Mrs. Hearst had made her decision, and

1. [Kroeber's first wife was Henriette Rothschild of Oakland, who died of tuberculosis in 1913.—Ed.]

2. [Waterman also made a major contribution to Yurok geography by mapping the Yurok settlements and place names. See the Editor's Preface and the Waterman maps reprinted in this volume.—Ed.]

with the fiscal year beginning July 1, 1908, her support dropped from an annual $20,000 to about one-tenth that amount, nearly all of which was targeted for Museum operating expenses. She continued occasionally to make gifts of specimens and works of art or of lump sums for Museum repairs or publication costs, but all other expenses were assumed by the University. The Department's budget became only one of many line items in the general University budget, and practically, that meant no research money. Kroeber and Goddard were continued in salaried academic positions, but Barrett, Sapir, and Waterman were all released. Putnam was continued for the one year remaining until he reached mandatory retirement age, and Goddard, seeing no future in California, went to the American Museum in New York. That freed some money and allowed Waterman and Nelson to return jointly as instructors and assistant curators, and they were able to continue their research on a smaller scale. All the staff now had heavier teaching responsibilities, however, and for Kroeber the changes of 1908-1909 marked something of a closure to one period of his life. His California collecting continued until 1917 but without the same intensity. Except for some material contributed by Waterman, the basis of Kroeber's chapters on the Yurok in his 1925 *Handbook of the Indians of California* (completed in 1917) was essentially what he had gathered from 1900 to 1908.

An even more significant indication of the change that occurred is represented in this volume of Yurok myths, some of it untouched even by Kroeber himself for over forty years. When he returned to the material, he did so with new questions and different emphases and certainly changed personal and professional perspectives. The result here is a document with considerable internal time depth, a valuable contribution to the biography of a man, the history of a discipline, and of course the study of a special people.

Timothy H. H. Thoresen

NOTE

The material in this sketch is abstracted from a larger work in progress, a book-length interpretation of A. L. Kroeber's anthropology. The primary source materials for that study are the manuscript collections in the University Archives and the A. L. Kroeber Papers, both collections housed in the Bancroft Library of the University of California, Berkeley, and used by permission. A more specific argument concerning 1900-1908 as Kroeber's "folkloristic" period appears in Thoresen (1973). A fuller discussion and complete documentation of the beginnings of academic anthropology in California appear in Thoresen (1975a). Below is a partial list of the published material on Kroeber and on the early years of the Department of Anthropology at Berkeley.

Dexter, Ralph W.

1966. Contributions of Frederic Ward Putnam to the Development of Anthropology in California. Science Education 50(no. 4): 314-318.

Freeman, John Finley

1965. University Anthropology: Early Departments in the United States. Kroeber Anthropological Society Papers 32: 78-90.

Hymes, Dell

1961. Alfred Louis Kroeber. Language 37(no. 1): 1-28.

Kroeber, A. L.

1915. Frederic Ward Putnam. American Anthropologist 17(no. 4): 712-718.

1923. Historical Introduction. Phoebe Apperson Hearst Memorial Volume. UC-PAAE 20: ix-xiv.

Kroeber, Theodora

1961. Ishi in Two Worlds: A Biography of the Last Wild Indian in North America. Berkeley and Los Angeles: University of California Press.

1970. Alfred Kroeber: A Personal Configuration. Berkeley and Los Angeles: University of California Press.

Putnam, Frederic W., and A. L. Kroeber

1905. The Department of Anthropology of the University of California. Berkeley: University Press.

Rowe, John Howland

1962. Alfred Louis Kroeber 1876-1960. American Antiquity 27: 395-415.

Steward, Julian H.

1961. Alfred Louis Kroeber 1876-1960. American Anthropologist 63 (no. 5): 1038-1060.

Stocking, George W., Jr.

1968. Race, Culture, and Evolution: Essays in the History of Anthropology. New York: Free Press.

1974. The Boas Plan for the Study of American Indian Languages. Studies in the History of Linguistics: Traditions and Paradigms, ed. Dell Hymes. Bloomington: Indiana University Press, pp. 454-484.

Thoresen, Timothy H. H.

1973. Folkloristics in A. L. Kroeber's Early Theory of Culture. Journal of the Folklore Institute 10(nos. 1-2): 41-55.

1975a. Paying the Piper and Calling the Tune: The Beginnings of Academic Anthropology in California. Journal of the History of the Behavioral Sciences. In press.

1975b. Typological Realism in A. L. Kroeber's Theory of Culture. Essays in the History of Anthropology, ed. Timothy H. H. Thoresen, The Hague: Mouton Publishers. In press.

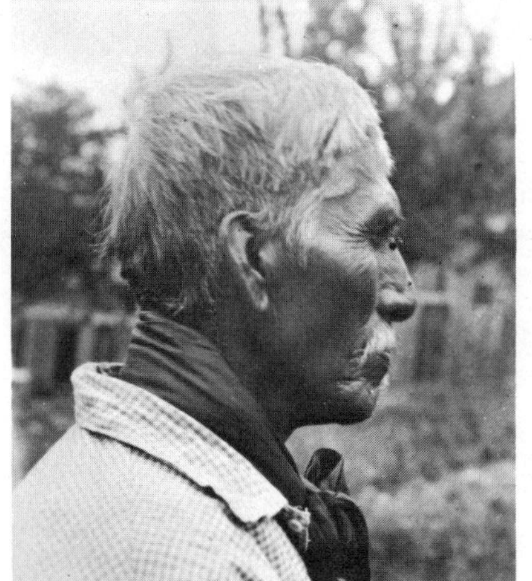

INFORMANT C
Stone of Weitspus, 1907

Alfred Kroeber, 1914

INFORMANT H
Dave Durban of Weitspus, 1907

INFORMANT N
Amits of Kepel, 1907

[Photographs of informants courtesy of the Bancroft Library, University of California, Berkeley. Photograph of Kroeber courtesy of Lowie Museum of Anthropology, University of California, Berkeley]

FOLKLORISTIC COMMENTARY

Yurok Myths is a major contribution to the study of native American oral literature, perhaps ranking in size and importance with Boas' monumental *Tsimshian Mythology* of 1916. Moreover, its inclusion of numerous informant biographies rather than just the narrative texts makes it almost unique in the annals of American Indian mythology scholarship. The vast majority of American Indian myth collections give little more than the names of informants, if that. In view of Kroeber's historic association with the superorganic concept of culture (Steward 1973:30), his emphasis upon individual informants—and the very organization of *Yurok Myths* by informant rather than by myth type—is all the more striking. While this arrangement does result in different versions of the same myth appearing in widely separated portions of the work, it does preserve intact the repertoire or repertoire sample of each informant.

It is a great pity that Kroeber did not write the elaborate commentary he intended. His rough indexes of persons and themes indicate that he planned to give detailed descriptions of all the dramatis personae of Yurok mythology. For each personage, major or minor, Kroeber expected to provide a synthetic composite synopsis of all events and allusions throughout the corpus. Thus, all the adventures of Wohpekumeu, the "widower from across the ocean," the culture hero/trickster responsible for stealing salmon and acorns for mankind, for regulating the flow of the river, for making natural childbirth replace women's death by Caesarian, and a host of other topographical and institutional innovations would have been put into a convenient summary chronicle. From such a summary, a reader unfamiliar with Yurok mythology would have learned that the licentious Wohpekumeu had only to look at a girl to make her pregnant, that he tricked his own son Kapuloyo into climbing a tall tree so that he could seduce Kapuloyo's wife (that is, his own daughter-in-law). Wohpekumeu's unbridled sexuality eventually leads him into trouble as one female victim, usually Skate (a creature of the sea) holds him fast and carries him back across the ocean. In similar fashion, Kroeber would have described the adventures of Pulekukwerek, whose name means literally "of downstream (end of world)" and "sharp (horned on buttocks)." Pulekukwerek and Wohpekumeu constitute the principal figures in Yurok mythology. Pulekukwerek survives a number of harrowing tests and slays a number of monsters.

Both Wohpekumeu and Pulekukwerek's exploits belong to a time period when the earth was inhabited by a race of beings called *woge*. The woge are small humanoid beings who reluctantly yielded the earth to mankind. There is an eerie sense of nostalgic sadness and loss whenever the woge are mentioned in Yurok myths. Inevitably, the woge withdrew into the mountains or across the sea or turned into landmarks, birds, or animals in order to escape close contact with newly created man. Yet the woge are still present in some sense, and they are depicted as being glad to be called upon (in ritual formulas and the like). Erikson has suggested (1943:261) that the childlike, innocent woge are "the projection of the [pregenital] state of childhood into prehistory," but whatever the original psychological reason for the existence of the woge might have been, it could be plausibly argued that one reason for their continued powerful emotional impact on the Yurok could be the acculturation situation. For just as the woge were sorrowfully destined to withdraw to escape humans, so the Yurok themselves may have felt like withdrawing to escape contact with Euro-Americans and their culture. Kroeber himself notes (F5, n. 1) "The woge are always represented as loath to leave their old haunts to which they were attached as much as the Yurok are to their homes." Kroeber failed, however, to see how closely some of his informants identified with the woge. For example, in one of the narratives told by Informant B, Tskerkr of Espeu, (B6*a*) we learn that the woge of Sigonoi refused to go off into the hills. "All the others went away, but these stayed on because they liked their town so much. So they remained the last ones, but were never ready to go. They were large men." In Kroeber's valuable sketch of Informant B, he is described as being robust, thick-chested, and possessed of a "massive frame." Since the woge are ordinarily perceived as small, childlike beings, the description of them as "large men" would appear to be idiosyncratic projection on Tskerkr's part. Moreover, Kroeber's careful account of Tskerkr's living in a solitary house which "was the only one still inhabited in the settlement" certainly supports the notion suggested here that the woge are in some sense the Yurok themselves, the original inhabitants of northwestern California who have slowly but surely been disenfranchised by the white man.

One reason why Kroeber was anxious to put the adventures of Wohpekumeu, Pulekukwerek, and the woge into pseudo-chronological order is that he felt that the Yurok were incapable of developing the tales "into a consistent and workable system" (A17, n. 3; cf. the end note to BB3). Kroeber never did completely repudiate his early remarks (1904:81, 97) to the effect that California Indian myths lacked the picturesqueness and dignity of other mythologies. Yet his search for system and consistency (cf. Thoresen 1973: 48) may have reflected his own ethnocentric bias rather than any deficiency real or imagined in Yurok culture. The data from these very Yurok myth texts suggests that there was considerable consistency in pattern and mythological system. The system may never have been articulated as such, for the Yurok had myths, not mythologists. It is mythologists, that is, individuals who study myths, who are concerned with extrapolating consistent mythological systems. The tellers of myths are content to allude to their mythic universe without worrying unduly about consistency. Few Euro-Americans are concerned about the two separate creations of man in the Bible (Genesis 1: 27; 2: 7, 22), one on the sixth day and one after the seventh day, or the creation of light several days before the creation of the sun (Genesis 1: 3, 16).

Kroeber's initial interest in Yurok mythology was classificatory and typological. In the intellectual heyday of grouping peoples possessing similar cultural traits or elements into common culture areas, Kroeber very early realized that Yurok mythology was quite distinct from the mythological systems of central and southern California. In an essay "Types of Indian Culture in California," published in 1904, well over half the discussion is devoted to mythology, and Kroeber made a convincing case for the distinctiveness of northwestern California (Yurok, Karok, and Hupa). Even in 1904, Kroeber knew or suspected the probable cultural similarities between northwestern California mythology and the mythology found on the North Pacific coast. Some of these similarities were spelled out in his 1920 essay on the same subject, entitled "California Culture Provinces." Kroeber's delineation of a Northwestern California cultural or subcultural mythological area has continued to be used, e.g., by Anna Gayton in her masterful survey "Areal Affiliations of California Folktales" in 1935, and by P. C. Holt in her valuable comparative study "The Relations of Shasta Folk Lore" (1942).

In the absence of a motif or tale type index for aboriginal North America (or even just for California or the Northwest Pacific coast), it is difficult to demonstrate the geographical provenience of all the narrative elements in *Yurok Myths*. Frankly, even if Kroeber had written a full-fledged critical introduction to the narratives, it is doubtful that he would have bothered to refer to Stith Thompson's six-volume *Motif-Index of Folk Literature*, the first edition of which was published from 1932 to 1936. Kroeber tended to restrict his comparisons to California or adjacent culture areas. For example, he is well aware that "Crane-leg-bridge" is a standard motif (A8*d*; A9; K3*b* and *c*), and he specifically observes (A8) that it has a "wide distribution in California." However, folklorists know this as motif R246, Crane-bridge, which is found in the Northwest Coast, Plateau, Plains, and Woodlands areas as well (cf. Stith Thompson, *Tales of the North American Indians*, p. 340, n. 227). By the same token, the origin of death usually involving a cricket (Wertspit) who for fear of overpopulation ordains permanent death or trods on a grave to keep the dead from coming back to life (A6*l*; F4*b*; P4*d*; X1*b* and *g*; Z3*a*) is not limited to the Yurok or even California. (For a possible Choctaw cognate, cf. Bushnell 1910: 527). Similarly, the "Theft of Fire" (D1x and y; X11; Z1) is motif A1415, an extremely widespread narrative in aboriginal North America.

One reason why full comparative annotations for this collection would have been particularly welcome is the demonstrated linguistic relationship existing between Yurok and Algonkian languages spoken by American Indians in the eastern and central United States (Haas 1958). Luomala in her detailed study of Sun Snarer remarked that the Yurok alone in California reported this tale, and she suggested the possibility that the Yurok text may represent a survival from a time period before the Yurok left the main body of the Algonkians (1940: 7, 19). However, generally speaking, tales are rarely bound by linguistic barriers—only one bilingual is required to transmit a story from one linguistic community to another. A cursory comparison of the present Yurok narratives with standard Algonkian tale types (Fisher 1946) reveals no obvious parallels, or rather parallels limited exclusively to the Yurok or other members of the Ritwan group. Yet despite the enormous complexity of comparative folktale scholarship, especially with narratives found on several continents (cf. Utley 1974), a close study of various single motifs in this Yurok corpus may well furnish some folkloristic support for what has been primarily a purely linguistic hypothesis.

Other features of *Yurok Myths* which are likely to be of special interest to folklorists include the re-eliciting of a particular tale from an informant and Kroeber's presentation of both versions, though unfortunately not always in full (cf. A15x and y; see also X14x and y). Perhaps even more important from the point of view of fieldwork methodology is Kroeber's judicious comparison between collecting a tale in piecemeal fashion, stopping long enough for an interpreter on the scene to translate each segment, with collecting the same tale in its uninterrupted entirety in Yurok and having it translated later, line by line (cf. D1x and y). Such experiments were far ahead of their time!

Despite the sophistication and insight of many of Kroeber's comments in both headnotes and footnotes, the reader ought to keep in mind that the fieldwork was carried out shortly after the turn of the century, long before modern folkloristics posed new theories and techniques to be applied to folklore data. One could well wish, for example, that Kroeber had attempted an analysis of the Yurok narratives along the lines of Melville Jacobs' *The Content and Style of an Oral Literature* or the sequel *The People are Coming Soon*. Jacobs, like Kroeber, trained in folklore by Boas, broke away from the literal "culture-reflector" theory of folklore (Dundes 1967: 66) to treat Clackamas Chinook myths and tales as projections of critical interpersonal tensions and rivalries. In view of the fact that the Yurok are one of the relatively few native American groups which have been studied from the vantage point of psychiatry (cf. Erikson 1943; Róheim 1950; Posinksy 1954, 1956, 1957; Valory 1970), it is too bad that we do not have the benefit of Kroeber's own systematic interpretations of the possible psychological implications of some of the narratives. For example, in view of the hypothesized partial anal-erotic basis of the Yurok concern with shell money and "pains," it would have been interesting to have had Kroeber's reaction to such narrative elements as squeezing a trout's belly to force out pebbles—which he does equate to dentalia or wealth (A20, n. 8) or the "evacuation" episode in "The Doctor Married at Turip" (C4*d*) in which the protagonist inside a sweathouse seizes the "pains" and tries to escape; since the entrance has been closed, "he escaped by the exit hole." Other possibly relevant details include Hummingbird's curing of Black Bear by flying through her, from mouth to rectum (C3*g*; cf. Erikson 1943: 287; Róheim 1950: 272) or the explicit connections made between cleanliness, garbage, and money (T3*h*). Such speculations might or might not have appeared reasonable to Kroeber in light of his exceptional knowledge of Yurok culture. He did remark once, very briefly, on the apparently anal character of the Yurok, but it was in his general textbook on anthropology (1948: 618) and not in one of his many detailed ethnographic studies of Yurok culture. Nor did he ever comment on the various psychoanalytic interpretations of Yurok data.

If Kroeber failed to provide an overview of the total Yurok mythological system and if he limited his analysis or interpretation to occasional ethnographic glosses, he did succeed in providing the crucial raw material which will allow others to attempt such overviews or analyses. There is no substitute for reliable data, and Kroeber's assiduous gathering of Yurok narratives affords both Yurok and non-Yurok alike a precious perspective on Yurok worldview and values, a perspective which had it not been recorded by Kroeber might have been lost forever.

Let me cite one brief example of an observation which Kroeber's *Yurok Myths* has made possible. In reading through this extraordinary narrative collection, I noticed what I think may be a Yurok predilection for the "middle." At first I thought it might be only an oral literary convention much like the motif of *two* wives, brides, girls (cf. T6, n. 11) or the consistent allusions to the ritual numbers five and ten. Whether the "normal" price for a wife of good family is ten strings of dentalia (F2, n. 10), or hiccups come in a series of ten (X11*b*), or the masculine ideal is ten orgasms in a single night (Posinsky 1957: 5), the "ten" patterning is ubiquitous in Yurok life and thought. Kroeber was well aware of the conventional five and the conventional ten, as he phrased it (A6 headnote; A14, n. 15), but I am not sure that he realized the paramount importance of the "middle" in Yurok worldview. The middle position is evidently a place of honor. A preferred house, for example, was specifically said to be in the middle (A12*a*; D6x*f*; J9*a*). Kroeber does remark that the middle house would normally belong to the leading man of the village (D6x*f*, n. 14), but he does not relate this fact to placing the best bows of a group in the middle (P5*a*) or the favorable regard for the middle of the day (A1*c*); A23*b*) or night (A16x*s*; R2*b*). Consistent with this pattern is a character's traveling in the middle of a river (C4*a*) or even the Yurok notion that there is "an ocean upstream as well as downstream from their country" (A11, n.12), which would, of course, place the Yurok homeground squarely in the middle. The "middle" is not only a place of distinction; it is also a place of danger. A girl is warned not to dig bulbs in the middle of the prairie (A7*a*). The sky strikes the sea in the middle (X13*b*). It was in the middle of the river that Crane drew up his leg and dropped an old woman to her death (A9*b*). In another tale, a being in the middle of the stream swallows every boat (Cl*e*). In still another, Coyote discovers that the roughest place in the river is the very middle (G4*b*; cf. X3*a*). From this textual data, we can see that it is reasonable from a Yurok perspective to imagine that the sun's path is a middle one (X10*c*) or that a metaphorical house might have its middle marked with a stripe of black with red on both sides (BB2*i*), just as the one marked gambling rod is banded with black in the middle where the hand covers it (T6, n. 28). The point is that with a single allusion to a middle position in a tale or two, one could not necessarily assume that such an allusion was part of a large-scale pattern. It is only from an examination of an extensive sampling of narrative texts such as this one, which Kroeber so painstakingly gathered, that one can begin to search for meaningful cognitive and symbolic categories.

The numerous introductory statements and prefaces in this volume are certainly no substitute for the critical apparatus that Kroeber might have offered us. But even without a definitive essay on Yurok oral literature, *Yurok Myths* will surely stand as a timeless memorial to the creative imagination of the Yurok people and the tireless labor of one of the giants of anthropology.

ALAN DUNDES

Boas, Franz

1916. Tsimshian Mythology, Annual Report of the Bureau of American Ethnology. Washington, D.C.

Bushnell, David I.

1910. Myths of the Louisiana Choctaw. American Anthropologist 12: 526-535.

Dundes, Alan

1967. North American Indian Folklore Studies. Journal de la Société des Américanistes 56: 53-79.

Erikson, Erik Homburger

1943 Observations on the Yurok: Childhood and World Image. UC-PAAE 35: 257-30l.

Fisher, Margaret W.

1946. The Mythology of the Northern and Northeastern Algonkians in Reference to Algonkian Mythology as a Whole. *In* Man in Northeastern North America, ed. Frederick Johnson. Papers of the Robert S. Peabody Foundation for Archaeology 3: 226-262.

Gayton, A. H.

1935. Areal Affiliations of California Folktales. American Anthropologist 37: 582-559.

Haas, Mary R.

1958. Algonkian-Ritwan: The End of a Controversy. International Journal of American Linguistics 24: 159-173.

Holt, Permelia Catharine

1942. The Relations of Shasta Folk Lore. Unpublished doctoral dissertation in anthropology, University of California, Berkeley.

Jacobs, Melville

1959. The Content and Style of an Oral Literature. Chicago: University of Chicago Press.

1960. The People Are Coming Soon. Seattle: University of Washington Press.

Kroeber, A. L.

1904. Types of Indian Culture in California. UC-PAAE 2: 81-103.

1920. California Culture Provinces. UC-PAAE 17: 151-169.

1948. Anthropology. New York: Harcourt, Brace.

Luomala, Katharine

1940. Oceanic, American Indian and African Myths of Snaring the Sun. Bernice P. Bishop Museum Bulletin 168. Honolulu.

1964. Motif A728: Sun Caught in Snare and Certain Related Motifs. Fabula 6: 213-252.

Posinsky, S. H.
1954. Yurok Ritual. Unpublished doctoral dissertation in political science, Columbia University.
1956. Yurok Shell Money and "Pains": A Freudian Interpretation. Psychiatric Quarterly 30: 598-632.
1957. The Problem of Yurok Anality. American Imago 14: 3-31.
Róheim, Géza
1950. The Yurok. *In* Psychoanalysis and Anthropology. New York: International Universities Press, pp. 270-290.
Steward, Julian H.
1973. Alfred Kroeber. New York: Columbia University Press.
Thompson, Stith
1955-58. Motif-Index of Folk Literature. 6 vols. Bloomington: Indiana University Press.
1966. Tales of the North American Indians. Bloomington: Indiana University Press.
Thoresen, Timothy H. H.
1973. Folkloristics in A. L. Kroeber's Early Theory of Culture. Journal of the Folklore Institute 10: 41-55.
Utley, Francis Lee
1974. The Migration of Folktales: Four Channels to the Americas. Current Anthropology 15: 5-27.
Valory, Dale Keith
1970. Yurok Doctors and Devils: A Study in Identity, Anxiety, and Deviance. Unpublished doctoral dissertation in anthropology, University of California, Berkeley.

EDITOR'S PREFACE

Alfred Kroeber left most of his manuscript of Yurok myths in typescript, but the section I have called "The Geographical Setting" and his biographies of Lame Billy and Tskerkr he left in handwritten draft.

Kroeber organized his manuscript so that the myths told him by a particular Yurok informant are grouped together. Each such grouping is preceded by a biographical sketch of the informant. Kroeber wrote two versions of most of these sketches, the first version usually genealogical and biographical, the second usually psychological. In order to supply the maximum amount of data about the informants, I have chosen to keep and combine both versions.

I have left the myths themselves virtually unchanged, except for an occasional punctuation mark. Almost all the parenthetical explanations within the tales themselves are Kroeber's own.

Kroeber was in the process of evolving a simpler system of transcribing Yurok words, but had reached only tale B14 in the revision of his footnotes. A specialist in the Yurok language was necessary if we were to achieve a general consistency in the later transcriptions, and so I called upon Dr. Mary R. Haas of the Department of Linguistics of the University of California, Berkeley. I would like to acknowledge her signal help in the publication of this collection. Realizing that Kroeber wrote his translations and did his revising over a period of many years, we made the decision to retain his spellings when in doubt. We consulted R. H. Robins' *Yurok Language* (1958) for the identification of certain plants and animals, but we did not attempt to adopt his system of transcription. Any definitions taken from Robins are acknowledged in the footnotes.

For scholars wishing to pursue Kroeber's orthography, the Bancroft Library of the University of California, Berkeley, has his notebooks with his penciled transcriptions, as well as his first and second typescripts of the Yurok myths. It was the second typescript which was used in the editing and typesetting of this book.[1]

I have renumbered Kroeber's footnotes so that they run consecutively, without gaps, for each myth. I have edited the notes for consistency of style, and for clarity where necessary, although Kroeber was such a fine stylist that his instinct for the right word or phrase was almost unerring.

Here and there I have added substantive footnotes in brackets as an aid to the general reader, since many of the works Kroeber referred to are now out of print and are likely to be available only in university libraries. Where Kroeber indicated that he intended to supply a cross-reference to another Yurok tale, I have silently supplied it. In a few places, where I could not locate a pertinent cross-reference, I have indicated that fact. I have added, in brackets, other cross-references of my own. And I have supplied, in brackets, information on Kroeber's marginal jottings, which he did not have time to incorporate formally into the body of his work. All such editorial insertions in the headnotes and footnotes are indicated by brackets and "Ed."

As both the Kroebers indicate, the Yurok myths have a strong geographical orientation. Readers who are fortunate enough to have the thirty-four maps of the *Yurok Geography* (1920) of T. T. Waterman will find it helpful to consult them frequently. For other readers, I have made a selection of the Waterman maps, retaining Waterman's spellings, which differ somewhat from Kroeber's but are readily intelligible. The map from Robert Spott and A. L. Kroeber's *Yurok Narratives* (1942), reproduced here as map 2, is an excellent general map, showing all the larger Yurok towns.

The photographs of three of the informants were taken by Kroeber himself. They were previously published in A. L. Kroeber and E. W. Gifford's *World Renewal* (1949), pp. 154-55, with the statement that Kroeber took them in 1907.

I would like to express my thanks to Marie Bryne of the Bancroft Library for her careful collating of the manuscript and her hospitality during the editing. I wish to express my appreciation to Geoffrey Brown and James Denton of the R. H. Lowie Museum of Anthropology, Berkeley, for compiling the information on the extant phonograph recordings of Yurok myths made by Kroeber and listed in the Appendix.

GRACE BUZALJKO

Editor, Department of Anthropology
University of California, Berkeley

1. Kroeber's second typescript contains the notation that it was typed by personnel of Works Project Administration Official Project No. 665-08-3-30, Unit A-15.

THE GEOGRAPHICAL SETTING

The intensive geographical setting of Yurok mythology must be followed on the map if a large part of the quality of the literature is not to be lost to the reader. But certain points recur so frequently that it may perhaps be worthwhile to fix them in mind in advance. Very often the detailed localization of a tale will then be self-explanatory.

Native names have been used throughout. Trinidad, being itself foreign, may sound nearly as appropriate as Tsuräu; and between Rekwoi, Meta, Weitspus and their accepted Anglicizations Requa, Mettah, Weitchpec, there is little to choose; but there is something incongruous in having a hero of antiquity pass by Smith River instead of Hinei, meet a companion at Johnsons, which is Wohtek, and steal light at the mouth of the Salmon River when the immemorial town of Segwu' there is to the inhabitants the center of the whole world; or to denominate Kenek, where Wohpekumeu grew out of the ground and practiced his deceptions, where Thunder and Earthquake dwelt, where the sun fell to earth, where the never-eating Pulekukwerek visited, and where all the race of old gathered to lament leaving this earth before the coming of mankind—to name this spot, dripping with associations, Tuley Creek, seems incongruous. To ninety-nine out of a hundred who turn these pages one designation will be as empty geographically as the other.[1]

The Yurok land consists of two lines, each stretching a scant fifty miles. One is a straight hilly coast, the other the Klamath River, winding only in

1. [Kroeber does, however, use English names for the rivers and streams. T. T. Waterman, in Yurok Geography, UC-PAAE 16:(no. 5): 196, explains that the Yurok did not usually name whole streams, but instead applied to the stream the name of some place on it or at its mouth.—Ed.]

short bends. The two lines meet at a sharp angle at Rekwoi, at the mouth. The upper end of the line of river is Weitspus, where the Klamath, which previously has been flowing south, turns with an impressive sweep to the northwest, and the Trinity comes in. The upper end of the line of coast as the Yurok reckon—it is down on our maps—is at Tsuräu, in the shelter of projecting Trinidad Head. It and Rekwoi and Weitspus were all great Yurok towns, and from them every spot in Yurok possession can be reckoned.

On the Klamath, halfway between Rekwoi and Weitspus, are Wohkero, Wohtek, and Ko'otep, almost a continuous town, and Pekwon, forming together probably the most populous group of Yurok settlements. Downstream from the cluster, the most important settlement is Turip, about halfway to Rekwoi. Upstream, about a third of the way to Weitspus, are Kepel and Sa', virtually one town, and Mūrek, just below and opposite. This is the region where perhaps the greatest number of Yurok were wont to gather annually, at the fish dam or weir at Kepel, whose ceremonies were concluded by dances at the great middle cluster. Two-thirds of the way up is Kenek, insignificant in recent generations, but the center of Yurok mythology. The rapids here are the most productive fishing place on the river.

The coast from Rekwoi to Tsuräu falls into four nearly equal stretches, marked by the towns of Espeu at Gold Bluff, Orekw at the mouth of Redwood Creek, and Oketo on Big Lagoon.

There were small settlements a few miles beyond each of the three pivotal points,[2] but the only one frequently mentioned is Omen, on the coast trail leading from Rekwoi north to the Tolowa. Facing Rekwoi was Wełkwäu, and opposite Weitspus, Pekwtuł, both on the southern bank and almost to be reckoned as suburbs of the larger centers.

Upstream on the Klamath the alien neighbors of the Yurok were the Karok. Their most important towns clustered about Ko'men (at Orleans) and Enek and Segwu', just below and above the mouth of the Salmon, tributary of the Klamath. These points are about eighteen and thirty miles from Weitspus. Of anything beyond, the Yurok as a whole have little knowledge or care.

Among the smaller tributary of the Klamath, the Trinity, and nearer, are the Athabascan Hupa. The foot of their fertile little valley is only six miles from Weitspus. The two chiefest Hupa villages are Oplego and Kohteł.[3]

Parallel to the Trinity and the lower Klamath, and to the west of their

2. [Meaning Tsuräu, Rekwoi, and Weitspus.—Ed.]

3. [Waterman, Geography, p. 255, notes that the Yurok, Karok, and Hupa each had their own names for the towns inhabited by the other two tribes. Some names were translations or paraphrases, but others were quite independent. Oplego and Kohteł, respectively, are the Yurok names for Hupa towns of Takimiłding and Medilding. See maps 1 and 2, and see also the tables of Yurok and Hupa town names in Kroeber, Handbook of the Indians of California, pp. 11 and 129.—Ed.]

course, is Redwood Creek, whose banks, and especially the intervening ridge of the Bald Hills, Tsulu, were frequented by an Athabascan people closely related to the Hupa: the Chilula. Their towns were unimportant and comparatively little visited by the Yurok.

Farther south, beyond Tsuräu, from the mouth of Mad River to Humboldt Bay and beyond to the lower Eel, were the Wiyot, a coastal people, but of slight intercourse with the Yurok of the coast, to judge by the scarcity of traditional references to their territory. North of the Yurok coast was a third Athabascan group, the Tolowa. Their central and possibly largest settlement was Hinei, at the mouth of Smith River.

The maps will help to fix this framework.[4]

A. L. KROEBER

4. [Kroeber's manuscript contained a diagram, drawn by him, showing the Yurok territory and that of nearby groups. However, two previously published maps, one from Waterman and one from Kroeber, seemed more informative and have been used here instead.—Ed.]

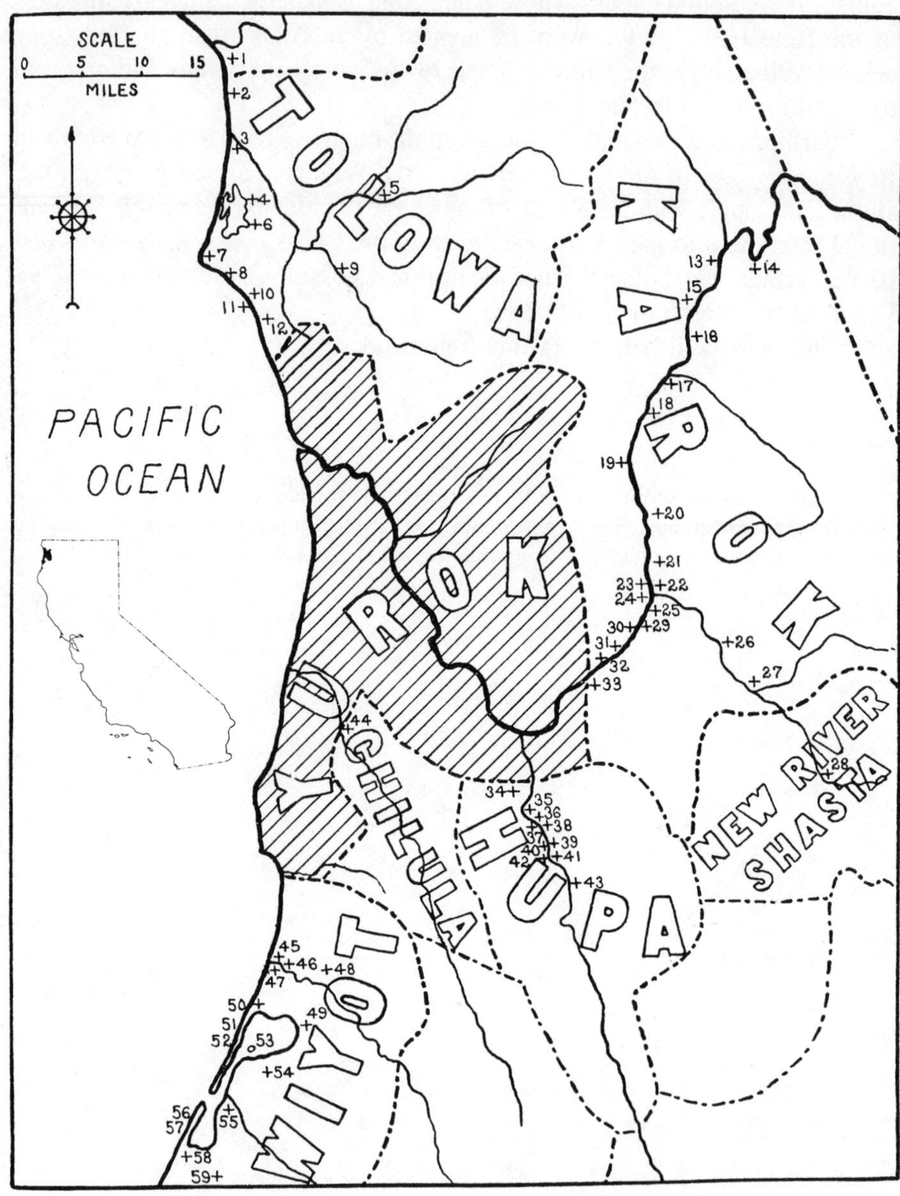

KEY TO MAP 1

1. rkr′
2. noro′rpeg
3. hinē′i
4. logeno′ʟ
5. hine′g
6. tolo′q̣^{w}
7. pēk^{w}tsū
8. ko′hpi
9. mistsi′ks
10. rʟ
11. ne′keʟ
12. osme′tsken
13. äko′nileʟ
14. äyo′omok
15. rä′yoik
16. häʟkutso′r
17. posī′r
18. äpye′^{w}
19. tsäno′ʟ
20. me′legoʟ
21. tū′noiyoʟ
22. higwoni′k
23. segwe′^{w}
24. e′nek
25. ma″a
26. sepola′
27. keski′ʟ
28. ke′per
29. nä′ästok
30. we′tsets
31. ko″ omen
32. olege′ʟ
33. oprgr′
34. plo′kse^{u}
35. oknū′ʟ
36. rgr′its
37. qrrwr′
38. o′plego
39. qä′xteʟ
40. rlr′n
41. pyä′ägeʟ
42. petso′^{w}
43. wo′xtoi
44. otle′p
45. ko′hso
46. sepora′
47. tegwo′ʟ
48. pegwe′
49. we′skwenet-o-tnä′^{w}
50. enikole′ʟ
51. rtr′qr
52. tepa′axk
53. olo′g
54. hike′ts
55. oknū′ʟ
56. weyo′
57. pi′min
58. le′plen
59. äyo′

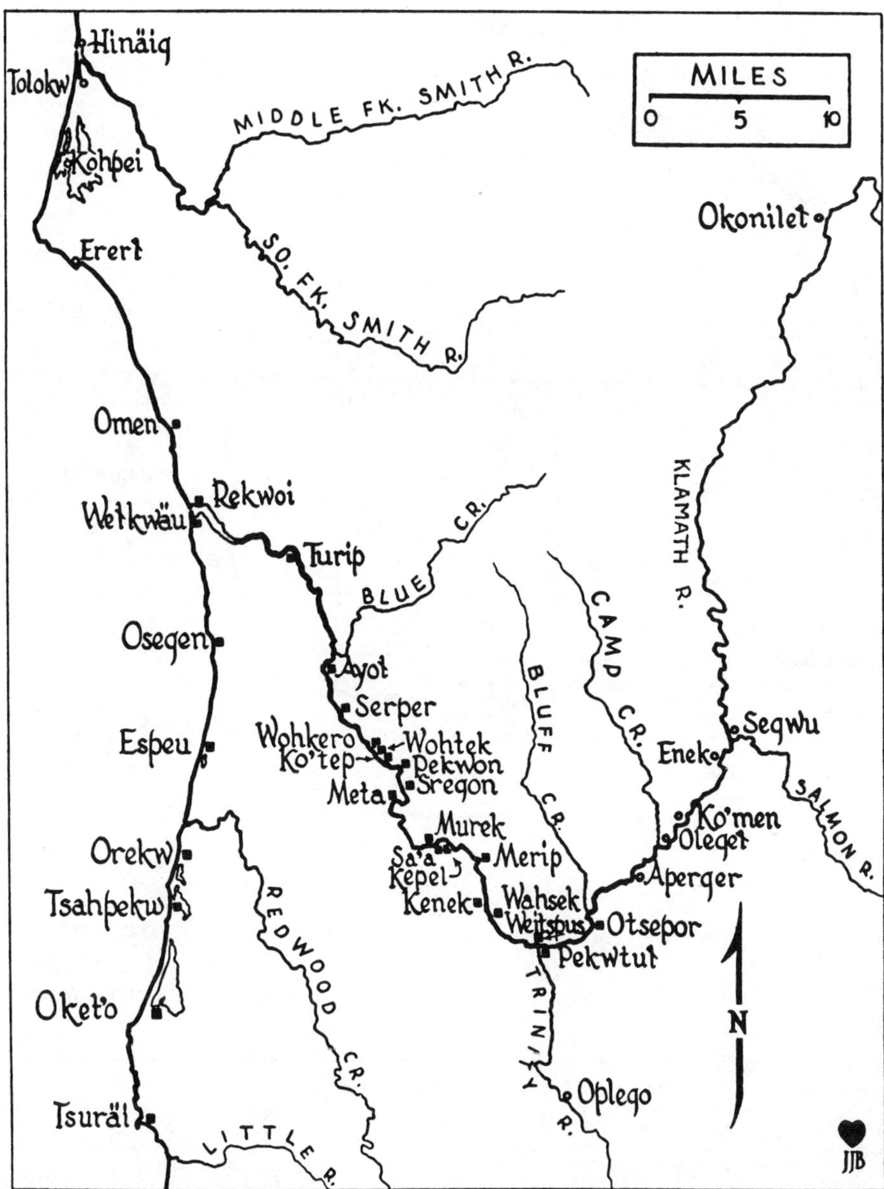

Map 1. (*left*) Northwestern California, showing distribution of Yurok place names outside Yurok territory. Inset map: California, showing the location of Yurok territory (shaded). (From Waterman, Yurok Geography, maps 1 and 2)

Map 2. (*above*) Principal Yurok towns, indicated by black squares, along the Klamath River and the northern California coast. Towns of the Tolowa, Hupa, and Karok are indicated by circles. The names shown for these are the Yurok ones. (From Spott and Kroeber, Yurok Narratives, frontispiece.)

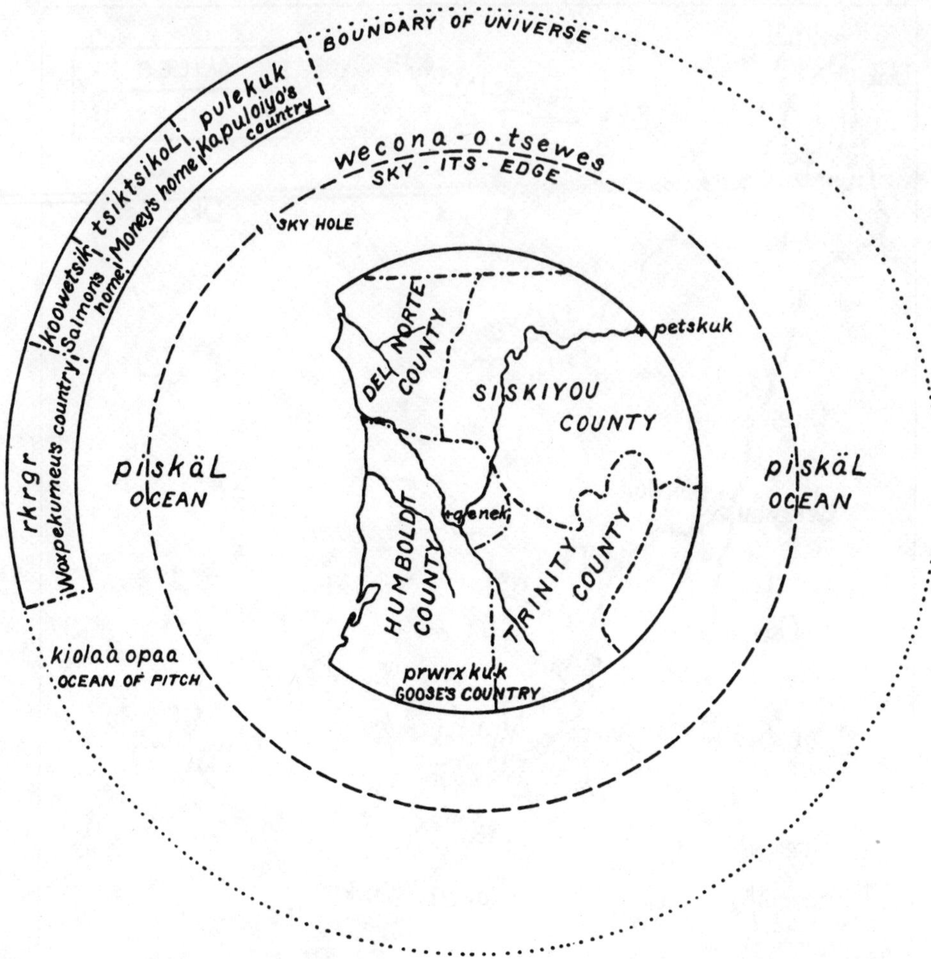

MAP 3. Diagram of the Yurok idea of the world. (From Waterman, Yurok Geography, fig. 1)

KEY TO MAP 4 (*RIGHT*)

1. itprpr', lake
2. ke'wet, nountain
3. egwole'q^{w}, open hill-side
4. egwole'q^{w}-higwo'n, acorn-ground
5. aro'ox-pets, scene of a ceremony
6. lo'-o-le'go pets, acorn-grounds
7. o-segä':wits, scene of a ceremony; hilltop
8. meq^{w}tege'n, fishing-place
9. o-tsīkits, fishing-place
10. aatemr'-haä'g, boulder at edge of river
11. meʟnega', fishing-place
12. t'rpr', fishing-place
13. to'hpr, fishing-place
14. haägola', fishing-place
15. neko'sit, fishing-place
16. we'spen, place
17. o-tegeke't wroi, creek
18. wiʟnega' wroi', creek
19. r'ʟr-pūl wroi', creek
20. kwo:lo'q^{w}, acorn-ground
21. wē'itspus, town
22. o:re'^{w}, fishing-place
23. rʟrgr', town
24. pek^{wu} tū'ʟ, town
25 honare'q^{w}, boulder near edge of river
26. pe''^{i}kar-o-re'^{w}, place
27. qoxtsemo'r wroi', creek
28. haägolo'k, place
29. lo'-o-lē wroi', creek
30. lo'-o-le'go, town; also called heyomu
31. o''oleq^{w}, acorn-grounds
32. slo''o, hillside
33. sä'är, acorn-grounds
34. pyegwelä'^{w} wroi', creek
35. ho''onokok, boulder in river
36. potsī', great rock in river
37. aiqo''o, Indian settlement
38. o-teyo', fishing-place
39. o-tsepo'r, Indian settlement
40. ro:moi', small flat
41. o-tlä' wroi', creek
42. o-lä'ig, acorn-ground
43. wo'xtoi, flat
44. tsī'poi wroi', BLUFF CREEK
45. tskr'i, place
46. häye'q^{w}, point of land
47. pe'ʟkoʟ, bar in river
48. o-keto'k, small plateau
49. pek^{w}tsū'ʟ-so, ridge
50. mī'lonets, place
51. megwimo'r, little rocks in river
52. megwi'ʟ-o-te'get, large boulder near river
53. o-wrgr'ts, boulder near river
54. re'kwoi, creek mouth
55. tso''ok wroi', creek
56. o-smemo'ʀʟ, Indian settlement
57. tesire'n, place
58. peli-kr''rts, place
59. o-slegoi'ts, Indian settlement

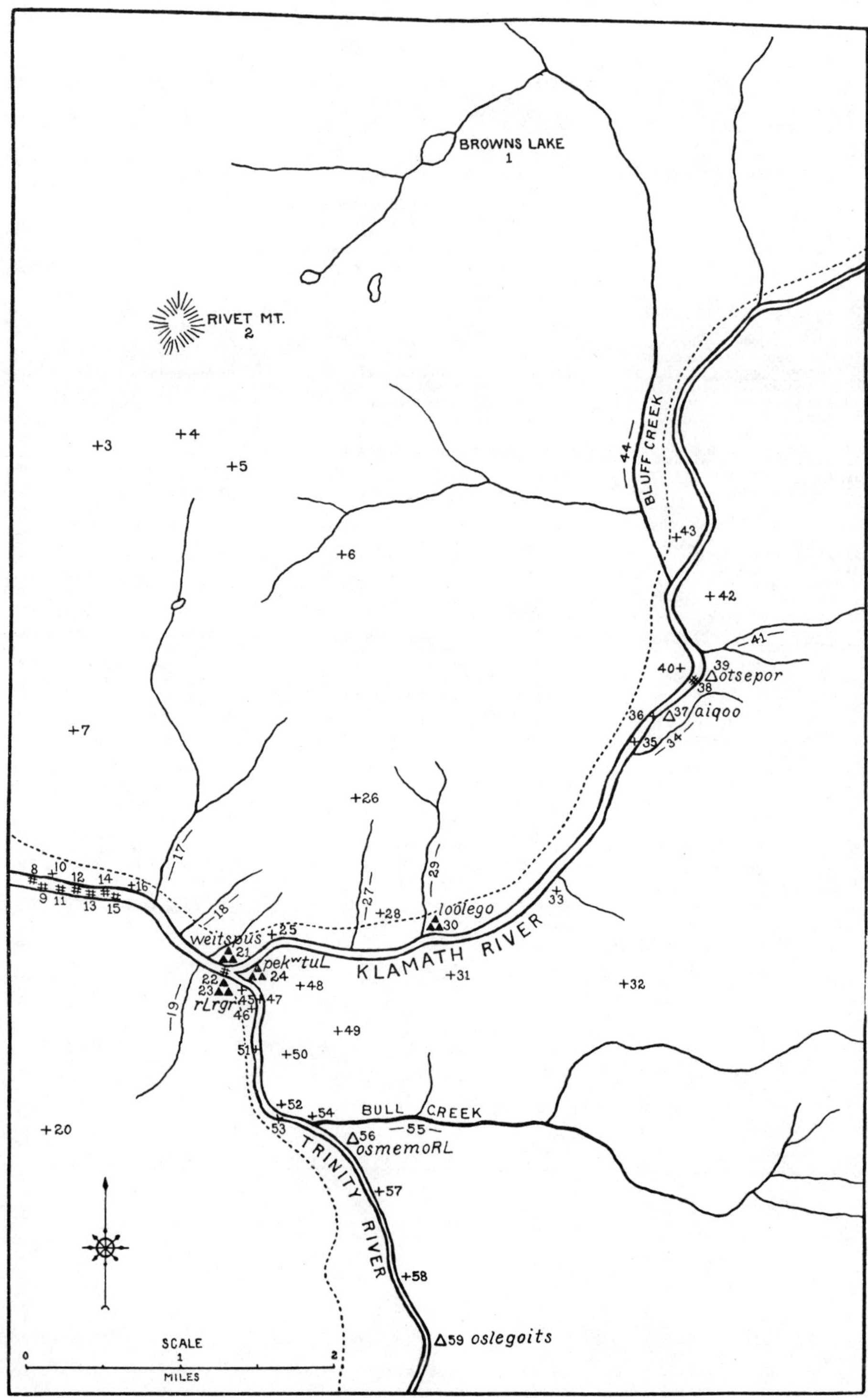

MAP 4. Weitspus and the junction of the Klamath and Trinity rivers. (From Waterman, Yurok Geography, map 25)

KEY TO MAP 5

1. tsrktsryr', fishing-place
2. qo'xtau, crag on hillside
3. qo'xtau wroi', creek
4. otskrgrū'n, flat rock in river
5. tsweyomū'we wroi', creek
6. teto'no wroi', creek
7. mū'ntsē haä'g, boulder at edge of river
8. we'ʟkwa^{w}-o-pa''a wroi', small creek
9. kne'tken-o-lo, large boulder at edge of river
10. kne'tkem-sio'ʟ, fishing-place
11. keyomo'r wroi', creek
12. olepo'ʟ wroi', creek
13. tsäp-o-sro'r, fishing-place
14. tsio:pī'ʟ wroi', creek
15. oro':wis, fishing-place
16. we''^{i} qem, site with house-pits
17. watsenē'gomek, snaring-place
18. hime'ʟ wroi', ROACH CREEK
19. hime'ʟ, town
20. nega'htūr haä'g, crag
21. hime'ʟ-hiqo' wroi', creek
22. tsegoro'k higwon
23. pre'grau', snaring-place
24. tse':korok^{w} wroi', creek
25. tsegoroq^{w}-hiqo' wroi', creek
26. tekū's-o-ke'pel, snaring-place
27. tsegoroko''ʀ, rock at edge of river
28. plo':lē wroi', creek
29. o'lē', fishing-place
30. no'htska, place
31. kya tsī's, fishing-place
32. ow𝓮' wroi', creek
33. no'htska, wroi', creek
34. rai'yo, place
35. m𝓮'rek, town
36. smeʀkito'ʀ wroi', creek
37. rkye'ʀ wroi', creek
38. wa''a, small sand bar
39. owī'ī gr, place on river bank
40. o'teräy, fishing-place
41. hiɴkelo'ʟ, place
42. we'ʀpe'q^{w} wroi', creek
43. knegwora', snaring-place
44. wohpe'iyo, snaring-place
45. segwo'ʀskoʟ, open hillside
46. megä'u, group of redwood trees
47a,b. me'tsep-rgr'its, clumps of brush
48. näko'-o-sre'goʀ, great rock in the river
49. sa''a, town
50. tepoläu' wroi', KEPEL CREEK
51. wogan, snaring-place
52. te'polay, fishing-place
53. ke'pel, town
54. merx'qwi, rock at edge of river
55. t'ū'lek, rock at edge of river
56. o-tre'ga', trickle of water
57. qr'mruk, place on river bank
58. rū'loiyo wroi', creek
59. o-kwē'go, tree
60. qe'nek-wone'^{w}-o-we''^{e}iqūn, acorn-place
61. o-wēga', acorn-place
62. ʟoko'ʟ-u-pa''a, lake
63. pē'tolo, acorn-ground
64. poʀkwe'ʟ, acorn-ground
65. mrkū'r, acorn-ground
66. meʀ-hīpets wroi', creek
67. o''res, fishing-place
68. wa'ase, ton
69. wa'ase-hipe'ts wroi', creek
70. wa'ase-hiqo' wroi', creek
71. sie'gweʟ, fishing-place
72. o-tlä^{w} wroi', small creek
73. qowi'tsik-o-loä'g wroi', creek
74. q'owitsiʟ-o-loäg, flat rock beside the river
75. hū'ūks-o-reqe'n wroi', creek
76. hū'ūks-o-rek, rock in edge of river
77. ole''ga wroi', creek
78. olēgī'k wroi', creek
79. me''^{i}kwets, acorn-place
80. o-sr'pr, acorn-place
81. lē'pin, acorn-place
82. kr'hprslek, acorn-place
83. o-pä''än, open country on hill summits
84. au''wo, acorn-place
85. me'rip-hiqo'-hi'gwonū, acorn-place
86. he'sīr, fishing-place
87. me'rip, town
88. regr'ogets, white-cedar timber
89. okē'ge, place
90. olī'īk, acorn-place
91. kne'tken-woäg, rock with fissure
92. rpryū'ʀʟ, cave in rocks
93. me'rip wroi', creek
94. myrgwr', fishing-place
95. wo'gi, fishing-place
96. tse'gwa, enormous rectangular boulder in edge of river; a fishing-place
97. ma''aga wroi', small creek
98. olo'k, fishing-place
99. ego''oloq^{w}, rock on the hillside
100. le'ta, fishing-place
101. otī'tr^{w}, fishing-place
102. oʟ-he'ʟku-o-legai' wroi', creek
103. oʟ-he'ʟku-o-legai', a large boulder
104. otrgr'p wroi', creek
105. wē'logets, fishing-place
106. mä'wä wroi', creek
107. heʟqwalū'ʟ, fishing-place
108. yogeyo'ʟ, fishing-place
109. aukwēya', settlement
110. aykwēya' wroi', creek
111. hä'äsqr''r-hiqo', fishing-place
112. hä'äsqr''r, fishing-place
113. egolo'ts wroi', creek
114. wor:o:''mes, fishing-place
115. osprwr'ts wroi', creek
116. qe'nek-pul, settlement
117. wo'koteʟ, acorn-ground
118. lo'htko, acorn-ground
119. qe'nek-heʟ, acorn-ground
120. na'hksau, acorn-ground
121. ro's-o-tū'k wroi', creek
122. o-tetqo'ʟ, fishing-place
123. okwē'go wroi', creek
124. tse'tskwi, settlement
125. tse'tskwi-hipe'ts wroi', creek
126. tse'tskwi-kes, fishing-place
127. nänepī'r, acorn-ground
128. wokote'l wroi', creek
129. herpūn amo', fishing-place
130. egwole'k wroi', creek
131. o-tsäū, fishing-place
132. pe'ʟkoʟ, fishing-place
133. qe'nek wroi', creek
134. qe'nek-hiqo', acorn-ground
135. o-slegoi'ts wroi', creek
136. rplr', fishing-place
137. qe'nek, town
138. okego' wroi', TULEY CREEK
139. mene''wots, fishing-place
140. qe'neqäs, large boulder in river
141. o'-tsäpimū'r, fishing-place
142. o-tsä'p, settlement

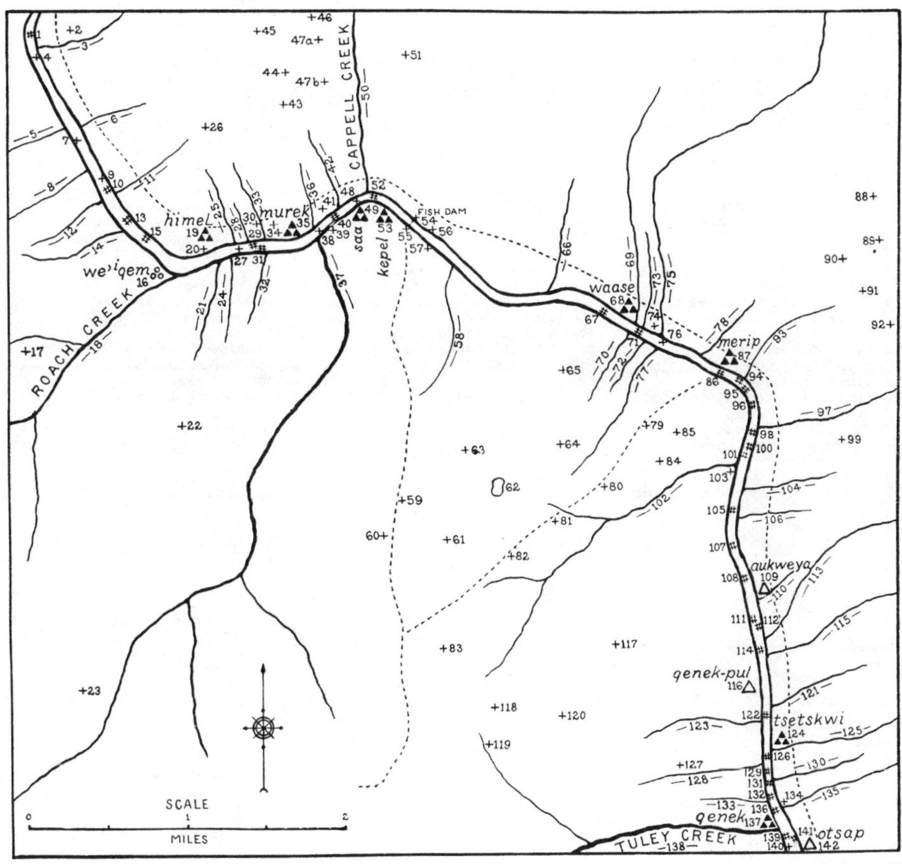

MAP 5. Kenek, Merip, Kepel-Sa', and Mūrek. (From Waterman, Yurok Geography, map 17)

KEY TO MAP 6

1. ʟkē'lik-o-le'pa, acorn-ground
2. orä'^{w}, acorn-ground
3. mr'ᴍ owe''e ikū', acorn-ground
4. pye'h-o-skē'go'o, acorn-ground
5. wr'sip-u-so'n, acorn-ground
6. wa'asinera', spring
7. äyoh, hillside
8. re'gok-o-yū''ū wroi', creek
9. o'men wroi', creek
10. o'men hipū'r, town
11. o''līk, small promontory
12. owrgr'ʟ, large sea-stack
13. he'ʟkus-o-le'gem, rock
14. kr'otskegī'm, sea-stack
15. o'n:ego, rpomontory
16. meʟmū'wim, rock almost submerged
17. orē'wok, hill
18. oke'gep, spring
19. yots-legai', ridge
20. kiʟ-o-mēyo', hill
21. tsmegi'ts-wesle'k-wo'ne^{w}, hill
22. otrgr'p wroi', creek
23. wo'gi sitso' wroi', creek
24. hirikūmr''^{w} wroi', creek
25. o'kwego oke'to, lake
26. o'men, town
27. tä'täiʟ, two sea-stacks, with channel between
28. rlr'gr, sea-stack, FALSE KLAMATH ROCK
29. pr'gris-o-tsī'guk, sea-stack
30. okwe'go, sacred tree
31. wo'giʟ-o-te'pon, hill
32. ä'spik-o-skū, spring
33. wä''ämok^{us}, hill
34. tahtosī'ts, hill
35. ä'kor-o-tep, knoll
36. otse'gep, sea-stack
37. ha'äg, sea-stack
38. sū''ū, fishing-place
39. melekoi'yo, small sēa-stack
40. mega', rock cliff
41. mo''o-o-tek, small sea-stack
42. otsnepä'^{w}, small sea-stack
43. orēgo's, large pointed crag
44. otspī'gr, rock on hillside
45. hr'wr''^{w}, hill
46. rnr'q, perpetual spring
47. otse'gep, landing-place
48. ro''o, a small rock
49. pkets-o-pe'gemū, small rock at water's edge
50. trpr', rock
51. re'kwoi, town
52. w'tspūs, point where a ridge enters the lagoon
53. plepē', point where a ridge enters the lagoon
54. tmr'i, settlement
55. tmr'i wroi', creek
56. petskus-o-re'tse, place
57. poiyowū'r wroi', creek
58. ūme'gwo, creek
59. pū'lik sr'nri, creek
60. he'ʟku sr, creek
61. nikurtsr'i, creek
62. tegwola'-o-tsäʟ, sand-spit
63. trkr'mrwr, large rock in sandbar
64. opegī''īyem, small sea-stack
65. ʟkē'lik-oʟ, small sea-stack
66. okne'get, large sea-stack
67. wä'ä^{w} son, small sea-stack
68. tsrähptsī'k, sea-stack, almost submerged
69. rlī'ʀq, crag
70. etskwokū''ūk, spring
71. ketso'k, berrying-place
72. we'ʟkwä^{w}, town
73. wahtsero', hillside
74. wo'hpi-oʟ, sand-spit
75. otwe'go, flat
76. ūpr'sr, a point of land
77. tselo'notep, camp site
78. otwego' wroi', creek and slough
79. tse'kweʟ, village or house site
80. hä''wo wroi', creek
81. seye'^{w} osle'p, acorn-ground
82. olī''ik, acorn-ground

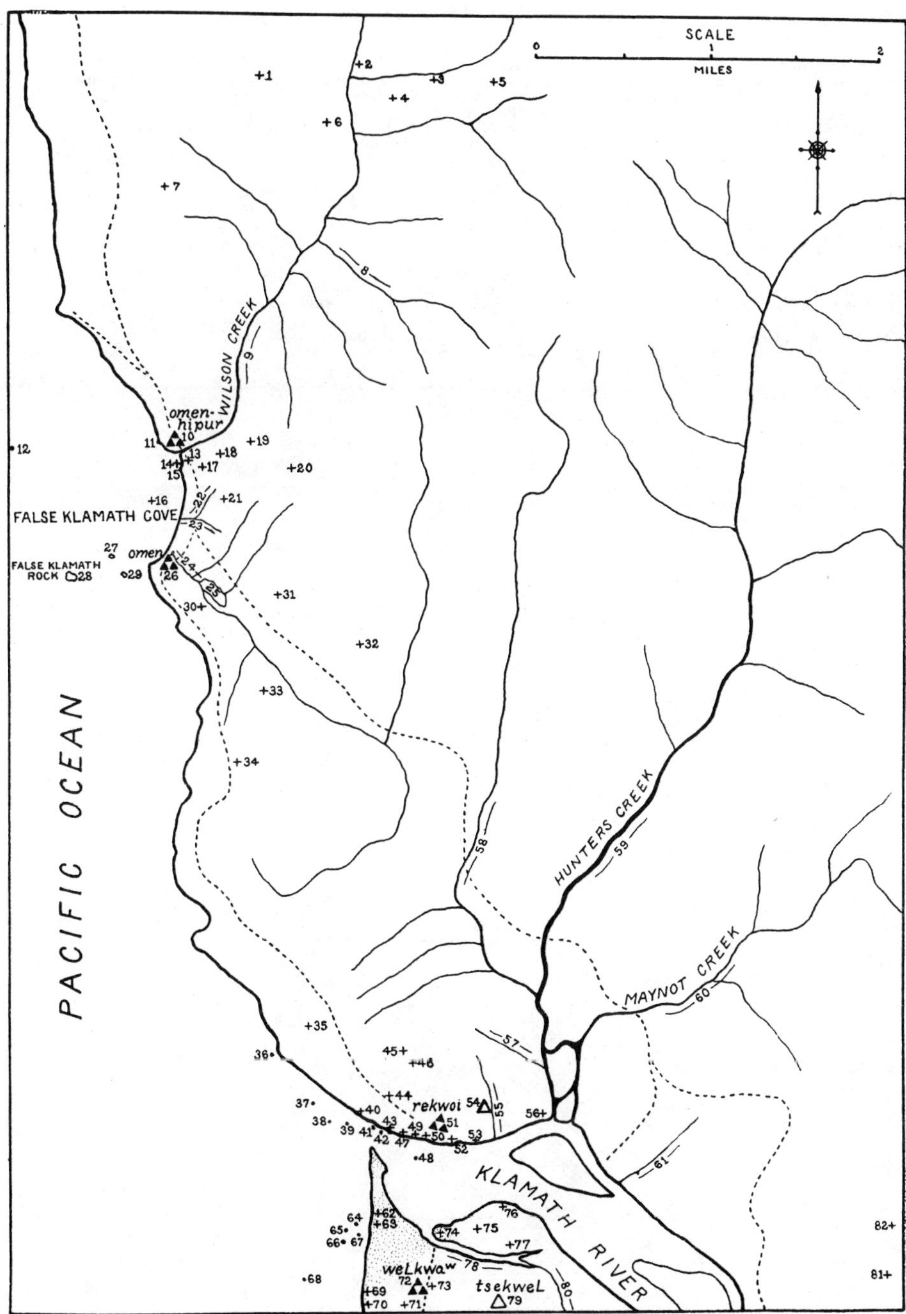

MAP 6. Rekwoi and the mouth of the Klamath. (From Waterman, Yurok Geography, map 5)

KEY TO MAP 7

1. nr′rts-o-po′peʟ, steep hillside with depressions
2. yots-o-kegē′i, narrow place on sand bar
3. pe′gwī, FRESHWATER LAGOON
4. toxteme′q^{w}, place at south end of Freshwater lagoon
5. tikwo′, promontory, SHARP POINT
6. pek^{w}te′ʟ, rocks
7. o-segenū′m, place on sand bar
8. hrgwr′′^{w}, town
9. r-ī′īk, rock
10. tsa′hpek^{w}, town
11. tsa′hpek^{w}-o-keto, STONE LAGOON
12. o-pego′ʟ, place
13. o-kegē′^{i}, sharp ridge
14. tso′tskwi, town
15. pr′gris-o-tsyē′guk, crag on shore
16. rock where Thunder lives
17. poi′xko-o-lep, dome of rock
18. os-o-ū′ūkweʟ, rock
19. tekwo′, tip end of lagoon
20. lega′, place on sand bar
21. pä′′är, town
22. o-sloq^{w}, town
23. kē′′^{i}xkem, Indian settlement
24. rgr′′ wroi′, creek
25. mä′′äts, town
26. o-ke′to, BIG LAGOON
27. nī′′wo, middle point of sand bar
28. nkeʀ numī′īg, place on sand bar
29. o-legwose′q^{w}, projecting sand bar
30. okege′to, place on sand bar
31. knegwolo′iʟ, place on sand bar
32. e′so, clay bank
33. pet′owo′′, place on sand bar
34. nrgr′-o-iʟ, point where beach ends
35. o-pyū′weg, town
36. tsī′k^{w} tsen, promontory into lagoon; SOUTH POINT
37. mä′ʀkwī, place
38. piɴpa, Indian settlement
39. owe′yek, point where cliffs get low
40. tspä′′är wroi′, creek
41. tspä′är, place
42. e′repa wroi′, creek
43. nryi′tmū′ʀɴ, place
44. nū′meroi wroi′, creek
45. to′loweʟ, sea-stack
46. o-le′′ɴ, sea-stack

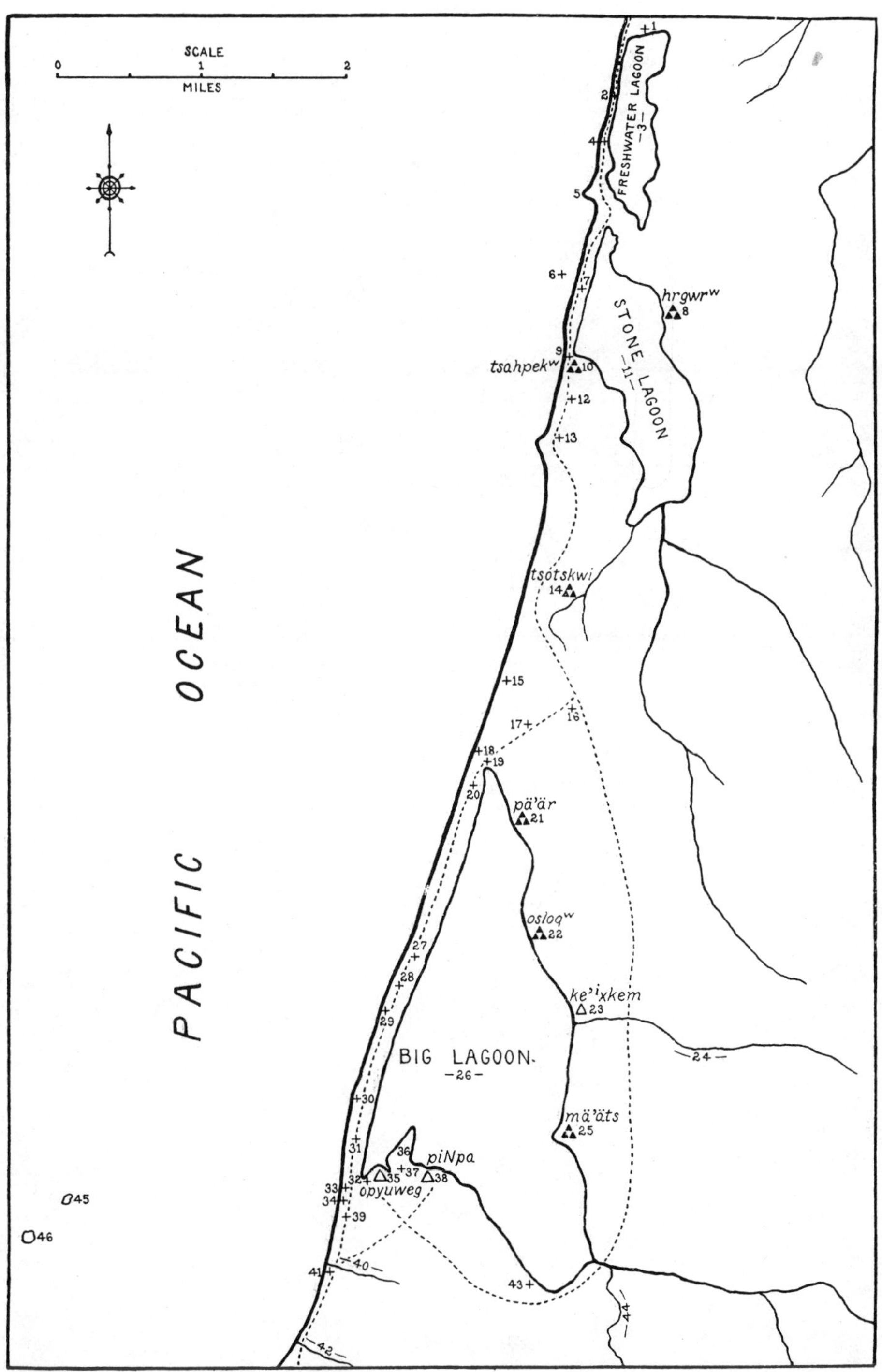

MAP 7. Freshwater, Stone, and Big Lagoons. (From Waterman, Yurok Geography, map 31)

Informant A

LAME BILLY OF WEITSPUS

When I knew Lame Billy in 1901, 1902, and 1903,[1] *he was probably forty to forty-five years old. His legs were entirely useless and at times swelled threateningly. He moved on crutches. I never saw him except in his house or close about it. In 1906 he was dead. His sickness probably was that from which most crippled and paralyzed Indians suffer who have been exposed to the same disintegrating influences of civilization as the Yurok: syphilis. Billy's family was an old one in Weitspus. Its house was that known as tsekweł,*[2] *and hence he was called K'e-(t)se'kweł. (Later he was known as Erperger-owa on account of his Karok wife from Erperger.) His lineage was neither notable nor contemptible. When he spoke of his father or uncles or grandfather, it was with pride. His maternal ancestry is not remembered. Three of his children were still living in 1940.*

Before he lost his bodily powers, Billy seems to have been active. He had been a good hunter, fisherman, and boatman. He had seen the world, as a Yurok undertands it, and mixed freely with Indians and whites. He was alert, inquisitive, a ready talker, and gifted with memory. He was well versed in myths, having learned them from his relatives in the house tsekweł.

The family wealth was in the keeping of Informant I. Billy owned chiefly arrows and Brush Dance feathers as well as two otter skins and a woodpecker

1. [On his manuscript, Kroeber queried the date 1903, and it may be an error. In Kroeber and Gifford, World Renewal, p. 133, K. says he knew Lame Billy in 1901 and 1902.—Ed.]

2. [Waterman, Geography, pp. 208-09, says that most Yurok houses had names. Some names were popular and were used in town after town, as a matter of convenience in referring to them. Only in very small towns were the houses nameless. See the translations of the house names in Waterman, pp. 209-13.

House names indicated family standing and respectability, and the names appear in the myths. "They tell us that the towns stood as they do now, house names and all, when the supernatural beings instead of the Indians were living along the Klamath" (Waterman, p. 209).—Ed.]

bandolier. He did not acquire dancing things to any extent, as his brother George did. However, when there was a dance at Weitspus, his Karok relatives from Erperger brought them a gray deerskin and a pair of black obsidians.

Billy's English was far better than that of the average fullblood of his age: ungrammatical, of course, but fluent and expressive. He commanded it more pliably than his wealthy townsman Frank, who was my usual interpreter. I need hardly say that Billy dictated his tales to me without intermediary. He took obvious pleasure in relating them, and the pay was welcome to a man deprived of practically all earning power. Several times he showed jealousy when I ceased coming to see him, in order to work temporarily with someone else.

In his person Billy was neat, and the house, especially that corner where he sat, was invariably clean and orderly. He must have chafed under his paralysis, although he never complained and kept himself as active as possible. He was handy with a knife, and usually had within reach a dance headnet in process of crocheting and a couple of curing wildcat or raccoon skins. In body he was of average height, rather taller than most Yurok, slenderly and well built and evidently once of more than average strength—a nervous constitution. His face expressed his individuality much more than it reflected his race. His nose was prominent and sharp, as in so many cripples; his eyes pierced brilliantly. His speech was illuminated with free and vivid gestures. He spoke well on any subject within his range: always to the point, and at once vigorously and with complete control. He was a man that would be listened to in any company. Suspicions, hostilities, and sullenness he no doubt felt like every Yurok. But he mastered his feelings with but little evidence of the repression that the Yurok in general are always visibly exercising. He was clearly a person of superior faculties.

Billy's powers as a storyteller rested on the combination of an excellent memory and a synthetic imagination. He was equally at ease in narrating a story of folktale type, of the hero order, a myth of the origin of institutions, or one of the conventional Yurok creator-rectifier-trickster traditions about Wohpekumeu and Pulekukwerek. The subject mattered very little, provided it allowed of treatment in his concrete and expansive manner. A bald incident he developed into a definite plot; a ready-made plot he interwove with others or with subsidiary ones into a complex construction.

He hardly ever hurries a tale, yet never drags one. The dialogue is lengthy, as in life, but does not become tedious because it unfolds the story; it is not inserted because of an inability to break away from mere reality. His characters talk because in mind he is with them and feels with them. The method is often epic in scale, yet always flexible. Where it is possible to compare tales, I find Billy's versions always longer, and I think more interesting, than those of other Yurok.

In addition to the power of weaving and enriching a plot, Billy possesses a definite gift of character portrayal. Each of his principal figures is something of an individuality. He is even able to take a stock character like the shifty Wohpekumeu and present three self-consistent and interconsistent aspects of his personality in three successive tales. Where he can contrast two or three or four characters in one story, he is at his happiest, and never lets pass such an opportunity for exercising his faculties of literary construction.

His personages command sympathy because they are quickly worked out into people. The hero of the average Indian tale is but the vaguest sort of character, and if our feelings go out to him it is only because of the situation in which he is. Billy's heroes and their friends and opponents maintain an invariable dignity of character. He rarely fails to invest them with an essential nobility, and is always striving, with the artist's refinement of device, to exalt and magnify them.

As to style in the narrower sense of the word, I can unfortunately say nothing about Billy's capacities. English, after all, remained an imperfect medium for him. He proved a poor dictator of Yurok text on the one or two occasions on which I tried him, and he was an unsatisfactory linguistic informant. Speech to him was a means, not a material for analysis; and my Yurok being more hampered than his English, he turned impatiently from it. If he had lived until 1906, I should have been able to record at least one of his tales in the full original on the phonograph for subsequent transcription and translation by others; but he died during my three years of absence from the Yurok.

One class of tales alone I never obtained from this informant: the narrative formulas with which the Yurok "make medicine." Whether he knew none or would not tell those he knew, I cannot say; I suspect the former.[3]

I have chosen Lame Billy's contribution to open this collection of Yurok traditions because it is on the whole the best artistically, not because it is the most representative. The reader who wishes a ready impression of normal Yurok mythology, both as to substance and manner, will do well to turn to any one of a half-dozen other informants. Lame Billy stands too far from the commonplace average.

A.L.K.

A1. Tsuräu Young Man

I put this myth first among those told by this narrator because it represents in well-developed form a kind of tale typical of the Yurok—what I call the institutional myth. On a pale and unadventurous film of plot are spread the origin of a civilizational institution or a series of them. The Yurok love to dwell on their institutions. Instead of symbolizing

3. [For an explanation of the difference between formula and myth, see the headnote to tale A1.—Ed.]

and systematizing them like the Pueblos, they have localized them and have made them expressible in terms of wealth.

A surprising proportion of their traditional knowledge, myths as well as formulas, is nothing but a recital of their own customs thinly cloaked in narrative. Some nameless individual of the generic *woge*[1] first did something—sometimes on the first trial, sometimes only after repeated attempts—that the Yurok do now. Thereby the practice was established for all time. If the custom involves belief in magic or the supernatural, a recital of how this happened suffices, with the aid of a nominal offering and some slight austerities, to bring about present results similar to those achieved in the first ancientness of time: we have a formula. If this practical application is lacking, the story is a myth.

Obviously children are scarcely capable of making this distinction. Most young people, the irresponsible among the mature, and even many of the serious-minded in periods of relaxation, share their attitude. Certain large elements of Yurok mythology are therefore of the order of folktales the world over. Any given myth is almost invariably a blend of the two strains. The barrenest magical formula has a semblance of plot; the tales told for amusement are likely to embody a reference to the origin of a feature of topography, the appearance of an animal, or some action customary among men. But the folktale element is generic, at least as regards its character; the institutional element is highly specific of the Yurok and other tribes of northwestern California. Its essential ingredient is perhaps the attention bestowed on the social practices of men—on Yurok culture.

The present narrator, being an artist, was never satisfied to tell anything baldly, but he was enough of a Yurok to feel thoroughly at home in an institutional myth. If its frame does not leave him quite the scope for character portrayal, for unusual event, as is afforded by other tales, that only means that the tone of the story is a bit subdued. His power of picturing human emotion is in no way cramped; and he finds ways of bringing personalities into relation with one another, without which his theme would seem barren. All that his tale requires for full appreciation is an understanding of the cultural milieu that is the warp of its fabric. [K. has a marginal notation to himself: "Work in dam episode, shame at R.," probably a reference to part *f* of the myth.—Ed.]

•

a. A young man grew at Tsuräu.[2] He had a sister. He told her (one) morning, "I should like to see a pretty hill be." What for?" she asked. "I always hear laughing when the wind blows from there. I almost hear someone laughing. That is why I want to make a good hill here. I want to sit on it that I may look about. There may be people somewhere. Perhaps they will see me when they come by."

1. [The woge are defined by Kroeber in myth A2, n. 6, as "a race more or less parallel to the human one"; they are "men of ancient days and somewhat enlarged powers."—Ed.]

2. Tsuräu is Trinidad, the most southerly Coast Yurok town, except for a small settlement at Little River.

He went down to the beach. He heaped up the sand with his hands and made the pile round, picked it up, took it in one hand, and set it down again. So he made Tsurewa.[3] When he had made it, he sat down on top of it. He said, "I wish you would be higher," and the sand grew higher. After a time he said, "I wish you would be a little higher," and the sand grew a little more. He looked around and said, "That is all."

b. Then he ran downhill to his house. He got a stool and took it with him to the very top and placed it well. Downstream[4] from it he set a white rock, across[5] a black rock, above[6] a red rock. Upstream[7] was the side to which he looked.[8]

As he sat, he thought, "I do not know what to do. I do not know what to make my stool turn to be." Then he began to know. He said, "It will be best if I make a hole here with a spring in it. I shall come here sometimes if I want woodpecker crests.[9] I shall wash my hands in that water and it will come to be (that I get woodpecker crests). I think that is how I shall make my stool. On the side here next to it I shall make a small hole. I shall come there if I want persons' money.[10] I shall come and wash my hands in that." Then he made the (two) holes and began to sit on his stool.

c. He sat still. The wind was blowing and he felt, he nearly heard, speaking. Then he quickly answered, "Yes, yes." Then he saw a stick standing near him. He began to think, "Is that stick talking?" He said, "Now that is what I want, because I am always lonely.[11] That is what I have been looking for. I should like to have someone to talk to me always." Then the stick said, "Go back to your house. It will be better if you go back. Build a sweathouse for me."

The young man went to his house. When he arrived he said, "My sister, do you know what a sweathouse is?" "Yes, I dreamed of it." "Well, I should like

3. Tsurewa is Trinidad Head, a rounded promontory, almost separated from the mainland, and forming a cove on which Tsuräu stood. The head is visible for long distances up and down the coast.

4. North.

5. Wohpäuk, west.

6. East.

7. South.

8. [Waterman, Geography, p. 193, says that the Yurok had no such idea as our cardinal points of the compass, north, south, east, and west. Yurok terms for direction and position are determined by the river that bisects their world, the Klamath. The fundamental Yurok concepts for direction are *pets,* upriver, and *pul,* downriver. The river, though it winds, follows a generally northwesterly course before flowing into the Pacific. By an extension of the idea, "downriver" also means northward along the coast.—Ed.]

9. The scarlet scalps of the pileated woodpecker, worked into dance ornaments by the Yurok and treasured as valuable. Even in recent years they have been bought and sold for a dollar to a dollar and a half each.

10. *Oł we-tsīk,* dentalium shells.

11. A sentiment frequent in Yurok tales. [K.'s marginal note: "Cf. paragraph 1."—Ed.]

to have that. Let us go outside. I will show you how to begin.'' Then they began to make it. In a short time it was made.[12]

Then he said, ''Now I can go back to my stool.'' When he came there, he saw that stick sitting on his stool. It had become a man. ''You have made it?'' he asked. ''I suppose you do not know me.'' ''Yes,[13] I do not know you.'' ''I will let you know my name. I can grow everywhere in the world. My name is Tohstek. Now I shall tell you what to do. I tell you now, here, because next time you shall not hear me anymore. Then you can do what I now tell you. You shall come here every morning and carry dry sticks (limbs) down. You shall sweat by means of them, in the sweathouse. As soon as you see the sticks burning, when you make a fire in the sweathouse, you will talk to that fire. You will talk to it continually. You will tell it what you want, what you want to become, that you want to become a rich man, or whatever else you want to be. If you want play and good times, tell it that.''[14]

''Yes, I will do that.''

''Tell your sister that I want her to come up here and gather firewood every middle of the day, and tell her that when she has piled up as much as she can carry, she is to talk to it, if she wishes to be rich or to see playing or anything else.''

''Yes, I will tell my sister that.''

''Now I shall tell you. For ten days come here every morning. Do not miss one day. You will see. You thought there were no gatherings for good times going on over all this world. If you do what I tell you, you shall see those festivals. If you do not fail in what I tell you, you shall have them all, but if you fail in it, you shall never have them, you shall never be near them. (If you do right) you will see people that are clean. Their caps, their clothing, and all that they use will be good. Now begin tomorrow. If you do that for seven mornings and wait, you will find something. You will find it in the path. Look well in the path every morning.''

d. Now the young man began to do so. Every morning he went to get sweathouse wood, and that young woman went in the middle of the day for wood. They never missed going. Then it was six nights, and he carried sweathouse wood. Then it was seven nights and he slept. Then he dreamed. He came somewhere. Then he saw a Deerskin Dance.[15] Then he thought, ''That is

12. [K's marginal note: ''Woman half!''—Ed.]

13. The Indian answers ''yes'' logically where we say ''no.''

14. Using the sweathouse is not only a habitual way of spending one's time awake and asleep, but one of the most efficacious means of attaining one's desires, if one ritualizes the gathering of the firewood used. [Only the men used the sweathouse.—Ed.]

15. One of the two varieties of great dances among the Yurok and their neighbors. The other is the Jumping Dance.

the kind of festivals I shall see.'' The next night, when he slept, he began to dream again. He saw a Jumping Dance. He awoke and thought, ''I think that is the kind of festival I shall see after awhile.'' The next night he dreamed and saw a Brush Dance.[16]

In the morning he started. He had nearly come to his seat. Then he looked about. He thought, ''Something has been at work here.'' The ground was clean. He saw one hair (fibril) lying in the middle of the cleared ground, a single fiber of woodpecker crest. ''I will take care of it,'' he thought. Then he kept it. When he returned, he left his wood outside the sweathouse. He went into the living house. He had ten wooden trunks.[17] He took the largest and opened it and put the one hair on the empty bottom. Then he went out, entered his sweathouse, and made a fire. That night he dreamed. It said, ''Do not open that trunk for ten days. After ten days wait until your sister comes in. Let her bring her wood first, and wait until she comes. Then open your trunk in the middle of the day.''

Then, on that tenth day, he told his sister to come into the house when she returned from gathering firewood. He said to her, ''Come and sit here.'' He took the smallest trunk, brought it (forward), and opened it. Then he saw it was full, entirely full of eagle feathers. He asked his sister, ''What is that good for?'' The girl said, ''Oh, there will be all kinds of festivals made with it. We shall have that kind of festival in time.'' Then he took another trunk and opened it. It was entirely full of *tsis-in-rego'* (long upright strands of sinew entirely covered with worked-in fibers of woodpecker crests and used as dancing headdresses). He asked her, ''What is that good for?'' She said, ''That is the kind with which we shall have festivals. They will have those festivals all over this world. I think that is what it is for.'' He opened the ten trunks. All were full, each of one kind. One trunk was full of long woodpecker-ornamented eagle feathers, another of fur forehead-bands (for the Deerskin Dance). He found deerskins and every kind (of ornament and valuable).

Then he opened the large trunk. He found twenty forehead-bands of woodpecker crests,[18] and there were (also) five white deerskins[19] in it. The woman said, ''I wish we had a little more. I wish we had two more of them.'' ''I

16. This is a much less pretentious affair, which can be held for anyone willing to pay the cost and irrespective of traditional locality.

17. Cylindrical boxes with a cover. They are long enough to hold feather ornaments, ride well in a canoe, and can be carried on land by a rope slung over one shoulder.

18. The chief ornaments worn in the Jumping Dance. In modern rating they are worth about seventy-five dollars each. [K. has a marginal query here.—Ed.] Probably no Yurok ever possessed twenty, though wealthy men, with the aid of their friends, no doubt could sometimes produce an even greater number at a dance.

19. Deerskins of unusual color—black, very pale, or mottled—were very valuable, and used in the dance which the whites have named from them. A pure albino skin was practically priceless; at any rate, it was not sold.

think that is against custom, for a man to have seven; they can show six in a dance, but it is against the way of doing if they have seven at once.[20]

Then he said, "I think this summer we shall go about. We shall go all over the world making festivals."

e. Then they went (upstream along the ocean, south to Mad River). They came to Kohso.[21] There they found a Jumping Dance. Then Tsuräu young man said, "Soon I shall have that kind also." Then the people of Kohso said, "You had better return; you can see nothing beyond here. There is nothing going on there.[22] But if you go back, you will not go far beyond Tsuräu before you find another dance of this kind."

Then he went (north) and came to Oketo.[23] He saw another (Jumping) dance there. He stayed there a little while. Then he went on (north).

f. They came near the mouth of the (Klamath) river.[24] He almost heard shouting. Then he told his sister, "Do you hear that shouting?" "Yes, I think there is another festival about here." Then they reached the hill above Wełkwäu.[25] They saw the river. He said, "Here is another river." He tried to look about. It was foggy and he did not see anything from there. So they went down.

They had nearly come to the town (of Wełkwäu) when he turned back. He trod back two steps and told his sister, "Stop! Look! See how clean they are (compared with our dress). I am ashamed." Then the girl went among the bushes; she wanted to look on, but she wanted no one to see her. She peeped out and thought, "I am ashamed to go." She said to her brother, "What are you

20. This probably means that nowhere in the ken of the Yurok had a dance ever been held in which more than six perfectly white skins could be assembled by any one party or set of dances. The total number extant among all the tribes of their world may have been a dozen or possibly two. There was a nominal taboo against what did not happen, anyway. Had any rich man and his friends been able to display seven—or ten—at once, I have no doubt they would have done so with alacrity. For any man, like our hero, to own five was a sort of dream.

21. Kohso is a town near the mouth of Mad River, where the Wiyot held a Jumping Dance, or at least one in which the woodpecker crest headbands were worn.

22. The Wiyot beyond Mad River made neither Deerskin nor Jumping Dances.

23. Big Lagoon. The largest town on it—at the southern end of the sheet—where a Jumping Dance was customary, is generally known simply as Oketo, though its proper name is Opyuweg, "they dance."

24. Orekw, at the mouth of Redwood Creek, another town with a Jumping Dance, is omitted.

25. Wełkwäu is the town on the south side of the mouth, as Rekwoi is on the north. In the past generation or two Rekwoi has been considerably the larger, but this condition may have been reversed more anciently, since Wełkwäu made a salmon new year's ceremony and traditionally a Deerskin Dance, and Rekwoi only a Jumping Dance, although this was longer maintained. The Klamath forms a wide tidal lagoon behind the bar that shuts it off from the ocean except at the mouth itself. This breach shifts occasionally from one side of the lagoon to the other; and it may be that the population followed the channel.

carrying to wear?" He said, "Yes, I am carrying everything to wear." She said, "Yes, so do I. I have my dress, my hair ties, my cap too. I have brought everything. We will change our clothes before we go there." Then they dressed beautifully and started to go on. He said to her, "Do not stand and look about, but follow me as I go right on."

As soon as the people saw them they did not look (at the young man and girl), being ashamed (at their splendor). They thought, "Here is a (real) man that has come from somewhere." The (two) did not go very far. They did not go near the crowd; but he told his sister, "Let us sit down." Then they sat.

A man went to them. He said, "Ayekwi! You are from Tsuräu?" "Yes." "There is a dance across the river." "I was ashamed to go. I thought I would stay on this side." "I will take you over." "Yes, I will go with you." Then he got up. That one said, "Well, let us cross. The dance will be over soon."

Now they were beginning the Jumping Dance on the other side of the Klamath (at Rekwoi). They could hear it on that side. That girl said to her brother, "What are you going to do?" He said, "I am going to make what we shall do. I shall be great when we come there. I shall be the first one. I shall make a good dance. Then I shall start from here upstream."

Now the people at Wełkwäu said to him, "Do you bring anything (to add to the dance)?" He said, "Yes, I am carrying ten woodpecker-crest headbands." "Yes, that is what I like." "Have you gone (to the dance) on the other side before?" "Yes." "How did you cross?" "I did not begin (dancing) on this side. I began on the other side. I gathered my people in one place there and then we started the dancing from that spot." "Have you two boats? Large ones? If three, it will be better." "No, I have only two." "Well, bring your boats here. We shall start (the dance) from here." He thought, "We shall dance right in the boat. We shall start like that and so we shall surpass them."[26] Then he made them go into the two boats, twenty of them, all wearing (his) woodpecker-crest headbands.[27] Then he said, "Now we start," and began to sing and dance in the boats. Then they went.

From Rekwoi they heard that and said, "Stop! Someone is coming from elsewhere. I can hear (the singing)." They looked across the river. Then the fog lifted and they saw them coming. Now the man[28] of Rekwoi came and looked about. He saw his food turned to stone, and some of it to ashes.[29] They were

26. The others had lined up somewhere about Rekwoi near the dancing place and had marched or danced in. He is going to have them begin in Wełkwäu and dance in boats all the way across the river. All these things that the myth represents as innovations are of course only faithful reflections of existing custom whose origin the Yurok know as little about as we—or less.

27. He had twenty headbands earlier in the story (*d*), but just previously has said ten.

28. Richest and most influential man in the town. He might be called a headman, but "chief" only by courtesy.

29. A reflection, as it were, of his shame at being outdone.

poor at Rekwoi now, and ashamed. They thought, "A (real) man is coming." They went down to the river's edge. Then some of the (Rekwoi) women turned to stone from shame when they saw that Tsuräu young woman coming—only one woman in the two boats. Many boats followed, but two were in advance, being danced in. They did not paddle them at all; they made the boats move by the leaping of the dance.

Now they landed and went up to the town. Then they (of Rekwoi) wanted to know where that man was from. They told them, "He is from Tsuräu." "Oh!" they said.

g. When they had ended the dance, Tsuräu young man said, "I am going on." The Rekwoi people said, "Do not go downstream.[30] There are no dances that way.[31] Follow the river and you will see many dances." The man from Wełkwäu said to him, "I will go with you, because I have been there." So he went with them upstream.

When they came near Wohtek,[32] they began to hear shouting. Then he said, "Now we are where they dance the Deerskin Dance." They sat down, those three; they wanted no one to see them. The one from Wełkwäu said, "Let us make a dance,[33] too. That is what we came for." Then Tsuräu young man said, "I think we will do it. We will go to the other side and dance across in a boat. That is how we shall do more than they.[34] That is something that they cannot do." "Yes, we will do that. Now let us hurry, for that dance will soon be over."

Then they started from the opposite side of the river in three boats. Whenever he called his boat: "I wish my boat were here," it was there from Tsuräu and all his property in it.

Now they reached the (Wohtek) side in their boats. The people wanted to know where they were from. Then they learned that one was from Wełkwäu, one from Tsuräu: there were only those two (men).[35]

h. When the dance was finished here, Tsuräu young man said, "I am going on. I want to go all over the world. I hear that the world has been made, but I think it is not all made. There will be sickness about if I do not finish it.

30. North along the coast, to the Tolowa.

31. This is not true. The Tolowa were wealthy, in Yurok opinion, and are (said) to have held a (Deerskin) dance, which would be absolute proof of riches. [Words shown in parentheses in this note were lightly crossed out by K. in his typescript.—Ed.]

32. Part of the cluster Wohkero-Wohtek-Ko'otep at Klamath Bluffs.

33. That is, a party entering or competing in the dancing.

34. Who dance only on land.

35. Who had equipped the dance and furnished the valuable paraphernalia for it. The dancers who wear them do not count; the girls may look at them, but a real man is interested in knowing who is wealthy enough to assemble so many treasures.

That is why I started out. I want to (finish) making (the world).''[36] ''Yes. When you come to Kepel you will see a great 'dance' (happening) there.'' ''That is what I want. That is not half-made. I shall make it. I want you all, from everywhere, to go there.'' They all said, ''Yes, we will go.''

Then he went upstream and came to downstream-of-Kepel, opposite Mūrek. There he stayed (for the night). That place was full of people. Then he said, ''In the morning we shall start. I shall make it in the morning.'' All night those people did not sleep, enjoying themselves.[37]

Next day they began to collect brush. He said, ''Let us gather brush and put it in the boats. Then let us go to see that weir. How many boats have we?'' Someone said, ''I think there are more than fifty here.'' ''Well, bring them together and put them next to each other. I am instituting it. You shall have this dance as long as the world lasts. You shall not lose it.''

He said, ''Let us try the dance,'' and first they held the brush in their hands and danced. He said, ''No, it does not look right. Put it on your heads. Now dance again.'' Then they put the brush on their heads and danced in the boats. Then it was good. The boats started, and, dancing, they went upstream until they came to Kepel, to where the weir was. Then they said to the persons of Kepel, ''You thought the dance was all made. You see that it was not half-made.'' The Kepel persons said, ''Yes, every day we wanted to see someone come. We knew it was not finished, because sometimes when we went down (to the dam or dance place) we got a headache or did not feel well. But when everything has been made, if a person comes to our fish dam he is well when he returns. Yes, this is what we wanted.'' He said, ''Let us go down to the river and make it now. All here are ready; that is why I brought them up.'' Then they went down to the river.

He said, ''Let us have ten boats on the other side of the river and ten on this side.'' Then they did it that way. Then they began to sing on the other side. Then they answered from Kepel. Then they began to dance in the boats and came to the dam. He said, ''When you reach the dam put the brush on it.''

i. Now there was a man about who looked as if he were foolish. Tsuräu young man asked him, ''Who are you?'' He said, ''You do not know me?'' ''No.'' ''I suppose you do not know my name?'' ''No, I do not know your name, nor where you are from, nor where you are going.'' ''I live downstream

36. Dances prevent pestilence, famine, flood. Earthqakes are due to their omission: the earth tilts and begins to slip. The great dances are at once the capstone of human life on earth and the buttress of the physical world. The Karok new year's ceremony which precedes the Deerskin Dance at Katimin—Segwu'—is called *isivsanen pikiavish,* ''earth making.''

37. The brief period when the great weir or ''dam'' is being erected and maintained at Kepel is one of games and jollity of every sort, ritualistic as well as informal, as might be expected from a gathering that drew visitors from the whole of Yurok territory besides a sprinkling from neighboring nationalities. [K. has a marginal note: ''But dam before Wohtek!''—Ed.]

from Kenek and have helped to make the world." Tsuräu young man thought, "I think I have heard about him. He is Coyote." That one said, "I will tell you my name. It is Coyote." "You had better help me. We shall have fun." "So be it."[38]

Then Tsuräu young man told the one from Wełkwäu, "Stay in the middle of the dam. Do not let anyone see you. Cover yourself up in the brush. I shall make it that someone comes there soon. I shall arrange what you will do." "What shall I do?" he said as he went to go. "When you see someone going by you, seize him; I shall cause him to pass by you."

Then he went to Coyote with a bunch of (iris) fibers for string. He said, "Coyote, do what I tell you." Coyote said, "Yes, I shall do it." He told him, "There is no fun here, no laughing. I should like to see them laugh before we go on to the next." "Yes." "Now I shall tell you what I want you to do. Go into the brush and make a beard of this string fiber. I shall give you a knife and the other things. Dress yourself well. What languages can you talk?" "I can speak many." "Do you think you can talk upstream language?"[39] "Yes, I can speak that well." "Well, let me hear you. Say, 'I am going home upstream.' When I ask you, 'Where are you going, old man?' I want you to say in upstream language, 'I am going home upstream.'"

Then Tsuräu young man said to four young men, "There is an old man sitting here. I think he is afraid. Perhaps he has done wrong somewhere and is afraid. I think he belongs upstream. Take him up in a boat. He is afraid to go by, fearing hurt might be done him." "Yes, we will take him up in a small boat." They went where they saw him sitting near the river. He had a quiver on one arm, a large knife in the other hand. They said, "Ayekwi, old man." He said, "Ha!"[40] "Where are you going, old man?" (In Karok): "I want to go upstream. I ran away with someone's wife. I am afraid to go by." "Old man, come into our boat. We shall take you by." "Ha!" "Yes, someone will do injury to you if you ran off with his wife." "Ha!" "Old man, you had better lie down in the boat (to conceal yourself)." "No, I shall watch carefully."

He took up his quiver of arrows and laid it on his thigh, took the knife in his right hand and held it up, and with the left he took hold of the edge of the boat. Then he said, "Now start!" Tsuräu young man said (to the crowd), "There is an upstream person who will go by here today." They looked down to the river and said, "He is coming. Four are poling[41] the boat. One is sitting up. He has a long beard, all white, and arrows lying ready, and a knife in his hand. Who will speak

38. *Tsuł.*

39. Karok.

40. Karok speech.

41. The Yurok paddle—except that used by the helmsman—is long and narrow. Probably a third or half of the Yurok stretch of the river can be better poled than paddled up, whereas in going downstream there is enough current to make the thick narrow blades suffice.

to that man going home upstream?" They said from along the edge of the water, "Old man, where are you going?" "*Tanipvaren*."[42] "Where do you live?" "Katimin." "Keep on, do not stop!" he whispered to those in the boat with him. "Good-bye, old man." "*Chimikuyak*,"[43] said Coyote.

Tsuräu young man went where the people were sitting. "What is the matter with him? He looks afraid. Perhaps he did wrong somewhere." One of them said, "I hear he has run off with someone else's wife. I think he is the man."

Then the Kepel man that owned the weir[44] called out (to the boat)," Pass through the middle! We have not finished it. It is not yet blocked. You can go through there!" "Yes," they said. Some of them knew that a man was hiding there on the weir; some did not know it. As the boat came near the middle of the weir, the old man in the boat watched closely, looking to both sides. "Do not stop![45] Go on!" he said.

The boat was nearly (at the gate in the weir) when that one who had hid himself on the dam stood up and said, "Why do you hold that big knife, old man?" "*Punositin*,"[46] he said, and began to stand up too. "He is the one that ran off with my wife! I know he is the one," cried the hider, and leaped into the boat. Coyote threw his knife into the water, saying, "You cannot have my knife."[47] All cried, "Stop them! The upstream person will be killed." Coyote threw his quiver into the water. "You cannot have that," he said. The four young men jumped overboard, and the two closed and wrestled alone in the boat. "The upstream person will be killed!" everybody shouted. "Stop!" they shouted. Coyote capsized the boat. They fought in the water and went under. Some wanted to stop them. "Swim to the other side! Run away, old man!" they shouted. They came out on the Kepel side. There was a little growth of brush there. Coyote leaped into it, tore off his beard, stepped out, and said, "Where has he gone? I could not hold him. I had to let him go." Some said, "Who is that that hid in the middle of the river?" "That was I,"[48] said Coyote. "I hunted for my wife all night. I knew that upstream man had her. I knew he was going to go upstream by boat. That is why I waited there."[49]

42. Karok: "I am going home."

43. Karok: "Good-bye."

44. The rich man, or *lo'*, of the place, who would boss the proceedings.

45. [K.'s marginal note: "Paddling now."—Ed.]

46. Karok: "I do not understand."

47. In the generation before 1850, a few Hudson's Bay knives filtered into Yurok possession through overland trade, and possibly also from ships that now and then made Trinidad. They were extremely valuable. The injured husband might be thinking more of damages than of revenge, in which case he would seize the knife to keep rather than to stab with.

48. He keeps up the game, eluding further pursuit by changing his appearance and pretending to be the pursuer.

49. This whole episode was apparently sometimes played at Kepel, perhaps an annual comedy.

j. Now Tsuräu young man had made half of the house[50] there, half of the dance. It took him two days to make it. When he had done, he said, "I shall go back to my house." The (head) man of Kepel said, "I want you to come when I start my dance each autumn." He said, "Yes, I shall be there." The one from Wełkwäu said, "That is the time that I shall come too." The one at Kepel said (to Tsuräu young man), "Do not walk downstream. I have ten boats. Take the best one. Keep it at Tsuräu."[51] "Yes, I shall go down in the boat," he said. Then he took the best boat in Kepel and went.

He stayed one night at Wełkwäu. The one there helped him to paddle the boat to Tsuräu. As he came to Tsuräu, everything looked good. His people were living there: they had grown while he was away. He had left only one house and one sweathouse. His people had taken care of them.

Next year he took all those people to Kepel. Every autumn, whenever they were about to make the fish dam, he went. He had one person (partner) who helped him to make his dance, one only: the one at Wełkwäu.

A2. Origin of Deerskin and Jumping Dances at Weitspus

This was previously published in Kroeber and Gifford, World Renewal, Appendix II, no. 8, pp. 117-20. [The notes were somewhat fuller in that journal.—Ed.] The myth is an institutional one, reflecting the dances as practiced, plus several tries at doing them a bit differently.

There are three characters, the instituter and two friends from Pekwtuł. These are made to travel, meet, converse, return, plan, and send word to each other, so as to build up a fairly involved plot in detail, in the manner characteristic of the informant; there is much moving about, but little feeling, and motivation remains external.

The main story (*a-g*) is the fairly bald instituting of the Deerskin Dance. Then follows (*h*) the somewhat more picturesque going off of the founder in his sweathouse, which leaps in stages up Rivet Mountain, thus instituting the Jumping Dance as a sequel. This portion resembles D6, but omits the episode of the girls (D6x*b, u*) and the long adventures at Dentalium Home (D6x*d-r*); the present part *h* is more narrowly institutional and has much lower emotional toning. The third part of our tale (*i-k*), about the going off of the Pekwtuł brothers, was told as a separate story, D5, by another Weitspus informant, though there the characters have nothing to do with instituting dances, being dentalia that determine where wealth will be greatest. The D5 story is simpler but more emotional; the sweathouse-moving of the present A2*h* recurs in it.

Thus it appears that Informant A wove three separately existing Yurok narratives into one (with liberal omissions where convenient), but preserved a thematic unity for his synthetic story by having all parts of it refer to the founding by the woge of the Weitspus world renewal and major dances.

•

50. [K. has queried "house."—Ed.]

51. He is making him a gift—something the Yurok are so chary of that it evidences great wealth.

a. He grew at Wespen.[1] He thought, "I have grown alone in this world." Once in the morning he thought, "I will walk upstream." He came to Weitspus. He saw tracks, and thought someone must live there. He looked across to the other side of the river. He thought, "I did not know this (Trinity) river before. I knew only one river. There is a fine sand beach below. I shall go to look at it." He went down, thinking, "There is another river here. It is a beautiful place. I am glad I grew (near) here. I shall make a dance here. I shall bring my house upstream."

He came to the sand bar and saw one sitting there at the path. He was a fine young man. "Where are you going?" that one asked. (Wespen young man said,) "I am going downstream to bring my house here. I want to make it that they will have dances here, because it is beautiful and they have two rivers. It is the first time I have been here. I always remained downstream." "Yes, I know that you were born there. I think you do not know where I grew." "No." "Look across to the other side.[2] I have a sweathouse there and a house. I grew there. I have a younger brother, a little boy. Well, go bring your house. Where do you think you shall put it?" "I shall put my house on this side (of the river)." "When you do so, I shall come across tomorrow in the middle of the day to see you." "Yes, it will be done by that time."

b. The next day (the other one) thought, "It is nearly the middle of the day." Then he came across (from Pekwtuł). He looked, but saw no house. The brush was thick all about. He walked upstream and downstream in Weitspus. Then he saw a house and the man (from Wespen) sitting outside. He said to him, "Where is your sweathouse?" "I wanted to know, before making my sweathouse, what sort I should have, and I waited for you. Now I shall make it quickly because I know that there are (human) people all along that (Trinity) river and all along this (Klamath) river. I want everything to be made when they arrive. I know now that we shall not remain here. There will be another kind of people in this world. We must hurry."[3] "You had better decide about your sweathouse today." "Yes, let us go."

Then they went to a spot near by,[4] and he said, "I will have my sweathouse here." Before he finished it, the sun had nearly set. He said, "Tonight we shall make a dance inside: the Jumping Dance. We shall wait until tomorrow in the

1. Wespen is about a third of a mile downstream from Weitspus. [See map 4, no. 16, in this volume.—Ed.]

2. To Pekwtuł.

3. Almost every other Yurok myth speaks of the great transformation as immediately impending. Taken literally, this would congest most of the events of their mythology into a few days. It is of course a stylistic device aimed at emotional heightening of each situation, such as is possible to a people at once unsystematic and devoid of exact time sense; an aesthetic exaggeration.

4. "The house pit behind Weitspus Johnny's house."

middle of the day. Then, if we hear that there is sickness, we shall change (the dance)."

Now it was sunset. Then they made a Jumping Dance in the sweathouse. They made it only a short time.

c. The next day, when it was nearly noon, a little boy came in. "Where are you from?" he asked him. "I live across the river. My older brother told me to tell you that sickness is coming[5] along the rivers. He said, 'Let him stop doing that with his sweathouse.'" "It is well. Tell him to come over again."

The little boy went and said to his brother (the Wespen man's companion from Pekwtuɫ), "He wants you over there again."

Then he (went across and) now saw a stone laid over the door of the sweathouse, so that the air could not come out. If it had come out, it would have made sickness. The one of Weitspus (Wespen) said, "Well, we shall see what we shall do. I have the skin of a year-old deer. It is fixed neatly and (the head is) stuffed with leaves." The one from opposite said, "I have other (dancing) things. I do not know what they are good for. Perhaps it will be well for us to put them together." "Yes, let us try it."

d. Then that one went to get his deerskin. When he brought it, he said, "This dance will be so. They will not begin in the morning. As long as this world lasts, if my dance is straight, they will begin toward evening. That is how it will be." Then toward evening they began. They began to make the dance from that place. They started down toward the sand beach. "How will they stand?" his friend asked him. "One will stand in the middle. He will face in the direction in which I grew (downriver). Some will turn to Hupa. Some will face upriver. So we shall reach all those places with the dance." "Yes," he said. And then they began to dance there.

In the morning his friend came over (from Pekwtuɫ) again and said, "That (also) did not go right. I think something bad will happen. Let us try the dance in another place."[6] "Yes. Let us wait until evening." Then they went to where the dance was to start. He said to them, "Try it (facing) downstream." Then they tried it. When they swayed their deerskins once, the sticks broke off where they held them. "I think it will be best if we bring it up to where my house is," he

5. This is a frequent Yurok concept, in and out of mythology.

6. The dance as now made was found by these instituters by trial and correction. Unsuitable paraphernalia were employed, the wrong place or time chosen, a faulty alignment attempted, and sickness, ill-ease, or other disadvantage resulted. When satisfactory consequences were finally obtained, they fixed as permanent the form of dance that had preceded them. This point of view, which is found in myth after myth, in those dealing with nature as well as those concerned with institutions, is evidently connected with the fact that the Yurok have little sense of creators or truly divine personages. Their woge, and even the individually named heads of these like Pulekukwerek, are a race more or less parallel to the human one; are after all only men of ancient days and somewhat enlarged powers.

said. Then they went uphill. When they came to where the dance place is (now), one of them said, "Let us try it here. Let the people go uphill; no one is to stand below. We shall stand in a row facing them, and hold the deerskins pointing uphill." Then they tried it so. When they saw it, they were happy. All felt good. Looking about, they saw everyone in the crowd smiling; some were laughing. The Weitspus young man said, "Well, how do you feel about it now?" "This is a good place. When I look away, I think that I see nearly the whole world, the day is so fine."

e. Now the little boy came from across the river. He said, "I do not think that, if I go where you want us to go, I shall be able to do without tobacco." "That is so," he said; "I do not know how they will give me tobacco after I am gone." "Well, I will tell you what I shall do. When I grew, I could talk the next day. Then I went out and talked to a rock. I know where it is. That is how I knew that they would always give us tobacco when they make this dance, if I brought that rock across to this (Weitspus) side. You, too, must find one." "Yes, I shall find one," said the Weitspus young man. Then the boy said to his older brother, "You find one too." "Yes, I will find it." The boy said, "We will bring them across and set them in the brush."

The next day they fetched their rocks across. They said, "Where shall we put them? We will put them farther up." Then they set the little boy's at one place.[7] They set his older brother's uphill; they counted how many steps away: it was eight steps. From there they measured downriver ten steps. The rock there belonged to Weitspus young man.[8]

Then the boy said, "How many (offering) places do you want?" "I want five," he said. Then they measured twelve steps downriver to the pepperwood tree. Then they returned and went four steps upstream from the first rock. There they set another rock, now covered. Then they went down to the dancing place. The boy said to his older brother, "Stand in the middle." To Weitspus (Wespen) young man he said, "Stand at the end. I shall stand here. Now listen. If any people ever forget what I say, it will not be good. If they do not lose what I say, this world will be good. Now you two listen to me."

Then they stood listening. The boy talked. "As long as the world lasts, this dance will be, and not one word will be mistaken. I want to leave this dance here. While the world stands, they will begin in only one way. They will go to my rock and speak to it and give me tobacco on it. We do not know where we are going, but we shall not live here. There will be others (in our place)."

Now he finished speaking. Then they began to dance. All were happy and smiled.

7. "In front of my house," said the narrator.

8. These rocks are no doubt among those addressed, with an offering of tobacco, when the formula for the Weitspus Deerskin Dance is spoken.

Next day, when they looked, they saw many people from the Trinity, from downriver, from upriver (come to watch). Weitspus young man thought, "That is the kind of dance I wanted to have."

f. Then one morning Pekwutł young man waited. He thought he should see them dancing. He did not see them. Next morning he thought, "I will go across and see. Something is wrong. They do not dance today." He came to Weitspus, to the dancing place, and saw no fire started. He went up, looked in the sweathouse, and saw no one. He went into the house, and saw no one there. He came outdoors again. Then he saw someone. He asked him, "Where is that one?" "He went away, I do not know where. He went last night."

In the afternoon, Pekwtuł young man said to his little brother, "Go across and make a dance. It is not good if we let two days go by. It will be that they must not miss a year. One summer they will have no dance; then the next year they must have it.[9] If we do not dance this evening it will not be right." Then the boy came across to below Weitspus. He began a dance that evening.

They waited four days, five days. Weitspus young man did not return. Sometimes the older brother, sometimes the boy, came across from Pekwtuł to make the dance.

g. Then one morning, sitting outside his sweathouse at Pekwtuł, he heard him (of Wespen–Weitspus) on the other side, bringing in sweathouse wood, and thought, "Now he has come back." He crossed and saw him sitting in his house. "You have been away long." "I was not here. I was not in this world. I was at the downriver end of the earth, at the very end. I know that it will be that I shall go off that way. I shall start tomorrow and come back in one day. It was a beautiful place where I was. You had better come with me."

"I do not think I shall go there. But I will ask my younger brother. Wherever my little brother wants to go, there I shall go."

"When I come back, tomorrow, I shall tell you what I shall do."

Then that one went back (to Pekwtuł) and entered his sweathouse. The little boy thought, "What is it?" He too went into the sweathouse. Then, after a time, his older brother talked. He said, "He is going to leave." The boy said no word.

h. The next day, at noon, the older brother went across and saw Weitspus young man sitting in his house. He (of Weitspus) said, "Well, I shall leave today. This my dance will be thus as long as the world stands. I shall take along my sweathouse, that is all." He looked at him and saw that he had a feather standing at the back of his head, and he held a Jumping Dance basket. Looking at him he thought, "How will he carry his sweathouse away? I do not believe it." He thought again, "He cannot carry his sweathouse." He said, "How will your dance be at the end?" "That is why I think I shall take my sweathouse. My

9. It is the usual Yurok practice to hold the dance at any one locality in alternate years.

dance will be a Jumping Dance at the last, when everything (else) is done.[10] I will make it so." Then he stood up and said, "Well, I go."

Then he entered his sweathouse. As soon as he began to look about in it, the sweathouse began to move, to turn. The one from Pekwtuł stood by outside. When he began to leap the Jumping Dance step inside, swinging his basket in his hand, the sweathouse flew up. Then it swung back to its place. Again he stood up and stepped and swung, turning, and the sweathouse flew up the hill. Then he made the Jumping Dance there for a little time. Then it flew farther up, to each dancing place, and the crowd of people followed. When he came to the summit where they dance, he stayed there for the night with his sweathouse. Then he gave them his instructions. He said, "Now, you Weitspus people, when you make this dance, do not eat below (in the town or on the way). Eat only when you arrive here."[11]

Then he went off with his sweathouse to the downstream end of the world.

i. Then Pekwtuł young man began to think, "Let me go off too." He went into his house and prepared his things. When it was nearly day he went outside. He went down to the river and stood on the spit between the two rivers. He stretched his hand downstream and thought if he felt wind against his hand he would not go that way. Soon he felt wind. He drew his hand back and stretched it uphill (north) and it was the same; then upstream and it was the same. Then he stretched it south (up the Trinity). Then he felt nothing. "I shall go that way."

He went and came to Oyegos.[12] He tried to sit down there. He did not feel well.

So he started again. He came to Alusei.[13] He tried to sit down there. He did not feel well, so he started again.

j. Then he came to Tepo'ohk where the Whilkut[14] live. There he stopped. Next morning, when it was nearly beginning to be day, he heard singing. He listened. Then he heard it again. He got up. He looked about and thought, "I shall have bad luck." Then he remembered: "Where is my brother? I forgot my little brother there!" Then he knew. He had left the boy still sleeping. Then he went outdoors, looking about, and thought, "He is the one who is singing, my little brother. I shall go back to where I grew, to get my little brother."

It did not take him long to return. He stood where he had had his

10. The Weitspus Deerskin Dance is followed by the Jumping Dance, held on the mountain behind the town.

11. All who dance, or go to watch, the Weitspus Jumping Dance may not eat from the night before until the last and highest dance spot is reached.

12. Oyegos is on Redwood Ridge.

13. Alusei is Liscum Hill, beyond, to the south.

14. The Whilkut were a Hupa-speaking group on upper Redwood Creek and lower Mad River. The Yurok had very little intercourse with them. Tepo'ohk was said to be inland from Eureka.

sweathouse (at Pekwtuł). His sweathouse was gone. Everything was gone. He sat down at the river. Then he watched if the Trinity would move. If it moved, he would see where his brother had gone. He saw nothing. He thought, "I shall stay here tonight. I may see him or hear him. Perhaps he will sing again tomorrow morning."

k. When it began to be day, he saw both the Trinity and the Klamath moving. He thought, "What is it?" He looked both ways. Before long he heard a dance coming on this side and on that side. Soon it was full day, and he saw a round fog moving down on the water, one fog down the Trinity, one down the Klamath. They were dancing in boats (inside the fogs). He thought, "I will stop them. I will speak first to the one coming down the Klamath." He said, "Stop!" Then they stopped in the middle of the river, but they did not come to him (at the shore). Then he said to the one on the Trinity, "Stop!" He said, "No, I will not stop. I shall go on. You thought I should not know where you were. You left me in the sweathouse, my older brother. You did wrong. Now I shall do something too. You shall hear of me. I too shall make things. Let me pass, my brother. You will know that you wronged me. But I shall live thus and have a name. You take a name too. Mine will be Kewomer.[15] Now I go." Then he asked the one in the boat on the Klamath, "What is your name?" "Mine is Kermerwermeri."[16]

Then his younger brother went on. Every evening he comes down the Trinity and his friend comes down the Klamath, and every evening they go downstream (and across the ocean) to where Wohpekumeu lives, and dance. Every morning they come back upstream.

A3. The Lo'olego Dance

This is also an institutional myth, but of less extreme type than the preceding ones. An insult offered to the hero's brother stirs the latter to attempt his achievement. Tsuräu young man (of A1) and Wespen young man (of A2) grow and wish for a dance and attain it because it is their nature to do so; they are clearly immortal woge, though thoroughly humanized ones. The Lo'olego hero is a man. The dance is already established; he merely adds a feature, and one that is not essential. A ceremony is a ceremony whether parties from three or from four towns appear in it. That Lo'olego came to participate is in the native mind not so much a fulfillment of the rite as a triumph for the family that proved wealthy enough to equip a dance party. In this sense the tale approaches hero stories, of which several are given below.

The pitying of the despised youth by a supernatural being is not only an idea familiar to most Indians as something that occurs constantly, but it is a favorite motive in myths of

15. Kewomer is usually the son of Kapuloyo and grandson of Wohpekumeu; see F2, for example.

16. Compare the invisible Kermerwermeri boatload of dancers at the end of D7.

the popular plot type. It enters also into clear hero stories, like that of Kewetspekw (A13).

For once the narrator tells his story in brief compass, and does not bring characters into relation to each other. The Weitspus people represent public opinion, first insolent, then ashamed, but a collective sentiment. The hero, his brother, and his father count only as a single personage: they are of one family, actuated by one motive, and they share in their triumph. The Long One, though kind, is wholly a monster; he does not even speak to the hero.

It is not without significance that a Weitspus narrator should throw himself with enthusiasm into depicting the discomfiture of his town by its little neighbor. It is true that the metropolis is merely rebuked for arrogance, not humbled in defeat. Yet local pride as such could not have been very potent to allow this story to be told with unaltered setting. The circumstance illustrates that, whatever sentiment might attach to locality, the town as such was rarely a true organ in Yurok society.

•

a. A young man lived at Lo'olego[1] with his brother. One summer he said to his older brother, "Go to Weitspus, so that we may make the fish dam soon, in a month, or less." Then the older brother went downstream to Weitspus. He told the young men, "Come up tomorrow (to help us). We want to begin making the dam." One of the young men said, "No. I know what you are thinking of." "No. We are thinking of nothing. We only wish to make our fish dam." But he kept saying, "I know what you are thinking." Then he said, "What do we think?" Then he told him, "(You think you can make a Deerskin Dance), but you cannot, because you have nothing." "Yes, that is so." That is all the young man from Lo'olego said.

Then he went back home. He did not go by the trail (along the river) but up on the mountain. He came to the very top. There he gathered sweathouse wood. He thought of what the Weitspus man had said. It made him angry. Then late, he came back. His younger brother thought, "What is wrong? He never did that before." He was crying when he went into the sweathouse. He cried so that he could hardly make the fire. Then he went down to the river and bathed. Then his younger brother said, "Did you go into the sweathouse?[2] You have been away long." "Yes," he said. Then he told what the Weitspus people had said. The other said no word. Then they made fire in the sweathouse all night.

b. In the morning, the old man, their father, knew what they were doing

1. Lo'olego is a small town 2 miles upstream from Weitspus. [See map 4, no. 30, in this volume.—Ed.] It and Kepel were the only places at which the Yurok built salmon weirs across the Klamath. The Lo'olego dam appears to have been of local importance only, and is much less frequently mentioned.

2. As we might say, "You went into the sweathouse, did you not?"

and said, "You are men.[3] You can make a Deerskin Dance if you wish to. If you do what I tell you, you will have all you want in not two years." Then the younger brother said, "Tell us what we are to do." "Bring sweathouse wood for ten nights.[4] I will prepare what you are to use."

Then they did that, both of them. They did not desist from carrying sweathouse wood. A young man from Weitspus came up to see about the making of the dam. He asked, "When do you begin?" They said, "We shall not begin. We are going upstream.[5] We go tomorrow. I think we shall begin (the dam) next month."

c. Then, for nine days, the old man prepared everything, and was ready, and the tenth day came. Then he said, "Which of you will do it?" The older brother said, "I will." "Come with me. I will show it to you," his father said. Then they went down to the rock Huksarekw.[6] They had a basket wholly smeared with pitch, and with its cover pitched. The old man said, "You can feel the hole under the water there. Go into it. Inside there is no water. You can make fire there.[7] You will have fire in your basket. But do not stay long. If water falls on your head once, come out at once. Do not wait and think, 'I will wait until it falls on me a second time.'"[8]

Then the young man went into the water and entered the hole and there was a ringing noise. Then he sat there. Now he felt water drip on his head. Then he thought, "I will wait for another drop." Then he saw something coming, a white one. He tried to rise but could not. His foot was fast to a rock. That which was coming had twenty horns, curved horns in a circle on its head.[9] It was as long as a log. It hooked him, held him fast on its head, and swam downstream. It swam to the mouth and across the ocean with the man still on its head.

They came somewhere and he heard talking. Then the one that carried him said, "I have brought him. He wants to make the Deerskin Dance and the Jumping Dance. He would like to have those dances." "Well, take him back

3. *Pegerk,* a man; also a real, able, wealthy, or brave man. Their father is not referring to their age.

4. The usual magico-ritualistic procedure for satisfying a wish.

5. Naturally they were keeping their purpose to themselves and did not wish a crowd of visitors about. An evasive or deceptive answer is habitual to a Yurok as soon as he has any business.

6. Huksarekw is a large rock in the river, between Lo'olego and Weitspus. The name means "sitting children."

7. To warm himself after his immersion.

8. A cave or cleft is pointed out near Tsuräu, on the coast, which people desiring good future—that is, wealth—were also directed to remain in only until water dripped on them once. [Cf. other such caves and instructions in tales T3 and X15.—Ed.] The cavity with submerged entrance at Huksarekw may be imaginary.

9. It was Knewollek, "Long One," the giant horned serpent of the water.

with you." He heard them say that. Then he thought he had been gone only a day, but he had been gone nearly a year.[10]

d. He had a sister. Once, in the morning, in spring, she went uphill to get wood. She was carrying her load, and sweated. Then she wanted to rest. She went to a spring and thought, "I will wash my face." Then she saw something lying there by the water, as white as could be. She thought, "It looks like a person." Then she saw that he was alive. She thought, "I will take care of him." Then he spoke to her with his hands. He held up his finger and pointed to his breast. Then he pointed down hill toward Lo'olego. Then he held up three fingers.[11] So he told her that he was her brother. Then she cared for him. She (went and) told her father, and they carried him to the house.

They told no one. They rubbed him all over with marrow. In about ten days his hair (?) grew and his hair (?) grew again.[12]

e. Then his younger brother constantly found money.[13] He always bought with it. The sick man had become well. Now it was nearly summer and they owned several white deerskins. They had bought them.[14] Then the old man prepared.

Now the Weitspus people came (to Lo'olego) to make the fish dam. After they had made (and used) the dam they went back to Weitspus and made the Deerskin Dance.[15] No one knew that there would be a dance (party)[16] from

10. The monster, in returning, went north from the place across the ocean, then east, and then swam down the Klamath, the narrator replied to a query as to the return route.

11. "I—am from Lo'olego—there were three of us brothers and sisters."

12. [Question marks by K. indicate possible omission or mistranslation.—Ed.]

13. Dentalia. *Tsīk* denotes these shells, but has about the force of our "money." The younger brother probably did not find money lying about, but it came to him, as the Yurok say, at every turn. Every venture proved lucrative. So, when a man has spoiled his luck, his dentalium shells leave him: he buys unwisely, fritters away his substance. The tsīk will not remain with him. [For a psychoanalytic discussion, see S. H. Posinsky, Yurok Shell Money and 'Pains,' *Psychiatric Quarterly,* 30: 598-632, 1956.—A. D.]

14. Ordinarily the Yurok say that white deerskins were too valuable to pass in trade. They were worth more, it would seem, than a very rich man's life. The selling family would lose its chiefest prestige. It is likely that most of them were never sold except when first bought by a very wealthy man from the lucky hunter who had killed an albino deer. At least, such is the impression the Yurok gave in their statements.

15. This passage proves that the Weitspus Deerskin Dance stood in much the same relation to the Lo'olego dam as existed between the Wohtek-Wohkero dance and the Kepel dam, and between the dances and First Salmon observances at Wełkwäu and Enek (Karok Amaikiaram). [K. had a notation, "see Hupa"; according to Kroeber and Gifford, World Renewal, p. 60, the Hupa did not hold their great Deerskin and Jumping dances in connection with the First Salmon ceremony at Xaslinding.—Ed.]

16. The richest man of each of the neighboring towns assembles his regalia and those of his relatives and friends at a distance and uses it to equip a party of young men who attempt to outvie the other parties in their song, movement, and especially the splendor and value of what

Lo'olego. Then they thought, "What is it with those upstream persons? No one has come." Then one who had been fishing at the dam said, "There are many people at Lo'olego. I hear that they will have a dance." "Oh, they cannot do it," they said.

Then once,[17] in the morning, they heard many people in the open flat near the river just upstream from Weitspus. Many boats were (lying) there. Then they heard a dance coming. The Weitspus people did not say a word, but went into their houses; the women, the men, and the old men. Some of the (other) people told them, "It is a good dance. They have three white deerskins. It is a beautiful dance." But not one Weitspus person came out to look at the dance. All stayed in their houses.[18]

f. Then the Weitspus people said: "Nevertheless I[19] think they will not be able to go up on the hill."[20] Then, when they had finished dancing at Weitspus and the people went up the hill, a dance came from Lo'olego up the mountain to Arohpets, and from there downstream to the place (of the Jumping Dance).

A4. Arrow

This tale may be of Hupa origin. It is wholly localized in Hupa Valley. It is another pure institutional myth, although all that it is concerned with are arrows, creek dams, nets, and boats. Clash of feeling, escapes, love, stirring events are wholly lacking. It is an able teller who can sustain interest in such a theme; and it is an unusual art that devotes itself to such unadventurous topics. The pride of Arrow in his destiny is well portrayed; and his young friend, who carries the thread of the plot, evokes, if not appeal, at least interest. Even Pyageɫ young man is more than a bare foil: one who can stretch a concealable little thing into a canoe is something of a man. In fine, though the key is low, there is distinct interplay of characters, and their emotions are dexterously if lightly indicated. The effect is heightened through the discussion by the personages (and by the people at large) of each other.

As usual in such stories, all the actors are nameless. They are also thoroughly

they wear and carry. The home village appears last in a dance. Thus at Weitspus, the towns of Wahsek, Pekwtuɫ, Lo'olego, and Weitspus competed.

17. The dances continue, for a short time daily, for ten or more days.

18. [K.'s marginal note: "Shame."—Ed.]

19. The usual number even when a mass speech is quoted, and logically. Each man speaks his opinion, not on behalf of a body.

20. The Deerskin Dance is made directly in front of the town. The Jumping Dance begins just uphill from Weitspus and proceeds by stages several miles up the mountain, where it culminates and ends. The Weitspus people in their humiliation console themselves with the conviction that the sudden wealth of the Lo'olego family will not suffice to furnish the second dance, for which the costumes are different. They are disappointed even in this last hope. It is not clear whether the narrator attributes their shame wholly to being surpassed or as accentuated by their previous taunts.

humanized. The future Arrow is a young man with a house and a fishing place, baskets, and paint. He grows only with a predisposition to his ultimate condition, as it were; and in the main he makes himself what he will be. Snipe is not even hinted at as being an animal until the story is over. When others take to the hills and the remote places abroad, he appears to become the bird because of a longing to remain close to the river by which he grew, fished, traveled, formed friendships, and lived his so satisfactory career. [K. has a marginal notation: "Personification of objects."—Ed.]

•

a. At Kererwer[1] was where Arrow began to be. A person grew (near) there (also). He thought, "I grew here." He made Socktish Creek and Mill Creek flowing (into the Trinity) opposite it.

Once, in the morning, he thought, "I will go down to the river." He came opposite the mouth of Socktish Creek and looked across the river. Then he saw something and thought, "What is that? I had better go see." Then he went across and looked. He thought, "I did not think that anybody was here. But now I feel it. It seems to me as if I could see somebody." Then he saw that someone had been at work on Mill Creek. He had made a fish dam. It crossed the creek, appearing pretty. He looked to the middle and saw that something was hanging there. Something was at the farther end also. Then he went close and looked down at the end near him and something was hanging there too. Three were hanging in three places. He thought, "I will go to see what are hanging." Then he found out: they were work (*rumitsek*) baskets. He thought, "Oh, that is the kind they are. There must be someone here who did that. I will look for him. He must live somewhere about."[2]

When he came to the top of Kererwer (hill), he saw someone sitting there. He looked at him a long time, thinking, "He looks like another kind of person." That one wore a feather on one side only, to the top of his head. He had grown thus. Then he thought, "I will speak to him." "Well,[3] you are sitting here." "Yes, but I shall not sit here always. You think I am only sitting; but this is where I live. Here is where I grew." "Have you never gone about here?" "Yes.

1. Kererwer is described as a hill in Hupa Valley, at its western edge, near the west-side village called Kererwer by the Yurok, Cheindekotding by the Hupa, and Socktish(?) by the whites. It was unoccupied in 1850. Socktish Creek flows from the west into the Trinity nearby; the mouth of Mill Creek is more or less opposite on the eastern bank. Apparently Kererwer is also used less specifically, since Arrow is described as growing at Kererwer and having his house on the hill, and after his departure his friend from across the river is spoken of as Kererwer person. At any rate, it is clear that Arrow grew on the east side and used Mill Creek for his dam, and that the young man who visited him came from the western side and transferred the dam to Socktish Creek whenever he pleased. [K. has a marginal reference to the map in Goddard, Life and Culture of the Hupa, and to Kroeber, Handbook, p. 129.—Ed.]

2. [K.'s marginal note: "Connect dam with arrow."—Ed.]

3. *Tsũł*.

At the mouth of the creek I have made what I was going to make. Did you not see it?" "Yes, I saw it. Well, I live on the other side." "Yes?" "I am going back now. I shall see you again sometime." "Yes, but I think that when you see me next you will not know me." "Who are you?" "After a time everybody will like me. Now it is the beginning, and I have not yet made myself. Soon I shall make myself as I am to be so that I shall look well. I will tell you what I shall become; when I see you again I will tell you that. I want to see you again."

b. He was beginning to think, "I do not look well. I have on one feather, but I had better have two." Then he went down to where his fish dam was, thinking, "Perhaps I shall find another feather at my fish dam." He looked but found nothing. Then he looked into one of his baskets and saw a feather there. Then he took it and put it on his head, from the top down on the opposite side. Now he was wearing two. Then he thought, "I think it will look better if I wear three. I think I should be better if I had three. Tomorrow I must go to my fish dam again. Perhaps I shall find another."

Then next day he went down to his fish dam and in the third basket he found another feather. The three feathers were different. One was red, one black, and the third different from both. He thought, "I think it is right that I did not find them all of one color. It looks better." Then he went to his house. He put the (third) feather on his nose over his forehead, and to the top of his head.

Then he thought, "Now if I paint myself it will be the last thing. I will go down to the middle basket and look in it." There he found something small, very red, and something that was black, and something blue.[4] Then he went up to the house and painted himself (horizontal stripes on the cheeks and legs).[5] Then he felt good and said, "I think that is all. I wish I were to see that one from across the river. I wish he would come today." He went out and sat down outside his house. Then he saw him coming up.

(The visitor) looked at him only a little[6] and thought, "That is the kind of person he is! I did not think such a one would grow as I now see."

c. Then that (sitting) one said, "Did you pass my dam below?" "Yes, I came by there." "Did you see nothing?" "Yes, I saw many fish." "That is good. Well, I am sorry for you. I always look across to the other side. You have made nothing at all for yourself. I do not know; perhaps you have provided for yourself, but I do not see it. I do not know what you will turn into, since you do not seem to care for anything. I pity you. I shall give you my fishing place. I shall give it and you shall live by that. Today will be the last day for me. I am

4. Modern Yurok bows and arrows are usually painted red and blue, but it is not known what pigment could have been used for the latter color before contact with Americans. Perhaps there was such a custom; or the story may be projecting the present into the past.

5. As arrows are painted with transverse bands.

6. Staring would probably be bad manners. The Yurok do not look one another in the eye much.

going away. All over this world people will be glad to see me. Young men will like me very much. Today is the last day you will see me. I shall give you my fishing place and you will use it. You will get your food from it. Come over tomorrow and see me start. I shall fly. Do you know my name? You must remember this place of mine. You must tell that I grew here. I grew here at Kererwer. I made this place myself. My name is Nerukret (Arrow). Few men will know that I grew here. A man who knows how I grew and how I made myself will always have good luck. Whoever knows how I began will be lucky. You must see me in the morning."

Then (that person) went back across the river. He thought, "I will not sleep. Perhaps he will leave during the night. I want to hear him if he goes." He did not sleep but sat outside the sweathouse all night, watching. In the morning he thought, "Well, I had better cross. I heard nothing last night. Perhaps he is still there."

Then he came to his house and saw him. He (Arrow) said, "Well, I am about to start. I will tell you what you must do. You must take care of this fishing place, that belonged to me." "Yes, I will do that." "Tell me what you will do if you catch nothing at the mouth of this creek?" "I think I will make a creek be on the other side, so that if I catch nothing here it will not be hard for me to move the fish dam across to the other side." "Yes, do that. That is good." "I will do it tomorrow. You say you will be everywhere and all will like you?" "Yes." "Perhaps you will lie outdoors in numbers when you become old." "No, do not be afraid of that. I do not know now where I shall go when I begin to be old. After a time I shall find where to go; but no one will know where I shall be. You will never find my feathers lying about in this world, not half of a single feather. When I feel that I am beginning to become old, then I shall find where I shall go. Well, now I shall start. You must keep up my fishing place. It will be good for you hereafter. Now come, let us go outdoors. There you can help me."

d. When they were outdoors he said, "Now stand downstream from me and I shall stand a little upstream from you. Now I will first go this way, upstream, and you must stand here until I come back." He turned (facing) up (the Trinity). "Now blow at the back of my neck, gently, so that I may start easily." Then he blew him gently and saw him flying upstream. So he stood there.

Then that one came back again. He said, "Now I know that I am right. Now I want to go that way (up the Klamath)." Then he faced in that direction. "Now blow on me and stand here. I shall come back." Then he blew, and before long that one came back. "I am right now. I know the whole world. This is the last time. But you must go down and make that place of mine as you will use it for yourself. I shall not return. I shall go downstream, down to the mouth and to the end (of the world). It is the last time you will see me." He believed him. Then he started. He thought, "It is the last time that I see him."

e. Then he went down the hill. He worked on the fishing place that he had left him.[7] Then he thought, "Let me make it on the other side too." Then he crossed to his house and made Socktish Creek. Whenever he wanted fish he went down to the river. If he had not caught many, he carried the dam across to the mouth of the creek on the opposite side. So he lived.

f. It was not ten days that that one had left, and he heard that all over the world everyone liked arrows. He thought, "That is what he said: 'All will like me.'"

Then once he thought, "Let me go upstream." Then he started and came to Oplego (Takimiłding, Hostler). He saw the young men carrying arrows. He thought, "You are carrying those arrows for pleasure. You do not know where he was born whom you are carrying, but I know it."

He went on upstream. He came to Kohteł (Medilding, Matilton). He saw them all carrying arrows and he thought regretfully of that one. "I know where he was born. I know how he left. I helped him."

g. Then a person there said: "There is a person living on the other side. We do not know him. We do not know how he lives. Every morning we hear him carrying sweathouse wood." Then he thought, "I will go there across the river."

Then he went across to Pyageł (Howunkut, Kentuck). When he arrived he saw a person sitting by his sweathouse. He went to him and looked at him. He thought, "He is a good-looking young man, tall and slender." He said to him, "You are sitting here?"[8] "Yes. Are there good persons downstream?" "Yes, there are many young men. Have you never been there?" "No. I somewhat wanted to go about, but I looked at myself and found that I had nothing to wear and to carry. I grew up poor. I do not know what I shall do for myself. I do not know at all." Then he was sorry for him. He said, "Is that so? Is that why you do not go about?" "Yes, that is why I do not go." "Well, I shall see you again tomorrow. I am going home now." "Where is your house? How far is it?" "Oh, it is not very far. I shall come upstream to see you again tomorrow."

Then as he went downstream on that (western) side of the river, while he was walking he pitied that good-looking young man. He thought, "Tomorrow I will provide for him so he may go about."

7. Characteristic omission of names. Arrow has been talking. The person believes him. Arrow starts. The person thinks it is the last time he will see Arrow. The person goes downhill to the fish dam that Arrow has left him. The simple English "he" is interminably confusing. Yurok speech may have a device for distinguishing; or, more likely, the listener may be supposed to be familiar with the thread of the story.

8. A polite greeting, not a request for information. Avowed curiosity might engender suspicion, but a comment on what is obvious is received with genuine satisfaction. It proves that one is not to be put on the defensive.

In the morning he started upstream and arrived. Then he saw that outside about his sweathouse it was clean. He looked in the sweathouse and did not see him. He thought, "I do not know where he went." He tracked him and saw that he had gone down to the river. Then he saw him there. He had something pretty[9] at the edge of the water, covered with brush. "You are here again?"[10] he said. "Yes, I have come again. I started this morning. What have you there?" "I have tried everything. Now I have tried this. Look at it," and he threw the brush off. Then he saw a very small thing there, as long as a finger. He said, "Yes, you have done well. You had better cover it again. I know what it is for."

Then they went up to the house. He said to him, "Come with me. Let us go downstream." "I am afraid to go downstream." "You need not fear. I will help you. You cannot always be here. You must go about and have pleasure." "If you think you can help me to prepare myself, I will go with you part way." "Yes, I wish you would come with me to where I live. I wish you would go downstream and see my fishing place. You must try to use what I have downstream." "Well, so be it."[11]

Then they went down to the river and took two paddles with them. They came to the water. Then Pyageɫ person thought, "Let me make it bigger." Then he took out the little thing that he had covered with brush, and stretched it. He said, "How long shall I make it?" Then he made it as long as a boat is. Then they started in it and came to Kohteɫ, and Kererwer person said, "We will get out here for a while.." Then they landed. Then they started again and got out at Oplego and stayed there.[12]

h. Then they started downstream again and came to his fish dam. That one looked at the fishing place. He said "Did you make it yourself?" "No." "Well, I must go back. It will be late." "Yes." Then he went back alone.

Then he thought, "Let me go downstream again to see my friend." Then he went to a Kohteɫ young man. He said to him, "I saw something good. Let us go downstream." They stopped at Oplego and took another young man. They came to the fish dam and saw Kererwer person there with his net. He had caught trout with the net, some on each side of the creek. Then he gave them some. He gave Oplego young man five, Kohteɫ young man five, and five to Pyageɫ young man. So they found where fish would be caught.

Next day ten went down from Oplego to see that, and ten from Kohteɫ, and five from Pyageɫ. Kererwer young man was in his house and looked down to the river and said, "There are many below at the fishing place. Let me take two

9. [K.'s marginal note: "Device-hinting."—Ed.]

10. Another greeting.

11. *Tsūɫ*.

12. [K. marginal note: "The two big towns."—Ed.]

more nets down and have one for the middle and one for each end of the dam." Then he took two more nets. Then he arranged them and said, "Now use these." Then they took the nets and fished and caught. In the middle of the day he said, "Let us stop and divide what we have caught and you can go home to eat. Come again in the evening if you like." Then he gave them fish until all had some,[13] and they carried them upstream. Then all learned where the fish came from.

An old man at Erlern[14] said to the people, "Go downstream to see. I hear someone is catching fish." "Yes," they said. "Wait until those from upstream[15] come," he said. Then they watched for them. When those came they said, "Where are you going?" "To the fish dam downstream." "We wish to go with you." Then they went with them and saw where the fishing was. Then Kererwer person told an Erlern young man, "You fish!" "Yes, I will try," he said. Then he fished. Then he liked fishing. He felt good. It looked well to him when he caught fish. In the evening (the owner of the place) said, "Now we will stop. You had better go home." Then he gave out the fish.

Old men said, "Did he make that dam himself?" Someone said, "No. But I do not know how he got it." Pyageł young man said, "I hear that someone else made that fishing place." Then some young men said, "Yes, I think so. He himself would not be able to find it out. Perhaps someone else made it to be there."

i. Then once an old man from Oplego said, "This is the last for you all. There will be another people." That day all went downstream saying, "This will be the last day." Kererwer person said, "Yes, I know. There will be other people. It is the last day for you, but not for me. The others who will be here will always see me. I shall always be about. I like this fishing place because I knew the one who left it to me. So I shall not leave it. You can scatter abroad, but I shall stay here and take care of my fish dam. As long as the world lasts I shall be on these streams."[16]

Then the next day they scattered and others came. Only Kererwer person did not go away. He is the little bird along the river, with a white neck. His name is Tseile'l.

13. They have been doing the fishing, but apparently it is he as owner of the fishing place and of the nets who distributes the catch.

14. Tołtsasding, a former village on the flat where the government school, west of the river, stands. The site was unoccupied in 1850.

15. [K.'s marginal note: "Pyageł."—Ed.]

16. The two large Hupa towns, Oplego and Kohteł (Takimiłding and Medilding in Hupa), on the east side of the Trinity, are drawn into the story, but Kererwer, Pyageł, and Erlern on the west side (the first and last abandoned in 1850, and Pyageł not very large) account for the origin of arrows, weirs and nets, and boats. [See map 1, nos. 37-41, in this volume.—Ed.]

A5. Obsidian

a. At Sakts'aree[1] he was a young man. Each morning he sat outside his sweathouse, looking. Then, once, in the morning, he saw something like fire coming down the middle of the river. Now he thought, "Tomorrow I will watch closely." In the evening he went down to his boat and laid his paddle in it.[2] In the morning he went to the river and sat. When he saw it coming, it looked like fire passing downstream in the middle of the water. Then he jumped into his boat, thinking, "I will catch it," and started after it. As soon as he was near, it sank; he could not see it anymore. Then he saw it repeatedly downstream, and pursued it, and each time it sank. At Mekwtegen[3] he thought, "I cannot take it," and desisted. He ran up on the rock at Mekwtegen and looked. Sometimes it crossed the river and then came to the nearer side again. Then it would move on downstream.

Now (having returned), he laid his paddle on the sweathouse and thought, "I will go to get sweathouse wood." When he was on the mountain, he wept continually. "I want to get it. I want to see what it is." He carried down sweathouse wood continually.[4] He only thought,[5] "I want to find it. I want it. I will watch for it." Then he came to Weitspus, thinking, "Downstream the river is wide, but here is a good place. I will watch whether it comes down the Trinity or down the Klamath."

b. In the morning he came upstream to Weitspus again, and watched. Then he saw the thing coming down the Trinity. "I shall catch it now. I shall set a snare for it there," he said. All day he worked making a snare, over on the other side[6] of the Trinity. Then he sat there (before dawn). When it was day, he saw the thing at the end of the sandspit between the rivers; then he knew that it

1. An uninhabited spot evidently between Weitspus and the fishing rocks Mekwtegen and Meɫnega mentioned below. [K. has a marginal note referring to an unspecified notebook of his and the spelling Hohsarek(?)—Ed.]

2. To have it ready. Paddles are usually kept on the house or sweathouse roof, as mentioned in the story below.

3. Mekwtegen is a fishing place on the north bank of the Klamath, 1 1/2 miles below Weitspus. Waterman, Geography, map 25, no. 8. [This map is reproduced here as map 4.—Ed.]

4. Always a meritorious act and, in practice as well as myths, the most usual means to attain any vehemently desired end. The wood should be cut from the tops of tall firs well up on ridges; it should be burned in a fire by which the devotee sweats; and he should weep and utter or think his wish during the whole procedure. This ritual is often continued for ten summer days, during which food restraints are observed and no water is drunk. The ritual practice is, however, only an accentuation of the daily habit of Yurok men.

5. He allowed no other thought to enter his mind. Intensive wishing is as important a means of attaining realization as are the hardships endured and the ritualistic observances.

6. The narrator is on the Weitspus side of the mouth of the Trinity.

had come down the Klamath. Now he left that place and went upstream from Weitspus and made another snaring place.

Then, in the morning, he watched for it from Pekwtuł.[7] He watched both rivers; but when he first saw it, it was (already) downstream from him, where the two rivers have flowed together. Then he thought that he might not be able to catch it. He crossed the river, took his snare, and went downriver to Mełnega.[8] There he made ready. He thought, "I will try once more. It will be the last time." He was still going up on the mountain every day to bring down sweathouse wood, weeping. He did not eat, for he wished so much to catch it.

Then (early in the morning) he sat down on a rock in the river at Mełnega. On the right he set his snare,[9] on the left a net. Now it was nearly daylight. Then he felt that it just touched his snare. He looked and found that only one place in the snare was not right. That is where it had passed through. Then he made that part as it should be.

c. In the morning he went there again. Now he had not been there long, with his snare entirely underwater, when it was not moving at all. So he waited. At last he thought, "I will stop. I will not try anymore. I will take out of the water what I have been using." He had seen no fire (passing). Then he drew his net into his boat; and then his snare. He thought, "Why is it so heavy?" Then he saw that he had caught something. The snare held it around the middle, and it seemed pretty. "That is the one I tried to catch!" he said. He laid it in the boat, and with a basket dipped in water. He thought, "Let me put in a little more water," and added until there was enough for it to swim about a little. Then he thought, "I will hide and see what it will do. It looks as if it were trying to move. It has been accustomed to swim everywhere." Then he sat down behind his boat.[10]

Soon he heard the water splash as that one moved about in the boat. Whenever it touched the boat, there was a ringing sound. The young man thought, "It is the one that I wanted!" Then he went to it and saw that it was running in the water like a salmon.

d. Then he spoke to it. He said, "Hi! I am glad I caught you. I am surprised to have caught you. I have thought about you for a long time and desired to catch you. I had no one to speak to. I was alone. That is why I caught you."

7. The town between the two rivers, opposite Weitspus.

8. A fishing rock near the south side of the Klamath, less than a quarter of a mile above Mekwtegen. It is no. 11 of the same map of Waterman and is diagonally across from and above the river's edge pictograph Abtemar-ha'äg (Waterman, no. 10).

9. The word for "snare" was not recorded. It may be a generic one meaning snare or trap, or any device for taking.

10. He was probably fishing off a rock at Mełnega. When he beached his boat nearby, he could squat on shore in the brush to watch.

Then he saw the water moving again. Then he began to know that it was thinking, "I will speak to him." Thereupon he said, "Yes, that is why I want to keep you, because I have no one to talk with." Then it said, "I wanted to go from that place where I grew. I thought no one would know what I was for. Now it is well: I shall be about the world. Sometimes I shall not live in a town.[11] Sometimes I shall live in a rich town, just one of me, or perhaps two. There will not be many towns where there are two of me; they will be few. But I shall be all over the world. This is the last time that I shall talk to men. You will keep me. I shall endure as long as human beings dance.[12] I shall be beautiful and valuable. I shall be worth much even if I am only a little piece. I do not like to tell you where I come from."

The young man said, "Let it be the same to you. I will keep you. If you tell me where you grew, I shall be able to tell people." "Well, then, so be it." "Well, what will you tell me?" "My name is Obsidian.[13] The name of the best of me is Red Obsidian,[14] Sokto. I grew upstream, not in the sky, but before one comes there. There is a cold spring there, Aterpr.[15] That is where I grew." That is the last it said to him.

e. Then the young man took it[16] up to his house. He is the one that caught Obsidian. If it had not been for him there would be no obsidian blades in the world.[17]

A6. Death

This tale was announced as relating to the origin of death, and, as this subject is usually related, Wertspit, the larval form of the Jerusalem cricket, is the principal agent. But there is curiously little about death in this version. Mole and Wertspit assemble followers and secretly go about in order to ruin what has been well established in the world; yet if human death is one of the results of their activity, it is only indirectly implied by the tale. Perhaps this incident, the oft-told kernel of the story, was so familiar to the teller that he slighted it, and elaborated events of more trivial consequence that lent themselves better to an active narrative. There is a constant going, coming, hiding, reporting, conferring,

11. Meaning "I shall be so valuable that there will be whole towns without one of me."

12. Which will be as long as the world lasts. For the exhibition of obsidian in dances, see Kroeber, Handbook, pp. 26-27, pp. 53-62 *passim,* and pl. 2.

13. *Nīgem*. The term appears to include any stone that is flaked, but obsidian is the most characteristic. Note that this is the first time in the story that it is mentioned what the animate thing is that the tale is about.

14. Most obsidian is black, occasional pieces verging to a translucent gray. A rarer and more prized variety is jasper-red, sometimes streaked with black. The red appears not to come in sufficiently large masses for the largest blades.

15. Not otherwise identified.

16. Toward the end of the story the narrator used the English "he."

17. Contrast, for the origin of obsidian, F1*p*.

questioning, and ordering in the tale. It is so narrowly localized for a story that purports to account for the institution of death in the world, and it takes so much for granted as understood concerning the vast evils intended and partly introduced by the plotters, that the tale must seem rather meaningless in theme to anyone not steeped in Yurok beliefs. It is clear that the narrator is, as always, far more interested in vivid, concrete action, or what he considers such, than in a logical setting forth of the philosophy of the world; the latter is mainly in the background of his mind. But it is there, and it not only gives the story a coherence but charges it with an emotional momentousness which the Caucasian reader finds it difficult to perceive in the six-mile journey between Weitspus and Okego and the discussions as to whether Mole has gone or may go or wishes to go here or there.

The number of personages is large for a tale of medium length. There is some boldness in joining Mole and Wertspit—who are the archconspirators but whose anatomical fortunes are chiefly dwelt on—with personifications like Ghost and Arrowhead, and the two poor little boys. The saviors are a conventional five—men from Weitspus, Okego, Kepel, Sregon, and Mūrek; but the last two are only listed, the third is no more than a messenger, and the true actors are the first two, with Weitspus young man the leader and Okego young man his assistant. In fact, the number of personages is too large for the plot; there are so many that the story is hard to follow. I have little doubt that the narrator built up this complication for his own satisfaction, just as he developed all the talk back and forth; and when the tale was properly ended he had his one hero visit the other to make sure that the two main evildoers did not escape or mitigate their punishment.

There is a thread of neighborly contempt running through this telling, of wealthy towns or great towns thinking poorly of little ones or suburbs. This is the reverse of A3, where sympathy is with little near-by Lo'olego against great Weitspus, though that is the narrator's natal town; but in A13, at the ending, Weitspus is boastful again: its men are dissatisfied at a day without fighting, surely a proverbial exaggeration. In the present tale the five on the side of right are one *otsin* or native of each of five different places, all but one rich and famous towns. Okego is a very small place, a suburb of Kenek, but the home of Grown-in-a-Basket, who wins over Kenek Earthquake and others at shinny in A14, and has a magical dog. This dog is mentioned in the present tale. He will not be needed, says his master, but the allusion establishes Okego young man as the famous hero victorious over Kenek.

Now on the other side, the instigator is Mole, elsewhere (F3) the ill-omened sister of Wohpekumeu at Kenek. Wertspit's home is not mentioned, but the others named are two from Wahsek, a small but well-to-do town between Kenek and Weitspus; two misguided boys from Wespen, a downriver suburb of Weitspus (not inhabited in historic recollection), which furnished the main hero for the origin of the Weitspus Deerskin Dance in A2; and Arrowhead and Ghost, who are, respectively, from the across-river towns of Erłerger and Pekwtuł. The pro-Weitspus bias of the tale, at the expense of most its neighbors, is evident.

These minutiae are gone into because they entered into the manufacture of this tale by informant A, when he combined, or recombined, standard but brief episodes about Mole, Wertspit, and perhaps Arrowhead and Ghost into a tale with a built-up plot with suspense involving an array of personages taking the sides of good and evil. It is in this side-taking that his local partisanship comes out. But it does help him to organize his plot; a dozen characters in so short a telling would be a confusion except for being arrayed in some such opposition. Moreover, on each side the personages are organized into a gradation in relation to the central theme. Protagonists of evil are Mole and Wertspit, known to every Yurok as favoring death; then Arrowhead and Ghost; then the Wahsek men, who provide the conspirators with a place to plot; and finally the erring Wespen boys, who are forgiven. On the side of good, the ranking is Weitspus, Okego, Kepel, Mūrek, and Sregon.

As regards the general structure of the society and culture, the question arises whether the local chauvinism here manifested contradicts my repeated finding that the Yurok town is not a politically functioning unit, not even in war ordinarily, except for smaller towns which may consist wholly of kinsmen. This finding stands: there are too many cases of a house standing aside in a feud on account of blood or affinal kinship, of shootings between coresidents of a town, of a house or two actively taking sides in fighting while the rest of the village remains neutral. The family or house, or the group of kinsmen in several houses, remains the only permanently functioning unit in Yurok society in all cases where law, control, tension, or violence are involved. At the same time, this fact does not prevent feelings of sympathy—or antipathy—from arising between people who see each other daily in the same settlement, or irregularly but frequently in nearby settlements. Successful neighbors are likely to build up warmer relations on the face-to-face level than kinsmen at a distance, though in times of stress the claims of the latter may take precedence.

I think there were minute local patriotisms and provincialisms constantly being built up among the Yurok. It could not well be otherwise among a people so attached to spots and localities. The present tale expresses a sample of such sentiments, and therein lies part of its interest. But these neighborly and parochial attachments do not so much contradict or upset the claims and obligations of law as they cut across them at a different level. They express the sentiments that the people indulged in when they were not at law or liability. Yurok law is refined into a specialized, precise system; but the Yurok were also human, and their lives were of course never wholly absorbed into functioning as machines in their system.

•

a. Wohpekumeu and Pulekukwerek made it that there should be another kind of berries every moon.[1] Then they went off.[2] Mole, Łkelikera, did not like that. He[3] came to Wahsek. Two young men there went with him. He went

1. That is, there would be easy food the year round. [For characterizations of Wohpekumeu and Pulekukwerek, see the Folkloristic Commentary at the front of the book—Ed.]

2. Left this world for Pulekuk, having finished their work. [Waterman, Geography, p. 193, identifies Pulekuk as a mythical place. Its name means, literally, "downriver-at"; it might be paraphrased as "at the north of everything," for there is nothing beyond it.—Ed.]

3. Female in other myths, sometimes described as the sister of Wohpekumeu. Always an

upstream to O'kun.[4] One lived there who had a friend at Knetken operu.[5] They both joined Mole. Then they all went down to Wespen.[6] There they found two little boys who went with them. That made seven. The eighth was Wertspit.[7] There were others from other places, I do not know where,—fifteen in all. Then they slept at Weitspus, hiding in the large rock just above[8] the town. From there they went to Hupa, but no one knew it.

b. Then someone came to Weitspus from Oplego (Takimiɫding in Hupa). He said, "Someone has come and spoiled everything—the berries, the hazelnuts, the acorns, and all. We think they have gone toward Redwood Creek, for we saw their tracks in that direction."

After two days they saw someone coming to Weitspus (again). It was a Kepel person. He said, "I came to tell you that we nearly had misfortune last night. We watched closely; that is why they did not altogether spoil our dam. Some sort of people were there and destroyed part of it." "Do you know where they came from?" "No, we did not see them, but we think they were many. They left their boats on the other side of the river. That is what made us think they were many." "We have heard that persons have been to Hupa and have ruined everything there: it might be they. You had better go back at once and stop at Okego. Get the young man there[9] to go with you and make him take his dog along."

c. Then the one from Kepel came to Okego. "Where is he?" he said. The old man said, "He is working blankets[10] down by the creek. Do you want to see him?" "Yes, I want to see him." Then the old man brought him, and the one from Kepel said, "I should like you to go with me to Kepel and stay there overnight. I want you to take your dog along." "Yes?" "Persons came there last night." "Well, there is no need of my dog going. I know who they were. You had better get others (to help you). Then we will follow them." "I think

---

animal of evil to the Yurok, and several times associated with Wertspit in the causation of death.

4. A spring at Pekwtuɫ (Waterman, Geography, map 28, *z*). The man, like the next, is later named by his town, not by the spring.

5. A spring at Erɫerger, downstream from the town. Knetken o-peru means "arrowpoint its-peru." [K. has a marginal note: "o-perei?"—Ed.]

6. A "third of a mile" downstream from Weitspus; three-quarters by Waterman's map 25, no. 16. [This map is reproduced here as map 4.—Ed.]

7. An underground larval locust, probably the sluggish, dome-headed, nocturnal Jerusalem cricket.

8. The rock is uncertain. There is no very conspicuous outcrop about the town, but Yurok landmarks depend on their associations as much as on any natural impressiveness.

9. Okego is at the mouth of Tuley or Tule Creek, immediately upstream from Kenek. The young man is probably the one told of in tale A14; compare his dog.

10. Dressing skins, probably.

that they are some kind of plants.''[11] ''I know it, and will tell you who they are. You have seen two at Wahsek and two from below Weitspus at Wespen: they are the ones. And I saw old Mole going by here; he came from downstream. He is the one that began it. Go to Weitspus and get them there to help you. I will go with you, and you yourself had better join in attacking them.''

Then Kepel person went back to Weitspus and got one man there to help him. He went to Mūrek and got one, and one at Sregon. He himself and the one from Okego made five. Then Okego young man said, ''Let us watch first at Wahsek. They might be staying there, since two of them belong there.''

d. They arrived at Wahsek in the middle of the day. There they saw a man standing about with a baby on his back.[12] Okego young man said, ''That is one of them.'' The Weitspus man said, ''Wait. Let me go to them first to find out how many there are.'' Then they went to a knoll uphill from the town to watch, but Weitspus man went to the creek. He said to himself, ''I shall say that I am coming from downstream.'' Then he saw five sitting outside a house. Some more were singing indoors. One of them asked him, ''Where do you come from?'' ''I am going upstream. I do not know how far.'' ''Oh, yes.'' ''How far is it to Weitspus?'' ''I do not know. Perhaps it is near, perhaps it is far.'' ''I should like to go to Weitspus to stay the night.'' ''Yes?'' ''I am afraid to walk the trail; I hear there are people about. Downstream I heard Hinei[13] persons (Tolowa) shouting, coming to attack. I was afraid, so I started upstream. If I go to Weitspus they will not attack me there.'' Then he went on upstream.

As soon as he was out of sight behind the nearest ridge, they all went into the house. ''Let us run off,'' they said. ''They are coming against us.''

e. Then the Weitspus man sat in the middle of the trail. He knew they would come by there. Before long he heard shouting. Someone was coming running. When he came up, he seized him. ''Sit down,'' he said. That one tried to break away, but he held him. It was Mole who was caught. He was caught by the wrist, and the Weitspus man turned it.[14] ''Sit down, sit down,'' he kept telling him, and made him sit. He saw another coming up, caught him too, and made him sit down. He was the one who was carrying the baby.[15] He caught another and another and soon had five. He made them all sit down.

Soon he saw Okego young man coming bringing two,[16] one with each

11. [K. makes a marginal reference to his original notes, which may have identified the specific plant.—Ed.]

12. Wertspit. The baby in its cradle suggests a woman; but my notes read ''man.'' See final paragraph of the story.

13. Xawunhwut (Drucker, Tolowa, map 2, p. 229), a large Tolowa town on lower Smith River.

14. Cf. n. 28.

15. Wertspit.

16. *Sic.* A moment later he enumerates five.

hand. The Weitspus man asked him, ''Where are the rest?'' Okego young man said, ''The others have changed into something. They will not be persons any longer. I brought that boy;[17] these two here I am bringing you because they grew in your place;[18] and these two are from across the river.[19] Perhaps they are your relatives. I brought them to show them (to) you to know what you want to do with them.''

f. Mole said, ''Wait! First straighten my arm.'' Weitspus young man did not look at him and spoke of something else. Mole said, ''Straighten me on this side.'' Again he did not answer him nor look at him.

Okego young man said to the two little boys from Wespen, ''What have you been doing?'' They said, ''This Mole began it. He went about in order to spoil everything.'' ''Yes?'' said Okego young man.

Then Weitspus man asked Mole, ''Do you think you will live and be good now?'' ''Yes,'' said Mole. ''Well, I will see.'' He heaped up sand, then said, ''Now sink in here and come out on the other side of the heap. Then fly[20] across the river and sink in the earth there and come out and throw up another ridge.'' Mole said, ''Yes, I wanted to be like that. That is why I ruined things.''[21] Then he went in(to the ground). Weitspus young man said to Okego young man, ''Stand on the other side (of the heap) where he will come out.'' So he stood there with a stick, and Weitspus young man blocked the hole Mole had entered with a stone. ''As soon as you see him emerging, hit him with your stick. I don't want to see him come out alive.'' Then he saw him about to emerge and struck him; so he went back to the other side and found this stopped. Then Weitspus young man told him, ''Now you will never come out. As long as you live you shall be like this.''

g. Then he spoke to the one carrying the baby. He took his quiver, drew out his arrows, and made an opening in the mouth[22] of the skin. Then he told him, ''Go in and come out at the other end. But hurry; if you stay inside too long, you will have no hair.'' Then that one entered. Then Okego young man made a hole in the ground, and they put the mouth of the skin to the hole. As

17. It is not clear who he is.

18. Wespen is reckoned as part of Weitspus, apparently.

19. Erłerger and Pekwtuł.

20. [K. has queried the word ''fly.''—Ed.]

21. Perhaps: I did damage in order to bring on a punishment that would change me into a form and habit of life that I desired but could not give myself; or: My inherent disposition is toward evil, and burrowing in the ground and ruining human life are both bad, so this sinking in just suits me.

22. The Yurok quiver is always a whole skin, with the mouth sewed up and the hind end slit open. It is the mouth of the animal skin, not of the quiver, that is here specially opened, so as to produce a sort of sleeve or tube. [Kroeber, Handbook, p. 27, says that quivers were usually made of otter or fisher skins.—Ed.]

Wertspit began to pass through, Weitspus young man lifted the quiver so that he would go through faster, and he slipped into the hole. Most of him was in the ground; only his hind end stuck out. Then Weitspus young man took away the quiver. Okego young man wanted to draw him out because he did not like to see his legs sticking out. But Weitspus young man said, "Don't! We shall see him like this. We do not want to see the whole of him. We shall not see his face, only the end that projects."[23] That is what this Weitspus young man brought about.

h. Then he looked at the two Wespen boys. He asked them, "What did you help to do?" "We only went along and looked on. We did not know what they were doing. He is the one who did it. He began it." "You did wrong." "Yes, we know it. We cannot say why we did it, for we knew that the world was all made."[24] "Well, where will you go?" "We want to return, for we have done nothing and only went along and looked on. We shall be good as long as the world lasts." Then the Okego young man told Weitspus young man, "You had better take them back home. They will become good now."

i. "Yes, I will take you along," he said, "but who are you?" addressing the one from Erłerger. That one said, "When I tell you, you will know me. I grew where I live. I shall tell you: I eat persons. I like to catch persons. When I enter persons' flesh, I live. Arrowhead, that is who I am." Weitspus young man said, "Go back to your place."[25]

j. Then he asked the one from Pekwtuł, "What is your place?" "I liked it where I grew. I lived there. So they found me there. I saw them (the woge) leave. But I thought, 'I shall be one who takes care of his own place as long as the world endures.' I do not know why I became bad. But as soon as these came by, I forgot what I had resolved before. Now I shall not go back to my house. I shall be a bringer of what is bad. If a man is to have bad luck, I shall be the first to tell him." He became Ghost.[26] "Well, you also can go along with me."

So Weitspus young man brought these four[27] upstream. Okego young man went downstream to his house.

k. That night Weitspus young man thought, "That Mole has become a different person. Perhaps he will go to Okego and say to that one, 'Straighten my hand!'"

Then, in the morning, he started for Okego. He arrived and told the young man, "I was afraid that he would ask you, 'Straighten my hand'; but do not do

23. The Yurok seem to be afraid to draw out one of these insects when its posterior and hind legs rise above the ground, or to look at its bald, bulging "forehead."

24. All instituted, finished, and therefore as it should thereafter remain.

25. As war exists in the world, Arrowhead is allowed to continue his existence, but the motive of the beneficent captor in permitting this existence is, cleverly enough, evaded. The same holds for Ghost.

26. So'o, ghost or skeleton.

27. The two boys from Wespen, and Arrowhead and Ghost, who are his neighbors.

it. Let it be as it is."[28] Okego young man said, "I heard crying last night. I think that was he." "Do not do it. He will be tired of living as he is; but do not make it for him."

l. Mole wanted to come out, but could not. Wertspit also wanted to emerge, but when he tried, only his (hind)legs came out (of the ground). Weitspus young man asked Wertspit, "What shall you do with your baby?" "Oh, it will fly about." Weitspus young man rubbed a little hole in the ground with his finger. "Put it in here," he said. "Now it will sleep." Then he brushed earth over it with his foot and patted it down.[29]

A7. No'ots

This is a true folk tale, well known among the Yurok (F6, J8, DD2) and told also by the Hupa (Goddard, Hupa Texts, nos. 2 and 4, pp. 146 and 160) and by the Karok. Its hero has a name, though this is sometimes given differently. The motivation is by simple emotions—avidity, disobedience, affection, shame, longing, suspicion, pursuit, anger. The end is an explanation—flocking seabirds and two bold rocks. Institutions and the customs of society are assumed as operative, not narrated from their origins. Supernatural events occur, but not perceptibly more or less than in the institutional myths.

The narrator is not at his best in this type of recital. True, he tells a fuller story than his peers, but a rapid unfolding is more in keeping with the popular nature of the plot than is his painstaking cumulative method of achieving effect. There is no opportunity for him to balance characters as he loves to. There are but two main characters, and interest between them is not wholly defined. This blemish indeed is inherent in the story, which, like most tales of wide appeal to the Indian, is concerned with events but is indifferent to characterization. With themes more congenial to his individual art, the narrator succeeds better in characterization.

A comparison of versions shows the tale to consist of three parts:

(1) The digging of the hero from the ground. (A separate story in Hupa.)

(2) His visits to the sky for acorns. (Omitted in the present version. His visiting of world renewal dances on earth is substituted.)

(3) Flight from his foster mother, and her pestle throwing. (The localization of this episode is usually the same, and rests on the allegation that Redding Rock is visible from Orleans Summit, which I doubt.)

Having only two characters given him, the narrator has elaborated his story first by inventing additional subsidiary personages, and second by repeating incidents cumulatively. The added personages—mostly vague—are: the old woman; "someone" in the girl's dream, *c*; Ko'men people who conjecture about the hero, *d*; his Weitspus friends, *d*; the Weitspus man who takes him to Hupa, *g*; the basket-weaving girl and the fisherman, *l*.

28. The sidewise-turned palms of the mole are a favorite subject of explanation in the mythologies of northern California.

29. Presumably a reference to some trait in the life history of the insect.

The elaborate step-by-step episodes are: prohibition to girl against digging in middle, then wonder, then disobedience, *a*; baby blown away, *b*; then found, *c*; hero's visit to dance at Weitspus, *d*; his arrival at Hupa after three tries, *e*, *f*, *g*; at Pekwon, *h*; at Rekwoi, *i*; his boat riding in spring, *j*; to Olege'l, *k*; down and back and over Orleans Summit, *l*; on ocean, *m*; girl's throwing of pestle halves from Summit and from Oyegos.

Except perhaps for the dance visiting, all these episodes probably occur in one or another version of the folktale, even, I would infer, the wind blowing out of the house against the baby coming in, though this does not occur in any other Yurok version known to me. What is distinctive of the present narrator is the way he progressively elaborates each of these episodes, whereas the ordinary Yurok, more swiftly moving in his recital, might merely allude to successive steps in an incident.

The blowing of the wind against the baby brought into the house rings as if it were part of the stock-in-trade of the mythology of the area, although it is otherwise unrecorded. The dream that the child is lying by the river is probably also part, although instructing dreams are not characteristic of Yurok narrative as they are not characteristic of shamanism. The being moved backward in trying to approach Hupa Takimiłding is almost certainly also not an invention of Informant A but was taken by him from some other existing context for weaving into his elaboration of No'ots. That leaves only the generalized idea of the hero's visiting a series of dances as this informant's presumably personal contribution of content. That it is such seems strengthened by the artificial rationalization that is No'ots's seeing of the ocean at Rekwoi which leads him to his final escape seaward.

That to trick his foster mother he doubles back upstream and then drags his canoe westward over Orleans Summit looks like a reapplication of the canoe route from the Trinity up into Pine Creek headwaters to reenter the Klamath (A13*y*).[1]

•

a. At Ko'men[2] a girl used to go up back from the river to dig bulbs. Then the old woman (her mother) said, "Do not dig bulbs in the middle of the prairie but along the edges." "Yes," she said.

Every day she went to dig. Then one day she thought, "Let me go to the middle and merely look around." So she went and looked. It was pretty there, as if something had been about, and the bulbs were thick. Then she returned to the house. In the morning she went out again. This time she went very near the middle. Close to it she found large bulbs and was glad.

Next morning she went and dug again. In the afternoon she was about to go home but could not (bring herself to start). She found too many bulbs; she liked them too well. So she came nearer and nearer the middle, finding very large ones. Now she thought, "I will keep on digging and go home in the evening." Then late in the afternoon, she found the one the old woman had spoken of (when she said,) "Do not dig in the middle of the prairie." When she dug it out,

1. [K.'s typescript indicated that he intended to supply other references from Hupa tales.—Ed.]

2. Ko'men is Karok Panamenik (Orleans). [See map 1, no. 31, in this volume.—Ed.]

this one in the very middle, she saw what it was, and did not want to take it. It was as long as a hand; above, it was like a bulb with leaves: at the lower end it was different.[3] But, after all, she thought, "Well, I had better take care of him.[4] I will carry him to the house."

b. Then the wind began to blow hard. She could hardly get back to town. When she tried to enter the house, the wind blew out from it so that she could not put her basket in at the door; it was driven back against her. The old woman came out and said, "What is the matter?" She did not say a word. The old woman continued to ask her, "What is the matter? You must have done wrong." "I think so," she said. Then the old woman ran up to the hill prairie. She knew where the root was and saw that it was gone. She ran back to the house and said, "What have you done with that baby?" The girl said, "I tried to bring it into the house and the wind blew it away." The old woman asked, "Where did your carrying basket go?" "It rolled down that way," she said. So the old woman looked for it, and the girl did too, all over the sand bar below the town, but could not find it. They found only the bulbs. So they stopped looking; they had been everywhere without seeing it.

c. Then they went to sleep and the girl dreamed. She saw someone. He said, "Why did you abandon that little boy? You took him. Now he will drown before daylight. He is lying close to the river." Then she awoke. She thought, "I dreamed strangely. I was dreaming about that boy. I had better go to see." Then she went down to the river, along its edge. She saw something lying by the water, very white. She took it and knew that it was the root (boy); he was nearly drowned. She came to the house and told the old woman, "Get up. I have found him. I found that root." The old woman said, "Well, we will take care of him. I know what we shall do with him. Now watch me, because this will be the custom." Then the girl saw her cut twigs, and twine them as long as her hand,[5] and work them neatly, until she had a basket cradle. Then she said, "Now we will put him in here to keep him."

d. After five days the root began to cry. Before long he was a little boy. When he cried, they could not stop him; so the girl took him up and carried him to the place where she had dug him out. There he played about over the prairie.

It was not yet a year and he was a man. Then he found what to do: he made many dances and good times at Ko'men. The people thought, "He has come from elsewhere: perhaps he will marry the girl." Only she knew where she had got him.

Once he went down to Weitspus to dance. Then the Weitspus people wanted him to go downstream with them to Kepel to the fish dam. So they went.

3. Unusual, portentous.

4. It was a baby.

5. Normal cradles are longer, but this bulb-baby was only hand-length.

When the Weitspus people began to gamble at Kepel they won all that the other side had; the young man from Ko'men did it for them. When they returned, the Weitspus people said, "We hear that they will have the Jumping Dance at Oplego.[6] You had better come back when they make that and we will go there." He said, "Good. When you hear that they are to begin, send me word"; and they agreed.

e. Then they heard that they had begun to dance at Oplego. So they told the young man, "Tell him to come; we are all going; they are dancing at Oplego." That one went to Ko'men, but the young man did not come the next day. So they left Weitspus without him. They knew what he thought, and they told a man who remained at Weitspus, "If he comes, do not let him go on. He cannot get there alone. Perhaps he could, but I do not think so; it is a very difficult place to reach if one has never been there before."

The next morning that man at Weitspus saw someone coming downstream: it was the young man from Ko'men. He said to him, "Where are you going?" He said, "I am going to Hupa to see the dance." That man told him, "Well, yesterday they all went from here. I do not think you will be able to get there, because you have not been before, I think." The young man said, "No, I do not know the country." The Weitspus man said, "I do not think you will be able to reach it. Many people from everywhere, some of them thinking they (truly) were men, have been unable to arrive. Then, when they could not reach it, they were ashamed. I am afraid it will be thc same way with you. But if you want to go, go." The young man said, "Is that so? Well, I think I can get there." "Well, I will set you across the river," the Weitspus man said.

So the young man started. Now he came to the creek downstream from Oplego. There he took a rest. When he got up to start he looked about. Then he thought, "Where am I? Where am I standing?" He was at the lower end of the valley, at the last town, at Oknuł.[7] He thought, "It is no use for me to try." Now he believed what the Weitspus man had said. Then he went back, passing Weitspus by night so that no one would see him, for he was ashamed. He returned to Ko'men.

f. Then he changed his clothes and started out again. He thought, "Let me try once more." When he was near (Oplego) he thought, "I will rest." Then, before he knew it, he was moving backward: he was again at Ergerits.[8] There is a spring there: it came from his tears as he cried, thinking, "There is no use my trying." Again he went back over the mountain to Ko'men.

g. The young men from Weitspus had felt it at Oplego as soon as he tried

6. Takimiłding in Hupa; "Hostler rancheria." [See map 1, no. 38, in this volume.—Ed.]

7. Honsading, the Hupa town at the foot of the valley. He had already gone above it, nearly to Oplego, and now finds himself carried back.

8. Ergerits is Hupa Miskut, which he has already passed. However, he did come closer to Oplego on this try. [K. has a marginal note: "disappoint."—Ed.]

to come. They were sorry for him; and some were a little angry because they had sent word up to him to go along with them (and he had not). Then, near the end, when there would be only two more days of the dance, the man (left) at Weitspus sent word upriver to Ko'men. He said, "Tell him to come down by morning." Then the young man got up at night, by daylight was at Bluff Creek, and arrived at Weitspus early. The man there said, "Do you want to go to see the dance? Tomorrow will be the last day." Then the young man was ashamed. He said, "I think I shall go when you tell me that you are going with me. I am ashamed, my friend. Perhaps you know it: I tried twice to get there." "Yes, I know it. Once, the first time, you came back by here at night." "Yes, that is so." "The other time you went by the trail over the mountain; I know it."

Then he (Weitspus man) said, "Well, let us go. I have a little boat. We will go in that and leave it at the lower end of the valley. It is time to go, for tomorrow will be the end." Then he looked for his medicine herb. He said, "You will go there carrying my medicine. I will make it. You cannot reach there without it. It is a very hard place to get to." Then he made his medicine. The one from Ko'men thought, "I had better make medicine of my own. How shall I do it?" Then they went.

It was evening when they arrived. As they walked, Ko'men young man nearly fell when the Hupa people looked at him (but he saw the dance).

h. Then from there he went downstream to Pekwon to see the Jumping Dance.

i. Next year he heard they were having the Jumping Dance at Rekwoi. He wanted to see how it looked there. They told him, "There is salt water there; it is the farthest town." He said, "I think I will go. I will go to Weitspus and see if they want to go too." Then he reached Rekwoi, going with the Weitspus people. He looked at the ocean and thought, "It is a good place for me." Then he began to know that that was what he was thinking of.[9]

j. When he came back to Ko'men, he bought a very little boat,[10] so long.[11] He thought, "What shall I do with it?" After a time he knew. He went to where the spring is now on the sandbar downstream from the town. He made that spring and put his little boat in it. Then he made himself a feathered headnet.[12] Every day he went down to look at his boat and ride about in it.

Then once the girl came down to Weitspus. They asked "Where is he?" She said, "Oh, he does not speak much to people since he has his boat. He is at that (spring) every day. That is why I shall go back at once." They said to her, "Yes, you had better. You must look out for him; for when we went to the

9. To know his ultimate nature or destiny.

10. Boats were sold, but it seems out of keeping for a magical hero to buy one.

11. Gesture.

12. *U-pergerim*. It is an ornament that hangs over the head and neck, not a net to confine the hair.

mouth of the river he came near staying there. He likes that place." Then she began to think, "He will leave me." She said, "I will go back now."

k. In the morning he was riding about on the river in his boat. She watched him. He came back to the house and she asked him, "What is the matter with you? If you do not feel well here it will be better if you go back where I got you. I shall not let you go away except to that place, because there I can see you whenever I want to." "I do not know," was all that he said.

Next day he went out and took his paddle and rode about on the river. That is why the river is crooked at Olege'l;[13] he made it so. Then from Ko'men she could see the feathers flying at his back: that was all she saw. Then she saw him return.

l. The last day that he went out in his boat she went to get firewood. Then he started. From outdoors she could not see his boat and went back to the house. She asked the old woman, "How long is it since he went away?" The old woman said, "He came in to get his headdress just after you had gone for wood and has not come back." Then she tried to follow him. At Operger[14] she asked, "Did you see him pass by?" They said, "No. You had better go back and track him, for he can carry his boat." She thought, "Yes, that is so." So she went back. She found that he had gone in his boat as far as . . .;[15] there he had turned back. At Ko'men a girl was making baskets at the river. She said, "Yes, I saw him riding about. He went up and down ten times, singing. The last time he went upstream." Then she went upstream thinking, "He has gone up." She went as far as . . . .[16] There she saw a man fishing. She asked him, "Did you see him pass by?" He said, "No, I did not see him." Then she crossed the river and went along on the opposite side, still looking. She came below the town. Then she saw where he had pulled his boat up over the sand. She saw that he had gone, carrying his boat, up onto Orleans Summit. Then she crossed the river again and ran back to her house, took her pestle, crossed once more, and followed him up the mountain to the summit.

m. When she looked toward the ocean, the first thing she saw as she came to the top of the ridge was the young man, just starting out for the other side.[17] She broke her pestle and threw one piece at him. She struck off half the feathers of his headdress, and they fluttered about: that is why there are so many birds on the ocean. Still he went on downstream along the ocean.[18]

n. Then she ran to Oyegos.[19] When she came up on that she saw him

13. Camp Creek, where there is a sudden bend; Karok Tishannik.
14. Karok Vonvirak, a town on the right bank.
15. [Name missing. K. has a marginal reference to his original notebooks.—Ed.]
16. [Again K. has reference to his notebooks.—Ed.]
17. Across the ocean. He was going to Pulekuk.
18. Northward.
19. On "Redwood Ridge," i.e., Bald Hills. The Yurok are rather indefinite about Chilula

again. She still had half of her pestle. She threw that and hit the other side of his headdress and knocked off the feathers. That was far downstream (north) near Smith River: the rock Pekwtso is her pestle: the first half had become Redding Rock.[20] Then she knew that she could not catch him. She let him go and went back to Ko'men. "Where is he?" they asked her. "He has gone. He left me," she said.[21]

A8. Married at Rumai

This was avowedly recorded as an abstract and may therefore not be considered for style. The narrator's manner of telling a story is much more expansive. Like most tales of danger, exploit, and revenge, this one was probably widely known to the Yurok, whereas few but the older men, or those of a thoughtful turn, would be interested in institutional myths.

Why the young woman held her husband is not altogether clear. Our impulse would perhaps be to attribute her act to affection: she did not wish him to perish with her mother. The Yurok more probably think of nothing but revenge. The old woman's urging that he should fish causes him almost to lose his life to the water monster; she must therefore have plotted to destroy him, and her daughter avenges his peril. The second old woman, it is certain, attempts revenge for her sister's death, until finally the hero puts her out of the way too. Had the story been recorded in detail, there would be little doubt as to the motives, which this narrator always brings out with clarity and often a delicate justness, though the average folktale, essentially concentrating on the action and among the Yurok sometimes on a suffused, generalized emotion, often enough neglects or contradicts its specific motivations.

To judge from the other versions (A9, K3, Q2), the present story consists of four obvious parts, each essentially a tale in itself, and possibly all of separate origin. Their central ideas occur in other settings. They are, however, neatly pieced together here, and flow advantageously as a single plot. The only break is formed by the third episode, which is usually told separately by the Yurok. It is indeed strung to the thread by an artifice, but an apparent one: the old woman wishes to eat of the great Eagle, just as her magically luring deer and her sister's desire for the Sekoyeu-salmon, have previously put the young man into danger. But he quickly fades from mention, and Screech Owl becomes the hero of this third episode. The close localization of the four plots in the region of the mouth of Bluff Creek and the interest in detail of the topography of the vicinity are, however, to the native mind an undoubted bond that tends to escape the

---

spots. Off the river or shoreline they seem to have difficulty defining localities. Waterman, Geography, p. 189, mentions Oyegos as in Chilula territory.

20. Off Orick, a bit north. "Ekwoneu" was heard here, for Sekwona. The north half of the pestle, Pekwtso, is the lighthouse rock off Point St. George, in Tolowa territory (Waterman, Geography, map 2, no. 7, and p. 187). [See map 1 in this volume.—Ed.]

21. His name was No'ots, the narrator stated when asked. The name seems to be from "two" and probably means "double." In F6 (which substitutes Megwomets for No'ots) it is a forked root that becomes a boy, as in Goddard, Hupa Texts, no. 2, p. 146—the mandrake idea.

civilized reader and may have contributed to their combination. On the whole, the welding of the discrete elements is the work of a nimble mind.

The active personages are unusually numerous, and had the story been preserved in full, it appears that their delineation would have been spirited. The hero, his devoted wife, the evil mother-in-law, her conspiring sister, the (Kingfisher) stranger who brings help in direst need, vainglorious Coyote, Screech Owl as great in accomplishment as small in person, the silent one from Kewet renowned in other tales, and long-legged, friendly Crane make a varied and lively company.

The concept of Crane-leg-bridge serving to kill a dangerous woman, regularly associated with "Married at Rumai" by the Yurok, has a wide distribution in California as the finale of Grizzly and Deer Women and their children.

•

a. A young man was married[1] at Rumai.[2] His mother-in-law told him to spear salmon. Where MacFarland's Creek flows into Bluff Creek, not far from the river, where there are still two footmarks, he stood to spear salmon. Then he harpooned the Sekoyeu.[3] Then he could not let go his salmon spear and was drawn into the stream. The water boiled and he was nearly drowned. A man[4] came and, seeing him about to drown, was sorry for him and gave him his song. When the young man sang it, the water became quiet. Then that person handed him a small salmon club. When he hit the Sekoyeu with it once, it died.

Then he carried it (the monster) to the house and the old woman cooked it. Soon he and his wife saw smoke coming from the house and heard cries. The young man wanted to go in to his mother-in-law, but his wife held him until the old woman was dead. Then they built a new house.

b. The dead woman had a sister who came to live with the young man and his wife. She made a deer on MacFarland's Prairie. The young man saw it and pursued it. He shot and seemed to hit it. The deer fell, got up, and ran off, so it lured him far into the mountains. At night he camped and ate (the deer). Then it

1. Probably "half-married"; a fully married man takes his wife to his home. But the myths do not always go into such technicalities of social status. [Waterman and Kroeber in Yurok Marriages, UC-PAAE 35:(no. 1): 1, 1934, explain that in full marriage the man "pays" for his wife and takes her to live in his house in his town, and the children are regarded as his. In half-marriage the man pays less for his wife and goes to live in his father-in-law's house or close to it, and is more or less under his direction; the children are then regarded as belonging to the wife's family. "Half-marriage is legitimate and carries no positive disapprobation; but it is presumptive indication of lack of wealth . . . in a society which equates wealth and rank."—Ed.]

2. Waterman, Geography, map 25, no. 40, Romoi, a small flat, 1/2 mile below the mouth of Bluff Creek, and opposite the settlement Otsepor. [This map is reproduced here as map 4.—Ed.]

3. A fishlike water monster.

4. This nameless and undescribed "man" is uncharacteristic of the narrator, and is probably the result of the tale's being recorded only in outline. In Spott and Kroeber, Yurok Narratives, no. 29, p. 238, the rescuer is Kingfisher.

snowed very heavily. For ten days it snowed. He had eaten all the deer except one leg bone and thought he would die. Then he burned the marrow of the bone, went to the spring, and sprinkled the burned marrow in, telling it to turn into fish. Taking string of hair,[5] he made a small net. This he made grow larger and caught fish with it. He ate of the fish until the snow was gone, and then returned home with a load of fish. Then he and his wife went to the spring and enlarged it to a lake, where there are trout now.[6]

c. Then the old woman said that she wanted to eat the one[7] that sat on top of Shelton Butte.[8] When the young man approached it, he saw that it had on it all kinds of feathers. Everyone came there to shoot at it. Coyote wanted to be the first to shoot. He would call out, "I almost hit it!" But his arrow could be seen landing very low down on the mountain. At last they asked Screech Owl[9] to shoot. He said, "I cannot hit it," but at last he consented to shoot. His bow was very small. He kneeled: the rock bearing the impress of his knee can be seen now. The man who knows that mark will have luck. Then he shot, hit that one, and it tottered. Now he from Kewet[10] gave him another arrow, for Screech Owl had only one. He shot again, hit it once more, and it fell and rolled down, making a slide along the mountain. It lay at the foot, across the river. When they went there, Coyote claimed one of the two arrows. They said to him, "If it is yours, pull it out." Coyote tried but could not draw the arrow. Then all tried and failed; but he from Kewet and Screech Owl each pulled one out with ease.[11]

d. Then the young man married at Rumai planned with Crane to kill the old woman. He said, "There is something nice for you across the river." The old woman was glad and asked him to set her across. He said, "I have no boat, but there is a man upstream fishing." When she went upstream she found Crane. He stretched his leg and told her, "Do not be afraid. It is safe. Many have crossed like this." She started to go over, but when she was just beyond his knee, he turned his leg,[12] and she fell off and was drowned.[13]

5. Either a string twisted out of his own hair, or possibly a string with which his hair was tied.

6. This might be Brown's Lake (Itperper of A13), Waterman, map 25, no. 1, or Fish Lake (Oketo of Pluɬ) of Yurok Narratives, no. 24, p. 224, and of G6, below. [See map 4 in this volume.—Ed.]

7. A gigantic eagle-like bird, whose feathers were "tails" or fur and feather coats from which the various animals or birds derived their appearance. This transformation incident is not included in the present abstract.

8. Shelton Butte (Mekaukh) is a sharp and rather high peak on the south (here east) side of the river, which makes a swing around its foot between Redcap and Bluff creeks. It is at the boundary between Karok and Yurok territory.

9. Pa'aku, a small owl. Cf. J9, Q1.

10. Kewet omewa; cf. A12 and C5.

11. Here follows the distribution of "tails" in standard versions of the episode.

12. Or jerked it up?

13. For another version of this incident, cf. the next tale.

A9. Crane at Bluff Creek

This is mainly a version of the last episode of the preceding tale, but A9 was obtained a year earlier as if it were a story in itself. However, it is differently motivated: an unclean old woman scares salmon away from a fisherman on Bluff Creek, so he hires Crane to kill her, by giving him a spear for a bill.

•

a. A man was fishing for salmon in Bluff Creek. When he caught nothing, he went to see what was the matter. Then he found an old woman bathing at the mouth of the creek. She was scaring the fish away (as they tried to enter the stream).[1] He wanted her to go away and clean herself, but she would not do it. Then he thought how he might kill her.

b. He said to Crane, "If you kill her I will pay you." Crane said, "Give me a long, sharp salmon spear,"[2] and the man replied, "I will give you that. Here. Try it on the other side of the river." Crane tried it out and was much pleased with his new spear (bill).

He said, "I will kill her. Take away your boat." The man put his boat elsewhere and then went to the old woman and said, "I have caught plenty of salmon for you. They are across the river." "Thanks," she said, and started to go to get them. When she came to the river, Crane told her, "Someone has taken away the boat." She said, "It is too bad. All the salmon will spoil. I cannot swim across." Crane said, "You can go over on my leg." She said, "You will not drop me off?" "No it is safe," he said. So she started to walk across. When she was in the middle, on his knee, Crane said, "You hurt me, you hurt me!" and drew up his leg, and she fell into the river and was drowned.

A10. The Giant

An obvious outline only, of a story intended to be told later.

•

At Redcap Creek[1] lived five brothers with their father and mother and sister. Their sister went out and did not come back. They thought she had died. After two years she returned with a baby and with five baskets made of dentalia. The baskets were filled with valuables instead of food. She told them that her husband was a giant, one of four brothers who stepped from ridge to ridge and

1. Deliberately? Or because she was menstruating? Cf. next sentence.
2. It became his bill.

---

1. The Karok settlement farthest downstream, or nearest the Yurok. [Kroeber, Handbook, p. 99, gives its Karok name as Wopum.—Ed.]

shouted loudly. Then her husband came. They gazed up at him and tried in vain to reach up to feed him. Then he went off with his wife. After a time she had another baby. Then she returned with one of her children, having been sent back home by the giant. He kept the other child.

A11. His Pet was Long One

Narrator's Introduction

An old man from Ho'peu, noted for his sweathouse (doctor-training) singing, came to Weitspus one midsummer. A woman at Weitspus was becoming a shaman. It was necessary for someone to go with her on the mountain for a night. This person must abstain from drinking water. Then her father asked my father to have someone go with her. So I went with her. On the way up, we stopped to make her a dress of maple bark. She told me, "Hold me fast if I start to go off somewhere (in my madness)." Then I made rope of maple bark, a fathom long, to tie her with, and carried it wound around my waist. Then on the mountain that night I sang (for her) and she danced. About the middle of the night she began to talk. Then I sang again and she danced until it was nearly day. Then she began to dance in a circle and, still dancing, went off. I ran after, held her, and as she was now out of her mind, tied her arms. Then, about sunrise, I succeeded in bringing her down the mountain as far as to the place where they make the Jumping Dance on Rivet Mountain. There she began to run. Halfway down the mountain, on the open prairie, she turned aside. I did what I could to keep her going straight toward Weitspus. Then we arrived, and I saw her father's sweathouse prepared like a house for the Brush Dance (the planks of the roof removed). People were waiting about the sweathouse. The woman did not go through the crowd but entered at the back and sat down and rested. Then I went to the river, bathed, and ate. After that I thought I would go to see the doctor-making dance which (had begun and) was still going on.

Then, toward sunset, coming to that sweathouse, I heard the old man from Ho'peu singing and stamping his foot. I heard what he sang and thought it must be a good myth.[1] Next day I asked him about his myth. "Which one?" he said. "I heard you singing about the man who lost his pet."[2] "Yes, that is a good

1. Why the old man should sing a myth or allude to it on this occasion is not clear, except that "any" song can be sung at the dance for shaman-making. Most Yurok dance songs are wordless. There is nothing in the story that makes it specially appropriate for the occasion. It does deal, it is true, with a monster that is sometimes a supernatural helper, but women doctors do not seem to enter into relation with the horned water serpent; their power resides in the possession of swallowed *telogel* or "pain" objects, not in communication with monsters.

2. The native word was not recorded here but is *ka'er*.

myth. I will tell it to you." Then later he said, "Sit down here. Sometime you will be sorry when you remember,[3] when you are alone on the mountain. And if you come downriver you will see its[4] trail there." Then he began to tell me the myth of the young man who grew at Espeu.

THE STORY

a. A young man lived at Espeu.[5] As soon as he was a little boy he wished to hunt. When he came back from hunting he would walk along the ocean. Then he would sleep. All summer for about two years (he did this). As soon as he was grown and could kill and carry a deer, he hunted.

b. Then once he went out again. He saw elk, and killed seven with seven shots. He thought, "I have had good luck." Then he went home. Then he walked along the ocean and back. Then he went inland. At a little creek he saw something. It was a nice and small (being), marked prettily on its back. "I had better take it," he thought, and caught it. Then it ran into his house and stayed there. Now he had a little (toy) boat,[6] about so long, into which he put water, and there he laid that thing, and it swam. Then he hid it away and cut two small pieces of elk meat and put them into the water. Then he went into the sweathouse. Next day he looked and the meat was gone. "That is why I kill so many," he thought.[7] Then he continued to do that. He constantly went hunting, killed game, and fed his pet.

c. Then the old woman (his mother) said, "What does he do, always killing deer?" And the old man (his father) asked him, "What do you do with the meat?" "Oh, I always give it away,"[8] he said.

Then he killed three deer and hung them in the house. The old woman said, "I will watch whether I can see anything come in." When it was nearly day, she

3. The Yurok are always being sorry for people, or wanting them to be sorry for themselves. More than once, when recording a song or story, I have been asked to remember the teller when he was gone; and once was literally entreated with tears to weep at least a little when I should hear of his death. This last was from a rich man noted for his sharp bargaining. There is no doubt that myths and songs contain to the Yurok an intense association of personality and its perishing. They evince a similar emotion in weeping at the climax of certain dances; and while this is said to be for their dead relatives who used to witness the same scene, it may be suspected that they mingle with their grief some anticipated sorrow for their own end.

4. The pet's (that is, the monster's) trail, at Hewego or Howego, as told in the story; cf. n. 15.

5. Espeu is at (Lower) Gold Bluff, on the coast 4 miles north of Orick and the mouth of Redwood Creek.

6. Several times mentioned in myths, and sometimes to be seen about the houses as toys.

7. The "thing" or being was a young Knewollek or water monster of the horned serpent type, living on game. It had intended to adopt the young man. Hence his success in hunting.

8. A typical Yurok evasion. He could hardly expect his parents to believe him, nor would he tell them about his supernatural pet.

thought she saw something above her sleeping place. Then she made the fire (blaze up). Then she could not see anything; but half the meat was gone. Then she continued to keep up the fire in order to not let that one eat any more.

In the morning the young man came into the house.[9] She said, "My son, I saw something come in last night, toward day." He answered nothing but went out and walked. He thought, "I had better let them know what I am keeping. They might do it an injury." He went back into the house. "You say something came into the house last night?" he said. "Yes." "Do you not know what I keep here in the house? Do not harm it. Let it eat the meat. That is what I hunt for."

d. Then the old woman allowed it to stay there all winter. Sometimes when she talked[10] to it, it was gone for two or three days. Then she was glad. Once she thought, "Let me hit it with my stick." In the middle of the night, she saw it eating the meat. Then she tried to strike it with her stick. It did not dodge, but she failed to strike it. Then she took a handful of coals, threw them, and hit it. Then it drew back and she heard it going off to the roof.[11]

Next morning the young man came in. He did not ask for it. He thought it had gone off and would come back. After two days, he asked, "Where is it gone?" The old woman said, "I do not know. I heard it go out. It is two days now."

e. Now he looked for it but could not find it. Then he went into his boat. He went twice around the world on the ocean[12] and could not see its tracks. He asked everyone, but no one had seen it. He spoke to every kind of being he met

9. He had spent the night in the sweathouse, of course.

10. Probably, scolded it.

11. And out of the smoke hole. [K. explains in his Handbook, pp. 78-82, that Yurok houses were built wholly of planks split from logs with wedges and more or less adzed. The walls were of planks set endwise into the ground, usually two rows thick. The side walls were low, but in the middle of the front and rear walls the planks might rise to ten feet. The sloping roof boards were laid on in two overlapping thicknesses, and the smoke hole was made by laying aside a board in the middle; it served as the only window. The doorway was a circular opening about two feet in diameter, cut near one end of the front wall. The door itself slid in a groove. Inside was a passageway that paralleled the front wall.

In the center of the house the soil was dug out for two to five feet and served as the working, cooking, eating, and sleeping area for the women and children. The surrounding shelf, at ground level, was a storage area. The men slept in the sweathouses, which were smaller structures. There was one sweathouse for approximately every three houses.—Ed.]

12. The Yurok frequently speak of an ocean upstream as well as downstream from their country. They also sometimes refer to the world-enclosing ocean here mentioned. Generally their ideas as to the southern and northern ends of that world, and of the peripheries of the universe, are vague or contradictory. Thus, there is a land across the western ocean, but it is also reached by going north along the coast. It may be the same as the land behind the sky in the north. Later in this story the hero reaches the sky by crossing the western ocean and then ascending eastward.

in the ocean, but none could tell him. He was so sorry that he cried as he went looking around the world. Then he came back without having found it. He did not eat, he did not drink water. He went into the sweathouse and lay down. The old man was sorry for his boy when he saw how he cried and looked and failed to find it.

f. Now, when the young man was asleep, he saw a little boy, who said, "I am sorry for you that nobody can tell you where it has gone. I will tell you. The old woman hit it. That is why it went away and no one can find it. Follow it in the morning. It stayed at a place where you will find me." When he woke he thought, "I have slept."[13]

Then he found its track behind the house. He followed it to the Klamath,[14] to Hewego,[15] where there is the mark of its crossing the river. Then he followed it up the ridge and along the mountains. He came to Fish Lake[16] and went into a house. There they told him, "Yes, it was here. It left two days ago. Do not follow it in this world, but go up to the sky."

Then he went back to Espeu. He thought, "Let me get my deer-hunting mask."[17] He took it, and went into the sweathouse, and took his pipe. Then they saw him go into his boat and out on the ocean with his hat[18] fluttering behind him. They thought, "He will not come back."

g. He crossed the ocean, left his boat, and went up to the sky. He traveled (eastward) across it. Then he found the one he was looking for. He knew it by its horns. There were many of them there, and they tried to deceive him, for the

13. That is, it was a dream, not reality, as I thought. [K.'s marginal note: "Dream motive, as in No'ots" (A7).—Ed.]

14. *Hierkik*, corresponding to approximate north (or to the right) when one is going downriver, is used in the sense of "on the Klamath" on the coast, that is, back inland. In both cases the general direction referred to is away from the water and not far from northeast; but the Yurok use no overt sun or compass directions.

15. Hewego is below Blue Creek, on the same side of the river: a narrow, steep gully down the mountain to the water's edge, which looks as if it might be the trail of a gigantic serpent. (Waterman, Geography, map 10, no. 19, has Howego, a flat on the left side, opposite a gash on the east bank by which Knewollek crossed coming from Espeu.) It is just above Erliken and something over 2 miles below Blue Creek.

16. Oketo (which means merely lake, lagoon, or any body of still water), a small mountain pond some half-dozen miles north or northeast of Weitspus; called Fish Lake by the whites. [See A8, n. 6, above.—Ed.] It is uninhabited except by spirits, thunders, and monsters. The dream boy was from there; hence his statement in *f*, "you will find me." It is inhabited by a whale in Spott and Kroeber, Yurok Narratives, no. 24, p. 224, and by Thunders in G6, below.

17. The stuffed deer head worn as a decoy by almost all California Indian hunters. The hero takes it along so he can provide for his pet if he finds it, or perhaps only for the sake of its associations.

18. Perhaps the deer head; but compare the feather-fringed net headdress in the No'ots story (A7*j*). Only women wear "hats" (basketry caps) among the Yurok.

others do not like to see a person. But that one that belonged to him said to them, "He is mine."

h. Then the young man said, "Well, let us go back." "No, I am ashamed,"[19] it said, and told him what the old woman had done. Then the young man could not persuade it and urged it otherwise. He said, "I want to live with you because I raised you. If as you came here you saw any place that you like, we will live there together." "Yes, I stayed at one place that pleased me. The door is large.[20] I should like to live with human beings. Because I was raised with them I should like to live where I can sometimes hear them talking." "We will go there. Now I am returning to get my things and leave that place (where I was born)." Then Long One[21] said to him, "Climb on my horns and sit. Do not walk."

i. Then it started with him. The young man thought it would go westward,[22] but it went eastward to the other ocean, and then back down the (Klamath) river to Fish Lake. "Downstream at the other end I left my boat," the young man said. It told him, "I will go there to get it, but do you go home and get your property. Put the things outside your house and I will take them."

Then he came back to Espeu. He carried outside everything that he had, a little distance from the house. Then he became tired. It was nearly sunset. He sat down where his things were. He lay down. At once he slept.

j. Then he awoke. He heard someone saying, "Wake up!" He looked about a long time. He did not get up. "Do you know where you are?" it asked him. "No," he said. "I made you sleep and brought you here. I carried you," it said. Then he found he was at Fish Lake. Then he lived there at Fish Lake. Those who were there helped them, advising them where there were bad places. "Here is a bad place where a man shoots whatever he sees," they said. So they told (those two) of everything, thinking that they did not know it already. So the young man from Espeu and the Long One he had raised as his pet lived there at Fish Lake.

A12. Kewet Omewa

This is a hero tale. I mean by this that it is neither concerned with the origin of an institution nor is it a story of emotion like the ordinary tale with a "plot." Its main interest is the delineation of a personality as revealed in his deeds. The accomplishments are part of the usual material of myths as known to all members of the group. Of course the ordinary man, among the Yurok as ourselves, takes story telling and story hearing too indifferently, or too naively, to trouble much about personality. The recital of an action

19. Another emotion the Yurok, and many Indians, are more ready to feel or acknowledge than we.

20. Enabling the monster to enter.

21. The first time that the story tells what "it" was!

22. The direction from which the young man had come in reaching the sky.

that is of a pattern with which he has become familiar substantially satisfies his literary need. The present narrator uses the same materials, but what his feelings evidently dwell on is the exalted nature of the personages. The incidents are a means, not a sufficient end in themselves.

The hero's traits are well brought out. He is reticent, self-communing, quiet, but master. This is not full characterization of the sort novels have accustomed us to, but it is definite and successful depiction of the status of a personality toward life.

The interweaving of the two chief characters is one of the favorite sleights of the narrator, and as dexterously done as usual. A good half of the story refers to Coyote, but Kewet omewa remains the undivided hero. We are told what he thinks of Coyote; but Coyote's acts and speeches are only related, scarcely what goes on in his mind. He is the stock Coyote of all Yurok tales, in fact, of all Californian mythology: amorous, greedy, avaricious, lying, vainglorious, servile, devoid of all upright self-respect. The usual device is to depict his cunning folly as succumbing in contest with sense, or to match his disposition against that of a restrained, wise, and benevolent companion. Both are simple devices. But in this tale Coyote is more than a despicable trickster. He does move his house. He is made a wonderful runner. Except for his lack of control, he would be a fit partner for Kewet omewa in his hazardous raids on the dentalium weir. That a person of such genuine abilities should be only a servant to the hero correspondingly elevates the latter.

Furthermore, there is no inconsistency of the type that sooner or later usually mars the Coyote conception in the longer tales of most other mythology. He is not improving the world in one episode, satisfying his gluttony in the next; or tumbling from foresight into insensate folly. This Coyote is invariably selfish, but though he overreaches himself he is never a fool; and he is frankly never concerned with anything but his own interests. The disjected character of the Coyote of central California lends itself much better to the stringing of a multifarious variety of incidents. Even Yurok mythology is not free from this tendency; see G2-4, J5-7. But the present tale makes of Coyote both a self-harmonious personage and one that contributes to the sympathy felt for the leading actor.

Finally, it is noticeable that Coyote, like the less conspicuous Cormorant, is wholly humanized. His temperament as a figure in the story is based on the character of the animal; but his motives, his actions, even his bodily shape, it may be gathered, are those of a man. He does not get his fur singed nor snap up gophers, nor is there any explanation of why his tail is scraggy. This personalized conception of him is rather regularly adhered to by the Yurok. Other Californians have him fluctuate between human and quadruped form, much as between trickster and hero.

•

a. On the top of Kewet[1] stood twenty-one houses. Ten were on the upstream side, ten downstream. A young man had his in the middle. This was Kewet omewa.[2] He told two of his young men, "Go get two poles, as long as

1. Kewet is Rivet (or Burrill) Mountain, which rises over 4,000 feet directly behind Weitspus.
2. Or Kewet o-megwa. It may mean "Kewet's owner."

you can find them in the woods.'' They came back, each with a pole. He looked and thought, ''Yes, those will be long enough.'' He said, ''Now set them up in front of my house, one at each corner.'' So they set them up there, and put three cross pieces on each. Then he thought, ''I shall wait until morning and see how it will be.'' He was lying in the sweathouse, listening from there. Then he began to hear pileated woodpeckers[3] outside. Soon he heard smaller red-headed woodpeckers[4] chattering.'' He said, ''Go look! I hear something chattering outside.'' One of them went out, came back, and said, ''Right here outside your house, all over one of those poles, are pileated woodpeckers; and on the other one, small woodpeckers.'' Then he thought, ''That is what I want, to have them fly here and sit on my house.''

b. That day he was sitting before his sweathouse. Then he saw someone come up the ridge from downstream.[5] He thought, ''It is a good-looking young man who comes. He has a quiver and bow and everything else.'' Then he asked him, ''Where are you from?'' That one said, ''I left where I lived, I do not know how long ago. I go everywhere.'' ''Yes?'' ''Where I lived there are few young men, and they have all gone away. I do not know where I am going.'' ''Yes? How far is it to where you were living?'' ''It is not very far. The place is called Kenek, where I stayed. All of them have left, and I have no place to go to. I have been looking for a place.'' ''Well, how will you move? Shall you move your house?'' ''Yes. If I call for my house it will be here in the morning.'' Kewet omewa thought, ''He is a man if he can do that.'' He said to him, ''Do you think you can run?'' ''Yes, I think I can run somewhat.''

c. Kewet omewa had something lying by him. He said, ''I wish you would go to the river for me and bring me some sand. I want to work at this.'' ''Yes,'' that one said (and started).

Soon he came back with the sand. Kewet omewa smiled and thought, ''He is intelligent: perhaps he has found sand somewhere on the mountain. I do not think he has gone (all the way down) to the river.'' He took the sand, looked at it, and thought, ''Well it looks as if it came from the river.''

d. Then he thought. He said, ''Well, I shall have to go to the ocean now. I forgot my paddle. It is lying in my boat there. I tell you, my friend, if you will get my paddle for me I shall always show you what to do.''[6] ''Where is your boat?'' ''Far downstream at the salt water. I have only the one paddle. Do bring

3. Birds whose crest or scalp furnishes the scarlet feathers so highly prized by the Yurok: the great pileated woodpeckers (*Dryocopus pileatus*) of California.

4. Smaller birds, whose scalps are valued at about a sixth to a tenth as much as those of the pileated woodpeckers, but used for the same purpose.

5. From Wahsek, the town next below Weitspus. The newcomer was Coyote, not named until *e*. [For the town names, see map 2 in this volume.—Ed.]

6. Give you directions, be your patron.

it up for me." "Very well." He started. Soon he saw him coming back. He looked and saw that it was his own paddle.

e. Then he thought, "I shall make him come and live here and tell him what to do."[7] Then he told him, "You had better bring your house up. You can live anywhere here." That one, Coyote,[8] said, "Yes, you will find my house here in the morning. I think I shall live at the upstream end of the (row of) houses. No, I shall be at the downstream end, that I may always look at the ocean." So he determined where he would put his house. Next morning Kewet omewa went out and saw the house there. Then Coyote lived there.

f. At Women[9] there were two girls, sisters. They had heard that there were two young men living on Kewet. "Let us go to see those young men," they said, and started. Coyote knew. He waited in their path, saw the two girls come, and spoke to them: "Where are you going?" They said, "We are going to that town.[10] We wonder if the young man there is at home." Coyote said, "I will go to see if he is home." "Yes, do," they said. "Wait here until I come back," Coyote said. He ran to Kewet omewa's house, drew out one of the long (woodpecker perch) poles, ran to his own house, set it in the ground at the corner, ran and got the other, and set it down too. Then he went back to the girls. He said, "Yes, he will be home soon. I will tell you where his house is. You will see a pole with pileated woodpeckers flying about it and another with small woodpeckers. Go into that house." Then they went on, but he stayed.

(When they arrived) the younger girl said, "Well, I have always heard that his house was in the middle. How is it that it is at the end?" The older one said, "Well, go by the poles. They are not at the middle house." Then they went into the house. It was good-looking, but in it they saw only one old woman. She said, "Where are you going?" The younger girl said, "Oh, we have just come here." They sat and heard many young men outside shouting and playing.

g. When it was nearly sunset a young man came in and sat down. "You have come?"[11] he said. "Yes," they said. Then they ate. Then someone spoke from outside: "Oh, Tsmegok!" That was Coyote's name. Then he thought, "They will find me out." Again they called him. Then he turned around and said, "You may make that dance."[12] The one outside had been sent by Kewet

7. Again, give him directions, be his patron.

8. The casual way in which the name is finally brought in shows that it is not felt to be essential to the story.

9. Women is Big Prairie, on the same ridge as Kewet, but farther from the river. There were of course no Yurok habitations here, any more than on Kewet. Waterman, Geography, p. 260, perhaps citing from the present tale, says that it is a "great open space on mountain back of Kewet," but that its location is uncertain. It is mentioned also in T4.

10. Kewet.

11. A greeting. It was Coyote.

12. He pretends to be the headman, issuing orders or granting permission. I do not know the

omewa to tell him to come and eat deer soup. He called, "Come and eat deer soup!" Then Coyote went out. The girls thought, "We should like to see it dark soon";[13] for they found that they had made a mistake.

h. When it was nearly day she awoke her sister. They looked out and saw the poles in front of the middle house now. She said, "I had heard that Coyote was about here also. He is the one who has done this to us." And they saw Kewet omewa sitting outside his sweathouse. Then they turned around and went home,[14] by way of Kenek.[15]

i. An old man was standing there. "Where have you been?" he asked. "On the mountain." "Why didn't you tell me? I know you have been put to shame, I know that house. I am an old man and I always go in there. No one else, no other man, can enter; it is too dangerous." "Will you take us there so that we may marry that young man? You shall be on Kewet also if you come with us." "Yes. I am going home now, downstream, but be ready in two days. You will see me here then." Then the two girls went home and got ready.

j. In two days they said, "Let us start. Perhaps we shall find the old man at Kenek." Then they saw the old man ready, painted up nicely, with a little red at the ends of his mouth. He was Cormorant.[16] Then they went. They came near the place. The old man said, "We shall get up there at sunset. They will all be in the houses. It will be the right time. He has ten brothers and sisters and a father and mother. Now when I go into the house, watch my feet. Do not look around you, but step in the same places as I. If you mistake my footsteps you will fall into the fire." "Yes, we will do that," they said.

Then the old man started to go in. "Come in, old man" (those in the house) said. The two girls only watched where his feet went and stepped in the same spots. The old woman said to one of the girls, "Come here and sit by me." The old man said to the other, "Sit by me." So they sat, one by each of the old people. Then they saw the young man with a little dog by him.

k. Cormorant had said to them, "When you are to cook, I will say, 'I am cold,' and put my feet by the fire. Then set the spit[17] between my toes, next to my big toe. You will find no holes[18] anywhere else to set the spits in, only four

meaning of Tsmegok, or Tsmegohk, which recurs in A18, though it is evidently derisive. Being called to eat deer soup seems also to be derogatory, perhaps because the soup is made from scraps or leavings.

13. [K.'s marginal note: "ashamed."—Ed.]

14. In shame.

15. "Went home, back to Kenek," my notes read. Billy would not be likely to forget that he had just brought the girls from Women, so I assume a misunderstanding and emend to "by way of." Possibly they were from Kenek but had come up via Women.

16. Or Shag, Tspega.

17. Cuts of salmon are broiled on sticks set on end before the fire.

18. The floor of this house is of stone, so that the sticks or spits can be set only in the sockets provided.

on four sides of the fire. I will spread my legs on both sides of the fire. When you have set in the spits, I shall draw back my feet." Now the old woman began to cut up salmon. Then old man Cormorant said, "I am cold from bringing my boat up in the water,"[19] and spread his legs. They did as he had told them and set the spits and broiled the salmon. When they had broiled it, the youngest of the brothers helped one girl take out the stick and the old woman helped the other. Then they all ate.

l. Next day Kewet omewa said, "You might go home in five days. We shall accompany you."[20] "Yes," they said. Old man Cormorant said, "Let us go to the ocean to fish." Kewet omewa sent three of his younger brothers with him. He told them to leave some of the fish in the boat: "Tsmegok can go and get them." The girls heard it. After a time they came back from fishing and said, "We left four fish and a paddle in the boat." "Somebody tell Tsmegok to bring them up." Soon Tsmegok came bringing the four salmon and the paddle. Then Cormorant thought, "He can indeed run fast. It is far off where we left the paddle."

m. After five days the old man of Kewet said, "Five of you take these girls home. Take ten girls with you from here to carry food to their house."[21] Kewet omewa sat and said nothing. He only asked, "When shall you come again? You must come back." One of them said, "Why do you not come with us?" He said, "No. Five of my brothers will take you. I never go anywhere. I stay here." Then the five young men took the girls home. Cormorant wanted to have them stay. He said, "They would like to live here. That is why they came." But Kewet omewa said, "After a while."[22]

n. Now Kewet omewa went off. He came back the next day. Then Coyote thought, "Why is it that the old man is not in the sweathouse?" Then he saw that the old man was eating.[23] Whenever he had bitten off[24] (the meat) he laid something down beside him. It looked pretty. "Does it taste good, old man?" Coyote asked him. "No, it does not taste good," he said. Coyote thought, "I should like to snatch one and taste it." Whenever Kewet omewa went away, the old man, after his return, always ate them and then twisted string. They were dentalia that he had. The old man ate out the meat, then measured off his string, strung (the shells) on it, and had money.

19. The Klamath in general is a swift stream, and in many places boats are poled, towed, shoved, or pulled by hand.

20. He is not refusing to marry them. In fact, the narrator explained, he did marry one, and one of his younger brothers the other.

21. Possibly they took them home with the bride price to be paid for them, but more likely it was only a good-will gift of food.

22. A great man is never hasty, particularly where gratification is involved.

23. No one ever eats in the sweathouse.

24. Or: sucked out.

o. Then Coyote said to Kewet omewa, once when he had come back, "I have been southward and have seen that kind there." (He wanted Kewet omewa to say, "Yes, that is where they grow.") Next time he said to him, "I have been upstream and have seen them." When he came another time, Coyote said to him, "I have been downstream and seen them there."

p. Kewet omewa used to go off and the middle of the next day came to a place where there was a fish weir with openwork trinket baskets (*rumitsek*) hanging along it. He always took one dentalium from each basket. But it was lonely for him. So he tried out all his brothers, to see if they could run fast enough to go with him. Starting from Kewet, they ran around the world, but he always returned far ahead of them. That is why he did not take them with him (on his dentalium trips), because they would be caught.[25]

q. Now he thought, "I will try Coyote. If I do not beat him badly he can perhaps come with me." So he thought as he was coming back from where the dentalia grew, feeling lonely. When he returned, Coyote said, "Did you not see someone's tracks in the path?" "No," he said. "I came along the path. I have been to that place," said Coyote. Kewet omewa asked him, "How many of them did you get?" Coyote said, "Oh, no. I did not want to take any. I went only to look at them. If ever I want to have any of those that you have been bringing I shall go to get them." Kewet omewa believed him and said, "Next time I go, come with me." "Yes," said Coyote, "but I shall not touch one. I only want to go along with you." Kewet omewa said, "I will tell you what we shall do. Let us run around this world and see who comes back first." Coyote said, "Yes." He thought, "I will do my best. I can (at least) stay near him."

r. Next morning they started from in front of their sweathouse, going around by the south and east and north and west. Then after a time they (at Kewet) saw them, the two together, and they came back to the sweathouse side by side. Then Coyote said, "I did not do my best." So Kewet omewa thought, "It must surely be that he will not be caught. I have never run my hardest when I took dentalia, and yet they (give up the pursuit after) following me only halfway."

s. In the morning he thought, "Well, I had better take him along today. I am always lonely when I go there alone." So he said to him, "Let us go." "Yes," said Coyote. Then they went. On every mountain they sat down and rested and talked. Kewet omewa thought, "That is the way I like it, to talk and enjoy myself." Before they reached the place he said, "Here is where we shall stay for the night. We shall arrive tomorrow after noon." Coyote did not want to lie down. He sat up listening to those who were shouting at the dentalium weir.

25. By the enraged owners of the weir and dentalia. (For dentalia in trinket baskets hung in a weir, see also A4.) [K. also has a marginal note to one Hupa tale but does not specify which.—Ed.]

Kewet omewa watched him. He thought, "Perhaps he will run down to that place (during the night) and leave me here."

t. The middle of the next day they saw them[26] all go home. They saw the last man go into his house. Then Kewet omewa said, "Well, now let us go. Do not take two, but only one from each basket," and Coyote said, "Yes, I do not want many. I want only three: one from this end, one from that end, and one from the middle basket." "Very well," said Kewet omewa. He himself always took twelve, one each from the twelve baskets hanging on the weir.

u. Now they got there. He took only one from each basket, saying continually, "Do not take too many." "Yes, I want only three," said Coyote. Then when they had gone halfway up the (first) ridge (on their return), they heard shouting: those people were pursuing them. Before this he had always traveled over one ridge before they began to follow him. Now he (and Coyote) arrived on the first ridge at the same time. At the next ridge Coyote was five steps behind. Kewet omewa waited for him, and they ran on. At the next ridge Coyote was ten steps behind. After five ridges he no longer saw Coyote, he was so far back. On the seventh ridge he waited and looked back. He did not see him coming. Then he thought, "I had better go on or they may catch me. I am afraid they have got him." After nine ridges he heard no more shouting. On the tenth he sat down and thought, "I am sorry. I am sure he was caught. I pity my companion. I had better go on." He started on his way.

v. Then he saw Coyote coming toward him from the direction in which he was traveling. "I ran around and ahead. They could not catch me," he said. "I thought you had been caught." "No, I thought they had you." "Where are those that you took?" "Here," said Coyote, and showed him his dentalia. Then Kewet omewa believed that he had not been overtaken.[27] They went on and returned to Kewet.

w. The next day Coyote worked. He made ten strings of his money out of dentalia.[28] Kewet omewa watched him. Then one day Coyote wanted to go to Ko'men.[29] Kewet omewa said to him, "Oh, do not go. There is one there who can do anything that he wants to." "Oh, I shall just go there (without engaging in anything). I only want to go to see the playing. I shall not carry anything there."[30] "Well, then go."

26. The dentalium owners.

27. He was caught and killed, but his blood returned to life. He then ran ahead in order to meet Kewet omewa and pretend successful escape. That the narrator does not mention that he was killed is perhaps due to the conviction which any Yurok would have that Coyote would not legitimately succeed in any enterprise. Whatever he asserted to his own glory would be invented or exaggerated.

28. That is, he had stolen about 120 shells instead of 12. Or did the dentalia multiply?

29. Panamenik, the Karok town where Orleans now stands.

30. That is, "I shall leave my money at home."

He went and in five days he had not come back. Then someone came from Ko'men. He asked him, "Where is he?" The Ko'men man said, "Oh, as soon as he arrived he began to gamble. He is still playing."

At last Coyote returned. "Well, you have been away a long time." "Yes, I saw all kinds of fun. I did not do anything myself but only looked on." "I hear that you gambled." "No, I did not gamble, but I saw many playing." "Where are the dentalia you had?" "I sent them back to where I got them."

x. Next day someone came from Ko'men. When they looked at him they saw that he wore a dentalium through his nose.[31] They said to him, "That is a pretty one you are wearing. Where did you get it?" He said, "A downstream person (Yurok) came and gambled away many." They said, "There is a man here who has been at Ko'men; perhaps he is the one." "I will see," said the Ko'men man. Soon Coyote came along polishing an arrow.[32] "That is the one," said the Ko'men person. "He brought much money with him. It is all about there now."[33]

A13. Kewetspekw

This is as patriotic a story as can be heard among the Yurok. Told by a Weitspus narrator, it has as its hero the legendary Samson of the town. He is named from the spring Wetspekw from which Weitspus drinks, and by whose appellation the community is sometimes known, as the American "Weitchpec" testifies. The hero's foes are from sites where no one lived recently whose friendship might be alienated by a recital of their defeats. The great Hupa village of Takimiłding, whose rich men brought their wealth to the Weitspus dances, is represented as neutral or friendly. The bad Hupa has his home at Oknul (Honsading), at the entrance to the valley, where a town once stood, a place uninhabited in historic time. Downstream, Kewetspekw's opponent was at Nä'gеł, an obscure little one-time town opposite Erner and the mouth of Blue Creek. The enemy might theoretically have been located there or just above at Oyoł, but here there were actual residents in historic times, who might have been offended by having their town named. Other versions of the tale put the foe further downstream at Łmeyekweł[1] (*łmei*, quarrelsome, vicious, oppressive), which was once a village, though a small one; here too the housepits indicate desertion for several generations.

It is to be noted, however, that the sentiment is one of local, not of national or racial, pride. The defeated include a Yurok as well as a Hupa; and the latter, for all his bad

31. A Karok and Tolowa custom. The Yurok and Hupa perforate the septum only after death.

32. A touch that is irrelevant to the story but adds vividness—more in the manner of a modern novel than a primitive folktale.

33. It has passed into many hands. Ten strings would buy a good wife or square a killing. To have so much money suddenly dissipated through a town would cause a sensation.

---

1. [K. spelled the name thus here, but queried it; in N1 he spells it Łemekweł.—Ed.]

disposition, must have been something of a man if he could drag and paddle his canoe over a mountain. His home town means much to every Yurok, but a conflict of his ethnic group with another, as of the children of Israel with the Philistines, is something he rarely rises to even in imagination.

The tale is told by the narrator at his most spirited. The hero comes into being modestly. Oppressions of his townmates move him, but he is peaceable, and detours his journeys to avoid a clash. New abuses greet his return. For half a year he says nothing but seeks a means. At last he finds a lake inhabited by supernatural beings who give bodily strength. That they are Thunders, the narrator does not at first find it necessary to specify, perhaps because his audience knows, possibly because the omission heightens suspense.

The swimming in a mountain pool at night is a custom familiar to all northerly Californians. With the Yurok, a woman becomes a shaman after occupying a stone seat on a mountain top. The occasional man who is ambitious for bravery seeks the lake. The narrator works climax into his description of the practice. The hero casts ten bundles of tobacco into the lake. On the seventh, thunder sounds faintly; on the eighth it rolls; on the ninth the water heaves with a roar; with the tenth the devotee leaps in, and his senses leave him. He returns slowly and quietly to consciousness. The mild old Thunder father stands over him and warns of his boisterous sons. There are ten, he says; he names the occupation of six; the story in its progress describes eight. Such lapses are immaterial to the narrator as against the effect which he is developing. So, later, the point of a messenger's achievement is that he travels to the mouth of the river and back between morning and evening; yet when those whom he convoyed are to make clear the terror inspired by the robber at Nä'ägel, the storyteller forgets and has them sneak by at night. As so often in this volume, discrepancies of number or time or circumstance, or of place when it is beyond the tread of Yurok feet, do not trouble a native narrator. He is intent on the thread of his plot, on the emotion of a situation; he forgets matters of fact or ignores them when it helps the story.

So here the cumulating power of the Thunders is the point. The first couple come in; the second clatter their sticks; the third shake the house and sit with bowed heads like men nursing a feud; the last rock and tip the structure and carelessly carry about with them the limbs of their victims. The story moves more rapidly with the climax: there is no explaining. "Here he is!" they shout, strike him with the carcasses, and he knows no more. European tales handle the return of the increasingly wild Wind sons with no greater vividness or more dexterous art.

The hero is given wealth and is astonished, an attitude that subtly establishes his native innocence of spirit. Every Yurok knows that he who would kill must have substance to settle claims. Kewetspekw seems to think of wealth as only the mark of the resplendent rich man, and so a Thunder has to explain to him that the valuables are to make him a man who can slay ten.

Slowly he prepares, careful to throw all onus on the wicked. His people gather property and display it to tempt the despoilers to a final outrage. He is warned that they are coming; he sends them word to leave him in peace. "Something is going to happen," the bystander begins to realize. "If he does come, you may bury me the day after," Kewetspekw tells him with indirect thrust. At the same time, he arranges everything to inflame the invader without having the responsibility fall on himself. When the great warrior arrives savagely and, infuriated still further by a direct but planned and legitimate refusal to settle for the loss of a henchman swept away in the river, he proceeds to despoil twofold and fivefold. The hero climbs out of his sweathouse and combs his hair as sign of his nonresistance. "Only do not take my one boat, friend," he modestly urges, to be insulted with the reply that if he spoke like a man he m·ght be one.

The clash breaks out where the attention has been focused. The canoe is seized, the hero pleads once more, it is drawn on. The long withheld action begins to reel out. One pull drags the boat away from the robbers. They rush forward, their bows snap and fall, the foremost is seized and hurled at the crowd. "Twenty are dead when that man stops flying." But the leader has been saved for the last. "Strong as a rock," he does not fall at the first attempt; Kewetspekw's palm does not turn his face homeward. They grapple; they pull, then push; neither yields; the hero's people stand looking. Then his might rises. He lifts the foe. It is not enough. Again he raises him, swings him clear, this time catches his foot, crashes him down once more to seize the other leg, and begins to split him. Slowly he draws him apart. "I grew without friends and need none now," he replies to the victim's appeals for partnership. Only when his own people intercede he lets go, and contemptuously sends the helpless foe home in the boat over which they fought.

But one such victory, as others relate the story, is not enough for the teller. There must be a second bad man overcome. And yet, though he exactly balances the first as a robber and terrorizer, his fate is not monotonously repeated. Kewetspekw sends for his friends from the faraway mouth of the river, to take them to Oknuɫ and recover their lost wealth from the cowed inhabitants. He learns from them that the second tyrant still plies his trade on their way; this time he takes the initiative. He paddles to Nä'ägeɫ and sends three followers into the town. A spirited conversation ensues between them and the strong man; the dialogue flies thick without the usual "said he" and "he said." The emissaries yield nothing. The Nä'ägeɫ leader in turn sends messengers to their chief below, who tauntingly misunderstands each repeated warning to leave—the last time construing it as an invitation to pillage the pillager! The home envoys can no longer ignore his studied answers and, beginning to fear, withdraw. But Kewetspekw is intent on precipitating the issue, and signals his fleet of waiting friends to come abreast the town as if to pass in open defiance. This brings the bully running down; and, like a real man, though a bad one, he wastes no time with retainers but makes for the hero himself. Kewetspekw falls once more into his seeming reluctance to violence, and shrinks back in his boat; but as the intimidator's hand first reaches to touch it—there is no dragging it over the sand this time—the wrist is instantly struck and the member falls to the ground. Playing with his victim, the hero slaps the hand back into place, only to pull out his entire arm. He meets no further resistance, and the vanquished leader himself shows Kewetspekw's trooping followers into his stronghold to restore what valuables they claim.

His work done, the hero discontinues his assumed voyage and returns home to send boats up and down the rivers to test the properly humble behavior of the vanquished; the boats return with reports of an unexampled peace. There follows the episode of the recovered Oknuɫ man's overland boat trip to save his pride in an intention persisted in, without contravening the orders of his new master. The story draws to a quieter close—a true finish, so often lacking in Indian tales, with Kewetspekw's expression of affection for his birthplace, and his enduring retirement into its spring—his head plume rising above it as the tree familiar since childhood to every inhabitant; and the end comes in a sudden exultant chord about the town that still boasts: "We have fought our day's work—let us to breakfast."

The characterization is no less artful than the plot. There is subtlety in differentiating three personages, all distinguished for the same quality of physical strength. The Oknuɬ man is active in his vocation, sends spies, leads out expeditions for plunder; he burns with wrath at an impediment; the one of Nä'ägeɬ sits on his rock exacting toll of the wayfarer; the hero is slow to move and always longing for peace, yet the swiftest when combat breaks; he is fertile in goading his adversaries, scornful yet moderate in victory, content with restitution, foregoing penalty for the greater triumph of conceded superiority. His followers exalt him no less than his opponents: the friend from the ocean, who can master a crowd of boats and yet leans on him for redress; and Tspega (Cormorant), who cuts a swift messenger's time in half.

•

a. He grew in the rock at the creek (spring) at Weitspus. That was his house. He was called Kewetspekw.

Then he always heard: "If they go to him, there is a man who takes away their quivers and arrows and other belongings. He lives at Oknuɬ[2] in Hupa." Sometimes a Weitspus person who had gone to Hupa said, "That Oknuɬ man abused me." Kewetspekw did not like to hear that.

Another man lived at Nä'ägeɬ.[3] He was the same kind; hostile[4] and wanting no one to come about. Kewetspekw heard of him and did not like it.

Now once he wished to go downstream to visit his friend. Then he went around to Redwood Creek and down it to the ocean and downstream[5] to Rekwoi. He feared to go straight downriver[6] on account of the one at Nä'ägeɬ. Then he heard from the Chilula[7] what that one did and how he robbed those who came by.

b. When he returned to Weitspus, he thought, "What is the matter today with (the Weitspus people)? They seem ugly-minded." He went into his house. "What is the matter with them?" he asked his father. The old man said, "I will tell you why it is. The bad one from Nä'ägeɬ came today and took all the quivers we had hanging outside the houses. And he took away five boats." "So?" said

2. Called Honsading in Hupa. [Many of the footnotes for this myth were indicated by K. as "not written or mislaid." The notes have been renumbered and supplied in as complete a form as possible. The larger towns mentioned are shown on map 2 in this volume.—Ed.]

3. Opposite the mouth of Blue Creek, which empties into the Klamath.

4. *Ɬmei*, "mean," a "bad man."

5. North along the coast.

6. On the Klamath.

7. Of Redwood Creek.

Kewetspekw. He thought, "He is always coming here to abuse them. I should like to know what to do. I will prepare. I will try to get ready this winter to meet him next year."

No one knew what he did. That winter he went about in the woods. Once the old man asked him, "Do you not notice something when you go about at night?" "No, I hear nothing, notice nothing." "I will tell you what to do. Make ten bundles of tobacco as long as that.[8] I once heard that if you find them,[9] it will turn out well. I know what you must do. Look around at Itperper.[10] There you will see water, a nice round lake. Wait there. Put a good stick in the water, and you will see it sink at once. That is the water you will wish."

Once Kewetspekw came home and said, "I found that water." "Now go there tomorrow. Take all the tobacco you have. Every little while put one bundle into the water. Then wait again. As soon as you put the last bundle into the water, follow it yourself."

c. Then he went there. When he arrived he threw one package into the water. When he had thrown in seven, he faintly heard thunder ringing. Then he dropped in the eighth and heard thunder. He cast in the ninth and saw the water shaking with thunder. When he dropped the last one, he jumped into the water himself. Then he knew nothing.

d. He heard someone waking him. "Are you asleep?" Then he had his senses. "Yes." Then that one said, "Come in the house." He looked and saw a house. They went in. Then the old man said to him, "My boys have wanted to see you. They know what those (two bad) men have done to you. They have been wanting to see you very much. I hear them talk of you. They will be glad. Wait until they come: they are ten. Hide under this. Do not be afraid of them in any case. Five of them are good, five bad. You will fear them, but there is no reason to be afraid. Now I will tell you where they have gone. Two went to gamble, (two to play shinny), two to the war dance, and two to war."[11]

Then he saw first those that had gone to gamble. They were young men. Then he heard shinny sticks clattering, and two more came back. Now there were four in the house. Whenever his sons came in, the old man said, "Ai! Stop! The one you always wanted to see is here. Go easy." He heard two more coming in. The entire house was shaking. The old man said, "Easy! The one you wanted is here." These had been at the war dance. They sat down with their heads on their knees, not looking about them. Their hair was tied up (for fighting), and they wore feathers and carried quivers. Then he heard them

8. A finger.

9. The Thunders mentioned below.

10. Half a dozen miles upstream from Weitspus and northwest from the river, in the hills. [See map 4, no. 1, in this volume.—Ed.]

11. So below, making eight instead of the ten specified; but actually the narrator accounts for only six here.

coming again. This time the house was nearly turned over, then almost tipped the other way. "Easy! The one you wanted to see has come," the old man said. Then he saw them come in. One of them was armless on one side. From behind the other's back, on each side, a person's foot projected that he was carrying. "Slowly! The one you pitied is here." "Yes? Where is he?" said he with the feet in his load, and drew out one (and then the other) of the human legs. "Here he is!" he shouted, pulling off his cover and striking him with one human leg and then with the other. Thus he gave him (supernatural strength). Then (Kewetspekw) did not know what they did to him.

e. But the old man knew. They laid him in the fire. They washed him. So they made new bones for him. Now they had done everything (they could) for him. Then they put one woodpecker crest in his hand and closed it so that he would not lose it. They put one dentalium in his other hand. And then they laid him out in the open at Itperper near the trail.

f. Now it was nearly day. Then he recovered. "I am alive in the open," he thought. Then he knew where he was. He looked at his foot and every part of himself and saw that he was not hurt. He looked in his hand and saw a dentalium. He closed the hand and looked in the other. There he saw a woodpecker crest. "I will go home," he thought. He got up, went, and began to feel well. He went on and felt better. He thought, "I should like to see a large white oak standing. I would try what I can do." Then he saw not far away a large oak with a fork higher than his head. "I will try that. I will see what I shall do," he said. Then he ran, leaped to the crotch, pushed both limbs with his elbows, and split the tree apart. Then he knew, "That is the kind of man I wanted to become." He smiled. "I will go to see him this summer."

He was (still) carrying the dentalium and the woodpecker crest in his hands. When he came to his house he opened his (cylindrical) trunk and laid the woodpecker crest in it. The dentalium he put into a large empty storage basket. Then he went to his sweathouse.

g. He thought, "I will sleep tonight." When he slept he dreamed. He thought he saw one of the Thunders, who said, "I have come to talk to you. Open your trunk in ten days and look inside. Wait another ten days and uncover your basket. You are well provided for. You will be able to do (your desire) whenever you wish."

Then in ten days he opened his trunk. It was full of woodpecker crests. In (another) ten days he uncovered his basket. He saw obsidians inside, and skins rolled full of dentalium (money), and other kinds of valuables, the basket full. He thought, "What are these for? I do not want to have good times (making dances like a rich man). I want something else."

h. That night he dreamed again. The Thunder said, "You need not think that. We knew what kind of a man you wished to become. That is why we gave you the woodpecker crests and the other things. Whenever a man injures your people, you will arise and kill him for it. You will kill ten men and pay ten times (in settlement) for killings." Then when he woke he thought, "That is what I wished. That is why they gave it to me: to pay for killing. That is good."

i. Then he began to talk to his people. "I want you to go about;[12] some upstream, some downstream, some on the mountains. Buy all the blankets you see. You who go downstream buy all the boats you can get. I will give you dentalia to buy them with." The next day five went downstream, five upstream; some on the mountains setting traps for fishers,[13] some to make bows and arrows. All bought, trapped, and made.

Then those who had gone downstream said, "We went to Serper; that is as far as we went: we were afraid of the man at Nä'ägeł." (Kewetspekw) said nothing.

Now it began to be summer. He told his people to make fine black quivers (of the fisher skins), and all made them.

j. Now it was summer. Persons came from Hupa. Two young men (from there) were standing at a distance and looking. Quivers hung outside the houses (at Weitspus); sometimes two, sometimes three; and there were (deer fur) blankets too.[14]

In the morning (Kewetspekw) said, "Where are those Hupa persons?" "We do not know. We see a (Weitspus) boat on the other side. Perhaps they have (used it to cross in and) gone home."

The one at Oknuł had sent the two to see if anything were hanging at the houses at Weitspus. He said, "I hear that many good things are hanging there. I will go to get them."

k. One morning Kewetspekw saw someone coming from Oplego.[15] It was his friend. He was sitting outside his house making a bow when Hupa person arrived. "I wanted to see you. That is why I came. I started early; I have eaten nothing." Kewetspekw said, "Let us go indoors and eat." Then his friend said, "When I came from where I belong, I looked at Oknuł and saw many people (gathered). I heard about it before, but I did not know where they were going. Now I have learned. Tomorrow, I do not know when, they will be here. They are going to rob you. Some of them have come from far. They were saying, 'I am going to my friends. I shall see if they have good quivers to give me, or boats or blankets. If they have, I will get them.' I felt sorry for you. That is why I came here. Hide the best things you have. Put them outdoors in the brush."

"Well, my friend, eat quickly and go back at once. Tell them not to come here, not one step. Tell them I say it." The Hupa person thought, "Something is

12. [K.'s marginal note: "Chief."—Ed.]

13. [Fishers are large carnivorous arboreal mammals (*Martes pennanti*) related to the weasel.—Ed.]

14. Airing or curing.

15. Takimiłding in Hupa.

going to happen." "If he wants to come down nevertheless, (said Kewetspekw,) let him come. And I want you to come the next day and bury me."[16] The Hupa person said, "Yes."

l. The next day they prepared food at Weitspus. He told them what to do if (the Hupa) should come. He told them: "Bring all boats over on this side. Do not leave one on the other side. Then if one of them swims, I will make him drown, so that the others begin to be angry. Have gambling going on in one place, and another game in another place, and elsewhere a shinny game." So they did, and in two places they were gambling, in one place they were playing shinny; elsewhere they were shooting at a mark. All kinds of games were being played.

m. Then they saw to persons across the river. One of the Weitspus men said (to another), "Where is Kewetspekw?" "He is in the sweathouse making arrows." He looked into the sweathouse and said to Kewetspekw, "There are two persons on the other side." After a time there were others across the river, and then more and more. Now one of them took off his moccasins:[17] He was about to swim across. Then they saw him swimming, for all the boats were on this side.[18] Then he began to sink. The last time they saw only his feet. Then Kewetspekw told one of his people, "One of them has drowned: now set them across."

The Oknuɬ people burned with anger; they felt ugly. When they saw one coming across (to them in a boat), some of them said, "We will kill him." Oknuɬ bad man said, "No. Let us first take away all they have. Then we will kill them. I know what to say. Let me cross first." Then he asked the one in the boat, "Is my friend[19] there?" "Yes," he said. "I am coming to see him." He did not say that one of them had drowned. Then they came across (with the Weitspus ferryman) and sat down on the sand beach. He told five of his men, "Go up to see him. I want my settlement pay, as much as I can carry: one of my men drowned here."

n. Kewetspekw asked one of his people, "How does he look?" "Oh, bad! He has his hair tied behind and a band over his forehead." "Why not? That is well." He told his people, "Let them take everything. Let them enter your houses and carry property into the boats: do not say a word. But when I am

16. Ironic, of course.

17. Moccasins were not always worn, but were sometimes mentioned as donned for travel. A go-between trying to arrange a settlement was paid a fee for his moccasin wear in traveling back and forth. Women often put on moccasins when they went to gather firewood. A war party may have wanted to arrive in the best of condition. [K.'s typescript had the second sentence of the note inserted by hand, with a notation to check it.—Ed.]

18. At Weitspus, where the narrator was telling the story. The refusal to ferry over any visitors or travelers would normally incur a claim; if the swimmer drowned, the claim would be the same as for a killing.

19. Kewetspekw, of course. Personal names are rarely used.

ready, I want you to be ready. Look at me and nothing more.'' He had his boat, a large, good boat, drawn far up on the land. He thought, ''That is where we will begin to quarrel,'' but he was (still) in the sweathouse.

o. Now he came outside and the five Hupa persons came to him. They told him, ''We want as much pay as we can carry.'' He sat with his hair loose, combing it with a stick.[20] ''Oh! You, my friend down below, should be ashamed to say that to me. I have not one woodpecker crest headband, not one string of dentalia. I have nothing. I cannot pay.'' ''Well, we will tell him.'' The five went.

They said, ''He will not give pay. He has nothing.'' ''Good!'' Oknuł man said, and got up and ran to the houses, and his people all came up. Some went into the houses, some took away everything that was outside. Still Kewetspekw sat combing his hair. He said nothing and laughed when they went by with a load. When they said, ''My friend, I am taking one of your boats,'' he said nothing.

p. Then Kewetspekw knew that they were going off with the last load. Oknuł bad man said, ''Good-bye, my friend. Down below ten boats are ready, full of things that I have taken.'' ''Say, my friend, do not take that boat there, my covered one. Do you hear? Leave that.'' ''Ha! ha! ha! So be it! If you say that more firmly, you will be a good Weitspus man.'' He stopped at the boat, laid on the ground what he was carrying, and threw the brush (covering) out of the boat.

Then Kewetspekw tied up his hair and said (to his people), ''Be ready. Have you your quivers?'' ''Yes,'' they said. Each one carried two quivers. ''Then run below into the brush.'' They ran down. Kewetspekw went down without arrows, without anything. They were dragging his boat toward the river. He said, ''My friend, I tell you, leave that boat here. Do not take it.'' Oknuł bad man said nothing. The Weitspus people were back in the brush, all with arrows. The Hupa people were still dragging the boat.

q. Then Kewetspekw caught his boat with one hand, saying, ''Stop, my friend. Leave my boat.'' He ran back a few steps pulling it with him. Then the Hupa wanted to seize him. They ran toward him. Some had their bows. When they drew them, the bows broke and fell in pieces. When they ran to take hold of him, he caught one by the arm, threw him, and struck twenty. Twenty Hupa were dead when that man stopped flying. Oknuł bad man came. He thought, ''I will fight him.'' Kewetspekw said, ''My friend, do not come near me. You had better go straight into your boat. I will set you over.'' Nevertheless Oknuł man went to fight. Kewetspekw pushed his palm against his forehead to turn

20. A leisurely indulgence after sweating. The hair was wet from the bath if not from the perspiring furnace; and while it was spread out on the stick or whipped by it to dry, basking in the sun was no doubt pleasant.

him around, saying, "Go home." Then he could not turn him: Oknuł man was strong as a rock. Oknuł man took him by the forearm and pulled. Then Kewetspekw found he was the sort of man who could seize people and draw them down with one pull. That is what he tried to do. Kewetspekw did the same. Then they pushed one another. For a long time neither could push the other. The Weitspus people stood, looked on, did nothing.

Then Kewetspekw became angry. He pushed his (opponent's) head, caught him by his tied-up hair, raised him, set him down, raised him again, swung him, caught his leg, set him down once more, caught both legs, and began to pull. He split half his body. Then that one said, "Stop, my friend!" Then Kewetspekw stopped. "What do you want to say?" he asked. "Be my friend. Let you and me be companions and allow me to go." "No. I want no friend." He lifted him, pulled again, split him farther. Still he talked. The last time he split him to the throat. Then some of the Weitspus men came up. "Perhaps he has learned something. You might let him go now." So (Kewetspekw) told four of his people, "Take him to Oknuł. If you find his people, let them carry him on up." After a time he saw the four coming back. They said, "We found a boatful of them up the (Trinity) river. They took him on up. He is still alive." "He will not die. I only wished him to learn something." Now they had taken all the property back out of the boats.

r. That night (Kewetspekw) thought, "I am sorry for my friend at the mouth (of the river). That one (from Oknuł) went downstream twice. He went with one boat and came back with ten, robbing the Rekwoi people." When it was nearly day he said, "Let us make a fire and all wash." Then they did so. He said, "I want two of you to go downstream to see my friend at Rekwoi. Let him bring up about twenty if they will come. (Tell him) the Weitspus men wish to go somewhere. If they come, I will tell them where I want to go."

Then two of them started. He thought, "They will be gone about two days." He asked them, "When will you be back?" They said, "You can look for us tomorrow. I do not think we shall be away two (whole) days."[21]

s. When it was nearly sunset, youths came. They kept saying, "Cormorant[22] has come back." Kewetspekw thought, "Those youths must be mistaken." Others said, "Cormorant will be here tomorrow or the next day." The biggest of the boys said, "No, I saw him coming back with a crowd of boats." Then Kewetspekw thought, "Perhaps it is he." He went outdoors, looked, saw many boats coming, and knew his own boat. He thought, "That is my boat. That is the one who started to go to the mouth this morning."

21. It is over forty miles from Weitspus to Rekwoi. The downstream trip can easily be made in a forenoon, but two days are generally reckoned to bring an empty boat up against the current, and three for a loaded one. It would be a light boat traveling fast that could complete the round trip in two summer days.

22. Tspega.

Then they arrived at Weitspus, and he distributed (the visitors) to all the houses.

In the morning he said, "I think it will be well if we go to see our friends. I hear they are rich. We will take away all they have and give back what was yours." So those from the mouth learned what he wanted to do.

t. Next day they started (up the Trinity). Soon they came to Oknuł. Then the Oknuł men went on top of their houses; not one of them stayed indoors. The (Weitspus and Rekwoi people) went in, took everything, robbed them of all they had robbed. They found everything, and took away all their boats. What belonged to Rekwoi they gave back to the Rekwoi people. Then they returned to Weitspus.

u. Now Kewetspekw asked how they had come by Nä'ägeł on the way up. "Oh, we passed at night.[23] It is impossible to come by that place in the day." He said, "Well, tomorrow I shall accompany you. I shall go downstream to Rekwoi."

Then the next day they started. He took ten of his men with him. They came to upstream of Nä'ägeł. Then he said, "Stay here. I will go ahead with three young men. Shout, so that they will know we are coming." Then they shouted and struck their boats with their paddles.

Then they saw someone sitting outside the sweathouse at Nä'ägeł but he did not come down (the bank). "Go to the town. I will stay here," Kewetspekw told his three young men.

v. The one from Nä'ägeł said, "Where are you from?" "We are from Weitspus." "Where are you going?" "We are looking for a good boat." "Tell him to go back. Who is he with you?" "Kewetspekw." "Where is he?" "Below." "Tell him he had better go back; not to go on downstream." "He wants to go to Rekwoi." "Tell him to go back. If he does not obey, I will do something to him. I do not want him to come about this place." "You had better go and tell him yourself. Perhaps he will do what you tell him."

Then the one from Nä'ägeł said to his people, "Tell him to go back quickly." Two of them went down (the slope). They saw him sitting in his boat whittling at his paddle. They said, "He wants you to go back. He does not like you here. He told us to tell you that." "Go up to the town and tell him to come to see me himself. If he wants very much to speak to me, he had better come down." "No. He wants you to go away." "Oh! He wants me to gamble[24] with him." "No. He wants you to go back." "Oh! He wants me to come to his house to eat." "No. He wants you to go away." "Oh! Now I know. You mean he

23. But they came with Cormorant, who is expressly mentioned as having left in the morning and returned before night!

24. Unfortunately, the lack of native text prevents our knowing whether puns of a sort underlie these deliberate misunderstandings.

wants me to come up and rob him.'' Then he allowed those two to go. They were afraid and thought, ''Perhaps he is a real man.''

w. Then Kewetspekw shook his paddle, signaling the Rekwoi persons he had left upstream to come down. Nä'ägeɬ bad man saw twenty boats of Rekwoi people coming downstream. ''What is the crowd here for?'' he asked. ''They belong with Kewetspekw. He is accompanying his friend to Rekwoi.'' Then Nä'ägeɬ man arose, ran down the hill, and came to the boat. Kewetspekw retreated to the stern as if afraid. Nä'ägeɬ bad man said, ''My friend, go back! I say so!'' Kewetspekw did not look at him. He looked down, (but) watching. He saw the other was going to take hold of the boat to pull it up on shore. As soon as he saw him touch the boat, Kewetspekw raised his hand and struck his wrist. ''My friend, let go of the boat!'' he said, and the hand and wrist dropped on the sand. Then he seized his arm, took the hand, put it on (the arm), rubbed over the wrist, and it was as good as before. Then saying, ''My friend, I had better teach you something,'' he pulled out his entire arm. Then Nä'ägeɬ man said, ''I think you and I shall be friends. You need not do anything more to me. We will go together.'' Kewetspekw said, ''I grew alone. I will go on like that. I have people enough.''

Then he asked the Rekwoi people, ''Has he robbed you?'' ''Yes, he came to Rekwoi often to rob us.'' ''Have you their property?'' he asked Nä'ägeɬ man. He said, ''Yes, I have it.'' ''Go up to the house and give it back to them,'' Kewetspekw said. ''All right,'' said Nä'ägeɬ man, and went up to the house and showed the property that belonged to Rekwoi and gave it back. If he had not done that, Kewetspekw would have split him.

x. Then Kewetspekw did not go on downstream to Rekwoi. He turned back upstream. He thought, ''Something may be wrong above. That upstream person is alive still. I had better go home.''

When he arrived at Weitspus, he saw that everything was peaceful. The next day he sent a boat to Hupa to see if anyone would annoy it. They came back. They said, ''Everything is well. We had very good friends at Hupa. We went past Oknuɬ and saw him.'' Then he sent some to go to the mouth. He wanted to know if anyone harmed them. They came back. They said, ''Everything is well. We went by Nä'ägeɬ and saw him sitting on top of his house.'' Kewetspekw thought, ''That is good.'' At first, upstream was the only way Weitspus people could travel and not be abused. If they went upstream (as far as) Hupa (or) if they went downstream, they were abused.

y. Then Kewetskpekw once heard the Oknuɬ man wished to go to Rekwoi. He thought, ''I will send one of my people to tell him, 'Do not come by here if you wish to go to Rekwoi. Do what I say. Go around.' '' Then the man started. He came to Oknuɬ. He said, ''Kewetspekw told me to say to you, 'Do not go downstream!' He said, 'Do what I say.' '' ''Tell my friend I am going downstream by boat,'' Oknuɬ man said. The Weitspus person returned and said to Kewetspekw, "He said, 'I cannot help it. I wish to go in a boat. I must go that way.'" Kewetspekw said, "I shall not let him. Let him not come. I do not wish to see him. I will do something if he come by, even if he comes at night." Then the man went to Oknuł again. He returned (to Weitspus) and said, "He will not listen. I urged him as best I could but he would not receive (the advice)."

Then Oknuł man began to think. He thought, "Well, I had better make a way for myself to go by, for I must travel by boat. I think I cannot endure not to go that way." Then he found what he would do. "Tomorrow I shall go by another way to see how far it is." The next day he started. He went up the creek (that now flows in) opposite where he lived. He took his boat up (the creek to) near the top of the ridge. Then he dragged it over the crest and down on the other side. Then he made another creek there (Pine Creek). He went down this into the (Klamath) river (thus traveling by boat without going along the rivers past Weitspus).[25]

Kewetspekw learned that he had gone. He saw a Hupa person. He asked him, "Where is he?" "He has just returned from downstream." "How did he go?" "He went in a boat."

Next day (Kewetspekw) sent one of his people. "Go see how he brought his boat downstream." They returned in the evening and told, "That ridge was not like this before. There is a creek that was not there. We looked at it and saw that someone had gone up in a boat. From this side (of the ridge) another creek runs down that was not there before. We could see where he dragged his boat over the crest and where he pushed it into the creek. He came out (into the river) downstream (from here)." So Kewetspekw found that that was how he had gone.

z. Then he said, "My people, I know where I shall go after this. I like my place so much where I grew, that I shall not leave it. I shall always see my people. I shall watch them." Now all those people scattered (to become woge). Some went to this mountain, some to that, and turned into other beings. No one stayed there except Kewetspekw. He went into the spring at Weitspus which is called Wetspekw. He lives there. The pepperwood tree is his headfeather. He made it that the Weitspus people were quarrelsome; that they did not like to eat until they had fought or had seen a fight.[26] They would say, "Let us breakfast now. We have fought."

25. The tumbling mountain stream would make such an ascent quite impossible even if sufficient water were added to it to float a canoe. The ridge must be almost 2000 feet high. The point of the episode is exaltation of the man who could perform such a feat—and yet is vanquished by the hero of the story. [K. has a marginal reference to Goddard, Hupa Texts, and to the Hupa god Yīmantūwiñyai.—Ed.]

26. The Yurok habit was to breakfast late and do as much as possible of the heavy work of the day before food rendered the faculties or the will sluggish. Fighting was the day's work of Weitspus, is what the allusion means.

A14. Grown-in-a-Basket

In this story the narrator has kept rather more closely to the folktale manner than is usual with him. The conception of the main character is of a kind with that of the hero tales, but the plot is a popular one, nor is it much altered. There is no development of any length added by the narrator, like the testing out between Kewet omewa and Coyote in the story of the former (A8) or the trip to Hupa in the tale of No'ots (A7). Even the dialogue is rather sparing. The only distinctive qualities are the vividness of treatment and the skillful welding of plot. The latter shows in the combination of episodes: the miraculous birth of the hero; his training; Coyote's revenge on Sun; Coyote's fall from the sky; the hero's feat of restoring Sun; his ascent to the sky and victory in the shinny game; and his escape from the flood. Characteristic, too, is the bringing in of Wohpekumeu and Pulekwerek, each with a definite function, though a very minor one. Most narrators would either have entirely omitted mention of their acts or would have attributed them to nameless nobodies.

[K.'s jottings indicate that he intended to expand this headnote to draw analogies between (*b-d*) Grown-in-a-Basket's birth and training, (*j-k*) his throwing Sun back, (*l-n*) Spider's taking Grown-in-a-Basket to the sky, where he wins shinny, *and* (*e-h*) Coyote's revenge on Sun and (*i*) his fall from the sky, concluding with (*o-p*) Wohpełtun's plan for the flood, but the survival of Grown-in-a-Basket.—Ed.]

•

a. Pulekukwerek, Wohpekumeu, Kewomer, Eagle, and many others were at Kenek. Everything had been made good in the world, and they were enjoying themselves. They played and gambled every day.

b. An old man was living near Okego[1] where the rocks are piled up. He lived there alone with his old woman. Whenever the old man was making a bow and drawing the sinew, he put the shreds together, and when he had finished he laid them in an openwork (*rumitsek*) basket hanging there. Once he looked at the basket and it was moving inside. He continued to put in sinew shreds. Again he saw it move. "What is it?" he thought. When he looked in he saw something lying there, something very small. The old man took it, laid it on his hand, and thought, "You will become a person." Then he laid him back in his place and strengthened the cord by which the basket hung.[2] Next day he saw that he was larger. Every day he grew. It was not long and he was a tall young man.

c. Then the Kenek people saw someone making smoke in the sweathouse at Okego. Now the old man always told him, "Do not go downstream. There

1. Okego is the great Tuley Rapids in the Klamath; also the name of a left-bank creek that comes in at their head, and of the mouth of that creek. It directly adjoins Kenek, the creek marking the upper limit of Kenek. [See map 5, no. 138, in this volume; also the mention of Okego and Okego young man in A6.—Ed.]

2. This touch—repairing the old cord because the basket is now a cradle—may have been part of one version of the folktale which Informant A utilized, but I suspect it is one of his embroideries of meticulous detail.

are many there (at Kenek)." A few of them saw him. They said, "A young man is living at Okego." Sometimes the young man went out. The old man watched, thinking, "Where is he going?" Sometimes he saw him come back. Then he learned where he always went: it was to Kenekpul,[3] at the edge of the river. There he sat and watched for the white duck.[4] He waited until he saw it just abreast. Then he started to run upstream while the bird flew. They would come to the sand bar at Okego together.

The next day he thought, "Let me try again." He heard them shouting at shinny at Kenek, but never went there. Then he saw (the duck) coming and thought, "I will start just even with it." Then they came up to the goal together. He thought, "I did not run hard. I will try again tomorrow," for he had not run his best.

Next morning he went downstream again. Then he saw (the duck) coming. He thought, "I will give it several steps lead and see if I cannot overtake it." Then he ran upstream and arrived and (turned and) stood and saw it (still) coming: he had beaten it. Then he thought, "This time I did my best."

d. In the morning he went downstream again. He thought, "Let me try something else," and took his bow and arrows. First he wanted to see how far he could shoot. So he shot, looked for his arrow, and found it on the open flat ("prairie") at Otsep.[5] The next day he went (to Kenekpul) again, shot, and started running. He came out on the (Otsep) prairie and the arrow fell as he got there. He thought, "Well, I did not do my best at the start. I think I can do better if I run my hardest from the very beginning. I will try again tomorrow."

In the morning he went downstream and shot again. He started and ran his hardest. Then he waited on the prairie: the arrow fell down. He had beaten it. So he thought, "Well, I think I can run." Still he heard them shouting at Kenek. Whenever he went downstream from Okego, he lifted with one hand stones that other persons could not handle at all. He thought, "I think I can do something. I shall be able to play shinny."

e. It began to be spring. A person at Kenekpul[6] had five children. In the

3. "Kenek-downstream," no. 1, "Coyote's house," on Waterman, Geography, map 22, his detail map of Kenek. I understood the house to have been somewhat more downstream. Waterman shows Kenek-pul on his general map 17 as a settlement, no. 116, nearly a mile below Kenek. [See map 5 in this volume.—Ed.] Waterman says that in mythological times an invisible ladder led up to the sky there (but for the present story, cf. part *m*). He also says that it used to be all one flat open place from Kenek-pul to Okego, and there people played shinny until the woge spoiled it (and there our hero races in *c* and *d*).

4. Murun. [See R1, n. 1.—Ed.]

5. Otsep is opposite Okego, slightly upriver, a fishing place and a settlement; Waterman, map 17, no. 142.

6. Coyote, though he is not named till later. His house was farthest downstream from historic Kenek (cf. n. 3); Wohpekumeu's was at the downstream and downhill (Tsoleu) edge of the

morning it was warm. He said, "Children, go out after seeds." They started and had come nearly to Onegep[7] on the other side of the river. Then it became foggy and began to snow. Two of them froze to death. Three of them came home. Then that person thought, "I will go to him who did that. He should not have done it. I know where he emerges in the morning. I will hit him with stones."[8]

f. He made ready sharp stones,[9] put them in his net sack, and started to the place where that one would come out. There he sat and watched. Then he saw him emerge on another ridge. Then he thought, "Well, I will go there tomorrow." So he kept following him back farther and farther.[10] He came to the end of the world.[11] Then in the morning he saw him come up out of the ocean[12] (and could not reach him).

g. Then he saw someone there. It was Mouse.[13] Mouse said to him, "Tonight is the last time you will see him." He said, "Yes, I shall be there tonight." "Yes, go into the sweathouse. That is the only way you can get him. I will help you, else you will be caught. I will make holes in their boats[14] so that they will sink, but you shall be able to go on." Now as they went toward the place (where Sun lived), Mouse pointed the way to him. He said, "Here you must remember not to take the clear path or you will go astray. Take the old trail and it will be well."

h. Then he went into the sweathouse. In the evening they came in, ten of them. The last one that came in was he.[15] He lay down close by him. When he lay down it was not dark (in the sweathouse). Then he began to tell how people were doing: he told all the news. One of them said, "I hear that someone lost two children; that they froze to death. Is that so?" He said, "Yes, that is what I saw." Then (Coyote) heard them laugh a little. Then he leaped on that (Sun) and struck him twice. Then he turned and ran out and fled. But before he knew it he

---

town; those of Earthquake, Thunder, Porpoises, etc., were back (inland) and upriver on Kenek flat, toward Tuley (Okego) Creek.

7. Unplaced; Waterman, p. 253, says the name means "where they always eat."

8. Coyote plans to kill Sun, whom he holds responsible for his children's death by shining warmly and then disappearing. The failure to name Sun is of course merely Yurok style.

9. *Lohłko*, cobbles or other stones split to sharp edges or points.

10. Each time he thought that the sun rose from the top of the ridge beyond.

11. *Wes'ona hostseiwes*, "sky's end." [The Yurok conceived of the sky as a solid net rising overhead but touching the ocean all around the edges of the world. See myth A16x *z-aa*.—Ed.]

12. At the eastern or upstream end of the world.

13. Negenits. They must be in the sky; cf. n. 17.

14. More usually in Yurok and other California tales, the mice gnaw bowstrings; but the following "will sink" makes boats indisputable in this passage, although how the pursuers would canoe after Coyote running on a sky trail is not clear.

15. The object of Coyote's search, Sun. Were there ten brothers, or just a conventional ten, or ten (instead of twelve) moons?

had taken the better trail. He ran along the well-traveled one. The nine[16] followed him but could not catch him: they had to let him go.

i. Then looking down from where he was,[17] he thought, "Well, I took the wrong path. I shall have to find what to do." He looked down again and thought, "Oh, it is not very far. I shall jump down." He spat and watched the spittle, falling. "Oh, it is nothing. I shall jump," he said. So he jumped. He went right through what he had spat on.[18] Then (as he continued) falling), he took out his heart, thinking, "Even if my bones are scattered I shall hold my heart in my hand." Then his bones dropped all about. He did not come back.[19] He was Coyote.

j. Then they began talking in Kenek. "What is it that it does not become day?" they said. Wohpekumeu was walking downstream from Kenek.[20] Then he saw something white. He went up and saw that it was Sun who had been killed. Now those who were strong went there to lift him and put him back. All of them went. Sometimes a hundred together tried to lift his foot but could not raise it. "It is all we can do," they said. "We shall have to endure (darkness). We cannot lift him back."

k. Someone said, "You had better try to get Rumitsek-onohsun."[21] But some said, "Oh, he will not be able to do anything." But one of them went after him. He came to Okego and asked the old man, "Where is he?" The old man said, "He is down at the river somewhere." Then that one went down to the river and found him. He said, "I have come to get you because we have found why there no longer is any day." Okego old man said, "I knew it. As soon as I heard that Sun had fallen, I knew that (Coyote) had done wrong. I think you should go. I know that you will not be able to do anything because there are many of them there and they are unable. Nevertheless you had better go." The young man said, "Yes, I will go. I am sorry it is so." Then he went with (the messenger).

When he came there where he saw Sun lying, he did not say a word. He

16. Sun of course was killed. How his being killed (as here and in J5*d* in his sweathouse in the sky) makes him fall at Kenek (or at Tsurău in DD13) is never made clear. Still, as interesting narrative, it is better to leave it vague than to clog the flow of the story with cosmographic explanations.

17. The sky.

18. Clouds. The "indirection" of mention is typical.

19. If "did not come back" means that he did not return to life, it is contrary to the usual Coyote tale pattern. The following "he was Coyote" perhaps means it was the end of his being a woge and that he became the animal.

20. Cf. n. 6. But the instituter Wohpekumeu is not usually mentioned in this connection. The narrator likes to draw on his repertory of personages much as he indulges in knitting together separate threads of plot.

21. Here at last we get his name: "Grown-in-a-*rumitsek*." This is a nearly spherical basket in openwork, usually neatly made, and serving to hold sinew, awls, spoons, and small odds and ends. More frequently the narrator calls him Okego-onohsun, "Grown-at-Okego," or simply "Okego young man."

looked at no one. He merely turned him over, lifted him with his left hand, put his right hand under him, and threw him up: (Sun struck) aginst the sky. Turning around, Grown-in-a-Basket looked at no one and went back. He did not see that many of them, in shame (at being so immeasurably surpassed), changed into rocks or bushes, and other things.

l. Now those that had been at Kenek went off to find another place to play in, for they were ashamed of Okego young man. Once, when he went to Kenek, he saw and heard no one. He wanted to know where they had gone: not one was left.[22] Then, upstream of Kenek, he met someone, a fine-looking young man. That one asked him, "Where are you going?" Grown-in-a-Basket said, "I am just walking. I am trying to find where they went." "You cannot go where they continually go. They have fled to avoid you. They used to play here, but now they have found another place where they play. You might as well go back to your house. But if you would like to see them play I will make it that you go there.[23] They ran away from you: that is why they are no longer here." Grown-at-Okego said, "I shall do them no harm. I would just like to see them play." "Well, we will do that. We will go there." Then he began to twist a string of spider web.

m. Next day he said to him, "Well, let us go." Then they went up on the hill to a large prairie.[24] When they came there he saw that there had been fires in ten places. Broken deer bones were lying about. "Do you know what this is for?" that person asked him. "No," said Grown-at-Okego. "They have been painting themselves (before going up to the sky). They took fat from the marrow of these bones.[25] Now, do you think you can shoot?" "Yes, I can shoot." Then he tied his string to the end of an arrow. Grown-at-Okego shot. Soon he heard it hitting the sky; he saw the string hanging down. Then Spider[26] said, "You see it is fast. We shall go up by it. Wait while I go." Then he climbed up.[27] Soon the young man saw something descending. It hung (above him), then stood there: it was a ladder. He climbed that. Then the ladder was drawn up again. Now he was right overhead.[28]

n. Spider told him, "You will see all kinds of men here, the best of them." Grown-at-Okego said, "That is good. They are the ones that I want to see." As soon as he came to where they were, some of them were displeased, for they knew him. He saw many kinds of persons there. When he arrived, some

22. Exaggeration; later, in *o*, after his return from the sky, he still finds a few of them.

23. The speech means: you cannot go there alone, but with my aid you can.

24. Probably one of the large open spaces that have given the Bald Hills their name. Or possibly the Women of A12*f*, and T4.

25. The marrow was used as grease to rub with the paint on face or body.

26. Again the name slips in unobtrusively after the hearer has pretty well gathered who the stranger must be.

27. Spider climbs up the rope of his own spinning and lets the ladder down for Okego young man.

28. In the middle of the sky.

of them said, "Go bring that young man here and let him play shinny." One of them came to him and said, "This will be the last game. We shall not bet any more after this. We have nothing left to bet." "I cannot play," he said. "Well, try it nevertheless." "Well, then, all right." Then he said to his friend Spider, "Get me the ball and I will hit it to the end of the sky." Then he struck the ball to the very end (of the sky) and won the game. As soon as he had beaten them, some turned from shame into one thing, some into another. When he saw that nearly all of them had changed, Spider said, "Let us go back." "Yes, let us go back," he said.

o. Now when he came back to Okego there were very few left at Kenek, and those wished to go off. Wohpekumeu was still there, but Pulekukwerek had gone. Wohpełtun[29] said, "Go on ahead; I shall be the last one to leave." So they all went. But he (stayed because he first) wanted to kill Grown-at-Okego. He thought, "I shall find some way of doing it." No one knew what he wanted to do. Then before they arrived where they were going,[30] Pulekukwerek[31] thought, "I did not ask (Wohpełtun) what he means to do. I had better go back and prevent him." So Pulekukwerek started back. But he found the river already risen (for the coming flood), and he could not go on.

p. When Grown-at-Okego saw the river rising, he knew that it was for himself. He went into the house, took a box,[32] emptied it, brought it outdoors, and laid it down with its cover near. Then he set his sweathouse on the cover and tied it on, and tied his house on the box. Then he entered the house, and the old man entered the sweathouse. Now the water rose. Then he heard something striking against the roof of his house. It knocked and knocked again. It was his house striking against the sky. The water was everywhere. That is why there are mountains and hills: they were made when the water ran off. Before there had been no hills: every place was level.

When the water dried, the house of Grown-at-Okego came down in the same place where it had stood before. It is the rock pile (at Okego) now.

A15x. Pulekukwerek, Pelin-tsīk, and Wohpekumeu

First Version

This is at bottom the normal Yurok Pulekukwerek monster-ridding cycle, boldly modified by the narrator's individual interests. It is first put into a frame of planning, talking, and cooperation between the chief hero and the less active but even more exalted

29. [K.'s marginal note indicated that he intended to supply a cross-reference here. This is the only mention of Wohpełtun in this collection.—Ed.]

30. Probably Pulekuk.

31. Pulekūkwerek, is here dragged in like Wohpekumeu in *j*, from sheer love of building a complex story.

32. The Yurok treasure box or "trunk" is cylindrical (probably for canoe travel), with some swelling in the middle. The lid covers one side and is lashed on.

Pelin-tsīk or Pelintsiek—"Great Money." Having had Pulekukwerek destroy or rectify the principal evils in Yurok land, the narrator is not content to stop, as the ordinary Yurok storyteller would, but lets his synthesizing fancy play on. Pulekukwerek returns only in order to start out again, this time with Pelin-tsīk's younger brother Tego'o, and to associate himself with Wohpekumeu.

The latter now becomes the chief actor, but with Pulekukwerek to counsel and influence him and the two Money brothers still further in the background. Wohpekumeu secures food for the world and escapes from the consequences of an amorous adventure—both in Karok territory. The others then go home, leaving Wohpekumeu to continue his less dignified roamings. All this last portion of the story has no connection with Pulekukwerek in the conventional Yurok telling, of which the versions C1, F1, and J3 are respresentative. The present narrator's coupling of the two cycles, or parts of them, is gratuitous, as it were, the expression of his desire for combination: he enjoys weaving a plot.

•

a. Pelin-tsīk[1] and Pulekukwerek were downstream. It is not known (precisely) where they grew. Pelin-tsīk used to fly downstream to the end of the world and back in half a day. Now one knew that he was passing. Once he came back and Pulekukwerek asked him, "Where have you been?" He said, "I was all over the world. I went to the right" (from right to left, anti-sunwise, up the Klamath, then northward and westward again). Pulekukwerek did not believe him. He had often gone in his thoughts. He had sat and sent his heart out and in one (whole) night he did not reach the ocean at the other end of the world. So now he did not believe Pelin-tsīk. Therefore he asked him, "Where were you?" Pelin-tsīk said, "I was at Rekwoi at the mouth of the river." "What did you see there?" "I saw one person there." He meant the rock (Oregos) at the very mouth of the river. "What did he say to you?" "He said nothing." Then Pulekukwerek knew that he had been there. He told him, "When you go again I want to go with you." Pelin-tsīk said, "It is well. When you hear my flute you will know that it is I."

Then once Pulekukwerek saw fog coming, moving along the coast. He thought, "What is it?" He went back[2] into his sweathouse and lay down. Soon he heard a flute and knew that it was Pelin-tsīk. He took out his pipe and laid it so that it pointed toward the mouth of the river. If it rolled to the left, Pelin-tsīk would be going on that side of the river. If it rolled to the right, he would be

1. Pelin-tsīk means large dentalium. Elsewhere in this collection the name has sometimes been translated "Great Money." In this tale he is a personage rather than a personification, so that the native appellation has seemed more appropriate. [For more details, see notes to B14.—Ed.]

2. When he has nothing special on hand, he spends his time in the sweathouse. He has looked out at the door, seen the fog, and now retires again.

going on the right (south) side. Then, as he watched his pipe, it began to rise and stood straight up. Now he knew that Pelin-tsīk was going above the river.

Toward morning he went outside to see where he would come from. Then he heard a noise inside the sweathouse. He looked in and saw that his pipe had rolled, still in its case, from the place where it had lain to a place near the fire. Then he took it, drew it out of its case, went outdoors again, and laid it pointing to the river. Then the pipe swung around crossways to the way he laid it, pointing north.[3] Then he knew that Pelin-tsīk would arrive from the north.

b. Soon Pelin-tsīk came. Then Pulekukwerek said to him, "You have been only half around the world. You went upstream, then you turned and went north and then back." Pelin-tsīk said, "How does he know? It is vain for me to say that I have been over the whole world, for he knows." Then he said, "Yes, I went by that way." Pulekukwerek said, "What did you see?" Pelin-tsīk told him, "I went to Rekwoi. There is something bad there. Whoever tries to cross gets drowned. Then I went upstream to Sa'aiɬ.[4] There is one who has a pipe which he gives people to smoke. As soon as they take it, it leaps into the crook of the arm and kills them. At Nä'ägeɬ I saw an old man splitting logs. He asks people to help him. Then he allows the log to close on them. I went on upstream. At Serper I saw two boys. They seesaw[5] with people. They swing them up and dash them against the sky. At Pekwon I saw two blind old women in a house of brush which turns to stone. From there I went to Redwood Creek. There an old man has a hook which he keeps moving about. Woodpecker crests and dentalia and deerskins are on it; but whenever anyone touches it, he becomes fast, and the old man draws him in. At that place I listened. There was no wind: everything was still, farther up Redwood Creek. But on the (Klamath) river at Kenek I heard something. I went there. There there are persons who kill with tobacco. And at Merip there is a jealous one who kills people. Then I went on upstream. At Weitspus I heard nothing. I listened up the Trinity and up the Klamath, but everything was quiet. Then I turned in a circle and came here. That is what I have seen."

Pulekukwerek sat thinking. He thought, "I will go to all those places where there is something bad and make it good. I do not think I shall be killed."

Pelin-tsīk knew what he thought. He said (to himself), "Well, let him.

3. *Hierkik,* at right angles to the flow of the Klamath, northeastward.

4. [Waterman, Geography, map 9, no. 50, shows Sa'aiɬ as a settlement about a half-mile downriver from Turip and on the opposite side. He says (p. 235) that Sa'aiɬ means "spirit people," who seem to have shared the town with its human inhabitants. In A21, n. 25, K. defines them as disease spirits; he usually spells their name as Sa'aɬ.—Ed.]

5. Probably "teetering" would be more exact. It is doubtful whether the Yurok knew a balanced seesaw. Apparently the boys had a tree bent over, and a victim was swayed on the tip of it. Then they let go the holding contrivance, and the victim was shot up as from a sling by the straightening tree. Cf. Goddard, Hupa Texts, p. 128.

I will follow him to see what he does.'' Pulekukwerek said, ''No, do not follow me. Stay here.'' So Pulekukwerek started and Pelin-tsīk remained.

c. Pulekukwerek came to Rekwoi. There he wanted to cross (the river at its mouth). The people told him, ''You will die. When birds fly so high that they are invisible to us, they succeed in crossing; but when we can see them, they always drop when they are above the middle (of the river). Everything that tries to cross is drowned.''

Then Pulekukwerek took a plank. He drew out his fire drill and made fire on the plank. Then he sat down on it (as if it were a boat) and began to cross. When he came to the middle of the river, the water boiled up all about him. Now he began to paddle hard. Then he ran to the bow of the boat and leaped. He reached the (southern) shore. But his boat was drawn down stern first. He ran up the hill and looked back. The land all about the mouth of the river was shaking, and the water was being thrown up. (When it quieted,) he went down again. (The beings who had sucked people in) had stranded at the bar across the mouth of the river. (The fire which they had swallowed with his boat had burned them.) He took them up and said, ''Well, you shall be good hereafter. You shall not kill men.'' He said that to each of them and put them into the ocean. There were ten of them.[6]

d. Pulekukwerek went upstream to Sa'aiɬ. The old man there said to him, ''Where are you going?'' He answered, ''I have come to see you.'' The old man said, ''It is good. You had better have a smoke.'' He got out his pipe and reached it over. Pulekukwerek had tied flat stones to his two hands, and held them behind his back. As soon as the old man reached him the pipe, he struck it with his other hand and killed the pipe. As he smashed it, he heard a noise. The old man fell over. He threw the pipe at him, and as it struck him his sweathouse fell to pieces.[7]

e. Pulekukwerek went on upstream. He thought, ''I wish I saw a gopher digging.'' Then he saw a gopher, killed it, and took it along. Now he heard somebody at work (at Nä'ägeɬ). Soon he reached an old man. That one said, ''I am glad you have come. I am too old to make what I want. Help me to work.'' ''Yes, I will try,'' said Pulekukwerek. The old man said, ''Go into the

6. The monsters may have been Kämes or of some other variety. It is characteristic of Yurok narrative to suppress both names and descriptions as far as possible in favor of dialogue and relation of events. Other accounts (including the same narrator's A16x *u*) place but one monster—a Knewollek or ''Long One''—in the river mouth. This has a logical advantage: the present version has one fire kill ten of the swallowers.

7. The narrator is rather clever in keeping the handling of this incident novel by merely adding to what the hearer already knows. The usual Indian manner is to give the warning in full and then to go over the same ground in relating the event, or to abbreviate the latter or assume it as having happened. This alternative between monotonous repetition and flat anticlimax has not, however, proved difficult for Billy to evade.

split of the log and move the wedge like this.'' Pulekukwerek went into the log. Then he said, ''Good: wait until I get it straight! I will tell you.'' But he went through the log and hid underneath it, leaving only the gopher in the crack. The old man drew out his wedge (to kill him). The log snapped to. Blood issued from it. Then the old man said, ''Well, he should not have come here (if he did not wish to die).'' Pulekukwerek, standing behind him, said, ''Old man, what are you saying?'' ''I said I was sorry. I thought I had made a mistake and killed you.'' ''No,'' said Pulekukwerek, ''you did not.'' ''Well, let us go to work again,'' said the old man. He began to be afraid. Then Pulekukwerek said, ''You go inside now and set the wedge, When you get it in place I will hold it. Then you can hit it.'' The old man agreed. He went into the split and placed the wedge. ''Well, I am ready,'' he said. Pulekukwerek drew out the other wedge, and the log closed. He asked, ''Old man, where are you?'' The old man said, ''I am within. I shall live here.'' Pulekukwerek said, ''They shall not kill people like this. When they open logs, they will find you inside.'' The old man became a large white maggot.

f. Pulekukwerek went on upstream to Serper. Before he arrived, he thought, ''I wish to kill something.'' He found a rat and killed it. When the two boys saw him coming upstream along the sand bar, they ran down to him. ''We are glad to see you, old man,'' they said. He went with them to where they had seesawed. ''Old man, come and play with us,'' they said. He consented. He went up on the seesaw, but sat down near the middle. ''No, that is not the place. Sit farther up,'' they said. ''Very well,'' he said, and moved farther out. ''How do you like it?'' they asked him. ''Oh, it is good.'' You had better go out still farther,'' they said. Pulekukwerek (moved out and) said, ''This is fine, with the wind blowing about. But do not swing it too hard.'' They said, ''Old man, it will be best of all if you sit at one end and we at the other.''[8] (He sat on the very end.) The second time, they swung (released?) it very hard and made his end fly up against the sky. But Pulekukwerek slipped off underneath. He left his rat in his place, and it was crushed against the sky. The boys said, ''He should not have come here.'' ''But where has he gone?'' they said. ''I don't see any bones.''[9] Finally the older brother said, ''Well, we must have killed him.'' Pulekukwerek thought, ''I wish they would both go out on the end.'' Soon one of them said, ''Come and help me, I cannot clean it off. His blood stinks.'' When they were both on the end, Pulekukwerek made it fly up. They are two stars in the sky, now, in the south.[10] Pulekukwerek broke up their seesaw and scattered it about.

8. This, contrary to what has been said in n. 5, rather suggests our type of seesaw. The narrator may have been vague because he had never seen the apparatus. It is unlikely that the Yurok ever constructed one in pre-American days.

9. Falling down from the sky.

10. [K.'s marginal note: ''Gemini?''—Ed.]

g. Pulekukwerek (went on upstream and) came to Pekwon. There a person told him, "Do not go upstream. Go to your right and you will see a house." So Pulekukwerek went uphill (toward Bald Hills and Redwood Creek). He saw a brush house, very prettily made. Inside, he heard pounding (with a pestle). He thought, "I will go in." He entered. On one side he saw an old woman, sitting making a basket. On the other side sat another old woman. She was the one who was pounding. She was pounding something white. Pulekukwerek looked at it. He said, "I should like to know what she is pounding." They did not know he was there because they were blind. They had stakes of bone, exceedingly sharp at both ends, lying close by. The one who was weaving the basket said, "Have you pounded it enough?" The other one answered, "No, it is not yet fine." "Give me some. Put it in my hand and let me feel it. Perhaps it is fine enough after all." Then she held some out and said, "Here." Pulekukwerek put out his hand and received it. The other woman's hand was extended in vain. "Where is it?" she said. "I gave it to you." "You did not give it to me." Pulekukwerek looked at it but did not know what it was.[11] It was white, like acorn flour.

"Give me some again. You did not put it in my hand last time," the one old woman said. "Yes, I gave it to you. But I will reach you some more. Here it is." Pulekukwerek took it again. Then the basket-weaving old woman began to know. She said, "Stop!" and threw her basket at the door. Then the door shut. She took her sharp bone; the older old woman took hers. Now Pulekukwerek saw that he would be killed. One of them said, "Someone is here." "Yes, try to catch him." They prodded all about the house. The old man (Pulekukwerek) tried to escape through the brush wall but it was (now) wholly of stone. He could not. Now he was caught. "I have him," one said. "I did not strike him, but I seized him." "Good! Let me feel how big he is. Ah! good! Give me the (basket) tray." The other brought the tray and Pulekukwerek was laid on it.

h. He kept his senses. He wanted to know what they would do to him. The old woman began to feel him again. She said, "Oh, sister! We have done wrong. I have heard about him. Have you never heard of him?" "No." "I have heard that a man would come who can do anything. He can make blind people see. I feel (his horns) on his rump."[12] "Yes, that is the one." "Let us try to make him alive again and find out who he is. Perhaps he can tell us." Then they poured water on his forehead. One of them said, "Man, have you your senses?" Pulekukwerek did not answer. They asked him again. This time he said, "Yes, I have my senses." The other one said, "Why did you come here?" Pulekukwerek said, "You treated me badly. I was told to come here to make your eyes good. That is why I came." "Do you think you can cure eyes?" "Yes, I do that." "We will let you get up." "I wish you would," said

11. Probably pulverized human bone. The narrator maintains suspense by not telling.

12. *Pulekuk-kwerek* means "downstream sharp" or pointed, with reference to this anatomical trait.

Pulekukwerek. He looked about the house. It had turned to brush again. He asked, "How far do you wish to see when you look about?" "I wish you would make our eyes the best in the world." "Yes, I will do that," said Pulekukwerek. "Well, I will begin. Where is the spring?" "It is not far from here." "Give me a basket. Yes, and another. I need two because there are two of you." "Good," they said, and gave him their two best baskets. Pulekukwerek said, "It will be warm today." He took a (burning) stick from the fire and said, "I will come in again very soon."

When he was outside he set fire to the left side of the door. Then he turned and set fire to the right side. He went around the house and set fire to it all about. The two old women began to feel warm. "Ihh! It is as he said. It will be warm today. I feel it. I am glad we shall have eyes." More heat began to come into the house. After a time one said, "I begin to smell something. They must be setting fire to the Bald Hills prairie.[13] They are burning it over, I think. I smell the smoke." Soon they knew: "The house is burning!" One of them burst and scattered. Pulekukwerek heard it. Then the other one burst. Pulekukwerek thought, "I have killed them."

i. He stood there and thought, "Which way shall I go along the ridge?" He went (across it and) downhill to Redwood Creek. He heard someone working. After a time he heard him singing near the stream. He thought, "Let me go to him." He stood not far away. "What is the old man doing?" he thought. He began to look at his face. He thought, "That is a wonderful one. He has (stone) mauls hanging from each pierced ear. He must be something of a man." That person had a pole, which now and then he moved up and down. The pole was hooked and decorated. All kinds of pretty things hung on it. Pulekukwerek thought, "Let me take some of them." But he looked on the ground and thought, "There are many bones here. They do not look like deer bones. Those are people's bones." Then he began to know. "He always catches them in this way." So he went to one side, thinking, "I will try to take hold of the end of the stick. I want to see it." Then he put out his hand. He nearly touched the stick. Then his hand was, as it were, drawn to the stick and almost fastened. "O! O! O! I missed him," the old man said. He began to move his hook about again. Pulekukwerek thought, "I will try once more." He held his hand underneath. The old man swung his hook, it touched the hand, and Pulekukwerek was caught. Then the old man moved along the pole until he felt Pulekukwerek's hand. "Ah! I am glad! I caught you," he said, seized him, opened his net sack, and put him in.

"I will go home now that I have him," he thought. As the old man started to run, the stone mauls hanging from his ears began to strike and clash. Pulekukwerek saw that he had three at each ear. It was not far before he saw a

13. Burnt over annually to keep it open and favorable to the growth of the annual plants whose seeds were gathered there.

house. Then he began to hear little girls crying, "Old man, come in, come in!" They were glad he had come with meat. He set down his load behind the house and asked, "Is the old woman inside?" "Yes, I am here," she said. "Bring me my knife," he said. "Where is your knife?" she asked. He said, "At my ear." The old woman said from inside, "I cannot find it." "Oh, it is right there at my earlobe," he said. He was speaking of places in the house.[14] She could not find the knife. Pulekukwerek thought, "I would like to see that knife lost." "Boys, come here," said the old man. "Watch him. I am going to get it myself." Then three boys ran out and the old man went inside.

j. The largest boy felt Pulekukwerek all over through the sack. "My brothers, he is nice behind, as sharp as can be." "Let me feel. Look! Let us open it a little." The old man was inside talking: he had lost his knife. Then the largest boy began to open the sack. Pulekukwerek thought, "A little larger, a little larger, a little larger!" The boys kept opening it until he was able to come out. Then he leaped out. The boys shouted, "He has run away! He has run away!" The old man came out muttering, "He has run away! He has run away!" He was angry. It was not far before Pulekukwerek was already nearly caught. He ran as fast as he could, but he saw that he would be caught. He thought, "I wish there were water here for me to jump into." Then he saw water, and said, "Let a large stump stand in the middle, hollow inside, so I can enter it and come out above." He leaped in, the old man close behind. Pelukekwerek swam underwater to the tree, found its hole, entered and went up inside to the top.

The old man went about in the water looking for him. Pulekukwerek knew that he was beginning to be cold. He was shivering, but still he tried to follow. Pulekukwerek thought, "Now I do not know what to do." After a time he stood up on the log. The old man was on the shore, very cold. As Pulekukwerek moved, the old man saw his shadow (reflection) in the water and jumped in to catch him. Then Pulekukwerek began to laugh. After a time he moved again, and the old man saw him. He became angry that he was still in the water (as he thought). He pulled off one of his stone mauls. "I will hit him with this," he thought, and threw it (at the reflection). Then he waited and saw that Pulekukwerek was still there. He jerked off another and threw it. "Now I think he will come out. I think I hit him then," he thought. Still he saw Pulekukwerek moving. "He is there still," he thought. One after another, he threw in all his mauls. Then he ran to get his hook. He came back, stood, and looked into the water. After a time Pulekukwerek moved. Seeing him again, the old man hooked the water everywhere. Again he waited. "He is still there." Then he thought, "I am too cold. I will rest and watch him." He lay down on the beach to warm himself.

Pulekukwerek thought, "Let him sleep that I may get away." Soon he saw

14. These puns of misunderstanding are like those in A13*v*.

him lying with his hand turned back (relaxed from the pole). He thought, "He is asleep. I will escape." He came from the tree, ran to where the hook was, and took it. The old man was still asleep. Pulekukwerek hooked him once with the stick and cut him in two. Then he hooked him again and again and cut him to pieces. He set fire to the scraps. Then he ran to the house. They were all inside. He put the hook to the door and set fire to the house at the back. The children tried to come out. They were caught on the hook. He killed them all. Then he thought, "Now I shall go on. I have killed them."

k. He had not gone far (upstream) on Redwood Creek ridge (the Bald Hills). Then he saw someone sitting on the path. "Where are you going?" he said. Pulekukwerek said, "I do not know. Shall I go on along the ridge?" "No, there is nothing on this ridge. You can walk along but you will find nothing about. I will tell you where to go. It is a dangerous place. A person cannot pass there. If he goes he does not come back. They never see him again." Pulekukwerek said, "Yes? Where is that place?" "You can go by this path. Before you come to the (Klamath) river you will find a town.[15] That is the place." "What is there there? Do you know what they do to people?" "I do not know. You will find it."

l. Now Pulekukwerek came uphill from Kenek. He was not far away. Then he smelled tobacco. As soon as he smelled it he almost fell down. Then he began to know. "That is how they kill people here. They give them to smoke. What shall I do? I will make ten (receptacles) of elkhorn." Then he made ten. All had a hole at one end.

Then he went on down to Kenek. He looked about outside the town and thought, "Many bones are lying here." He knew they were people's bones. They said there, "A good-natured-looking man is coming." They said to him. "Stay here tonight, and tomorrow go on where you are going." He said, "Yes, I will stay for the night." They asked him, "Will you come into the house?" He said, "No, I never eat food." (Thereupon they started to go to the sweathouse.) They began to whisper to each other, "We will kill him." The ladder to their sweathouse was slippery. Pulekukwerek put down his heels, cut into the ladder with them, moved down a step and sat on the place he had cut, and so descended. Then they thought, "What sort of a man is he to come in here without being killed?"

They said to him, "Old man, will you smoke?" and he said, "Yes." He smoked and drew the smoke into the smallest of his hollow elkhorns (all of which he had swallowed). They asked him where he came from. They said, "We should like to hear the news."[16] He told them, "I do not hear much." One after another all ten of them gave him to smoke. After he had smoked eight

15. This is a bit literal, seeing that Kenek is on the edge of the river bluff.

16. They are making conversation in order to keep him smoking instead of going to sleep.

times, he felt very bad. After the ninth pipe he nearly fell over. Then, when it was nearly day, he smoked the tenth and caused the smoke to enter his last hollow elkhorn. He said, "I want to go outside." He could hardly reach the creek. He put his feet into the water, drew out the pieces of elkhorn, and saw they were burned full of holes. The last one was worn very thin. He put them into the water, washed and broke them, and scattered the pieces. Then he went back into the sweathouse.

m. Now he drew out his own pipe. As soon as he lit it, two of them began to go to sleep. He said to them, "You had better smoke with me." They took the pipe from him, but each soon let it fall. Every one of them dropped asleep. Pulekukwerek thought, "I am sorry for them. They have done wrong but they are good people. If I revive them they will help me make the world (right)."[17] Then he awoke them. He told them, "I want you to be good. Do not live as you have been doing. I shall come again. Now I want to go back where I came from." But they said, "No, do not go back yet. There is another town, Merip. That is the last place. Then go on up from here." "Well," Pulekukwerek thought, "I had better go see the man there."

Then the youngest of the ten at Kenek said, "Old man, you will not come back if you go there." "How is that?" said Pulekukwerek. "I will show you what to do if you will take me with you," said the boy. Then Pulekukwerek took him and they went (downstream).[18] After a time the boy said, "This is as far as I can go." Pulekukwerek told him, "No. Go on. Do not be afraid." "Well, my

17. In the usual versions of this episode, the ten brothers—they are the Ka-sumig-or or Kegor or Kenomer or porpoises—are quite colorless except for being bad. When they fail in their own efforts to kill Pulekukwerek, they send him to Merip (as in F1*k*) in the hope that the jealous one there will have better luck against him. The variation which the present narrator introduces is probably original with him: Pulekukwerek converts his hosts and they help him reform the world. There seem to be two psychological impulses involved. One is that the ordinary folktale dwells in simple antitheses of good and bad, of hero and villain—of "leading man" and "heavy" in the parlance of our theater. Billy, as an artist, does not put up with this aversion toward even the more elementary subtleties. To him a colorful story must contain a variety of characters, and some element of the unexpected as regards personality. His second motive is a certain passion for nobility, a tendency to exalt his actors: The way they gather allies and associates brings out their own greatness. Parallels may be found in many of Billy's tales: the relation of Coyote to Kewet Omewa (A12), the repentance of Segwu' old man in "Wohpekumeu at Segwu' " (A23), Oknuł fierce one's success in taking his boat over a mountain after his defeat by Kewetspekw (A13*y*), and the Wełkwäu companion of Tsuräu young man (A1). Billy has an instinct that magnanimity enhances a hero far more than would his mere stamping out of a fallen opponent.

18. All Pulekukwerek versions agree in moving upstream. The switch to the Bald Hills between Pekwon and Kenek is only a lengthening of the way, not a change of direction. Yet the versions are also unanimous in putting the smoking at Kenek before the Merip episode, though this order takes the hero temporarily a few miles downstream.

uncle,[19] I will watch you. Give me your heart and go." Then Pulekukwerek gave him his heart[20] and crossed the river.

n. He came to Merip and found the door of the house open. He went inside. The boy was watching him from across the river. Pulekukwerek found only a woman in the house. He said, "Are you here alone?" She said, "Yes. You should not have come. Why did you?" He said, "I have come to see my friend. Where is he?" She said, "He has gone to Kepel. You had better leave at once. He will be back soon." "No, I want to see him," said Pulekukwerek. "I will stay for the night if he wants me to." The woman thought, "He will be dead soon."

Then they heard a paddle being laid on the roof of the house. The one outside did not speak but went around the house. Pulekukwerek was sitting near the woman. The man came in, looked, took an arrow, and prepared to shoot. "My friend, you cannot kill me with that arrow," said Pulekukwerek. The people at Kenek had told him to say this. Then the man drew out another arrow, and another. He drew out eight, and nine. Then he took his last one. "That is the one," said Pulekukwerek. "Now shoot me right here. If you hit me here or here I shall not die, but if you hit me here in the heart I shall be killed," and he bared[21] his breast. But the man did not answer. He shot, and Pulekukwerek fell. "Take him out and throw him away," the man said to his wife. She dragged him out but did not throw him down. She was sorry for the elderly man.

The boy was looking on from across the river. He said, "That is Pulekukwerek." When the woman had gone into the house again, he came over with the heart, put it in Pulekukwerek's hand, and struck him. Pulekukwerek got up. He went down to the river and drank. He crossed, and came back in a boat, calling, "My friend, where are you?" The jealous man came outside. He thought someone else had come. He went down to the river and saw Pulekukwerek laughing. Then he too began to laugh. Pulekukwerek said to him, "My friend, you will be like that. As long as the world lasts, you shall sit on top of a rock and laugh. You will be Merits-atser.[22]

19. An expression of affection, presumably. The Yurok word for "uncle" covers the same primary relationship as the English one.

20. This keeping of his heart for him by the boy during the following encounter is peculiar to the present tale, and is in line with the variation discussed in n. 17.

21. Or "pointed to it."

22. A small bird. Merits is a form of Merip. A number of the concrete touches that usually enliven this incident are left out by the narrator: the jealous one's poisoning of people whose footprints he finds near his house; Pulekukwerek's embracing the wife (or wives) in order to rouse him to fury; his leaping through the smoke hole when shot; and above all the fact that the jealous one's arrowhead is flaming, and that from it the rattlesnake subsequently derives its poison. In spite of all these omissions of visually concrete acts, Billy makes the episode lively through his interest in persons and their relations.

o. Pulekukwerek returned to Kenek. They saw a Weitspus person coming, who said, "Someone is coming who will not be stopped. He eats all that he meets as he comes downstream. Yesterday he was at Weitspus." They asked, "On which side of the river is he?" The Weitspus person listened and said, "On the Trinity (or south) side," because he heard a dog barking there. Pulekukwerek thought, "Pelin-tsīk did not tell me anything about him. He must be very bad." Then he went into the sweathouse. The people were afraid that that one would come the next day. Pulekukwerek said, "Do not be uneasy about him. I shall make everything in this world good in time. Run off in the morning, and I shall speak to him." Then, when the sun rose, they all went off.

Pulekukwerek had got a woman to heat stones for him. He had asked, "What kind of a person is he?" The Weitspus man said, "I did not see him, but I hear that he has a mouth reaching to his shoulders, and teeth outside, and eyes on the side of his snout." Then Pulekukwerek got two young men to bring him sticks and split them and fasten them on himself as if they were teeth. Now he felt that that one was coming. His fire with the stones in it was large. Inside of himself he had put a vessel of stone, and he had on his false teeth. He stood on top of the house looking upstream.

Then he saw that one standing at a distance and looking about. "Come," he motioned to him. He approached and Pulekukwerek went down from the roof to meet him. "Where do you come from?" Pulekukwerek asked him with his hands.[23] The other one signed, "I come from there. I eat up people." "Is that so?" "Yes." Then Pulekukwerek said to him in gestures, "Let us go together." That one nodded in assent. Then Pulekukwerek signed to him, "Let us go indoors." They went in and Pulekukwerek pointed to a stool. Then he pointed to one of the hot stones and invited him to eat. That one refused. Pulekukwerek let his hand fall backward (in surprise). "You will die somewhere if you do not eat one," he said. "Look." Then he ate one himself and urged him again. He reached him one and that one swallowed it and the stone came out through his throat (and he died). Then Pulekukwerek took out of his body the hollow stone he had used. He called to the people, "Come back. I told you that I would talk with him. Now look in the house." They looked in a saw a large monster (in human form, a Sa'ał). That was the last of the bad things that Pulekukwerek destroyed.

p. At night Pulekukwerek said, "Well, I shall go. I am going to make the world good." Then he went back to Pelin-tsīk. He said to him, "You had better come with me." Pelin-tsīk said, "What shall you do?" Pulekukwerek said, "There will be another people. Those who are in the world now will leave. I

23. This gesturing is of interest because of rarity of communication by manual signs in native California. Apparently the Sa'ał do not speak.

shall make them go away." Then Pelin-tsīk told Tego'o,[24] his younger brother, "Go with him." So Pulekukwerek and Tego'o started. Pelin-tsīk said, "I shall come later.

q. Pulekukwerek and Tego'o came to Kenek. They found Wohpekumeu there. "Where is he from?" Pulekukwerek asked. They told him, "We do not know where he came from. We saw him sitting outside the sweathouse." Then Wohpekumeu said to him, "I think you do not know me." Pulekukwerek said, "Yes, I do not know you." Wohpekumeu said, "I know this one's brother, Pelin-tsık. I am the one who knew him first. I am able to tell you what you are thinking. I will help you. What do you say?" Pulekukwerek said, "Well, what am I thinking?" Wohpekumeu said, "What you think I think too. I am thinking that I wish to make the world good. You also think the world is not good enough and that you will make it so. We think the same."

Pulekukwerek thought, "How did he know it? It is true. I came here to make the world so that human beings will live." He said, "Another kind will live here. We had better first find what they will eat." Wohpekumeu said, "Yes, let us do it tomorrow." Then he said, "The older brother of this one here has started to go about the world." Pulekukwerek thought, "If it is true, he is wiser than I, because I left (Pelin-tsīk) and knew that he would follow."[25]

r. Next day, Pulekukwerek said, "I do not think he will come," but Wohpekumeu said, "Yes, I will make it that he will come." Wohpekumeu sat outside and played his flute. Then Pulekukwerek thought, "He knows more than I." After a time Pelin-tsīk came. He sat there. "Where have you been?" they asked him. "All over the world," he said. "Upstream they have food, and in the south different food, and where we come from they use tobacco. But there is one place, not far from here, that I was hardly able to leave, so much did I like what I smelled there. I flew about and wanted to smell it again. I want people that we are going to make to be, to have that sort of food." Wohpekumeu said, "How far is it?" Pelin-tsīk said, "It is not very far away. It will take a day to go there." Wohpekumeu said, "I shall go tomorrow." Then Pulekukwerek thought, "Well, let him go." Pulekukwerek asked, "Who lives there, men or women?" "Two women," said Pelin-tsīk. Wohpekumeu said, "I shall go in the morning."

s. Then, next day, he started. He came to the mouth of the Salmon.[26] He found the house and the two women. They said, "Old man, stay here for the

24. Dentalium money of the largest size, or next to the longest, that is, twelve pieces to a string of arm's length.

25. This balancing of separate characters and matching of conversation is what the narrator loves. Passages of this sort are probably wholly of his inventing. There is certainly almost no trace of them in the stock versions of the same tales told by most Yurok.

26. Probably to the town of Enek (Karok Amaikiaram), to judge by other versions and the Salmon New Year's rite performed there.

night." He said, "Yes, but I never eat." He looked in the house and saw acorn storage baskets. They said, "Well, old man, will you eat acorns?" and he said, "Yes." They said, "Will you eat salmon?" and he said, "Yes." It tasted very good to him. He thought, "I will not harm them. I will not take anything away (now). Then when I come back I shall get everything." He wanted to know where the salmon and the acorns came from. He said, "I will be here again in ten days. I shall bring salmon and acorns with me." But he did not know what they were. Then he went back downstream to Kenek and told them.

They said, "How shall you get those things?" He said, "I shall find them." Pelin-tsīk said, "Good. If you obtain them it will be good in the world. I know where Darkness is and we will get him too." Then Wohpekumeu stayed there four (*sic*) nights before he (prepared to) return. Then he said, "If we get those things the world will be good. I know it, for I ate them." Pulekukwerek said, "Do you know what you ate?" Wohpekumeu said, "I do not know what it is, but I know its name. One is called 'sa'mon,' another '*keko'o*,[27] another hazelnuts,' and another kind 'lamprey eels.' "[28] Then Tego'o asked him, "Is that all you ate?" Wohpekumeu said, "Yes, I ate only four kinds of food." Tego'o said, "I think those women have more than four kinds." Wohpekumeu said, "They must have many kinds. I saw that they had large baskets, very large baskets. There must be something in them." Pulekukwerek said, "There is one above all that we must obtain: the one that they keep in the house and catch in the river. We must get the one that is called 'salmon.'" Wohpekumeu said, "Yes. I think it will not be hard to find out how to get it." Pulekukwerek said to him, "You had better go back tomorrow." Wohpekumeu said, "Yes, I shall go tomorrow."

t. In the morning he started. He followed the trail over the hill to Otsepor[29] carrying his quiver. Then he found a madrone tree. He took bark from two limbs. Then he spoke to the two pieces of bark. He said, "When I speak to you in that place to which I am going, then turn into what I tell you to turn into. When I say to you, 'Be salmon,' then turn to salmon." He went on. He saw something hanging and knocked it down with a stick. He opened it and there were two little round things inside. He told them also to turn into what he ordered them. He told them to become nuts. He put them also into his quiver. Then he looked for white-oak bark. He said to it, "When I speak to you, turn into acorn-meal bread." Now he was looking for something round. He had come to the hill above the place to which he was going and saw the house below him. He felt bad that he had not found anything round. He thought, "I had better

27. [K. has queried whether this should be *teko'o* or *rego'o*.—Ed.]

28. [Kroeber, Handbook, p. 85, notes that lamprey, commonly known as eels, ascend the Klamath in great numbers and are prized by the Yurok for their rich greasiness.—Ed.]

29. Otsepor is a little town at the mouth of Bluff Creek, the last Yurok settlement up the Klamath.

cut out something round.'' He took a piece of wood and began to whittle it. Then a bird came carrying something in its bill. It sat above him. It was a Jay. Wohpekumeu said, ''Drop what you are holding,'' and Jay[30] dropped it. It was acorns. ''That is what I wanted,'' said Wohpekumeu. Jay had known that Wohpekumeu could not find acorns anywhere. Therefore he had stolen them from the women and brought them to Wohpekumeu.

Then Wohpekumeu came and sat down outside the house. The two women inside began to feel that he was there. The older one said to her sister, ''Do you feel anything?'' She said, ''Somehow I feel that somebody is outdoors.'' ''You had better go and look,'' said the older. Then the younger went out, saw Wohpekumeu, came back, and said, ''There is someone outside.'' The older sister said, ''Go and speak to him.'' Then she went out again. She said, ''Where do you come from?'' Wohpekumeu said, ''I have come back again.'' She said, ''Oh! Is it you, the one who stayed here one night? Come inside.'' ''Yes, I will enter,'' said Wohpekumeu. He went in. Then the older sister said, ''No one, and I know people all over the world, has ever come into our house. No one has ever wanted to come in except you. I am glad that you have come.'' Wohpekumeu said, ''I go everywhere, all over the world. That is my kind. I go into houses, but I have not seen so fine a house as yours. Nevertheless, everywhere they all use the same food as you do.'' Then they did not believe him. They said, ''If they use the same food as we, they are well off.'' ''Yes, so they are,'' said Wohpekumeu. Then they got up and brought food. They gave him hazelnuts and lamprey-eels and acorns (and salmon). ''Eat,'' they said. ''We want to hear news because you say you have been all over the world.'' ''Yes, I have been everywhere,'' he said. ''I will eat.'' Then he turned where he sat on his stool and reached for his quiver. He said, ''I think you had better take some of my food.'' He drew out the madrone bark and said to it, ''Be salmon.'' Then he laid it next to their salmon, and it looked the same. Then he gave them his acorn meal (bread) and his nuts. ''Eat this,'' he said. The younger sister took a nut, cracked it, and found it was the same as their own hazelnuts. The older sister thought, ''Perhaps it does not taste like our salmon even though it looks good.'' So she tasted his salmon and found it was good and liked it. They broke the acorn-meal bread, and each of them ate some. Everything tasted just like their own food. Then they were ashamed and believed him. The older one said, ''They must (already) have made it how those human beings are to live.'' ''Yes, they have provided for it,'' said Wohpekumeu.

u. Now Wohpekumeu began to think where the acorn trees might be. He thought that if he felt something in his head, the trees were growing in the sky. If he felt something in his buttocks, they would be growing on earth. Then he found out: he felt it in his head, and knew that the trees grew in the sky.

30. [K. has queried whether this should be Blue Jay.—Ed.]

Now, before this, the women had always brushed away the leavings and carefully cleaned up after they had eaten.[31] Now they did not do so any longer, for they thought it unnecessary. Then Wohpekumeu said, "Well, what do you wish to hear about?" The younger sister said, "I want to hear where they obtained their good acorn trees." Wohpekumeu said, "I have never been there myself, but I know where they get their acorns. They go straight up to the sky." The women thought, "It must be that they have them, for he knows." "Where did they get their salmon?" they asked. He said, "I think I know that too. They cannot get them in the river, but one person has them all in his house. He alone has them all, I do not know where." "We are the ones," they thought. Then at once he knew that it was they who had the salmon.[32]

Now they went to bed. He lay in the middle. He did not sleep. Then the older sister moved. Wohpekumeu pretended to be asleep. She said to her younger sister, "Get up and get some acorns. He is asleep. He will not awake until you come back." The younger woman started to go out quietly. She said (to the older), "Go down to the river and get a salmon so that he can eat dried salmon when he goes." Wohpekumeu was watching. "I will find out where they get them," he thought. When the younger sister had gone out, the older one took a (glowing) stick from the fire and put it (close) to Wohpekumeu's leg. He did not move. Then she thought that he was sound asleep. She climbed up a ladder (onto the terrace in the house) and went behind storage baskets. Then he heard water running. Then she came back into the pit of the house, took a net, and went outdoors. Wohpekumeu got up, climbed back on the terrace, looked, and saw a box full of salmon. He overturned it, and all the water and salmon were poured out and ran down into the river. Then he broke the box and scattered the pieces. Before he went, he took his quiver, laid it in his place, and said, "Be a person." The older sister heard a noise, came back and looked. She saw him sleeping and thought everything was well. He ran down to the river and took her net. Then he knew that the other one was coming. She had her burden basket full of acorns. Slipping behind her, he tipped over the basket so that the acorns were spilled out of it and rolled down into the river. Then he ran back into the house and said to his quiver, "Be a quiver and arrows again," lay down, and pretended to be asleep.

The younger sister came and said, "Somehow my basket tipped and all the acorns rolled out." The older one said, "Is that so? I too thought I heard a noise, but the man was asleep here all the time." They went up to where their box was, looked for it, and found that it was gone. Then Wohpekemeu woke up. They told him, "Someone has been here and destroyed our salmon box." Wohpekumeu said, "I know him. He is from the south. He wants no one but himself to have salmon. Therefore he goes about and destroys those of other people."

31. As part of their policy of concealment of food.

32. He reads their minds when they react to his suggestion.

v. Wohpekumeu was still thinking, "I must find out where they keep the acorn tree and how to go there." He said, "I think you had better go now where your acorns are, up to the sky where you get them." They said, "But we like our house and the things we have here." Wohpekumeu said, "I will take your house up for you wherever you want to go." The younger sister thought (in her mind), "I do not think you will be able to do that." But Wohpekumeu said, "Do not think that. I am able to do it. Go up to that place, and in five days I shall come back here. I shall be able to follow your tracks."

Then he left them and went back downstream to Kenek. He told the young men to make an (A-frame dip) net and catch salmon in the river. Now they went fishing and caught salmon. He told the Kenek women, "Go out in the woods and look for round things on the ground." They went out and saw the round things, gathered them here and there, brought them back, cracked and pounded them, cooked the meal, and it tasted good.[33]

w. Then Wohpekumeu said, "Do you know when Pelin-tsīk will come? I do not think you know." Pulekukwerek said, "No, I do not know." Wohpekumeu said, "Well, I know it. He is now going all around the earth in this direction (from right to left). He will soon be here." Pulekukwerek went outside the sweathouse and began to smoke. Then Pelin-tsīk arrived.

Now he and Wohpekumeu went upstream (to Enek) to the house of those women. It was closed. Wohpekumeu went in and saw everything arranged beautifully. He came out again. Pelin-tsīk said, "I have found their tracks. They are right above here. Now we will take the house up. You will not be able to go all the way. You can go only part way, but you may start with me. When you feel the wind blowing, you will be able to go no farther. Then let go of the house, and I shall take it on alone." Now they started up. Then Wohpekumeu heard the wind. He went on until he felt it blowing. Then he stopped and went down and returned to Kenek. Pelin-tsīk went on up with the house. He set it down and asked the women, "Where do you want it?" They said, "Right over here by the acorn tree (*homono*, tan oak)." They said, "Are you the man who was with us when our salmon were taken away?" He said, "No, that was another. He was not able to come all the way up. Only I could bring your house up." "Well, come to see us sometimes," they said. "Yes," he said. When they went inside to look at the house, and he was going about outside to arrange (its boards), he broke off branches from the tree and hid them. Now he too came back to Kenek. He told them what he had done and what the women had said. He showed the branches that he had broken off. Pulekukwerek took them, pounded them to dust, put it in his hand, and blew it off. "Now there will be acorns all over the world," he said. In the morning there were oaks everywhere on the hills.

33. Here they have acorns derived from those he spilled upriver at Enek; but rounding of the plot requires a journey to the sky, so the possession is overlooked and the quest continues.

x. Then Pulekukwerek saw that Wohpekumeu was not staying with them in the sweathouse. He was where the women were. Pulekukwerek thought, "He will not be my companion and go about with me making the world over." He said, "How shall we make it in this world? I think that all these people will go away and that there will be others." Then Tego'o said, "Yes, I think that will be good." Pelin-tsīk said, "I am going back." He was afraid his wings might become dirty.[34] He said, "Come and tell me what happens. I want to know what you do. Go on upstream and up the Trinity and north; but do not go south.[35] That is where Wohpekumeu came from. I saw his tracks coming from the south. That is where he must have grown." Pulekukwerek said to him, "I am coming down soon to where you are. You can depend on it. I shall finish making this world and then I shall come." Then Pelin-tsīk and his younger brother Tego'o went off downstream.

Then Pulekukwerek said to Wohpekumeu, "How do you think it will be? Will they always live like this?" Wohpekumeu said, "Yes, I think it will always be like this." Pulekukwerek said, "No. These here will go away. Others will come. Every man and every woman will say what kind they will be hereafter. They will go, some here and some there, and some will fly away. Then others will come."[36]

y. At Kenek they told that there were ten young men at Ko'men[37] who shot at strangers with too little provocation. Then Pulekukwerek wanted to render them harmless. He asked Wohpekumeu, "Do you think you can change them (to birds and animals)?" Wohpekumeu said, "Yes." Then the two of them went upstream. Pulekukwerek said, "If I go on without looking back, follow me." Wohpekumeu said he would do so. Then they came to Weitspus. Many people were outside about the town. Pulekukwerek went through among them to the sweathouse. Then he looked back. He saw Wohpekumeu sitting with a group of women. "I thought that is what he would do," he said.

In the morning they went on upstream, and Pulekukwerek again told Wohpekumeu to follow him, and he promised. Then they came to Ko'men, and again there were many people about, men and women. Pulekukwerek went right on to where a young man was sitting outside a sweathouse. Without having turned aside on his way, he sat down by him. The other moved a seat for him, and only then Pulekukwerek looked back. He did not see Wohpekumeu. Then he saw

34. Pelin-tsīk is rarely described as doing anything. At most he travels—in this tale by flying—and talks. In a sense he is superior to Wohpekumeu and Pulekukwerek, who often execute his wishes, whereas he never moves to carry out theirs. The touch about fearing to soil his wings has subtlety.

35. Probably *wohpauk,* which sometimes means south as well as across the ocean. [See A1, n. 8, for an explanation of Yurok directional terms.—Ed.]

36. Here Pulekukwerek knows more, just as before Wohpekumeu surpassed him. The narrator carefully distributes credits among his personages.

37. Orleans, Karok Panamenik.

where a crowd of women was making baskets. Someone was sitting with them. It was Wohpekumeu. Then when Pulekukwerek saw the sister of the ten hostile young men sitting among them, he was satisfied, because he knew that now the ten brothers would be changed and made harmless.[38] Then he saw the girl trying to pull one of the arrows out of Wohpekumeu's quiver.[39] Thereupon the ten men, her brothers, rose up, went into their house, and brought their bows.

"You had better escape. They will kill you," it was said to Pulekukwerek. "Oh, that does not concern me. I have nothing to with that. He is the one. I have nothing to do with him. I met him on the road and he came with me. He lives downstream at Kenek." So Pulekukwerek said. But when they warned Wohpekumeu that he was to be killed, he ran off. The ten pursued him. When he looked back, he saw that they had nearly overtaken him. Then he said, "I wish there were a tree with a hole in it." Then there was such a tree before him and he jumped into it. "I wish it would grow together," he said, and the tree grew together. The hole had closed up. The ten came up but could not find him. At last they went off.

z. Then Pulekukwerek thought, "I think I can find him." He followed the tracks, which stopped at an oak. He looked about. "Where are you?" he said. "I am here," said Wohpekumeu. "You cannot get out," said Pulekukwerek. Wohpekumeu told him, "I know it. Get the birds to come, especially the woodpeckers, to take me out." Then the birds came, ten of them, and pecked at the tree. The last one that came was the pileated woodpecker. He worked best of all and pecked hardest. Soon there was a large hole, and Wohpekumeu emerged.

He said, "I will make you all as you would like to be." He built a fire and prepared. "How do you wish to be?" he asked one. "I want woodpecker crest[40] on both my shoulders." Wohpekumeu made him so. Then he asked the next and the next, and made each one so. Crow said, "I want to be woodpecker crest all over my body." When he asked pileated woodpecker, he said, "I want woodpecker crest from my forehead to the back of my neck." Wohpekumeu made him like that.

Then Crow asked again to be woodpecker crest all over. He said it again and again. Wohpekumeu became angry. He said, "Very well, I will do it for you. Close your eyes, and when I have finished, fly as far as you can before you look at yourself." Then he blackened him with coals. Crow darted up, flew a long distance, and opened his eyes. When he saw himself black instead of bright red, he was angry. He came back, but found that nearly all had gone; for Wohpekumeu knew that he would return (and had warned them). But Crow saw

38. They would be jealous, there would be a conflict, and then they would suffer change.

39. In play, provocatively.

40. That is, scarlet feathers. *Tsīṣ*, woodpecker crest, is a precious material to the Yurok, as pearl or ivory is to us, rather than being thought of as a part of an animal body.

two little boys, ...[41] They too had been decorated with woodpecker crest, but he pushed them into the ashes and spoiled most of it.[42]

aa. Pulekukwerek thought that Wohpekumeu was running after women too much. He told him, "I am going back to Pelin-tsīk. Stay here and enjoy yourself. Go about with women all you like. Then when these (immortals) go off and human beings live here, come downstream and tell me, and I will come and we will finally make the world good." Wohpekumeu said, "Very well." Then, next day, Pulekukwerek went off downstream in his boat.[43]

Wohpekumeu remained and went everywhere, associating with women. After a time, Pulekukwerek said to Pelin-tsīk, "Go up and see what he is doing." Pelin-tsīk flew upstream, flew back again, and told him that Wohpekumeu was still pursuing women. Pulekukwerek said, "It is what I thought. Well, let him get through with that. Let him have enough."[44]

A15y. Pulekukwerek, Pelin-tsīk, and Wohpekumeu

Outline of Variant Version

This is a synopsis of the last portion of the same myth, told by the same informant a year later. It was not recorded in full, but an abstract was jotted down with a view to comparing the substance of the two versions. It will be seen that they are far from identical. The narrator not only combines his episodes quite differently but uses other incidents in the second rendition of the same episode. With all the definiteness of feeling which he has for a story as a complete whole, as something finished, it is evident that he did not carry each tale in his mind as a crystallized unit of distinctive content, but that he improvised as he went along, satisfying a craving for workmanship in rounding each version off. The same conclusion as to fluidity is to be derived from the two versions given of the making of the sky in the following tale (A16), as well as from a comparison of them with the present story.

•

41. [Omission in typescript. K. has a marginal notation referring to his original notebooks.—Ed.]

42. Over the decorating of the rescuing birds, the narrator has quite forgotten that the purpose of the expedition was the transformation of the ten Ko'men men. Also, the big pileated woodpecker, the chief source of tsīs, is forgotten among the birds, or taken for granted. See A15y *c*.

43. To the end of the world. The boat is a bit surprising.

44. This deliberate refraining from a conclusion is something that few narrators would indulge in. It suggests an attempt to arrange myths in a system or ordered cycle. For instance, the two tales of Wohpekumeu's love adventures—A21 and 22—would follow here; then his departure from this world; then his return in 23. But while the narrator feels no impulse in this systematizing direction, he never goes farther than to place the tale he is telling against a background of his people's mythology as a whole. The background is never consistently arranged. And even the individual tale varies from one to another recounting, as what follows proves.

a. Wohpekumeu had gone to Hupa, Pulekukwerek accompanying him. At last Pulekukwerek succeeded in bringing him back to Kenek.[45]

b. Then they started to go upstream to Ko'men. There a girl lived who never left her house, although dances constantly took place before it (to tempt her out). Wohpekumeu hid a little distance upstream from the town for five days. He took a hundred of his pubic hairs, laid them on the ground, and told them to rise. They got up as young men, all alike, a hundred of them. They painted and dressed themselves, and he told them to make the war dance. Then the people of Ko'men said, "Another party is coming," and the hundred arrived and danced. Then at last the girl looked out of her house. Wohpekumeu was dancing in the middle of the line of hundred and smiled at her. The people began to suspect him as Wohpekumeu. At last her oldest brother said, "He is Wohpekumeu." The latter told his hundred young men, "Fly up!" and they flew off as birds. He ran, and when closely pursued took refuge in a hollow tree.

c. He was rescued (as told in the previous version, except that it is added that): Pileated Woodpecker found the hole still quite small when he arrived and with two strokes enlarged it enough for Wohpekumeu to emerge. Wohpekumeu offered to give Crow woodpecker crest over the upper half of his body, but Crow wanted to be entirely red. Wohpekumeu painted him black while his eyes were shut, and told him to fly to a high dead tree and look at himself.

Afterwards, Wohpekumeu asked what had become of his hundred young men. He was told that they were along the river, a flock of small birds. They are called *Wohpekumeu-tegin*.

d. Then Wohpekumeu and Pulekukwerek went back to Weitspus. There Pulekukwerek lost his companion and heard that he had gone to Pekwtuł. Crossing to look for him there, he heard that on seeing a girl laughing he had gone on further. Pulekukwerek became angered and left. At Kenek he found only Pelin-tsīk.

e. Wohpekumeu's son Kapuloyo had already gone downstream. Following him, Pulekukwerek saw him at the mouth of the river, with a basket and a dentalium purse, waiting for a companion from Rekwoi. Pulekukwerek was on the opposite side at Wełkwäu. Taking his flute he played and caused two dentalia to come back, *wetskāk*, the smallest, and *tsīk weilul*, the largest. Pursuing Kapuloyo, Pulekukwerek overtook him. Kapuloyo missed his dentalia and thought his father Wohpekumeu responsible, although it was Pulekukwerek.[46]

45. To desist from his amorous pursuits.

46. The usual account (as in F2) makes Wohpekumeu the pursuer, Kapuloyo having fled with the money of the world because of his father's seduction of his wife. Wohpekumeu then recovers some of the money.

f. Wohpekumeu became tired of being about the world, and, following after the others, found them gone from Kenek. He went downstream to the mouth. There he lost their tracks and turned southward (instead of north). As he traveled along the beach, he saw lying girls. At last, beyond Tsuräu,[47] he could no longer resist and went to one. She carried him into the ocean.

g. The salt water seemed like a prairie. At last they reached houses on the other side. An old man there said, "I am sorry for you, that you were left behind." Now a fog came, and Wohpekumeu hid in a basket. Ten canoes arrived, invisible in the fog, making the Jumping Dance.[48] Kapuloyo and Pulekukwerek were in them. Wohpekumeu showed himself, and they became ashamed, the fog reappeared, and they vanished. Wohpekumeu sent to them to say, "We were once together. Let us be comrades now." Then Kapuloyo was persuaded and returned. From that time on they all danced every day. The place where they lived was called Tsīktsīko'ł.[49] The old man and the girl who had seduced Wohpekumeu across (the ocean) were Tsīktsīko'l old man and Tsīktsīko'ł girl.[50]

A16x. Pulekukwerek Travels and Makes the Sky

FULL VERSION

From the Yurok point of view, this is a more recondite story than the last. It is more artificial, with elements of personal source outweighing the content of national origin. The first half, after which I have named the whole, has very little "action." A nameless boy, Wetskāk the smallest dentalium, Pulekukwerek, and Megwomets the food-giver confer, predict, and travel upstream, inspecting the places that are already satisfactory and those that need improving. The boy having recounted the latter, Pulekukwerek again starts out, this time alone, to attend to his tasks. Their execution is, however, passed over, except for the extermination of the monster at the mouth of the Klamath—and this episode the narrator has also included in the preceding story (A15*x*). Then Pulekukwerek turns aside to get the sky and stars made, an incident related in some detail. Further riddings of evils he delegates as subsidiary to a nameless friend on the river, and goes to the upstream end of the world to secure sleep for the world. (Compare the tale after this one, A17.)

This part of the story is hurried again.

47. This would be on Wiyot shore.

48. The narrator has used this idea, of the dance coming to Pulekuk in a fog, in another story, A23*h*.

49. Dentalium Home. The shells grow thickly at Pulekuk.

50. Most versions make her Skate.

It is an uneven tale, but notable for two things. The first is the number of cooperating personages, each with a definite role, so that they never constitute a mere company acting as a unit: Pulekukwerek, the boy, Wetskāk, Megwomets, Sky-Possessor, Wełkwäu old man, the dam maker at Kepel, Wohpekumeu, the guide from Segwu'. The second point of interest is that the narrator was able to improvise so complicated a whole with so little repetition of episodes that he used in other connections.

Further discussion of the tale's structure follows the narration. [K. has a notation: "Needs picture from notebook."—Ed.]

•

a. At the end of the sky[1] a boy grew. He found that there was sickness about. He thought, "I wish to know all the world.[2] I want someone to talk to me." Then he changed his mind and thought, "I had better sleep. I think I shall dream." He lay down in his sweathouse. When he slept, he dreamed.

b. Someone was outside.[3] He thought, "That is the one I want. I want to see him." The person came in and said, "I am sorry for you, that you grow alone. I shall tell you what to do. You do right to have a sweathouse. But I shall tell you what else you will have. Come outside." So the boy went outside. He looked about. He thought, "I am not asleep." "Yes, you are asleep. I will tell you how you to live. You shall build a house." "What is that?" "I will help you to build it." So he built it thus (with one ridgepole). The boy said, "It does not look well." "But you cannot live alone. We will build another one." Then the person built another house. He made it thus (with two ridgepoles). "That is how it will be all over the world. I have been there. I have gone about. Houses will be like this as long as this world lives. Poor men will have this kind of house; a rich man will have that kind there.[4] You and I will establish it so."

c. Then the boy thought, "I had better know who that is, where he comes from." He said: "I will go with you. Where are you from? Who are you? I

1. *Wes'ona hestsei,* "the sky across the ocean," the narrator called it. It is where the edge of the sky comes down to meet the ocean. *Wes'ona* means both "sky" and "world." Cf. A14, n. 11.

2. [K. first had "words" here, changed to "world," and queried.—Ed.]

3. This would seem to be the beginning of the boy's dream. The statement a few lines below; "Yes, you are asleep," confirms it. But from here on until *q* everything is related as if it were an actual happening, not a dream. To be sure, at the end of the journey, the boy wakes up in his own sweathouse, as if the dream ended there. But the references to what he sees at Rekwoi (*i*) and Erner (*k*) are as to real events. Again, if the dream is in the nature of an anticipation or prophecy, it fails, since the events in the second half of the story are almost all new, not a fulfillment of what has been touched on before. I admit to being in the dark. Cf. n. 24.

4. The normal Yurok roof had two ridgepoles and three pitches. A house built like ours, with a single ridge, was spoken of as a poor man's house. [For more details of house construction, see A11, n. 11.—Ed.]

grew here myself. I thought I was the only person alive." "You think you grew. You would not have grown if it were not for me. I am the one who grew first. That is why I know all the world. I shall make this world as it will be (hereafter), before I tell you what I myself shall turn to be." "No, tell me now." "Very well. But do not say it. If anyone asks, do not tell. There are many people all over the world who wish to know who I am. But I will tell you what I shall become. When this world is all made, then I shall turn into human persons' dentalia." "Yes? What will be your name?" "There are many kinds. I will tell you now how many kinds of them will grow. There will be. . . .[5] That is the last one. They are five. But these are not I. They are the ones I shall not turn into. I shall become one that is far behind them (the smallest in size and value), a pretty one. I shall be called Wetskāk. Now we had better start out in the morning." "Yes."

d. The boy was glad that he was to go all over the world, but thought, "I do not believe I shall be able to walk." That one said, "No, you need not think that. You can sit on my back, because I want you with me." "What shall we use?" "What for?" "What shall we eat when we travel?" "We shall eat nothing. We shall use tobacco, that is all." "Have you some of that thing? I do not know it." "It is only a short distance to where one lives (who has tobacco). We will take him along with us." "I do not think he can go. He is an old man."[6] "Oh, he can go. I will tell you his name." "Yes." "He knows. He knows more than I, that old man. He uses only tobacco. His name is Pulekukwerek. That is his name." "Yes? I did not know that. I knew no one."

e. They came where (Pulekukwerek) lived and saw many houses. "Count them! Those are the only houses you will see. This is where Pulekukwerek lives. We will take him with us." He counted. There were twelve houses. He heard talking; and when he went into the sweathouse he heard talking outside. He tried to see the persons but could not. He only saw Pulekukwerek, the old man, making a pipe in the sweathouse. The old man said, "Perhaps you would like to go along?" The boy said, "Yes, I should like to go with you." "Yes, I will take you. I shall show you how they live in the world." Then he said, "I think we had better start. I must go to see my friend."

f. When the boy had come into the sweathouse he saw a little stick, pretty, nearly white. Pulekukwerek said: "I had better let my friend know I am

5. [K. refers to his notebooks for the names of the dentalia. A15y, *e*, above identifies *wetskāk* as the smallest and *tsīk weilul* as the largest. See also Kroeber, Handbook, pp. 22-25, esp. the table on p. 23, which lists the five (non-personage) dentalia as *kergerpił, tego'o, wega, hewiyem,* and *merostan*.—Ed.]

6. Here he knows that the man is old; in the last paragraph he has said that he thought himself the only person alive.

going." He touched the stick. "Oh, my brother, I am going." Then the boy saw the stick move, get up, turn into a person. Then that man spoke. "Ayekwi, boy! You do not know me?" "No, I do not know you." "Well, look at me, so you will know me." The boy looked. He was carrying something on his back but the boy saw no packstrap or cords across his breast. He saw holes through his shoulders, and cords in those. That person had a net sack on his back. He said: "You need not say 'How did he come to look like that?' I never take them off, I grew like that. I shall let you know my name. My name is Megwomets. In this world you will see many people. All are my friends. I keep food for them and give them everything (to eat). Do you see my back?" Then the boy looked at (the sack on) his back. He saw salmon, lamprey eels, acorns, all seeds, berries—everything edible in that sack. "I keep that for my friends. I take it and throw it abroad and it grows for my friends. I do the same with salmon. I am that kind of person. Why do you wish to go about?" "I want to know the world." Pulekukwerek said, "There is sickness." Megwomets said, "Well, take him around the world. After a time we will make it (right). We will let him know the land." "Yes" (said Pulekukwerek), and the boy said, "Yes, that is what I wish."

g. Megwomets said, "Did you hear talking outside?" "Yes." "Those are not (human) persons. I will tell you know what they have changed from. Over all the world people are making arrows. All over they are making bows. As soon as arrows are worn out, they turn into men and come here. That is the kind of persons of whom there are many outside. Now as we go about, you will see all the people. Of the young men, some have two hundred and some three hundred arrows; but you cannot find one old one lying outdoors. When you come to a town you may look about. But you cannot see one arrow because when they are old and they throw them away, they turn to men who come here. That is the kind you heard talking outdoors." When he looked there, that boy, tears came into his eyes; he was sorry. Pulekukwerek said; "You need not be sorry about that. As long as this world is alive it will be thus."

h. Then Pulekukwerek said, "Well, let us start." They started. They ran nearly a whole night. "It is nearly sunrise and we shall come into a town. Do not say anything. Some men are inquisitive. Some may want to find out who we are. Do not tell them." The boy said, "Yes."

They came to a town. "Now, boy, count how many those houses are." Then the boy counted them as soon as they arrived. He counted fifty-one houses and fifty-one sweathouses.[7]

7. This would be about twice as many houses as any historic Yurok town contained. Sweathouses are always less numerous than houses, about in the ratio of one to three. An important man, however, is almost certain to have a sweathouse of his own.

Then they sat down outside a sweathouse. Some were making arrows, those young men; some a bow; some painted a bow; some rolled string; some made nets. Then the boy looked about. Outside some of the houses, ten quivers were hanging full of arrows; some had a hundred arrows in them, some more. The boy looked around to see any old arrows lying here or there. He saw none. Then he cried. Pulekukwerek said, "You need not be sorry."

Then he said, "Well, we will go on." The people tried to ask where they were going. "Oh, we are only going about." The people did not know who they were; they did not know where they came from.

i. They traveled for half a day. Then the old man (Pulekukwerek) said, "Perhaps you wish to go where they make boats." The boy said, "Yes, I want to go there." Then they turned up the (Klamath) river. Now the boy found that there was the river. He heard pounding, pounding. Then he saw they were making boats. In one place they were making ten boats. Ten men worked. He looked across stream, and another ten men were working there. That was at the mouth.

They started to cross. The people there stopped them. "Do not cross. (Even) a bird cannot fly above the water. It is compelled to fall in the middle. You must go about to come to the other side. Pulekukwerek said, "Well, it is useless to try to cross." But he thought, "I will come later and make it right." He thought that, but he did not say it.[8]

j. Then they went upstream (on the north side). They came to Terwer.[9] He who lived there, an old man, made Pulekukwerek (and his companions) stay for the night. The three (travelers) ate no food. They only smoked. They came indoors, and Pulekukwerek talked and looked at those who were eating and kept on talking. Some said, "Where are they from? We do not know where they are from. It is useless to ask them."

Now the old man told them how some persons there were becoming bad and made it bad to travel. Pulekukwerek said, "Yes?" "If you go upstream (the old man said), do not go to Erner.[10] It is a bad place." "Very well," said Pulekukwerek.

k. Next morning they started. Pulekukwerek said, "I will go ahead. You follow. I hear that it is a bad place." As soon as they saw Pulekukwerek coming, they did not look, five men sitting outside the sweathouse at Erner. They looked on the ground. When Pulekukwerek reached them, they looked at him only for a moment. Pulekukwerek thought, "I wish you would look at me. You would forget that you are bad. You will be good-natured." One

8. This saving up of an episode complicates the plot, which is what the narrator wants.

9. Terwer is a good-sized creek coming in from the north some 5 1/2 miles above Rekwoi, at the Klamath's second-to-the-last right-angled bend. There is a flat at the mouth, a favored campsite, where there may have been a pre-1850 town.

10. Erner was a town at the mouth of Blue Creek, important until the flood of 1861-62.

began to look at Pulekukwerek. Pulekukwerek laughed and that man began to laugh too.[11] Then Pulekukwerek said, "What is it? How do you do it? How did you come here? I saw no tracks on the sand beach." "Well, we never feel good," one of them said. "How do you keep alive?" One of them answered, "I do not know." "Don't you eat?" One said, "No. We do not know how to eat." Don't you drink water?" "No, we know nothing about drinking." Then Pulekukwerek told the boy, "Go to the spring," and gave him a (basketry) cup, and the boy went to the spring. The boy reached Megwomets the filled cup to hand to those five men. "Now drink this," Megwomets said. Then they all drank a little, those five, a very little. Megwomets told that boy, "Take a piece of salmon from my back." Then he took a bit of salmon, only one swallow of it; and one acorn, one bit of lamprey eel, and a little of all seeds (and gave it to them). They ate.

When they had finished, Megwomets said, "Now, you, I will make a net for you. Go down to the river and catch salmon. Go uphill in autumn and you will find many acorns. You will be good-natured men all your lives. You were bad because you did not know how to eat."[12]

l. Then they started upstream from Erner and came to Wohtek. The people there tried to make them stop, but Pulekukwerek said, "No, we hurry."

They came to Pekwon. The boy wanted to go to the sweathouse (which is connected with) the Jumping Dance. Megwomets talked to the sweathouse. The sweathouse answered him. That was all they did there. They started on again.

m. There was Wohpekumeu. Pulekukwerek thought, "I want to be where he is. We shall stay at Kepel one night." They came to Kepel and heard shouting as they were making the fish dam.[13] The boy thought, "That is what I want to see. I am glad to hear it." When they arrived, they saw a man sitting outside a sweathouse. "Ah! I am glad to see you. Sit down." He took out his pipe. "Have a smoke," he said. That old man (Pulekukwerek), this is where he got tobacco. All the way he had seen no one that had tobacco, and now he came to Kepel and an old man had tobacco and a pipe. The old man (of Kepel) said, "Boy, you had better smoke, too. It is nothing bad. All is good and undisturbed and they are making much fun. We will take you down to where they are playing as soon as we have smoked."[14] The boy took the pipe and

11. [K. has a marginal reference here to the episode at Merip in A15.—Ed.]

12. This curious episode has no known parallels in Yurok tradition.

13. [For a description of this great annual ritual at Kepel, see Waterman and Kroeber, The Kepel Fish Dam, UC-PAAE 35, 49-80, 1938.—Ed.]

14. A great man must not be hasty. He is probably *lo'*, the ritual master of the dam.

smoked. Pulekukwerek had already smoked. Then Pulekukwerek thought, "Well, he is a man. He smokes." Then Pulekukwerek gave the old man his own pipe. He said, "You had better smoke this."

When they finished, the old man of Kepel said, "Let us go down to the river and see my fun."[15] Then they went down. They saw the fishing place (the dam). It was nearly done. The old man said, "You had better stay here tonight." Pulekukwerek said, "Yes, we will stay." Now they remained there.

n. Then the old man told them, "I will tell you. I know where you are going. You must not travel above (Okonile'l).[16] That is where you should turn back." Pulekukwerek thought, "How did he know where we were going? How did he find out so quickly?" "There are bad places where this world was not made right. I wish you would come again, and I will go with you and we will make it right." "Yes, that is what we travel for" (said Pulekukwerek). "Yes, I never go about. I attend to my fun down at the river here. Do not stop where . . . is,[17] for that man never comes here." "Good, we shall not stop there." "Boy, do not think anything about that place; there is much play there, and many young men, but go on without delaying there."

Then (in the morning they went on upstream and) came to Kenek but did not stop except for a very little time. The young men there urged the boy to stay. Megwomets did not stop at all but went on. Then soon (Pulekukwerek and the boy) went on too.

o. At Tohper[18] they saw people playing. The boy wanted to stop, but (his two companions) did not wish it. Megwomets said, "You will see many good times not far from here. Before long, you will see two rivers coming together. They make a dance there on the water, and they have many good times." Then the boy thought, "I must see that."

When they reached Wespen[19] they heard shouting. "Now you hear it." The boy said, "Yes, I hear." As soon as they came to the place (Weitspus), they looked down to the sand beach between the two rivers and saw many deerskins. The boy asked, "What is it?" Megwomets said, "Yes, this is the place. They have much fun here." After a time, the people entered boats and danced in them. The boy sat. When he turned Pulekukwerek was looking at him and saw tears dropping out of his eyes. "You are not sorry for that?" "Yes, I am sorry for those people. When they (first) made that kind, how did

15. The games, gambling, lovemaking, and jollity that accompanied dances and especially the ceremonial making of the Kepel salmon weir.

16. Okonile'l is Karok Inam, the last world renewal site upriver.

17. At Kenek. [For the omission in the typescript, K. has a marginal reference to his notebooks.—Ed.]

18. Tohper was said to be Butte Camp, above Wahsek.

19. Wespen is the downstream outskirts of Weitspus.

they come to think 'I will have that'?'' He thought, "How did they grow? They knew something when they were born.'' Therefore he cried.[20]

p. They stayed there one night. The people urged them, and the boy wished to stay. They took them across to Pekwtuł. There they remained for the night. They sat down outside a sweathouse. As soon as (the owner of the sweathouse) saw them he said, "Sit down. I am glad to see you here.'' Immediately he took out his pipe. He said, "Smoke.'' Pulekukwerek thought, "Here is another one who is a man.'' That one said, "I have that sort of good times here. I made (established the dance), but I did not make it (wholly) right. I wish you would come back and we will make it good. Do not go up (the Trinity) here. It is a bad river. All bad herbs grow there. On this side upstream (up the Klamath), that is the way for you to go.'' "Well, we shall go on to Enek[21] in half a day. We shall travel without stopping on the way.'' "Yes, you had better go there. There they have made it too (established a great dance), but they have not yet made it right. You will see that it is not good at all.''

q. Then (in the morning they went on) to Enek. They had not made it right when they made the land[22] there. Pulekukwerek knew it as soon as he arrived. They thought that they had made everything well, but they had not.

Next morning Megwomets said, "This is the last day of our going upstream. Let us begin to go back.'' The boy had already forgotten where he grew. He asked, "Where are we from?'' "You will know it when you wake up tomorrow. You will know then where you grew.'' The boy thought, "It must take a long time to go there. I have already forgotten.'' When they lay down, Pulekukwerek said (to the boy), "Lie in the middle. Do not be in a hurry to get up. Do not look about quickly when you wake up. Rise and look around you slowly. Perhaps you will wake up where you grew.''

The boy awoke. He did not look about. He heard a bird singing outside. Then he was sorry.[23] "Every morning I used to hear that where I grew.'' Now he looked around. "It looks like my own sweathouse.'' Pulekukwerek watched him. The boy stood up, went out, and saw his two houses that he had built. Then he knew that he was again where he grew. Then he rolled around. His tears swept the ground clean outdoors and then in.

r. Now Pulekukwerek and the boy had found all the bad places. They were speaking of how they would make them right. Then old man Megwomets said, "I shall not travel again. I shall give food to my friends, but stay here. If you tell me, I shall throw something (abroad) outdoors, but I shall not go with

20. Typical Yurok sentiment—or sentimentality?
21. See A15, n. 26.
22. [K. has queried "land.'' Perhaps it should be "dance.''—Ed.]
23. Homesick, filled with longing remembrance.

you any more." That is what he does now. He asks, "How are my friends?" "Oh, they are poor. Food is hard to get." Then he throws food. "How are my friends? Have they to eat?" he asks. "Yes they are eating acorns. They have enough." "That is good," he says. Now he never went any more. But the boy came with Pulekukwerek again the last time they went upstream. Then Pulekukwerek destroyed everything bad that he had seen and made everything right in the world.[24]

s. Pulekukwerek thought: "That boy, I think I will ask him how many bad places we went by." He said to him, "How many bad places did we pass? Do you know?" "Yes, I know. I know them all from this place here where the arrows live. Nearest here I know there is a place where no one will camp." Pulekukwerek thought, "Yes, that is so." He asked him, "How do you know?" "I saw many bones of people lying there. I think that is a bad place to camp.[25] Then here is another bad place, Kohpei.[26] Whenever they see a person come there, they want to play with him. If he will not play, they kill him. That is what is dangerous there." Pulekukwerek thought, "Yes, that is what I too think." "There is another place (further on but still) downstream from the mouth of the river. I saw an old man there working wood.[27] Then here is another place at the mouth of the river, where persons cannot cross. And there is another place near Wohkel.[28] A person cannot pass there in the evening. In the middle of the night it is good, but in the evening he cannot go by." Pulekukwerek said, "Do you know what makes it so?" "Yes, I know. If he goes by, he will not see anyone, but he will hear something roaring behind him. If he looks back, he will see a person's head rolling, only the head. Then he will fall." Pulekukwerek thought, "Yes, I think so too."[29] So the boy went along upstream (in his mind), counting all the bad places. Pulekukwerek said, "That is all, I think. Now stay here and I will go about to see. I will try to destory each of those dangers. They are all bad." "I think you will not be able to do it." "Well, I shall go to see."

24. Everything to here is in the nature of a reconnaissance, or, as discussed in n. 3, it may have to be taken as a dream of the boy. Billy and I broke off work at this point, to resume another day. This fact may have contributed to the comparative irrelevance of what has gone before to what follows from here.

25. These four incidents are passed over in the remainder of the story: the place of human bones, the playing (spearing?) at Kohpei, the log-splitting (at O'men?), and the rolling head at Wohkel.

26. Kohpei is the Tolowa town at Crescent City.

27. The reference perhaps is to O'men, where other versions have Pulekukwerek overcome an old man who catches passersby in a split log.

28. Wohkel is downstream from Terwer, and on the opposite side.

29. This is the only reference in the recorded body of Yurok tradition to the concept of the rolling head or skull, which is so widely spread among the American Indians. It is a pity that Lame Billy forgot or saw fit to suppress his relation of the incident.

t. Then Pulekukwerek prepared. He wanted (and made magically) a small bow as long as his finger and two or three arrows. He put them away in his body. He took four small stones at the water, and put them away. He went about and got a stick as long as that,[30] and another one so long[31] and so wide,[32] and made them neat. "The boy said, "What are you going to do with those?" "With this one I shall shoot where I camp first. With these stones I shall hit the old man at Kohpei. Then he will no longer be about. With this I shall hit the old man farther on. This stick[33] I shall use at the mouth of the river because I cannot cross otherwise." "What are you going to do with them?" "Do you want to know?" "Yes." Then Pulekukwerek took one stick, turned it two or three times between his hands, and soon fire burned up from between the two pieces. "Now, boy, wait two days until morning. I shall stay at Kohpei one night; I shall stay at the mouth one night; in the morning I shall cross over. Then you will feel it. The whole earth will shake. I shall kill the one there." The boy was sorry for him (Pulekukwerek). He thought he would be killed. Pulekukwerek said, "Oh, you need not think that, boy. I shall not be killed."

u. Then he came (to Rekwoi).[34] "I shall cross the river," he said. They told him, "Oh, you must not try." "But I am traveling south along the ocean." "You had better go upriver and then back." Pulekukwerek thought, "I will not do that." He went outside[35] and down to the river and looked. He saw the water piling up. He stripped the bark from an alder and made a boat of it, a small boat. He went into it to try it, and the boat stood without moving. Then he laid wood into the boat, and stones, and brush, and set his fire drill. He turned, and made fire. Then, when he saw that it was blazing well and (the stones were) hot, he went into the boat and started. They all ran down (from the town), saying, "That one is crossing." They were all sorry. "He is gone," they thought. He had nearly come to the other side. Then he ran to the head of the boat and jumped out to the (farther) shore. As soon as he was out, the boat moved backward and down into the water. He lit [it] and ran uphill to Wełkwäu. Seeing no one, he sat down in front of a sweathouse and looked

30. Gesture.

31. The length of the forearm and half as much again.

32. Two fingers' breadth.

33. Fire drill.

34. The two dangerous places on the way south to the mouth of the Klamath are not mentioned again and are supposed to have been passed over by him; the same holds for the rolling head at Wohkel, which Pulekukwerek would later encounter on going from the mouth upstream to Kepel. The omissions may be due to the narrator's desire to come to the river-crossing episode, which he has held in abeyance for some time; see n. 8. [K. has a marginal reference to A15x.—Ed.]

35. He has probably gone into the sweathouse immediately on arriving.

back. He saw something moving in the water and making it leap. The land was shaking. He thought, "I caught him then." When it was nearly sunset, the shaking stopped.[36]

An old man there said to him, "You came by boat?" "Yes, I saw many salmon. Let us go and spear." "Oh, we cannot go there." "Yes, it is good now. I crossed this morning." The old man believed him and went out with him. They speared salmon. Pulekukwerek said, "Now it is good. I am the one who made it so."

v. Then the old man said to him, "Now that you have killed this one, I will tell you that there is only one (other really) bad place. There are many dangerous ones, but that one is the only (very) bad place. I tell you only this. You must stop nowhere to sleep, but go straight to Kepel in one day. That is as far as you should go. There is one lives in Kepel: send him on upstream and come back yourself." "Why?" "It is easy to make good those places where there are bad people. You can do that later. Now there is only one (other) thing I do not like. I think you do not know where he lives (who is concerned with that). I know where he lives." "Yes? Where is that?" "Look up. When I look up, it does not seem well. I can see nothing. I want to have it that in the evening we can see the moon and stars. We never see them now. I know the one who can make this." Pulekukwerek thought, "I believed I was wise. I did not think we should have that. But it will look well if we make it."

w. In the morning he started and went (straight upstream) to Kepel. He said (to the one there), "Go and destroy all the bad places at which there are bad persons. Ruin them all. I wish you to travel about. I shall return." The one at Kepel said, "Yes, if you leave me all that you are carrying." "Yes, and I will tell you what to use to destroy them. And when you come to where Wohpekumeu lives, try to spoil what he has made."[37] "Yes, I will do that."

In the morning Pulekukwerek returned. He came to Weɬkwäu. The one there said, "Well, I shall go with you. I shall show you where he lives. He does not like to see people. He goes about, but no one ever sees him. I know where he lives. I know he will do it if you talk to him, because I know him. This earth formerly lay like this (in the shape of a circle adjoining a smaller one). Now it lies (in shape) like this (circle). It is round. You do not know that, but I know it. He is the one that went about and made it that the earth is round."

x. Then all that Pulekukwerek knew was that he entered the boat. The one from Weɬkwäu told him to enter and not look, not to know where he was going. So he did not know where they went. But it was not very far.[38] Then the

36. The narrator has told this episode before, in number A15x *c*, and somewhat differently: then there were ten monsters.

37. Evidently he looks on Wohpekumeu as an untrustworthy person, who, being influenced almost wholly by erotic considerations, is as likely to institute the world badly as well.

38. Long.

one from Wełkwäu said, "You can look about slowly," and Pulekukwerek raised his eyes and looked. He saw a sand beach, a wide beach. That land looked very different.[39] Both came out of the boat. He held the boat with one hand and told Pulekukwerek, "Go right into the middle house. He is in there now. He is there half the day. If he is not inside when you enter, he will come again. Perhaps you will find him inside. Do not obey if any person tells you to stop. Do not do it, but go straight on. All will tell you to stop, but if you stop you will never find that house." Pulekukwerek thought, "I will do that."

He started. He looked at the house, thinking, "I will not lose it." Someone said, "Hello!" "Yes," he said, but did not look around. "Come here. It is a hot day. Rest." He went on, not looking, not answering. Another said, "Stop. See this!" Pulekukwerek did not look. Another said, "Ho! Come, shuffle the gaming sticks once," where (there was the sound of) gambling. "Yes, I shall be with you soon," said Pulekukwerek and went on. "Look! They are starting a footrace!" they said. He went on. In another place a person said, "Stop! Those persons are about to wrestle! Stand here!" He went straight on without looking back, without looking aside. He heard shouting behind him, but looked only at that house.

Then Pulekukwerek knew that he had walked half a day. At first he had thought he was near the house. Now (at last) he was outside it. Then he saw every kind of play going on. He went right in by the open door; he did not look at that playing. He entered.

y. The one there, who wore a long falling headnet,[40] saw Pulekukwerek. He did not speak to him. He reached out to a stool and touched it with his hand. Pulekukwerek went and sat on it. Then he saw that that one had sticks behind him, so long,[41] five of them, netting shuttles.

Pulekukwerek took out his pipe and prepared to smoke. There was nothing there, no fire, and the floor was smooth. Pulekukwerek took out his fire drill and turned it. It burned. He lit the pipe and gave it to him to draw at. He took it, sucked once, and spoke. "You are the kind of man I like to see. I have never seen one like you." Pulekukwerek said, "I shall live with you if you will do what I wish." "Yes, it is well. Whatever you say I shall do." "I will tell you. I have gone halfway (over the world). I want to make all this world good. Then I thought and looked up, but could see nothing. I wish we had fog close by (above). It would look well." "Well, light another. Then we shall go out and you will tell me what it is that you wish to have." So he gave him another pipeful, for Pulekukwerek had grown with his hand full of

39. They are probably across the ocean, beyond the sky, where the ocean is calm, the land a wide, treeless beach.

40. *Pergerei*. [K. has a marginal notation, "Hupa," without further details.—Ed.]

41. About a yard. This is extreme. The Yurok shuttle—which was often made of elkhorn—ran to a foot or little more in length. But then this string must weave the sky.

tobacco. It was never gone. He always had it with him. Then that one smoked and talked. Then he put the pipe into its skin case and handed it back. Pulekukwerek said, "You can keep it if you do what I tell you." "Good. Let us go out."

They went out. Pulekukwerek said, "If you can make that, it will be called sky.[42] If you can make it, in the evening we shall see something good. We shall call that stars." "It is good. I can make that (the sky), but that other I cannot make. Even if you give me the stars I cannot make them (be there)." "If you will make the sky, I will make the stars," said Pulekukwerek. That one thought, "I will do it."

z. He took string. He laid it like this. He fastened each end to a stick. "Now watch," he said. Then he tied a string from here (the right) to here (halfway between the right and the lower end). From there he again tied a string to the middle. "Now light your pipe," he said. Pulekukwerek set his fire drill. He tried, but it was too windy. Then he went inside the coil at the (lower) end here. There he got fire and lit his pipe and came to where that one was standing (where he had last fastened his string). "You think your pipe[43] will help?" (said Pulekukwerek). "Yes, that is the only way we can make it. Now give it to me." He took the pipe, drew it well, went to the middle, put its opening over the cross of the strings, blew, and it spread out. Then he went to the right end, put the end of the string into the pipe, blew, and fog came out and spread. Some are black now and some white. They are clouds. They are tobacco smoke blown out by him. Then he went here (to the lower end), put the end of the string into the pipe, blew, and the smoke came out and spread. Then he went across here (to the left end) and blew.

Then he told Pulekukwerek, "You try it here (at the loop at the upper end)." Pulekukwerek said, "No, I am afraid to spoil it. Do it yourself. I shall make the stars, that is all." Then that one saw that it was about to be finished. He had wanted it ruined. Therefore he had asked him to blow. If Pulekukwerek had done so at that one end, it would all have been spoiled; but he was too wise. Then that one went back again here (to the lower end) and blew at it again (not blowing at all from the upper end). Now the smoke spread out over the whole[44] and covered it all. So he made it well.

aa. Then he said, "Now what are we going to do?" Pulekukwerek said, "Now we will raise it. But wait. I shall make the stars." Then Pulekukwerek lit his pipe to make the stars. He drew long, blew the smoke into his hollow hand, threw it down, blew in his hand again, threw the smoke downward, again and again, and made the stars. He said, "We cannot see them (well) in

42. *Wes'ona*.

43. Pulekukwerek's own pipe—but he has just handed it to the other.

44. [K.'s typescript had "hole" here; he changed to "whole" and queried.—Ed.]

the day. At night we shall see them well. Now let us put it up." "Yes," he said, and they raised it. First they pulled out the stake here at the side (near the lower end). They put that right in the middle. Then he drew out the stake here (at the right) and set it in the middle of the loop at this end (above). He drew out the stake at the opposite side and put it inside the coil at the end (below). Pulekukwerek said: "You will have no stakes here at the two sides?" "No, it will move this way, up and down all the time. Then the ocean will move continually.[45] If this did not move, the ocean would always lie still; but if this moves, then the ocean will constantly move up and down, and will look well."

Then they raised (the whole fabric). They pushed it up. Just once they pushed it, then they heard a clap above. "Now wait until evening; then we shall see."

In the evening they said, "Well, let us go outdoors[46] to see. Let us look at the stars." They looked up. Then they saw the stars. That one said, "Oh, it is beautiful!" Pulekukwerek said, "That is what I wanted."[47]

Pulekukwerek tried to get him to go about with him, but he said, "No. I do not think I can go about." In the morning, Pulekukwerek returned.[48]

bb. Then he went to see the one at Kepel. He came to Kepel. The one there said, "They are dangerous for those who travel. Many things are bad. The tobacco is bad; (here or there) if a man sleeps it is bad; if he drinks water it is bad." Pulekukwerek said, "I can make it right if you will come with me."

The next day he said, "Well, I will go with you." At night he talked to the people in the sweathouse. He said, "The one at Kenek is good. He knows every kind of play. He can make any kind of food grow. He can make anything be that he wants. He thinks of it and it grows." Pulekukwerek said, "Whom do you mean? Kapuloyo?" "No, Wohpekumeu." "Yes." "I think it is best if we take him with us." Pulekukwerek thought, "If he wants to come and is well-behaved, let him go along with us."

They started from Kepel and came to Kenek. There they saw every kind of play going on. There were many young men, Hupa people, upstream people,[49] downstream people.[50] All were having good times there. The Kepel old man said (to Wohpekumeu, whom they found at Kenek), "This is as far as I can go, this place here. I am afraid something will ruin my play place. I want to go back in the morning. You go with him." Pulekukwerek said, "Yes, I

45. The sky comes up and down, pounding the ocean and making its waves.

46. Having nothing more on hand to do, they have retired into the sweathouse.

47. The episode of making the sky was recorded from this informant on another occasion. This other version immediately follows the conclusion of the present story, as A16y.

48. Presumably to Wełkwäu, with the one who had brought him across the ocean.

49. Karok, *Petsik-la*.

50. Yurok, *Pulik-la*.

wish you would come with me. I want to make all this world before I go off." Wohpekumeu said, "Then I will go with you. If you return, I shall return with you. I will go with you as far as Segwu'.[51] That is as far as I will go with you. Then I will come back."

cc. In the morning they started. They came to Segwu'. Pulekukwerek wanted someone to go on with him. He wanted to go farther upstream. Wohpekumeu said to one, "Let the three of us go."

They started. (On the way the two others) said (to Pulekukwerek), "We shall leave you outside the sweathouse and return." He said, "Yes, I will go in." When they arrived, Pulekukwerek entered the sweathouse, and they turned back downstream. They only showed him the bad place and went back immediately.

Then those there said, "What did you come for?" Pulekukwerek said, "I came because I thought it was not well. I want men to sleep and wake up and feel good. If they do not sleep they will not feel good." They said, "Oh, yes. We always sleep here. You will see night come. We shall sleep. Next morning we shall get up and feel better." "Oh, that is what I want." "If you go with this one people will sleep. Any night, anywhere, they will sleep." Pulekukwerek saw a little black boy there. He asked his name. "His name is Tskierka."[52] As soon as Pulekukwerek asked him, "Boy, do you want to go with me?" the boy laughed. He said again, "I think, boy, you had better go with me." The boy said, "Well, I say to you that there is no need in my going, for after a time some will not like me, although some will like me very much." "What will they like you for?" "Well, I will tell you how it is to be. A lazy woman will like me very much. She will want to sleep even in the day. And a lazy man will like me. He is the one who will sleep constantly, even in the daytime." Pulekukwerek said, "It is well. Let it be so. But come with me."

dd. Then he took Tskierka along with him. At every town he came to, as they went downstream, he stayed overnight. At every town, after they had talked, all went to sleep. He did not tell anyone what kind of boy it was that he brought. He took him all over this world. He took him to all the small towns, here and there and in other places; and then he brought the boy back to Segwu'.[53]

•

51. Karok Katimin, a little upstream from Enek, which was the limit of Pulekukwerek's reconnaissances earlier in this story and the scene of Wohpekumeu's food-stealing exploit in the last.

52. Sleep. His home was at the upstream end of the world. Cf. nn. 53 and 55.

53. He returns him to Segwu', though he got him upriver from there. The Yurok was often hazy or indifferent about Segwu', Okonile'l, and beyond; they are all near the edge. It is a hurried ending, as if the narrator had tired. Virtually the same episode, but told of Night instead of Sleep, constitutes the following tale, A17.

There is one unexplained break in the personages of the story. In *b* the unnamed boy hero dreams of someone who builds him a house; in *c* this person announces himself as Wetskāk dentalium, who has caused the boy to come into being; in *d* Wetskāk invites the boy to ride on him when they fly; in *e* Wetskāk takes him to Pulekukwerek, who also invites him to come along. But with *f* a stick turns into Megwomets, and it is he who accompanies Pulekukwerek and the boy on the first trip upriver as far as Enek (in *q*). Wetskāk is not mentioned again after *e*!

Did the narrator assume that he had made it clear that Wetskāk turned into the stick that got up as Megwomets? (It would be contrary rather than in accord with Yurok mythology to identify these two.) Or is Wetskāk the boy's alter ego? Or did the narrator, when it came to introducing Megwomets, forget all about Wetskāk? Or is the whole section *b-q* to be considered only as a dream of the boy, as discussed in nn. 3 and 24? I do not know the answer, but it is clear that the narrator slipped at least one cog.

The whole story tends to displace person by person. Pulekukwerek is absent in *a-d*. The boy lasts through their journey, *e-q*, and then keeps on a couple of paragraphs longer (*r-t*), discussing past and future with Pulekukwerek. Megwomets formally withdraws from all further travel in *r*. With *u*, Pulekukwerek begins a new journey. In this he performs one exploit alone, at Rekwoi; several others that have been promised—like that of the rolling head—are never mentioned again. Except for a dash to Kepel to give instructions to the dam-maker, *v-aa* are concerned with Wełkwäu old man taking him to Sky-Possessor, the latter making the sky, and Pulekukwerek making the stars. After that, in *bb-cc*, Pulekukwerek goes upriver beyond Segwu' and brings Sleep into the world. This is exceptionally loose-jointed construction.

In summary, the story breaks down thus:

(1) *a-e*, boy, Wetskāk, and Pulekukwerek meet.

(2a) *f-q*, boy, Pulekukwerek, and Megwomets travel, without dangers or monster riddings. The trip is, as it were, made to inspect conditions and to instruct the boy.

(2b) *r*, Pulekukwerek destroys the evil he has seen.

(2c) *s-t*, boy and Pulekukwerek reminisce and plan.

(3a) *u*, Pulekukwerek kills Rekwoi monster alone.

(3b) *v-aa*, Pulekukwerek, Wełkwäu old man, and Sky-Possessor, and the making of sky and stars.

(3c) *bb-cc*, Pulekukwerek brings Sleep.

A16y. Making the Sky

VARIANT VERSION

As in the preceding myth (A15), part of this tale was separately recorded from the same informant—this time a year earlier. It proves again to be a decided variant, showing that this narrator often improvised his stories by weaving several incidents around a theme. It is not likely that he had heard and remembered two separate versions of the episode, since the tale of the weaving of the sky is not widely known among the Yurok.

It is clear that what he had in mind was the weaving in a peculiar shape, and that a certain Sky-Possessor and Pulekukwerek were concerned with its origin. In the version that follows, Sky-Possessor, far from having to be induced against his will to construct the sky, makes it of his own initiative.

The narrator boasted to me of his unique or unusual knowledge of this theme, and said that many years before he had dictated it to Jeremiah Curtin. Curtin's Yurok myths must have bulked rather large and included a number from Lame Billy. Curtin's manuscript seems to have been lost. If it is ever recovered and published, it will probably present an interesting third version of this episode. Incidentally, if this Curtin material were available, it would be of value also in furnishing a check of the personal equation of the collectors. [Jeremiah Curtin (1835–1906) was an ethnologist and linguist noted for his collections of Irish myths and for his studies of the Slavs and of the American Indians, especially the Seneca. He also collected myths from several northern California Indian groups.—Ed.]

•

a. Sky-Possessor[54] made the sky. He made it of string, like a net. He thought he was the only person (in existence). Starting out, he traveled in a circle halfway, stopped, made his rope, and returned. Then he started the other way (i.e., in the same direction, but circling to the other side), and went as far as he had gone before. Then he turned sharply. After a time he thought he had gone too far. He was lost. He turned again and went on.

b. After a time he began to smell tobacco smoke. It came from Pulekukwerek. Then he knew that he was not alone in the world. He found where Pulekukwerek lived. At that place he turned once more, and finally came to the place where he had first left the end of his string.

c. The next day he worked at the sky. He brought the string across, back and forth like a net, singing as he went.

d. Then he went to throw it up. He took it in two places, at the end from which he had first started out to travel, and at the place where he had first turned aside before he reached Pulekukwerek. Then he threw the woven string up, and the sky was there. He had walked about it in such a way that he could take hold of it in the places where he did. He had traveled that course on purpose.[55]

54. *Wes'ona megetoł*. *Megetoł* is usually translated as "keeper" or "owner."

55. The narrator added: Beyond where Sky-Possessor made the end of the sky, is where Sun, Wind, and Night lived. When Coyote arrived there and killed Sun (cf. A14), he did not go back the way he had come. After crossing the river, he followed the path along which Sky-Possessor had first gone in a semicircle. Then he found himself in the sky. He did not know how to come back. At last, seeing the clouds below him, he took them to be the earth (thought it an easy fall), and dropped down, but (the distance was so great that) he only reached the earth as scattered bones.

A17. Pulekukwerek Obtains Night

This is a variant of the last episode of A16x, which was recorded a year earlier. Night is substituted for Sleep as the object of search. Cf. A16x, n. 52.

•

a. After Wohpekumeu and Pulekukwerek had obtained water[1] and salmon[2] upstream, they went upstream once more.[3] It was never dark, and they wanted to bring night.

Now they stopped on the way. Wohpekumeu tried to make himself invisible. He approached Pulekukwerek from behind as he sat smoking. Pulekukwerek knew that Wohpekumeu was behind him. He said, "You are behind me. I do not think you will be able to make yourself invisible."

Wohpekumeu said, "I will try again. If I cannot do it this time, I shall return. Close your eyes and open them again." Pulekukwerek shut his eyes. When he opened them, Wohpekumeu was not there. It was a small place where they were. A very little thing, a pebble, was lying there. Then Pulekukwerek said, "I do not think they will be able to find you. Perhaps this is you." Then Wohpekumeu stood there once more (in his person) and they went on upstream.

b. Now they came to Segwu'.[4] Here was a sweathouse into which ten men and an old man went with a boy.[5] Whenever the boy entered, the sweathouse became dark. The ladder was smooth. When they asked a person to come in, he always slipped and fell into the fire. Thus they killed them.

1. See A18.
2. See A15x *t-v*.
3. This glib reference to a supposedly well-known order in which the great rectifications and institutions of the world occurred must not be taken too seriously. Billy, with all his active synthetic imagination, was too much of a Yurok ever to develop the tales into a consistent and workable system. He was only playing with transient suggestions of systems. The conflict between the last two tales and their variants proves that all he was trying to do was to work out a story that should be a rather intricately harmonious whole while it was being told. He achieved complexity by allusions of this kind, and by bringing in characters that are not necessary to the plot: but he never troubled himself to square one story seriously with another. Had the Yurok had a written literature, or were men of Billy's type of mind common among them, we might have had this mythology, and especially its Pulekukwerek, Wohpekumeu, and Pelin-tsīk portions, worked into a cycle with parts that fitted. Billy went somewhat further in this direction than the rest of his countrymen, but he never really grappled with the task.
4. Karok Katimin, just above the mouth of the Salmon.
5. In A16x *bb-cc*, Pulekukwerek and Wohpekumeu go upstream beyond Segwu' to the end of the world to find Night or Sleep. Here Night lives at Segwu'. The difference is great—logically—between a place that lies beyond the sky and one that is thirty miles away from one's home—a town, moreover, that one may have repeatedly visited in dance time; but mythologically, the variation is of much less moment.

But Pulekukwerek had sharp points on his buttocks and under his heels. So when they came to the sweathouse, Wohpekumeu took hold of Pulekukwerek's hair and lowered himself down and did not fall, and made himself very small, and hid.

c. The ten men were eating supper in the (living) house. Now they entered their sweathouse. When the boy came in, it became dark. He lay close by the ladder.

One of them said, "Whiff, whiff. It smells strong." Then another, Sun, said, "It is because I helped to bury a man that died." Soon another one said, "It smells too strong." Then Sun said, "It is because a woman's child died and I buried it today. I have not yet washed." Wohpekumeu heard all they said. He did not know where Pulekukwerek was.

d. Then Pulekukwerek came to the sweathouse. They told the boy, "Go out and tell him to come in." The boy told him. Pulekukwerek stepped on the ladder with his heel and made a deep mark and then sat down on it, then on the next notch, and so descended without falling. He asked, "Where shall I lie?" The ten were surprised.

He said, "I will tell you why I have come. I have come to get a boy that you have, Night. We have made salmon and we have made water. We have arranged everything. This is the last thing to be done.[6] We want to make it dark in the world so that people may sleep and so that it will not be too continuously hot. That is why I came and brought my companion with me."

e. "Yes, I am here," Wohpekumeu said. Then those men became afraid. Someone had come in without their knowing it; they had not seen him. Now Pulekukwerek took out his pipe and began to smoke. He made them nod and sway.

f. In the morning, he and Wohpekumeu went off with the boy. The old man[7] waited there at Segwu' for them to bring the boy back. Wohpekumeu went over the world with the boy, downstream to the ocean and back to Segwu', all in a day, and returned him to the old man. Then the boy said, "Now I know the way, I can go alone." From that time on it was dark every night.

g. Then Wohpekumeu took Sun up through the sky, down to the ocean, and back underneath. He showed him the way, and from that time Sun traveled that road. Before this Sun had stood at one place.[8]

6. The thing in prospect is always the only one that still remains undone.

7. The owner of the sweathouse, presumably.

8. This tale flowers with inconsistencies: Sun has always "stood at one place," and yet he comes home and tells of his experiences in helping to bury two people. It becomes dark when the boy Night enters, but Sun is in the sweathouse too. Wohpekumeu takes Night over the world in "a day."

A18. Pulekukwerek Obtains Water

The idea of this story is simple. Water, which is personified, is lacking in the world. Pulekukwerek gathers allies to obtain it. The last one succeeds in outrunning Water, who is then taken through the world and makes springs. This bald explanatory theme of origins the narrator has taken and worked into a true plot, with a dozen personages. They cannot be called individualized characters, but each has his role and a definite relation to the others. Coyote–Tsmegok, Kewet omewa, Wohpekumeu, and Kerernit are all the heroes of separate stories or cycles, such as this narrator delights to weave into new tales again and again. The result is a constantly moving tale of two thousand words on a subject about which the average Yurok would have spoken a few hundred.[1]

•

a. Pulekukwerek started from where he lived at the end of the world,[2] downstream north, far beyond Kohpei.[3] He did not know where to go. He saw no people and walked south along the beach.

He looked about and thought, "Here will be a good place for me to stop. Perhaps I shall stay a moon, perhaps longer. It looks to me as if I saw that something had been here. Perhaps something has been about. Let me make a small (sweat)house to sleep in.

Then he thought a little. "I do not know what this place is called." After a time he knew what it was called. "This place is Knäwi."[4]

b. Now it was nearly sunset. He heard someone working down at the ocean. He said, "That is what I thought, that there might be someone about." He went out[5] and looked down to the beach. He saw a person there with a wedge and a maul, pounding. He thought, "I will go to see him." He came nearer. Then that one looked at him and said, "Well, are you here? I have been waiting for you. I heard you would come. That is why I prepared all this wood, for I thought you would want to know what we shall use to live by. I do not know what to use."

Pulekukwerek did not answer. He wanted to hear what he would say. That one went on: "It will be best if we use that thing. We shall use it always if we get it. (Having it, we shall never fail.) All over the world they will not live well if we do not have it, if we do not get it for them. As for myself, I

1. [K.'s marginal jottings indicate that he intended to expand this headnote: "Add epic breadth . . .; various characters and abilities; range over world; confer, send, plan; active participants: P. leader; W. goal; Knäwi instigates; C. wins race; K. omewa cause of win; W. advises C.; others runners, incl. Falcon . . .; sister stays."—Ed.]

2. At Pulekuk.

3. Kohpei is the Tolowa town at Crescent City.

4. Knäwi, "long," is the flat, far-projecting headland Point St. George, north of Crescent City, in Tolowa country.

5. From his house or sweathouse.

cannot go where it is. I have gone to the end upstream. As you go on, you will find the river. I have been to the end of it and did not find that thing. I went to other places. Only in one place I heard a little noise; somewhere I think I heard it."

Then Pulekukwerek answered; "Yes. Do persons live anywhere in the world?" "Yes, there are persons, many of them. If you start from here, before you get to that place where is that which I want, you will hear twelve languages."[6]

c. Pulekukwerek said, "I think you had better come with me." That one said, "Yes, but let us build fifty-four houses. That is what these planks[7] are for." Pulekukwerek said, "I think when we come back we shall see everything built. Let us put all the wood together, and when we come again we shall see all the houses standing." Then he agreed.

d. Pulekukwerek said, "Now you had better tell me what we are going to get, so that as we travel I shall not become tired. I know nothing about it. I thought that as long as this world exists we should live by what I use, by tobacco, by that alone." "No, it would not be well: a man would not feel well (with only tobacco). But that (other) one is fine. If you bring it here, sometimes in summer if a man uses it, he will feel good, very good, because it is cool. In winter it will be warm, and a man using it will feel well too. Its name is Water.[8] Pulekukwerek thought, "He must be a good one. We had better go." That one said, "We shall walk for ten days. We will take others with us from along the river. We want to go there with five (companions.)"

e. Well then,[9] they started, and came to the mouth of the river. Then Pulekukwerek asked if any young men lived there who could run. The Rekwoi people said, "Yes, there are many young men who can run fast. Ten of them will go down to the beach. Watch, and the one who passes the others shall go with you." "Yes, that is good," Pulekukwerek said. Then they took them down to the beach; and one of them ran ahead of the others. Pulekukwerek said to him, "Come with me." He said, "Yes, I will go with you. Only I want to

6. This is on the verge of poetic exaggeration, like the fifty-four houses in the next paragraph. The Yurok knew more or less of Tolowa-Chetco Athabascan, Yurok, Coast Yurok, Hupa, and Chilula Athabascan, and Wiyot; and they probably occasionally heard at a foreign dance, where strangers met, Shasta, Konomihu, Chimariko, and Nongatl or Saya Athabascan. They may have been aware that there were such tongues as Modoc, Wintun, and Mattole Athabascan. But they certainly preferred on the whole to have no dealings with the more remote of all these speakers, and to think in their wish fantasies of the world as ending before their territories were reached.

7. Which Pulukwerek had heard being split with his wedge. [K. has a marginal reference to A16*h*.—Ed.]

8. *Pa'*.

9. *Tsuł*.

tell you how far I can run. I can run over ten ridges.[10] That is as far as I can run."

They started upstream. At Wohtek[11] they wanted another man. They did not find him. All the young men ran, but the one from Rekwoi beat them. So they thought, "We had better take none of them."

Then they came to Kenek and saw many young men. They wanted one there, so they selected ten and they ran, but the one from Rekwoi beat them all.

f. Then somebody thought, "There is one who can run. That one down[12] there can. Let him come up and try." Some said, "Oh, he cannot run. He is not fast." Pulekukwerek sent two youths after him. The people said to the youths, "Do not go to get him." But the one who sat there and had thought of him said, "Youths, go get him." Two youths ran down. They saw the old woman in the house and asked, "Where is Tsmegok?"[13] "Tsmegok is not at home," said the old woman. "He started this morning to go up to see his relative." The youths went back to the houses at Kenek. "He is not in the house," they said. Pulekukwerek said, "Where did he go?" They said, "He went to see his relative."

g. Wohpekumeu was sitting by, not saying a word. Pulekukwerek asked him, "Where does his relative live?" Wohpekumeu looked a little and said, "Ehe! I do not think that it is his relative whom he went to see. He went to the one who lives up there on Kewet.[14] I think he went there to eat good food."

Pulekukwerek looked about, saying, "Who of you travels fast?" One of them said, pointing, "I think this one can travel fast to bring him." "I wish you would go after him, young man," Pulekukwerek said. That one said, stretching and shaking his wings, "Yes, I will go," and when he flew up, *zzzzzz!* he was out of sight. Soon, *zzzzzz!* he was back from the mountain.

h. Immediately a man was coming, below where the boats were. Pulekukwerek thought, "That must be the one who has come from the mountain." He saw that he was a good-looking man, well built. He said to him, "My friend, do you think you can run?" "I do not know. Perhaps I

10. Northwestern California is a country not of mountains but of long parallel ridges with a north-northwesterly trend.

11. At the community which has been variously called Johnsons, Klamath, and Klamath Bluffs, about halfway from Rekwoi to Weitspus.

12. A little downstream from Kenek.

13. In the tale of Kewet omewa (A12), this is a name applied derogatively to Coyote; the meaning of the word is not known. In that tale Coyote also lived a little downstream from Kenek, and was a friend or client of Kewet omewa. Yet farther on in the present story Coyote appears in addition to Tsmegok! And toward the end they are again treated as one person: see n. 30.

14. Kewet omewa, of the mountain behind Weitspus.

might start and fall down."[15] "Well, run against this young man here. Start from a distance and run to here." "Well then,[16] come on." Those who had run and had been beaten before were ashamed now. Then they (two)[17] went to Okego[18] and started from there to run to Kenek. Pulekukwerek and all the young men stayed.

Immediately that young man sat down by Pulekukwerek. After a time the one from Rekwoi came. "I did not run very hard," said the one who had come (in first). "Come with me," said Pulekukwerek. "Yes, if you will tell me what you are going to do, I will go with you." "Yes, I will tell you. I am going after the one that is called Water." "I shall ask my relative to go with us."

i. He went back to Kewet to tell the young man there. He said to him, "Come with me to go with the one who is going to get Water." That one (of Kewet) said, "I do not think you can do it. I know that place. I pity you. But I like you, and I shall go part way with you, for I know you will be caught there. If I give you my foot, if you use my leg, then they cannot catch you. I know what day you will arrive. On that day I shall be at a place part way. You will see me there. Now you can go. I know that one. I know he is good. I have heard him ripple. I know he is something of a person. I know he is somewhere in that place." So said the young man on Kewet. Immediately (thereafter) his friend (Tsmegok) arrived at Kenek (on his return). He said, "Well then, let us go."

(*j.* Then Wohpekumeu said to Pulekukwerek, "Do you know the one to go with you?" "No." "He lives below here, downstream. His name is Coyote. That is the one to go with you. Did you ever hear his name before?" "No, but that makes no difference. Any kind of person can go with me if I know that he can run." So they got Coyote.)

k. Then they wanted to find someone else who could run. Pulekukwerek stayed there. The one from Rekwoi went to Hupa. He and Coyote went to Hupa to find someone there; Pulekukwerek stayed at Kenek and waited. In a very short time he saw them coming downstream, three of them, and Pulekukwerek said, "I saw it." The one from Rekwoi said, "We found one. We started to run. He and Coyote ran even, just even." "How far did you run?" "Over ten ridges." "That is good." That one was from Kohteɫ.[19]

l. Now they had three (*sic*)[20] men. Pulekukwerek wanted two more.

15. Modesty, perhaps ironical.

16. *Tsuɫ.*

17. Tsmegok and Rekwoi young man.

18. Tuley Creek, at the upstream end of the Kenek terrace.

19. Medilding, "Captain John's ranch" of the Americans, the largest town in the upper half of Hupa Valley.

20. Actually four: Rekwoi young man, Tsmegok, Coyote, and the one from Hupa, not

They (went upstream and) came to Segwu'.[21] They asked if one was there who could run. The people said, "There is no one here; but the one who lives on that rock there,[22] he who looks old,[23] is the one that can go with you." "Bring him here. I want to see him," said Pulekukwerek. Then they went and brought him.

Pulekukwerek said, "You know where I am going?" Then that one, Kerernit,[24] said, "Yes, I was there five days ago. He did not yet ripple loudly. Wait until summer. Then, when the days are hot, you can hear him rippling. It will be easy to catch him. He can speak. I do not know where his house is, where the door to it is." Pulekukwerek said, "Well, we will wait."

m. So they waited until the hot days came. Then they went to a place downstream from where he was,[25] and stopped. There was a wide level plain. He lived in the middle of it, the one they had gone to get. Then in the morning they saw Kewet young man sitting there: there they found him.

Pulekukwerek said (to the others), "You had better stay here. I shall go to see that one in the place where he is. I shall try to talk to him. I know how to open his door."

n. Then Pulekukwerek saw his door. He saw a young man and a girl inside. Pulekukwerek went in. He took out his pipe to smoke. Those two did not know fire. Pulekukwerek turned his drill, made fire, and lit his pipe. They began to be afraid and said, "Something of a man has come here."

Pulekukwerek said, "Are you not sometimes lonely?" The young man said, "Yes, sometimes. There is one thing: I do not go about. I should like to go about, but I am worth nothing. That is why I do not show myself." Pulekukwerek said, "You had better come with me." He said, "No, we cannot go. We cannot even go outside our door here." Now Pulekukwerek urged him with his best words. "If you do that it will be best." But he did not accept his words. Pulekukwerek offered him all kinds of enjoyment. "I will make every kind of fun for you." But, no, they would not do it.

o. Then Pulekukwerek began to be a little angry. Then Water said to him, "I will tell you what makes it that I do not want to go. I should be worthless. Both of us, this my sister and I, will be worthless. If a person likes me too much, if he craves me, he will be poor.[26] That is the reason. Now I will tell

---

counting Kewet omewa. If Tsmegok and Coyote are identified as one person, the count is correct.

21. Karok Katimin.

22. The rock or peak that the Karok call A'u'ich, which towers above Katimin.

23. Because he is immortal.

24. Karok Aikneich, the true falcon or "duck hawk." See C3.

25. Presumably they went upstream but not quite as far as his house.

26. Restraints as regards food, drink, sexual gratification, or bodily ease are necessary to success in life, particularly as regards the acquisition of wealth. A man who drinks as fast as he is thirsty will drink bad water, in tabooed places, and never become rich.

you what I shall do. I am going there to that (upstream) end (of the plain), and from there I shall start to run to see if you have any that can catch me. I shall run ten times, in a circle, and if any of them can catch me in the middle,[27] I will go with you and take my sister with me."[28] "It is good," Pulekukwerek said. "You will run only five times, because I have only five (companions)."

p. Now the one from Kewet said to Coyote, "Do not run first. Be the last one." So Coyote just sat there. The one from Rekwoi ran first. He was beaten badly. Water ran around ten times,[29] the one from Rekwoi only three times.

Then the Hupa person started. He ran around five times while Water ran around ten times.

Then the one from Segwu' ran. This time Water (had to) run faster. He ran ten times, the one from Segwu' seven times.

q. Then the one from Kewet said, "My friend, use my foot." Then Coyote said, "Yes."[30] Pulekukwerek said to him, "My friend, do the best you can. It looks (as if) we have come here in vain." Then the one from Kewet said, "I do not think so. I think that if my friend does not overtake him, I will." He stood up. "Get ready," he said. "Get up, Pulekukwerek, he is coming to catch you. Start, or he will catch you!" Then he made Pulekukwerek get up.

As they started, his friend (Coyote) nearly caught (Water). At first he ran in a circle (instead of crossing the plain for a start). Then Water began to get ahead of him. Then old Coyote began to run faster. He nearly caught him. Now they had run only three times around when the one from Kewet said, "My friend, run a little faster. We are about to start to return." As he said that, Coyote snapped[31] and seized him (Water).

r. "Now what?" said Coyote. Water said, "I will go with you." Then, as they went downstream, Pulekukwerek did the same everywhere and did not omit one place: everywhere he made him sit down and there was a spring. Then persons found that there was water. It tasted good to them. In the morning everyone went to wash. Pulekukwerek took him all over the world.

s. Pulekukwerek came back to Knäwi. There he found the fifty-four houses standing. There they kept Water. They kept him there always, and there was good water there. Water's sister they did not take away. When they caught him, she asked her brother, "When do you think you shall come back?" "I do not think I shall come back," he said.

27. Of the race-course, presumably, not of the plain.

28. This does not happen.

29. He ran in decreasing spirals, ending at his house in the center. He started at one side of the plain, and they from the opposite side.

30. Coyote and Tsmegok are identified here. It is Coyote to whom Kewet omewa lends his foot, which he has previously offered to Tsmegok.

31. This is one of the rare occasions on which the narrator allows his wholly human conception of Coyote to lapse.

A19. Pulekukwerek Institutes Blood Money

This tale compares with F1*p*, J4, P3, and Y1. It differs from them in being built up through interplay of characters. It is Pulekukwerek who institutes settlement, but it is Wohpekumeu who sees him act strangely and kill, who tracks him down, and offers the compensation. Pulekukwerek acts out the part of a hiding killer, almost disabled by the death wishes of the grieving kin. The results of the interaction of these two well-known personages is that the incident, bold in itself as a precedent in law, is animated into a narrative plot.

In the vivid touch, the act that can be visualized, the present narrator is not superior to his fellow countrymen. Indeed, he has nothing like the dentalium shell that sucks in half the sky, or the killer cowering under the last plank of his blown-away house. He is unusual in the skill with which he can take the standard episodes and characters of Yurok mythology and build them up into much more elaborate constructs of a literary nature, including dialogue that strongly savors of the realistic.

•

a. Wohpekumeu was going downstream. Looking back, he saw a man following. That one carried a quiver, drew out arrows, held them in his teeth, took his bow in his hand, and looked about him. Wohpekumeu thought, "He looks like Pulekukwerek." He watched him. He saw him approach a man and shoot. The man fell. Then that one went on.

b. Wohpekumeu followed his tracks. He came to a large tree and the tracks stopped. Wohpekumeu looked on this side and on that of the tree but could find no more tracks. Then he heard someone above him. "Here I am." Pulekukwerek was in the tree. "Why did you do that?" asked Wohpekumeu. "I did it in order that they may not kill each other too much, that they may not kill all the time," said Pulekukwerek. "Take this and go and tell them to accept it in settlement." He gave him dentalium money.

c. Then Wohpekumeu went where they were mourning for the dead man. He said, "Accept a settlement. He will give you woodpecker crests and boats and money, whatever you like. Ask for what you want and he will pay you." Then they were persuaded and said, "I want this and that," and received it.

d. Now Pulekukwerek said, "I have made it that it is good. Now they will not kill often.[1] When they do kill one another, they will settle for it and that will be the end. If anyone does not pay he will die in ten days.[2] Even while they were crying I nearly fell off the tree. I was so weak[3] that I could hardly hold my place."

1. It would cause financial ruin.
2. The vindictive wishes of the mourners are operating against the slayer.
3. From their tears and black hearts.

A20. PULEKUKWEREK FOUNDS HINEI

The action of this tale is low in key even for an institutional myth, and yet it is sustained by a semblance of plot. Individual characterization is not attempted, except for the ever-beneficent Pulekukwerek, but the action is carried largely through a mass of dialogue. The things accounted for are the Tolowa town of Hinei, its wealth, its local manner of fishing, its connection with Turip, and the use of boats on the ocean. The scene is more Tolowa than Yurok.

•

a. There was a large house at Hinei.[1] There a young man grew. Whenever he went about he saw footprints. Then he thought, "Someone must be here every night. I will track him." Then he went southward (along the beach), following the tracks. He came to a stick standing in the sand. "Let me go to look at it," he thought. Then he saw a string extending from its top and leading over the beach into the ocean. He thought, "I will draw it out." He pulled but felt something at the end and thought, "I had better let go."

He went back to his house and took his pipe. He looked at it long, thinking, "I will take my pipe with me and I will try to find someone. I know where I will go.[2] I hear someone lives there. I will try to bring him here." Then he started north from Hinei.

b. Then he came to Nororpek.[3] He saw someone on the other side of the stream who at once came over for him. The young man thought, "I will not go into the boat. I will first learn who he is that has come to set me across." As soon as he arrived he said to him, "I am going only as far as this side. I shall not cross, for I came to see you." "Yes? You want to see me?" "Yes, I came to see you, if you are Pulekukwerek." "Yes, that is my name." "I came for you. Yesterday morning I found something on the beach. I wanted to draw it in and take what was on the end."[4] "I know what you saw. It belongs to me. The

1. Hinei or Hinäig, probably the most important and wealthy town of the Tolowa, near the mouth of Smith River, 25 or 30 miles north of the mouth of the Klamath. Relations between Hinei and the Yurok towns on the Klamath from Pekwon down were close. Hinei's Tolowa name was Xawunhwut. [See map 1, no. 3, in this volume.—Ed.]

2. North along the coast; *pulik,* downstream.

3. Nororpek is the mouth of Chetco River, a few miles into Oregon (Waterman, map 2, no. 2). For most of the Yurok the known world ends here. Beyond are only the sky and Pulekuk. [Again, see map 1 in this volume.—Ed.]

4. This story, like most told by Lame Billy, was recorded without the *ole'm,* "he said," with which the Yurok normally preface each direct quotation. Very likely this is the result of his animated narration, which my pencil had difficulty in keeping up with; but it may be a stylistic peculiarity of a vivacious recounter.

stick that you saw is mine. The string leads across southerly."[5] "Is that so? Tell me what was on the end." "I will tell you. It is what I fish for. Trying to catch it, I always go about, and it was my tracks you saw. I will go with you to my stick."

c. Then they went to where Pulekukwerek had his stick on the beach. When they came they saw it leaning over and swinging. Pulekukwerek took the stick and began to draw the line in. Soon they saw a "trout"[6] leap. Pulekukwerek said, "That is what I wanted to catch. Now hold the line and I will take it off." The young man took over the line, and Pulekukwerek caught hold of the trout. Then he took out from it the bone gorget.[7] He said, "Now I will press its belly, and what it ate will come out. Then we shall let it go again." When he squeezed it, they saw little objects come out. The young man thought, "They are white stones. It has been eating pebbles."[8] Then they put it back into the salt water and saw it dash straight away, the water spraying about. It flew on as far as they could see. Pulekukwerek said, "I suppose you can take care of what we have here?" The young man said, "If you put it in my house I shall care for it." "Where is your house?" "It is not far." "I will go there."

d. Then they went until they saw his house. Pulekukwerek said, "I have always been about here along on the beach, but I never thought that you were so near (by on the river)." "I have lived here a long time." "Have you no kinsmen (cousins)?" "Yes, I have friends: two brothers; but I am alone here." "Where do they live?" "Up the (Klamath) river." "How far?" "When you come to the mouth, go upstream until you reach Turip." "I know that place. It does not seem good that you should be here alone. You had better bring your friends here." "Do you think that you will be able to go there and bring them? You may tell them that I said they were to come." "Yes, I will go. But tell me how this place of yours is called, so that when I come to them they will know that I am speaking the truth." "Call it Hinei."

e. Pulekukwerek started. He came to Turip. There he saw a neatly made house. At the river was a boat with a paddle lying ready in it. But he saw no person. He thought, "I will go in." So he entered. He saw two young men. The younger one said, "I feel that someone is coming in." The older one

5. "South" the narrator said, either for *perwer,* south, or for *wohpauk,* which denotes the direction about at right angles to the course of the lower Klamath, or roughly southwest.

6. *Mīs.* Trout are *regok.*

7. "Salmon bone," my notes read, probably meaning a bone implement for taking salmon. However, the known northwestern hooks are of quadruped bone pointed and angled, or cut out curved from shell or bone, not mere double-pointed bars. Compare Goddard, Life and Culture of the Hupa, UC-PAAE 1, pl. 13 and p. 25, and Robert F. Heizer, Curved Single-Piece Fishhooks of Shell and Bone in California, American Antiquity, 15 (no. 2): 89-97, 1949.

8. They probably were dentalia; compare the subsequent prediction (in *e*) of wealth.

looked up and said, "Old man, come in." "Yes, I will come in, but then I must go back where I came from." "Are you traveling upriver or down?" "I was traveling upriver from Nororpek. I have seen your friend: he came to where I lived. I was sorry for him because he is alone. That is why I came. It will be a good place where he is. A man that grows there will always be rich. He will never have bad luck, because of what I caught this morning and gave him to keep. As long as the world lasts it will be thus: everyone born there will be rich. I wish you would go to live where your friend is." "What is that place called? Where is it?" "It is downstream at Hinei. It is a good place." Then the older one said, "We are sorry for him. But we have prepared everything around here, believing we should always live here, and I think we cannot go." Pulekukwerek said, "You had better try. Come today; you can return tomorrow if you do not find your house in Hinei. Stay the night with your friend, and when you awake you will find your house." The younger one thought, "He cannot carry this house." He said to the older, "Let us go." So they went along with Pulekukwerek, not believing him and thinking that they should be coming back to Turip the next day.

When they came to Hinei, they saw everything well arranged around the house. Then Pulekukwerek thought, "I will go back to where I live. They will not return (to Turip), but find their house here." He said, "Well, I am going. If there is anything you want, come for me." The young man of Hinei said, "Yes." Then Pulekukwerek said, "Good-bye. Perhaps tomorrow you will go back."[9] "Yes, if we do not find our house here we are going back, but we shall always live here if in the morning we see our house. Yet even if we return we shall always be friends. Hinei and Turip will be friends as long as the world lasts." "Yes, so it shall be," said Pulekukwerek.

f. Then he went to his house (at Nororpek). He waited a day and saw no one. The next day he saw no one. He began to think, "Perhaps something is wrong. I will go and see." Then he thought, "No. They would come to get me if something were wrong." Next morning he sat outdoors and looked across the stream. Then he saw five young men coming. One of them looked like the young man from Turip. "I will set them across. They have come to see me," said Pulekukwerek. So he ferried them over the stream. They all spoke to him[10] and were glad and went up to his house with him. They said, "Old man, tomorrow we go back. Tonight we will stay here, but in the morning you must come with us. There are many people at Hinei now. I wish you would stay there a night and make the place good. We want it so that we go down to the

9. Concealed irony, of course. The great Pulekukwerek does not doubt his power to produce their house.

10. A sign of friendship, as one of the first symptoms of ill-feeling on the part of a Yurok is the maintenance of silence.

river to fish, every evening and again in the morning. We have tried that but cannot do it." "Is that so? Well, I will go with you in the morning. I will make it so because you wish to live in that way." "Yes, that is how we wish to live. We want to catch fish; we want nets and boats." Then Pulekukwerek began to work at something of bone. They looked on and thought, "It will be good."

g. In the morning they went. Pulekukwerek carried his pieces of bone. They came to Hinei. Pulekukwerek said, "How many of you want to fish at once?" They said, "We should like five boats to fish together." "Well, I will make it like that," said Pulekukwerek. They went to (Smith) river, and he made five small canoes, each with paddles and nets. He also took long poles and on the (double, forked) ends set the harpoon points which he had made of the bone. Then he said, "Well, now you had better try it out, for this is how you will live. Once in the morning, once in the middle of the day, and once in the evening you will go out. You will fish three times a day."

The five boats started with nets. Then Pulekukwerek said to two strong young men, giving them the harpoons, "Try to use these. When you see a salmon coming, spear it." Then they began fishing. The boats went upstream, and the two stood on opposite banks. One of them saw a large salmon and speared it. They could see the salmon leaping and being drawn in by the harpooner. Then he on the other bank speared one, and those who were fishing with nets began to catch them. Looking up to the town, Pulekukwerek saw many people watching. Then they landed from the boats, and those in the town came down and carried up the salmon.

Pulekukwerek went to the house and said, "Well, now I am going." They said, "Yes? Well, we will go with you part of the way. From there you can go on alone." So Pulekukwerek went back to Nororpek. He said, "Send for me if there is anything wrong." Then he arrived at Nororpek.

h. After five days he thought, "I need not wait for anyone to come for me, for that place is now all made." So he went of his own account. When he came to Hinei, they were just returning from fishing. All were glad to see him. Pulekukwerek alone did not eat: he only smoked tobacco. They asked him to eat but he would not. Then he said, "How is the fishing?" "It is going well. We always catch them." "Well, this is the last time I shall be here. Have you not gone back to Turip?" "Not one of us. We have never even thought of going back." "Well, I will tell you that where you lived at Turip there is a large town again." Then the older brother from Turip said, "Well, that is good. We shall not return, but we shall have friends there. There is only one thing that I regret. I had finished my paddle and a little canoe that I was going to use." Pulekukwerek said, "I think it will not take me long to go there if you want that boat." They said, "You cannot pass by (with it) at Rekwoi." "Oh, yes," he said, "I can go. Let us arrange that you wait for me at O'menwo,[11] this side of Rekwoi. I will go past Rekwoi alone."[12] Then some said, "It is dangerous. Boats never go on the ocean." But some said, "Oh yes, he will be able to do it."

Then Pulekukwerek went. Five of them waited at the (appointed) rock at O'menwo. Now they saw him coming over the ocean in the boat. It was the first time that a boat had gone on salt water.[13] Soon he reached them. "I told you that the old man could do it," they said. Then he took the boat into Smith River. Thereupon he said, "Now I am going."

A21. Wohpekumeu at Weitspus

For an erotically motivated story of the trickster, this has an unusual tone. The ordinary narrator's interest is in either Wohpekumeu's devices or in his foilings. Billy has his mind so full of his hero's greatness that he makes him considerate, helpful, restrained, and even patient; that he should be forgiving would hardly be conceivable to a Yurok. He desires a woman, indeed, but without indecency, and he more than pays his way. The tinge of contempt with which Wohpekumeu is often spoken of by the Yurok is thus wholly lacking in this tale. It is characteristic of the narrator's imagination that his heroes must be free of any touch of baseness or pettiness.

The result is that Wohpekumeu the inveterate woman chaser is here made into a restrained, magnanimous hero, who gives, and patiently waits for a return, until he is definitely fobbed off—a very un-Yurok Wohpekumeu indeed. This departure from the norm seems to be a purely personal whim of the narrator. (Compare tale E1*f*.)

Formally the myth is scarcely institutional, except in the might-have-been sense: whatever is made in it by the hero is undone again and no one is better or worse off. In vein, however, it belongs to the institutional class of tales.

The tale is a mine of cultural information on how the Yurok talked, approached each other, gathered food and gave it, slept, made love, behaved afterward, watched, and waited—all this because of the narrator's passion to tell his tale slowly but realistically.

11. I cannot place O'menwo nor etymologize it. It suggests the town of Omen (or O'men) at Wilson Creek, 4 or 5 miles north of the Klamath mouth. This would be a reasonable distance for people who had already come all of 20 miles. But if it was a question merely of avoiding the mouth, Rekwoi had an embarkation and disembarkation beach cove, Ostsegep ("where they customarily land"), about 1/2 mile from the bar (Waterman, map 5, nos. 36 and 47). [See map 6 in this volume.—Ed.]

12. The reference seems to be not to the monster in the river, which presumably had already been destroyed by Pulekukwerek (A16x *u*), but to the passage of the river mouth and to ocean travel, which had never yet been attempted. The mouth tends to be rough and there are several rocks close in.

13. Navigating the sea with their blunt-ended river-evolved canoes is looked on as a serious achievement, even by the Coast Yurok, and they observe taboos and take out women or corpses only under certain conditions.

a. Wohpekumeu was living at Kenek. He started out, thinking, "I will go to Weitspus." He came to Hagolots.[1] There he sat down on the seat[2] and looked toward Weitspus and saw many people playing about.

He went on and came to (the house) Okriger[3] (in Weitspus). There he saw (two young men sitting before their house. They said to him, "You have come upstream?"[4] "Yes," he said. "I thought this morning that I would go upstream to Weitspus." They said, "You have done well to come. We are glad. You can go down to the river with us in a little while and help us." Wohpekumeu saw young men at the bar.[5] One of those with him said, "That is where we try to catch fish; but we cannot get many." The old man thought, "I will go down and help them fish. I will make them catch all they can carry." After a time he said, "Well, when shall you begin to fish?" They said, "We are going soon." He asked them, "How do you catch salmon?" Then they showed him a small scoop net,[6] a very small one, only so large.[7] "That is what we try to catch them with. Sometimes we take a few," they said.

b. Now they went down to the river. The old man (Wohpekumeu) said, "I have a net here. Let us use that." They said, "Good. If you have a net we shall use it." He put his hand into his quiver and drew out a net. Then he said, "I want two sticks[8] as long as that." Then they cut the sticks for him. He said, "Now let us take a small boat."[9] They said, "Very well." He told them, "Let

1. "Butte Camp Ridge," on the south side of the Klamath between Kenek and Weitspus. I suspect it is not far from Po'toyo, Bloody Camp (Waterman, Geography, map 23, no. 12).

2. Either a resting place there or one of the seats used by shamans in their night training on the mountains.

3. Okriger was mentioned as if a town, but I conjecture it to be the house in Weitspus where they tie up their hair and fix up for dancing (Waterman, map 26, no. 16, and p. 258), which he calls Erkigeri ("rkīgri") and Spott calls Erkīger or Okīger in Kroeber and Gifford, World Renewal, pp. 87, 91. In Weitspus it is one of the houses farthest downhill in the town.

4. Making conversation. Billy, with his love of concreteness in what concerns human relations, frequently delays the progress of a tale to indulge in realistic small talk.

5. This is a wide crescentic beach, now largely of boulders and torn up by placer mining, but formerly covered with gravel or sand. (See Waterman, pl. 11.) The river rushes by it in a strong sweep and without eddies and at some depth, so that the reach is unfavorable for taking salmon. Weitspus fishes on the other side of the river or above and below the town. I have never heard that seines are used in this stretch; the current is likely to be too rapid. Wohpekumeu's seining here is probably of a piece with the salmon running up the creeks: it would have been pleasant to have it so, and from the wish sprang the tale.

6. Such nets, on an oval or kite-shaped frame, are effective in a small stream, and at certain special places on the Klamath, such as the foot of the fall at Enek. The Yurok in general used them very little. They would certainly bag very few fish with them at Weitspus. Compare tale L1*b*.

7. Gesture.

8. For the ends of the seine, so it can be held stretched to its full width.

9. A large boat, being wider, deeper, and heavier, is less easily handled and probably less convenient for fishing.

us start upstream (from Weitspus) and fish down.'' He showed them what to do. ''You stand here and you there.'' Then one of them swam in a semicircle with the seine,[10] and the other held his end at the shore. When both ends were brought to land, the old man[11] danced in the water. Then he said, ''Lift it out.'' They got a big haul. Then they went on fishing down the river, and before they had got far the people of Weitspus saw them and ran down to look on. By the time they were in front of Weitspus everyone had come down to see. When they landed, their boat was nearly full of salmon. The old man said, ''Well, I do not own the fish. They are yours. Divide them so that everybody has some.'' Then the two brothers divided the salmon and every house was full of food.

c. Wohpekumeu stayed there that night. Next morning, when the sun was up, he said, ''Let us fish again.'' They said, ''Yes, let us,'' and he told them, ''I will go with you.'' As they started to go down to the river, Wohpekumeu said, ''Tell them that if any women want salmon they are to come down for them.'' So the two brothers called to the people that if any women wanted salmon they should come and get them. Then they fished, and the women began to watch to see if they caught many that they might be given. When they saw that they caught very many indeed, they said, ''Well, let us go down for them,'' and all went down. As they came down to the water, the fishing had stopped and the boat was entirely full. The old man sat down and looked on while they divided the salmon. Everybody got some, even those from across the river. They liked Wohpekumeu because he knew how to fish.

d. In the evening they went out again, and more men and more women came down to where they landed. Wohpekumeu looked all the women over. He saw that the most beautiful one lived in the house where he was staying. Then he began to speak to her.[12] He stayed there a long time, wishing to marry her. She said, ''Yes, if you will first make that by which we are to live.'' ''Well, you shall see,'' said Wohpekumeu. But he thought, ''I do not know what to do.'' The next day he thought of something. ''I will go downstream to the next creek,'' he thought. He went there and worked, down by the river and up the hill, looked about, and said, ''It will be level prairie from here to Weitspus when I get up in the morning.'' He made many bulbs (of Brodiaeas) be in that prairie.

e. That evening they did not catch many salmon because the old man was not with them but working downstream. They[13] said, ''We did not catch many, only a few.'' He said, ''Is that so? Well, come downstream to the creek tomorrow. You will catch salmon there.'' They said, ''How shall we take

10. ***Hełkuerego***. [But K. has a reference to his notebooks.—Ed.]

11. Wohpekumeu, as before.

12. Making proposals.

13. The two brothers, his hosts.

them if we see them?'' He told them, ''I will make it for you.'' Then he worked two things, one for each of the young men.[14]

In the morning they went downstream with him. They said, ''What are you going to do with these things?'' He said, ''Take long sticks. Put these toggle-heads on the ends and tie them with string. When you see a salmon, harpoon it.'' Then they came to the stream and saw many large salmon. They killed all they could see. Coming back upstream to Weitspus, they said, ''We caught many.''

f. Then soon all the people from Weitspus were going there to spear salmon. The old man came, looked on, and thought, ''There ought to be another creek. There are too many of them for one creek.'' Then he went downriver to Pulik-weroi.[15] He made that to carry salmon also. Then he told them,[16] ''Go farther downriver, to the next creek. There are salmon there too.'' The two brothers ran downriver. They did not look at the many from Weitspus and from across river who were fishing at the upper creek. As soon as they came to the lower creek they saw many salmon.

Now Wohpekumeu saw many young women coming to carry home salmon. When it was nearly sunset he looked and saw many of them digging bulbs in the prairie. Some of the people knew that he was Wohpekumeu and thought, ''He will live here. He wants to marry.'' They all had abundance of salmon.

g. It became spring. The young women said, ''Let us go to gather clover[17] on Pekwtuɬ Ridge.''[18] Then they all went. After a time they returned. Only the one that Wohpekumeu desired did not return. She came home very late. Then she would not speak, not as usually.[19]

14. Salmon harpoon toggle heads. The vague allusion is often favored by the Yurok because the listener is supposed to know what is referred to, but I suspect Billy used it also as a device to heighten my suspense while listening to him. The ordinary harpoon has two heads, not one. The narrator is inexact, not ignorant of the implement; or his ''one for each'' may be short for ''a pair for each.''

15. ''Downriver stream,'' a descriptive name for the occasion. The Yurok several times told me that in the woge time the salmon would run up the little creek that flows through Weitspus. The reference to the prairie, however, indicates that the creek first improved by Wohpekumeu in this tale was the small one about a third of a mile below Weitspus (Waterman, map 25, no. 18, Wiɬnega weroi. [See map 4 in this volume.—Ed.] This would make the *ad hoc* named ''Pulik-weroi'' be the larger creek Otegeket weroi (no. 17), which runs a quarter or a third of a mile farther downriver but is still in convenient reach.

16. The two brothers.

17. *Nepoyets.*

18. The ridge between the Klamath and Trinity, with the town of Pekwtuɬ (or Pekwteu) on its nose. Waterman, Pekwtsuɬ-so', map 25, no. 49. [See map 4 in this volume.—Ed.]

19. ''Did not talk good,'' the narrator said, referring to an unwillingness to converse because of growing unfriendliness.

Once in the morning she said to her two brothers, "Put me across the river. I want to dig roots." Then she did not come back until late, when the sun was nearly down, and did as before: she did not speak when she came.

h. During that summer, when Wohpekumeu came out from the sweathouse in the morning, he saw wood piled at the house and thought, "She has been early to get wood." Now this girl used to go out; one did not often see her in the house. She would go down to the river to make baskets and sit where no one saw her. The old man was watching.

i. All the young women were sleeping on the bar; it was too warm to sleep indoors. He would leave the sweathouse to bathe in the river. On his way back,[20] if some of the women were still awake, he would talk with them, looking about for this girl; but he never saw her. One evening he thought, "I will look for her again tonight. I will leave my pipe in the house so that I shall have to go in during the night."[21] That night he went down to the river, spoke with the women, kept watch, and did not see her. When he was again in the sweathouse he said, "Ah! This is the first time I have had bad luck. I have left my pipe in the house. I do not think I shall be able to sleep without having smoked." One of the old men said, "Go get your pipe if you know where it is." "Yes, I know where it is," said Wohpekumeu. He went to the house and said, "I forgot my pipe." The old woman said, "Yes, you forgot your pipe. Come right in and get it if you know where it is." Wohpekumeu came out again at once; he had not seen the girl in the house. He thought, "I must look for her in the morning." When it was nearly day he went outside and looked everywhere. He did not see her come: only tracks upstream. Then he concluded: "She has not come back to town at all. She has gone for wood from the place where she slept, and will come home from there."

j. Then he saw a boat on the other side of the river and knew that someone had crossed that morning. Then he went across to Pekwtuɬ and asked who had gone after sweathouse wood[22] that morning. The old men said, "No one has been to get sweathouse wood except one man, and he slept here." Wohpekumeu said, "Well, I had a boat on the other side of the river, and it has been taken to this side; someone must have crossed this morning." They said, "We heard someone at daybreak. Perhaps that was the one." Then a young man said, "I know who it is. I felt last night that there was a person about. Therefore I did not feel well and did not get sweathouse wood this

20. The fire is made in the evening. When it has burned itself out, the inmates may bathe. Then they return to sleep without blankets in the warm sweathouse.

21. So strict was the separation of the sleeping quarters of the sexes that even an old man's entry into the living house at night was open to misconstruction—against which the hero is discreetly guarding.

22. This shows that in spite of frequent loose statements about men "always" bringing in sweathouse wood as a semiritualistic office, they by no means did so regularly.

morning.[23] He lives upstream on the Trinity." Then Wohpekumeu thought, "That is why she always crosses over here and never has a good word for me when I come. I will watch again."

k. In two days he found out more: he knew everything. Then he said to her, "I have learned what you are doing." She did not answer. Then the other young women talked to her. They said, "Why do you like that other man? This one is good. He makes everything." "Well, let him go away. He has made everything," she said, "and I do not like him. He has finished here and made it how we shall fish and dig roots." Then Wohpekumeu said to her, "I am not going away. I shall leave only when I see that you have gone to that man's house. As long as you stay here I shall stay."[24] He knew what he was about to do.

l. Then one morning the girl did not come home, and they found that she had gone up the Trinity to the young man there. Wohpekumeu still stayed. Some of the young women tried to be friendly with him, but he would not meet them. When the sun set he had prepared. He thought, "I shall go back downriver to where I live." When it was dark he went out. He went to the prairie that he had made and spoiled it. He went to the creek beyond and spoiled it for salmon; then to the creek below and ruined that. Only small trout are left in them. In the morning the people got up and found that their prairie was destroyed. Some went to the creeks and saw them spoiled for salmon. Some went to the river to fish but did not catch one. All the old men and old women of Weitspus hated to know that the girl had married the other one and that Wohpekumeu had gone away. They were angry because the old man had been fooled after he had been so good to them.

m. When it camc to be autumn the wind began to blow. Some knew, "That is he who ran away with the woman." Now the wind was always blowing at Weitspus; it blew very hard at the spring Wetspekw.[25] Then he in the spring[26] scared him away: he said, "What are you good for?" Wind[27] said, "I shall be good as long as the world lasts. You will see I sweep off every place. I shall sweep everything here." But he (Wind) was afraid of coming to

23. Another confirmation. Perhaps the young man did not like being watched by a stranger during the operation. However, a rigidly imposed ceremony would not be omitted for such a reason.

24. He will not undo his work until her rejection of him is made final by openly living with his rival, whom she has been visiting of nights.

25. The spring at the upstream end of Weitspus from which the town drew its drinking water. River water is ordinarily avoided by the Yurok, and Weitspus Creek was inhabited by a Sa'ał disease spirit.

26. Kewetspekw, hero of tale A13.

27. Tserhkeruk.

the spring, so now there is not much wind there; but where the houses are in Weitspus, the wind is always coming there.[28]

A22. Wohpekumeu at Hupa

This tale also puts Wohpekumeu in a good light, though he is scarcely as benign as in the last. Here he is distinctly self-centered in his purposes, and not above concealing his identity; but he is a good deal of a man, and his actions are scarcely underhanded. If he ruins girls, most of them are after all only Hupas, whereas in the previous tale, when it came to the narrator's native Weitspus, the hero showed himself as full of good will as anyone might like. It is another evidence of the skill of the informant that in each tale he is able to bring out another aspect of the same personage's character and maintain it consistently.

•

a. Pulekukwerek and Wohpekumeu came downstream from Ko'men[1] to Weitspus. There Pulekukwerek lost him. He thought, "Where has he gone?" They told him, "He is across the river at Pekwtuł." Pulekukwerek crossed and, seeing a man, asked him, "Did you see Wohpekumeu?" "He is across the (Trinity) river at Erłerger. He heard a girl laughing and went there." Pulekukwerek turned away. He thought, "Let him enjoy himself. I shall go downstream to where I live. Perhaps after a time I shall come back to him, perhaps not." So he went.

After a time Wohpekumeu thought, "Where has he gone? I will go to the creek below." He saw a man fishing there. It was Tspega, Cormorant.[2] He asked him, "Have you seen Pulekukwerek?" Tspega said, "Yes, I saw him going downstream in a boat. I think he has gone off home." Wohpekumeu thought, "Well, I will follow him."

He came to Kenek.[3] Off the trail at a spring he heard a girl laughing. Then he turned there. He found many girls and enjoyed himself. He did not know it, but he stayed five days. Then he tired of it. He thought, "I will go elsewhere before I follow my companion: I will go to the Trinity." Then he went across the mountains.

b. He came out on Bald Mountain,[4] looked up the (Trinity) over prairie

28. Weitspus is windy, lying on an open terrace in a bend of the Klamath with the Trinity coming in opposite. Even the Karok know that Wind married there. But the spring Wetspekw (*y* on Waterman's map 26) lies in a hollow at the upriver end of the town.

1. Orleans, Karok Panamenik.
2. Tspega is a favorite character of this narrator; see A12 and A13.
3. His own town. That he should try his seductions there seems strange.
4. Overlooking Hupa Valley from the north or downstream end.

and valley, and saw many young men and women in the flat below digging roots. He thought, "There are many of them; I am glad I have come. Let me hurry and go to them." Then he came to the flat at Oknuł.[5] He thought, "This is where I will enjoy myself before I go on upstream." When he came there he looked about but saw no one. He walked about but could not find one person. He thought, "Someone has tricked me. I do not know what to do—whether it will be best to go on or to go back up on the mountain and look for them again."

c. Then, recrossing the river, he went uphill once more. He laid himself a rock, sat on it, and looked up the valley again. There were more people now than before. Wohpekumeu thought, "Whoever did that played a good trick on me. But I have always thought that I too was a man. I shall try it again and do my best. I will prepare here and sing for myself. When I rub my hands one kind of plant will come into each of my hands. With these I shall make medicine. Then I shall be able to approach them." Then he made himself ready (as he had said). After that he laid one plant on each side of his seat. He said, "After a time there will be another people here. If one of them knows my two plants, and where my seat is, it will be well for him. I shall leave them here, and if he knows them, he will have good medicine for women.[6]

d. Then he went on. He thought, "I have nothing to carry. I want something to carry. I wish I saw a basket full of seaweed."[7] Then he saw a basket; it was full. He took it and carried it over his shoulder by a string. When he crossed the river again, he saw that those he had seen were still there. This time they had not disappeared. Then he thought, "What language shall I speak to them? I will talk Omimos[8] to them." He called, "Come here. I will give you seaweed." He gave each of them a cake, but the basket never held less, never became empty. "Well, I will go on," he said.

e. He came to Kererwer[9] and saw many people. He crossed to Ergerits,[10] went on upstream to Oplego,[11] then back to the other side and upstream to

5. Hupa Honsading.

6. A formula may underlie this episode. [K. has a partly illegible marginal note: "Love . . ."—Ed.]

7. A purplish seaweed (*Porphyra,* etc.), eaten on account of its salt. It comes in flat pads or dried cakes, about a foot across. It would be quite desirable to a people so far inland as the Hupa.

8. The Athabascan language spoken by the Hupa, Chilula, and Whilkut. (The Tolowa form of Athabascan was known to the Yurok by another name.)

9. Hupa Cheindekotding. [Notes 9-15 were incomplete in K.'s typescript. I have taken the spellings shown here from Kroeber, Handbook, p. 129.—Ed.]

10. Hupa Miskut.

11. Hupa Takimiłding.

Erlern.[12] From there he went on up to Kohteɬ[13] and then to Pyageɬ.[14] Now his seaweed was nearly gone; his basket felt light. He thought, "I will go a little farther upstream and stop; it is nearly sunset." Then he came to (above) Petsou.[15] He thought: "I will stay here. In the morning I will go back down to see the girls." Then he slept there that night.

f. Next day he thought what to do. He decided: "This is what I shall do. I will make a good sand bar at the river here. I will cause a rock to be in the water, with one hole for suckers, one for trout, one for lamprey eels, one for sturgeon, and one for salmon."[16] That day he made all that. He made the rock with the holes partly in the water and partly out. Then he slept again.

In the morning, he went to look at his (fishing) place. There were very many fish. He thought, "That is how I wished to do it. Now I should like to have someone to let them know about it." Then he saw a small boat with three men in it. He thought, "I wish they would come upstream as far as here." Then they came near. He called, "Come across!" They said, "There is an old man on the other side. Let us go to him." He said, "Where do you live?" They said, "It is not far. Where do you live, old man?" "I live here. I catch salmon. Have you no fish?" "No." "Bring your boat in and I will give you some to take home." He gave them sturgeon and salmon and suckers and lamprey eels and trout. Then they went back with their fish to Petsou. "Where did you get the fish?" they were asked. "There is an old man there who has many." "You had better go up again tomorrow." Next day they went there once more. Soon they returned with their boat full of fish of all kinds. They divided them and told (visitors from Pyageɬ) how they had got them from the old man.

Then in the morning many went up from Pyageɬ. Next day they came from Kohteɬ. In five days they were coming from the downstream end of the valley and sleeping on the bar where Wohpekumeu was. Soon the girls and young men were sleeping there, and all night the old man chased them about. In the morning the girls all went home: in the evening they came again.

g. Wohpekumeu thought, "Perhaps they will find out who I am.[17] I am afraid of that." There were five girls, the prettiest in Hupa, who used to come

12. Hupa Toɬtsasding.

13. Hupa Medilding.

14. Hupa Howunkut.

15. "Above" is not in the text, but what follows shows that he must have gone upstream beyond the town. Petsou is Hupa Djishtangading, the farthest town upstream in Hupa Valley.

16. [K. has a marginal note: "Abut(?) order of importance."—Ed.]

17. When the girls were discovered to be pregnant, which usually happened very soon when Wohpekumeu was involved.

every night. One evening they did not come. In the morning the old man thought, "I shall be found out today. I will divide my catch early and go away and spoil my fishing place." So he divided his fish, overturned his fishing place, and left.

Then young men came[18] to where he had been, but he was gone. They tried to track him but could not. If he had gone in a boat he would have been seen, but no one had seen him. Then they knew that he was Wohpekumeu.

h. He went on up the Trinity until he came to Hanatep.[19] There he saw a girl. Then he wanted to stay. He said, "How do you catch salmon?" They said, "We take them in the river, but it is hard. Sometimes we catch two or three, that is all." "Oh, I will make it so that you will catch them," he said and went out. They heard a noise at the river. Then he came back and said, "I have made it so that you will have salmon. I shall stay there tonight. Come down in the morning to carry up the fish," he said to the girl. "Yes, I will come in the morning," she said.

In the morning she awoke, went down to the river, looked, and saw the old man sleeping by his fire.[20] "It looks as if he had not fished," she thought. She went to him and said, "Are you asleep?" He said, "No, I have just lain down. I have got through fishing. I think I caught as many as you can carry." He stood up. Then she saw many fish. "Here they are; put them in your basket." "How did you catch them?" "Come. I will show you how I caught them." She went close to the river. Then she saw a long rock extending. It had two holes in it. Wohpekumeu pushed the rock into the water and raised one end. Then the river ran over (the other end) and fish entered the holes. "That is how I catch them," he said. "Yes," she said. "Now you may go back," said Wohpekumeu. When she stooped to lift up her basket Wohpekumeu was standing before her[21] and she could hardly raise it; but she returned to the house. Wohpekumeu did thus every day.

i. Then one morning he saw someone coming from Hupa. The one from Hupa said, "We had heard that one had gone all along the Klamath and had had to leave, for he is the one, I heard, that ruined all the finest girls. He ruined them in Hupa also. We do not know where he is gone, but his name is Wohpekumeu." Then he thought, "That is I." That night he thought, "They will find me. I had better go away. But I will leave this fishing place for these people. I shall leave it for them to use as long as the world lasts. That is what I will do for them." He went down to his fishing place and put it in order and

18. To collect damages or inflict revenge.

19. Probably in the valley above Hupa which Willow Creek enters. The inhabitants spoke Hupa and are included among the Hupa.

20. A man who fished at night kept a fire on shore to warm himself at intervals if he stayed awake, or to sleep by.

21. Evidently this was when she became pregnant.

spoke to it. "You will be here. There will be another people. They will call on me here. They will say 'Wohpekumeu is the one who made it thus at Hanatep.'"

j. In the morning they found that he had gone, so they knew that he was the old man. He went down the Trinity in a boat. He could no longer go anywhere else because now they knew him everywhere. So he went on down the Klamath. When he came to the mouth he tried (unsuccessfully) to learn where Pulekukwerek had gone, to which side of the mouth he had turned. Then Wohpekumeu went southward.[22]

A23. Wohpekumeu at Segwu'

I have used this title because of the ultimate theme of the plot. "Wohpekumeu's Return" would have been more distinctive, because all the events occur after his supposedly final departure from the world. But that title would suggest a prophecy of his coming back in the future, of which no Yurok thinks.

Wohpekumeu is here depicted in still another aspect—that of the deliberate world improver. It is not merely that an impulse leads him to do what is good; he ponders and cherishes and finishes his task. His character is much more like that of Pulekukwerek than his usual one. For once he is thinking wholly of humanity and not at all of erotic satisfaction.

The story is remarkable for dealing explicitly with human beings and not—as is normally assumed in tales—with the prehuman woge of the mythical period. But it conforms to type: the people of Segwu' after all are cannibals, go underground, and carry their houses off as if they were woge; and those of Ko'men voyage nightly across the ocean.

Five themes are interwoven: Wohpekumeu's watching over the new human race; his giving of medicines; the dance relations between Ko'men and Pulekuk; the stamping out of cannibalism at Segwu';[1] and the institution of dances there. The dexterity with which these are brought into connection is admirable. The Ko'men incident seems at first to be only a loosely inserted episode, as at bottom it is; but it finally leads to a renewal of reference to Segwu' and of Wohpekumeu's interest in it and the rehabilitation of this important town. Even the scout Hahkwełtsin, who seems dropped from sight after the first paragraph, reappears toward the close to help fill and round out the tale; and Pulekukwerek and Kapuloyo, minor thought their functions are, are brought in without a wrench.

•

22. Here presumably would follow the incident of Wohpekumeu's finally yielding to the temptations of Skate and being carried by her across the ocean to join the other immortals.

1. Segwu' is Karok Katimin, on the Klamath a mile or so above the mouth of the Salmon River, perhaps the most important town of the Karok and reckoned by them the center of the world. Yurok myth tends to associate Segwu' with evil. [K. has a marginal notation: "Footnotes need redoing."—Ed.]

a. After Wohpekumeu had made everything[2] here[3] and all of them[4] had gone away, some far downstream to the end of the world[5] and some on the mountains,[6] and after these people that are here now had begun to grow, Wohpekumeu lived at Pulekuk. He wished to hear of this world. He asked Hahkweɫtsin,[7] "How are they getting on?" Hahkweɫtsin said, "Some of them look sick. Some are very thin. Some are well, but some are not; and some cannot eat at all." Wohpekumeu said, "Try to find out what is the matter." Hahkweɫtsin agreed. Every night he came by here.[8] In the morning Wohpekumeu said to him, "You are here again?" He said, "Yes, I am going back. I shall go for a little to every town and I will find out why they are sick. I think they never will be well, for they eat bad food." Wohpekumeu said, "Yes, that is what I thought as I looked from here." After five days Hahkweɫtsin came back again to where Wohpekumeu lived. But he did not see him. He asked "Where is he?" "He left the day before yesterday. I do not know where he went," they told him. Wohpekumeu had started to come here.[9] No one knew it. Nobody here knew him.

b. He came to a town. "Where are you going?" they asked. "I am going upstream until I see salt water." "Where are you from?" "I am from far downstream. I grew there." "Do not go upstream. It is bad there. Those who go never come back." Wohpekumeu said, "Yes. I think I will turn back." Then he went outdoors but left some medicine in the house. "What is the matter?" he had asked about one who was sick there. Then he had given him medicine and had caused it to grow outdoors there.[10]

Then he went on up. In the middle of the day he saw someone lying in the path. He looked and saw that it was a fine young man asleep. He woke up. Wohpekumeu said, "What is the matter with you?" He could scarcely speak: "I am sick." "What is it?" "I am sick. I can hardly walk." He was thin, nothing but bones. The old man (Wohpekumeu) said, "I will help you." That one did not believe (that he could). "Try to get up," he said. Then that one got up. He washed him. He made him drink water. That was all he did for him.

2. "Making everything" means ordering the world, not creating it.

3. In the world of human beings.

4. The people of prehuman times.

5. Pulekukwerek, Pelin-tsīk, Wohpekumeu, No'ots, and others at Pulekuk. [K. adds in a marginal notation Megwomets and Kapuloyo.—Ed.]

6. The woge who remained as spirits in the hills or became animals.

7. [Wohpekemeu's scout and messenger. K. queries whether the name should be spelled Hahkweɫtsin or Hohkweɫ-.—Ed.]

8. That is, went up the Klamath.

9. After all, Wohpekumeu is too great a personage to be dependent on the report of his messenger. He can act on his own knowledge.

10. The narrator is inserting details which he forgot to mention two or three sentences before.

Then he waited. Soon the young man began to speak. Then he asked him, "How did you become sick?" "I grew downstream not far away and thought I would go upstream. I had gone part way. Then I began to feel sick from those who use bad food."[11] "Yes?" "Do not go up, old man. You will not come back." "Yes?" "It is a town on the south side.[12] Go there if you wish, but if they give you anything to eat do not take it." "Yes."

c. Then the old man crossed the river. He came to a town of many houses. There were many men about, all of them thin. He went to the sweathouse and sat outside it. An old man came to him, looked at him, but did not know who he was nor where he came from. He asked him, "Where are you from?" "I am going upriver until I reach salt water." "I think you will not be able to do it. Look at all these young men. Sometimes they only go over that ridge and the wind blows from upstream (and strikes them). That is what made them so. It is a bad place. Do not go there." "Yes? What are you doing for these young men?" "I sing for them, that is all." "You give them no medicine?" "No, I can find no (herb) growing here." "I have some here in my quiver. I think it will help them. Go indoors and bring a basket. I will crush my plant and give it to them to drink." He gave it to the sickest one, who was so thin and feeble that he could hardly walk over to him (and cured him). Then he scattered the plant about, and it began to grow. He said, "After a time you will all use it. Now I think I shall go back." But he did not mean to go back. He went downstream a little way, turned and went upstream again.

d. He came to Ko'men.[13] He saw no one about. Then he sat down outside a large house. Inside he heard them talking. After a time an old woman came out. She said, "Someone is sitting outside." Then the man (of the house) came out and spoke to him. He said, "I thought we should never see anyone again. No one has been here. It is a bad place. I do not know where they have gone, those of whom we hear that they made everything in the world. Perhaps they did not believe that this would be a bad place." "Do you know where they went?" "No. When they made everything through the world, it was the last time that they were seen. I know them: I know of Wohpekumeu and Pulekukwerek. I am always wishing that they would come back." "Well, send word to them by me. I live near them." "Tell them that we shall do whatever they say." "You think you will do it?" "Yes." "Do you think you can go down there[14] every few nights? They make the Jumping Dance nightly." "Yes. If Pulekukwerek says it, and Wohpekumeu says it, we will go down every night." Wohpekumeu thought, "That is what I like." He said,

11. The effects of the cannibalism and poison-eating practiced at Segwu' are infectious at long distances.

12. That is, east.

13. Orleans, Karok Panamenik.

14. Not only to the mouth of the river but across the ocean to Pulekuk beyond the sky.

''I will tell you what I shall do. I will give you a medicine to drink which I have in here. Give me a basket.'' Then he gave them all to drink and scattered the medicine (herb) about. He said, ''In future, when you are sick, use this medicine. I tell you to do so.''

Then that one asked him, ''Where are you going?'' Wohpekumeu said, ''I am going upstream until I see salt water.'' They said, ''Do not go. It is bad. One who goes there never comes back. You will find it so.'' ''Well, yes, I will turn back. But you must wait. Pulekukwerek and Wohpekumeu will come.'' ''We shall be ready. We will go down to them every night.''

e. Then he went downstream, turned about, and went on up. He came to a ridge and heard shouting.[15] He looked upstream and saw dances going on. He thought, ''I will try it. I will eat the sort of food that they have.'' He came to them. There were many of them. All of them spoke to him.[16] Some said, ''Come to eat.'' He said, ''Yes.'' He went into a house and they gave him to eat. He knew what kind of food they gave him. Still he ate it. Then they gave him another kind and he knew what that was but ate it. Then they gave him another kind and he knew it. He looked at it and thought, ''I know what it is.''[17] He ate all that they gave him. Then he said, ''I am going.'' They said, ''Yes, go.''[18]

He went on. Then the old man (Wohpekumeu) began to feel that his legs were heavy. ''That food did it,'' he thought. He went on; he hardly walked any longer. He lay down. Then he got up again. He thought, ''That is what makes it.'' He came to a spring. Then he drank, pounded his medicine, and drank that. Then he began to be well. He thought, ''Now I have found how to do it.''

f. Then he turned back to the same town. He had made food which he carried in his quiver. When he came, they asked him, ''Where did you come from?'' He said, ''I come from upstream. I am going down.'' ''Did you see any sick men on the way?'' ''Yes, I saw one asleep on the trail. An old man.''[19] ''Yes, that is the one. But you had better eat before you go on.'' ''Yes.'' He had his quiver close to him. As soon as he took food that they gave him, he put it into his quiver and said to it, ''Eat it,'' and the quiver swallowed the baskets of food; and he took out what he had put in it and ate that, and the people did not know. He gave them back their baskets and the remnants of food. Then he said, ''Now I am going.''

g. He went, sat down, took his drill, and made fire. Then he took that

15. At Segwu'.

16. In greeting.

17. The failure to mention it here seems to be a device of the narrator to work up the suspense. So we may conclude from his subsequent deliberate specification of the evil food.

18. Said not in brusqueness, as might seem to us, but in polite farewell.

19. Meaning himself. He has changed his appearance, no doubt.

food out of his quiver, put it in the fire, and said to it, "Be nothing. Then it will be well. If people are sick they will use my medicine. It will not be so bad as it is now. I will put you into the fire." So he burned it.

He went on down. He saw many people. All of them looked well. He told them, "Continue. You will not be sick any longer." Then those upstream, where they had given him bad food, found that he was Wohpekumeu. But he came back to Pulekuk.

Then he told Pulekukwerek, "I have found it. There is only one place where they did that. The wind from there was causing the sickness. But I ruined their food. I put it in the fire. And I did something else. There is a town. It is a good town, the best in the world. I caused it that they will come here every night to make the Jumping Dance. That will make ten dances."[20] "Yes," said Pulekukwerek.

h. Then Wohpekumeu sent Kapuloyo[21] to tell the people of Ko'men to come. Kapuloyo went up. He said, "He sent me. He wants you to come." They said, "We are waiting. Our boats are ready. We are glad." "Well, I am going back now," said Kapuloyo. They said, "No, go with us tonight." Then Kapuloyo agreed. When it was dark they went downstream to the ocean and across. "Now that is what we shall do every night," they said. Now nine dances had come one after the other to where Wohpekumeu was. Then he heard the tenth and knew it was they. He saw no persons, only a fog coming.[22] The fog spread and entered the house. Wohpekumeu said to Pulekukwerek, "That is the sort of people we like to see." He saw Kapuloyo with them. In the morning the man[23] from Ko'men said to Kapuloyo, "Do you not want to stay where I live and own the dance?" Wohpekumeu said, "You had better do that."

i. Now once they came late. In the morning, when they were going to start to go back, Wohpekumeu asked them, "Why were you so late?" They said, "Some young men came to our town. We did not want to bring them along because we knew they were of those who used to make bad food." "Yes. Do not bring them here. Let them go their own way," said Wohpekumeu.

Then the last time[24] they came Wohpekumeu said, "You have been there where they used to be at the bad place?" One of them said, "Yes, I have been

20. Dances are held in parties or sets that try to outdo each other. There were nine such at Pulekuk (five is about as great a number as is reported for any Yurok dance); Ko'men was now contributing the tenth.

21. His son.

22. Other versions of the episode speak of the dancers' feet being visible under the fog.

23. The rich man of the town. Americans usually call him "chief"; the Yurok say merely *pegerk,* "man," and in speaking English occasionally venture on "king."

24. This does not mean that they ceased coming, but "the last time until then" or "finally."

there. There is hardly anyone there. Each takes away his house. I do not know where they have gone, whether to the mountains or elsewhere. There are only fifty[25] houses left.'' Before that there had been a hundred. Wohpekumeu said, ''Do not go to them. Let them go off.''

j. Then he saw Hahkweɫtsin again. He asked him, ''How are they?'' Hahkweɫtsin said, ''I know everything, for I go over the whole world in half a night seeing everything. But all I see is their tracks. Each time I (come I) find one more house gone. They are not to be seen, but I can tell where they have gone.'' Wohpekumeu said, ''That is what I wanted. I made it that way. They fed me with dead persons' bones. Then with dead snake. And then with old women's flesh. That is what they gave me to eat. I burned that food. That is why they have gone away. Let no one go there until they have all left.''

The last time[26] he saw Hahkweɫtsin, that one said, ''There is only one house left. It is the last one.'' Then Wohpekumeu thought, ''I will go to see because it is the last one.'' Then he started.

k. When it was nearly day he came there. He saw one house. He saw only one old man in the house. He looked at him. The old man did not speak. Wohpekumeu said, ''What is the matter, old man?'' There was no answer. ''Something is wrong with you,'' he said again. The old man did not answer at all. Wohpekumeu said, ''I am sorry for you. It looks as if there had been many houses here. I saw many pits outside. What is the matter? I think you are a bad old man.'' Then he said, ''Yes. I want someone to do something for me.'' Wohpekumeu said, ''I will do it. How do you want to be?'' ''I want to be as I was before.'' ''Well, show me.'' Wohpekumeu had a white-oak ball (gall) which he had taken from a tree. He said, ''I am the sort of man who can do anything. Now look. I shall take out my heart and put it back again. You do the same.'' He opened and spread out his chest and (took out and) put back his heart. The old man said, ''I think I shall not be able to endure it.'' ''It will not hurt you,'' said Wohpekumeu. He had the ball hidden in his right hand. He wanted to change that one's heart. ''Let me do it to you,'' he said. Then the old man drew out his heart and Wohpekumeu put in the oak ball. The old man did not know it was done.

l. Wohpekumeu sat down opposite him. He thought, ''I will speak to him.'' He said, ''Old man, how do you feel now?'' ''I feel good. I think that now I shall soon find how to live here.'' ''Yes,'' said Wohpekumeu. He asked him often, ''How do you feel, old man?'' ''I feel good,'' he said. Then the last time he told Wohpekumeu: ''Now do something for me. I shall be a good

25. The average number of houses in a Yurok town was half a dozen. Twelve to fifteen would make a notable settlement, and the greatest did not contain over twenty-five or thirty. Inmates seem to have averaged seven or eight per house. This informant mentions 51 houses in A16x *h* in a dream sequence, and 54 in A18 *c*.

26. As before.

person here. I had many people once; but I had thought that I would go away from here in the morning." "Where were you going to go?" "(With) my people (who) have gone straight below." "You had better stay here. After a time persons will come, and you will have many people again. You are the head man. You can make your own dance here—any kind you want. There are four kinds: the Deerskin Dance, the Jumping Dance, the Brush Dance, and the Adolescence Dance.[27] You can hold any kind you like." "I will have all kinds."[28] "It is well. You shall have any kind you want. I will leave them all to you." Then Wohpekumeu went back downstream.

That town was Segwu'. Now they hold all those dances there. They keep them there as Wohpekumeu told them. But that was a bad place once, Segwu'.[29]

27. A dance for adolescent girls was made by the Karok and Hupa but not by the Yurok.

28. A Brush Dance, whose inception was in private hands, might be made anywhere. The Deerskin and Jumping Dances were associated with world renewal rites normally held only at certain places; very few of the largest towns made both—Yurok Weitspus and Kepel-Wohkero, and Oplego (Takimiłding) in Hupa. Ko'men (Panamenik) did not; it made only the Deerskin Dance at its own New Year. But it and neighboring towns also owned the right to put on performances of the Jumping Dance at Enek (Amaikiaram) in Karok some months after the First Salmon world renewal rite there. This was the farthest upriver the Jumping Dance was made. Segwu' (Katimin)'s New Year or world renewal, like that of Ko'men, could be followed by a Deerskin Dance. The town could be said to possess a Jumping Dance only by the inclusion of Enek, which is a mile and a half away; and the Yurok-Karok attitude is against such effacing of local particularity. Enek, after all, had its own rite with its own name, sweathouse, sacred places, and procedures. The informant is letting his characters exaggerate a bit.

29. [K. has a marginal jotting: "Informant half Karok? from where? Yurok disprise Segwu' dance? not allowed there?"—Ed.]

INFORMANT B

TSKERKR OF ESPEU

Tskerkr, a robust veteran of seventy to seventy-five when I knew him between 1902[1] *and 1907, had been born at Espeu (or Gold Bluff) and was living in the remnant of his wife's native town of Orekw, near American Orick, facing the ocean at the south side of the mouth of Redwood Creek. Their house, in fact, was the only one still inhabited in the settlement. Tskerkr was thus a typical Coast Yurok in origin as well as life. Born before the coming of the white man, he had remained a complete Indian at least in spirit, and still frequented his sweathouse in spite of spending most of his time huddled over an iron stove and sleeping in a bed in an American frame house, whose windows were nailed down and before which a fierce mastiff lay chained.*

Here he lived out his blind and thick-chested age, flanked and partly controlled by a narrow-souled wife and a daughter-in-law who for sheer meanness and gratuitous hostility was one of the most extraordinary persons I have ever dealt with. If he knew a little English, he did not speak it, and our dealings were wholly through Weitpus Frank (my Informant G).

Of Tskerkr's ancestry and youth I know nothing.[2] *His women would have kept him reticent had he possessed any inclination toward personal communicativeness. His body and carriage showed him to be much of a man. His narration was direct and incisive; that his feelings were powerful was evinced by the uncontrollable sobs into which the associations of his stories repeatedly shook him, when his massive frame would struggle and heave for minutes. He would have been an impressive and satisfying friend, divorced from the vindictive women to whom his infirmity subjected him.*

Tskerkr's stories carry as distinctive and high a quality as Lame Billy's; but his manner is antithetical. His plots are not welded but flow in a thin, insistent, tenacious stream. He hammers monotonously but intensely at his theme. There is no interest in character, and but little in the balance or struggle of personalities. His hero's emotions engage him above all else. Around some

1. [K. queries whether this should be 1901.—Ed.]

2. [For the biography of his sister, Ann of Espeu, see that of Informant BB, below. For explanation of Tskerkr's name, see tale F1, n. 19, below.—Ed.]

undying desire for a home, a locality, a lover, a pet, a dance, an escape, the tale is built. The effect therefore is lyrical, whereas Lame Billy's is epic, or in dialogue approaches the dramatic. Sorrow, regret, longing, homesickness suffuse almost all of Tskerkr's tales. He understands pathos and the poignancy of situations; events that do not contribute to these emotions have but little meaning, and he omits or slights them.

It is probably no mere accident that the best narrators in this volume were both disabled men: one a cripple, the other blind. Billy seems to have been a man of action until his infirmity turned his thoughts inward. Tskerkr must have been passionately introverted all his life.

B1. The Dance at Espeu

In spite of the brevity, this is a myth and not an abstract, and typical of the narrator's condensed style. Tskerkr's interest is centered in a single person or family group. Other personages are introduced only as they contribute to the theme of the plot, never to round out a number or to introduce balance or variety. Incidents are used with the same economy and single-mindedness. The teller cares not in the least for character as such, for the quality of the individual personality matching another personality. But he feels intensely the emotions his personages feel as they experience and do what he tells of them. He does not indeed often say in so many words that now they are happy and now dejected. His method is to tell what they did, how they waited, what they said aloud or to themselves. This little story may seem very barren of emotion to a civilized Caucasian who does not know what dances and beautiful wealth and the country across the ocean mean to a Yurok. Yet there is evident feeling in the motivation that leads the brothers to destroy rather than use again for profaner purposes the boat that has brought them through danger to miracle and a glorious achievement. The same high pressure of sentiment runs through the tale, and through all others told by Tskerkr.

There is a touch of local affection in the subject. Espeu took part in the Orekw Jumping Dance, but held none of its own. The narrator brings out how this custom arose not from the insignificance or poverty of his birthplace, but because it was foreordained that dances should eventuate well only in certain places. Orekw was one of these spots, Espeu was not, but its inhabitants had vindicated their ability to hold a splendid dance if the circumstance of fate had allowed.

•

a. There were four woge at Espeu.[1] Then the oldest was ashamed because they did not make the Jumping Dance. So he began to try to make it. He went

1. Espeu (Waterman, Geography, map 29, no. 14), at Lower Gold Bluff, where a creek breaks through the continuous cliff to form a tiny lagoon some four miles north of Orekw, was the principal Yurok settlement on the coast between the mouth of the Klamath and the mouth of Redwood Creek. It was the narrator's birthplace. [See also map 2 in this volume.—Ed.]

back on the hill to make a boat, at Sepola-usahs.[2] When he finished his boat, he took it down to the salt water. Then he started to go across the ocean[3] with his brothers. He arrived at the other side of the ocean at the end of the sky. There he stopped. The sky was coming down and hitting the water and rising again. There were four of them in the boat. Then when they saw the sky rise, they began to paddle. Then the one at the stern was almost caught as the sky descended, and a piece of the end of the boat was cut off.[4]

b. Then they came to land. Where the beach was sandy they landed. Then very many red-crested woodpeckers came to the boat and covered it,[5] and they cut off their heads, and kept only the heads.[6] Now the boat was full of woodpecker heads.

Then they returned. They went through as they had come. They waited while the sky was falling. When it rose they passed through. Then it was just daylight, when they landed at Espeu.[7] Then they broke up the boat, for they did not want to use it any more. They thought that they would have used it only across the ocean.

c. Then they made their woodpecker crest headbands. They had seven to begin the Jumping Dance with.[8] Then they found that it was not well to begin to make the dance at Espeu. They tried it there, but it was not well.[9] So when they danced they brought their things to Orekw to dance with.

2. Boats were usually hollowed out of fallen redwood logs close to the water, but the bluffs at Espeu are timbered only on top, in fact probably, so far as the redwood is concerned, only some distance back from the edge. It is not known where Sepola-usahs is. It may be well up on a ridge, where none but mythical persons ever built canoes. [For details on Yurok boatbuilding, see Kroeber, Handbook, pp. 82-83.—Ed.]

3. *Wohpauk,* west.

4. Characteristic narration. Why mention that they got through when the hearer expects that fact or perhaps knows it already? So only the start and the closeness of their escape are described. The picture of woge straining under the falling edge of the sky is left to the imagination.

5. The birds sat on it so thickly.

6. For the valuable scarlet crests.

7. Spirits of the past and present usually cross the ocean and return in one night.

8. A considerable but not exaggerated number for one household to own. Perhaps the emphasis is on the "begin." All Yurok dances work very gradually up to a climax of display. A dance that commenced with seven of these bands would end in an astounding burst of magnificence. Seven headdresses would contain from 280 to 350 scalps. A Yurok is probably familiar enough with numbers, particularly when they concern valuables, to feel at once that a boatful of birds' heads—if "boatful" is to be taken literally—would be much more than enough for seven headdresses.

9. A frequent Yurok motive: A dance or institution is tried out in a certain place or manner, does not function properly—usually in a way not specified—and is then tried again until it is performed as it is known in custom, when it is perfect. Thus the actual dance of the district was made at Orekw, not at Espeu.

B2. Long One Was His Pet

This story compares with A11 and B6, and also with T5, U2, U3, and CC1. It is fuller than the preceding tale by Tskerkr, makes use of dialogue, and directly names the emotions felt; it clings even more insistently to its undivided and ever-accentuating theme.

•

a. It was at Espeu that he lived who owned the Long One.[1] He hunted constantly at Plek'en.[2] There he found it when it was little. When he saw it, he thought, "It is pretty. I shall try to keep it." He wanted to see how large it would be when grown. Then he brought it to the house and made a box for it and kept it. At first he did not know what it was.

He was always hunting. When he killed deer or elk, he fed a small piece of the meat to his pet. When he came again, he always saw that it had grown. Whenever he went to hunt, he said to those in the house, "Do not go back on the terrace[3] among the baskets." None of them knew that he had it. As it grew, they could hear something moving, but none went up to look at it. Then, when he returned and went indoors he sometimes gave it a whole shoulder of deer. It took only a short time to eat that. Every day he saw it had grown. Then he changed its box because it had grown too long. Those in the house did not like it. They were afraid of it. But he only told them, "Do not go near it."

b. Then he went to Redding Rock[4] for sea lions. He brought home sea lions and hung them up in the house. Then toward morning there was nothing hanging there. It had eaten them all during the night. He always told them, "Do not go near it." That was all he said. He never told them what it would do. Then he would go hunting again. Sometimes he killed three elk. Then when they in the house had eaten once, that would be all they had of those elk because this Long One took all the rest; only the bones it left. Then his younger brothers did not like it. They never told their older brother, but talked among themselves. They did not like it that they could not have meat when he killed elk; but they were afraid to tell him.

Then he did not keep it in a box any longer. It was too large. It had grown very long. At night it went on top of the house and lay there. It watched like a dog. It reached about with its long neck. Sometimes they saw it reach out far and then draw back its head. Then when daylight came it crawled into the house and hid itself.

His two younger brothers liked women and married, but their oldest

1. Knewellok, the horned water-serpent monster.
2. A cliff a mile or two north of Espeu (Waterman, Geography, map 29, no. 10).
3. The ledge or shelf at ground level which surrounds the interior pit of Yurok houses.
4. [Sekwona, a large rock about 5 miles offshore.—Ed.] It is visited for mussels in tale B7.

brother, the one who had this pet, did not want a woman.[5] They hated it because it ate too much, for it ate all the elk and sea lions and they had of them only once. At first he had thought it would be pretty because it was so small. That is why he had kept it. He did not know that it would grow so much.

c. Then his younger brothers told him, "What will you do? You had better let it go." Then their oldest brother said, "No. I want what it wants." "Well, we are afraid of it. When it starts to go out of the house it reaches to the fireplace. Sometimes it looks as if the whole fire were swallowed. That is why we are afraid. So I tell you, can you not make it go?" "No. I cannot consent now. I will tell you what I must do. I must speak to it myself. It will do what I tell it."

Then he went hunting again. He killed ten elk. When he came to the house he went to give it a whole piece (animal?). Then he stood and looked at it eating and spoke to it. He said, "My brothers do not like you because you eat too much." It said, "It is well. Do not say any more. I think tonight will be my last night here." "Tell me where you are going." "No, I shall not tell you." "I should like to know where you are going. I want to keep you because I have had you so long. It is only my brothers who do not like you."

He went hunting again. When he came back he was carrying a deer. He left the deer outside. He did not hear it in the house and thought perhaps it had gone. Then he entered and asked if they had heard it moving. They said, "Yes, we heard it all night." Then he saw it lying still. It said, "I have been waiting for you. Because all who live here do not like me, I will go now." "Tell me where you are going." "No, I shall not tell you." "I wish you to tell me." "No." "If you do not tell me, I shall look for you everywhere." "No, do not do that. I should be angry at you." "If I see you anywhere I shall take you away." "No, do not do that. I speak to you now because tonight I shall go away."

d. Then he went to bring sweathouse wood. He did not hunt that day because it had said that it would go that night. He went north of Espeu to get sweathouse wood. Then he thought that he heard something moving somewhere and said, "I think it has gone." He came to the sweathouse and made the fire.[6] He was in the sweathouse only a short time. Then he went into the house. He looked where it had been and saw that it was gone. Everything it had had was gone. And it had not told him where it went.

Then he went back into the sweathouse. He was angry at his brothers. He stayed in the sweathouse all day.[7] He did not eat. Then those in the house came out to get him. They asked him to eat but he would not go. He was sorry that it had gone, and he remained in the sweathouse.

Then he started to look for it. He looked everywhere; upstream (south) as far as Oketo, and uphill (inland) on Bald Hills; but he did not find it. He

5. His affections were entirely centered on his pet.
6. The action is religious and cannot be interrupted until the fire has burned down.
7. Sulking, according to Yurok practice.

searched far downstream (north), thinking about his brothers, angry at them. He thought, "They were the ones who did not like it. That is why it wanted to leave. Now I think I shall not stay. I will go away too." He was crying constantly, looking for it. He thought, "It was so easy for me to kill deer and elk, for it ate them itself and wanted me to kill them." So he thought and was sorry. Sometimes people saw him. They did not know him, for he did not look like himself. His eyes were swollen because he cried all the time.

e. Then he lay in the sweathouse with his head near the exit. He was sorrowing. Then it came. He saw it outside the sweathouse.[8] It said, "It is too bad that you are sorry for me constantly. You will not find me by seeking. I saw you when you were looking for me, but if you want to see me, do not go far away. I am at Prairie Creek.[9] Come to see me in the morning. Come early. I will leave you ten elk. You will find them in the prairie, so come early."

Then in the morning he started early. He came to Prairie Creek. Then he could hear it. There was much noise. Then he knew: "That is the place where it is." He went on. He knew he had found it at last. Then he came to the prairie. He looked at the ridge on the other side and saw it lying on the tops of the trees. Then he went there under the trees and spoke to it. He said, "Come down, because I have come to see you." The trees there are short, flat on top, because it always lay on them.

f. Next morning he came again. He saw it on the trees again and called to it, "Come down." But it did not come down. He cried constantly for he wanted to see it and talk with it. Now it was the middle of the day. Then he became angry that it did not descend to him. He thought, "I will kill it." He set on fire the trees where it lay. They began to burn. When Long One burned, "pitch" dropped like rain from the tops of the trees. It was its oil. At last it fell down. So he killed it himself, he who owned it.

B3. They Live Beyond the Sky

Most American tribes know a story of forbidden love, but to have one end happily is startling. The narrator thinks so passionately of his beloved Espeu that he cannot bring himself to attribute final misfortune to any of its inhabitants. His tale moves swiftly along the single theme; each repetition, like the refrain of a ballad, drives in the gathering

8. As he looked up through the exit.

9. A stream a dozen miles long, flowing from the north into Redwood Creek at Oräu, 2 1/2 miles above its mouth. The long meadow after which Prairie Creek is named is on the stream's lower course, nearer Espeu than Orekw, and like all such open spaces must have been a productive hunting ground before guns were fired. The Yurok kept such "prairies" cleared by burning, and they may have originated in fires set by man. They and the grassy hillsides tend to return to brush, since the U.S. Forest Service forbids burning over. [K. queried whether the area had been made an elk reserve. In the 1970's Prairie Creek State Park contained California's last remaining herd of Roosevelt elk.—Ed.]

feeling further. It is a poignant story. The brother silent and preparing to leave as his sister comes back to him, his longing to wait as she follows, his unwilling request not to set over the unnamed but so well-known one who travels after him are powerful touches.

•

a. At Espeu lived woge. There he (had) kept that little Long One. There was a woman there and a man. Then she lived there with her own brother. Then it was bad, they said. So they learned that it was bad if a man married his own sister.[1] Then one came from the sky to get that woman. He paid much for her. Then they learned that he was Thunder. Then, when he had bought her, she went with him to his house.

Then her brother constantly went to bring sweathouse wood (ritually). He was sorry because she had left him: so he went to bring sweathouse wood.

b. Then once he saw his sister coming. Then he went into his house and took out his trunk. Now the woman came into the house. She saw her brother putting arrows into his quiver, and a woodpecker-crested ring around his head. That was all he took. But he did not speak to her at all. Then, when he had taken what he wished, he went out.

She had been told by her husband, Thunder, "If you take a lover, it does not matter where you go, I shall destroy you, for I can go everywhere. There is only one place I cannot follow you: I cannot overtake a person beyond the sky." Now when she saw her brother go out, she followed him.

c. Then he came to Osegen.[2] He looked back and saw her coming along the beach. He thought, "I shall not stop. I will go on."

When he came to the mouth of the (Klamath) river, he crossed. He said to the one who ferried him over, "Someone is coming behind. Do not take him[3] across." When he was up on the hill above Rekwoi he saw her coming on the other side of the river.

Then he came to Omen. He said again, "Someone is coming after me, but do not set him across."[4]

1. [K. notes: "might be cousin."—Ed.]

2. North along the coast between Espeu and the mouth of the Klamath at Rekwoi.

3. Yurok is indeterminate as to sex in the nouns and pronouns. English "her" gives a specific meaning that is lacking in the original and greatly weakens the passage. Inclusive Indian words like "house," "make," "see," and the like are the despair of the translator, who in many passages knows that they mean "home," "establish," or "perceive," but hesitates to use these terms because of their connotations which the native equivalents do not carry. Here, on the other hand, is a case of the generic word having far the greater force, and English being deficient in compelling a choice between "him," which is inexact and perhaps misleading without an explanation, and "her," which is so bold as to wipe out most of the emotion contained in the sentence. The geniuses of the languages fail to coincide.

4. Omen is at Wilson Creek, barely large enough to warrant ferrying except in winter. Perhaps it was customary to canoe around the mouth rather than to wade the stream. [K. explains in C1 that a traveler is always ferried across for the asking; he does not take the boat himself because the residents want the boat brought back.—Ed.]

Then he went on. When he came to Smith River[5] he said, "Someone is coming behind. Do not set him across."

He went on and came to Erkier.[6] The one who ferried him asked, "Where are you going?" He said, "I do not know where I am going, but I am going on. Do not set him over who comes behind. Do not speak to him." He did not know where he would go, but he went on because he was afraid of Thunder. Sometimes he was sorry for her who was coming behind him alone, and turned around. Then he thought, "I will keep going."

d. Now he came to the next place,[7] thinking about the woman following him. Then he said, "Someone is coming behind. Do not set him across." "Where are you going?" "I do not know, but I am going on." "Well, you cannot go farther. Look! That is where the sky comes down." Then that man thought, "I think this is where he will overtake me." Then there were many birds about, geese, which flew through to the other side. There was an opening large enough to pass.[8] Then he stayed there a little while watching to see how he might go through. Then the woman came up with him. She said, "Well, I think we shall both be killed. Thunder always says, 'It does not matter where you go, I shall follow there if you go off with a man.'" So she said to her brother. Then they saw the sky rise. Then they leaped to the other side. When they were there, the sky came down again.

Then that night they heard Thunder running,[9] but he was on the other side.[10] Then they saw that the land beyond was level and like fine sand. I have not heard that they came back, that man and his sister. It is where they live now.

B4. Sky Condor

Several things combine to invest this tale with an atmosphere of strangeness. The first is the lack of expressed motivation, which for some time obscures the action. This factor is discussed more fully in the notes. The second is the manner of telling the story almost

5. Probably at Hinei. The territory is Tolowa.

6. Erkier is the farthest named place, though some Yurok namings stop at Nororpek, at the Chetco River in southernmost Oregon. Erkier or Erkyer is also named in B5*d*; it is Robert Spott's Okyer at Rogue River mouth, in Spott and Kroeber, Yurok Narratives, p. 202. [See map 1 in this volume, nos. 1 and 2.—Ed.]

7. Unnamed, because the edge of the sky is in sight. The Yurok world ends almost immediately beyond the land known to them by experience. They evidently liked to think of it as thus shut in. A vague great beyond seems to have given them a sensation of discomfort.

8. The sky hole through which the geese fly is mentioned by Waterman, Geography, p. 190, and shown on his fig. 1, which diagrams the Yurok idea of the world. [This is reproduced here as map 3.—Ed.]

9. Roaring, which is the result of his running.

10. Other side from them, that is, on the side of the world of men. They are now safe in Pulekuk or Tsīktsīkʊ'ɬ, Dentalium Home, or Erkerger, as the sandy, beachlike land of the next sentence indicates.

wholly through pronouns instead of by names. At the risk of fatiguing the reader, this trait has been retained as characteristic, except for a few designations added in parentheses. A third feature, which also produces some effect of remoteness on a civilized person, is the silent and patient persistence with which the robbed Sky Condor follows his treasure and adheres to the spot of its secretion. There is definite pathos evoked here.

•

a. Two young men grew at Espeu. They went out on the ocean. One of them would not look at the other; turned away. "What is the matter?" he asked. "Nothing," said the other. "But it looks as if something were wrong with you." "No," he said. But his lip was hurt, cut upward on the side. Then they returned, when his lip began to hurt. They prepared to make a fire in the sweat-house. Then the younger said to his older brother, "I should like to have you die." "Yes? But I shall not die, for I am not sick." The younger said, "I nevertheless should like to see you die. I will show you how."[1] Then he told him, and the older one did so. Now he lay there. His younger brother did not bury him at once. Then he thought that he would bury him. He brought him southward along the coast. There were two rocks off shore. It was about (on) them that he had been hurt on the lip. He thought, "I will bury him there." He had prepared to bury him there: that is why he brought him there now.

b. In the morning the younger one went to see his brother where he lay buried. He arrived, took out what was above him,[2] looked down, and saw him. Then he himself descended and stayed with him. After a time he looked up. He saw many birds in the sky. He saw them approaching. There was Raven, who said, "I am a man, not a bird." "It is well." He saw many more birds. Some had woodpecker crest on their heads. At last one came who was woodpecker

1. The civilized hearer is almost certain to get off to a wrong understanding here. It is not in the least a case of unnatural emotions, but a rather matter-of-fact situation which the Indian's ellipses endow with a certain mystery for us. The brothers are poor. The younger wants the older to *pretend* to die in order to bury him in a grave which is really an ambush from which they may be able to wrest from the great supernatural Sky Condor his precious woodpecker-crest-covered stick, and so become wealthy. The cut lip seems merely to have furnished the suggestion, or perhaps the excuse, for the pretended sickness and death. The motives and even the facts are never explicitly set forth: one gets them casually, by indirection. I made sure by a question, after the story was finished, that my interpretation was correct, and was rewarded by one or two additional details. My interpreter probably was somewhat surer in his mind than I, but preferred to ask Tskerkr rather than risk his own guess. An older and religious-minded man would very likely have made at once a correct estimation of what was happening in the story, but I imagine that a native child would have been as baffled or misled as a Caucasian ignorant of Yurok civilization.

2. A layer of sticks, lightly covered with earth, that is, the eagle-catching pit familiar to so many American tribes.

crest from his middle up.[3] Another one arrived last and was about to lift the dead man out of the grave. The younger brother said to him, "Slowly! You may take him out, but do not hurry." Then they delayed.

In the morning he started out again early and stayed there with his brother in the ground. Then he saw Raven coming again. He said, "It is well. I am a man and know.[4] When you see that which he has, that which he will use to pry them[5] out, you will see that it is woodpecker crest all over. That is the one to take. But if you see that it is somewhat short, do not take it." "Yes," the younger brother said. Soon he saw him[6] come. But he did not come near. Raven said, "Now he is approaching." Then he looked. He saw what he had. Raven said, "That is the one to take." "Yes, I will take it." It was wholly of woodpecker crest. When he saw him coming with that stick to pry out his eyes, he lay still and that one thought him dead. When he put the stick to his eyes, he pulled it away from him, he that had died. He was not really dead. He had made himself like that in order to take the stick away.[7] Then all the others flew up and went off high; but the one of the stick went only a little distance and stopped.

c. Then he went home with his younger brother, carrying the stick—he that had died. Then they saw that one come after; but they went on. When they had gone farther, he came near. The one that had died was afraid: he thought he would overtake them, and told his younger brother, "Take the stick." He looked back and saw he had come closer. He said, "Hide it when you get home now." They had nearly arrived when he saw him right at his back. Then (the younger brother) went into the sweathouse and hid the stick, lifting a slab at the rear of the floor. The older one went uphill to bring sweathouse wood. When he came back, he saw him[8] sitting outside following his stick. He did not speak to him, but only began to shove the wood into the sweathouse. Then he made a fire. Then he saw him come in. He did not speak, and that one sat in the sweathouse by the fire.

d. He started out for sweathouse wood again. When he returned, he saw him sitting outside again. He thought, "I think that is how I will kill him: I will make a great fire. I think I can kill him that way."[9] When he was about to start

3. We must translate by naming a species, which of course makes for incongruity; but to the Yurok *tsīs* (woodpecker crest) is merely a precious and beautiful substance.

4. What you wish and how to attain it.

5. The eyes of the corpse, as specified below.

6. The owner of the desired stick, Sky Condor. Tskerkr is again following his and the Yurok bent of beginning with pronouns and perhaps naming the person or thing subsequently.

7. This explanation comes so belatedly as to cause the suspicion that the narrator may after all have concealed the situation with intent. Until this moment the older brother has lain as if actually dead, all the talking having been done by the younger.

8. Sky Condor; he still has not been named.

9. One does not of course use open violence on supernaturals.

the fire he saw him come in again. Now he started the fire. Whenever it became hot, that one shook his wings. Then the fire ceased and all the wood was consumed. He thought, "I had better get more wood." So he went up the hill again, and started another fire. Still that one sat in the sweathouse. He did thus the whole of that day, but did not kill him.

In the morning he began again. He did the same all day.It was Sky Condor who had had that stick.[10] As he started the fire again, he came to think, "Well, I will give him back his stick after I have had a fire for ten days, if I do not kill him by then." Only he and Sky Condor were there. The younger brother was not in the sweathouse when he made the fires.

He continued for four days. When he made fire, he saw water running from his mouth. He sat only above where they had hidden it under the floor. He never left that spot. So he had no chance to remove the stick elsewhere. All the time his feathers remained whole. They never burnt, no matter how hot it was.

Now he had had a fire all day for seven days. When the fire in the sweathouse was very great he rolled about from the heat; yet he never killed him. He thought, "If I cannot kill him in ten days, I will let him have his stick." Then his younger brother came in. He said, "Why do you not give it back to him? He will not be killed. It will be best if you give it back." "No, I will not give it back." "Since you cannot kill him, it is best thus, that you give it back to him, so that he will go away." "No," he said. But (Condor) never talked; he only sat there. Then he said no more to his elder brother.

He stayed with him in the sweathouse. He made a fire again. Now it was nine days. He had tried every kind of wood for the fire. He thought, "Perhaps I might kill him in this way," and changed the wood. He began to think, "Perhaps I shall not be able to kill him." That one stayed with him in the sweathouse, day and night. It was nine nights.

When it began to be day, he heard him move a little. He had sat on the spot where his stick was hidden; he had come there at first and remained. Now he heard him shaking his wings. Then he said, 'I think you had better not try to kill me. I see that you want to kill me with fire. I do not like it: I will tell you why. I want my stick. I shall stay here. I shall not go back even if I do not get it. Therefore I tell you this now. It is best if you come with me. Whatever you wish you shall get if you come with me; for you cannot kill me. That is why I tell you this."

e. Then it was the tenth day when he started the fire again. Sky Condor said, "Do not make a large fire. I will tell you why. I think we shall go off tonight. That is why I say to you, 'Do not make a large fire.' " "Where will you take me?" "Anywhere. Wherever you want to go, I will take you there." Then

10. The withholding of the name of course is capable of literary effect; but if such was at all sought, it is largely neutralized by the disconnected way in which it is revealed.

after a time, when he stopped feeding the fire, he said, "I think I shall take you to the sky." The young man said, "No, I do not think I will go to the sky." "Very well. Tell me where you wish to go and I will take you there. Now I shall make you so that you will know how to go." "Very well." Then he drew off his wings and, beginning at the little finger, put feathers[11] on him up along the arm. Now he saw that he had two sets of wings, one over the other. Then he found he would travel in this manner: by having feathers.[12] Then he[13] said, "I think we had better have a new fire this evening because we are going." Then his younger brother came. (The older one) said to him, "I think I am about to go. I am going with him. Do not think that I shall die: I am only going away and shall come back sometime." "Where are you going?" "I do not know. He has not told me yet. But it is well."

Now it was ten days; he said, "We go tonight." "It is well." But he never told where they were to go. Then they (got ready) to start. He wanted to see how he would be able to travel. "I want to try to fly." Then he tried for a little and came back. "I do not think I shall make it." "Wash once more." "Very well." Then he washed himself. "Now start again and see how you go." Then he started from north of Espeu. He came back. "It is right now. I can do it." So they prepared to start. Condor said, "I will tell you what you must do. Get on my back. Hold me, but move your wings too." "I do not want you to leave me somewhere; it was you who wished to take me." "No, I shall not abandon you." "Very well."

f. So they started. They went. The young man held to his back. Condor told him, "Shut your eyes. Do not try to look. We shall fall down if you try to see. Do not open your eyes even if you hear a great wind. I pass through places of violence; but do not be afraid; you cannot be killed." Then he shut his eyes. At times he felt a strong wind. Sometimes he felt nearly turned over, so great was the wind. But he never tried to look, because he had told him beforehand, "Do not think, 'I shall fall off.'" They went on, but Condor never told him where they were going. He merely carried him off like this. They kept on. He stayed right on his back. He did not try to open his eyes. They went on with his eyes shut. After a time he heard a sound, as of something coming down on the ground.[14] Then he felt they were not moving any longer, but he never looked. Then he heard a sound again and felt Condor start. They went on.

They arrived somewhere. "Now get off me," (Condor) said. So he got off and felt he was on the ground. "Open your eyes," he said. He opened his eyes. Then he was in Pulekuk. He saw only little breakers coming in from the ocean;

11. "Wings" and "feathers" seem to be the same in Yurok—at any rate in Yurok English.

12. Condor draws off his own wings and puts them on the man, who sees that Condor has had two sets and that he himself is to learn to fly.

13. Condor.

14. Condor has alighted either to rest or to pass under the pounding sky.

they were not as here, but very small. He looked at the beach and saw that it was altogether (composed) of human beings' money[15] of all sizes. Condor said, "Do not try to touch that money: leave it!"

g. Then the young man looked farther on and saw that at a distance it looked nearly like soil.[16] "That is where we will go and then return." "It is well." So they went to the middle of that land. There he saw *wetskāk*[17] lying about. He said, "Now you can gather: but take only one." It looked as if there were two (dentalia) joined. "That is the one to pick up: take that!" So he took it.

"Now I will take you around the other way to go home." So he carried him that way, beyond the sky, around its edge. "Whenever I know that we have come (abreast of) Espeu I will turn straight off, and you must do the same as before: shut your eyes." So he did. Then he felt in some places that it was rough: the wind blew, and it was very cold. Then they came home.

(Condor) told him: "Now put it in a small storage basket,—put that (piece of *wetskāk*) money in and keep it there. Every five days look inside. You will see that it is full. Then change it: put it in something else." "Very well." "Now do not lose it. Every five days when you change it, you will have your basket full of money. You will have all you want. When you have enough, then do not change the basket any longer. And come up to see me sometime; for I am going to the sky." "No, I shall not know how to go there. I will stay here." "Very well. But do as I tell you about money." "Yes." "Now I am going." Then he went to the sky.

B5. Earthquake and Thunder

[K. has a marginal reference to tale BB3.—Ed.]

•

a. There were many at Espeu. It was when they were about to go away. Then Earthquake thought: "How will it be about the earth?" Thunder came and said, "It will be best if I help you when you shake." Earthquake thought: "Perhaps it will not amount to anything if he helps me." Thunder said, "It will be well, for I shall be running all over the world, and it will be good like that." Earthquake said, "Well, I shall tear up the earth." Thunder said, "That's why I say we will be companions, because I shall go over the whole world and scare them. Wherever I know people live, I shall go, upstream or across the ocean, for

15. [Dentalium shells. K.'s typescript indicates that the notes he had intended for the rest of the story were mislaid. He has a marginal reference to M2.—Ed.]

16. [Cf. the description in B3*d*.—Ed.]

17. [The smallest dentalia. See A15*e*.—Ed.]

I bought something to be seen at night; at Pulekuk[1] I bought it." Earthquake said, "If I see the earth tilt, I can level it again. That is what I shall want to do." Thunder said, "I will begin to run. Listen." So he began to run, and he listened. It seemed as if the sky began to fall, so hard did Thunder run, and leaped on trees and broke them down. Earthquake stayed still to listen to his running. Then he said to him, "Now you listen: I shall begin to run." He started. He shook the ground. He tore it and broke it to pieces, because he did not wish us[2] to be about. All the trees shook;[3] some fell. Earthquake lived at Espeu, at the south of the town: that was his house.[4]

b. Then he started to go to Osegen along the beach.[5] He began to run and all the trees fell because he tore up the ground. Thunder was almost frightened. Earthquake was about to start from Osegen. Then Thunder came. Earthquake said, "I shall go around this world. You do the same in the sky. I shall begin now." Thunder said, "Yes."

They came to Rekwoi and could not cross. There was no boat. Then he began to shake the earth, thinking it would move together from the two sides of the (Klamath) river and he could cross. Then he was unable. Then at night Thunder began to run in the sky. Earthquake saw him. It was like day because of the flashes. Then he thought: "Well, I shall have a good companion." Sometimes when he shook, the earth nearly met, but the river washed it out again. Now when it was night he shook again, and Thunder was running too. Thēn he saw that the earth came together. So he crossed, and arrived at Rekwoi, and stayed there a little. Then he heard Thunder (come) running. Thunder said; "You thought you would not have a good companion. Now when you shake the earth, I too begin to run. That is how I will help you when we are companions. We can go about the world." Now it was night again at Rekwoi. Then they saw many birds, and thought, "That is good."[6]

c. They started for Omen.[7] They went inland from the beach, to where it

1. The downstream or northern end of the world. The narrator did not know from whom Thunder bought the lightning. He called Thunder "Słohkoł" in place of the River Yurok "Łohkoł."

2. The human race. This sentiment rather conflicts with his later promise to preserve the earth. Perhaps he was angry at the impending depärture of the woge. They are always represented as regretful but yielding to an irresistible and unexplained fate.

3. "As you see someone shaking an apple tree."

4. At Yegwoł-u-kwäp (Waterman, Geography, map 29, no. 19), at the south end of Espeu lagoon. The River Yurok usually put Earthquake's house at Kenek and sometimes give him another house at Sumig, or Patrick's Point, on the cost. [K. queries "= Kewet?"—Ed.]

5. Between Espeu and Rekwoi.

6. The reference of this passage is obscure.

7. Two or three hamlets about the mouth of Wilson Creek, half a dozen miles north of Rekwoi. [See map 6 in this volume.—Ed.]

looks level, as if there had been a stream:[8] that is because Earthquake traveled there. They came to Omen. Then Thunder began to run. One could hear him all about, sometimes not loudly, because he seemed far off. Then Earthquake thought: "Well, I shall take him to be my companion." He said, "I will take care of these human beings. Whenever I see the earth turn up on one side, I will make it level again."

Then he went on from Omen. Before he started he shook the ground. Wherever they stayed he did that before he started. Sometimes he shook it hard. Then he came to Kohpei.[9] Then he looked back and saw the earth all torn behind, and the trees sunk into the ground: sometimes one could see their tops, nothing more. Now Thunder too ran, whenever Earthquake ran. So he thought again: "He will be a good companion: I will accept him." Then he saw two men. They said, "I heard you were coming. So I thought I would go with you. I wanted to see you." "Yes, I am coming," Earthquake said. "Well, I heard that you are the one who levels the earth," they said. "Yes," he told them.

At night they started from Kohpei and came to Hinei.[10] Whenever they started, Earthquake ran. The two woge went with them. They said, "Well, it will be right when you see the earth tilt, for you level it, because if it tilts upright all human beings will be killed. So when you see it beginning to lie sloping, make it level. And Thunder will do the same in the sky; so you will have a good companion."

They started from Hinei; always they traveled at night. The two went with them. They came to Nororpek.[11] They saw a great rock. The two said: "Let me see you shake that rock." "Very well," he said. Then he began to shake. Thunder too was running. Then they saw that great rock fall. "Well, you are strong," they said to him. "When you see the earth tilt, you will be able to level it; now I believe it, because I have seen this rock fall."

d. Then Earthquake came to Erkier, the last town of human beings.[12] He was traveling at night; only once he had traveled by day. Then he tried to

8. Where the highway from Klamath Bridge to Crescent City goes up Hunter Creek, a western affluent [of the Klamath] and through a sort of pass which may be an old channel of the Klamath. The Yurok still regard Omen weroi, Wilson Creek, as the original mouth of the Klamath, which was later put where it is now, at Rekwoi; cf. X14.

9. Kohpei is the Tolowa town at Crescent City. [For this and the following place names, see map 1 in this volume.—Ed.]

10. Hinei, near the mouth of Smith River, is the most important Tolowa town.

11. Nororpek (or Norerpek) is at the mouth of the Chetco River in Oregon. The people here were Athabascans, but are usually reckoned with the Chasta Costa instead of the Tolowa. The Yurok seem to have no separate word for them.

12. That is, the last known to the Yurok. Erkier (or Erkyer) is named in B3, and is called Okyer in Spott and Kroeber, Yurok Narratives, p. 202. It lies at the mouth of the Rogue River. Beyond is Pulekuk and the sky.

shake the earth again. He felt it was as if it did not move. He shook harder. Then he felt it move a little. He hardly heard Thunder. Then he wished to know, because he scarcely had heard Thunder run. He said, "What is wrong?" Thunder said: "This is as far as I come. I cannot go beyond, because the sky descends."[13] He could not pass. But Earthquake looked at it. Thunder saw him nearly penetrate, tearing the earth. He said: "You will penetrate if you wish; but I, I cannot." Earthquake said: "Well, I shall see you again." Thunder said, "You will see me far off to *hierkik.*[14]

"Very well," Earthquake said to him.

I cannot name the place because I do not know:[15] but Earthquake passed through to it. Then he saw ocean. He thought: "That is a good place." The two told him: "No. You will see pretty places where we are going. This is not pretty." Now Earthquake was listening for Thunder but heard nothing. He went a little way, listened again, and heard nothing. He began to shake the ground. Then it was as if he nearly heard Thunder. He shook harder, and really heard him. He thought: "It is well. I have my companion with me. I shall try to go around the world."

e. Then he started: but the two continued to go with him.[16] Then Thunder met them. He said: "I wanted to see you again before you went on, because I wanted to know if you would do that: level the earth if you see it slope; for if it tilts, it will kill all persons. But if you care for it, it will lie level. And I will do the same in the sky. That is why I came to see you, because perhaps I shall not see you again for some time. So we will talk here to agree what we will do." Earthquake said: "Let it be so."

Now that is thc reason Earthquake goes to different places because in the beginning he did that, and did not encompass the world in one day. It is thus with him now: he cannot go entirely around in a day, so he goes part way, and as it were spends the night. In some places he shakes the earth hard, in some he shakes it a little. For he did that in the beginning and does it now.[17]

13. *Wes'ona oliken.*

14. Northeast from where the narrator is speaking. At Weitspus, where the river flows west, it denotes the north. The generic meaning seems to be: at right angles away from the river or coast, on the righthand side as one looks downstream.

15. Perhaps the passage should read: Thunder could not name the place where he would meet Earthquake because he did not know the country beyond.

16. Such nameless, unmotivated, and inactive companions, who . . . merely Yurok mythology. [Words missing here in manuscript. K. has a marginal notation: "A w'd = W & Pul."—Ed.]

17. This paragraph is characteristic of Yurok reasoning when tying up past events with the present condition of the natural world. Yurok logic seems less involved to us when they are "explaining" their institutions.

B6. Deer Was His Pet at Sigonoi

This tale, while not specially notable, is in the informant's own manner. A passionate, unceasing longing is again the motivating impulse that leads to the piling on of incident after incident, without anything sensational occurring. Even the ascent to the sky is treated as something comparatively commonplace alongside the hero's mastering obsession. Of peril or true adventure there is none.

•

a. At Sigonoi above Freshwater Lagoon[1] lived woge. There they had their old town and made their spring a little distance up the hill. All birds were afraid to go by there. Whenever they approached on the beach the woge drove them away. So no kind ever went past the house.[2] These woge did not go off into the hills. All the others went away, but these stayed on because they liked their town so much. So they remained the last ones, but were never ready to go.

They were large men. They wore elk skins and these were like small blankets, so big were the men. They were called Nerernits o-po'pelin.[3] They killed all sorts of game where they lived: sea lion, deer, and elk. That was what they lived on, their meat. But now they were almost ready to go off because all the others had gone. This was the only place where (woge) still lived, the last place.

b. Then one morning they thought they would go out to Redding Rock.[4] So they went. When they had gone halfway, a wind began to come up. Some of them in the boat wished to go back, but the one of them who had wanted to go wished to keep on.[5] Then they consented. When they had gone a little farther, they saw a great wind blowing on the other side of the rock. So they all sat down in their boat and waited, thinking perhaps the wind would die down.

1. No Yurok settlement on Freshwater Lagoon is known. Sigonoi is the point that separates Freshwater and Redwood Creek lagoons. Near the foot of its southern slope I have found midden and bones. Waterman, Geography, map 31, no. 1, describes the north end of Freshwater Lagoon as "steep hillside with depressions," and gives it the name Nererts-o-popeł, about which see n. 3 below. [This map is reproduced here as map 7.—Ed.]

2. "Houses," the interpreter usually said, but seven people, all related, would normally occupy only one house. If one of the brothers, on marrying, built himself a separate house, it would usually stand very close by and have the name of the ancestral house site. The reference to the birds not passing is obscure: the narrator knew but was content to be elliptical.

3. Nerernits o-po'pelin, which I would translate as "large Coast Yurok (Nererner)," corresponds to Waterman, p. 264, no. 1, which he hesitantly translates as "giants where they lived" or "blankets where big."

4. To get mussels or hunt sea lions. Redding Rock is the site of the next tale.

5. The Yurok canoe is basically a river craft and not very seaworthy. The ocean, being entirely open, can blow up very rough along this coast.

But it did not die down. The boat began to run downstream.[6] They did not paddle: it went before the wind and they only steered it straight. Then the oldest one in the boat cried. He did not know where they were going: that is why he cried. But the boat kept on. They all talked; they continued to talk. Then the oldest said, "Perhaps it is in this way that we shall go off, for anyway we were the last to remain. The others have gone, all of them. Perhaps it is for this very thing that we stayed till the last. But nevertheless it cannot be helped," . . . [7] for the wind was blowing very hard and the waves coming as great as breakers, and they were crying in the boat because they thought they would drown. Then the oldest said, "Do not cry. I think it will be well. I think it is because we stayed in our place so long that the wind is blowing us. This great wind will take us somewhere. But my pet that I have, that is all I cry for," he said. For he had left it at the house. Then their boat ran to Pulekuk.[8] There they landed. That is where they came to because of the wind carrying them.

c. Now the oldest one cried constantly for that which he had left, he was so sorry for it. One day he spoke to his brothers: "I am going back because I must see my pet. If I reach our town, I will bring everything here when I return. I will take the women and the houses[9] and the sweathouse. But I shall not return at once." They asked him, "How shall you go?" "I shall walk," he said. They had thought he would go back by boat.

Then he started overland.[10] He thought constantly of his pet; sometimes he began to cry. He did not think of the women whom they had left in the houses: it was only his pet that he thought of.[11] For if there was anything he wanted, his pet brought it to him; anything he wanted to eat it got. Therefore he thought much of it.

d. He kept going on.[12] He came near a place where there was a large stream.[13] Then he heard shouting, but would not look. They continued to shout to him. He thought, "I shall not go where they call me because perhaps they will not let me go on.[14] Those shouting were woge. He knew when they shouted that it was they. He thought, "I will not go to them because they will try to stop me and I want to get my pet." He came to the stream and thought,

6. North.

7. [K. has a marginal notation indicating an omission in the typescript here.—Ed.]

8. The downstream or northern end of the world. It is sometimes specified as being beyond the sky, but as often as not narrators forget about the passage through.

9. See n. 2.

10. They went by boat; he returns by following the coast south.

11. The affection or craving is obsessive and excludes love of women and children.

12. Southward.

13. This might be Rogue, Chetco, or Smith River, but the narrator did not name it.

14. Not that they would detain him forcibly, but he would be compelled to resist their urging to stay.

"I do not know how I shall cross." Then he put his foot on the water and his foot remained on top. Then he made another step and again his foot was on top of the water. So he crossed that river and went on. He never stopped crying. He came to the top of the hill at Rekwoi and saw the (Klamath) river. He thought, "Here is another river!" Then he heard shouting. He thought, "I will not go there, for I want to go home. All my brothers are well. They are satisfied because they have a place to live, the place where I left them."[15] Then he crossed the river at Rekwoi in the same way.

e. He came abreast of Tskermerwer.[16] When he was on the sloping shore opposite,[17] he saw someone on the rock. Then someone shouted. He looked but saw no one. It shouted again. Then again he saw somebody on the rock. He thought, "I want to see him." He ran down to the beach. Looking out at the rock he thought, "I cannot reach it: the breakers are coming in. Nevertheless I will try." He made a step on the water. Then he walked on it. As soon as he had crossed the breakers, he began to run. He ran just as he would on land. When he reached the rock he saw that it was as if there were steps on it, good broad steps. He climbed them. When he came on top he saw a person by a fire. The top of the rock was hollow: that is where he had his fire. That one there asked him, "Where are you from?" "I do not know where I come from. Our boat ran far away. We landed there. I left all my brothers where we landed, but I came back by land. A strong wind blew us there." "I saw it. The pet, the one you have, came. It came along the shore but not out to here. Now the woge always go across southwestward.[18] Look at this rock. It is yellowish. That is where they smoke. When they have smoked, they knock out their pipes on it. That is why it has become yellowish. And that is why I stay here. I take care of the place where they smoke. No matter where they come from or where they are going, they come here. They have to smoke here before they go by."

f. Then he went back to the land from the rock. Then he (went on and) saw a person. That one said, "I know you are going to your own town. You ought to go off somewhere like us. We too lived in our town but we left it to go away." He said, "No, I too shall go somewhere. I shall not stay in my town. But I want to see the women and my pet. My brothers have a place to live." Then the one there said, "It is well. Go on." That place was Meleyu.[19]

15. Whereas I am not satisfied and must push on.

16. A large rock off the bluff near Wełkwäu, rising out of the sand beach or ocean according to tide and shifting of the bar. Waterman, map 5, no. 63, calls it Terkermerwer. [This map is reproduced here as map 6.—Ed.]

17. *Hierkik*, on the land side of, inland from, on the mainland abreast the rock.

18. *Wohpauk*. They go nightly to dance.

19. Waterman, map 9, nos. 9 and 10, gives Meleg, a seastack and creek, 2 1/2 to 3 miles south of Terkermerwer. [For this and the following place name, K. has a notation to check his notebooks.—Ed.]

Then he came to Na'niig.[20] There again he saw a person who spoke the same. He asked, "Are you going off or shall you stay at your place?" Again he said, "I shall go away; but I want to see the women." "Well, good. Then go." Then he started from Na'niig.

He came to Womets.[21] There he saw a person who asked, "Where are you going?" "I am going back to my place." "I do not think it is right that you stay about here. You should go off somewhere to a hill to live." "I shall go, but I want to return first. After that I will go away somewhere." "Look at this sweathouse before you go." That one blew out[22] and then he saw the sweathouse. It was beautiful. On both sides of the door it had woodpecker crests. A pole stood[23] before the door like a dead tree. He saw that that tree was covered with woodpecker (crests),[24] large ones and small ones. Then he thought, "This is the first time I have seen that."

Then he was anxious to go on to reach his town. So he started again and come to . . . .[25] When he was near the beach he saw his own place. Then he felt sorry as he went along the beach.

g. Then he came to his town (Sigonoi). He saw no one about. He stood outside for a little time before he went in. The door was shut. He opened it to go inside. Then he saw that his wife had cut her hair because she thought he had died. He saw his mother sitting there. He called her, "Mother." The old woman began to cry; she thought someone was mocking her. He said, "Everything is well. I have come back."

Then he asked for his pet. The old woman said, "It is gone." He went up to where he used to keep it. Then he saw indeed that it was gone. Then he looked where he had had his spring and saw that that was gone too. The old woman told him, "The pet took good care of me. Some days there were five deer swimming in the lagoon; sometimes ten.[26] Look at this hill.[27] It made

20. Waterman, map 9, no. 14, Nōmig, a promontory, 1/2 mile south of last.

21. Womets is Waterman's Womots (map 9, no. 17), an open hillside something over 1 mile south of last and 2 miles north of Osegen town.

22. Like blowing away fog or smoke, or like an offering of tobacco crumbs.

23. "Dry wood was growing." Cf. the posts planted before the house of Kewet omewa in A12*a*.

24. Following the precedent of A12, the post was, I suspect, covered not with crests but with living pileated woodpeckers.

25. "North of the mouth of Redwood Creek." [For the omitted name, K. has a reference to his notebooks.—Ed.]

26. Which could be killed without difficulty from a boat.

27. The hill separating Freshwater Lagoon from the lagoon at the mouth of Redwood Creek. The hill is a spur whose end has been cut off square by the surf, and is perhaps a quarter-mile wide at its base. (See Waterman, map 30, but his contours for the hill are too low by nearly half.) From 1923 to 1928 I had a cabin on the flat acre or so on top, right back of the bluff. The State Highway Commission then lowered the surface some 8 feet for a turnabout and viewpoint.

that. It talked before it went away. It said, 'Now I will make this hill because that is the way I shall come when I want to come here. Whoever lives in this place will not lack meat. I shall watch. I shall let him get meat easily whenever he wants it!' Now look to the other end of the lagoon. There is another hill there. It made that too."

h. Then the man said, "Now you women must go where my brothers went. Go in advance of me. But I, I must find my pet before I leave. I want to speak to it. I want to tell it to take care of whoever lives about here, and let them have game to hunt." The old woman said, "Well, it was speaking here." "When was it here last?" "Two days ago it came. It was going to come again tonight. But now it will not come, I think. It is angry at you because you left, because it thought you had gone away for always." He said, "No, it was because a strong wind came and took us." She told him, "I know where it lives now, but I shall not tell you." "I shall find it for myself. I know all the places about. I shall go everywhere to find it. I shall stay until I do find it." His mother said, "It said that it knew that you would come. It thought you would come here and take away everything, the houses and the sweathouses and the spring. That was why it was angry at you. That is why I do not think that you will see it. But if you wish to see it you may try." He said, "I must see it before I go." Then the old woman told him where to go; and he went. He cried constantly because he wanted to see it.

i. Then he came to the place that his mother had told him of. When he was there he saw that the ground was swept off clean like a floor. He sat down there and cried. He had sat only a short time when he saw a ladder descend from the sky. Then he ran up the ladder. When he had climbed up and got off (in the sky), the ladder came up also. Then he asked him who took it there.[28] "Where shall I go?" That one said, "You will see what you want there." "Yes? That is what I wish." "They dance there as in the Jumping Dance. When the dance has come three times, then, the fourth time, you will see the one you want to see. It comes to help the dance. That dance is made by bull elks, and by this one in the sky which is covered with woodpecker crest; and fishers[29] sit on the horns of the elks. They will smell you because you come from below and it is different in the sky; but that will not matter." Thus he told him. "Now that dance is coming." Then he saw it come. He watched. He saw the one he wanted to see, helping the dance. All the elk danced. Then his pet said, "I smell a person." So the man said, "I think you smell me." But he

28. Unclear. The one who took the pet to the sky? The one who took him up by the ladder? [Again, K. has a marginal notation to check his notebooks.—Ed.]

29. [Fishers (*Martes pennanti*) are carnivorous animals related to the weasel.—Ed.]

stayed there nevertheless. Whenever they lowered their horns and bowed their heads in the dance, then he could see the one he wanted to see. As they put their heads down, he saw the fishers climbing about on their horns. Then he wanted somehow to speak to his pet. It was a deer, a buck he had caught when it was young. Only from its neck up it was different: its head was covered with woodpecker crest. Now he thought how he should speak to it. Then he came close and put his hand on it. The pet said, "I think you want to speak to me." "Yes." "I saw you return. Nevertheless, I wish you would go. You are the only one still staying. Everyone else has gone." "I do not want to tell you, 'Come with me,' but I should like to see you come with me to the old place." "Yes, I should like to speak with you again before you go away. I will come; but I shall not come with you now. Go, and I will come tomorrow." Then the man went back; he went back that day. The ladder went with him. He let the ladder down and so he returned.

j. When he came back to his house he saw his old mother. "Did you see it which you wanted to see?" she asked. "Yes, it is coming tomorrow. It said, 'I shall come down to see you before you go. Whoever lives in this place will not lack for meat, even though you no longer live there.[30] Whoever lives there, I will do that for them.'"

Then the deer came from the sky. It said, "Come, sit down close to me, because I have come only for a little while. I am going back again. I want you to do as thc others have done, and go away from here." "That is what I must do; but I wanted to tell you, whoever lives here, do not let him lack meat." "I will do that. Now where are you going?" "I am going to Pulekuk." "I shall be here always. Whoever lives here will not lack meat. I shall look out for him, I myself. Sometimes I will bring him two (deer). I will make it be so." "It is good. Now I am starting to go." "I will go too. Do not leave anything: take away everything you have. Take the water you used. Take that too." Then the man went back to Pulekuk.[31]

The brothers were four. They had all gone in the boat. Two of them were married. They had a mother, but the old man, their father, had died before. So there were three women that went to Pulekuk, and four men. That is all the people there were in the place. Some of the spring the oldest brother took with him, but some of it he left.

30. Narrator's inaccuracy. The pet has said nothing of the kind. The hero himself has had the matter on his mind, but only broaches it to the pet the next day.

31. The story ends here. The paragraph that follows is elucidation in answer to a question from me.

B7. Married at Kweihtser

a. There was a young man at . . .,[1] who went after sweathouse wood constantly. Redding Rock[2] came from up the river:[3] that is where it is from. Now they went to get mussels[4] at that rock; there were five in the boat. When they came to the rock, three of them climbed out on it, and two stayed in the boat. When they were ready to go back, two of them looked around[5] for the other one who had landed (with them). After a time they saw him and shouted, "We must start for home." "No," he said. They entered the boat and shouted again, thinking he would come, but he did not come. Then they went back onto the rock after him. But they found him standing with his feet grown fast to the rock so he could not be moved; and his hands were grown fast too. Then the four of them started to return without him.

Now he began to shout. Then they stopped and went back and one of them leaped out on the rock and went to him. Then he saw that he had turned into rock further up (his legs), and that his hands were stone to the wrists. So they were about to leave him again, and started off in their boat, and had gone farther off, when he shouted again and they saw him moving about on the rock and calling, "Come back. I want to go in the boat." So they returned. Then they found him fast to the rock again and turned to stone still farther. Again they went off and saw him moving about and he shouted, and again they returned because he called to them that he wanted to go with them; but when they came to the rock he was fast again and now was stone nearly all through.

As they went off they heard him shouting once more, and again it looked as if he were free, but when they came there, they found him fast again. Then they threw onto the rock for him what they had in the boat,[6] and their sealion harpoon, and made him a fire,[7] and left him, and returned to land without their mussels. They they landed downstream[8] of the mouth of Redwood Creek.

1. [Omission in typescript. K. has a marginal notation referring to his original notebooks.—Ed.]

2. Sekwona, or Sekwoneu, 94 feet high, about 5 miles offshore. See A7*n* and B2*b*.

3. It was a woman's pestle thrown from Orleans Summit, in Karok territory, as usually told; cf. A7*l*. This piece of information, however, is a digression of a sort that Tskerkr rarely allows himself.

4. Mussels are larger at this outlying islet than alongshore.

5. Although the rock is conical, its surface no doubt has irregularities.

6. The mussels they had taken, which would serve him as food.

7. They may have carried a wrapped-up fire drill, or some firebrands on a bed of earth (this might be hard to protect from spray, except that trips were usually made early in the day before the wind sprang up). The ocean is cold even in summer, and paddlers could not conveniently wear deerskin blankets.

8. North.

b. Then the old woman at . . .,[9] whose son it was they had left on the rock, cried for him. He had had twelve baskets of tobacco. So she began to put them into the fire (daily). She had put in eight.

c. Now it was nine days: then he thought he heard a boat coming. Now as he lived on the rock, he had made living places for himself:[10] three holes. When the wind came from downstream he went into the hole on the other side, but when the wind was from upstream he went to the opposite side. So he slept on that rock. Now it was nine days and he heard something. Then he saw something hugging the rock. It is a very great rock, but that thing wholly embraced it. Then he took his flint knife and cut off its fingers[11] and heard them fall into the water. Perermer[12] was this one that had clasped the rock.

d. The next day, when it was ten days, he heard someone saying, "Paddle." Soon he heard them break off mussels. He looked out over and saw a man prying mussels with a long stick.[13] That one said to him, "Come with us." But he thought, "I have nothing to wear." Then he who had told him to come threw him a blanket to wear. When he jumped into the boat from the rock, the water was rough. They told him, "Shut your eyes! Do not look!" But he peeped and saw that the boat was covered with woodpecker crests on its front crossbar.[14] They kept telling him, "Keep your eyes closed! Do not look! Even if you feel the boat moving fast, do not try to see. Sometimes you will feel water entering the boat, but do not look." He did not know where they were going. After a time he felt water splash in; he felt the boat running fast.

e. When they landed, they said, "Well, brother-in-law, get out. Now you may look about." Then he saw he had come home. Then he went up to the house to see his mother, and called her, and the old woman began to cry, for she thought she had lost him and that he would never come back.

Then he went to Kweihtser[15] on Bald Hills.[16] There he was married. Those who lived there were the ones who had wanted him to stay on the rock because they knew that thus they would get him for themselves.[17]

f. Now when he left to go on Bald Hills, he told his mother that he would

9. [Omission in typescript.—Ed.]

10. Apparently he petrified and lost his motion only when they returned to rescue him.

11. Fingers, hands, claws?

12. This monster Perermer is not known from other sources.

13. This would be safer than bringing the boat alongside and touching the rock in the open sea, even on its lee side.

14. *Umeihtsep*: the withe under which the rope for towing, etc., passes; it is called the necklace. [K. has a notation querying this definition.—Ed.]

15. I have no further reference to this Chilula settlement. Kweihtser is its Yurok name.

16. Tsulu, whence Tsulu-la, and our "Chilula," the Athabascans of Bald Hills ridge and middle Redwood Creek.

17. [Meaning those who wished him fastened to the rock and who later recued him.—Ed.]

come back. So he did come back for her. Then in the morning (the people there) could no longer see one sweathouse, and one house was gone. He had taken his sweathouse and his house and his mother to Bald Hills.

B8. A Flood

[In a marginal jotting K. notes that this narrative is given in Kroeber and Gifford, World Renewal. The version there (pp. 102-103), by the same informant, differs in wording but contains the same essential elements.—Ed.]

•

a. There used to be a settlement at Siwitsu[1] just north of Orekw. Then it happened that there almost came to be no people (left in the world) on account of (what happened at) this settlement. For an old man and his brother went into the sweathouse to sleep. But a man was outside, and when they slept, he went in and tied their hair together. Then he went out and shouted, "They have come! Somebody will be killed! They are going to fight!"

b. Then the ocean began to turn rough (from the anger of the old men).[2] A breaker came over the settlement (of Siwitsu), washed the whole of it away, and drowned everyone. Then all the people of Orekw ran off to the top of the hill, wearing their woodpecker-crest headbands:[3] they were afraid.

c. Then he at Orekw who knew the formula for the sacred sweathouse there[4] ran to Oketo,[5] for now the water was already all around Orekw. He

1. Siwitsu (or Siwetsu) (Waterman, Geography, map 30, *x*, Sigwetsu, place on flat) is on the sandbar that separates the sea from Redwood Creek lagoon. It is perhaps 300 yards north of Orekw. About 1901-1906, Tskerkr, the narrator, had his sweathouse a little beyond there, guiding himself to it by a furrow that had been plowed from door to door. The choice of site was probably dictated by proximity to clear bathing water in the lagoon; a blind old man could hardly venture into the surf. There could not well have been a town on so exposed and low a spot. Every few winters a storm is likely to wash over it. It is probably a house site, and is ordinarily counted as an outlying part of Orekw. However, Tskerkr kept speaking of it as a town. It is mentioned again in DD8. [Waterman, p. 262, says that at least two houses and one sweathouse once stood on the site.—Ed.]

2. This is ellipsis in vigor: given the setting, the listener is left to imagine both the event and its consequence. When the old men started up from the outcry and bumped each other's heads, they probably considered themselves already attacked, and struggled fiercely in supposed self-preservation. As they could not pursue him who had victimized them, they caused the ocean to rise in flood and overwhelm the world.

3. A great ceremony—a Jumping or Deerskin dance—may be held outside its normal time and place in order to stave off an impending catastrophe: pestilence, flood, or earthquake. Even as they flee, the Orekw people have danced with the Jumping Dance accouterments.

4. The formula for the Orekw Jumping Dance, spoken in this sweathouse.

5. Oketo [or Opyuweg] is the chief town on Big Lagoon, about 10 miles to the south, where

looked into the sweathouse at Oketo. There was the one who knew that formula.[6] He spoke to him, but that one did not answer. Four times he spoke to him. Then he said, "Were they drowned?"[7] "Yes, I saw them drown," said he of Orekw, "but I am afraid the water will cover the whole land."

d. And now the breakers were already dashing against one side of that sweathouse (at Oketo). Then that one began to speak his formula[8] in that sweathouse. He had to do it hastily; therefore he used old boards to make the fire.[9] Then the ocean went down.

B9. Married Across the Ocean

This is one of the most fully worked out tales of Tskerkr, and of the type characteristic of him, both in form and content. The omissions make the motivation difficult for any but a Yurok to understand, and yet a tenacious adherence to a narrow line of action dictated by a single purpose stands out visibly. A similarity to B3 is evident.

[K. made a number of marginal jottings, indicating that he intended to expand this headnote, drawing parallels to both A1 and B3: "(1) Hero wavers? she wavers? (2) Incest motive, but condensed. (3) Loon woman pursuit, log? Repeat log incident."—Ed.]

•

a. In Tsuräu[1] he was a young man. Constantly he went to bring sweathouse firewood. And his sister[2] always made baskets, sitting on the plank over the door of the sweathouse.[3] When he began to make his sweathouse fire, only then she worked at her basket. Then she always left her materials, and the young man saw them lying when he came out. Now he constantly went for sweathouse firewood. The woman did not know where he got it; sometimes

another Jumping Dance is made. [See map 7 in this volume.—Ed.] Evidently the Orekw formulist felt that his ritual was insufficient to stay the flood.

6. For the Oketo dance.

7. Those of Siwitsu who were responsible for the flood.

8. "Make the medicine," that is, start a fire, speak the formula, and offer incense.

9. Most unritualistic, but sanctioned by the emergency. He should have gone up a hill, climbed to the top of a fir, and hacked off branches. To use old house lumber is enough of a profanation to indicate the acuteness of the crisis. [K. has a marginal reference to *sahsi'p*, Ceanothus. For this plant, see B13, n. 2.—Ed.]

---

1. Or Tsuräi (Trinidad), the native town. [See DD10, below, for another setting.—Ed.]

2. A kinswoman, not a blood sister.

3. *Wilepo*.

she looked, but did not see. Then at last she found he went to Tewoleu.[4] That is where he got his sweathouse wood. So she made baskets, and he did nothing but go for sweathouse wood, and became very thin, because he fasted[5] and drank no water. Then the woman wondered, because he did that constantly. She said; "Why do you always get sweathouse wood?"

"I like to do it, nevertheless," he said. "Yes," she said, thinking he might say that he went with such and such a purpose in mind; but he did not tell her. Now he continued doing so while he was becoming a fully grown man,[6] and she a woman. Then she thought; "Let me to get firewood." Now the young man went to one place only, the summit of Tewoleu. There he looked at the hole[7] and always cried when he saw it. He only looked about on the rock, and thought how beautiful it was, and then cried more.[8]

b. Now the woman thought; "I will do the same." So she did the same: when she went to bring firewood, she cried on the peak of Tewoleu. She only went to get firewood, only that, and the young man stayed in the sweathouse. So she now did as he did, but formerly she had not gone to get wood.[9]

c. Now the young man was lying inside the sweathouse. Then he heard a boat land. "Where do they come from?" he thought. Then someone[10] said, "They have come to buy the woman who constantly goes out for firewood." But he did not know from where they had come. Now he who had come by boat bought the woman. The young man accepted the money for her. But before he took the wealth, he did not ask where he had come from. He who

4. Tewoleu is Trinidad Head, the rounded promontory close to Tsuräu. It is a landmark for long distances on shore and at sea. In A1*a*, it is called Tsurewa, which is also what Waterman, Geography, map 33, no. 11, calls it.

5. Ate only thin acorn gruel.

6. He was outgrowing being *tsines,* a youth.

7. Cf. A1*b*.

8. The crying while gathering sweathouse wood was for good fortune, presumably wealth, as any Yurok might do at an elevated spot that tradition told him was favorable. The train of feeling connected with the beauty of the place seems to be: the spot is pretty; he who once lived here must have been fond of it; if I am sorry for him at no longer living here, he will be sorry for me and will help me; if I cry, he will know I am sorry for him. The motive of the frequenter is therefore a practical one. He is thinking of dentalia, not of scenery. But he makes the natural beauty a part of his ritual chain because he feels the beauty. A Yurok will cry as if his heart were breaking while he is cutting or carrying sticks, and, when the fire in the sweathouse has burned out, he will go about other business in the most composed way. The whole performance is a narrow ceremony, but the summit he visits, like almost every spot connected with his religion, is often aesthetically impressive even to the Caucasian unaware of its associations.

9. That is, she now brings it as an ascetic rite accumulating merit. The former daily getting of wood to keep the house warm or to cook with does not count. The women's fuel gathering is much less frequent than the men's and much less intense, probably because it is associated only with the living house and not with the sweathouse.

10. A townsman.

had come by boat offered enough; that was all,[11] and the young man thought, "It is well," and was satisfied.[12] Then only later he knew where that one had come from: he came from across the ocean.[13] Then the woman thought she would go along with him, because that was her house now. So she went there, across the ocean.

d. Then he began again to get sweathouse wood; because he was sorry after he sold her, therefore he got sweathouse wood again. Every day from now he did not stop sweathousing, because he thought she would not come back, that he would never see her again, because it was so far. That is why he cried constantly[14] while he was bringing sweathouse wood, even though he had been paid much. He did nothing else. Where she had sat on the sweathouse making her baskets, there he always went and sat.[15] Then he would be sorry and go for wood again. So he always did. Then once he thought he would stay in his sweathouse. He was lying inside. Then he saw a boat coming toward the beach. He thought, "It looks like him to whom I sold her." He kept looking and saw it was he. Now they[16] came to the foot of the bluff and were out of sight. Then he leaped from his sweathouse, ran into the house, seized his arrows and his necklace of *terkutem* dentalia,[17] and ran off: he did not (stop to) see the woman.[18]

e. As he ran from Tsuräu, he went downstream.[19] He came to Oketo[20] "Where do you go?" they asked him. "I am only traveling," he said. And he went on. He did not want to see the woman, that is why he ran. Then he saw

11. That is, no questions were asked. A man who tendered much for a woman must necessarily be of family and repute, even if personally unknown.

12. So the story, whose motivation is consequently not clear to any but a Yurok familiar with the type of tale. The narrator, on being asked, subsequently explained that the young man agreed to take the payment for his "sister," thinking that she was fond enough of him to wish to stay with him and would object to his acceptance. But she was willing to go, and, disappointed as he was, there was nothing for him to do but conclude the transaction. But he was angry at her, and hence fled when she returned later. That a woman should remonstrate against her own marriage when the tender is honorably large is something that the Yurok ordinarily do not refer to.

13. *Wohpauk,* directly across. It is also possible to reach the land across the ocean by going far enough north along the coast, *pulekuk*; cf. n. 30. But they are two separate places, not one; cf. n. 29 and fig. 3 (Erkerger, Wohpekumeu's country).

14. The weeping is ritual, but personal grief may contribute to it, and, conversely, the grief is no doubt often induced by the weeping.

15. A touch of sentiment, affectionate and nostalgic.

16. From the boat.

17. *Terkuten* are dentalium fragments used in quantities in bead necklaces, not as measured money.

18. Absence has changed his anger to grief; the sight of her now revives the anger.

19. North along the coast.

20. Big Lagoon. No doubt Opyuweg, the principal town on its shores, is meant.

that she was following, but kept on. When he came to Redwood Creek, he saw it running out[21] (into the ocean) and they ferried him over. Then he said; "Some one is following: do not take him across.[22] Even though he wishes it, do not ferry him." Then the woman came. "I want to cross," she said. "No, I will not ferry you," the Orekw person said. Then she picked up small stones, white ones and black ones, into her hat, half full, and threw them across, and ran over the stream (with them), and on. Looking behind, she said to the pebbles: "Fly up, do not sink in the water." Then they were gulls,[23] some of them black, some white.

And the man went on, and the woman. Sometimes he saw her behind, sometimes she saw him ahead. At Osegen, at the top of the trail, he saw her coming along the beach, and he went on. At Welkwäu, he asked to cross (the Klamath), but they denied him. Then he urged, and at last they said; "Well, we will ferry you." So they took him across. "Someone is coming: do not ferry him," he said. "Yes," they said. Then they saw her coming. She wished to cross. He with the boat said, "No, I will not ferry you." Then she did as before with the pebbles, and threw them over, and herself ran over, and again the stones flew up (as gulls).

Now at Rekwoi, she saw someone sitting, a little black one: it was Mink.[24] He said: "Do not follow him, because he will not let you overtake him, for he became angry that you went away. You cannot catch him. You had better stop." "Well," she said, "nevertheless I must follow. Perhaps I shall overtake him." Then when she came near the lake at Omen, she saw him across the stream, going on; but he did not see her because she was still in the woods.[25] And when she came to Smetsken,[26] on top of the hill, she saw him on the beach below, and tried to go faster. But the young man saw her, and he too went faster. So they went. Sometimes he saw her near, sometimes far off. He went from Kohpei,[27] he came to Hinei, he was ferried over (Smith River). He said again, "Do not put her across." But the woman knew what to do and crossed again. She thought, "I shall not stop. Perhaps somewhere he cannot pass: then I shall overtake him. I will not give up, but keep on," and he too

21. Possibly merely a concrete visualization. In summer, however, the surf sometimes throws a sand beach across the mouth of the stream. Then no boat is necessary, but when the bar breaks, one ferries again.

22. Gender is not distinguished in Yurok. He does not say that it is a woman who follows him.

23. *Kegosne*.

24. One of the few animals introduced by this narrator.

25. He is rounding the promontory north of Wilson Creek. She is perhaps a half-mile or more behind (see Waterman, map 6). The Omen lake is Okwego. They have come nearly fifty miles from Trinidad.

26. Some five miles south of Crescent City. They are now in Tolowa territory.

27. Crescent City.

thought; "I shall not stop." So he continued, sometimes seeing her far off, sometimes close by. Then he went faster, and when she looked, she saw him very small because he was so far; but she followed.

f. Then he reached Pulekuk[28] and stopped. "Well, let her come," he thought. The woman came. She laughed, though she was afraid of him, for she did not wish him to be angry. So they stopped there and made camp. At night as they were lying, he saw that she was asleep. Then he looked for a log, and laid it in his blanket, so she would think he was sleeping still. Then he went off, and she did not see him. She looked for his tracks, but could find none. He had gone to Wohpauk, and she could not see his tracks because they were in the water.[29]

g. Then she took off her hair tie and threw (one end of) it downstream.[30] It flew only a little distance and fell. Then she threw it upstream, and inland,[31] and it was the same. Then she threw it across.[32] Then it was as if it were a string that ran out of itself. Then she learned: "That is where he went." Then she threw it again, that tie, and went across on it.

h. So she came to Wohpauk. then she saw one coming, one with thin legs.[33] He said: "It is well that you have come. He who arrived before you is at the houses. That is why I wanted you to come, because I saw him. Tonight I will go with him to fish—for they kill many people here to feed the dentalia with.[34] Therefore I wanted to see you, to tell you that." "Good," she said. And when she came into the house, the old men called out that she would be married to one of their sons. She heard, and said nothing. Then a young man came in, one of the old man's sons, and sat down beside her.[35] Then after a time she saw the young man, her brother, enter. There were two women in the house. Those who lived there said to him; "Those are your wives."

i. Now he with the thin legs said to him: "Let us fish tonight." Then they went down to the beach. He told him; "Do not fall asleep. Many die thus: they sleep and do not awake." Then he got a small log, and laid it in his

28. Pulekuk is "downstream" at the end of the world.

29. Here Wohpauk is across the ocean from Pulekuk, as it is from this world, whereas they are usually described as adjacent.

30. *Pulekuk,* both a direction and a place at the end of that direction. She is throwing farther in this direction, beyond the end of it!

31. *Perwer,* south, and then *hierkik,* inland.

32. *Wohpauk* or *wohpau,* west; like *pulekuk,* both a direction and a place.

33. Weak or short legs? See n. 39 below.

34. This looks as if a trap were being laid for the hero, but what follows shows that he is only to be protected from the fate that befalls ordinary visitors. Perhaps too the feeding of strangers to the dentalia is a trait of Dentalium Home or of Pulekuk, not of Wohpauk.

35. He married her. What became of her first husband, the one also from Wohpauk, who bought her, is not said. The people among whom she and her "brother" married had wanted them to come to them; that is why, unknown to themselves, they had come to Wohpauk.

blanket, so that the thin-legged one would think he were sleeping, close to the fire. Every little while the thin-legged one would look around at him. Then he thought he saw him sleeping. Then he thought; "Alas, now he is killed and cannot arise." So he came over and tried to wake him. "Get up," he said. But he never moved, because it was only a log. Meanwhile he[36] was at the fishing place and caught many dentalia, large ones. Then he went up to the house.

j. But this woman who had followed him went out and said to herself: "I wish I saw my carrying basket and my wedge."[37] Then she looked down and saw them. She took up her basket but saw no wood anywhere.[38] Then she thought; "I wish I saw wood, madrone." Then she saw it, and cut it, and carried it to the outside of the house, and split it, and piled it. Then they had much firewood.

They are living there now. The thin-legged one was Cormorant.[39]

B10. He Walked on the Ocean

[K. did not write a headnote for this tale, but made these jottings: "Water/ocean walking theme: B9 river cross, pebbles."—Ed.]

•

a. At Tsuräu he started to come toward here.[1] When he left they told him: "There is no one there. They have all gone to Pulekuk.[2] You will see nobody." "Yes. But I am going," he said, and started. Then he came to Redding Rock.[3] Then he heard a dance. "I think that is where they all went," he said. He saw someone looking out from a sweathouse; he said: "Come in." "No, I am traveling. I only wish to stop a very little." Then he sang, like this.[4] He sang because he had been asked to enter. "I am going," he said, and went. "When you come back, stop and enter," they said. "Yes," he said. So he went on.

36. The hero.
37. For firewood-gathering, as in her old home at Tsuräu.
38. The countries across the ocean are often described as treeless meadows.
39. Tspega, Cormorant or Shag.

---

1. From Trinidad northward along the coast. The narrator is speaking at Orekw.
2. The northern end of the world. The time is that just before the appearance of the human race, as the woge are leaving. There is nothing in the story that has to do with this change; in fact, the hero returns to this world. The allusion appears to be introduced only because of the strong emotional appeal which the idea of the departing woge always exercises on the Yurok.
3. Sekwona. It is 94 feet high, about 5 miles offshore, somewhat north of the mouth of Redwood Creek.
4. The song comes into the tale. It consists of two long notes, the second lower. It may represent flute playing.

b. He came off Espeu,[5] as far offshore as Redding Rock stands out. He was walking on the surface of the ocean. There he sang again.[6]

c. He went on. The wind was blowing now. He could see the water beginning to heave a very little.[7] At Rekwoi too he did not come to land, and sang again. Then as he was about to go on, he looked around. He thought, "Alas, I see no path." As he thought thus, he looked around again. Then he saw a path, a little path on the ocean, of foam: sometimes it lies in a row. Then he went across.[8]

d. When he arrived, he began to go around, (in order) to return.[9] Then he saw a person. "You had better stay." "No." "But stay." "No." Nevertheless he stayed a little. They said: "You had better stay with us because we have singing. You do not know it, but we wished you to come to us.[10] That is why you came. I will tell you what to do: play the flute." "Well, then, I will stay," he said. So he remained.

e. Then he wished to go again. They wanted him to stay to play on the flute for them. They knew what he was thinking, as if they heard him tell it. He said: "I think I had better return. I do not wish to stay here always." So he started. And he came back (to Tsuräu.)

B11. He Started from Me'noi

This was told as if it were a myth, but it is almost certainly a curing formula.

•

a. At Me'noi[1] he started. He saw a sick person in the house. He came to Melei,[2] and saw a sick one. He came to Namig[3] and saw one there, sick and

5. Tales B1-5 relate to Espeu.
6. A different song.
7. This description appears not to be introduced for its own sake, but as preliminary to the foam by which he later finds his way.
8. Westward across the ocean to Wohpauk.
9. Wohpauk is apparently continuous, in some tales, with Pulekuk, which is reached by going north; and one can return from it to this human earth by going south, then east, and north again; or from Wohpauk north to Pulekuk and thence south along the actual coast.
10. This motive is favored by the narrator; cf. B7 and B9.

---

1. Me'noi is an offshore rock, covered with bird guano, a mile south of Wełkwäu at the mouth of the Klamath; Waterman, Geography, map 9, no. 6. Several of the places mentioned are rocks, and none are Yurok towns. The personages are spirits of former time. The journey is southward along shore.
2. Another rock, but onshore, said the informant. It is Waterman's Meleg (map 9, no. 9), there shown offshore, about a mile south of last.
3. A promontory 1/2 mile south of the last; Waterman, map 9, no. 14, Nomig.

very thin. He stayed only a little and went on. He went farther upstream and saw someone sick at Womets.[4] He did not stay long. He came to Hostsegep[5] and found a sick person. ''I wish you would try somehow to cure him,'' one said to him. ''I know nothing,'' he said. ''Where did he come from?'' that one asked another. One who knew him spoke his name:[6] ''Me'noi he is from.'' That one said again; ''Help me with this sick person.'' ''No, I have no herb, I know nothing,'' he said.

He went on. He came to Oknäu[7] and saw someone sick, but did not wish to stay long. Therefore he said; ''I know nothing, I have no herb, I cannot help you.'' Then he went on.

b. When he came to Oskig[8] he saw someone sick. They said; ''Help us! He is about to die, he is so thin.'' ''Yes,'' he said. Everywhere he had seen sick persons he had refused, but now he consented.

c. He went on and came to Tohtemekw.[9] He looked ahead. Two were going now, one before, he behind. He saw the other nearly at Tsahpekw.[10] Nevertheless, he thought he would overtake him. Then he went on.

He came to Okegei.[11] ''Make medicine for us,'' they said to him. ''No, I cannot stop,'' he said. ''Oh, you will overtake your companion. He is the one who gave me a little medicine and said you were following,'' they told him. ''Very well,'' he said.

d. He started again and came to He'wo'[12] and found someone sick. They

4. ''On shore, several miles south of the starting point, approaching Osegen.'' It is Waterman's Womots (map 9, no. 17), 1 1/4 miles south of last and 1/4 mile inland, ''an open hillside'' between two small creeks called Smerkitur and Amonek.

5. ''South of Osegen,'' but Waterman, map 9, no. 23, has Ostsegep 1 1/2 miles south of last but still 3/4 miles north of Osegen. The name means ''landing'' and was applied to many spots.

6. That is, designated him by where he was raised or married. His personal name would hardly be spoken so freely.

7. ''In the timber south of Espeu, Gold Bluff.'' It must be more or less back from the shore. There is no rock there. Waterman, map 29, no. 20, has ''Oknew, landslide high on mountain,'' south of Espeu, about 1/2 mile inland and 7 miles south of Ostsegep.

8. Near the north side of the mouth of Redwood Creek. The old trail followed the bluff. The spot is on this trail where another crosses it leading from the former town of Otmekwor on the lagoon over the bluff and down to the beach. Waterman, map 29, no. 29, shows it as on the oceanward side of Otmekwor and 3 1/2 or 4 miles south of Oknäu.

9. On the beach, south of Freshwater Lagoon. Waterman, map 31, no. 4, puts it 1 1/2 miles south of Oknäu. [This map is reproduced in this volume as map 7.—Ed.]

10. The town on the west side of Stone Lagoon; Waterman, map 31, no. 10, places it 1 1/2 miles beyond last. The travelers do not stop here; perhaps the town is thought of as not yet inhabited.

11. Near Tsahpekw, 1/2 mile south of it. Waterman, map 31, no. 13, describes it as a ''sharp ridge'' or headland.

12. ''On Big Lagoon.'' Waterman, map 31, no. 19, Tekwo, is at the northern tip of Big Lagoon, about 2 1/2 miles south of last.

said; "Give me of your medicine." He said, "I am hastening. I cannot stop." They said; "Do you not see him who goes ahead? As for him, it was well: he made medicine for me. But now you follow: that is why I want you."[13] He said; "Well, I wish to overtake him, that is why I hurry." That one said to him; "You will overtake him. He is not far." "Very well, then," he said, and made his medicine. Then he started, thinking to overtake him.

e. He came to Pa'ar[14] and looked. Then he saw his companion turn off to go up the hill. He saw him going on Sumig[15] flat. So he went on. At Sumig he asked where he had gone. "Do you not see him? He is there, only a little way off. But I should like you to give me medicine for this sick one." He said, "I am hurrying. But I will tell you what I will do. I will stay here. Then I can always make medicine." "It is good." There were three houses on Sumig. They are rocks now, at Melekwa:[16] they were houses then. They said to him; "I think you will find him in the next house. He went there." He saw him and said; "I thought I should overtake you here, because this is where I belong." The one who lived there said: "This is my house. Look about you." He said; "This is the one I sought. I tried to overtake him and here I caught up with him." Then he stayed, in that rock.[17]

B12. Why There Are No Deerskin Dances on the Coast

This story was told in answer to a query why the River Yurok and Karok and Hupa made both Deerskin and Jumping dances, whereas the Coast Yurok held only the latter. It is clear, however, from the substance and manner, that the informant already had the tale in mind and that it has not been materially colored by the question. It paral-

13. The two travelers are already working complementarily, though they have not yet met face to face.

14. "Between Big Lagoon and Patrick Point." This must be Waterman's map 31, no. 40, Tspä'är, a tiny creek coming into the ocean over half a mile south of the town of Opyuweg at the southwest corner of Big Lagoon. There is also a town Pä'är, Waterman, no. 21, on the inland side of Big Lagoon, to the northeast. This name agrees with Pa'ar of the story, but context places the spot at Waterman's Tspä'är; either he or I misheard or was confused.

15. Here, the Patrick's Point peninsula; specifically, Sumig is Patrick's Point itself; Waterman, map 32, no. 11, 2 miles southwest of last.

16. On the Sumig peninsula (Waterman, map 32, no. 14, a crag inland from the point proper). Compare the next tale, B12. Along the coast the distance from Me'noi is 26 or 27 miles; from Wełkwäu and the mouth of the Klamath, 1 mile more.

17. The narrator elucidated: The Me'noi person traveled like a formula-and-herb doctor on the way to cure. The companion went out to get the Me'noi person to follow him to Sumig, where he was wanted to cure. The herb he used is *kekusa,* a white-flowered composite, creeping in the coast sand. Hot steam from it is used to cure badly emaciated people.

lels A1. It is the only tale in which Tskerkr of his own accord mentioned either Wohpekumeu or Pulekukwerek.

•

a. At Olog[1] he began, he who wanted to make Deerskin Dances. He said; "I should like to see that dance here." They said; "No, we do not want that kind of dance here." "Very well," he said, and took his dance with him.[2] "But I should like to see Deerskin Dances about here."

Then he came to Peweyu.[3] There he wanted to make the dance. They said: "No, it will not be well to have the Deerskin Dance here." He who had the deerskins said; "It will be well if they make it here. Everyone will be glad to see it." "No," they said, "it will not be right."[4]

Then he came to Tsuräu. "Well, that is why I came, to have a Deerskin Dance," he said. "No, I do not think it will be well," they said. "Nevertheless, I should like to see it. You ought to have it," he said. "No, it will not be good. No one will like it. We do not wish it," they said. "All the way from Olog I tried and everyone said, 'No, we do not want it.' But I think it will be well to have it here." he said. "Well," they of Tsuräu told him, "we shall not help you." He stayed for a time at Tsuräu.

b. When he went, he came to Wokseyu.[5] Then he saw two men. They

1. Olog is the Yurok name—it means "floating"—of an important Wiyot town opposite Eureka, on Gunther Island (Waterman, Geography, map 2, no. 53). [This map is reproduced here as map 1.—Ed.] There was a dance held here, but of a different character from any Yurok ceremony. Olog is about thirty miles south of the most southerly Yurok settlement at Tsuräu (Trinidad). The Yurok seem rarely to have visited much farther into Wiyot territory. The route of the story is northward along the coast, first through Wiyot territory and then through the principal Coast Yurok towns. Some of these make Jumping Dances, which are reckoned of equal grandeur, but Deerskin Dances were held only along the Klamath and Trinity rivers, where the population was denser and wealth more concentrated. At Orekw, at the mouth of Redwood Creek, the journey turns inland and cuts across to the Klamath at Wohkero, where the hero, of course in accord with the fact of custom, finally succeeds in helping to establish the ceremony so dear to him.

2. That is, his bundle of dance paraphernalia, as appears below.

3. Peweyu was said to be near the mouth of Mad River,the last important Wiyot town. Its name is more frequently given as Kohso or Sepola, where a Jumping Dance was made, more or less in the Yurok manner. See Kroeber and Gifford, World Renewal, p. 104. Waterman, map 2, gives, on the north side of Mad River in order up from the mouth: no. 45 Kohso, no. 46 Sepora, no. 48 Pegwe (equals present Peweyu), with no. 47 Tegwoł on the south side opposite Kohso. [See map 1 in this volume.—Ed.]

4. Whatever is not established by custom is wrong, is the native reaction. Historically, Mad River made no Deerskin Dance, so it would have been wrong to have it, and this sentiment is projected back into the minds of the people of woge times.

5. Wokseyu was given as an open prairie, not far from the pre-highway wagon road, about two miles north of Tsuräu. It is Waterman's Woksei (map 32, no. 34), resting place on trail, 1/2 mile inland, about halfway from Tsuräu to Sumig (Patrick's Point).

said; "Well, what are you carrying?" "I have deerskins," he said. "Let us try to dance here," they said. "We two can begin to dance (while you stand between us and sing.)" "Good, let us begin," he said. Then they dressed and mounted the skins. So they began. Then they did not dance well. It was as if something were wrong. He tried as best he could to sing, but it seemed as if he were not singing right: he almost forgot his song. Then he said; "I do not think it will be good to have the dance here;[6] we will not have it. Let us undress. I will arrange my pack."

c. They started and came to Olen.[7] They stopped only a very little and went on, for they saw no one.

At Sumig[8] they went up on the flat. At Melekwa,[9] by the trail, on the big rock, they saw two men sitting. He said: "I come because I want to see you also have the dance." But they said to him, "No, I saw you. You tried it. You saw for yourself that you lost the song, because that sort is not good about here. It will be best not to have it." He said, "I thought it would be well." But they said: "No, we do not want it."

d. He arrived at Oketo.[10] "Well, I have come with a Deerskin Dance," he said. They said, "That is not good here. We will not have it." "Very well," he said, and started again.

e. He came to Tekwanuł.[11] There he looked inland across the lagoon, on the hill, and saw many people. So he thought: "I will go." Then he reached Tsahpekw. There they said, "We are about to go." "Where are you going?" "We go to see the Deerskin Dance start across there." Then he began to cry to

6. A major dance goes well and is efficacious only at certain spots. Myths frequently relate how the final site is found by trial. Theoretically, no Yurok would dream of holding a Deerskin or Jumping Dance at a place not established by custom.

7. "Close to the ocean, a little south of Patrick Point." It is Waterman's Ole'm (map 32, no. 10), a camp site, at the head of the cove extending back along the north side of Patrick's Point promontory itself (no. 11, Sumig) and at the mouth of the creek (no. 21, Opermerg weroi), named after blue basaltic pebbles.

8. Sumig is the generic name for the whole of Patrick's Point. The promontory was camped on but not permanently inhabited by the recent Yurok, and yet the myths frequently give it inhabitants.

9. Melekwa is a large rock at which myth B11 ends. It was said to be also called Opergeryotł. From this point south, the old trail was said to cross the peninsula a half-mile or so inland, instead of following the edge of the ocean, as it does further north. Waterman, map 32, no. 14, Melekwa, crag, beside trail. The second name may be for a second rock in the group, since myth B11*e* speaks of the rocks as being three houses once.

10. Oketo or Opyuweg, the large town at the southwest corner of Big Lagoon. It had a famous Jumping Dance; see B8.

11. Tekwanuł was said to be a little south of Tsahpekw, the town on the west side of Stone Lagoon. Waterman, map 31, no. 19, and p. 265, has Tekwo or Tekwanuł, tip end of Big Lagoon. This fits with looking across (Big) Lagoon at Hoslok, on the east bank. Waterman, no. 22 and p. 265, describes Oslokw as a former town where the firs stand in line abreast, like Deerskin dancers. [This map is reproduced here as map 7.—Ed.]

himself. "I tried and nobody wanted it. Well, I will go and watch that dance. He looked across (the lagoon) and saw they were beginning at Hoslok. They had many white skins. Then he went over to see. Those about to begin the dance were with Wohpekumeu. Now he who had come was angry. As they were commencing, "That dance they shall not have here,"[12] he said, and blew out[13] toward them. Thus he did. Then they all remained standing on the hill. One can see them now, those firs, standing like a Deerskin Dance. Wohpekumeu had a cane. It is there still, a fir, because he was ashamed that his dance had been stopped.[14]

f. Then he started again, but inland, toward the Klamath. He came to Olege'l.[15] Then he saw they were beginning to have the Deerskin Dance. Many said that they would make it there. Then he was as it were angry, because he had come far, and no one had listened to him: that was why he was angry. And he did the same. He stopped that Deerskin Dance.

g. Then he started for the Klamath.[16] He came to Wohkero.[17] Then he heard that they were about to begin a Deerskin Dance there. "That is what I wanted. I like to hear that; for this is a different place from the coast." Then they began and he saw their dance. He said: "Good. That is what I want. They will have that dance here."[18]

B13. Oka Young Man's Deer Brush

a. At Oka[1] a young man always went to hunt. He saw no deer. But he continued hunting. There was no grass there, nor any open prairie. He

12. A Yurok is always easily envious.

13. *Upahsoyolemek.*

14. The Chilula of Redwood Creek point out the cane of Yimantũwinyai. Goddard, Chilula Indians of Northwestern California, UC-PAAE 10: (no. 6): pl. 41, 1914.

15. Gans Prairie, some miles up Redwood Creek from the mouth. It was a camp site frequented in acorn-gathering time by the people of Orekw and vicinity, but not a permanent town. The traveler's direction is still north rather than inland. The Orekw Jumping Dance ended on this prairie; the name I got for it from Robert Spott was Megwił Olege'l, "where the elk play or dance" (Kroeber and Gifford, World Renewal, p. 101). [It is not the Olege'l mentioned in A7*l*.—Ed.]

16. Cutting further inland from Gans Prairie.

17. Part of the populous complex Wohkero-Wohtek-Ko'otep. Its Deerskin Dance was connected with the sacred fish dam rites upstream at Kepel. It is the furthest downriver of authenticated Deerskin Dances.

18. Wełkwäu, which legendarily did have a Deerskin Dance, though it is on the coast, is not mentioned in this myth from a Coast Yurok. (See Kroeber and Gifford, World Renewal, pp. 99-100.)

---

1. A high, reddish, rather bare ridge, more or less parallel to the lower Klamath, some miles back from its right bank. It is visible from the river at several points downstream from Blue Creek.

thought, "Perhaps the reason I see no deer is that there is no grass here. They do not like it (as a place) to live because there is nothing to eat." He liked to hunt, yet he never saw a deer. Then he wished to go far upstream where the river came from, because he found no deer where he was hunting. Then he started. When he arrived, he saw a bush.[2] The deer had been eating its leaves. Then he wanted to take it. The bush had seeds. He wanted to take the seeds home to plant.[3] Then he took them. He planted them. The brush grew. The deer came to eat the leaves. Then he thought it was good.

b. Every morning at daybreak he listened. Yet he never heard any birds cry. Then he thought, "Perhaps there are no birds about because there is no grass." And it never blew there. He thought, "Let me go back again." He wanted to bring wind, too. If he found it, he would take it with him, for he had planted seeds of the brush, and thought that if he got the wind, it would be all finished and he would be satisfied. So he went to where he had got the seeds, because he was always thinking of the birds, always wishing to hear the birds when he awoke,[4] yet never hearing them. So he traveled upstream. When he arrived, that was the only place where he saw birds: he had never seen them where he himself grew. Omo'ohpeyo,[5] that is where he found the birds and the seeds, the only place at which he saw birds. Then he brought them downstream. In the morning he listened. Then he heard the birds outdoors. He thought, "That is how I like it. I am glad to hear them."[6]

Then he began to think about the deer again. He thought, "If I go and bring more of that seed and plant it, it will grow." So he went and got it and planted it. Then when he went about, he saw deer tracks; yet he had never seen deer tracks before.

c. Then he thought, "It will be best if I make a spring, for perhaps the deer do not like it that there is no water here." There were no deer (yet) about where he lived because there was no water. So again he went upstream, to get water. Then he got it. Then he went up on the mountain and made a spring for his deer. Then he saw deer tracks[7] and thought: "It is good." So when he brought the water, the birds were glad, for that water was from upstream. And the deer were glad. He heard all the birds shout; therefore he was satisfied. He thought, "That is how I like it, to hear the birds shouting on all sides." He felt

2. *Sahsi'p* or *sahsi'm*. It is locally called wild honeysuckle but may be Ceanothus, buck brush. Its leaves are used with a deer hunting formula—perhaps this tale.

3. Although wholly nonagricultural as regards subsistence, the Yurok are familiar with the idea of sowing from their little ridgetop plantations of tobacco.

4. There is probably a real "feeling for nature" here but, as so often, coupled with a practical desire. If the birds sang and the place were animated, the deer would be more likely to frequent it.

5. Not otherwise known; perhaps a mythical place.

6. The wind that was to be brought is forgotten.

7. Double repetition. The deer came to eat the brush after his first journey, and after his second planting he has seen their tracks.

well when he heard them. That is why one hears birds now because of that: If this young man had not tried to have birds about, one would not hear them, for that is where he got them, where he got those seeds. All of them went to that place,[8] and all the deer also. That is what he desired; it was what he thought it would be well for. Therefore he brought the spring too. So then he got them all; because if it had not been for him, if he had not gone to bring them, none of them would be.[9]

B14. Money's Journey

Except for its monotonous insistence on a narrow theme, this story is not particularly representative of the informant. But it is a most characteristic Yurok myth. It exemplifies the significance of wealth, the craving for it that lends to its personification, the tendency to specify carefully the amounts possessed, and the comparative indifference to plot in many serious myths. Ethnologically the tale is of value in showing how the Yurok rated the leading families of their principal towns. It is rather remarkable that this tale of the wealth of the river and the poverty of the coast should have been recorded from the mouth of a Coast Yurok. [K. has a marginal reference to Spott and Kroeber, Yurok Narratives, no. 36, and to D5x and y below.—Ed.]

•

a. Money[1] had a name, every one, even the small ones. They came together in one place, at Rekwoi-so,[2] to talk over how they would go about to persons. That is where they were going to make their names. All the beings[3] came to where they would talk. Great Money[4] was there too, because there would be a name for everyone. Then they were about to begin. Each one spoke his name, each little money. The largest one, Great Money, said, "It is good.

8. Perhaps: Came downstream into the Yurok world.

9. What begins as a specific formula ends as an origin myth of wide applicability.

1. The word "money" is used in this rendition for "dentalium shell," Yurok *tsīk*. The shells were money to the Indians as much as gold is to us; but since the quality of money cannot be made to attach, in Caucasian usage, to a word such as "dentalium," this term has been avoided.

2. Uphill above Rekwoi, overlooking the mouth of the Klamath and the coast to the south.

3. The Yurok usually say "birds" in English in this context, probably because they do not know the generic word "animal." But the context frequently shows that they include in it quadrupeds, spirits in rocks, and other beings.

4. Pelin-tsīk, literally "Great Money," the largest size of dentalium shell, which among the Yurok is nearly 2-1/2 inches long. However, the name Pelin-tsīk belongs to myth and is generic; it is not used in wealth transactions as a specific designation of size, as *tego'o* is. [In money transactions it would be called *kergerpił*, according to Kroeber, Handbook, p. 23.—Ed.] Pelin-tsīk appears in several tales as one of the creators or instituters; cf. tales A15, D5, T1, X3, and Y1.

We shall call you what you called yourselves. I will go (along the Klamath) upstream. You little moneys go (south) along the coast;[5] let the large ones go up river." Now Great Money was not his name. He had a name, but Great Money was what everyone knew him as. Then it was time to start. Then the little moneys came in this direction.[6]

Great Money said, "I shall go upstream. You little moneys are going in that direction, but I shall not go there. I am going along the river, because I think it is better there, on the river. Wherever someone lives, as it were a (real) man, there I shall live. That is why I do not want to go on the coast, because there will be more property on the river, and where they keep much property, there I shall live." When he said, "It is well," he saw them start, going up the coast and up the river. So they all went.

b. Now Great Money came to Ho'peu.[7] Tego'o[8] wanted to go in there. Great Money said, "No, I do not think we will enter at Ho'peu, because the people there will be poor. It will be best to enter at Turip."[9] The other said, "No, I do not think it will be good there. I think Serper[10] will be best." Great Money said, "No, Serper will be poor. I think I shall not go into a house there. We will go on by."[11]

They came to Wohtek.[12] Then Great Money said, "I think this is a good place to enter." It was as if one travels and steps into a friend's house: that is how he wanted to do. Tego'o said, "Good. We will go in. But I think Ko'otep[13] is the best."

5. *Perwer*; sometimes also *Petskuk*, but that would be confusing here.

6. The narrator is speaking at Orekw, on the coast 20 or so miles south of Rekwoi.

7. Ho'peu is a smallish town (Waterman, Geography, map 9, no. 37), on the north bank, 3-1/2 to 4 miles from Rekwoi, just above the last right-angle turn of the Klamath.

8. The second size of dentalium shell, of which twelve went to an arm's-length string. Sometimes *tego'o* seems to be used for the largest size; see n. 4 above.

9. Turip was the largest town between Rekwoi and the Wohkero–Ko'otep–Pekwon cluster. It is on the south side of the stream, about 8 miles from the mouth, on a flat in a bend of the river.

10. Serper is on the northeast bank, perhaps 18 miles above Rekwoi and 4 below Wohtek (Waterman, map 10, no. 72). It was a small settlement. Erner and several other small towns have been passed by unmentioned in the story.

11. Turip counts as wealthy among the Yurok. Perhaps Great Money had his way and they turned in, although the narrator does not so specify. Or perhaps his intention to stop is sufficient to rank it above Ho'peu and Serper.

12. Wohtek is a large town on the north-northeast bank of the river, named Johnsons on account of a store but known to the Post Office for some years as Klamath Bluffs. It is just upriver from Wohkero, which for the purposes of this tale seems to be included with it. Wohtek was largely populated from Ko'otep, 1/2 miles above, after this town was washed out in the flood winter of 1861-62. (For all three towns, see Waterman, map 11.)

13. Ko'otep was almost adjacent to Wohtek, and until its flooding seems to have had more houses than Wohtek and Wohkero combined; but Wohkero was the scene of the Deerskin and

Then he said, "What is your name?" Great Money said, "I cannot tell you my name. I will tell you when we have completed. I am on the way now: therefore I cannot let you know my name.

c. They started from Ko'otep and went to Sregon.[14] At Sregon they went in.

Then they started upstream. Tego'o talked. "I am sorry because of the small money on the coast." Great Money said, "Well, that will be good, for there they will have no large money. They will have small money. But at Pekwon they will have large money."

Tego'o said, "Well, what is your name?" "No, I shall not tell you my name," Great Money said. Now Tego'o was as it were angry, though he said nothing, for two or three times he had tried to learn his name. He said, "I told you my name at first, but you will not tell me yours." Great Money said, "I shall tell you my name when we have finished. There will be large money about Sregon and Pekwon." "Very well," he said to him.

They started from Sregon. He said, "I do not think I shall enter at Nohtsku'm and at Meta.[15] But I will go in at Mūrek."[16] The other said, "You ought to tell your name, so that they will know you." He said: "No, I will not (yet) call my name, for if I tell it, perhaps I shall not leave again. Perhaps I should stay there, because if they knew my name, it would be as if they held me. Not everyone will know my name: only men,[17] no one else. I shall tell it to you when we have finished, but now we are continuing to travel." Then when they entered the house at Mūrek, [18] they left large money in it.

Jumping dances attached to the Kepel dam. Ko'otep had no dance. The following sentences show that the two Moneys entered both Wohtek–Wohkero and Ko'otep.

Strangely, there is no mention of a stop at Pekwon, less than a mile upriver (Waterman, map 11, no. 54), which was perhaps the largest of the four towns and had a World Renewal sweathouse and a Jumping Dance of its own. This omission must be due to a slip of memory, since Great Money twice prophesies riches for Pekwon after leaving Sregon, the next stop.

14. Sregon is more than 1 mile above Pekwon and less than 2 above Ko'otep, still on the north-northeast bank (Waterman, map 11, no. 90). It was never very large and had no dance, but is always spoken of as wealthy.

15. Two moderately sized towns above Sregon, both on the more shaded and less favorable west-southwest bank. Nohtsku'm is about 3-1/2 miles above Sregon, Meta about half as far (Waterman, map 11, nos. 147 and 118).

16. Mūrek, 3 miles above Nohtsku'm, is a large town, religiously subordinate to Sa'-Kepel, which lie just upstream from it across a bend of the river. Mūrek may be about 8 miles above Wohtek.

17. That is, "rich men," "real men."

18. [K. has a notation: "From here, footnotes not redone, Aug. 1950."—Ed.] The narrator is very far from implying that every house in the villages mentioned was made wealthy. The reference undoubtedly is to the house of the richest family in the town, with whose repute every Yurok would be familiar. The head of such a house might well be designated a chief if the attitude of Yurok society were more political and less economic.

They went on. "I will leave some money at Sa'."[19] The other was sorry again on account of the small money that had gone along the coast. Great Money said, "It will be well. I know that the little money will pass through up the coast. But we shall have many friends along the river. We shall enter into many houses. At Wa'soi[20] we will leave money." Tego'o said, "Well, you ought to tell your name, so that they may know you." "No, I shall not tell it. I said that when we had finished I would name myself," he said.

d. They started.[21] They came to Kenek.[22] He wanted to leave some money there.[23] He said, "When we come to Wahsek,[24] we will leave three pieces[25] there. It is too bad: they are all going off.[26] It looks as if we were late, coming too slowly." "Well, it is bad, but speak your name; I too would like to know it." "Why do you wish to know it?" "So that all may know it." "I shall say to you always that you will learn it when we have finished."

They went on again.[27] At Weitspus they left three pieces. Then they started to cross to Pekwtuł.[28] Tego'o again tried to learn his name, but he would not tell. Then Tego'o thought, "Very well, since he constantly says he will tell me when we have finished, it is well." When they came to Pekwtuł, those there said, "All are leaving. You almost came too late. If you had come one day after, you would not be able to go off. But it is well: you are just in time. Well, let us go into the sweathouse for the night." Great Money thought, "Well, yes." Then that night they all went in.

e. Great Money said, "I think this is as far as I shall go. I think I will return from here. Have all come into the sweathouse?" He who had the sweathouse said, "Yes, they are all in." They were many. All wished to hear what Great Money would tell. He said, "Whoever is sorry for me[29] at Weitspus will

19. Sa' and Kepel form a continuous settlement on a terrace on the south-southwest bank. Together they constitute one of the largest communities on this side of the stream. At Kepel the famous fish dam is made; the sweathouse connected with it is in Sa'.

20. Wa'soi is a small town on the north-northeast side, about 1-1/2 miles above Kepel. [See map 5 in this volume.—Ed.] It contains a rich old man, whose family wealth probably goes back at least several generations.

21. From Wa'soi, where, as at Sa', they had turned in.

22. Kenek is a very small town, except in mythology. It has had no wealthy man in the historic period.

23. And did leave it, presumably.

24, Wahsek is a moderate-sized but rich town, 3 or 4 miles below Weitspus.

25. "Pieces" stands for a suffix attached to numeral stems when dentalia are counted.

26. The departure of the prehuman race is referred to. If all such allusions were taken literally, about half the events of Yurok mythology would have to be construed as happening simultaneously.

27. From Wahsek, where they must be understood to have gone in.

28. Or Pekwteu, on the nose between the Trinity and the Klamath, directly opposite Weitspus. It is much smaller than Weitspus but is also wealthy.

29. That is, remembers me, pities me, and cries for me while bringing in wood for the sweathouse fire.

always have money. That is why I asked if all were in the sweathouse. I want everyone to hear what I have to say. At Pekwtuɬ it will be the same: Whoever is sorry for me, and goes out for sweathouse firewood, will have money. Now I shall start early to return. But I want no one in this sweathouse to sleep, because I wish them all to see me leave."

Then Tego'o said, "You ought to leave your name." Great Money said, "Why do you wish to know it? You ask me constantly for it. I shall tell it to you when I start to go off. For[30] just then some money will go to Hupa and upstream."[31]

f. Now it was the time when he was about to start, early in the morning. Great Money said, "I want to know if all are awake." "Yes, we are all up," they said. "Well, some money will go upstream of here, and some to Hupa. But I shall go a little farther upstream, only a very little, because I wish to see how you[32] go, since I myself am returning." Tego'o said, "Well, why do you not tell your name? I thought you would leave it when you started?" Great Money said, "Yes, that will be right. Now all follow me from the sweathouse. I shall go first." Then he went on the flat place at Pekwtuɬ.[33] He looked behind at the others coming: one he missed, he could not see.[34] Then Great Money said, "Well, I will shout here, because I want them to hear me from Weitspus too. That is why I will shout. Hu! Ke-näɬ-tamir,[35] that is my name!"

B15. Wohpekumeu's Departure

With all their traveling along the Klamath, Wohpekumeu is rarely made by the Yurok to journey south along the coast, and Pulekukwerek never, except on finally leaving this world. It seemed to me that the Coast Yurok might have tales of their own about these heroes, and I therefore asked Tskerkr. Of Pulekukwerek he knew nothing that related to the coast towns. He did know a Wohpekumeu tale, he said, and told the following, the central incident of which, about Wohpekumeu's departure from this world, is known to every Yurok. Only the introductory portions have true local reference.

30. The Yurok often use "for" and "because" when causal connection is not strict. The prefixes evidently have a wider meaning than our conjunctions.

31. To the Hupa and Karok, who live next above on the two rivers that flow together at Pekwtuɬ. [The Hupa live along the Trinity, and the Karok further up the Klamath. See map 1 in this volume.—Ed.]

32. It seems he is speaking to the pieces of money that are to go upstream; or perhaps the Pekwtuɬ people are to fulfill his function as they go farther up the two rivers.

33. "Where Canyon Tom has his house now." [Waterman, pp. 256–257, says that Canyon Tom was a half-Hupa who lived in the steep canyon above Weitspus, in the six-mile stretch below the first Hupa village. He took part in the Deerskin Dances at Weitspus.—Ed.]

34. The reference to the missing one is obscure.

35. "Both sizes (of money)," the interpreter translated. *Ke-* is "he of," *-näɬ-* is "two," and *-tamir-* is one form of the suffix on numeral words denoting dentalium shells. Evidently the name is a joint one for Tego'o and himself.

The story is entirely out of Tskerkr's manner. It is told without his usual passionateness, even without feeling. He is clearly but little interested in this drifting, unattached, and fickle-minded hero, with his love affairs and tricks. He tries indeed to make him a sort of reformer, but pallidly. He can only repeat that Wohpekumeu's mind is set on bettering the world; the means used remain unspecified, the dangers encountered unconcrete. It is not a subject that lends itself to the Tskerkr type of treatment; and it never acquires unity, energy, or even interest.

Lame Billy's three Wohpekumeu tales—A21 to A23—are also concerned with episodes in this personage's career. But Lame Billy cares about character, and succeeds in presenting three different phases of Wohpekumeu, each clear and self-consistent. Moreover, he is always under the inward compulsion of exalting his hero whoever he may be, of sympathizing with him as a personality. Tskerkr's sympathy is for a hero's situation, for his longings or attachment to place, home, kin, pet, or possession. He depicts his heroes as successful, although tried; but as obscure instead of preeminent; and usually as nameless. In honoring my request to tell about Wohpekumeu, he abandoned his peculiar vein and fell back on customary myth material with which he was familiar, but which was without real appeal to him; and the tale emerges without special quality of telling. [K. has this additional marginal note: "Hooks in *a, b, c* ex Pul. Salmon eye trade in *g* new."—Ed.]

•

a. Wohpekumeu started southward from the mouth of the river. He came to the top of the hill at Womets.[1] There he sat and rested. He had heard that it was bad to go south, that there were three places where one could not pass through: that was why he wanted to go. Then he went on. The first place was Tekta-'otemets:[2] there (was the first bad place, where) they caught people with a hook. But he had medicine and they could not see him: so he went by.

b. Then he came to Otmekwor.[3] No one ever went there. He said, "I want to go by." They said to him, "No, you must not."[4] Nevertheless, he insisted. So they said to him, "Why do you wish to go?" He said, "I am the one who makes this land good: it is therefore that I want to go." They said, "You had better not go. Even if we let you by, you cannot pass the other place." "Well, if I do not succeed, another one will come after me. He will

1. "On the coast four or five miles south of the mouth of the Klamath," Waterman, Geography, map 9, no. 17, shows Womots, an open hillside 1/4 mile or so inland, on the coast trail at a point where another trail strikes east toward McGarvey Creek and the Klamath.

2. Tekta-'otemets is Waterman, map 29, no. 22, Tekto-oktenets, a swamp associated with a small creek flowing into the ocean at Poiyura, Mussel Point, 1-1/4 mile south of Espeu. The catching or fishing for people with a hook was perhaps like that of the two blind women whom Pulekukwerek destroyed on Bald Hills (F1*g*).

3. Otmekwor is on the north side of the lagoon of Redwood Creek, facing Orekw (Waterman, map 29, nos. 30 and 32).

4. An obscure sentence about the town of Tsahpekw follows here.

come tomorrow. If I do not go by he will go by, and they will not stop him." He meant Pulekukwerek. Then Wohpekumeu (went, and) was not injured by them, and came past that place.[5]

c. He went along the beach. At Orekw he thought, "I shall be killed before night. I wish this sand were better so that they might travel here more easily hereafter." It was (ahead) at Tsahpekw that they always fished with a hook and caught people. When they caught anyone, they threw him inland[6] over the hills and so killed him. (On his way there,) Wohpekumeu came to Freshwater Lagoon. He thought, "I should like to see water here. I should like a lake here." That is how the lagoon came to be there: it had been salt water before, but he made it a (fresh) lake. He kept on and looked ahead and saw Stone Lagoon. He saw someone there, but nevertheless he went on, although he thought that he would be killed. He did not wish to destroy anyone nor to fight, but he wanted the land to be good. Now he rubbed his hands and threw into the lagoon[7] the black epidermis[8] that came off. It became trout. So he came to Tsahpekw. On top of a sharp rock (there) he saw someone standing, as if he were fishing. Wohpekumeu made medicine and was not seen. Thus he passed by. He let that one be: he did not destroy him. He only wanted to make the land good.[9]

d. When he had gone by Tsahpekw he kept on. He thought, "I wish the beach were sandy." He went on a little and saw it was sandy. When he had gone on a short distance farther, he found a woman. Nevertheless he went on and did not think of her.[10] He was thinking only of making the world (better). He went on and saw another woman. He thought nothing of her also, but went on. Then constantly he saw women, but went on along the beach. Then he saw two women coming along. So he had companions. He thought, "Well, I will go along with them." So he went on with them. He thought, "I wish that beach were longer," because now he had companions. When they came near Oketo,[11] the two women turned off from the beach. They were both pregnant (from him).

e. Wohpekumeu went on. He found another woman on the beach but thought, "I will go on." He went and after a short distance found another one.

5. It is not clear whether his threat of Pulekukwerek suffices or whether his own power enables him to overcome theirs. The whole episode is unusually vague.

6. *Hierkik*, "back" as the Yurok translate it.

7. Stone Lagoon, which he is approaching. The town of Tsahpekw is on the western side near the ocean (Waterman, map 31, no. 10). [This map is reproduced here as map 7.—Ed.]

8. *U-meseum*.

9. That is, he permanently broke the evildoer's power, of fishing for people with his hook, by withstanding the power once.

10. This is remarkable self-restraint for Wohpekumeu, in Yurok eyes.

11. Or Opyuweg, the principal town on Oketo or Big Lagoon, at its southwest corner, not far from the ocean.

She was young. Then he thought, "Well, I will take her." So he took her. Then the salt water rose and the breakers came up the beach but the woman would not let go of clasping him. More water came and she turned and took him into the ocean. So she carried him away.

f. Then they came to the other side of the ocean.[12] They came up on the beach, and the woman said, "This is where you will live. We want you here. That is why I went to get you. I think you will have to remain here; you will not be able to go back." But he would not speak. He did not know where he was, and he was blind because when the woman took him they went under the salt water. He did not go about; he stayed in one place. But she that took him away was not a woman. She lived in the ocean: I never heard that she lived in a town. She was Skate.[13]

g. Now Wohpekumeu thought, "I wish someone would come"; but no one came. He was blind. Then at last he heard them coming. There were four of them, Salmon. Wohpekumeu began to speak to them. He said, "I saw you when you started from where you live at Kowetsek.[14] As soon as you started I saw you." They said, "You see very far. Our eyes cannot look as far as that. We see only a short distance." One of them said, "I should like to trade my eyes for yours." Wohpekumeu said, "No, my eyes are too good." But really he could see nothing. Then he was about to trade his eyes with Salmon when another one came and said, "I should like to trade with you." That was Steelhead.[15] Then Wohpekumeu said, "Very well." First he took out his eyes. Then Steelhead did the same. He gave his eyes and Wohpekumeu could see well. Then he made medicine for fog. He wanted to escape that they might not take their eyes away from him again. Then it became foggy and he ran off. They did not see him again. Steelhead cried because he was blind and his eyes hurt him.

B16. Great Money in the South

Tskerkr was too old and emotionally set to learn to dictate to writing. Inasmuch as his unusual faculties made it desirable to secure from him at least some Yurok text as an example of his style in its completeness, speaking into a phonograph seemed the only

12. Wohpauk, after which Wohpekumeu—"across the ocean widower"—is named.

13. Nospeu.

14. Kowetsek (see C2) is the home of the salmon, also across the ocean, but apparently conceived as more nearly due west of the Yurok world, whereas Wohpauk seems to be somewhat south of west; at any rate, Kowetsek is north of Erkerger, Wohpekumeu's place in Wohpauk, on Waterman's diagram of the Yurok idea of the world (Waterman, Geography, (fig. 1). [This diagram is reproduced here as map 3.—Ed.]

15. *Tskoł*. [Steelhead are large, silvery trout which, like the salmon, travel upriver from the ocean to spawn.—Ed.]

medium. I was without apparatus the last time I saw him, but arranged to secure from him several myths and formulas on my return. Even the pay was stipulated. Dr. Waterman took the trouble to fulfill my part of the contract, and so the University of California came to possess some cylinders in Tskerkr's voice. Unfortunately, they promise never to be of much use. Tskerkr could not bring himself to utter the formulas so that they are continuously audible. Long habit prevailed against every request and pressure and even against his own willingness, with the result that nearly every sentence trails off into a whining mutter from which a Yurok ear is about as inadequate as our own to disentangle the articulate words. The myths, recorded, which the old man was wont to pronounce audibly, are not quite so bad; and with considerable effort Mrs. Catherine Goodwin was able to make out nearly all of one and to English it. The profit, however, was not very great. There is very little action, much dialogue, an irregular attribution of this to the characters, a deal of repetition, and as much omission, so that the thread of the story remained as obscure to Mrs. Goodwin as to myself. It is a case of Tskerkr at his most elliptical. It may be that his mind had become disordered in senility during the two years since he had worked for me, or that this one audible story happens to be unusually deficient in motion; but I suspect also that my interpreter Frank used to profit in his renderings by sitting in the physical presence of the old man, and was thus able to hold the clue of each tale, so as to supply the most disconcerting omissions; and that perhaps unconsciously he suppressed some of the baldest repetitions. From the point of view of a civilized audience, he therefore probably improved the foregoing tales, but at the cost of diluting their characteristic narrator's flavor, which it would have been historically desirable and aesthetically interesting to have preserved in its fullness. To do what may be thought worth while, without dealing unduly in the unintelligible, I give the opening passage of this myth. I omit marks of quotation in the hope that the adroit reader may be able to supply them with less sense of bafflement than I.

•

Now this is how it was: he grew at Pulekuk, he grew, Goose; that is where he grew. That is where he lived, Great Money. That is why it is so, that they sometimes go home to Perwerhkuk.[1] That is how he travels, although he grew at Pulekuk, this Great Money. I think now that I see you. What makes me live? Now you see my children all going south (to Perwerhkuk), all my children. The geese are my children. I do not go with them: I stay here (and) wait for them to come back—my children. Although my children are thin while they are here at Pulekuk, when they go to Perwerhkuk they become fat. For a woman lives there. And now I shall go. I shall go to see my child, (my) one (child). He will stay here. And Great Money said, No, No, I shall take all of

1. Perwer is south along the coast, Perwerhkuk the southern home of the geese. [See Waterman, Geography, fig. 1, the diagram of the Yurok idea of the world. It is reproduced here as map 3.—Ed.]

my children to Perwerhkuk. You are to stay here. I shall go to Perwerhkuk, said Great Money. He said, Very well, very well. So then he started. His children had left. And he said, Take all my children, said Great Money. For their mother lives at Perwerhkuk—his wife; his wife lives at Perwerhkuk, the great Abalone:[2] she is the wife of Great Money. They are thin when they are here where I live, for I myself do not know what to do (to care for them), for I am a man, said Great Money.

What glimpses of plot there are here become fainter as the story progresses into a maze of new elements and repetitions. Great Money lives at Pulekuk, the downstream end of the world reached by following the coast north. His wife Yer'erner, Abalone, who tries to fly to Pulekuk but is too fat, is at Perwerhkuk, the corresponding southern end. The geese who travel back and forth seem to be their children; but the relation of the geese to Goose at Pulekuk, and of Goose to the unnamed person who has but one child and talks with Great Money, is problematic.

It is drizzly and foggy when the geese fly, and they are told to fly over the ocean and by night, because on land the woge harass them. Their mother in the south always sweeps the ground clear for her brothers to alight. The children speak like their father when they are with him, but when they return they talk Ner'er'ner, southern Coast Yurok.

2. Abalone (*Haliotis*) comes to the Yurok from the south. In Spott and Kroeber, Yurok Narratives, no. 36, most kinds of shells travel north, some both north and south, but Yer'erner, Abalone, go only south.

Informant C

STONE OF WEITSPUS

Stone was usually called Megwollep, formulist. He was also called K'e-segwa'akweł, which means that his father was from the Karok town of Segwu' (Katimin). His mother was evidently married there from Weitspus, but her house is not remembered, nor is it known how Stone came to return to his mother's people among the Yurok. Possibly his mother was from the house ple'ł; at any rate, that is where he later lived.

He was not married, but lived illegitimately with a woman of the house petsku. She was called Stūn-wer, Stone's mistress. They had no children.

Stone had some valuables. He owned a red obsidian twelve or fourteen inches long, three dance baskets, two ringtail-cat aprons, five or six deerskin blankets, five bone whistles, and four dentalium bead necklaces, not engraved but of good quality and therefore usually worn by one of the middle dancers. Stone also used to borrow for dances two white deerskins and two silver-gray fox skins from his Segwu' relatives.[1]

C1. Pulekukwerek

This is a typical Pulekukwerek monster-ridding story, lacking the account of his origin and broken off before its conclusion, but containing most of the stock incidents known to every Yurok: the split log, the horned serpent at the mouth of the river, the poison smokers at Kenek, the jealous one of Merip, the Sa'ał killed with hot stones, and the blind women on Bald Hills. The only incident foreign to the strict Pulekukwerek cycle is that of Kewet young man beating Earthquake at shinny (in section *p*). The whole story

1. [For an account of the Weitspus Deerskin and Jumping dances and of Stone's role as formulist, see Kroeber and Gifford, World Renewal, pp. 66–80.—Ed.]

is popular tradition, lacking in religious tone, and told reasonably well, but without particular zest or skill. It was the old man's first narrating to me, and the result is more conventional than in subsequent years.

•

a. Before there were human beings, Pulekukwerek tried to make boats. He tried many kinds of wood, but when he put them into the water they did not last. They cracked or wore out and became useless. He began to believe he should not be able to make a boat. Then he thought of redwood. When he tried it, the boat was good.

b. Now, when they made boats, sometimes, as they split the log, a man was killed. It was a dangerous thing. Pulekukwerek thought, "Perhaps I can make it that they split without killing anyone." Now he came to Omen, where they were working: a log was about to be split in half. He also saw many human bones lying about. The one who was working said, "It is good that you came; you can help me." Now Pulekukwerek saw that this man was glad when people came because he was trying to catch and kill them in the cleft. He would tell them, "Reach down into the crack and hold the wedge." Then he would draw the wedge out and crush them. So he drew out the wedge on Pulekukwerek, and the log closed. But Pulekukwerek was not caught; there he sat close by. Then that man said to him, "Why did you let go of it?" Pulekukwerek said, "I don't know how to do this work." That one said, "Let me show you. This is the way to hold it," and he reached in. "I don't yet understand," said Pulekukwerek, looking down into the crack where the other was setting the wedge. "This is how," he said, showing him again. Then Pulekukwerek drew out the wedge, the log snapped together and that one was killed. Blood oozed out all along the crack. Pulekukwerek blew out and said, "This is how it will be. They shall use redwood for canoes, but they will not be killed in splitting it."

c. Pulekukwerek went on to Rekwoi. Then he began to hear shouting. Coming out on the hill above the town he saw people playing. They were playing with a ball of wild pumpkin (manroot), throwing spears at it from two sides. When he came down to them they said, "Play with us." They used to kill by telling a person, "You are from elsewhere: play against us," placing him opposite, and then, as he watched the ball, throwing their spears at him all at the same time. Pulekukwerek answered, "I do not know how." They said, "Well, try. That is how one learns." "Well then, yes," he said. So he stood over against them. As the ball rolled past, they all threw at him. But none of them struck him. Then he threw his spear, and it went entirely through one of them. Then he blew out and said, "This will no longer be so. People will not be killed when they play at the rolling ball."

d. He prepared to stay the night at Rekwoi. When he entered the sweathouse, women sat in it working at baskets and deerskin dresses.[1] The sweathouse was full of people, men and women together. Then, when they came and brought wood, he said, "Throw in much." They said, "We do not throw in a great deal." "Well, nevertheless, throw in much," he told them. Then he built a great fire. Some of the women said to him, "Do not make the fire so large." He answered, "Oh, it is well to have the fire big." He made it burn as much as he could. It became exceedingly hot inside. Soon the women were rolling about in distress. Then they began to run out. Now Pulekukwerek sat inside alone, singing to himself. He blew after the last of the women, and said, "A woman shall not come into the sweathouse. They will sleep in the house. They shall not be in here with the men."

e. Then he remained at Rekwoi another night. In the morning he said, "Ferry mc across."[2] Now there was a being in the middle of the stream which swallowed every boat. People were always drowned, unless they went far upstream to cross. So they said to him, "We cannot ferry you over. They always drown here." He said, "I think I shall be able to cross safely if you will take me." But they told him, "No, we cannot." "Well, all right then," he said. He took the ridge board off a sweathouse,[3] and carried it down to the river. They went along, thinking, "Let us watch him crossing. He will surely be drowned." Then they called up to those in the town, "He is making a fire in his boat." Then they saw him out on the stream. His boat was so small and low that it looked as if he were sitting on the water. But he sat unconcernedly, paddling a stroke only now and then. Soon the salmon began to leap. They leaped all about him. He came to the middle of the stream, where the water was heaving and turning. More salmon were leaping about him now. Then they thought that he seemed to begin to be afraid: he suddenly paddled hard. When he had passed the turmoil and began to near the shore, he jumped to land, leaving his boat in the stream. When he turned, he saw one end of it standing up out of the water. Then it disappeared wholly. It had been swallowed. Pulekukwerek went up the slope toward Wełkwäu. Then he saw the salmon leaping again. The water was waving and surging. When he arrived at

1. A sweathouse is a taboo to women on ordinary occasions, as one of our men's clubs might be.

2. A traveler is always ferried for the asking. He can claim damages if denied. He does not ferry himself, unless the residents are away, because they will want their boat brought back.

3. This board is usually the gunwale or a piece of bottom of a broken boat. The convexity covers the joint of the two slopes of the roof.

the houses of Wełkwäu, he saw that something was floating in the middle. It was Knewollek, the Long One. It was dead from swallowing the fire in the boat. Then he went back down to where it lay and saw that it had many sharp horns. He drew it to shore, but it was so long that when he had one end high up the slope the tail was still in the water. He cut it into many pieces. He threw the heart (north) to Crescent City. There is a rock in rough surf there now.[4] The lungs he threw south to beyond Big Lagoon,[5] where there is another rock and a dangerous place in the water.

f. Then he went on to Espeu.[6] Here was another man who killed people in logs. He said, "I am glad you have come. Help me to work." "I do not know how," said Pulekukwerek. "Well, learn. I will show you. Do thus. Place this wedge while I hold it from above." As Pulekukwerek felt him begin drawing the wedge away, he leaped out of the crack, and sat on the ground. "Why did you do that?" said the man from the top of the log. "I told you I did not know how," Pulekukwerek told him. "Well, I will show you again. Do it this way. Now when you feel it begin to move, move it along." Suddenly Pulekukwerek drew out the wedge on him. He was killed. Then Pulekukwerek blew out and said, "They shall not kill people here in canoe making."

g. That is as far as Pulekukwerek went along the coast. From here he went back to the river, and upstream to Kenek. He had heard that this was a dangerous place. Eleven porpoises[7] used to kill people by taking them into their sweathouse and giving them tobacco. Now he came to a rock near the trail upstream from Kenek. He climbed up on this rock and looked toward the town. It was evening, and the people were all at supper. Then he slid himself down the rock and gouged marks on it with the points on his buttocks.

h. After that he cut eleven sticks of elder, pushing out the pith, and swallowed them. Then he went to the town and entered the sweathouse. The floor was of fine slabs of stone, he saw. He sat down in the best place.[8] As he leaned back and stretched to lie down, he broke the slab under him. Now the youngest of the eleven porpoises came in and felt about.[9] He thought, "Who

4. And "a lighthouse on it"; therefore probably Point St. George, or perhaps Crescent City roadstead.

5. "Beyond Big Lagoon" might be Patrick's Point, off which there are sea stacks.

6. Lower Gold Bluff, on the coast south of Rekwoi and Wełkwäu. Few accounts of Pulekukwerek have him travel south of the Klamath at all.

7. *Kegor* or *kenomer*. The former seems to be the common word for porpoise; the latter is usually employed in the narration of this incident and seems to refer to the porpoises as residents of Kenek. [K. has a notation to check this.—Ed.]

8. The lying places in the sweathouse were graded as more and less desirable, and visitors were assigned to them according to rank and esteem.

9. The sweathouse is dim in the day and totally black at night.

has been here? This slab is cracked.'' It was the oldest brother's place. The others came in one by one. When the oldest brother entered, they said to him, ''Your sleeping place has been broken.''

i. Pulekukwerek was lying to the side, pretending to sleep. ''Who is this man?'' they said. Some answered, ''I do not know.'' Then one of them asked him, ''Are you asleep?'' ''Yes, I have been,'' said Pulekukwerek. ''Well, you had better have a smoke,'' they said, and the youngest held out his pipe. Pulekukwerek drew two puffs, and the pipe was burned empty. The smoke entered an elder stick in his body. The next brother said, ''Try my pipe, too.'' He took that, and then another and another, until he had smoked all eleven. The oldest brother's pipe nearly killed him. Its smoke almost perforated the last elderwood box. Then two of them went out and said to each other, ''What sort of a person is this whom we cannot kill with our tobacco?'' ''Well,'' said the other, ''Tomorrow we shall overcome him with a great fire.'' Thus they killed people who might survive their tobacco.

j. Then in the morning they built a great fire in the sweathouse. As soon as it bcgan to burn down a little, they put on more wood. It became exceedingly hot inside. But in time one after another of them had to run out, until Pulekukwerek was left alone in the sweathouse, singing. Then he too emerged, walked slowly down to the river, and bathed.

k. Then they said to one another, ''What shall we do? He is a hard one to kill. But let us try again. When he is asleep in the sweathouse let us lift the boards off the roof and drop a stone on him.'' Soon Pulekukwerek said, ''I shall stay in the sweathouse and sleep today.'' After a time a man peeped in and saw him asleep. Even those outside could hear him sleeping. Three of the men brought a large stone up from the river. Carefully they opened the roof of the sweathouse, just above where he lay. Then they rolled the stone over the edge of the hole. But Pulekukwerek moved aside and the stone fell in his place, just missing him. Then they said, ''Since we cannot kill him, let us be his friends. Let us get him to (try to) make it good at Merip.'' So they gave up trying to kill him themselves. Pulekukwerek blew out and said, ''They will not kill people here any longer, either by smoking or by large fires.''

l. Then Pulekukwerek went downstream to Merip. The Porpoises said to him, ''The man there is extremely jealous. When he goes out he paints his wives' faces. When he comes back he can see if anyone has been going by even across the river: some of the paint has come off their faces.'' The Porpoises sent him down hoping that he would be killed, for the jealous one of Merip was powerful and had killed some of them.

m. When Pulekukwerek was near Merip he thought he would take out his heart and put it on[10] one of his fingers. He put it on one of his fingers, and it shook. He took it off, put it on another, and it shook again. So he knew that he would certainly be killed if he left it there. He placed it on all his fingers (in turn), and on each of them it shook. Then (he) did not know what to do. He put it on all of his toes, and it shook. Only when he put it on the last one, the little toe, it did not shake. Then he knew that that was the place for him to have it.

n. He came to Merip and entered the house. Only the two women were there, weaving baskets. He sat down between them and took hold of each with one of his arms. They said, "Let us go!" But he continued to embrace them. "Where is my friend?" he asked. "He will come soon," they said. He kept holding them, for he wanted to make their man angry. Soon he heard him coming. "Enter!" he told him. Then the man saw him holding his two wives. He sat down opposite, but facing the wall in anger. When he turned, Pulekukwerek saw him take an arrow, part of the head of which was flaming. They of Kenek had told him, "When he draws an arrow only part of whose head is on fire, say to him, 'Do not use that one! It will not kill me.' He has eleven burning arrows. Make him use the best one. When he takes the one that sets the bow afire, tell him, 'That is the one!' So Pulekukwerek said, "That is not the one! It will not kill me." Thus he said to that man sitting directly opposite him, while he still held fast the two women. Then the one of Merip drew another arrow. A little more of its head was flaming. Again Pulekukwerek said, "It will not kill me." He said that ten times. Then the man took out his last arrow, and the bow began to burn. "That is the one! That will kill me," Pulekukwerek said. He released the two women, protruded his chest, and said, "Shoot me right here." Then that one shot and Pulekukwerek fell, twitching and jerking. The women got up and went out, the man followed. Pulekukwerek, still twitching, bounded up on the drying frame. There he lay awhile. He thought he was about to die. Then he leaped through the smoke hole on the roof. From there he bounded to a rock above Merip; his blood can still be seen on a stone nearby. From there he bounded upstream and across to Kenek.[11] Then he sat up, took out the arrowhead, and was well.

o. Then he showed the (arrow)head to the Porpoises. They said, "Good. It is what we wanted." So he gave it to them. It was a large flint, and they wanted to work it over into smaller arrow points. They asked for somebody to do this, but everyone refused. At last Kwar'erei[12] agreed. He went on the roof,

10. Or "in."

11. Two or three miles.

12. A small, black-eyed bird. [Robins, Yurok Language, p. 214, identifies it as a towhee.—Ed.]

laid down a deerskin, padded his hand with buckskin, and began to flake. Whenever he pressed off a chip it flamed. Then the people heard laughing indoors, and one of them went in to look. He saw snakes, ants, and wasps inside: they were about to go off and become animals. Now they stood looking up, and whenever a spark burned through the deerskin and the roof and fell down, they ran with open mouths to catch it. Then Porpoise seized Grass Snake[13] and said to it, "What are you doing? Grass Snake said, "We are catching these sparks because we wish to keep them." Porpoise said, "You must not want that: it is like poison." He took the bit of flaming flint away from him. But Rattlesnake hid his burning chip in his navel: that is why he is so vicious now. Yellow Jacket[14] also had got some of the flint and succeeded in keeping it. Now the Porpoises also were almost ready to go off.

p. Those at Kenek used to play shinny with Earthquake. They always lost because Earthquake would cause the ground to heave and wave on both sides of him so that his opponents could not run. Now a stranger came with a dog. "Well, my brother-in-law," said one of the Porpoises, who had two unmarried sisters. He always said that: whoever beat Earthquake was to marry the two girls. "Play shinny here," he told him. "I do not know how," said the young man. "Well, nevertheless you might play." Kwar'erei also came down from his roof and urged him. When they had all spoken to him, he consented to play. Then one of the Porpoises withdrew from the game and said, "Here, take my stick." "No, I have one of my own," said the youth, who was the youngest of ten brothers from Kewet,[15] and whom they were all watching. Then Porpoise said to him, "When Earthquake has the ball, follow him. Do not try to pass him, for at his sides the ground heaves and you cannot run. Where he himself travels it does not heave: therefore follow in his tracks."

The dog which the youth from Kewet had brought with him was covered with sores. Now he took angelica root, put it in a basket, and poured the water on the dog's back. Then the sores fell off, and he was woodpecker crest all along his back. The youth said to him, "When he drives the ball through the air, get in its way. Cause it to strike you and drop." Then they played, and the dog was invisible. Soon the youth got the ball and carried it to his goal and won. He was the first one who had beaten Earthquake. So he married the two women.

q. Now a person came from upriver and said that a Sa'ał[16] was coming.

13. [Probably the harmless garter snake, *Thamnophis sirtalis*.—Ed.]
14. [A small, ground-nesting wasp (Vespidae) with a painful sting.—Ed.]
15. Rivet Mountain above Weitspus.
16. A disease-bringing spirit. [Cf. A15x *b* and A21 *m*.—Ed.]

Many had died already. Pulekukwerek said, "You had better all go away. I shall stay." So all the Porpoises went off, while Pulekukwerek stood on a house. He drew out his head until it reached nearly to his arms' length and was pointed at the end, with eyes near the end and the mouth reaching back to his shoulders.[17] Looking upstream, he saw someone coming: it was the Sa'ał. He called to him, but the Sa'ał went on, and did not answer. Again Pulekukwerek called: "Come here! I want to see you." Then Sa'ał came. "Where are you going?" said Pulekukwerek. Sa'ał pointed about in a circle. Pulekukwerek said, "Well, I do that too. I will go about the world with you." Sa'ał agreed. Pulekukwerek said, "Come into the house first," and brought him in. He had put new cooking stones into the fire. They were red hot by now. Then he said, "I always eat one of these before I go. You too had better take one." Sa'ał shook his head. "Take one," said Pulekukwerek, "I always eat them. It keeps me from getting sick. Come." Sa'ał was afraid and refused. Again Pulekukwerek urged him. Then when he still would not, he himself ate one. He had swallowed a hollow elkhorn; so now, picking up one of the stones, he let it fall into his mouth and was unhurt. When he urged Sa'ał again and again and he still refused, he took up a hot stone, went to him, and said, "Open your mouth!" Then he threw it in. At once he saw smoke coming out of his throat. Then the stone burned out through his belly and Sa'ał fell over, twitched, and was dead. Then the Porpoises came back to the town.

r. Now Pulekukwerek was told that on Bald Hills prairie there were two blind women whom no one could escape who passed. When a person entered they caused the door to close on him, and he was as unable to move as if he were stuck in pitch. Then the old women would feel around until they caught him, put him in a basket, and cook him. In this way they destroyed people. Pulekukwerek went there. Then he heard the noise of pounding. He went in quietly. One of them was crushing (what looked like) grass seed. "Is it nearly done?" asked the other. "I don't know. I will give you some to taste," said the first, and held some out in her hand. Pulekukwerek reached over with his hand, took what she gave, and saw what it was.[18] "Why don't you hand it to me?" said the other, older woman. "I gave it to you," said the first one. "No." "Well, I will give you some more." Again Pulekukwerek took it. "Well, let me have it," she said. "I gave you some twice!" "No, you gave me nothing." They began to quarrel. Then one of them said, "Perhaps there is somebody in the house." Then the door closed.

When Pulekukwerek tried to escape, he could not move. Soon they caught him. When they felt him over, one said, "Perhaps this is he of the eye

17. He was making himself look like a Sa'ał.

18. Human bones pounded like grass seeds.

medicine."[19] "Yes, I am he," said Pulekukwerek. "Well, it would have been too bad.[20] Here, take the basket," they said, and caused the door to open for him. He said, "I want two baskets, one for the medicine for each of you." They gave him the baskets, and he went out. He piled stones against the door. He heard the pounding going on. Now he set fire to the house, first at one end, then at the other, then all around. The old women smelled the smoke. "There must be a prairie fire off somewhere," they said. Then they heard the flames roar. "The house is on fire!" they cried. "It must have been he who said he had eye medicine." They tried to crawl out but could not. The roof caught, and soon the whole house was blazing. Then Pulekukwerek heard a popping, and then another. Their entrails had burst. The entire house burned up. Pulekukwerek blew out. He said, "You will kill no more people. No one will be destroyed here."[21]

C2x. The Salmon and Kowetsek

VERSION FROM PHONOGRAPH DICTATION

This is not a proper myth, but an endeavor by the informant to satisfy my request in 1902, for an account of the origin of salmon. He told in brief outline the episode, familiar to every Yurok, of Wohpekumeu's theft of the concealed first salmon; supplied another snatch, of the institutional myth type, about the salmon run; added some non-narrative folklore about the great head salmon Nepewo and his home Kowetsek across the ocean; summarized a formula, associated with Wohpekumeu, for luck in salmon fishing; went on, at somewhat greater length, to tell the story which explains the origin, or constitutes the kernel, of the formula spoken at the annual First Salmon or New Year's ceremony at Wełkwäu at the mouth of the Klamath; and finished with interlardings of description of the ritual and taboos. There is no formal unity to the account, but it seems to be much the sort of thing which a Yurok might now and then have told his son or nephew as they lay in the sweathouse.

●

a. It was at Enek[1] that they first made salmon. Two women lived there. There were no salmon in the world when Wohpekumeu came. He entered and

19. They recognized him by his horns.
20. If they had killed him who could restore their sight.
21. Incomplete.

1. The Yurok name of the Karok town of Amaikiaram, small but sacred, and situated on the west ("north") bank just downstream of the falls below the mouth of the Salmon. A New Year's ceremony for salmon and a Jumping Dance are made here in the spring. The attribution to this place of the first salmon, which is common or customary in Yurok belief, is therefore natural.

saw them. One said to the other, "What shall we eat?" She said, "Go up on the terrace."[2] She climbed up while Wohpekumeu sat and watched her trying to conceal what she did. She had a box with water and salmon inside. She took one out. Then they split it, put it on sticks, and broiled it. Wohpekumeu put his hand into his carrying case[3] and said, "I shall eat my salmon." They looked and saw him draw it out. It was really alder bark.[4] They thought, "Where did he get his salmon?" for they were the only ones that owned salmon and had concealed them. Wohpekumeu watched, thinking, "Let me learn with surety whether it is they who keep salmon, for I have never seen it before." Now when they cooked their salmon they put angelica root[5] into its mouth before they set it by the fire, that they might not have bad luck. Then they said, "Let us go out."

As soon as Wohpekumeu saw that he was alone in the house, he went hastily (to) where he had seen them take the salmon. He found the box, tipped it over, and ran out. The water flowed to the river.[6] Wohpekumeu ran upstream. The two women pursued him. They were about to catch him when he saw two tan oak trees.[7] He jumped between them, saying, "Spread apart: they are about to overtake me." When he was between, they closed around him. The two women went around outside, unable to reach him.

b. Then Wohpekumeu said, "Let the river run downstream," and he blew downstream. That is how the river comes to flow. Before there had been none. Wohpekumeu said to the river, "First of all, a great salmon must come up. He will be the salmon chief. They shall never catch him with nets. They shall catch only the little ones."

Every spring the great salmon has to come first, and all the little ordinary ones follow him upstream. He is called Nepewo. The place downstream[8] from which he leaves is Kowetsek. That is where he lives. When he comes from there he runs right up the middle of the river, so he is never caught with nets. When he comes to Enek he circles around in the river several times, looking at the place.[9]

2. *Melku*, the peripheral part of a Yurok house at ground level, as contrasted with the sunken center.

3. *Egor*: a piece of skin folded once lengthwise and with a stick attached along each edge. The skin is dried in bent position, and springs naturally together after opening. The whole article has much the external shape and size of a quiver, but is carried clamped under the arm.

4. Slabs of dried salmon have much the rusty color and texture of alder bark.

5. *Wołpei*. Of all herbs and roots it is the greatest stand-by in Yurok magic, especially of the more ritualistic sort.

6. That is, to where the river would be.

7. *Homono*.

8. Across the ocean.

9. The natal spot of his species, so to speak.

At the beginning the woge wanted to have salmon run up only one side of the river, so that they might be sure to have salmon there, but only there. Then they tried it thus. But they never caught anything. Then they changed. They thought, "Let them come upstream on both sides." Now they began to catch; so they knew that now they were coming upstream the right way. In some places the water eddies upstream. That is the salmon's resting place.[10] There he does not have to swim; the water carries him up.

c. Wohpekumeu, because it was he who made the river, went up to see how it ran. He saw many people along it, but all were afraid of him. They did not want him about because whatever woman he saw he took. So he came to the end of the river, to Petskuk.[11] Then he came downstream again. All along the river he saw nobody. They had all run away from him. They did not want to see him because he always desired women. Then he went on across the ocean to Kowetsek. There he saw those who had lived on the river but had gone there because they feared him. They saw him coming. They saw him across the river,[12] and one shouted, "Here he is again." Wohpekumeu sat down at the river. He thought, "Why do they fear me? I never do them harm." He took a stick, set it up in the water, and thought, "I will make my fishing place here. I will teach them how to catch salmon." Then his medicine[13] began to talk behind him. He looked back and took it: it was fir needles. He rubbed and crushed them between his hands over the water where he was going to fish, and as the needles fell and touched the water he saw the salmon begin to leap there.

d. There was a young man at Wełkwäu. Every day he remained in the sweathouse. They always saw him asleep[14] and thought that he remained (there) constantly. But he was not always there. At night he would go off. He went to Kowetsek. There he saw many people. They stood along the river holding salmon harpoons. He saw them: that is how human beings learned to use salmon harpoons. He thought, "I would like to take that home." Then he spoke to the headman there, and the headman said, "If you want to learn this thing, stay here and I will tell you how to use the medicine." So he stayed.

10. *Woegolok*.

11. "Upstream," here as the name of the eastern end of the world.

12. Imaginary worlds have a way of being replicas of this one, and the Yurok world is built around a river.

13. The herb, leaf, or root used with a formula.

14. The northwestern Indians, especially the older men, have a faculty of spending indefinite periods lying in a somnolent condition, although this does not seem to prevent them from rousing their full faculties on occasion. Nothing much would have been thought of the young man's appearing to sleep day after day and night after night.

They went down to the river and saw Nepewo coming.[15] The headman stood ready, holding his spear. The one from Weɫkwäu stood by him. The headman said, "Watch me." When he saw the great salmon moving slowly along, he motioned as if to thrust, but held his harpoon back. Then he began to talk to Nepewo. He said, "I wish many salmon would come. I want no one to have ill luck, but all to do well. I want no one to be bitten by rattlesnakes. I want no sickness to be. Let everything grow well, acorns and grass seeds, and other things."[16] While he talked, he poised his harpoon, pointing it at Nepewo, who went on slowly. But he did not strike, and the great salmon went on his way. It was him that he had addressed.

Then, after he had let Nepewo escape, the headman went to the mouth of the river and watched for other salmon. As soon as he saw one, he speared it. He said, "If you catch salmon thus at the mouth,[17] do not use a wooden club to kill them. Take a stone and hit them on the head. If you use wood it will be bad: you will not catch more. But upstream everyone will use wooden clubs. And if you catch salmon at the mouth, bury them in the sand. Do not let them lie out. Even if you catch twenty, bury every one. Let only the tails stick out."

Then he from Weɫkwäu saw him carrying that salmon away. He saw that when the headman of Kowetsek started to go to his house, he carried the salmon in his right hand. Then when he came to a certain place he changed it to his left hand. Across the stream were many men, all shouting about the salmon. Now they came up to the house, and he was about to cut up his salmon. Then he took angelica root and rubbed it between his hands, letting it drop into the fire. Then as he cooked, the smell was good. Not everybody might eat of the salmon cooked like this. If a man had slept with a woman the night before, he might not even remain in the house when this was being done or he would become sick, for the angelica was medicine.

Then he saw how they did with their salmon harpoon, keeping it outside the sweathouse. He learned this at Kowetsek: that is why they do thus now at the mouth of the river. The night before he was going to use his harpoon, the headman rested it on a stick.[18] He said to him, "Always point the spear toward me[19] before you are going to use it; set it up like this and talk to it."

15. The entire performance is that which occurred annually at the mouth of the Klamath—transferred to the mythical place across the ocean.

16. This prayer, if the series of blunt requests can be so called, evidently forms part of the formula recited at the Weɫkwäu New Year ceremony.

17. Of the Klamath.

18. The front end of the harpoon is supported on an upright stick; the berth [?] rests on the ground.

19. Toward Kowetsek, west.

Now the man who is to spear the next day does not sleep. All night he throws angelica into the fire in the sweathouse and talks to his harpoon outside so that he may have good luck. And he must have a man ready to eat his salmon when he has speared it. And if he sees a woman bathing in the creek, naked, he will not spear, but goes back. It is difficult to harpoon the salmon, and necessary to make the medicine first. Thus they do at the mouth of the river.[20]

Then he of Weɬkwäu went to Kowetsek again. He wished to learn more, because there were not many salmon. When he arrived he said to the headman, "There are not many salmon at the mouth of the river." Then the one of Kowetsek said, "It is well. This time I shall give you more. At first I did not believe that you were going to do what I told you, but now (that I see you are in earnest) I shall give you more of the medicine that I use; and you must feed him enough at Weɬkwäu; feed him with angelica." He meant the (sacred) pipe in the house at Weɬkwäu which helps to bring the salmon. This is alive. If one sees it he might think it is only a pipe, a wooden pipe with a little stone bowl; but it is a person.[21]

When he who is going to make medicine at the mouth of the river has taken the salmon, it is carried up to Weɬkwäu and sliced. There the man who is to eat it is ready. He has stayed in the sweathouse for some time, getting sweathouse wood daily. Now the salmon is cooking with angelica root, and he begins to eat. The headman at Kowetsek had said, "If you eat the entire salmon you will always be lucky. If he who eats this salmon eats it all, he will have fortune all his life." But no one ever eats the whole salmon at once; it is too much for him, for it is too greasy. Many men have tried, because he of Kowetsek spoke thus, but no one has succeeded.

Now perhaps he who has eaten it wishes to go southward. Then he has to wait five nights before he starts along the coast. If he wants to go downstream (north along the coast), he must cross the river to Rekwoi and stay five nights before he travels. That is because the salmon has been caught and cooked with medicine, and therefore the medicine is inside him. After five nights it is well; he may go. But if he is to travel upstream, it is only three nights that he need wait before starting.[22]

Lamprey eels were also first made at Kowetsek. If one catches them at the mouth of the river, he must cover them with sand. But if he who has killed a person goes out to gaff lamprey eels there, he does not bury them, so that he may leave hurriedly at any time. Such a man is constantly looking about him

20. Here the narrator has lapsed from mythical narrative into outright description of ritual. He returns to his story in the ensuing paragraph, only to leave it for explanation once more.

21. This pipe is so powerful as to be very much dreaded by the Yurok.

22. The reason for this lightening of the taboo is not clear.

because he has killed:[23] therefore he lets his eels dry lying on the sand. Also, he does not string them through their mouths but carried them off in his quiver.

•

After dictating into ten cylinders, Stone said that he had forgotton to say that Wełkwäu young man brought one sacred pipe from Kowetsek and then made a "partner" or mate for it at Wełkwäu. Also he left something "like his picture" (his shadow?) at home while he traveled to the end of the world; it was thus he saw the pipe at Kowetsek. Less clear is the following: They did not recognize him at Kowetsek and were going to harpoon him. When a salmon came, he speared it. Though they lay in wait for him, they could not kill him there.

C2y. The Salmon and Kowetsek

A SUMMARY ACCOUNT

An interpreter-Englished version of this tale, obtained from Stone in 1902, was printed in Kroeber and Gifford, World Renewal, Appendix II, no. 9, pp. 120–23, though with different letter designations for the sections.

Portion *d* (*f* in World Renewal), telling the origin of the First Salmon rite at Wełkwäu, was redictated by Stone onto phonograph cylinders in 1907, and subsequently transcribed into Yurok and English, but it proved repetitious and without content additional to that of the first version; consequently the translation has not been included here.

C3. Falcon

This is more definitely an animal story than the Yurok generally tell. It is somewhat in the Karok vein, and in fact it is likely that it is a composite of Karok and Yurok episodes. The swift duck hawk or gerfalcon who is the hero is always associated by the Karok with the peak A'u'ich (Sugarloaf), which overhangs the Klamath and a little upstream from the mouth of the Salmon, in the heart of their territory. A ledge near the summit of the little mountain has been the meeting place of individuals of this species probably from time immemorial. The Karok believe in consequence that the pair of *aikneich* hawks homing on A'u'ich are immortal, and that they go off only to take away their young of the year. The bird has deeply impressed their mythologic consciousness. It is of significance that Stone, the narrator of this tale, was half Karok in ancestry, and in fact that his father was from Segwu' at the foot of A'u'ich. On the other hand, the first parts of the story are not only localized in Yurok territory but are explanatory of natural features there. These first incidents are therefore likely to be of

23. He is uneasy because avengers may at any time appear.

Yurok origin, though whether they have always attached to the *aikneich-kerernit* hawk cannot be affirmed.

However mingled its elements, the tale is well organized. The concentration on the career of the hero produces an inner unity of plot. This following out of a life history to its achieved completion is in the accustomed vein of serious Yurok story-tellers. The variety of animal characters, abundance of explanations of topographical features, rapidity of development of action in each episode, lack of emotional tension, and inclination to an unaccentuated humor are typical of popular or fragmentary narration. Most of the incidents are indeed mentioned in Waterman's toponymy (see the footnotes). However, they are here strung together into a consistent Kerernit saga, specifically characterized by almost exclusively animal (or at least subhuman) personages.

•

a. Kerernit[1] grew at Orekw.[2] The Pelicans[3] lived near him. Gull[4] was his friend. Then Kerernit's children died. He said, "I want no one to catch smelt (surf fish) here, because my children have died."[5] Soon he saw many boats. The Pelicans were coming to fish at Orekw. Then Kerernit sent word to Gull, "Go and tell them that I shall not let them fish because my children have died." Gull went and told the Pelicans. They said, "We cannot stop now; we have come and we must fish. How big is his mouth?" Gull said, "Oh, he has only a small mouth." The Pelicans said, "Well, let him come. We are going to fish. If he does not like it, tell him he can begin to fight." Gull went back to Kerernit. The Pelicans said to one another, "Let us attack him. We have large mouths and can swallow him. When you see him, open your mouths."

Now they say Kerernit coming, and prepared to fight. The first Pelican opened his mouth. Kerenit flew straight into it and shot through him. The next one opened his mouth, and Kerenit went through him. So he killed them all. That is why he moved away from Orekw, because he had killed many of them.[6]

1. Kerernit (Karok Aikneich) is the duck hawk or gerfalcon.

2. [K. has a marginal query whether the wording should be "in sight of Orekw." He notes that Waterman, Geography, map 33, nos. 24 and 25, has Kerernit start at Trinidad.—Ed.] This localization on the coast does not necessarily go back to a Yurok source. The Karok and Yurok had some knowledge of all of each other's territory, and Orekw would stand out as a place where a dance was held. Nevertheless, the color of the first two episodes suggests a Coast Yurok origin.

3. Takwus.

4. Kegosne.

5. A characteristic state of mind: I have suffered; therefore my dignity is hurt if others find profit or pleasure in my sight.

6. Vengeance would be taken on him.

b. He went on toward the river, but first he stopped at Melego.[7] Someone was already living on the other side of the rock, but he thought, "Perhaps they will not trouble me." He went to hunt sea lions and sometimes caught ten. When the one on the other side of the rock saw him bringing them ashore, she came and took away eight, lifting them like salmon: she was exceedingly tall. Perhaps she left him two of his ten sea lions. Keremit was displeased. He said to his wives, "Next time I think I shall hurt her. She does not do right. She always takes away my sea lions. She leaves me two, or sometimes only one." His wives said, "No, let it be. Do not mind. She is large and you are small." Then he thought, "Well, perhaps."

c. Now he went hunting again and killed ten. He (had) said to his wives, "This time I shall do her an injury. When she takes them away from me, sometimes she carries them herself, and sometimes she has me help her put them on her back." As soon as he landed he saw her coming. She took eight sea lions and prepared to carry them on her back. Then she called to Keremit, "Help me to rise with my load." He was ready with a stone. As she began to get up and the pack strap drew her forehead back, he struck her. He beat her head again and again until she was dead. Then he ran and said to his wives, "I have killed her. Let us close the house." Their door was of stone: they shut it. Soon they heard it shake. Then it rattled harder. They heard the water strike it; each time it moved. Now his women said, "I told you not to hurt her." Soon they heard waves dashing far up on the rock in which was their house. Then when he seemed to hear the water falling from above,[8] he opened the door and leaped out with his wives.[9] They were breakers[10] who were pursuing him because he had killed one of them.

d. Keremit went on to upstream from Nohtsku'm, where there is a large rock by the river at Knetkenolo.[11] He put his house right on that rock. He also made a fish dam there. He did not wish any salmon to pass: he made a waterfall so high that they could not leap it. People had to drag boats up over the rocks and set them in again above. The sloping stone is smooth now where they drew them up, and there are holes in the rock which held the posts of his

7. Melego is a large rock "a mile or two" south of the mouth of the Klamath. See Waterman, Geography, map 9, no. 9: Meleg, a sea stack, over two miles south of the mouth; and a reference to the present myth. The name refers to offal or refuse.

8. Between breakers of the surf.

9. "Wife" the interpreter has said up to this point, possibly through inaccuracy, since two wives are mentioned beyond. Or the narrator may have been inadvertent.

10. *Aihpo*?

11. Knetkenolo is on the north side, about halfway between Nohtsku'm and Mūrek. See Waterman, map 17, no. 9, with a summary of the same incident. [This map is reproduced here as map 5.—Ed.]

dam. Below, he put a large rock to sit on and watch the fishing at the dam: he called it Otskergerun.[12] Then the old woman Black Bear,[13] his wife, thought she would be the first to try the seat. It was flat only on top, and the sides sloped steeply. She went too far, her feet slipped, she slid down, struck below, and her excrement flew about. One can see it now on the rocks.

e. Now they did not like him to have his dam there, because there would never be salmon above. And Kerernit heard the noise of the breakers from the ocean.[14] He thought, "Perhaps they will come up after me. I had better move farther upstream." Then he went on up to Merip and built his dam over again. He thought, "Well, this will be a good place to have dances and jollity." So he sent Fish Hawk[15] to Kowetsek[16] to bring a flat rock to gamble on. Owl and Blue Jay and many others were with Kerernit. Then Fish Hawk returned but could not carry the rock quite to Merip. It was too heavy, and he dropped it just upstream of Wa'asei: it is there now.[17] Blue Jay, who was dressing a deerskin on a stone by the river, just downstream from Merip, left the skin there. One can see where she left it: the stone is spotted on top.

f. Now there was no one upstream who could eat salmon because of the dam at Merip. There was a powerful person at Oknuɫ[18] who wished to go down to Merip and tear up the dam. So he started, and many with him, ready to fight. But Kerernit was away at Kowetsek and did not see them. When he came home his dam was gone. Then they told him how the vicious one of Oknuɫ had come from Hupa and torn it down. Kerernit said, "We shall go and fight for that." They prepared for war and started.

g. At Koitsoperekw[19] they stopped to eat salmon. Hurhurhurtsim[20] brought an acorn. Half of it was eaten off, but he brought them one end of it. Coyote also came with half an acorn. They threw the two pieces in the fire and they burst. Then much acorn meal fell down: it covered everything about. Old

12. Waterman, map 17, no. 4 (same incident). Otskergerun is nearly a mile below Knetkenolo.

13. Tsireri.

14. Mythologic exaggeration. The surf cannot possibly be heard so far inland. The place is more than twenty miles from the mouth by river, and twelve air miles from Orekw, the nearest point on the coast.

15. Tseikwatsekw.

16. Kowetsek is across the ocean, where the salmon live.

17. Waterman, map 17, no. 74, Kowitsik-oloäg, with the same incident. [See map 5 in this volume.—Ed.]

18. Oknuɫ is Hupa Honsading, the town in Hupa Valley farthest downstream on the Trinity, that is, nearest the Yurok.

19. On the hills above the north or downstream end of Hupa.

20. A bird.

woman Black Bear and old woman Grizzly Bear, Kerernit's wives,[21] helped themselves greedily. He said, "Eat slowly"; but they would not. Then they began to grunt, for they had eaten too much. He said, "I told you not to eat so much. I knew you would get sick." Their bellies swelled. Hummingbird[22] began to dance to doctor them. Then she (?) said, "Open your mouth," and when Black Bear opened it, Hummingbird darted in, flew through her, and emerged, and Black Bear was relieved. So they got well again.

h. Then they started again. Now they had come nearly to Hupa, and from the prairie on the hill could see the whole valley. So they said, "We had better sing." They sang that they might not be hit by arrows. One of them began, the others joined in, and all danced. When they finished they said to Hurhurhurtsim, "You sing." They knew that his was the best song.[23] So little Hurhurhurtsim sang and they danced. Soon they heard a wind. Then they danced harder. After a time they could hear the wind breaking down trees. Then someone was crying. It was old woman Black Bear frightened by the wind and running off downhill. Kerernit was ashamed, blew after her, and called "Do not come back to me! Stay in the woods!" Then they heard another crying: it was Grizzly Bear. She also ran downhill and Kerernit called out, "Do not come back." So these two live about in the woods.

i. When they came to Oknuɬ, they did not find that man. After he had destroyed the dam he was afraid of Kerernit and made his house in the water. Kerernit and his companions saw him and his wife sitting on top of his house.[24] Coyote wanted to be the first to shoot him. "Watch! I shall hit him! Look! Look!" he said as he shot, but his arrow flew only a little way. Before he knew it Coyote had shot away all his arrows. Then Kerernit shot. He struck the side of the house, but not the man. Then he and his wife jumped off and hid behind the stone (house). They shot at him over the river, but he remained hidden behind. Finally he went underwater. They could not reach him. So they all returned downstream to Merip.

j. When they arrived they counted their number and missed Fish Hawk. Kerernit thought, "He must have been killed somehow on the way." They searched everywhere. Now they had been everywhere without finding him. Then Kerernit went up into the sky. There he found him. He said to Kerernit, "I came because I have a grandmother here." So Kerernit returned.

k. Kerernit got ready to move upstream again. He did not like to remain

21. Women accompanied war parties to cook.
22. Tsegemem.
23. Most effective against arrows. Its power made the wind rise.
24. A rock in the river.

at Merip because he had lost his dam. Then he went to A'u'ich.[25] There he made himself a new dam, for he thought that here he would finally live.[26] He made a fishing place on this and on that side of the river: one was his and the other for Fish Hawk. His house he built on A'u'ich. He carried salmon home in a new way, because it was so steep to where he lived: he made a bridge of poles and scaffolding from his fishing place across the face of the cliff to nearly the summit, where he had his house.

l. He made it that they fish differently in that place. He did not use the same dipnet as downstream here. He took shorter sticks and made a net for scooping.[27]

m. Now Grizzly Bear came back to Kerernit. He had given her up, but she lived with him there at A'u'ich. However, he had another wife, Barnacle.[28] Then Grizzly Bear said to her, "Let me louse you." Barnacle consented. Grizzly scratched her head instead of really looking for lice. Barnacle cried, "You hurt me!" Grizzly did not wish to louse her: she wished to kill her. She threw into the fire whatever she found in Barnacles's hair. It would burst and shoot about, fire was scattered around the house, and Grizzly Bear ran off in fear.

n. Kerernit used to go downstream to see his sweetheart. Then a little boy, Tsega,[29] was singing, "I want him to come back: I shall eat *nôris* roots." Grizzly Bear heard it and caught him. "Why do you always say that?" she said, scaring him. The boy said, "Kerernit went far downstream to see his sweetheart, and will bring back *nôris* roots." That is how Grizzly Bear found out that he had a sweetheart. She went down to the river, pulled out the stake at one end of his dam, and the whole of it was swept away. She had been angry at her husband; but now she was afraid and thought, "Let me run away." So she started off with all her property on her back. Just as she got out the door, she saw Kerernit coming, but he did not see her.

25. A precipitous and striking conical peak around which the Klamath winds just downstream from Katimin (Segwu') and upstream from the mouth of the Salmon. The Karok name is here retained. The Yurok equivalent was given as Segwem, which seems derived from Segwu', or may be an error for it.

26. The Yurok conceive of a life as established on a spot. Settlement there gives final repose and marks accomplishment of natural courses. This attitude is reflected in tale after tale; and in life by the custom of dying where one was reared.

27. Such a net is used by the Karok of this section. The frame is kite-shaped and is plunged into holes at the bottom of falls, whereas the usual larger "dipnet" has a triangular frame and is set in an eddy.

28. Nererger.

29. A small riverbird.

When he came to the top of A'u'ich he did not hear the (usual) noise of roaring from the river falling over his dam. Then he knew that something was wrong. He came into the house and asked, "What has happened to my dam?" The little boy said, "Your wife destroyed it." "Where is she now?" "She has gone away." "Where did she go?" "I do not know; but she went out." "How long has she been gone?" "She had just left when you came in." Kerernit took his bow and arrows. He went out and looked over Segwu'. There he saw her with her load. Angrily he aimed, shot, and saw her fall down crying. The ground is bloody where she was hit, and Grizzly Bear is a rock there now.

o. Then Kerernit married the downstream woman. Whenever he has children on that ledge on the cliff of A'u'ich, they cry for five days. When they are large enough, they all come down to his fishing place. Then he takes them downriver to the place in which he was married.[30] He does not keep his children.

p. Once while Kerernit was taking his children away, a man went to look at his house. He sat in a wood-carrying basket, while his friends carefully let him down from the summit by a rope of hazel withes. Then he found feathers of many different kinds before Kerernit's house. There were many large woodpecker crests. He took what he wanted and they drew up the rope again. Then he related, and they saw, what he had got; and they returned (home). That man became exceedingly rich. No one had ever been at Kerernit's house before, so he was able to take whatever he liked.[31]

C4. The Doctor Married at Turip

This tale has more of the emotional quality of good Yurok tales than most of the others told by this informant. It is typical in dealing with the life history of an individual, or rather, a pair of individuals—their longings, endeavors, and satisfactions—and the plot incidents are developed with reference to them. The story begins with two subsidiary themes, whose proper relation to the main theme is skillfully established.

The main story is related to that recounted in Spott and Kroeber, Yurok Narratives, no. 23, "The Doctor from Repokw." Its localization is the same: Rekwoi, Turip, the mountains above Blue Creek, even the whale there; and the tragedy is the same, but in the former version the doctor's two brothers play no important role. That narrative seemed to me a legend of human beings rather than a myth about woge. The present version, however, is connected with the episode of the sea lion, who institutes

30. Katimin. [K. has a marginal reference to Orpheus.—Ed.]
31. This paragraph is legend pieced onto the myth.

custom and is therefore a woge. Hence it is fitting that the doctor does not die either, but goes to live with the spirits. The whole tale remains on the plane of myth.[1]

•

a. It was a person of Sa' who made it that the eyes are taken out from salmon caught at Akierger[2] opposite Erliken.[3] They throw away the eyes of salmon only at this place. The one who caused this to be, used to go downstream, making himself like a sea lion. He came to Rekwoi, where they always like to spear sea lions. They saw him, ran to harpoon him, and struck him. He tried to escape. Many men were holding the line, when it broke. He swam out into the ocean and leaped about, splashing. Soon they saw him coming back. They said, "It is the same one! See how he leaps!" He went up the middle of the river to Erliken. There he swam into their nets, but felt them in time and swam out again and was not caught. Then he went onshore where they fish. He thought, "This is a good fishing place. I was nearly caught. I am glad that I tore away. It will be best if they take out the eyes from salmon here. Perhaps they will have good luck if they do that."

b. He was nearly dead from his harpoon wound.[4] All the doctors tried to cure him, but he did not get better. He was unable to rise. Then he heard that they were beginning to make the Deerskin Dance at Wohkero; but he lay and thought he should die.

c. Now a man came up from downstream (Rekwoi) with two slaves to go to the dance.[5] Below Wohkero they begin the Jumping Dance near the river, but not everyone may dance. They question and they say to this and that one, "You may dance." If a man has paid very much for his wife, his children are not allowed to dance. If he has paid only dentalia, it is well: his children may

1. [K.'s manuscript has a number of jottings indicating he intended to expand this headnote: "Welding of 3 themes—(1) sea lion, (2a) slaves—sulk—seize pains/give—shark, (2b) [Yurok Narratives] #23 mainly concerned *her* acquisition of power, (3) marry, force (?), lost/short. Man gets pains—dr. practice—on shark—1 yr. after marriage—sleeping on bar."—Ed.]

2. Waterman, Geography, map 10, no. 17: Erkyierger, a fishing place. Eyes are gouged out of salmon caught here, and they must be cooked the same day. There is a swift current here, known as Lamb's Riffle.

3. Waterman, map 10, no. 14. [Erliken is a town about 3 miles downstream from the mouth of Blue Creek.—Ed.]

4. He has apparently come home to Sa' now.

5. Here begins a second thread leading to the main story. [Kroeber, Handbook, p. 32, explains that Yurok men sometimes entered into slavery when they were unable to pay claims for acts of violence or the destruction of property. On the present manuscript K. has a marginal note giving the dance place as Plekseu (?) or Helegäu, 1 mile downriver from Wohkero.—Ed.]

dance. But if he has added woodpecker crests, his children may not dance.[6] Thus they always select the dancers there.

Now this one from downstream arrived with his two slaves. Then they said, "No, they cannot dance. They are slaves." Then he said, "Well, I think we had better go home." He had heard them say, "They cannot dance because they are slaves." So he went downstream with his two slaves. He sat in the middle while they paddled; and he cried, thinking of how they had been prevented from dancing.[7] When he came to Blue Creek he said, "Land here." Then they brought the boat to shore. He said, "I shall stay somewhere tonight. Take the boat down, but tomorrow bring it up and wait for me at Sa'. I shall meet you there."

d. Then he went up (Blue Creek), crying continually. He came to a brook flowing into Blue Creek and followed that. Then he saw trout. It was late and he thought, "I had better make camp." So he stayed there for the night. He caught five of the trout and, twirling his fire drill, cooked them. He found that they smelled like angelica root.[8] Then he began to think again about his slaves that had been sent out of the dance, and he cried more. He did not eat, and sat up all night without sleeping.

Early in the morning he started. When he had gone a short distance he saw small tracks. He followed them uphill. He continued until he came to a spring. There he saw something arranged for a seat. It was a whale's vertebra. Whale ribs were lying about. Then he knew that that was where they sat when they bathed in that spring.[9] From there he followed the tracks again. He was going on a trail now. Finally he saw a sweathouse. He heard them dancing inside.[10] Then he thought, "I will jump in." Then he jumped into the sweathouse. They were dancing for a woman who had begun to be a doctor. Then he seized the pains[11] and started out through the small door. They had closed the entrance as soon as he came in, but he escaped by the exit hole. When he came outside he knew nothing more. He was as if crazy. After a time he found himself nearly at the top of the hill above Sa', saw where he was, and

6. Others add that he may not dance if too little or nothing was paid for his mother.

7. His identification with his slaves suggests the familial status of these.

8. An omen of the supernatural events to follow.

9. To obtain supernatural power.

10. They were spirits; the mountains along upper Blue Creek are famous for them. The Yurok of course do not live in the mountains.

11. The *telogeł* or small animate objects which in the body of an ordinary person cause disease but in the body of the shaman, after proper "cooking" and domiciling by ritual, give her clairvoyance and the faculty of curing. The dance is part of the means used to accustom to each other the pains and their host.

knew where to go. He turned down to the river, found his two slaves waiting for him in the boat, jumped in, and lay down. They paddled him downstream.

e. As soon as he came to where he lived, to Knewole,[12] he went into the sweathouse and they began to make the doctor dance for the pains he had stolen from the people on the hill. He told his younger sister, "Take them. I give them to you."[13] Then she took the pains,[14] and they danced. After a time she controlled the pains and was a doctor.

f. Then she thought, "Let us go to Kohpei."[15] So she and her elder brother went. At Nekeł,[16] they found a dead shark on the beach, full of maggots. The woman thought, "Let me try if I can make it well." She danced around it. Sometimes she would suck it and then dance again. Now she saw the shark beginning to twitch; and when the tide was high it swam off, cured. Then she knew that she would be a good doctor.

g. Nevertheless they went on to Kohpei. They did not stay there long. When they came back to Rekwoi they found two men from Sa' to bring her to doctor him who had been speared and was about to die. She went upstream with them, for they paid her many dentalia. When she came to Sa' and saw him, he was very sick, and so thin that only his bones remained. Then she began to treat him. After a time she smoked. Then she danced again. Then she sang. Then she found the harpoon head in his body. The other doctors had not been able to see it. She sucked it out, and he became well.[17]

h. Now a man from Turip bought this doctor for wife. Her brother did not want to sell her, but the one from Turip offered so much that he took the price and let him have his sister. She did not want to go, but they paid so much that her brother had to let her go. Yet he told her husband, "Do not try to sleep with her: she has just become a doctor."[18] Then he agreed, and he went upstream with her. Now she considered, "It is well," and lived with her husband.

i. At last he thought, "I will sleep with her. It is over a year since we

12. Spoken of as if it were a part or suburb of Rekwoi, but probably the name of a house, like repokw in Spott and Kroeber, Yurok Narratives, no. 23. The word means "long." Waterman, map 8, no. 17, gives knäu as a house, which also appears several times in the Narratives.

13. Women, not men, are Yurok doctors.

14. Swallowed them.

15. At Crescent City; a Tolowa town.

16. In English, Nickel Creek, at about the southern limit of Tolowa territory.

17. Ordinary doctors do not usually suck out projectile points or treat wounds, but this patient was a spirit who had turned himself into a sea lion, and the harpoon point may have been supernatural too.

18. Supernatural and sexual activity are of course incompatible.

were married." He took her down on the sandbar[19] and slept with her. Then he fell asleep. After a time he knew that she was gone; but he thought, "Perhaps she went to get wood." It became nearly noon and he had not seen her. Now he knew that something had happened. So he started for Rekwoi, thinking, "Perhaps I shall find her there." When he arrived, her brother said, "No, I did not see her. She has not come here." Her husband said, "We went down to the river to sleep together. That is where I lost her." Her brother said, "Well, I told you not to try to sleep with her for a long time. But I think I know where she is. She has gone to the place where I seized the pains. I will go there. I cannot tell you when I shall come back, but I shall return."

j. He went upstream with him in his boat. Then he went uphill to where he had taken away the pains from them. Then from a distance he heard dancing in the sweathouse. When he came outside, he knew that his sister was dancing. Then he thought, "I will jump into the sweathouse and take her along." So he leaped in. As soon as he entered, the door shut, but he went out by the small exit, dragging his sister with him. Then he from Turip saw his wife coming back down the river. But her brother did not leave her there. He took her with him to Rekwoi to dance.[20] Then her husband followed her down from Turip and helped in her dance. After that she went back with him.

k. After nearly a year he tried to sleep with her again. The same thing happened. During the night she disappeared. He went to Rekwoi once more and told his brother-in-law. His brother-in-law came with him and went up in the hills again. There he saw his sister in the same place. But the people there said, "You shall not take your sister away this time. You will not be able to. She will live here. You can live here too and have a wife. Let her have a husband.[21] Both of you are not to go back." Then he said, "It is well." That is where they live now, he and his sister.

C5. Kewet Young Man Plays Shinny with Earthquake

This story is a formula and is recited to make the three players on one's side win. The players' legs are painted white.

•

19. Since the Yurok do not cohabit indoors for fear of driving wealth away from the house, they are constrained to sleep with their wives or sweethearts in the willows at the back of the bars along the river; and this is convenient only in the dry summer months.

20. Presumably the *remohpo* or doctor-training dance. She evidently had received an additional pain while with the spirits in the hills.

21. [K. queries whether "a husband" should be "her husband."—Ed.]

a. Earthquake[1] grew at Kenek. Five young men lived on Kewet Mountain: they came to Kenek to play double-ball shinny. Looking at the flat[2] there, they saw a crowd of people. Then a man asked them into his house. They (the Kenek people) were thinking of the five, "If they win they will take our women away." Then the youngest of the Kenek men invited those from Kewet to play shinny. Now one of the five from Kewet had a dog that was all covered with sores. When he poured water on its back, all the sores vanished and its skin was smooth. Then they handed shinny sticks to their visitors, but these said they had their own. Their friend advised them, "Don't run well off from your opponent (but step right where he treads), for he is Earthquake, and when he plays he shakes the ground."

b. Now Earthquake gave the double-ball to Kewet young man to hold in his teeth and drop it to start the game;[3] and there was a great crowd watching. Now those from Kewet had very short striking sticks, less than a forearm long.[4] Then their player scratched the ground in upriver direction,[5] picked up the loose dust, then drew his stick through his hand, and though it was of greasy-stone it stretched. So he made a scratch downriverward, did the same, and his shinny stick was full length.

c. The Kewet dog stood where Earthquake would throw the ball to.[6] His owner told it, "Whenever you see the double-ball coming, stand high and block it." But Earthquake did not see the dog. Then the Kewet player dropped the ball beside where he stood and struck. As he took it,[7] all shouted, thinking he would win. And he took it only once and carried it to the goal.[8] Then his

1. Yewoł.

2. The Kenek river terrace is fairly high and rather extensive.

3. The center players stand shoulder to shoulder, and as soon as the ball drops both try to hook the string. There is no blade on the stick, only a slightly curved point. [Stewart Culin, in Games of the North American Indians, U. S. Bureau of American Ethnology, Vol. 24, 1902–03, pp. 664-665, describes the Yurok game as played with "two bottle-shaped wooden billets . . . , 5-1/2 inches in length, with a knob at the end and two lines of bark left at the center, tied together with a piece of twine . . . ; accompanied by two long slender sticks . . . , 33 and 35 inches in length." Culin illustrates the billets and a stick; the latter he had obtained from "Wichapec Billy, 57 years of age, who had used them in matches . . . Money was put up, say five dollars on a side. Matches were formerly common between Hupa and Wichapec." Billy is probably K.'s informant A. I am indebted for the Culin reference to Frank Norick of the Lowie Museum of Anthropology, Berkeley.—Ed.]

4. Bad narrating; they were of *permeryer*, greasy-stone, but this comes out only below. Usually these tiny shinny sticks of legend are a span or less in length.

5. As we would say right and left, the Yurok thinks in terms of river flow.

6. The double-ball is mostly cast by its string, not struck like our shinny balls or hockey pucks.

7. Caught it on his hook end.

8. I believe it is allowable to run with the ball on one's stick. At any rate he got it to the goal

Kenek opponent sat down off to the side, holding his stick before his mouth,[9] ashamed, and went off to the hills and was called At-Kenek-he-plays-shinny, Kenek-erlergerł, Sandpiper.[10] Now Earthquake stopped playing, because he was ashamed too, since no one else had ever won from Kenek. But the Kewet player, the youngest brother of the five, took the two girls as wives that had been staked; they were in a house by themselves.

d. Now the youngest brother started to go to Sumig,[11] and his brother-in-law from Kenek went along. When he came to Johnson Lyons' place on the Bald Hills, at Umekweł, he smoked. Then he knocked the ashes out of his pipe: they are rocks there now.[12]

e. He went on to a place, I do not know what it is called,[13] where he smoked and blew out tobacco,[14] and said, "I wish I would see two whales," so that those who lived at Sumig would go after them,[15] and he could take the place. When he arrived at Sumig, there was no one around; all were busy about the whales. So he took the houses.

f. When those from Sumig returned, they asked, "Why do you stay in our houses?" "We came," he said. "We thought we would stop here and take the place." Then they began to fight. Those from Kenek became afraid, because even though they ran behind rocks, when the Sumig people shot, the arrows went right through. Nevertheless the Kenek people took the place, and those who had lived at Sumig went off.

g. The Kegor, Porpoises, are the children of Kewet young man.[16] They said, "We cannot raise our heads out of the water: only the backs of our necks show.[17]

Kekenomer means "living at Kenek"; they are the five brothers from Kewet Mountain.[18]

---

line. But if he did that on the first try, what part did the invisible dog play in the blocking of the cast of an opponent who never got started? Also it was Earthquake who could not see the dog, but Sandpiper who was defeated. Either the telling or the interpreting is careless about omissions and contradictions.

9. Hand before mouth is a familiar Indian gesture of embarrassment, but the stick is new.

10. Or Snipe?

11. Patrick's Point, on the coast between Trinidad and Big Lagoon.

12. Umekweł may mean "his pipe ashes."

13. Such ignorance or forgetfulness of locality is unusual.

14. As an offering to spirits.

15. As the Yurok do not pursue whales, he must have wished for whales on the beach or in risk of beaching themselves, an event that would certainly empty the town.

16. I suspect a misunderstanding.

17. This fits porpoises, but its relevance is unclear.

18. The etymology may or may not be sound, but I query the origin on Kewet. [Cl, n. 7, gives Kenomer as the name for the porpoises of Kenek.—Ed.]

Informant D

BILLY WERK OF WEITSPUS

Billy Werk was a tall, gaunt man of perhaps sixty when he recited most of the following narratives for me in 1907. He lived in the native house adjoining that of Stone (Informant I), the megwollep *or formulist for the Weitspus Deerskin and Jumping dances. This was Billy's wife's house, nī'kerwerk, "close-to-the-dance place,"*[1] *and he was therefore presumably half-married to her. He belonged to the house hiwo or hiwohp near the upriver end of the town, and was brother of Weitspus Doctor (Informant E) and of Billy Wilson, the legal father of Informant J. Billy Werk's Indian appellation was from his home: K'e-hiwo'h. This was a high-family house, and Hiwo'kege'i was a great doctor of a preceding generation. It was the sweathouse of hiwo which an inmate of woge times took away with him to the northern edge of the world (as recounted in tale D6), resting it briefly on its way uphill at ten spots at which the Jumping Dance ritual is performed.*

In spite of the family wealth, the brothers owned nothing in the way of valuables. All that Billy brought into the house into which he half-married was a shell dress which later on his daughter wore. Even then people talked about its being a dress of hiwo. Billy himself went about in rags, and his house was furnished meagerly for an old-style Yurok one. He had evidently not learned to do white man's work, or perhaps had become too old for it, and cash was scarce. When the 1901 Deerskin Dance broke up in a quarrel because too many obsidians had been saved out for the last performance, and Stone, the megwollep, *became sulky and refused to speak the formula for the Jumping Dance to follow, Werk was tempted by the four dollars which I had collected*

1. House 15 in Waterman, Geography, map 26, but the adjacent 14 is nameless in Waterman and was presumably an "annex" or extension. In my day, 15 was a pit and Werk lived in 14, next to which stood 13, ple'l, the home of Stone.

and contributed for the formulist's efforts, and undertook to recite the ritual, which he probably more or less knew but not formally or perfectly. This brought Stone around, and he officiated.[2] But Werk had already spent part of *the fee at the store for some flour and a shirt—a rather pathetic illustration of poverty in a time which had become dollar-economied even for the Indians.*

In 1906, having considerable load and expecting more, I went downriver with two boats, and engaged Billy to steer the second. He asked for advance wages to buy his wife food while he was on the trip; but next morning some of the money having also gone for whiskey, he was unable to start. After some hours he sent word that if I could let him have some of my "soap medicine" (Bromo-Seltzer) for his headache, he would be ready; and, having blinked this down and tied a red strip of rag around his lank gray locks, he managed his canoe with complete control, a picturesque figure as he stood up in the stern for each riffle.

He was a peaceable man who got into no troubles. He knew the medicine formula for deersickness, wer-neryermer. *He also knew songs for deer hunting and was in demand for them. He always kept a boat. The only work he did for white people was as a boatman. He was also a good fisherman and with his brothers had four fishing places near Weitspus.*

His unkemptness, and the fact that he seemed to enjoy no particular esteem for knowledge among his townsmen, led me to neglect him unduly, but he proved an excellent informant, both as to substance and manner, and I ought probably to have secured more tales from him.[3] *As a narrator he is concrete, orderly, unrepetitious, and to the point. His stories move along concisely and with interest.*

Narratives D1, 2, 3, 5, and 6 I secured on the phonograph, also writing down for guidance an outline of the interpreter's translation. These narratives were later Englished phrase by phrase from the cylinders by Catherine Goodwin.[4] *The first of these myths I wrote not only in outline but in full English at the time; and the two renditions are here reproduced as D1*x *and D1*y. *They are followed by a comparison which shows the differences to be in substance rather than form; that is, the narrator varied more from telling to telling than the two differently circumstanced translators varied in faithfulness or style.*

D1x. Theft of Fire

interpreter's version

a. They were living at Kenek. They had no food that we use now, only pitch for acorns and alder bark for salmon. There was not yet a river. It was

2. Kroeber, Handbook, p. 58.
3. [See also tale DD4 at end of book, for a fragment told by Informant D.—Ed.]
4. [Kroeber added in the margin "and others!" but did not specify who they were.—Ed.]

always night; there was no daylight as now. They had no fire. Whenever they wished to cook food, they put it into the armpit. Many lived there at Kenek: Wohpekumeu was there, and Earthquake, and Thunder, and Kenek-erlergerɬ,[1] who played shinny, and the (small hairy) Ant (Harputs). All they did was to play shinny. But they did not like the way it was, for it was always night.

b. Then Megwomets[2] said, "Let me go around this world to find daylight. If I do not find it in this world, I will go to the sky. I will attempt it."

Then he arrived there above, and saw that it was light as it is here now. So he went back from the sky to Kenek. Those there said, "Did you find it?" "Yes, I saw it," he said. "Where is it?" "It is in the sky." "Well, then, how can we bring it down here, do you think? For we must have it." They asked all who lived there, but all said they did not know, that it was very difficult.

c. Wohpekumeu sat in his house and never came out: he did not care to see the playing. Now they had talked for one year. Then one of them went and told Wohpekumeu, "Well, now, we have found fire, for everything is up above. But we can in no way obtain it, for the people there are too many. He who saw it says that he could not at all come close. He saw it from far." Wohpekumeu said, "Well, I am able."

d. Then he went to all the birds to tell them to help. "I will tell you what we must do. We will stand at intervals. Let one stand there (and one there). I will enter the house. But that which I take, to the first one that is standing, I will hand it to him."

e. Then they started. Megwomets went along to show them where he had seen it. They said, "Let us first see the place." Then they came where they could see from, and saw that town.

f. Then Wohpekumeu thought, "Let me appear like a woman." Then he changed himself. He put on a (double) dress and a new deerskin blanket and carried a burden basket. Every kind (of food) was in that basket, salmon and acorns. He was about to start so as to arrive when it was just evening. Now it began to be night in that (place) above. Then he told them where they should stand and wait. Then he went.

g. When he arrived, he saw there was only one sweathouse. Then he stood outdoors a little while and looked about, for they had all gone (into the house) to eat and he wanted to see. Then he entered. Now there were many persons inside, eating. He went straight in without halting, carrying his basket. As he entered, he saw an old woman sitting on the left (of the house as one enters). Now he carried his basket to where the old woman sat. All

1. [Kenek-erlergerɬ is tentatively identified as Sandpiper in C5*c*.—Ed.]

2. [Megwomets is a bearded dwarf, the food-giver—Ed.]

looked, but no one spoke, because no one knew him;[3] but all stopped eating. Then he saw a man sitting in the middle, a large man, shining and clear.

h. Now the (men) all went out to go to the sweathouse (for the night). The woman (Wohpekumeu) looked about. He saw two *rumitsek* (openwork) baskets hanging. He saw something almost like light in them. Then he knew that one of them contained fire and one daylight (*ketsain*). Whenever he looked about in that house he saw a sort of daylight in the basket, but the other he saw was constantly bright, the one that held fire.

Then now it began to dawn, but he had not slept, the one who had come there. He had waked the whole night. Now he stood up carefully. The old woman was sleeping. He went to the entrance and softly opened the inner door.[4] Then he opened the outer door. Then he reentered the house. Then he softly walked to take the baskets. Then carefully he went out. As soon as he had emerged, he ran. But he left in the house all the (woman's) clothing he had been wearing. When he was outdoors, he became a man, for he had taken off the clothing. He had not gone halfway from the house to where the first (of his companions) stood when he heard shouting behind. The fire owners were following him. Nearly they caught him.

i. Then he reached the person who was standing nearest. He gave him the baskets. He was Eagle (Tohteɬ). Then they pursued him. Whenever they drew near, he swerved to the side, then to the other.

Then he came to the next one, who was Pigeon (Hemi'). He ran. He too swerved, but they pursued.

The next was Chicken-Hawk (Tspegi). He too fled.

The next was Long One (Knewollek, a water monster). As far as they had carried them, there was daylight. He leaped straight into the river.

Next was Ant. He too ran swiftly.

Then Hummingbird (Tsegemem) took them.

Then Kenek-erlergerɬ took them. And he was nearly caught.

j. The last was Frog. When (that one) was almost caught, Frog received (the baskets). He leaped. He went on by leaping. And he too was tired and nearly caught. Then he threw the baskets into his mouth and leaped into the water. Then it began to be dark again.[5] They who pursued did not see where

3. The Yurok pronoun is indeterminate as to sex.

4. At the head of the ladder from the pit or at the partition forming the wood storage chamber. Recent old-style houses sometimes contain such inner doors, but they swing on a leather hinge. The ancient method of hanging them is not known.

5. The same should have happened when Long One dived. The narrator was then evidently on the point of so saying, since he stated that until then the flight had taken place in daylight. However, either he or the interpreter neglected to complete the remark, or it was deliberately omitted because the darkness cannot well be brought on until the pursuit is to be ended.

they were going. Then they stopped where they were in the darkness: the pursuers all went home.

Frog emerged again. When he had emerged, he looked about, but saw no one. Then he brought out his baskets from his mouth. Then he spat (the fire) into willow roots. That is why they make fire with the drill, because he spat into the willow.[6] Then there was fire and there was daylight as now.

D1y. Theft of Fire

VERSION FROM PHONOGRAPH DICTATION

a. They lived at Kenek. Every kind lived there, Megwomets, Wohpekumeu, Ant, Earthquake, Thunder—they played shinny constantly—and Kenekerlergerł. They scarcely had daylight. And they did not like that, the dark. So they were talking about it, saying, "What can we do? We do not like the darkness."

b. And Megwomets said, "I will do the traveling." They said, "So be it, may you." He said, "I am going around this world. And if I do not see, I will go around the sky."

And he went up in the sky, and found much light there. And in plain sight was a house; there were so many persons there that when anything flew overhead it almost fell down. And he did not go farther, but returned to Kenek. And they asked him if he had seen. So he said, "Yes, but I can do nothing. I cannot bring the light here."

c. They talked about it for a whole year. And there was one seated in the house who did not hear[7] anything about it—about what they did. He never looked there, that one, at them playing shinny. All day they played shinny: he never came out and watched them. So once they said, "Let us tell him. Let him know too." Then they told him. They told him that it was thus, "and we can do nothing."

So they talked much. And they said to Earthquake, "Can you break[8] it?" He said, "No." Then they asked Thunder, "Can you break it?" He said, "No." They asked everyone that was there, "Can you break it?" At last Wohpekumeu said, "Anyhow, I will go. I think I can do something about it." That is how he came to go.

d. Now they decided who was to go with him. Then they told him who was to go with him. Thunder was to go along, Chicken Hawk (Tspegi), Pigeon

6. The usual Yurok material for making a fire.

7. It was Wohpekumeu.

8. [K. queries whether the word (here and below) should be "bring," as seems likely.—Ed.]

(Hemi'), Kenek-erlergerł also, Long One[9] also, Hummingbird (Tsegemem) also, Long One also.[10]

e. Now they started; and Megwomets said, "I will show you the way"; and they arrived. They saw where there was much light; and persons were living in full sight. There were so many there that whatever flew over fell down. "How can a person approach them?"

f. Then Wohpekumeu said, "I will go. I will go as a woman. I shall appear a woman." Then he tied his hair, took his blanket, took a burden basket and a basket dipper, put acorns in the burden basket, and salmon. And the salmon was only alder bark, and the acorns pitch.

g. Now it was dusk when he arrived, almost dark. The persons were indoors. Then he opened the door. "Why, someone is coming in." And no one spoke a word as he entered. All thought, "Where has she come from? What a pretty woman!" And he[11] passed around behind the old woman[12] and set his load down; he passed on around. They finished eating. No one spoke to him.

h. They all went out. He looked about. And he saw two *rumitsek* baskets hanging, and inside it was fire, and daylight in the other. And in the middle of the night he did not sleep. And he saw one of the baskets bright on each side, and it was becoming dawn. And then it was almost day when he got up. He opened the door very carefully and went under and took one of the baskets. Then he leaped outdoors and started to run. He ran as fast as he could. He had not gone far when he heard them shouting. And they followed him.

i. They had about caught him when he gave the basket to Eagle. Eagle dodged under them and came to a hollow and left (the basket) there in the hollow[13] and ran to the next hollow. Now he had passed over four ridges, and on the fifth ridge they were so close that they could touch him.

And he gave it to Pigeon. Then Pigeon took it. Pigeon went so fast they barely saw him. And he had gone over seven ridges, and they came so near him they could touch him.

And then he gave it to Long One. And he went into the water. He began to swim. And now he had gone over five ridges.[14]

And then he gave it, then he gave it, to Hummingbird. They did not see Hummingbird at all (he went so fast), because he was so small. And they went

9. Knewollek, the water monster.

10. *Sic*, repeated.

11. "He" and "she" are the same in Yurok.

12. Of the house.

13. Obscure. The basket is carried farther.

14. While swimming! As far as five ridges; the Yurok use ridges as we would use miles.

as far again as before and caught up with Hummingbird and got so near they could touch him.

And then he gave it to Kenek-erlergerɫ. "They are beating us!" They began to pursue him down this river.

j. And he sat down and gave it to (Water) Ant (Harputs). And he jumped into the water: they had caught up with him. Then they heard only water splashing. It became dark. They were running about in the dark. Only then did they go back. Nowhere could they see him.

k. Then, a long time after, he came up out of the water, and it became light again. And he took (the fire) out of his mouth, he spat it out, did Ant: he spat it on a willow. That is why they get their fire drills from that. So it was thus ever afterward as it is now: formerly it was dark.[15]

Comparison of D1x and D1y

The first version was obtained by the usual method of the narrator's telling it in paragraphs to the interpreter, who retold each for the literal recording of his rather slow English in my longhand writing. A few days before or after, the narrator dictated the second version into the phonograph, without interruption other than that caused by insertion of new cylinders. Several years later, this dictation was Englished, this time phrase by phrase, by Mrs. Catherine Goodwin, the phonograph being halted while her translation was written down. As Weitspus Frank[16] was translating much larger passages than Mrs. Goodwin, and as his English was distinctly of the picked-up kind, whereas hers was fluent and expressive even though somewhat colloquial, the double translation should have served as a check on Frank's interpreting, which I relied on for so many of the tales in this collection. Frank's version ought to be the inferior one. The question arises whether the stylistic working over I have given his jargon English has brought it measurably within par of Mrs. Goodwin's version. I must leave it to the reader to judge this question. I cannot see any great difference. The two translations appear to preserve nearly equally the Yurok sentence structure, the Yurok order of words, so far as this can be retained in English, and to employ a similar vocabulary.

The interpreter who carries a whole passage in mind before he renders it is more likely to forget an item or incident than he who handles sentence after sentence. Frank's version, as here given, contains not quite a thousand words, as against a little less than nine hundred in Mrs. Goodwin's. His statements are often a trifle less compact, but it is clear that he cannot have omitted much substance.

15. Characteristic looseness: separate baskets for fire and light; only one is taken, but its theft results in giving the world both fire and light. The enterprise seems to be motivated by the dissatisfaction of the Kenek people with playing shinny in the gloom. [For another version of the myth, see X11.—Ed.]

16. [K.'s usual Yurok interpreter in the field.—Ed.]

Frank has a total of 11 speeches, Mrs. Goodwin 19. It is not likely that the informant, Billy Werk, changed his manner to this degree between his two recitals. The difference must be laid to Frank, who evidently was at greater pains to preserve the substance rather than the manner of relation. On the other hand, names, usually reduced to a bare minimum in characteristic Yurok storytelling, occur only 21 times in the free translation, 29 times in the phonographic record. It is clear that on this point the original Yurok has lost less of its peculiarity in Frank's rendering.

The phonograph record contains some passages that do not appear in Frank's translation. Such are:

There is only one house where daylight is kept, and what flies over it almost falls down.

Those at Kenek ask Thunder, Earthquake, etc., to undertake the theft.

Wohpekumeu names those who are to go.

The daylight owners wonder at Wohpekumeu.

Eagle flies into a hollow.

Eagle flies over 5 ridges, Pigeon over 7, Long One over 5.

But it is probable that these are not translator's omissions, since the Frank version contains elements which the narrator did not speak into the phonograph:

Those at Kenek cooked in the armpit.

Wohpekumeu posts his followers at intervals.

He waits in front of the daylight owners' sweathouse.

There is a shining man in the house.

Chicken Hawk is one of those who flees with the baskets.

There is daylight until Long One dives.

It seems therefore that, although Frank may have forgotten to give one or more minor allusions, on the whole he rendered with accuracy as to incident, and that it was chiefly the narrator who altered his tale at each telling. That this alteration occurred is clear from two transpositions. The free translation mentions the salmon meat of alder bark and the acorns of pitch at the very outset, the phonographed story only in about the middle, after Wohpekumeu has disguised himself as a woman. This cannot be a transposition by Frank, because he translated the initial installment of the story before he listened to the middle. Second, while the order of runners is substantially the same, the final escape is attributed in one version to Frog, in the other to Ant. There can be no error of record on this matter because each actor is mentioned by name in its version at least twice. Moreover, the Frank rendering, which makes Frog finally successful, by no means overlooks Ant, who is included in the enumeration of inhabitants of Kenek at the outset of the tale, and later takes the baskets from Long One and carries them to Hummingbird. It is clear, therefore, that the story was altered in Werk's own mind during the few days between his two tellings of it, much as Informant A's two versions of stories (A15x, y, and A16x, y) told a year apart vary. In short, many Yurok, although ready to recite myths without notice, are not so familiar with them, or so habituated to telling them in a definitive form, that they can repeat them unchanged even in substance.

With such variability of content proved, there is little that can be charged to

Frank's deficiencies as conveyor. The finding also argues that the largest body of tales included—those by Informant A—have not been seriously distorted in presentation, since Lame Billy was his own narrator, and commanded a more exact English than Frank.

D2x. Crane, Quail, and Pigeon

First Version

a. And now, Crane was going. And he thought, "I will go into the valley, I will go to dance in the valley." For he heard there was a girl there who was about to be adolescent. There were two women there: that is why Crane went. He made himself a pipe. So Crane made his pipe: he had it, made with woodpecker crest; he would smoke it when he arrived. And he came to the valley. He saw the house at a distance, one house alone. He had all the animals as his companions, the animals that are about. And they rehearsed below the house. And they came up and went to the house, and they entered. And Crane went straight to the fire. And he (had) said, "You must say this to me: 'Wohkotsimohkoi,' when you see me smoke. And one of you stay by the door, the one who is to say that, (until) after we begin to dance." And then he finished smoking, and Beaver who was there with his sister said, "Wohkotsimohkoi." And he looked up. And then (those there) looked, and they saw that his pipe was trimmed with woodpecker crest.

b. And they made (the dance) themselves, those that were there, the people; and they prepared to dance themselves. And they danced five times, so many people were there. And now day began to break; it began to be day. Then Crane thought, "Let us dance again." And they went off and rehearsed, preparing to dance. Not until then did they see the two. And there were those two, two persons together there. And he painted himself, Quail: he painted himself with what they use in the house (soot). And then the other one (Pigeon) came, and painted himself with yellow clay. They had only one feather left (to put on themselves): that is why Quail has a feather on his head; that is why he has a feather.[1] And Quail thought, "Let me sing." And they said,[2] "So be it." And another[3] wanted to sing second[4] to him. But Quail said, "No, I will second myself." So Quail sang the song:

1. [The California quail has a short black topknot curving forward on its head.—Ed.]
2. They answer his thought because "think" and "say" can be expressed by the same word.
3. Pigeon?
4. A nearly monotone accompaniment or drone, scarcely audible when the principal singer's voice rises to a climax, but maintaining the rhythm in the intervals during which his melody dies away.

(A wordless melody)

So they continued to dance. Then they said, "Put it behind." And they put it behind; they put it behind them.

(A song with words unintelligible to the translator)

c. Then only did the two women come out. Now they went, those women, to where Quail was, and where Pigeon was. And they[5] continued to dance there, to dance. And now they thought, "We will stop, we will go home"

d. So they (started to) go home: they went outdoors. And the women came with them. And they went down (the bank), they went down. And Crane said, "We will go in this boat, my boat." And the women said, "No. We are going in the boat that they[6] came in." There was a boat there, a very small boat. Now they went home.

e. And they emerged at the ocean, they came out on the ocean. And then Crane said, "Let us go down under." So they said to him, "Go ahead!" And he went down, and traveled around down in it. He had taken a woman's hip dress with him.

And they said to Quail, "Now you go next!" And he dived down. And he walked on the bottom. He did not come up for a long time. And he brought the dress up, and they saw that the shells on it were alive.[7]

f. And they thought, Now let us start our boats. And Crane said, "I hope the wind blows." He sang a song to make the wind blow. And the wind blew. It blew so hard that Crane's boat began to founder. And at last it did founder. And the small(er) boat went along as if nothing were wrong. So now they all got into the little boat: Crane's boat had foundered. So they went across the ocean, those.

g. And the women, one of them was the large red-crested woodpecker, and one was the small red-crested woodpecker. That is why there are so many of them there.[8]

D2y. Crane, Quail, and Pigeon

NOTEBOOK VERSION IN ENGLISH

This is the notebook version in English. Only supplements or discrepancies are cited.

5. Quail and Pigeon.
6. Quail and Pigeon.
7. The purpose of the diving appears to have been to cause the bare deerskin skirt to become ornamented with shells.
8. In the land across the ocean, where wealth is fabulously abundant.

a. Crane is Merkwteks. The dance place is at Se'pola, ''prairie,'' on Salmon river. (A girl's puberty dance is actually made by the Karok, Hupa, and Shasta, though not by the Yurok.) Coyote wants to accompany Crane. The women remain hidden, have never emerged; the dance is to draw them out. The adolescence dance is ''like'' the Yurok brush dance: they begin outdoors, but dance indoors. Instead of ''wohkotsimohkoi'' the word is ''metsomes,'' ''smoke!'' Instead of Beaver, it is Letkwel (?) (probably Oriole, a yellow bird, smaller than a flicker, which builds a sacklike nest), who forgets to call the signal until Crane is already knocking the ashes out of his pipe. Coyote has sung for Crane.

b. Two of the visiting party, Quail (Yegom) and Pigeon (Hemi') disappear and are finally found in the firewood alcove. Pigeon paints with ''mud.'' Quail sings twice. The ocean bird Tsegin wants to sing ''next'' (second?), but Quail refuses.

c. On the first song the women are heard stirring in their hiding place; on the second, they come out.

d. Crane, the headman, objects that Quail and Pigeon's boat is too small. The women tell him that they are going with the young men, not with him.

e. At Rekwoi they enter the ocean. Crane suggests ''swimming'' (diving). and Quail tells him to go first. He comes up and drops clamshells (for the women's dresses) into his boat. Quail brings up live clams. Then they know that Crane has taken his shells down hidden in his belt. He had hoped to drown Quail. There is no mention of a dress being taken under water.

f. Crane makes the wind so that the women will be frightened and enter his big boat. But it is driven back and capsizes, and he and his men are taken into the little boat. They reach Wohpäuk across the ocean. The women are Ko'koneu and Terkerit, the large and small redheaded woodpeckers.

D3x. Moon and Frog Formula for Wounds

interpreter's version

[K. did not specifically identify the versions of D3. I have indicated that D3x is the interpreter's version because of the direct quotations in the accompanying footnotes, which appear to be the narrator's in answer to questions K. raised at the time he wrote down the interpreter's version.—Ed.]

•

a. The one who always travels at night was going along when all at once they attacked him—*o'rawi,* lizards, *merus'isle*,[1] crows, various birds tried to

1. ''Like a lizard, longer, fat, yellowish.'' [Perhaps a skink?''—Ed.]

kill him. When they hurt him, the moonlight became dark. When they killed him, he was cut up: only his blood could be seen.

b. Now he had two wives, Frog and Grizzly Bear.[2] When they saw him attacked, (Grizzly Bear) sometimes seized five of them at once; nevertheless, they succeeded in killing him.

c. But Frog followed; he had told her, "Follow behind." She had *tuptup* herb in her *tseilo'* basket.[3] Those who killed him ate his flesh, his bones, everything. But she, wherever she saw his blood, dipped that tuptup into it and shook it off into her basket. Grizzly Bear just returned and sat down, but (Frog) kept coming with her tuptup, wherever she saw his blood. Just one madrone leaf was lying there; she did not touch it. Five times she came and did that, five times she went back. Then she picked up the madrone leaf and wiped it around, and no longer used the tuptup. Then he began to be a man again, a living man, all restored.

d. Frog said, "If any person is shot, do thus: 'Huhuhuhu, I have come to see you.' Use tuptup, wherever he is wounded, use that. Use it for my medicine, mine, Kelkwerterps and Lotso."[4] Now a person (*olôlekwiso'l*) has got shot and wounded. "That is why I come to you, for your medicine." "Yes? I did not see anyone coming. I have medicine for that. Well, I will give it to you. Huhuhuhu," and she dipped with it. "Well, my medicine is good, for they killed my man, completely, and ate him all up, even the bones, so I could find (only) his blood, (and yet he recovered). Therefore this man who was shot will not die from it. But I have another medicine."

e. Then she[5] drew out the madrone leaf (from dress, belt, or pouch), put it on the wound, and rubbed it on. With every word, she spat on his wound a little, and said, "You cannot be killed. You will get well. Though they always kill my man, he always recovers from this medicine."

"Have you tobacco?"[6] "Yes, I have it." "I want it. I am giving you my medicine; I want tobacco for it. It is not for me, that tobacco, it is for my man." Then (the person) gives her tobacco.

Now when Moon (Wanauslei) gets the tobacco, he says, "Good. That is what I like, for it is hard to secure. And I will help you because you give it to me. Now I use water (with my medicine), but not much. Where he is struck, put on two drops and rub them on."

2. Lotso and Nikwits.

3. *Tuptup* "grows in creeks, like ferns, but long." [Robins, Yurok Language, p. 260, identifies it as the sword fern. Robins, p. 274, defines *tseilo'* as a fancy basket.—Ed.]

4. Frog's two names.

5. Frog; also, description of what the imitating formulist does.

6. *Ol-w-ohkum*, human beings' tobacco.

That is Moon's medicine. Then (the formulist) puts a little water on the wound, and the madrone leaf on that, and ties something over to hold it in place: just one leaf. It is left on as long as it will stay; or if they see healing, they can take it off.

f. Only Raccoon helped Moon when he was attacked.[7]

D3y. Moon and Frog Formula for Wounds

VERSION FROM PHONOGRAPH DICTATION

a. Moon did this, Moon that travels at night. It happened that one of the times he was traveling something attacked him, this Moon. This is what they did to Moon: they ate him up. Those who did this were those that are here, those called *o'rawi*, the lizards, the crows, all kinds of animals.

b. Now he was married to Frog and he was married to Grizzly Bear: those were the two wives he had. And she seized five at a time, Grizzly Bear. She killed them, but still they ate Moon, ate him up. That is what they did to him.

c. So this is what Frog did: she walked after him with her burden basket on her back. For wherever there was a drop of his blood she gathered it on a leaf of tuptup. And they would eat him and would see that he was eaten up: they ate him bones and all, and did not leave even a drop of his blood. And then they would go away, they who had done this. And then she would go there, Frog would, and would turn her basket over in that place. There was just one madrone leaf there. Then she would begin to go around the basket and beat it all around, down to the edge. She went around it and then she went off. And then immediately she would come from there and begin hitting the basket again. She went around it again and began hitting the basket again. She went around it again and went away again. She would do that five times, beating the basket. And she would lay the leaf aside and would pick up what was lying there. And then she wiped the leaf off like this. She wiped it off all over. She did not leave anything to rub off. When she wiped it off like this, she saw he was so. He was so again.[8]

d. And this is how they speak to Frog, saying, "Ha-a-a-a! Now pity me! A person, a person[9] they have hurt. They have hurt a person. That is why I come to ask you to pity me."

7. "This formula is to cure wounds, not to end eclipses; there is none such. But because Raccoon helped Moon, now when there is an eclipse, people who have raccoon skins hang them on sticks on top of the house."

8. Moon was himself again.

9,10. In these lines, 9 designates the human patient, 10, Moon. The nondesignation by noun or name is characteristic of Yurok narrative.

And Frog says, "I will, person. It is as I thought. He[9] does not seem to get well quickly. I knew that something was wrong. That is why I tell you, person, that that is how it is with me; it happens thus to me, person. For we travel together: for it is he. There is nothing wrong. Everything is peaceful, when suddenly those come and attack him. And this is what they do to him. And they tell me to stand away from him. And I travel behind. And this is what I have with me: tuptup. There is a drop of blood falls on it. And I take the blood. That is all I do. Therefore I tell you, person, he will not die, since you have told me. For this is my herb, this, that they call tuptup. That is what I gather up his blood with. It makes no difference if he loses every drop of blood. I turn my basket upside down: that is what I do to him who is with me. And then I go off from the basket and sit. 'What shall I do for him?' (I think). And then I go again to the basket, and I go around the basket. Five times I do that. And then I drop my herb the tuptup.

e. "And then I pick up what is lying here, what persons call madrone. Then I wipe him all off with it. 'Why, he is coming to! And he is as he was!' That is what I do. That is why I tell you, person, he[9] will not die. For the human person[9] will be just like him,[10] as he is, and he[10] is as he was. Thus I do for him. Thus I do for him, thus I always do.

f. "Therefore I tell you, person, the person[9] that walks on this earth will be like him,[10] for I have carried him through. Therefore I ask you, have you carried him through?"[11]

And the person says, "That is enough."

The person says, "It is not mine. It belongs to the one who is with me; and he says, person, that it is the one. That is what makes me glad, for at times I have almost given up hope. For I have here herb, and water. That is why I ask you, person, to help me. I have only a little herb. Only take my herb and rub it all over, for that is what I do. I rub it on myself:[12] that is what I do. That is why I tell you, person, it[13] will not hurt him. Therefore I tell you, person, let me rub it on myself."[14]

That is what they do. That is how they speak to the leaf when they put it on.

D4. A Formula for Salmon

interpreter's version

This is a description of magical practice rather than a true formula, but it was given as

11. Obscure: succeeded in saving? Or: have you brought me tobacco?
12. Or: I myself rub it on?
13. The wound.
14. The attribution of the dialogue in this paragraph is not clear.

the latter and is included here because of the narrative fragment in the last paragraph. The whole was also recorded on phonograph cylinders.

•

a. Long ago, when the salmon ran, they did not do as now; so people took no salmon, and many starved. They they came to do like this: When one has sung and tied the dipnet to its frame, he moves as if to set it in the water but draws it up again. Then he looks across the river, sees the salmon traveling there, and says, "I see that trail of theirs: it is white." Thereupon he looks to the middle of the river and likewise sees a trail. Then he moves again as if to set the net but raises it, looks downstream on his side of the river, and says, "I see another trail along this side. I see that trail leading into my net." Holding the net, he says, "I see a trail underground (*noltsoarek*). I know all your trails." Only then does he really put his net in. He may not draw it up until a salmon has entered it, because he has prepared it with a formula.[1]

b. When he is about to make his net ready, he begins at the middle of the upper crossbar[2] and sings and ties his net on along to the left, and down the long (left) pole to the lower crossbar. There he stops. Then he goes back to the upper bar again (and sings and ties on the net) along the right (half of the frames). They call that singing and speaking *rekwoi.*[3] "I wish to enter (the river) from the ocean," (it says).

c. The small Tserhker salmon with the wide tail is the one who (first) sang that, in the sweathouse in Kowetsek.[4] He followed the fishes into (the sweathouse), lamprey-eels, sturgeon, and all kinds. This Tserhker entered last. The owner of the sweathouse, said, "There is no room for you to lie down." But as soon as he entered, he lay down right by the foot of the ladder,[5] this Tserhker. After a time he knew that they all slept, so he began to sing. Then one lying at *melku*[6] said, "Ah, you have begun to sing! You are always doing that; I do not like it." It was Sturgeon, Kohko, who said this, for he wished to sleep.[7]

1. "With medicine," he interpreter said, although no herb, plant, or tobacco is used, and the "medicine" consists only of the words that are spoken and sung.

2. The dipnet frame has the shape of a capital A closed at the bottom by the addition of another horizontal stroke.

3. The same as the name of the town at the mouth of the river. The meaning is not certain, but it may refer to an entrance.

4. The mythical home of the salmon across the ocean.

5. The least desirable place.

6. A place in the sweathouse, the corner farthest from both entrance and exit.

7. [K. has a marginal query about whether the tale is incomplete. He also has a note: "Add compar. *x* and *y*"; but the typescript did not contain a second version of D4.—Ed.]

D5x. The Dentalia Leave from Pekwtuł

interpreter's version

[For the theme of the younger brother forgotten and the moving of the sweathouse up Rivet Mountain, compare this tale with A2. For the journey of the moneys, compare it with B14.—Ed.]

•

a. At Pekwtuł[1] is where they lived, five brothers; with a boy, the youngest, they were five. Now they were about to go off, back into the hills.[2] And they were talking together about starting the next day in the morning. Now one of them (the oldest) slept next to the boy in the sweathouse, at the place *atserger*;[3] but when they got up early, he forgot him (in the dark sweathouse).

b. Now they had gone up on the ridge above Pekwtuł, and stopped for a little. Their quartz rocks for cutting themselves when they gathered ritual sweathouse wood they set in a row across the trail (and they are there now). Then they began to talk: "We do not all want to go to one place. Let us separate here." The oldest said, "I shall go across the river on Kewet."[4] The others said they would stay in the hills on their side of the (Klamath) river, in different spots. That is why it is good now to gather sweathouse wood above Pekwtuł because they see it and bring the man luck.

c. When they were ready to start, one said, "Where is the boy?" None of them knew; they had forgotten him in the sweathouse. (The oldest) one said he would go back after him. They said, "Well, then we shall not know where you have gone, because when you return you will not find anyone (of us) here." "All right, but anyhow I want to get him."

d. So he ran back down; but when he came partway, he heard him crying, at Slo'o.[5] The boy was taking the sweathouse along: he moved it by a stick[6] in the exit door. And he sang thus: (Song). His older brother heard him, but he could not overtake him. Sometimes as he came on a hill, he saw him on another (ridge) going on over it, and singing, "Alas, my brothers, nevertheless I am going south."[7] All his brothers could hear him now.

1. [Pekwtul is a town across the river from Weitspus. See Waterman, Geography, map 25, no. 24, reprinted here as map 4.—Ed.]
2. To make way for the human race.
3. By the exit, in the far corner.
4. Kewet is Rivet or Burrill Mountain, behind Weitspus.
5. [Waterman, map 25, no. 32, shows Slo'o as a hillside about 2 miles east of Pekwtuł and its nearby ridge.—Ed.]
6. *Tse'gi'l.*
7. *Perwer.*

e. Then the boy waited a little, and saw his brother coming, the one who was following him. And he said to him, "Well, I shall wait for you. I will take you along. I thought I would not, because I was sorry (angry) when you left me in the sweathouse, all my brothers going off and none remembering me. But now I shall take you."

f. So those two arrived across the ocean.[8] That is why the dentalia are so short in that direction,[9] because it was the smallest one that went there. And the oldest, Tego'o,[10] went on the mountain behind here, on Kewet; that is why dentalia are long here (at Weitspus).[11] But the others went (east) uphill from Pekwtuł.

D5y. The Dentalia Leave from Pekwtuł

VERSION FROM PHONOGRAPH DICTATION

a. At Pekwtuł they lived; five persons they were, living at Pekwtuł. He made the fifth one, the boy. Now one night they thought, "Well,[12] let us go back into the hills." Then they thought, "Yes, yes."[13] All of them thought, "Yes."

b. Then in the morning they got up and went out. Now they started to travel, to travel uphill, uphill above Pekwtuł; at that Peihpergers Sitting in a Row[14] they arrived; they brought them there, those *peihpergers*.

c. Then (one) said, "And where is the boy?" One said, "He is still asleep in the sweathouse." Then (the oldest) thought, "What shall I do? Well, I had better go to see about him, that boy." So about that smallest one he thought, "I will go back to him." And he said, "Let us not all go off together; we will separate here." And the largest one was going to the ridge[15] on this

8. Wohpäu (*sic*).

9. *Perwer*, south along the coast (which leads to Wohpäu?).

10. [Cf. tale B14, n. 8.—Ed.]

11. He must have gone finally to Kewet after first accompanying his little brother across the ocean; at least so by our logic. To the Yurok it may be enough to produce the result that the boy *intended* or *started* to go south, and the oldest brother to Kewet. In magical thinking there might be no perceived conflict between going there and across the ocean at the same time.

12. *Tsūł*.

13. *Tsū*.

14. Peihpergers (or Peihpegos) Ore'woreken, a place on the ridge above Pekwtuł where there are white stones in a row. *Peihpergers* is quartz used for scarification in the sweathouse penance. The five had brought their cutting stones with them.

15. *Ukōtsa'*. The narrator says *kihiyok ukōtsa'*, because he is narrating at Weitspus. This ridge runs up into Rivet Mountain.

side (of the river), to the ridge of Weitspus. Then he said, "I will go down to see my little brother." They said, "Yes,[16] but perhaps you will not bring him back."

d. So he went down. Then, when he had come partway, he heard him across the river, where he had gone, still inside their sweathouse, crying, that boy. And he thought he would sing; this is how he sang, that child:[17]

Tsūweɫ tsī'tse perwerhku kisôtok.
(Good-bye, brother, south I go.)

Across the (Trinity) river he followed him. A little farther on he heard his singing. One ridge[18] more he went and heard him over the hill. Having gone over, he followed him. All of them heard him, wherever they went, back up on the hills, and he went on until he came to where he lives now.

e. There he finally stopped and talked with his (older) brother. He said, "You have followed me far. Well, I will go with you; I will go with you."[19]

COMPARISON

The phonograph dictation is not wholly complete. Perhaps the narrator, having given the substance of the events, did not think it necessary to start a new cylinder for what little remained. The phonograph text is the briefer version of the two, and more repetitious at that. Motivation, geography, and final outcome are all more explicit in the interpreter's free translation; the native text takes so much for granted as to be hard to follow, except for a Yurok steeped in his people's folklore. Some effect is no doubt lost by my inability to grasp the finer shades of meaning in Yurok; but it is clear that the phonograph version remains elliptical as to fact.

D6x. Origin of the Weitspus Jumping Dance

TRANSLATOR'S VERSION OF PHONOGRAPH DICTATION

[An abstract of this myth was published in Kroeber and Gifford, World Renewal, p. 117.—Ed.]

a. Here is where the sweathouse stood, below here.[1] There were two

16. *Tsū.*
17. *Hūksa*, child.
18. *U-krerertser* (cf. n. 15, *ukōtsa'* = ridge) here used as a generic term for a short distance of travel, perhaps about as far as one can ordinarily see; similar to "one bend" in the river; sometimes equated by the Yurok with a mile.
19. A word is indistinguishable at the end of the record, but the dictation is obviously incomplete.

1. The narrator is speaking at Weitspus.

persons (who used it). One was a young man who lived here at hiwo,[2] and the other lived in the house wogi.[3] They were both wealthy. Therefore they used to have Deerskin Dances constantly,[4] so wealthy were they. Then one year they began to desire women. They used to cross to Pekwtuł:[5] they maintained sexual relations with two girls there. So a few years went by.

b. Then one night one of them had crossed over twice, and he said, "Let us go over (again)." And he said, "Very well," said the young man of wogi. And so they went over (again); and not until then did he (of hiwo) tell (his companion) what had been done to him. He told him that he had been struck with her apron (by the girl). So (instead of going to the girls as usual) they went straight on past to get sweathouse wood; and then (having recrossed to Weitspus and entered their sweathouse), they made fire (there). Then he said, "Let us do something that people do not often do: (for) I have been treated shamefully."

c. Then they continued (for some time) to gather sweathouse wood. And one morning they said, "Now let us leave." And they went uphill (behind Weitspus). They did not know what they would do. They came a long distance (from where they had started). Not until then did this happen to the young man (of hiwo):[6] he began to sit and take long rests (from weakness). Next day they went on again. He became so that his friend had to carry him (on his back). Their legs became red as blood.[7] So (it was) one night, and in the morning he said, "I shall leave you. I shall leave you. I cannot carry you farther." So he left him there. And before he left him, that one (of hiwo)[8] began to cry, thinking, "He has abandoned me!"

d. Now there was only one (more) mountain ridge to go over, from where he had left him (to the ocean at the northern edge of the world).[9] And he saw from there, he saw from there. . . .[10] So he went on to the ocean, and saw

2. Or hiwohp or higwo or hiwohk, "in front" or "close to the river," Waterman, Geography, map 26, house 22, higwop. It is the narrator's natal house.

3. Or wogwu, "in the middle," Waterman house 17, near both 16, erkīgeri, "where they tie their hair up (for dancing)," and 18, opyuweg, "where they dance."

4. This probably means, not that they made them at all times or when they wished, but whenever the stated occasions came. At least it would mean this in historic Yurok life.

5. Pekwtuł is the town opposite Weistpus, between the Klamath and the Trinity. [Waterman map 28 shows the placement of the six houses there.—Ed.]

6. My conjecture.

7. Perhaps from being scratched by travel through the brush, as D6y says, or from lacerating themselves with quartz, *peihpegos*, cf. D5y, n. 14.

8. My conjecture.

9. Or possibly the Pacific so far north that Pulekuk was near.

10. The word on the record is inaudible.

the waves were small. He saw exceedingly much money[11] there and gathered it. Then he raised his head and looked toward Pulekuk and thought he saw someone coming. He looked long. The person kept approaching. And he said, "What is he doing?" He could see him throw something into the water, and then put his hand into his basket again.[12] At last that one was close. Then he (of hiwo) went farther away from the shore and dug a hole on the far side of a log and crawled into the hole and buried himself.

e. The person was quite near now. Then he saw that it was a woman. She came straight to where he had been. (There) she looked about and then started to come where he was. She was still some distance from him when she said to him, "I am glad that you have come, my husband." She came directly to where he was, (this) woman, and dug the sand away from him and took him out, the young man, and said again, "I am glad you have come, my husband." Then she said, "I shall put you in my (carrying) basket," and she put him into the basket. And then she told him, "I wanted you to come. I was the one, I was the one, that wanted you to come. I did not want your companion to come. You are the only one that I want." That is how she was talking to him. He did not answer her, for he saw from a distance that there was a veritable fog of smoke, there were so many people (where she was going).

f. So now they had come close. Then he saw how they lived:[13] there were ten houses (in a row). She went to the middle house.[14] And an old woman spoke (from) indoors and said, "Have you brought my son-in-law?" And she said, "Sweep the house before I bring him in." So (the old woman) swept the house, and she brought him in. It became dusk. Then they heard someone entering. When he got to the door, he said, "I am glad you have come, my son-in-law."[15] There were ten brothers. The oldest said, "Sit by me." and they sat together.

g. Now he had seen when he first came in front of the house that the ground looked white.[16] And now his pipe case[17] began to speak. It said, "Keep yourself in control! Do not eat when they offer you food." And they set before him what they wanted him to eat. And they finished eating, but he would not eat.

11. Dentalium shells.

12. He—or rather she, as it proves—was throwing a line and hook with human bait into the ocean, and putting the dentalia she caught into her pack basket.

13. How the houses were grouped.

14. This would normally belong to the leading man of the settlement.

15. *Sic*; perhaps for "brother-in-law."

16. Obscure on the record, and the translator queried the word. If white, it probably was human bones; cf. part *m*.

17. Or tobacco pouch.

h. He said, "Brother-in-law, let us go to the sweathouse." And he said, "Very well, very well." Then his pipe case said, "I will go in first. I will go in and see how it is in there." What he had as a case was a weasel skin. So it ran to the sweathouse, this pipe case, and came back from the sweathouse and said, "When you first enter the sweathouse and feel the level (floor), sit and crawl." So he entered. And he said, "Have you come in, brother-in-law?" And he said "Yes." Then he said, "I will make it warm for you. Sleep by the exit hole;[18] that is where I sleep."

i. The case had already told him, "Do not smoke, (else) you will die." Then they said to him, "Let us smoke, brother-in-law." And he said, "No, I smoke only occasionally. I shall not smoke for some days now, at least five days. And I have my (own) pipe case."[19] There was a spot before the fireplace, and they had it so that when one came into the sweathouse one would slip (there) and slide into the fire: that is how one would die. And if one did not slip into the fire, they would cause him to smoke (to kill him).

j. And it said, "Now do not sleep," said the case. "For after you fall asleep they will take a firebrand and blow coals into your eyes." Then he did so. When he became very sleepy, the case would scratch him and say, "Awake. Now when you go for sweathouse wood in the morning, I will precede you and see how it is. I will go and find a place for you (to cut wood): for one dies there (where they wish you to gather it)." So it went ahead to look where he was to get the sweathouse wood and returned.

k. So in the morning at break of day he got up. His case preceded him. And it said, "This is the place to cut your wood." And before he arrived, he heard someone crying. And the case said, "Do you know who is crying?" He said, "No." And it said, "It is your former companion who is crying. He is crying at Wogitsateg."[20] Only then did he know it was he. And he brought his load to the sweathouse and threw it down there. Then the old man said inside, "I am glad, son-in-law." And everyone of the brothers said, "I am glad, brother-in-law." And they took the wood in. It almost filled the sweathouse, and some was still left outdoors.

l. Then he came into the sweathouse, and his case said, "Put only two sticks into the fire. If you put on more than two you will die." Then he did exactly as he was told: he put in only two sticks. So he finished making the fire. And the case said to him again, "Do not eat anything, but go and bring more sweathouse wood, for if you eat you will die." And he did just as he was told: he went after more sweathouse wood.[21] There was only one of them left

18. [*Atserger* or *ertserger*.—Ed.]
19. Which contains tobacco.
20. Wogitsateg, unidentified; Wogusitsa in D6y.
21. Bringing in sweathouse wood is an act valuable and meritorious in itself.

in the sweathouse, the one who was to wait for him.[22] He threw the wood down again and made new fire. And he had finished making the fire. Then he went and bathed. And when it came time to make a fire in the evening he went for more sweathouse wood: it was just dusk[23] when he stopped making the fire. Then the pipe case said, "Now they will ask you to go out and catch salmon: that is what they will (subject) you to. But do not eat before you go, (even) if you wish to eat."

m. And they had supper; and they said to him, "Will you not go fish for salmon, brother-in-law? Let your wife go with you." So the young man said, "Very well," and went to fish for salmon. The woman was with him. Only then did the woman say, "He'e'e'e, my husband! I shall help you. For I too do that:[24] I throw men into the river. See, that is why there are so many bones here; for we take their flesh and use it for bait;[25] that is why we do that. So he'e'e'e', now I shall help you." And the case said, "I too shall help, I too shall help."

n. Then they came down to the river and saw there (what there was). He went to one of the large holes that were there. And she said, "You will have to go to that hole first and drive a stake[26] and then come to the holes on this side." There were ten holes. And then she said, "My husband, come here!" For she had with her *kwokitel*.[27] And then she bathed him all over with the *kwokitel*; on his forehead she rubbed it, on his feet she rubbed it. She said, "Now you must look constantly at a certain[28] place."

o. When it began to be day—she was sitting by him, the woman—he saw two flashes. And she said, "Did you see, my husband? For it[29] is coming." "Yes, I saw." And she said, "That is it. Your heart will beat with fright, for your feet will stick to the ground and your hands will stick to the ground: you will become paralyzed and it will carry you along." And she gave him more (*kwokitel*) to rub on himself, and he rubbed it on.

p. And they saw it coming nearer. Each time it flashed it was approach-

22. To receive the sticks as the bringer passes them in. The entrance is so small that is somewhat inconvenient for a single person to haul the wood inside.

23. This shows that sweating was by no means always an after-supper affair, and that ritual sweating and the heating of the sweathouse at night to make it warm for sleeping are separate operations. I have seen Yurok going from the sweathouse to bathe—which means they had had a fire—toward the end of a sunny afternoon.

24. I too do mischief like my brothers, and my work is this.

25. For dentalia.

26. For a wier or net, or to hold the catch?

27. A plant used as medicine or charm.

28. The narrator is wavering between narrative and quotation.

29. The monster that was to destroy him. It is typical of the Yurok manner that it is neither named nor described.

ing. Thus they saw it emerge very close by and he felt himself being dragged down by the hands,[30] and did not regain consciousness until he was about halfway.[31] Then he thought, "I will let go," and let go. And then he tried to draw it out, and the woman leaped and began to help him and the pipe case began to help him. And then they succeeded: they raised the net out of the water and he said, "Strike it just once," and tried to lift it out of the net. But the woman said, "This is the way to lift it out," and lifted it out by taking hold of each end, and put it into (one of) the large holes. And then she said "Come here! Come and warm yourself."[32] And he looked and saw that (the hole) was full already; and it was not long until they were all full. And then the woman said, "Let us go home, my husband."

q. It was day now, and he went directly by (the house on his way) to get sweathouse wood. He was still hearing him cry not far off, his companion. And across the river (at Pekwtuł) they constantly laughed all day, thinking that he was dead. "Because he was so sure of himself, that is why he died," that is how they laughed, (those two) girls.

r. Then he finished having his sweathouse fire, and the pipe case said to him, "Now you can eat if they ask you, for they will do you no harm now. Eat now." Then he did as he was told, the young man, he did as he was told: he ate. And then he said, "I am going back. I am sorry, for I can hear him cry not far away; that is why I am going home." But they said, "No, for we want you here. That is why we wanted you to come, for we do not wish you to return." And he said, "No, I must go back." And then all the people came in, the people that lived in the other houses. And he said, "I cannot leave my sweathouse: that is why I am going home." And again, they said to him, "No, for you will have to live here." And he said, "No, for you did not wish my friend to come—that is why he is not here. For I shall not leave him. That is why I am going home." And they said, "You may go home. You may bring your sweathouse and bring your friend here."

s. And it seemed to him that he ran only a short distance: he was only one night (on the way). That is why the ridge is like that at the place (called) "Egor[33]-Lies-Turned-Over." For when he arrived there he heard (his friend) crying; he had been crying before he arrived there. The ridge extends upstream, for that is the direction in which he ran. And there is a black oak in plain sight: he ran by that black oak on one side and ran by the hill. When they had first gone out (he and his friend), he had taken a feather with him.[34] Now

30. Which were holding the net.
31. To the bottom?
32. In night fishing, a fire is kept up near the platform.
33. A cylindrical basket, ornamental, carried in the Jumping dance.
34. A word is lost here.

he thought he had been gone only two days, and he had been gone two years. At last he saw him coming on his way to get sweathouse wood: the man[35] was directly downhill from him. He heard him before he reached him: it sounded like hitting against a tin.[36] For the feather had become a living thing, and its name was *hohotsin*,[37] the feather; and it was a white *hohotsin*. He[38] seized him as he was packing sweathouse wood; and he cried and said, "He has me now." He took two steps and cried again. And then he (of hiwo) leaped down and said, "It is I, my friend," and stepped up.

t. And then they went to the sweathouse (in Weitspus) together and built a fire. And he said, "Do not by any means tell them that I want you. For you are not to know what we shall do tonight: that is what is to happen to us tonight." And he brought sweathouse wood ten times. And so it became night.

u. And they began to get ready: they were about to take away (their) sweathouse. They (in other houses) could hear the sounds in the sweathouse: they could hear them from Pekwtuɫ. And they[39] said, "Listen! It seems as if we could hear something. Let us go across and see." And they came to this side (to Weitspus). They[40] had the sweathouse door closed and the exit hole also: "We do not wish anyone to come in." And the girls came to the exit door and sat one on each side of its pit. The girls did not think they were visible, but they could see them from inside the sweathouse; they saw them come there. They[41] had not been there long when they disappeared: only their basketry hats were left. Then the people came: but they had not been there long when they felt the ground move, and they went away (in alarm).

v. And they saw the sweathouse move, and saw it rise out of the ground.[42] And the first place at which it rested was at this rock downhill from us here.[43] And then it rested again at this rock uphill from us. And next it went all

35. His friend whom he had left behind.

36. The simile is of course a modernism. It is not clear what was making the noise. Possibly it was the breaking of boughs to serve as sweathouse fuel, or more likely the feather for dancing was leaping.

37. *Hohotsin* was heard as *hurhurtsin* in D6y; it is the name of a bird. [Cf. C3, n. 20: *hurhurhurtsim*.—Ed.]

38. "They" says the translation: perhaps the hiwo young man and the *hohotsin* feather together.

39. The two Pekwtuɫ girls.

40. The two young men.

41. The girls.

42. All but the roof of a sweathouse is underground.

43. The narrator is pointing from where he speaks at Weitspus. The ten places at which the sweathouse rested, and of which this is the first one, are those at or to which part of the formula is spoken, tobacco offered, and a brief dance made, on the first morning of the Jumping Dance, which is devoted to a slow journey of three or more miles up Kewet (Rivet) Mountain behind Weitspus. Here at last the story becomes ritualistic and refers to its title.

the way (across the Klamath) to Po'toi.[44] Then they brought it back toward here and let it rest uphill from us here. And they raised it again and caused it to go to Egor-ole'geläu.[45] And they raised it from Egor-ole'geläu and took it to Skoyamu. And they raised it from Skoyamu and took it to Mur'n. From there they took it to Arupets.[46] And from there they took it to Opyuwegpets.[47] And they took it again from Opyuweg(pets?); they took it to Osegawits.[48]

D6y. Origin of the Weitspus Jumping Dance

OUTLINE OF INTERPRETER'S VERSION

To save space, only variants from D6x are cited: * denotes increments given only in the present English version; †, items found only in the Yurok text on the phonograph (D6x). As usual, the free translation (y) is a little fuller. Matters taken for granted in Yurok were explained by the interpreter. On the whole, the two versions conform very closely.

(*a*) †No mention of wealth and making Deerskin dances; *but the young men dance in their sweathouse. (*b*) One *morning the one from hiwo tells his partner he has been struck by the girl and wants to *return to Weitspus. Thereupon they go after sweathouse wood on the hill *behind Weitspus, not †behind Pekwtuɬ. (*c*) They do this for *ten days, (*q*) *the girls watching and laughing from across the river. *The one girl has told the other that she has whipped him. *Then one morning they no longer see smoke from the young men's sweathouse. (*c*) The young men have gone *over Kewet, far, for *five days. Then one gives out, and his friend carries him for *five more. When he too is exhausted, and his legs *scratched by brush, the friend leaves him, *with his consent.

(*d*) After his abandonment, *he becomes stronger, and after one more ridge sees the ocean; †no mention of small waves. Looking *hesi-pulu* (northwest or north?) along

44. A spot high uphill *south* of the river, a tree at which is addressed from one of the nine ritual stops north of the river. [For alternative spellings of this and other dance spots, see D6y.—Ed.]

45. Evidently the same 'Egor-Lies-Turned-Over' mentioned before.

46. [Cf. Arohpets in A3*f*.—Ed.]

47. Opyuweg, "they dance (the Jumping or Deerskin Dance)"; pets, "upriver from." The ninth place danced at is actually more or less east or upstream from the final one, which, as the scene of two days' dancing, would naturally be known as Opyuweg. Osegawits, in D6y called Osega'weɬ, is on the top, not far from Opyuweg, on the Wahsek side of it; the Wahsek party danced there before coming to Opyuweg. (See Kroeber and Gifford, World Renewal, p. 79, no. 11, n. g.) Waterman shows Osegawits on his map 25 as no. 7, but much too near the river. [See map 4 in this volume.—Ed.]

48. Although this story ends with an enumeration of the Weitspus Jumping Dance spots, it is really a myth. It contains no invocation or request, as a formula would. Other lists of the Jumping Dance places on the way up the mountain are given in World Renewal, p. 79, as cited above.

the shore, he sees what at first looks like a stump but is a person. He hides behind a log and covers himself with sand, (e) *still clutching the dentalia he has found on the shore. The newcomer uses a *pole, line, and hook (*ulertkerł*), catches something, and throws it in *a pack basket; sees *the young man's tracks on the beach, follows them; the young man sees it is a woman. She sets her basket down, puts him in, carries him, tells him *she made his partner become sick. †No mention of smoke from her town. (*g*) The ground is white *from bones. (*h*) The sweathouse floor is **permeryer* (greasy-stone). He is asked by his brother-in-law to sleep at ertserger* so they can emerge early and get wood. (*j*) †No mention of weasel's scratching him awake so they cannot blow coals into his eyes. (*m*) *They kill people to use flesh for dentalium bait. (*k*) On hill he hears his friend crying at Wogusitsa (Wogitsateg in D6x); near Weitspus. (*l*) Weasel hears them in sweathouse *saying they have tried three ways and perhaps cannot kill him. (*m*) *The salmon are great dentalia. (*n*) †Wife rubs him with *something in her hair, †not *kwokitel*. †No mention of driving stake in hole. (*o*) *She warns him of flash just before dawn: *that is Great Dentalium coming from west about to enter net. *He is to keep moving on his feet, (*p*) *and slide hands along net poles, so as not to get stuck fast and be drawn under; (*o*) *fishing scaffold timbers also rubbed. (*p*) *The ten holes are behind the scaffold. (*o*) No mention of †two flashes, †being paralyzed, †losing consciousness. (*p*) He *cannot lift the catch, but woman does easily. †No mention warming himself.

(*r*) People from other houses *urge him to stay. (*s*) Finds friend at ägo'r-olegeleu. †No mention of feather or *hohotsin* here. *He is on limb of black oak when he seizes his friend's load. Calls him *brother, †not friend. (*t*) Tells him to *keep his return secret; but they get sweathouse wood ten times! (*u*) At night, dance; the girls hear, come across. †Incident of girls being seen from inside sweathouse but not knowing it is not mentioned. People come, *but both doors of sweathouse shut, as never before during dance. (*s*) Returned youth on way had *found a feather, *put it on his hat (!); that was what his friend first heard, rattling pleasantly. Feather becomes a white *hurhurtsin* bird, *in sweathouse. *If heard at ägo'r-olegeleu now, is good luck, though invisible. (*u*) Girls' hats only left; they disappeared *because ashamed.

(*v*) Sweathouse stops:

Rock under large pepper tree in Weitspus
Rock a little uphill and upstream, at edge of town
Po'toyo, across river at Bloody Camp, *former Deerskin Dance place
Upriver a little and above second; first dance stop
Ägo'r-olegeleu
Skoyomor; a dance stop
Murm, in prairie; a dance stop
Arohpets
Near final dance stop
Apyuwe, main dance place
Osega'weł, on top, where formerly those from Wahsek also danced

The interpreter's version does not specify which youth has the adventures on the northern ocean, though one would expect it to be the one from hiwo, who was struck. In answer to a question after the tale was finished, the interpreter reported it was the one from wogi, contrary to the way I understood the text. The interpreter was himself from wogi, the narrator from hiwo.

D7. Origin of the Several Deerskin Dances

[This account was first published in Kroeber and Gifford, World Renewal, p. 113. —Ed.]

•

At the upriver end of the world[1] is where they first made the Deerskin Dance and the Brush Dance and Gambling by Guessing and the Girls' Adolescence Dance and all the others. The Deerskin Dance was on one side, all the short dances on the other. Then they wanted to bring the Deerskin Dance downriver, because they did not have it here.

So they arrived at Okonile'l.[2] He was in a hurry to go on, the one who was bringing it; so he started a Deerskin Dance there, but they did not use deerskins. They held brush instead, but nevertheless they called it a Deerskin Dance.

Then they went on downriver and came to Segwu'.[3] The evening they arrived, they danced on the water in a boat; then they went up to the town to see if they wanted to dance there also. So they said, "It is well; we can begin here." And they went back down to the river to bring their regalia, and began, but some did not like it; nevertheless, they began. It was as now, when the dances are nearly the same but not quite alike, at this town or that; so here at Segwu', by the time they finished, they were not doing right. It was like a war dance when they stopped. They were dancing in a circle holding the poles of the deerskins upright.

Now they came down and arrived at Olege'l, Camp Creek.[4] There they

1. Petskuk.

2. Karok Inam, at Clear Creek. It has a world renewal ceremony, and the dance is often listed as Deerskin, but is actually of surrogate type with otter or fisher skins or brush. Hence the myth mentions it slightingly.

3. Karok Katimin. The dance here is sometimes a full Deerskin Dance, sometimes an imitation. The way the poles are here said to be held suggests the Hupa manner. Katimin also dances the war dance at New Year.

4. Karok Tishannik, near Panamenik and associated with its ritual. The Yurok say that the Karok use skins other than of deer in the Deerskin Dance. (Enek, Karok Amaikiaram, is omitted, in spite of a world renewal, evidently because its dance is Jumping, not Deerskin.)

danced well. They used various kinds of skins here: white deerskin and silver fox.

Now they came to Weitspus and began to dance. They stayed longer here.[5] As they began to dance they stood facing upriver, but it was not good. Then they faced across the river, but it was not right. They faced downriver, but it was not right. Then they stood facing uphill, and everything went well.

Now they arrived at Kepel.[6] The people there wanted that dance, so they began to dance it there, and went on (to finish it) to Wohtek.[7] Now here and from Weitspus on they used all kinds of regalia and feathers; but at the beginning they had not worn everything that ought to be used in the Deerskin Dance. And also as they traveled along from one place to another, they danced in a boat. From each town where they danced they took a man, and put him in a boat on each side, and in the middle boat they danced as they went downriver (three boats altogether).

Next they came to Rekwoi and spoke of dancing there. The man who was head said, "There are many Deerskin Dances upriver now; let us begin a different dance here. I think we will make the Jumping Dance, and we must do that inside a house."[8] So now they had two dances: the Jumping Dance and the Deerskin Dance.

From there they went (out on the ocean) dancing. Now Wohpekumeu shouted from behind, "Anyway, take along my son";[9] but their boat kept moving and was already far from shore. Then Wohpekumeu threw his son as if he were a stone, and he lit in the boat. He was called Kapuloyo, the one who was thrown.

Then they went across the ocean to Wohpäu in the boat, taking the dance there. Now they dance there every night in Wohpäu.

From the upstream end of the river they go every night to Wohpäu to see that dancing. Almost every night one can hear the mice laughing, and the frogs, because they are glad that they are traveling on the way to the dance.

(It was three boats abreast that crossed the ocean the first time, but a

5. Ten days or more, as against a maximum of five among the Karok.

6. The fish dam world renewal rite at Kepel ends in a Deerskin Dance below Wohkero.

7. Wohtek is mentioned because after the flood of 1862 Wohtek was built up by refugees and became larger than Wohkero.

8. Pekwon and its Jumping Dance are omitted, though it and Rekwoi—in fact, Orekw and Oketo on the coast too—are reckoned as "siblings." These four Jumping Dances were danced mainly indoors; but the upriver outdoor Jumping Dances are usually finales to the Deerskin Dance. Although the two are usually considered equal in splendor and importance, this myth deals with the world's Deerskin Dances.

9. Evidently an ellipsis: they had refused to take Wohpekumeu himself. The woges' running away from him is a favorite motif.

single boat goes down the river nightly. The one who first carried the dance downriver is called Kimełholemonioł.)[10]

The interpreter added that the boatload of people who go down every night are called Kermerwermeri,[11] and that they are not the same people who first carried the dances down and across.[12]

10. "He or they by whom we exist," a generic term in ritual for the instituting spirits or woge.

11. Cf. A2*k*.

12. [K.'s typescript also contained a handwritten list titled "Origin of the Deerskin Dances": (1) Oko'nile'l; (2) Segwu'; (3) O'lege'l; (4) Weitspus; (5) Kepel; (6) Wohtek; (7) Rekwoi; (8) Wohpekumeu; (9) Kapuloyo; (10) Wohpäu; (11) Kimełhôlemoniôł; (12) Kermerwermeri.—Ed.]

INFORMANT E

DOCTOR OF WEITSPUS

Weitspus Doctor, when he narrated these bits, was a slight, gaunt-looking, elderly man, who looked half-starved and was poor also from the Indian point of view. I came to him very early in my career among the Yurok because he was a friend of interpreter Frank. The informant, called K'e-hiwo'h, was of hiwo in Weitspus, a house of good standing; brother of Informant D, Billy Werk; and paternal uncle of Informant J, Julia Wilson.

Doctor was younger than Werk. He was not a medicine man; the name Doctor was given him by the whites. He also did not dance much. He used to work occasionally for ranchers at scything and hoeing, and he always kept a horse. He married a woman from Pi'npa on Big Lagoon on the coast.[1]*They had no children. At dances, Doctor's wife used to wear four dentalium necklaces, two in front and two behind, which came from her husband's house, hiwo. People would comment half-audibly, saying, "She never said that she brought necklaces with her from Pi'npa." Apparently a woman was to be equipped by her own family with the things she wore, and was not to use hereditary property of her husband's family.*

With a little development, Doctor could probably have done somewhat better as a narrator, and yet it is evident that he was neither well informed nor a natural storyteller. His tales are bald strings of episodes, or isolated bits. There is little organization, detail, or liveliness, and no indication of even concealed religious feeling. The first tale is a disorderly and sketchy attempt to present some parts of the Wohpekumeu cycle; the second, a Coyote tale known also to the Karok; the third, an animal trickster story of a type that adult Yurok generally are little interested in; and the last, a local explanation connected with an unusual and morbid fancy.

1. [Elsewhere in the typescript K. says that she was called Hiwo'pison.—Ed.]

E1. Wohpekumeu

a. At first there was no one in the world but Wohpekumeu. There was no salmon and nothing to eat. Now he wished to find what human beings would eat. He went upstream to the sky. There he found people. He made salmon (meat) out of red alder (bark) and entered the house where they lived: they were two women. He heard the sound of water in the house. He said, "Well, I shall eat my salmon," and took out his alder. Then they, who had real salmon, said, "We may as well let him have some." He said again, "My mouth is sore around the lips (from cracking acorns)." They answered, "We have that kind, too." So he found out (that they had food). Now one of the women went out for acorns, he did not know where. The other one he caused to fall asleep, for he wanted to look about the house. When she slept, he searched and found the place where they kept their salmon. Then he broke the box, and the salmon flowed out. That is why there are salmon in the river. Then he seized some acorns and ran off.

b. The two women pursued him. He ran until he becamc tired, saw a tree with a hole near the ground, leaped in, and said, "Come together, so that they may not see me." So the hole closed and they could not find him.

After a time he thought, "How shall I get out?" Then he heard Tsegetsil[1] tapping the tree. He called, "Help me to get out! If you cannot, get others to help you." Then different woodpeckers and other birds came. He told them, "Chip it open that I may come out." When they released him, he caused them all to sit down. He asked one, "What sort of feathers do you want?" When they said, "Red on the head," he would give it to them. Whenever he had decorated one, he would say, "Fly off," and it flew away.

c. Then Crow said, "I want to be woodpecker crest[2] all over. Whoever kills me is to be a rich man." Wohpekumeu said, "I will give you half. You shall be woodpecker crest from the breast to the top of your head." "No, I want to be like that over my whole body," Crow said. Then Wohpekumeu said, "Very well. Shut your eyes." Now he took charcoal, crushed it in his hand, rubbed it all over Crow, and said, "When I tell you to fly, then fly up and light wherever you want." Crow was thinking that he would be scarlet. Then Wohpekumeu told him, "Now fly up." So Crow flew, lit, opened his eyes, and looked at himself: he was entirely black. Then he returned and saw Tsegetsil still there. The upper part of his body was red. He caught him, threw him in the dust, pushed and rubbed him around, and spoiled him, so that Tsegetsil now has only a little red on his shoulders.

1. A small bird of woodpecker type.
2. This to the Yurok suggests not a part of a bird, but a beautiful and precious substance.

d. Wohpekumeu was living at Kenek. There was much snow. It had been made by others. He thought it should be spring or summer, but still the snow lay deep. Then he saw a blue jay with hazelnuts in its bill and began to know what time of year it really was. So he made himself snowshoes, and came upstream on them. That is how people came to have snowshoes. They (the other woge) had caused the snow around his house in order to starve him to death: he was disliked for his desire of women.

e. Wohpekumeu never stayed long anywhere but always traveled. It was he who first made this world.[3] Women did not like him because he pursued them so much. At Orleans,[4] where he fished, there were two women whom he desired. They heard a war dance coming, but thought, "It is Wohpekumeu,"[5] and did not come out of their house to see it. Wohpekumeu wished to live there, but because they would not have him he went off.

f. He traveled through the world in order to make it better, but wanted to be paid by being given women. He went through Hupa and made it fine. He found women there (who would have him): that is why that valley is so good.

g. At Weitspus he said, "I will make it that salmon run up the creek (into the town) if I can have seven women." But the women of Weitspus would not have him: therefore salmon do not come up the creek. Everywhere he was driven off because people disliked him.

h. At first there were no human beings in the world. There were a different kind, like dentalia, but persons. They went off because Wohpekumeu was about to change the world.[6] They said, "We are going away. Whoever knows us will always have good luck."

E2. Coyote's Thirst

a. Coyote wanted to get himself dentalia. He had heard that it was only necessary to carry strings for them if one went to the place where they grew. Then on his way he saw a sweathouse; there was fire inside. Outside he saw

3. The Yurok frequently utter this statement. It is partly loose formulation, a popular singling out of the most conspicuous personage in their mythology. In any event the phrase must be understood as referring to an inception of human institution and occasional purposeful finishing touch to nature, not to a creation of the physical cosmos.

4. Either Ko'men or Olege'l, Camp Creek.

5. As it was; or rather, a party of young man he had made from his pubic hairs, according to fuller versions, H1 and X5.

6. That is, the great change was impending which would replace the woge and animals by human beings.

baskets standing with something in them. He drank it. It was sweet, and he found it was crushed berries.[1] Then he went on.

b. Now he became thirsty. He went on until he heard water; he seemed to be near a creek. Then he ran toward it, but before he arrived the stream had dried up. He went on. Again he heard water. He saw it. Then he thought, "Let me throw my deerskin blanket in and suck out the wetness." But the stream dried up before the blanket fell into it. He went on, still intent on finding the dentalia. When he heard another stream running he pulled the foreshaft out of an arrow and shot, hoping that the socket might hold a little water. But the creek dried before the arrow reached it.

c. Then he followed the stream-bed down and at last came to the river. There he drank.[2] His feet slipped, he fell in, and was drowned. The one in the sweathouse, whose berries he had drunk, had caused all the streams to dry up.

E3. Owl and the Geese

a. Geese were traveling. Owl said to them, "Your father was my great friend. Stay here for the night!" (After they consented,) he said, "There are many about who hate me. They might try to injure you for that."[1] Some of the Geese slept in his house; some slept in the sweathouse with him. When he knew that they were asleep he got up and felt these over. When he thought he had found the fattest one, he killed him. In the morning he cried, "I told you that I have enemies and that perhaps one of you would suffer!"

b. But when he went into the living house and saw that some of them there were even fatter than the one he had killed, he was sorry. So he said, "I should like to go with you." Then he traveled with them, picking out those that he would sleep with when they made camp. He said, "I will sleep with you, and with you," as they flew along strung out. Then he flew with the two fattest of the Geese before and after him. When they broke up their line, he suddenly seized these two, dropped out from the flock, and flew off home with them.

1. To steal food is contemptible; to make away with the drink set aside by a sweating man to break his thirst is despicable. The crushed berries were probably gooseberries.

2. Also a sign of lack of self-control: the Yurok do not drink river water, which may have been infected by menstrual blood, abortions, dogs, corpses, or other poisons. Anyway, one who was setting out to acquire money shells would be the last to drink at all.

---

1. An avenging party was likely to be indistriminate.

E4. They Lived at Roktsu

A woman and her daughter lived alone at Roktsu.[1] She always sent her daughter out to bring her mushrooms; that was all she would eat. She remained lying all the time. Sometimes she had her daughter turn her over. Now the girl was outdoors eating (gathering?) peppernuts.[2] Then her mother called, told her to stand above her, and turn her over. As the girl took hold, her mother seized her and tried to cohabit with her with a penis that had grown on her.[3] The girl tore herself loose and ran off. When she came to Weitspus, in her fright, she was still holding the peppernuts. There she threw them away. That is why there are many pepperwoods about Weitspus.[4]

1. A Chilula village on Bald Hills or near Redwood creek.

2. The pungent nuts of California laurel, *Umbellularia californica*, called "pepperwood" in the region of the Klamath, Eel, and Russian rivers, "bay" or "bay laurel" south thereof, "myrtle" in Oregon. The tree grows up to 60 feet high.

3. Grown mushroomlike, no doubt, from her exclusive fare.

4. Or perhaps Erlerger, which she would reach first, as being on the near side of the Klamath and Trinity to her coming from Bald Hills.

Informant F

MACK OF WEITSPUS

I do not very clearly remember as a person this elderly informant, who narrated to me in 1902. His house was oslok in Weitspus. This was the house of his father, who was full-married to a Tolowa woman from Hinei on Smith River. Mack was therefore called Hineis-or. His mother brought a shell dress with her into the family.

Mack seems not to have been married. First he was the werres, *or sweetheart, of a woman of the house tsekweł in his home town. By her he had three children; their mother used to be called* kohô, *mother of bastards. Later she married a man of the house nī kerwerk, also in Weitspus. After that Mack got into a similar relation with a woman at Merip who was partly from Sregon. He had no children with her. He died and was buried at Merip.*

There was a story that an ancestor of his, perhaps a grandfather, owned an uma'a *for bewitching,*[1] *but that this was inherited by another relative. Mack made no medicines and was no singer except of deer songs, but he was a good hunter. He sold all the family treasures except two woodpecker bands.*

His stories may be described as fairly orderly, commonplace, and lacking in specific literary quality. They represent very well such nationally current myth material as the average old Yurok would know, and are told with average skill. There are no serious confusions but a few obscurities, a good many omissions, some oversights subsequently corrected, little motivation—and that crude. A number of these defects and mediocrities are pointed out in the footnotes. It is significant that, although in the main this undistinguished narrator told the things that every Yurok knows about the stock heroes Wohpekumeu, Pulekukwerek, and Megwomets, three of his tales are downright institutional in type.

1. [See F1, n. 37.—Ed.]

F1. PULEKUKWEREK

a. At Pulekuk,[1] Pulekukwerek grew. He heard about what there was here[2] and thought there were too many bad places. They said that at those places a person was always killed, in canoe-building or somehow. Pulekukwerek thought, "I should like to go there and see them. I will go." Then he started.

b. He came to Hinei.[3] There he learned that there was a place where they made boats. He arrived there, at Hinei-hir,[4] and saw a man working on a boat. That one said, "Ah, I was wishing for someone to help me!" "Yes," said Pulekukwerek. He saw him splitting a log. The one who was doing the work said, "Climb inside and try to pry it farther; it is only half-split." Pulekukwerek had heard that he customarily killed people by having them go into the crack to arrange the wedge. So he said, "I do not know how. You had better show me; then I will go in." The man consented and went into the split of the tree. Then, because he had always killed others that way, Pulekukwerek drew out the wedge on him, the tree closed, and he saw his blood come out. That is how he stopped it that men were killed this way here.

c. He went on upstream and came to Omen. When he arrived he saw a man working, and when he came close saw that he also was trying to split (a redwood) for a boat. He said, 'I am glad to see you. I am unable to split it alone. I want to make a boat but cannot split it because there is no one to go inside and arrange the wedge. I wish you would help me." Pulekukwerek said, "I do not know how." The man said, "I can tell you how to do it." Pulekukwerek said "It will be better if you go in and show me while I look on and see what I shall have to do." "Very well," the man said, and went in. Then Pulekukwerek pulled out the wedge, the tree came together, and he was killed. Then Pulekukwerek said, "Now they shall not kill a man when he is working on a boat. A boat will be the right sort of thing to use on the water, and nobody shall be killed by means of it. Whoever wishes to make himself a

1. The downstream end of the world, reached by following the coast north, Pulekukwerek, in coming from there to the country of the River Yurok, follows the coast southward. The interpreter added that Pulekuk is also "across" the ocean; which, though to us inconsistent, is generally affirmed by the Yurok.
2. In the world of human beings, that is, the Yurok and their neighbors.
3. On lower Smith river, and perhaps the largest Tolowa town.
4. Hinei-behind, Hinei-inland-from.

boat will be able to do it alone."[5] Then he blew out.[6] He did that in these two places, at Hinei and at Omen.[7]

d. He went on up along the coast and came to Rekwoi. There he saw many people playing. They had a *tekwuskei* root, which they were rolling downhill.[8] When he arrived, they said, "Join us!" When the man there[9] saw a stranger he always told him, "Go right there below me." He would make him stand in the middle (of the course on which) the ball was rolling downhill. When it came to himself, he dodged it, for whenever it touched anyone on the leg or body it killed him; but as it rolled by he would spear it and make it roll against the stranger below him. Pulekukwerek saw how it was. Now that man said to him, "Go in the middle, down below, and strike it there." But Pulekukwerek said, "No, I will do that afterwards. First let me have your spear and you stand below. I want to try it." The Rekwoi person had never seen him before and thought that he would not know. So Pulekukwerek took his spear. The ball started and he saw it coming. Then he struck it with his spear and it rolled against the Rekwoi person and broke his legs and killed him.[10] Then Pulekukwerek blew out. Hc said, "They shall not kill men in this way. Let little boys play this.[11] It is not for killing people." So he made it to be. Now boys play that kind and the place in Rekwoi is called Oregok.[12]

e. When the ball had stopped rolling down, he said, "I want to go to the sweathouse." A Rekwoi man said, "We never go into the sweathouse because the women are there." Pulekukwerek said, "Well, I want to go in neverthe-

5. This argues skill and experience in halving logs which are up to 4 feet across. De facto I have not heard of assistants to habitual boat builders.

6. Blowing out is the normal beginning of formal ordainments. It may be related to the ritual offering of tobacco crumbs blown off the palm by human beings in invoking woge spirits.

7. Omen is the northernmost Yurok settlement. The duplication here of this split-log incident at Hinei and Omen recurs in tale C1 and is thus established as "standard" for the complete Pulekukwerek cycle. It is the only incident that the same narrator seems to repeat. The localization, however, varies: C1 gives Omen and Espeu instead of Hinei and Omen. Nä'ägeł in A15x, and Kenek in J3 (this probably erroneously, since there are no redwoods so far upstream) are also given as sites of the incident.

8. The hill manroot, *Echinocystis origanus*. The game, *oregok*, was played semiceremonially at Rekwoi, and at about two other Yurok towns; a proper hillside is necessary. Apparently the manroot crushes whom it rolls on.

9. The one in charge of the game. In other versions, the local man spears the visitor instead of spearing the rolling root. [Cf. C1*c*.—Ed.]

10. It is characteristic of the present narrator that he has his hero evade the test. More usually, in this as well as other incidents, Pulekukwerek is made to undergo and escape the danger before he subjects his opponent to it.

11. It is also played by adults, more or less ritually.

12. The rolling began near the southwesternmost house in Rekwoi, called oregok from the game; Waterman, Geography, map 8, no. 23.

less." That man told him, "The women say, 'You men must not come in.' They do not want us in the sweathouse." Pulekukwerek said, "Well, I am going." It was in daytime. Now he went and saw two women. They had shoots and fibers and were making baskets. He stayed only a short time and went out. He went to the top of the hill and gathered sweathouse wood. When he had put his sticks together ready to tie up—he knew how much he would carry—he thought, "I wish I saw a chicken hawk (*tspegi*) light on this tree." Then he saw a chicken hawk coming to the tree and caught it in his hand. He hid it[13] and said to it, "The reason I want you is that I wish you to help me. I am about to make a fire in the sweathouse. I shall tell you what I want you to do." He took it along with him. When he came to the sweathouse, he passed the sticks inside. One of the women drew them in. Then he entered and started the fire. The woman said, "Do not put on too much wood. We do not use much. We put in only a little, just enough to sweat by." Pulekukwerek said, "Well, I shall not put in too much." Then he told the chicken hawk, "Go (to the part of the sweat house) where these women are. Go right above them, stretch out your wings and beat down with them." He told him this that the heat might be fanned down on them.[14] Soon he saw the women rolling about because they were too hot. Then they could not stand it any longer, even though it was only a small fire. They started to go out; it was too hot for them. They emerged and lay in the open because they were so hot. Pulekukwerek said to himself inside, "Women will not stay in the sweathouse hereafter. Let men be in the sweathouse, and no others." Then he blew out and said, "Women may not come into the sweathouse any longer." So he prevented it. Therefore women no longer enter the sweathouse. Only when one is about to be made a doctor do they come in.[15]

f. After he had finished in the sweathouse at Rekwoi, he wanted to cross the river. "I want to go to the other side," he told them. "No, we never go over," they said. They never crossed there: that is why they would not ferry him over. If they had to go to the other side, they went upstream to cross. Then those of Rekwoi thought, "Well, let him die (if he wishes). Let him go." They said, "I have a boat here. You can take it yourself if you wish." Pulekukwerek said, "Very well," and went down to the river. He knew about the thing . . .[16] because he had heard that one never crossed there. Then up at the town they waited, watching to see him cross. For a long time they did not

13. Under the piece of deerskin which Yurok men usually wore about the hips as a loincloth.

14. With the exit—ventilator and door closed, the heat (and smoke) are stifling, and the occupants lie with their faces close to the floor. Any fanning of heat downward might well be insupportable.

15. They are actually admitted to the partly dismantled sweathouse for the doctor-making dance in which the woman novice's *teloget* pains are tamed and cooked.

16. Water monster, usually specified as a *knewollek* or "long one."

see him come (out from the shore).[17] They only saw a little smoke by the river. At last they saw the boat coming; he had a fire in it. Before he started he had made the fire and had put stones into it; they were red-hot. Now he began to cross. They watched him from the town above. They saw him going. When he had nearly reached the other side, they saw his boat almost stand on end. Then Pulekukwerek leaped to land, and they saw the boat go down; they did not see it any more. Pulekukwerek went only a short distance; then he saw that one floating which had swallowed the boat. The hot stones had killed it. That is why Pulekukwerek had done so: he knew he could kill it in that way. Then he blew out and said, "It is well. Anyone will be able to cross here. No matter where a stranger comes from, nevertheless he will go over."

g. He started from Rekwoi and came to Ploksäu on the Bald Hills.[18] When he got there he heard them pounding acorns in the house; it sounded as if there were two of them. He wished to go in, so he entered softly. When he was inside he saw two old women, both blind. They were pounding *heiwanek* seeds. One of them said, "I do not know whether (the meal) is fine enough to eat." The other said, "Give me some and I can tell." So she handed it to her. Pulekukwerek was in the house unknown to them, and he took earth into his hand. When one said, "Here, I will give it to you," and the other reached out her hand across the fireplace, Pulekukwerek dropped the earth into her hand, and she put it into her mouth. She said, "It does not taste like *heiwanek*. Well, I will give you some of mine." Then the other one reached out her hand and Pulekukwerek dropped earth into hers. Then they said, "I think someone must be in the house." Now they had heard of Pulekukwerek that he was good to cure eyes: when people were blind Pulekukwerek could make them well. One of them said, "Perhaps it is he who is in the house. I heard that he was coming this way." The other said, "No, I think not. If it were he he would have spoken." So with a stick, like a spear,[19] with which they killed people, they struck all about the house. Soon they felt him impaled.[20] One said, "Oh, it is too bad! Perhaps it is he who is good to cure eyes." The other said, "Well, we

17. The edge of the river at the Rekwoi boat landing is under the slope and not visible from the town. His delay was due to his stone-heating.

18. Near Stanhoff's place, on Bald Hills. In Yurok the hills are called Tsulu, in Tsulu-la or Chilula country. Ploksäu is given by Waterman as Plokseu (map 2, no. 34), but his location of it seems too near the Trinity River. [Also, he shows it in Hupa rather than Chilula country. See map 1 in this volume.—Ed.]

19. *Wetskerkr*. The word was later applied to pitchforks and became the nickname of Informant B. Waterman, p. 218.

20. He could not escape because the stone door of the house closed on him, but the narrator forgot to mention this detail.

can tell by his buttocks,'' for they had heard that his buttocks were sharp.[21] Then they felt him. ''Yes, it is he!'' The other said, ''Well, it is too bad. It will be best if we try to revive him.'' So they made medicine for him. He was lying there; after a time he began to come to; soon he was well. ''Are you he who can doctor bad eyes?'' they said. ''Yes, that is I,'' said Pulekukwerek. ''We want you to cure our eyes because we are both blind.'' they said. Pulekukwerek said, ''Yes, I will do it. Can you not let me go out a little while before I begin?''[22] ''Yes,'' they said. So he went out. It was summer, and everything was dry. Pulekukwerek thought, ''Let me set fire to what is around the house and burn them.''[23] Then he set fire to it. The two women inside heard; it sounded like fire somewhere. They said, ''They must be burning the prairie where they gather seeds.''[24] But it was their own house that was burning on all sides. At last they knew that it was on fire. Pulekukwerek stook outside watching. When the house was consumed he heard two pops. The two old women had burst as they burned. Then he blew out and said, ''People will not be killed by heiwanek seeds.'' The old women were themselves called Heiwanek. People had died of those seeds because they were too dry and long and when the old women fed them to persons they stuck in their throats and killed them.[25]

h. Pulekukwerek started to go. He turned[26] and came down to the river at Kenek. There it used to be bad. The Ka-sumig-or[27] lived there. They were porpoises.[28] Because they went to Sumig, they are called Ka-sumig-or, but they had grown at Kenek. They smoked: when (some)one smelled the tobacco

21. He had two little horns on his buttocks, whence his name, Pulekuk-kwerek, ''down-stream sharp.''

22. Again the narrator is vague; the usual motivation is that he must go out to find the herb which he needs as medicine for them.

23. The same sort of ellipsis; here he just sets fire, without blocking the exit or heaping up fuel, as in other versions.

24. Burning over the prairies kept the brush down and made seed-beating easier and more profitable the next year.

25. I do not know the seed. [Robins, Yurok Language, translates it as wild oats.—Ed.] It seems the women were ***heiwanek*** plants, or became such; but this ending of the usually rather vivid episode seems unduly rationalized. In other versions the two women pound up the bones of people they catch in their house, and hence are cannibals.

26. He has previously turned off the main avenue, the Klamath, to go up on Bald Hills. Now he is turning back to it.

27. From Sumig, Patrick's Point on the coast. The going of the porpoises from Kenek to Sumig is frequently mentioned. They are also called Kenomer. Their house pit is still shown: Waterman, map 22, no. 13.

28. ***Kegor***.

from across the river it killed him. Pulekukwerek had heard of that and therefore came. Now they had eaten supper; soon they went to the sweathouse.[29] They were ten brothers. In the sweathouse they talked with one another. They told the youngest one, "You give him your pipe first." Now Pulekukwerek had provided where the smoke would go inside of him. He had taken (hollowed) elderberry sticks and swallowed them, eleven of them. He thought that when he smoked he would put the smoke in the sticks; but he concealed this. Now the youngest brother gave him his pipe. Pulekukwerek smoked it. When he was through, he gave it back to him. Another gave him his pipe, and then others. So it went on. He always drew out the stick (full of smoke) and threw it away because it was nearly eaten through by the time he finished a pipe. They continued to give him their pipes. The oldest brother had the strongest tobacco. That is why Pulekukwerek had provided eleven sticks; he thought he would put this one's smoke into two. Now it came the oldest one's turn, and Pulekukwerek drew his smoke into the two (remaining) sticks. But when he had smoked his pipe, he felt it in his throat; it nearly burned him.[30] Then he handed him back his empty pipe. Then they said, "Well, let us go bathe before we sleep. It is too hot in here."[31] When they had gone, Pulekukwerek blew out and said, "They shall not kill men with tobacco. Let anyone smoke it."[32]

i. Now they returned from having bathed. They had talked. They had said, "I do not know where he is from. When people only smell (our tobacco) across the river it kills them; but he smoked them all and was not killed." Now they pretended to sleep. After a time they heard him snore as if he were blowing a flute. Then they began to talk to each other again. They wished to kill him asleep. One of them said, "I think we should open a hole just above where he is sleeping." Then they did that and went after a big stone. It was all that two of them could carry. They went on the roof of the sweathouse and held it over where they knew he was sleeping and let it fall.[33] Pulekukwerek just turned aside a little. He knew they were going to let the stone drop and turned aside, and it missed him. Then they knew that they could not kill him. They thought, "Well, we will let him go." They carried the rock out. Pulekukwerek knew all about it, but did as if he had been asleep. In the morning they saw that the stone slab floor was spoiled: where the rock had

29. To spend the evening and sleep. They take their guest with them.

30. Really, it burned him so that the pain was nearly intolerable.

31. This comment indicates that the Yurok did not usually bathe after the evening sweat, but ordinarily went to sleep in comfort (they were naked) in the sweathouse.

32. The implication is that this is the origin of the use of tobacco—another rationalization. Pulekukwerek had always used tobacco.

33. It was a matter of lifting aside four or five boards in the sweathouse roof; nothing is nailed, pegged, or tied.

fallen, there was a hole. Pulekukwerek said, "It is too bad! It looks as if something had fallen here. The slab is spoiled." He put his hand on the floor, rubbed the place, and they saw that the slab was smooth again. They thought, "What sort of a person is he? Where does he come from?"

j. He started from Kenek to take a stroll upstream. He came to a rock, climbed on top of it, and slid down. He cut the rock.[34] They saw him doing it. He slid a number of times from the top: thus he gouged it as it is. Then he said, "The reason I do this is that if anyone has sore eyes he can come here and take the dust from this rock. Or he can take a sharp stone and cut this rock; and the dust will be good for the eyes." So the people use this for sore eyes.

k. Merip was another bad place. A man lived there who had two wives and was excessively jealous of them. Even if he saw a footprint on the sand on the other side of the river he was jealous. He would place his poison on the footprint and so kill the person who had passed. Everybody was afraid and would not go there. Those of Kenek wished to send Pulekukwerek, because they knew that they themselves could not kill him. So they got him to go downstream. He came to Merip,[35] went into the house, saw the two women inside, but did not see the man. He sat down between the two women, putting his legs on their laps. They said, "Oh, it is bad! I am a married woman! My husband will be here soon." "Oh, that is all right," said Pulekukwerek. He continued to sit like that. After a time he heard a noise outside and the women said, "Now he is coming, I think." But he remained sitting as he was. Then he saw the man come in. As he entered he looked and then went to the other side of the fireplace from Pulekukwerek. There he drew out an arrow. He had ten of them. The first one he took out had the point almost burning. Pulekukwerek said, "No, not that one. You can't kill me with it." Now he had taken out his heart and put it into his little toe.[36] That man kept drawing out his arrows. When he took out the sixth, Pulekukwerek saw that the flame at the point was larger. But he said, "No, you cannot kill me with that one. Take the best one you have." Then he drew out nine, and the flame was still larger. When he pulled out the tenth, he nearly burned himself. Then Pulekukwerek said, "That is it! That is the one that will kill me!"[37] He put his

34. With his horns or points. The rock is a small fraction of a mile upstream from Kenek, near the trail but off the river in the timber, and it is disappointing both in size and in conspicuousness of the scratches, after all the talk by the Yurok about it.

35. Waterman, map 21; and plate 7 for the rock into which the jealous one turned. Merip is 3 miles *down*stream from Kenek, on the opposite side.

36. As several times before, the narrator has forgotten a point which it becomes necessary to go back to before a consequence is clear.

37. Pulekukwerek wanted to get it away from him, to break his power. Minute flaming arrowheads, it should be said, shot secretly at people, are the fatal mechanism of witchcraft of the ***uma'a*** or "Indian devil" type.

fingers to his breast and said, "Shoot me here, right in my heart!" That one shot. Pulekukwerek fell over. That one had (apparently) killed him. After a time he saw him move a little. Then he saw him leap to the drying scaffold (hanging from the roof). There he lay a while and leaped again, upstream and uphill to Egolok.[38] From there he jumped once more, to Kenek. There he drew the arrow out of himself. Then he took his heart and put it back into his body.

l. He thought he would make arrowpoints from the (large) flint (head) that he had drawn out. He went on the roof;[39] that is where he worked. Then from there (he) heard something. He thought, "It is as if I heard laughing and talking somewhere." But he continued working. After a time he heard that it was in the house. Then he came down to see those inside. He saw there were a lot of little ones, rattlesnakes and ants and yellow jackets. When a piece of burning flint fell, they opened their mouths (to catch it). Pulekukwerek had not known that the flakes from the flaming flint would burn through the roof. He jumped on Rattlesnake and tried to take the chips away from him, but Rattlesnake held his head down[40] and hid them, for he knew that Pulekukwerek would take them away. That is how his head comes to be so short and flat, and he is venomous: this is how he got his poison.

m. Now Pulekukwerek blew out and said, "He will not any longer kill men with that poison of his downstream there at Merip." This is how people began to be jealous: because K'e-merip, the one of Merip, was so jealous. But Pulekukwerek stopped people being killed because of it.

n. Whenever Pulekukwerek stopped anywhere and destroyed what was evil there, they always told him, "There is another bad place upstream." So he heard at Kenek that at Ko'men[41] there was a woman who killed men. Now he always went off during the day. Those of Kenek did not know where he was. He went and got himself hollow elder sticks, ten of them. Then he started to go upstream. He had heard: "There is a pretty woman there, but whoever tries to cohabit with her, she always kills the man in that way." So Pulekukwerek went there to Ko'men with his hollow elder sticks. When she saw him she said, "Come into the house." He entered, stayed only a little while,[42] but

38. Ego'olokw (Waterman, map 17, no. 99, "rock on the hillside") is on the Merip side, nearly 1 mile from Merip and perhaps 1/2 mile above the river. [See map 5 in this volume.—Ed.]

39. A "house" was specified, although other versions mention the sweathouse, which a man would be more likely to sit on while working.

40. Had his head stepped on by Pulekukwerek in other versions, to get his spark of poison away from him.

41. Orleans; Karok Panamenik.

42. Probably he went to the sweathouse as usual.

at night came back in.[43] "You had better sleep with me," she said. He agreed. Now she was eager because she wanted to kill him; but he was reluctant. "Nevertheless, I'll try it," he thought, and covered his member with one of his hollow sticks. Then he could hear like something being cut up. He withdrew slowly, so that she might cut it all to pieces. After a while he did not hear it any longer, and she got up to go the creek and wash. That is when Pulekukwerek put on another elder tube. When the woman came back into the house, she was eager for intercourse again. So he did the same way. And every time she had wholly cut up the elder and no longer felt it, she got up to wash. After nine times, when he had only one more elder, it was beginning to be daylight. He went to her again, because he had ten of the hollow sticks. As soon as they finished, she went out and down to the river to wash; it was full daylight then.

o. When he saw her going there, Pulekukwerek ran off because he had no more hollow stems. He ran downriver. They were having the fish dam at Kepel; and when he came to it, he said to Thunder,[44] who owned the north end of the dam, "Someone is pursuing to kill me; catch and hold that one!"[45] "Yes," said Thunder. So Pulekukwerek crossed on the weir; when he got to the middle, he saw the woman coming. Thunder tried to keep her back. "It is a bad place to cross," he said. "It is against the rule for a woman to cross on the weir." But he could not hold her, so let her pass. So Pulekukwerek kept on running downriver. When she had crossed, those owning the Kepel side of the weir, the Earthquakes, Yewoɫ. ten of them,[46] tried to hold her. Then this sky (*wes'ona*) seemed to be falling, because the world[47] was shaking so much from the Earthquakes being angry, trying to stop the woman. And Thunder shouted from across the river, "Let her pass," for he feared the sky would fall from so much shaking.

p. So Pulekukwerek ran on, and the woman after him. Then he reached his home, Pulekuk, and the old woman there, his mother.[48] Now the woman

43. To accomplish his mission.

44. Or Thunders?

45. Yurok is noncommittal between "him" and "her."

46. There were ten Earthquakes, the informant said, as elsewhere ten Thunders are often spoken of; but this may have been a statement of general information, not a part of the story. Earthquake and Thunder are often associated, as at Kenek, and again on the coast; cf. BB3.

47. The sky and world are distinguished, but are called by the same word, *wes'ona*; or perhaps more accurately, the sky and the land together constitute the world.

48. According to Goddard, Life and Culture, p. 75, and Hupa Texts, no. 1, p. 123, Yimantuwinyai, who corresponds mainly to Wohpekumeu but also performs some of Pulekukwerek's feats (there is no separate Hupa deity equivalent to the latter) is born from the ground at Kenek, and (Texts, p. 134) ends by going to the downstream ("north") end of the world to his grandmother, who somehow seems more appropriate for a great culture-hero than a mother.

from Ko'men was ashamed because she had not killed him; and she thought, "Well, anyway, let me live with him." And she was no longer trying to kill him; but he did not like it, because she had killed many men at Ko'men that way and tried to sleep with him too; so he was going to go off. "I would like her ruined,"[49] he said to the old woman. "Can you do it somehow?" "Yes, I can do that," she said. Then she said to the girl,[50] "I want cooking stones[51] from the room, early in the morning,"[52] So in the morning she went to bring stones. "When you come back, get wood," the old woman told her; and then, "Fetch water too." So she brought everything that was wanted. Then, "Stand on top of the house," she ordered her. "Now set your foot on one side of the smoke hole,[53] your other foot on the far side,"[54] and she did so. Now the old woman had a great fire in the house, and the stones in it. Then she threw the water on the fire, and the steam rose to where the girl stood, and the stones cracked (and flew up). Then she heard something cracking up there where she was standing across the smoke hole; so she was killed. Now she had obsidians in her; that is how she killed men, by cutting them up with those. When she burst, the black obsidians flew upriverward from here (at Weitspus) and fell there. That is why they have that kind there,[55] in some places,[56] because of

---

However, as appears below in *q*, and in F3 and F6, the present informant has Pulekukwerek, Megwomets, and Wohpekumeu all originate underground, the first two being dug up by a bulb-gathering woman, a motive which ordinarily applies to No'ots as the Yurok tell it (see A7 above) and to his Hupa counterpart Hahowilwał (Texts, p. 146; Megwomets is Yinukatsisdai in Hupa). Whether this is an individual confusion on the part of Informant F, or a proper variant stream of Yurok tradition, I do not know.

49. "Hurt," the interpreter rendered it. For once, Pulekukwerek is far from heroic; but the Yurok have bungled the story, compared with the way it is told elsewhere (whence the technical name vagina dentata for the episode), where the hero breaks out her teeth with a stone pestle. The Yurok substitution of the hollow elder covers (taken from the Yurok poisonous tobacco story) is weak; they leave the hero defenseless. He can escape but not overcome her.

50. Though the informant called her a women in the tale, he said her name was Ko'men umä'i, Ko'men girl, when asked afterward. *Umä'i*, like Hupa *keltsan* and Karok *ifapi*, does not mean maiden, as it has at times been translated, but a young woman who has not yet borne a child.

51. Stream cobbles up to the size of a fist.

52. As the old woman (*perei*) of the house, she has authority over her daughters-in-law. See Spott and Kroeber, Yurok Narratives, no. 18, p. 206.

53. Which is simply one board laid aside in the middle tier of roofing.

54. To straddle, and open her genitals.

55. The Yurok know that obsidians, especially the big black ones, come from upriver. On the other hand, no quarry of red osidian is known within Yurok territory; the statement in the next sentence means only that such obsidians are found in possession of human beings along the river.

56. Here and there, because large ones are few, rare, and valuable.

when she burst. But the red ones fell around here along the river: that is why they have red obsidian everywhere hereabout.[57] Then the old woman said, "Now they will buy wives with those, if they have them; that is how they will do. And they will be good for all kinds of things. If they kill a man, they can settle for it with that kind. And when there is a Deerskin Dance, they can dance with them too."

q. (Asked about the old woman, the informant added:) A woman had been digging (Brodiaea) bulbs since early morning. When it was nearly sundown, she made another hole in the ground. Then she saw a baby come out: he called her "mother." That is how Pulekukwerek grew.

No, Megwomets is a different man. He was born in the ground too, but he went off south along the coast.[58] And Wohpekumeu grew in the ground; but he had a sister.[59]

F2. WOHPEKUMEU

a. Wohpekumeu lived at Kenek.[1] There were no women there. He wanted them but could find none. All about here he could not see one. Then he started upstream.

b. He came to the sky, at the (upstream) end of the world. There he saw a house and went in. He saw men, ten of them, and no one else, except one girl. She was just old enough for a husband. Then at night they said, "Let us go to the sweathouse," and went in. Wohpekumeu desired the girl but would not say so because there were so many of them. So he went into the sweathouse with them. In the morning he saw the girl going after wood. He thought, "I will follow her. I shall let her go ahead." Then she went. When he tried to follow her he could not find her at all, though he went everywhere. At last he thought, "Well, I must go back," gathered sweathouse wood, and carried it downhill, because he could not find the girl. When he took up (the load of)

57. See note before last. Perhaps one reason why this vagina dentata episode is so bungled here is that the Yurok are more interested in the institutional values and uses of obsidian blades then they let themselves be interested in sex details. Pulekukwerek, the great monster destroyer, is really a quite unsuitable hero for this tale, because, as the Yurok say, he always smoked but never ate food and never had intercourse; he lived in the sweathouse when he was not traveling. So he is miscast in the role, and the monster girl has to be destroyed by his old mother.

58. This is the story given as F6.

59. And this one is F3.

1. His home, according to all Yurok accounts, and according to occasional statements the place of his growth, although most versions, like this one, are silent on his origin.

wood, a pileated woodpecker[2] lit on it. Wohpekumeu came to the sweathouse and passed the wood in. When they took it they caught the woodpecker.

He stayed there ten days but did not find the girl. Every day he brought down sweathouse wood. Ten times he passed it into the sweathouse, and each time that they took it in they got a pileated woodpecker. So they had ten woodpeckers, one each. Then they did not know what sort of a man he was. They had never seen such a man before.

c. The eleventh day he went out after sweathouse wood again. He had gone only a short distance from the house when he heard someone chopping wood.[3] He thought, "I will go to see." Then he arrived and found the girl. He said, "I have wanted to see you for a long time but have never found you." She said, "Yes? I cut wood here every day." He said, "I have never seen you." So he sat down and began to talk to her. After a time he said, "I want to speak to you because I like you." Soon he sat down close to her and wished to toy with her; but she would not let him. He said, "Why do you not let me play with you?" She said, "No. I am afraid to have children because they will cut me open." When a woman was to have a child then, they always cut her and the child was born, but she died.

Far off there was a large hill. Wohpekumeu said, "Let us go there. No one will see us." She said, "No, it is too far." He said, "You will not know it if you go." She said, "No, it is too far. I cannot go there." But Wohpekumeu said, "Wait only an instant." Then shortly she knew[4] that she was on the hill: she found herself there. He said, "I told you that you would not know how you went there." She said, "Well, it is good." He said, "You will return the same way: you will not feel that you are going." Then he caused her to return[5] in the same way.

d. Now he went back to the house with her. After a time she cooked for them and they ate. It began to look as if there were something wrong with her. The ten men saw it. By the time they had finished eating the woman began to be ill.[6] She cried and said, "My belly hurts me." They began to think, "Perhaps it is Wohpekumeu. Perhaps that is he." The girl cried more loudly, and they knew it was he. They made a bed for her and she lay down. Then they seized Wohpekumeu and were about to kill him because their sister was to have a child. He said, "Let me go!" "No," they said. He asked, "Let me go

2. *Dryocopus pileatus*, the species from which the large and valuable scarlet crests are obtained.

3. Dead or fallen wood was split with maul and elkhorn wedge, or broken across.

4. That is, he deceived her into thinking she was there. So in other versions, although what follows makes it look almost as if the meaning were that he actually transported her.

5. In fact or seeming to her?

6. With the pains of labor.

outdoors. I will make medicine for her." "No," they said again. The girl cried again, and they were on the point of cutting her open. Then Wohpekumeu took ashes (from the fireplace) for his medicine, because they would not let him go outdoors (to find an herb). He put ashes into water and stirred it: so he made his medicine. Then he had her drink it. As soon as she drank they heard the baby crying. It was born safely: a boy. Wohpekumeu said, "I think they will nevermore cut women open. They will not do that way. Let them make medicine. Then it will be well."[7]

e. Now they were in the sweathouse. Then the boy came[8] and called for his father. "Where is he?" he said. "He is in the sweathouse," they told him. Then the boy came into the sweathouse. Next day Wohpekumeu thought he would pay for his wife and child.[9] Then he paid them five strings of money (for the woman). Then he put down five more strings of dentalia for the child.[10] He said, "I am paying for the woman. I want it to be thus. I do not wish to see anyone have children for nothing. He will have to pay. If he does not pay and has children, they will be worthless. They will always cause much trouble."[11] Then the people thought, "It is well." It became (instituted) thus because Wohpekumeu then said so.

f. Wohpekumeu thought, "I will return." The ten men said, "You had better take your wife with you." He said, "No." They told him, "Then take your boy." But he said, "No." "Take him," they said. "He is your own. Take him along." "Well then, all right," he said. The ten men gave the boy a quiver, and he started with his father. But Wohpekumeu did not want him. He hoped to find women wherever he went: therefore he did not wish to have his boy along.[12] He thought, "I will take him with me and kill him." He knew a bad place on the way, a lake. (When they came there) he said, "It is hot. Let

7. This episode is the basis of that one of the childbirth formulas most widely known to the Yurok and their neighbors. Here it is reduced to an incident in a tale. The magic value of a formula resides in its exact recitation in a particular form, including specification of the original locality, under the proper circumstances, and with the application of a certain herb or other substance.

8. He grew to half-maturity at once. Other versions so specify; this one implies the fact.

9. To legitimize the marriage and offspring.

10. The "normal" price of a wife of good family was ten strings of dentalia plus other property. For seduction resulting in a child, the penalty was about half, or nearly so. If the father claimed the child, he paid for it separately. After that, only a small balance remained due if he wanted the woman. Of course, the brothers have already had ten woodpecker crests from him, but that was like currying favor and making him welcome to stay.

11. Bastards and lowbred people are troublemakers from whom no good can come, the Yurok think. They treat them with contempt and an inequality that must tend to bring about this result.

12. The women would think Wohpekumeu older.

us swim here." The boy said, "Yes," and took off his clothes.[13] As soon as he entered the water he disappeared. Wohpekumeu did not see him any longer. Then he was glad and went on. He had not gone far when he heard someone behind him. He looked and saw that it was his boy. He was carrying a different quiver and around his head he wore a band with woodpecker crests.[14] He was larger: he was almost grown up.

g. They went on. They came to Nastok.[15] Then Wohpekmeu thought, "I will tell him to shoot a ground squirrel here." They heard a noise above the trail, and the boy went up to shoot the ground squirrel. Then many rattlesnakes attacked him. Wohpekumeu saw him killed by them. He went on, thinking, "I shall not have to take that child." He was glad to see him killed. He thought, "But if he comes again, looking just like me, then I will take him." Now Wohpekumeu's quiver was different (from those of other people) and his hair was covered[16] with woodpecker crests. He thought, "If he has a quiver of the same fur as I,[17] and woodpecker crests on his head, I will take him." He went on and had gone far. Then he heard someone coming behind him. He looked and saw his boy. He saw that he carried the same sort of quiver as himself, and was ornamented in the same way. Then he thought, "I shall take him, I like him now." Then he went downstream with him. They came back to Kenek. They arrived late, after it was dark. He had his house nearer the river than the (other) houses of Kenek.[18] There was no woman in his house.[19]

h. In the morning women went to the creek to bathe. One of them reported, "I saw a young man. I have never seen him before. He came with Wohpekumeu, but I do not know where he came from." Soon the young man thought, "Let me go back from the river and see who lives behind our sweathouse." But Wohpekumeu stayed in the sweathouse. Then the young man came to the Kenek sweathouse carrying his quiver. Those inside saw him and told him to come in, and he entered. They did not know where he came from.

13. At most he would be wearing a piece of skin about the hips, and possibly moccasins and a necklace.

14. *Ma'aku*, a stuffed ring of deerskin with three or four of the scarlet scalps sewn on. [K. has a marginal reference to Kroeber and Gifford, World Renewal. Later, in Informant Z's biography, K. spells this as *ma'äk*.—Ed.]

15. Six miles upstream from Orleans, in Karok territory. Waterman, Geography, map 2, no. 29, Nastok.

16. Probably they grew on or were fastened directly to his hair, possibly attached to headgear.

17. The narrator is awkward in his vagueness. There is no effect to be got out of the lack of concrete specification here.

18. Wohpekumeu's house was downstream from the three or four houses that constituted the historic town of Kenek; those of the Porpoises, Thunder, Earthquake, etc., are upstream and farther back from the river. Waterman, map 22.

19. His name means "widower of Wohpäuk."

One of them said, "Can you make arrow points? I have flint, but have not worked it into points." The young man said, "Yes, I think I can make them." Then that man went into his house and brought the flint into the sweathouse on a basketry plate. The boy took it. He let the flint lie before him for a long time before he took it up. Then he put the contents of the plate into his quiver. He who lived there thought, "Why does he not work on it? He said he would make them for me." He watched him. Then the young man took up the plate and poured the flints out of his quiver. Then they saw that they were worked beautifully, though they had been unable to see him making them. Then he handed them back and went out to go to his father. They spoke about him, saying, "He is a good young man." But they did not know where he was from; they had not seen him before. One of them said, "I did not see him working them; nevertheless he made them beautifully." Another said, "Let us tell our sisters to take him for a husband." Then they went into the house (and told the girls). The girls said, "Yes, we will do it."

i. Now old man Wohpekumeu heard that his boy was going to marry the girls and that they liked him. The old man was not pleased to hear that. He went out, downstream from Kenekpul,[20] thinking. He did not want his son to marry the girls.[21]

He thought, "I wish I saw a good boat." Then there was a large boat there, a newly made one. It had just been burned.[22] Then he wished, "I should like to see an old woman and an old man and boys." Then there was an old woman sitting near the boat, and an old man, and two boys, and a baby basket decorated with dentalia. Wohpekumeu said to them, "Put me into the basket cradle and hold me, for I do not like my boy to marry those girls. Take me into the boat. When you come opposite Kenek, hold me facing the town so they can see me, because the two girls are at the river leaching acorns." Then the old people said, "Yes," and started upstream in the boat. They went up on the farther side of the river.

Wohpekumeu said, "When the boat is opposite the town, speak loudly, so that they will hear you and come out to see." Then they spoke loudly and all (the people of Kenek) came out of their houses. The two girls were right at the river. They said,[23] "Someone has come from downstream with a new boat. It is pretty baby that they have. Look at its basket cradle!" The boat continued on upstream. Soon it was above and they could not see it any more. Then they

20. Kenekpul is downstream from Kenek, as the name indicates. Waterman, map 17, no. 116, has it nearly a mile below Kenek.

21. The motivation may have been desire or envy, or again the wish to maintain the appearance of his own youth.

22. The Yurok depended more on fire than on adzes to hollow a boat. A new boat would show charring.

23. To those up the bank in the town?

heard shouting upstream and more cries. Then they saw the boat floating downstream capsized. The old man and the old woman flew up and became birds, but the baby floated down in its basket cradle.

j. The two girls, still leaching acorns, saw it struggling on the water as it floated. One of them said, "Take off your clothes and jump in and catch it." Then the other went into the water, took hold of the basket, and brought it to shore. Now the baby cried. Only when she held it facing her did it stop. Whenever she held it at her side it began to cry again. Then she said to the other girl, "You hold it. I cannot make it stop crying." Then the other one took it. But the baby did the same: it cried until they held it facing them.[24] Then they said, "Oh, it is Wohpekumeu, I think," and threw it, basket cradle (and all), into the water. Then he freed himself of the cradle and climbed up the bank on his hands and knees: he was the old man again. He went up to his house. Then both of the girls (were about to) have children. Wohpekumeu had done that because he did not wish his boy to have the girls.

k. Those living back of him[25] in the town did not want the old man about because now both girls were with child. They wished to kill him. But they knew that they could not kill him in any ordinary way, for he would always revive. They began to say, "We can kill him only if we make the ocean come and cover the world. We can kill him only if we drown him." But Wohpekumeu never went out of his sweathouse.[26] Then they sent the long-billed Pipir to his sweathouse to try to pierce it from all sides, that the water might enter it. Pipir tried to make the holes but could not, for the sweathouse was of stone inside. So Wohpekumeu stayed inside.

l. But one day he thought, "Let me go to hunt." In the woods above Tuley Creek[27] he had set deer snares. Now he went to look at them. While he was there, the water rose. Then the piece of ground on which he was, floated. For ten days the water covered everything; there was nothing to be seen above it. Then those at Kenek thought, "By this time, I think, he is dead. He must have drowned." Then the water fell. Then Wohpekumeu returned. When they saw him coming they knew that they could not kill him. Therefore they went off to the coast to Sumig.[28]

24. In order to cohabit with them.

25. Ka-sumig-or, Thunder, and the others lived both upstream and farther back from the river on the Kenek terrace.

26. In self-protection.

27. Tuley (or Tule or Tulley) Creek, Okego weroi, comes into the river at the upstream end of Kenek. It is 7 or 8 miles long, rises in the open prairies of Bald Hills, and flows down a forested slope. The terrain should be an excellent hunting ground. Waterman, map 22.

28. Sumig is Patrick's Point on the coast between Big Lagoon and Trinidad. This final home makes them the Ka-sumig-or. They are also called Kegor, the Porpoises.

m. Now Wohpekumeu's son was married and had a boy. Then Wohpekumeu said to him, "Go up into the woods. There are young chicken hawks in a tree. You had better get them." Then his son climbed the tree. His name was Kapuloyo,[29] and his boy's Kewomer. When he was on the tree Wohpekumeu thought, "I wish the wind would blow." He wanted to take his son's wife, that is what he wanted. Then the wind began to rise. Kapuloyo held fast to the tree as it swayed. As he held onto the limbs, he felt that they would break under his feet and hands.[30] He stayed on that tree for ten days. Wohpekumeu thought, "He must be dead now. The wind has blown ten days, and he has not come back." Then the wind stopped.

n. When Kapuloyo descended,[31] he heard a woodpecker calling. He went (toward the noise), and when he came below where the woodpecker had cried (from up in the tree), he saw someone standing: he was blind. He spoke to him, and that one answered. Then he thought, "It is my boy." The boy said, "I am blind. Wohpekumeu has taken your wife and made me blind."[32] Kapuloyo said, "Wait a little." He began to cry. When he looked where his tears had fallen, he saw a hole full of water. He took some of it and rubbed it on Kewomer's eyes. Then the boy's eyes were well again.

o. Now he told him, "Go to the house and get my tobacco." The boy said, "I myself[33] threw your tobacco into the fire; but there is one basket left, the best one." "Well, get that," said Kapuloyo, and the boy ran and got it. Then Kapuloyo said, "We will go off somewhere."

Kewomer had a cane. He pointed downstream, and the stick just reached. Then he pointed upstream, but did not have to stretch his arm out all the way.[34] Then he knew that that direction was the nearest to the sky. Kapuloyo said, "I think that is where you will go. You will go upstream because that is the nearest." Therefore that is where Kewomer lives. Then Kapuloyo told him, "We shall always meet across the ocean where they dance the Deerskin Dance every night. When you come, come along the river and take away from

29. Until now the narrator has not thought it necessary to name him. From here on, three people of as many generations are involved and the lack of names would make for confusion.

30. The narrative is too condensed. Presumably the lower limbs must have been blown off, as in almost all other versions, else he could have climbed down at once. Usually he descends by using chewing gum made of pitch (cf. J2*c*) or is helped by Spider. [K. has a notation to check these variant versions. I do not find a Spider version.—Ed.]

31. Another omission: How did he come down?

32. With his semen, in other versions.

33. The most intimate belongings of the dead are destroyed by fire or exposed on the grave.

34. The interpretation given is not wholly certain. My notes read: "downstream the stick stretched all the way" and "upstream his arm did not stretch." The theme of measuring to the sky recurs among some distant tribes, such as the Mohave and Pueblo.

every town the valuables that the people use when they dance.[35] Then I will meet you there.'' Kewomer said to his father, ''You do the same downstream.'' ''Yes,'' he said, and then they went. Now Kapuloyo stretched out his hand, and all money[36] and valuables came into it. Kewomer did the same.

p. Now the woman[37] went and told Wohpekumeu in the sweathouse, ''The boy came and got (his father's) tobacco.'' Wohpekumeu came out and went into the house. He looked for his money and saw that it was gone. Then he said to the woman, ''Go to the other houses and tell them that if they have money they had better look at it.'' She went, and they looked for their money and saw that it was gone. Then Wohpekumeu followed Kapuloyo downstream. Whenever he came to a town he asked the people whether they had recently looked at their money. Then they looked where they kept it, and always said that it was gone.

q. When he came to Wełkwäu[38] he had not caught up with Kapuloyo, and all the money (in the world) had been taken away (by the latter). Wohpekumeu thought, ''It will not be well if there is no money along this river. We must have money because a man is to pay for a woman if he wants to marry her.'' All those at Wełkwäu also found that their money was entirely gone. They found only one small piece, . . .[39] in a purse. It shouted, ''Take me too!'' Then Kapuloyo stopped for a little on the hill above Rekwoi, wishing to take this little money too. He held out his hand, but it did not come to him. Wohpekumeu said to it, ''Cry, 'Take me,' and then I shall overtake him. Keep calling, and I shall cross the river.'' Kapuloyo did not think that Wohpekumeu was following him. When Wohpekumeu arrived uphill from Rekwoi, it began to be foggy (around him) and Kapuloyo could not see him.

Standing on a little hill by him were two baskets full of money and valuables. When the fog cleared he saw Wohpekumeu coming. Then he ran on hastily and forgot the two baskets.[40] He left them and they are there today.[41] That is why we have money: if Wohpekumeu had not overtaken him, we should not have any. Then Wohpekumeu threw short money[42] along the coast

35. This also is not clear. As Kewomer is to come to dance, it might be that he is to take the deerskins, woodpecker crest bands, and the like, or their spiritual counterparts, away from mankind to use them each night. However, his father simply robs human beings of their money in order to leave them deprived, and he may be asking Kewomer to do the same. The ideas being allied, the narrator probably did not sense the latent conflict!

36. Dentalium shells, *tsīk*.

37. Kapuloyo's wife, whom Wohpekumeu had taken.

38. At the mouth of the river, on the south side, as Rekwoi is on the north.

39. Omission in typescript. [K. refers to his notebooks, querying whether the one piece was a *wetskāk* (the smallest dentalium).—Ed.]

40. But took away the load he had on his back, so that Wohpekumeu recovered only part of the theft.

41. As small mounds.

42. [For the gradations in value of money, see Kroeber, Handbook, p. 23.—Ed.]

to the south. He said, 'It will be bad if they have large money there.[43] They must have short pieces.'' And he arranged how people would do with money. He blew on a woman and said, ''A woman will be worth money. If a man wants to marry her, he will pay with money. And if a man is killed, they will receive money for him because he who killed him must settle.''

r. Then he went back to the towns, to Rekwoi and Wełkwäu, but found no one there. They were ashamed because their money had been taken, and they had all gone away, some back on the hills and some elsewhere. Wohpekumeu began to cry because he had been left behind and did not know where to go. Then he went southward along the beach. He cried constantly because he had been left alone.

When he had gone far, he saw a woman lying at the edge of the ocean. He continued to go and cry. Then he stopped a little; but he thought, ''I will go on. I was left here because I always wanted women. That is why I stayed behind.'' So he went on again. But after a little he saw another woman lying on the sand, more beautiful than the other, and finely dressed. Then he thought, ''I might as well take her, since I have been left anyhow.'' Then it felt to him as if she were moving. Soon she was at the water's edge, and then in the water. She floated like a boat, moving across the ocean. Wohpekumeu could not free himself from her. He thought, ''Well, I must.'' So she carried him across the ocean. She was Skate.[44]

F3. Mole

Wohpekumeu, like Pulekukwerek and Megwomets, grew from the ground. He had a sister. She is the one that lives in the ground, the mole, Łkelikera. He told her, ''Come, you had better go out.'' But she did not want to come. Then he hurt her[1] because she did not want to come out. He said, ''Now if you come out of the earth you will die. All you will do will be to live underground.''

F4. Origin of Death

a. The woge were ready to go off into the hills. They began to discuss. Some said, ''If (people) are very old, let them become young again.'' Others said, ''There will be too many. They will not have room in the world. They

43. All Yurok accounts credit more valuable money to the River than to the Coast Yurok.

44. Nospeu. The way in which dead skates thrown up by the surf sometimes lie flat on the beach perhaps led to the choice of this fish to serve as the seducing woman.

1. Twisted her hand?

had better live only once.'' The (first ones) were going to have them live twice. Then the others agreed, ''Let it be so.''[1]

b. Now Wertspit[2] said, ''I have lost my children. They have died.'' Just then they were about to start to go to the hills. He said, ''Well, I shall bury my children. I shall make it that (people) shall not come back and be young again after they have been old. They shall not be able to do that, because I shall bury my children. What brought it about that I lost my children when we were all ready to move away? Now if people die, they shall die. They shall not come back.'' He is the one that made it so; for he lost his children at the time they were all going to where they would stay.[3]

c. It was ten brothers who had talked about this thing, considering what would be best.[4]

Now he of Kepel[5] wanted it that if anyone died and was carried along the river in a boat, they were not to take him by Kepel except (behind his back) over land. They were to take a dead person around behind, on the shore, even when there was no fish weir erected.[6] When they came to the creek Owiger downstream from Kepel,[7] they were to begin to carry the body over the land to upstream of Kepel, at Kermuruk; there they might take it into the boat again.

d. And (they arranged that) if a corpse was brought upstream, it was to lie with its head downstream until they came to Erner.[8] When they passed Erner, they would have to turn its head upstream.

e. And when they came near Merip they were to carry it behind the large rock at the water's edge. One who knows how can bring a corpse by this rock in a boat; only not everyone knows how. He puts two feathers on the cross

1. Those in favor of rebirth were about to prevail.

2. The Jerusalem cricket.

3. The motivation is: grief for his children, sense of loss, of injury, the wish to make others suffer also.

4. They are no doubt the ten spirits resident in rocks along the river who are successively called on in the formula for purification from corpse contamination (Kroeber, Handbook, p. 70). (Some versions of the formula increase the number of spirits up to 18 and 22; cf. H2 below.) Wertspit was not one of the ten spirits; he merely undid their work. Neither were Pulekukwerek, Wohpekumeu, Kapuloyo, Kewomer, or Megwomets concerned in the matter one way or the other, the informant said in answer to a question.

5. The one of the ten brothers who belonged to Kepel. This and the next three paragraphs are a recital of corpse transport taboos in the disguise of the myth of their origin.

6. This is the great Kepel weir, constructeed at the beginning of a world renewal rite and Deerskin Dance (Waterman, Geography, map 17). According to Waterman (p. 249), the objecting spirit went into the rock Merhkwi (map 17, no. 54) at the dam site. The tabooed stretch runs from Owiger (no. 39) up to Kermruk (no. 57). [See map 5 in this volume.—Ed.]

7. And upstream from Mūrek.

8. At the mouth of Blue Creek, 15 miles above the mouth of the Klamath. The head-direction rule is also observed for the redwood used in rebuilding the ritual house for the Jumping Dance at Rekwoi.

withe at the bow, as if it were a man. After a short distance he takes the feathers off again.[9]

f. (And they ordained that) when one came to downstream from Kenek, just upstream from Kenekpul, one would have to take the corpse by land to Otsep upstream from Kenek. That would be the last place. From there one could go on by boat uninterruptedly.[10] When one arrived, after taking out the dead body, one would have to turn the boat over in the water and leave it like that the remainder of the day and all night.[11]

g. The woge went back on the hills because they knew that human beings would live here.[12] That is why Pulekukwerek went along the river to Kenek, Merip, and other places (destroying dangers), because he knew that human beings would live on the river. He wanted them to live there. He knew that the woge would move back (to the interior).

h. The woge said, "If a person wants to tell me something, let him come up (into the hills) in the evening and stay all night. Let him take tobacco with him and angelica root, only those two. And he must be careful of himself before he does that: he must get sweathouse wood, and drink no water, and go with no women. Then I shall answer him if he calls my name; but if he does not do that, I shall not answer him; and if I answer him, he will have what he tells me that he wants. And he may not eat in the house with the others. He will have to eat his food (separately) for ten days."[13]

9. The objecting, anti-death rock is Tsekwa (Waterman, map 17, no. 96). Waterman says it is just opposite the town of Merip; his map shows it on the southwest side, 1/3 mile upstream. My recollection is that it is at the river's edge on the northeast side. The reembarkation place (on an upriver trip) is given by Waterman as no. 103, Oł-hełku-olegai, "person ashore customarily carried." This is 1/2 mile above his no. 96. Women also might not pass before the face of the rock. About 1901, my guide and interpreter unloaded his wife just above the rock, and she passed behind it and rejoined the boat a bit below it. Perhaps the length of the detour insisted on was less for women than for corpses.

10. Waterman, map 17, gives, for this portage of over a mile, numbers 116, 140, and 142, being respectively Kenekpul, Kenek-äs, and Otsep. My recollection of Kenekpul is as being nearer Kenek than he shows it. Kenek-äs is on the southwest side, just above Tuley Creek and the Kenek rapids. I too was told about the spirit in the rock gathering the bones of all who drown in the river.

The three spirits or rocks mentioned in both of the death-purification formulas outlined in Handbook, p. 70, are, respectively (in *downstream* order, as the formulas always run, contrary to the order in this myth) (1) Otsep and Okegor at Kenek, Tsekwa at Merip, and Owiger below Kepel-Sa'; and (2) Okegor, Tsekwa, and Merhkwi above Kepel, and Owiger below Sa'. [Cf. also X8, below.—Ed.]

11. To purify the boat from corpse contact.

12. Added in answer to a question. The reason is the one usually given; but it conflicts with the reason stated in the informant's tale F2—at least for the woge at the mouth of the river, who went off from shame at losing their money to Kapuloyo.

13. This paragraph also is merely custom put into myth form by having its origin told. The narrator added the following in amplification:

F5. Origin of Adultery

a. The woge were moving away. At Turip they all came together. The woge who lived downstream were ready to go. They said, "Now that people are coming, let us go!" But they were a little slow, for they did not like to go at once.[1] And they all wanted to get ready and start together on the same day. Then now they were ready, all in one place. There was no one left anywhere else: every other place was deserted because they were all at Turip. No one was any longer going about.

b. Then they saw four persons coming, traveling underground. They all went toward them and said, "Where do you come from?" Those four said, "We came from upstream." They asked them, "Who are you? What is your name?" One said, "My name is Adulterer.[2] A person who is thus will be killed. That is why I have come away." Another said, "Hired murderer,[3] that is I. If a man wishes to kill someone he comes to me and says, 'I want you to watch that man and tell me where he goes,' and I say, 'I will do that.'" They asked the third, "What is your name?" and he said, "Salmon-wizard.[4] I stop the salmon from coming upstream." There is a root growing in the mountains which will stop the salmon. If no salmon run, there is perhaps a person down-

---

Formerly, when boys were old enough, men would talk to them thus: "Go to get sweathouse wood. Then you will always have money, and no one can make you a slave. But if you are poor, someone may sometime make you a slave (because you cannot pay a debt or claim)." All wealthy people knew that. If one went to these wealthy persons, one could learn many formulas and myths. Those old men said, "Go at night to the top of the hill. Stay all night. Take angelica root and tobacco, and shout into the night. Perhaps you will say, 'I am poor now! I should like to get money somehow! I wish you would help me, you woge!' Shout like that all night and throw the angelica into the fire. Do not drink water when you are about to do that. When you are going to do it, you must bring sweathouse wood for ten days and drink no water. Drink only acorn soup. Sometimes you will shout three or four times in such a place. Then you will nearly hear an answer. That is good, if they answer. You have (had) your tobacco by the fire. Then you see that your tobacco is gone: The woge have it." All the rich people know these things. The mountaintop up from the Jumping Dance place above Weitspus is good. There is a seat of stone there, like a chair. One sits there and has a fire nearby and shouts. Downstream, too, are hills that are good. But if a man desires women and girls much, the woge will not accept him. He will always be a poor man and a worthless one if he thinks of women.

---

1. The woge are always represented as loath to leave their old haunts, to which they were attached as much as the Yurok are to their homes.

2. Herermtser.

3. Wernerygerkr.

4. Pererkwerter. The root or being used for this "salmon famine" witchcraft is called *pererkr*, and its peculiar properties are discussed in Spott and Kroeber, Yurok Narratives, pp. 202-03 and 208.

stream who has that medicine, and then people go and try to kill him.[5] The fourth was called Uma'a.[6] Now these four men came there.

c. Then they took those four upstream to Heremts-olok[7] and shoved stones down their throats and threw them into the river and put a large rock on them. They thought they had killed them. Then they said, "Well, let us start now."

d. So they were ready to go. Then they saw those four coming again. Thereupon they caught them and took them to Heremts-olok once more and threw larger rocks on them. Then they started to go to Turip again, those woge. When they had gone a little way, they looked across the river and saw them coming swimming, to land. Then they let them go: they thought, "We cannot kill them."

Now when anyone commits adultery with a married woman, even if no one sees them, it will be known somehow. It is like that because then the woge did not (succeed in) kill(ing) those four. Therefore people are slain for adultery.

F6. Megwomets' Birth and Departure

a. He grew at Ko'men.[1] An old woman lived there with her daughter. The girl always went to dig bulbs. Her mother kept saying, "Do not come home late. When you see that the sun is about to set, I want you to come before that. And if you see a bulb growing into a double stalk, do not take that one." She tried to learn from her mother why she should not dig the double kind; but the old woman would not tell her. As it became late, the girl was always wanting to dig that sort of root. Then once she thought, "Well, I will try it," for she wished to know what she would find if she dug a (double-stemmed) bulb late. Now the sun set; then she dug it. Then she saw a little boy baby coming out of the ground. As soon as he emerged he called her mother. She ran off, but the boy followed. He came after her into the house, kept calling her mother, and she was ashamed.

b. Now he became a young man and built himself a sweathouse. But he saw his mother only at night. If he went to see her in the day, he never found

5. Explanation; a lapse from myth.

6. Uma'a, "Indian devil" in colloquial parlance: a wood spirit associated with the means of deadly witchcraft, minute flaming arrows which people can acquire.

7. "Adulterer-olok." Waterman, Geography, mentions it on p. 236 without locating it, and his reference may be taken from the present tale.

---

1. Orleans; Karok Panamenik.

her because she was away somewhere. One morning he thought, "I will hide and watch where she always goes." Then he hid. Now it was autumn, and every evening when she came home he always saw her carrying a load of acorns, all large ones. He had gone everywhere, but never could find such acorns. He himself carried acorns,[2] but they were not large like hers: that is why he wanted to watch her and learn where she went.[3] So now, he saw her go off with her basket just at daylight. He followed her, far behind, watching her. She did not go very far from her house; then she stood. Soon he saw her go in a circle. Then something like a ladder came down from above. So he learned that she went to the sky on the ladder and there got her acorns, those large ones.

c. When she had first found him, she did not want to take him. She had said to the old woman, "If he kills the white deer that I see in the sky I will have him for my son." The old woman had told this to the boy, and that the white deer was half-covered with woodpecker crests. That is why he now wanted to watch her again.

d. Then he saw her go out as before, stop, and walk in a circle. After a time he did not see her any longer: she was gone. Then he went to where he had seen her stand. He thought, "Let me try it." Then he tried. Then he saw the ladder descend. He climbed it. When he got up on top there was a fine prairie, and he could see all around. Now he saw many deer bones lying there. He looked another way and saw many (white and woodpecker-crested) deer standing. And he saw a trail, and thought he would follow that, but did not see anyone. Soon he came to where he saw people, but not his mother. He hid himself again, and saw the people come to a great oak. Now his mother was with them.

e. Then one of them said, "Shake the limbs and throw down acorns." She said that to Blue Jay. Soon (the young man) heard shaking up in the tree. Then the women set out their carrying baskets underneath, and the acorns fell in. Soon the baskets were full. Now they went home. He followed them.

f. When he came to the ladder, he saw the (white) deer to one side and thought, "Let me kill one of them." He had a tiny bow of greasy-stone.[4] As

2. Megwomets, a bearded dwarf, otherwise described as carrying about acorns and other seed foods, which he causes to yield bountifully. This propensity, however, has no intrinsic connection with the present story, whose hero in other versions is not Megwomets. [See n. 11 below—Ed.]

3. This rationalized motivation is not followed up in the story, which quickly reverts to its customary folktale hero type.

4. *Permeryer*, a black, hard, smooth stone found as boulders in the river. The name means simply "greasy." A Hupa counterpart is translated "blue-stone" in Goddard, Hupa Texts, p. 344n.

he was about to use it, he pulled on both ends with his hands and it drew out long. Then he shot a deer. He began to skin it, took the skin, and the meat too.

g. When he came home he saw that his mother was already there. Now she said, "Oh, it is my son! Let us make a good fire and roast that deer." But he looked angry. He did not like to hear her say that because she would not have him as son before.[5] Only the two women ate of the deer; he did not eat of it, but went into the sweathouse.[6]

h. Next morning he did not come into the house but went down to the river. He made a little boat for himself, entered it, and began to sing. There were then many Kämes monsters, and whatever went on the river was drowned (by them). Therefore he sang, and when the Kämes heard his song they were afraid. And he made himself a close-woven headnet,[7] and wore that in his little boat. He was angry at his mother because at first she had not wanted him. He wanted to leave her for that, and had killed the deer only in order to make her sorry (when he left).[8] So now he started downstream in his boat.

i. She looked for her son and saw a little boat going downstream. As soon as she saw it she knew that it was he, for there were no other boats then. So she ran back into the house to get her pestle. She followed him downstream, but never caught up with him. At the mouth of the river she saw him out on the ocean. It was on account of his singing that everything (evil) was afraid of him and that he was able to go downstream. If one rides only on one small board and sings that song he will not be drowned.

When she could not overtake him, she still had the pestle in her hand. She threw that after him. She tried to strike his boat,[9] but just clipped the feathers at the (flying) end of his headnet. Then the seagulls came into existence from these feathers. That is why they call Redding Rock Sekwona: it is the pestle.[10] She had carried it from her house in Ko'men.

j. But he did not return. His name is Megwomets.[11]

5. A Yurok is always ready to be insulted and to cherish the wound.

6. Where a man in anger usually betakes himself, to lie in silent and undisturbed hate.

7. Such as are worn in the Deerskin Dance. They hang down behind and are feathered at the end. See Goddard, Life and Culture of the Hupa, pl. 7, right. See also Spott and Kroeber, World Renewal, p. 70.

8. Unlovely, but typical Yurok psychology.

9. In her, too, hatred predominates.

10. *Sekwona*. The rock is narrow, 94 feet high, and pointed, about 5 miles offshore, a little north of the mouth of Redwood Creek, about abreast of Mussel Point, 17 miles north of Trinidad Head and 13 miles south of mouth of the Klamath. The Indians assert that it is visible from the summit above Orleans, and some versions have the woman hurl her pestle from there.

11. The name is given as No'ots in most versions. See F1, n. 48; also A7, J8, DD2, and Goddard, Hupa Texts, no. 2, p. 146. And for Megwomets in another context, see A16*x*.

F7. Origin of Cohabitation

a. There was a girl living on the river, I do not know where, alone. No one else was about, she slept with no one; nevertheless, she began to be pregnant. She thought, How can it be? From what am I going to have a baby when I have not slept with anybody? Then she had a child, a boy.

b. The boy cried all the time. Even though she tried to hush him, sometimes she had to give up and just lay him down and let him cry. Then she would think, "Well, anyhow, nobody made him." But after a while she would feel sorry and take him up again. But when he continued to cry and cry, she put him down again, like throwing him away. "I can't take care of you," she said. "I try but I can't. Maybe you want female genitalia, maybe that is what you want to eat, that is what you are crying for." And when she said that, she saw the baby stand up by himself; he went to her and had intercourse with her. Then he sang: "That is the kind I like to eat, woman's genitalia."

Now he was grown up: then he was Meihkwet:[1] that is how he came to be.

1. Penis, with the indefinite prefix *m*-, "someone's," in the abstract.

INFORMANT G

FRANK OF WEITSPUS

[In Kroeber and Gifford, World Renewal, p. 133, Kroeber says that Frank[1] *was his "interpreter and vademecum from 1900 to 1907. He was about forty or forty-two when I first knew him. He was of the house wogwu in Weitspus (Weitspekw), which was probably the leading one of the town in promoting Deerskin and Jumping dance regalia and hospitality. Frank was matter-of-fact, unimaginative, practical, and reliable, not much interested in ideas. He preferred to transmit faithfully what more interested and better informed old men imparted; and I used him as informant chiefly to chink gaps that appeared in their information. Hence his own data are somewhat fragmentary."*[2] *Frank was the younger brother of Dave Durban, Informant H. Frank was the actual father of Robert Spott, who was later adopted by Captain Spott of Rekwoi, husband of his father's sister.—Ed.]*

G1. BEGINNINGS

a. At first Wohpekumeu[1] wanted to make the river run upstream on one side and downstream on the other. But it was too hard to do; so the river was made as it is now.

b. He also wanted to make it unnecessary to carry things. Baskets were to be filled and set in a row. A person was to start walking and the baskets were to follow him one by one. This also did not work well and was given up.

c. At first people were to eat pitch instead of acorns; but this did not do.

d. And there was no fire. Wohpekumeu had planned that people were to

1. [In other writings K. referred to him as Weitchpec Frank, using the Anglicized form of the town's name.—Ed.]
2. [For another fragment told to this informant, see DD6 at end of book. For an analysis of Frank's work as an interpreter, see D1 and D6, above.—Ed.]

---

1. "The woge," anonymously, most Yurok would say generically.

do without fire. People were to cook by holding their food in their armpits. That is why it is warm and hairy there now.

e. Then fire was obtained by Inchworm. He went to him that had the fire. Throwing some of it into his mouth, he started back. He had it hidden inside his body. That is why it shines from inside his body when he is seen at night. He stretched from one ridge to another until he came back. So he brought fire.

G2. Animal Shapes

a. Coyote came from upstream. None of the birds had feathers.[1] A great eagle had them all: he sat on Shelton Butte.[2] Everybody came from all over the world to get his feathers. They shot at him, but none of their arrows reached: the mountain was too high.

Coyote came downstream with his otter skin (quiver) full of arrows. ''Now stop,'' he said. ''I am about to shoot. I can hit him.'' Next morning he began. ''Now! Now! Now, I shall hit him! Look! Look!'' he said, as he saw his arrow flying straight up toward the eagle. But soon it dropped short. So he shot all day, and his otter skin was empty.

b. Next day all began to shoot again. At last the great eagle was hit and fell.[3] He rolled down almost to the river. Then they said, ''We will all go there together in the morning. Let no one go before the others. The rich shall have the best feathers, the poor the small feathers.''[4]

c. Coyote thought he would be the first to reach the bird. He made up his mind to get up first and go alone. The others were all sleeping around him. Then, to keep awake, he took a sharp stick and placed it under his head. But he slept nevertheless, and when he awoke, the stick had pierced him: he had not felt it. The others had already all gone off. They had come to the great bird and distributed its feathers and hair. There was one old tail that none of them wanted. ''Let us leave this for Coyote,'' they said.

Now Coyote thought, ''Well, I will follow them.'' When he came to the bird, they were all gone, and there was only the one old tail left. He took that and stuck it on his back. That is his tail.[5]

1. Nor had the animals fur or tails. The Yurok say ''birds'' in English, probably because they do not know ''animal'' or ''quadruped.''

2. A sharp peak overlooking the Klamath at about the Yurok–Karok boundary.

3. That the marksman was the little owl, and how he succeeded, the narrator has evidently forgotten. [See A8*c*.—Ed.]

4. In other versions, the earliest get the best, which fits in with the tenor of the story. The narrator may have been influenced by belonging to a wealthy family. And there is always the Yurok implication that the wealthy are abstemious and will rise early, while the man who sleeps late is indolent, greedy, and uncontrolled, and will remain poor.

5. What sticks out from this mangled fragment is Coyote's part. It is characteristic that three of this informant's tales are about Coyote.

G3. Coyote and Sun

a. Coyote was in his house[1] without food. It was winter and raining. Then the sun shone. He sent his child[2] on the prairie to gather seeds. Then the sun disappeared again, and it rained and snowed. When the child did not come back, Coyote went and looked for it. The snow was nearly knee-deep. He called but could not find him. He thought, "It is too bad." He went back home, angry that his boy was dead. He wanted to kill Sun, who had done it.

b. He went to the river and split stones to sharp edges. He got a large basketful of them. Then he went to the place where he had always seen Sun come up. He went early, so as to be sure to catch him. He took a stone in his hand, with the basket set before him, and waited. At last Sun came up behind another hill. "Well, that is strange," he thought. "I have always seen him coming up right here." He went to the next hill and slept there. Again he waited, and Sun came up farther off. So he went farther and farther until at last he starved to death.[3]

c. He jumped into the river and drifted down. He stranded at a town. Two women came to the shore to gather wood. Seeing a good dry alder log, they went to split it. They drove in a wedge. "Here, what are you doing? Don't do that again," said Coyote, leaping up, as they started back, one to each side.

G4. Coyote and His Grandmother

a. Coyote lived with his grandmother. He brought in no food, did not help her, but was always traveling around. "I am the one to go ahead," he kept saying. His grandmother became angry: she would cook for herself while he was away, and there would be nothing when he came home. Now once she was boiling acorn soup and had just put the hot stones in, when he returned. Seeing no place to hide the basket, she sat on it and covered it with her dress. "I am hungry," said Coyote; but she told him she had no food. Finding acorn shells lying there, he began to eat these. Meanwhile the soup boiled under her. "What is that? It seems I hear acorns cooking," he said. "No, it must be something outdoors," she told him. Soon he said, "What is the noise down there? What have you under your buttocks?" "I am just flatulating," she said. But he seized her, pulled her off, saw and snatched the basket of soup, ran off, and ate it.

1. Unlocalized.
2. "Children" in other versions; cf. J5, for example.
3. In other versions he attains his revenge.

b. Coyote came where they were eating moldy acorns.[1] They gave him some. He said, "I like these. I have been eating only white ones and am tired of them. How do you make these?" They told him, "Fill your boat with acorns and go downstream to Kenek where the rapids are bad. The water that splashes in will wet the acorns and make them like this."

Coyote went back to his grandmother. He told her to carry her acorns down to the river. She asked, "What for?" He told her, "I shall make them black by carrying them down over the rapids. I have an (old) boat there with one gunwale broken out. I shall use that." She said, "No, you will lose all." But he said, "If you do not carry them, I shall do it myself." Then she thought, "It is no use: he will do it anyhow." So she brought the acorns down to the river, and he filled his boat with them.

Now, when he came downstream near the rough water, he climbed out of his boat and stood on the rocks to see where the river ran the swiftest. "They told me to take the roughest place," he said. Then he thought that it was roughest in the very middle. So he paddled there. As soon as he reached the place, he upset and went under. He lost all his acorns. At last, far downstream from the rapids, he came to the surface again and climbed ashore. Beyond him he saw his boat being carried down.

c. Across from Weitspus ferns are thick on the hillside. Coyote, having no food, took his grandmoher there to gather the roots to roast. He said, "Go on uphill and uncover them with your digging stick, and I will gather them as I follow." She said, "I can pick them up as I dig them." But he angrily told her, "No," and she said no more. As she went uphill digging, her backdress lifted as she stooped. Coyote kept peeping at her from below, while moving his hands about as if gathering fern roots. "What are you looking at?" she asked. "Oh, I am looking to miss no roots," he told her. She was watching him sidelong. He crept up closer, almost touched her legs, jumped, threw her down, had intercourse with her. "Well, let us go home now," said Coyote.

G5. The Bastard

Two men were sleeping in the sweathouse. A bastard tied their hair together. Then he called out, "A deer is swimming by." They started up but felt their hair caught. Each thought the other was holding him and began to fight. When they found what he had done, they said, "Hereafter a bastard will be born speechless."[1]

1. They are stored wet or in water and turn dark, "moldy," and sweet (probably tannin-less).

1. Probably: shall not be permitted to speak before his betters.

G6. KEWETSPEKW

a. There was a man of Weitspus. Another man took his wife away from him. He was sorry, went to the mountaintops, and cried. He went into the river that a Kämes[1] might take him into its house and make him strong. He went into lakes, but was not accepted by any monster.

b. Finally, when he jumped into Fish Lake,[2] he found himself in a house. An old man and an old woman were there. The old man said, "You are the one we have been looking for. We have heard you crying. We will give you what you want. Do not be afraid of anyone that comes in. Hide in the old woman's blanket." Then he hid under her blanket. On top of the house a mountain lion was watching.

c. There was a crash and the house shook. "Easy! Easy!" said the old woman. They had ten sons who had gone away: some to see a feud settled, some to gamble, and some to do other things. This was the first one coming back. Then there was a harder crash, and the house shook more. "Easy! Easy, my son!" said the old woman. This one also came in and sat down. Each time one of them lit on top of the house, there was a louder crash and the house shook and swayed more. After lighting on the roof they came in by the door. The tenth one made the house sway back and forth. He nearly turned it over. Again the old woman said, "Easy! Easy!"

Then the (Weitspus) man, peeping out from under her deerskin blanket, saw that he who had just come had a human being's feet sticking out of his quiver. He had gone to see the settlement of a feud, they had begun to fight again,[3] and he[4] had killed this one and taken him away as if he were game.

d. Then the old man said to them, "The one that we have been looking for so long is here, the one we have heard crying on the mountain. Let us make him strong." Then they took their knives, but could not cut him. They took stone war clubs[5] and beat him until he was dead. Then they made medicine for him, and he came to life. The old woman put stones into the fire. When they were red-hot, the strongest of the ten took them in his hand and crammed them down the man's throat. Soon he disgorged the stones again. Then they said, "Now you are nearly done." They told him to take gravel and throw it against the planks of the house. The gravel went through. So they said, "Now you are complete."

1. [A water monster.—Ed.]

2. Oketo, some five miles back from Weitspus in the hills and upstream. It houses powerful spirits, usually called Thunders, and it formerly contained a whale. [See A8*b* and Spott and Kroeber, Yurok Narratives no. 24.—Ed.]

3. As not infrequently happened.

4. Or perhaps, "*they* had killed one and *he* had carried him off." But again, he may have joined in the fight just for the fun of it.

5. *Kawaya*. About a foot long, with two blunt edges.

e. Then the old man put a small dentalium shell into one of his hands and a small woodpecker crest into the other. He told him, "Close your hands and do not open them until you come home. Then put the money into a purse and the woodpecker crest between two boards. When you kill a person, you will be able to pay for him." Then the man lost consciousness.

f. He revived at the edge of the lake and went home. He saw his father and mother. He said, "My mother!" The old woman began to cry. "Who calls me mother?" she said.[6] He said, "My father," and his father began to cry. Then they asked him, "Who are you?" He told them that he was their son. He had been gone a year. He thought he had been away only one day.

g. Then he put the piece of dentalium money into a purse and the woodpecker scalp between boards. After a time he looked at them. The purse was full of large dentalia, and between the boards were many scalps. He took out his (original) small money, put it into another purse, and laid the little woodpecker crest between other boards. So he kept doing. Now he was very powerful. When he killed a man he was able to pay for him at once. He was so strong that he could take hold of a man's thighs and split him all the way. If he pulled at an arm he pulled it out. If he threw gravel at a man it went through him. Before, when his wife was taken, he had been angry but afraid to do anything: now he killed many people.[7]

G7. Crippled at Okpis

a. A man lived at Hanatep, on the Trinity above Hupa. With ten companions he went to hunt at Blue Creek. When they came opposite Pekwon Creek, some of them thought it was Blue Creek but some of them said not.[1] Then they agreed and went on downstream to opposite Blue Creek. There they said, "Now we have come to the place. In the morning we shall go across and hunt on the prairie."

Next day they went there. They did not see any deer and went back to their camp without having killed any. They made medicine,[2] put angelica on

6. It tears open the wound of grief, and done with knowledge lodges a claim for heavy damages.

7. A merely gloating ending, instead of the usual retribution to the bully who had wronged him, as in A13, N1, and Yurok Narratives, no. 25.

---

1. They were foreigners from a distance, and the two creeks are alike and come into the river at similar angles. But the relevance of the confusion is not clear, unless it is the beginning of the magic influence which is exerted on them.

2. Spoke a formula and used an herb.

the fire, painted themselves, and went to the prairie again. Now they saw many deer. "Now we shall shoot them! Follow me and we shall kill every one," said the man. When they began to shoot, he fell down. He had broken his leg, and he was lying on the ground. They tried to carry him, but whenever they took him up he nearly died and they had to set him down again. They tried to take him on a litter of poles, but again he nearly died and they had to put him down. Then he said to them, "You had better go back and leave me; carry the deer off." They agreed.

b. Then he saw two women coming. They said, "We are glad to have a husband." He said, "No." They said, "That is how you came to break your leg. We like you. Live with us." "No, I want to go home," he said. "No, we want you to marry us," they said. "We shall carry you away." Then he agreed. "We shall carry you on our backs," they said, "to where we live." Then he sat down in their seed-carrying basket, and the women took him to their house.

When he entered the basket to be carried, he was not sick any more, but he could not move: it was if he were stuck fast with pitch. They cured him at their house. They told him that if he tried to go home he would break his leg again. They lived in the hills north of the river by Blue Creek.

c. Then he said, "I want to see those who came with me. I want to tell them to go back home." They said, "We will go with you," and he agreed. So they went to where he had made camp in the brush, but found no one there yet. Then he saw them coming. He told them, "Go home. I shall stay here. I am married now." His people told him, "No." But he said, "Go back. When you make a dance, I shall come up to see it. When you hunt, make medicine of angelica and paint yourselves: then you shall kill deer." His people said, "Yes." He told them, "If you see a fog at Oplego,[3] it will be I who am coming there. If you see birds entering the house, do not hurt them. It will be I. That is how I shall come back. When you see fog, you will see me returning to where they dance. Now I am going away. Good-bye."

The women were called Weterreks neigemen.[4] He is Okpis alkekwerer.[5]

3. Takimiɫding, the scene of the greatest dances in Hupa. A return in fog to see the Jumping Dance is mentioned in Kroeber and Gifford, World Renewal, pp. 61, 65.

4. "They-carry-seed-gathering-baskets," *terreks*.

5. "He-broke-his-leg-at-Okpis," Blue Creek prairie; Waterman, Geography, map 10, no. 82.

Informant H

DAVE DURBAN OF WEITSPUS

[*Kroeber and Gifford, World Renewal, p. 154, describes Dave Durban as the "rich man of Weitspus, that is, oldest surviving male of the house accounted the wealthiest in the town and therefore taking the initiative in the making of the Deerskin and Jumping dances there. This privilege and responsibility were shared by his younger brother, Weitchpec Frank, who served as Kroeber's chief guide and interpreter." Frank is Informant G.—Ed.*]

H1. Wohpekumeu's Departure

a. Wohpekumeu grew at Kenek. He went upstream to Ko'men,[1] for he had heard there were two women there who never looked at men, never went out of the house; so he desired them. He thought, What shall I do? Then he pulled out his pubic hairs, threw them on the ground, and they turned into young men. Then he made the war dance with them. But it was no use: the women still did not come outdoors. Again he pulled out his hairs, threw them down, and made the Brush Dance. But the women stayed in the house.

b. He saw he could not do it that way. He said, "I wish there were a very small boat." There was a pond,[2] close by the house: now a small (toy) boat floated there. He said, "I wish I wore beads." Then he had a necklace on. He went into the boat and cried. (Song)[3]

One of the women said, "It seems like a baby." The other said, "Yes,"

1. Orleans; Karok Panamenik.
2. Or backflow from the river; perhaps a pool behind a gravel bar. Orleans is the first place upstream on the Klamath containing enough flat land to be describable as a valley.
3. The narrator sings Wohpekumeu's crying here. It is a wordless melody.

and looked out: then she saw a baby. Both wanted it. So they went down and reached and took it up. At once both became pregnant.

c. He went on upstream, far up. Then he met someone, who said, "Where are you going? Where you have come from? Everyone has left.[4] You have nearly come too late (to find us) here." So he went downstream again, sorry, and crying. (Song)[5]

d. When he came to Kenek he saw they had all left. The place was spoiled and thrown all about. A large storage basket was thrown in the river.[6] He went on downstream. In some towns only two or three people remained. He was sorry and cried; he said he would no more take up with women. Then he passed a lying woman but went by because he had said he would have no more to do with them.

e. When he came to the mouth, he did not know which way to go. He pointed his cane inland,[7] and then downstream,[8] but these did not seem to be the right ways to go. They said to him, "Your son Kapuloyo has gone to Pulekuk; you had better follow him." "No, I do not wish to. I will go south."[9]

f. Then he went south, still crying. So he came again to a lying woman. Then he went to her. Now she clasped him with her thighs and carried him across the ocean.[10]

H2. Death and Purification

Informant H dictated a version of the death purification formula into eighteen phonograph cylinders. The following is an outline of the text.

As each place (spirit in a rock) is addressed, the formulist stamps his foot. He does not strike the sweathouse post, as stated in some other versions. On reaching the tenth place, at Weitspus, he blows out tobacco crumbs, and the mourner is washed with *hegwomes* root infusion. The same is done again when the eighteenth and last rock is addressed.

•

4. Because he always pursued their women.

5. Also rendered by a song. Its only word is *pasikemkosonawok,* "I will no longer pursue them."

6. Now a rock with a hole in it, in the Kenek rapids. Waterman, Geography, map 22, and pl. 8, fig. 1. Waterman writes *paxtek,* I *pahtekus*; the name means a Xerophyllum-decorated storage basket.

7. *Hierkik,* inland or northeast.

8. *Pulekuk,* downstream and north along the coast.

9. *Perwer,* south along the coast.

10. *Wohpäu,* whence his name, "Across-widower."

a. The eighteen spots given by the informant, and their identification in Waterman, Geography, are shown in the table.[1]

The narrative includes the following:

b. Spirits 12, 13, and 14 were those who wanted dead human beings to become young again. When their wish did not prevail, they became angry and insisted that no corpse should pass in front of them. Spirit 14 was particularly irritated, and said he was sorry he had not made it that corpses would be carried over the land even farther than above Kepel.

c. Another who was disgruntled and hurt went off with the plant *hegwomes*, which was to purify mourners. But the spirits at Weitspus and Rekwoi (10 and 18 of the list), went after him and recovered (knowledge of) the medicine.

18 Places	Identification in Waterman, Geography
1. Ayomok	
2. Okonile'l (Karok Inam) at Clear Creek	
3. Otskergun, rock at Hikwanek (Shamnamkarak)	
4. Oskergun-hiko, opposite last at Enek (Amaikiaram)	
5. Otskergun-hipurayo, uninhabited, on east side, less than a mile below last	
6. Wetsets-käs, down at the river from Wetsets, a town 2 miles above Orleans (Karok Panamenik), on east side	
7. Olege'l, Camp Creek (Tishannik)	
8. Otsepor weroi, Bluff Creek, Yurok Territory	map 25, nos. 44, 39
9. Houks-arek, "children sitting," rock in river, 1/2 mile from Weitspus	map 25, no. 25 (misspelled)
10. Oräuw, rock on south side of river opposite Weitspus, a bit downstream from Erłerger; here the mourner is washed	map 25, no. 22
11. Otsep, a big rock at the river and a settlement, diagonally across from and above Kenek	map 17, nos. 141, 142
12. Kenek-äs, rock at edge of river near Kenek, above mouth of Tuley Creek	map 17, no. 140

1. These eighteen spots are given in less detail in Kroeber, Handbook, p. 70.

13. Tsekwa, fishing place opposite and above Merip	map 17, no. 96
14. Awiyer, on south edge of river, between Sa' and Mūrek-hiko	map 17, no. 39
15. Nä'ägeɬ-hiko-wonek, uphill opposite Nä'ägeɬ, a hill at mouth of Blue Creek	map 10, no. 39, probably Ni'oɬoɬ, conical hill
16. Turip-hiko, Sa'aiɬ	map 9, nos. 52 and 50
17. Ho'peu-pulekw, downriver from Ho'peu	map 9, no. 34, a small creek
18. Oregos, pillar at Klamath mouth, at foot of Rekwoi	map 5, no. 43

INFORMANT I

DOMINGO OF WEITSPUS

Domingo was given this name by an allotment surveyor. He was from the house tsekweɫ in Weitspus and was therefore known as K'e-(t)se'kweɫ. His wife was the widow of his brother Jones. He married her two years after his brother's death. Domingo had no children with her. Jones did, but they died.

Domingo was a famous singer for the Deerskin, Jumping, and Brush dances. He also knew many deer songs and was a good hunter. After Stone and then Billy Werk died, Domingo was megwollep, *or formulist, for the Weitspus dances once or twice before they were given up. He was not a relative of Stone but probably was selected by him or his successor, Werk, as dependable.*

He owned the property of the house tsekweɫ: two gray deerskins, a pair of black obsidians reaching to above the elbow, five of the tandem eagle feathers called ɫeges, *deerskin blankets, and Brush Dance feathers and arrows. He acquired nothing of his own to add to these inherited valuables. On his deathbed there was a squabble about them between his wife and his niece, Sunny Bosky. He raised himself on his pillows, pointed to the trunk which contained the property, and said that the things were not his, but belonged to the house tsekweɫ. Thereupon Sunny Bosky took the trunk away.*

I1. Turip Young Man and His Dogs

a. At Turip he grew, a young man. Ten were his dogs. One was long old, of his dogs. He always hunted, the young man. Now he was no longer any good, that very old dog. Before[1] the sweathouse he always lay. Then they were about to leave (the world). We[2] were about to live here, the (old) dog dreamed. Thus he dreamed. They were about to leave as soon as it was day.

1. *Kwenomet.*
2. Human beings.

He got ready, the young man, to come out from his sweathouse. Then he looked at the dogs. He was standing,[3] standing right up, that old one. He[4] always ground up, what he ate he always ground up for him (because he had no teeth left): that is how he ate, that old dog. It was the only way he fed him. So he went out (from the sweathouse). He said, "Hei! I must leave." He entered the house;[5] he took (his) quiver. Then he crossed (the river). Then he climbed Sa'aiɫ[6] its ridge.[7] He took along the dogs. They went up, the young ones. The one who was old went first, the old dog. He had been lying, this dog; (now) he followed the ridge, that dog,[8] going first. So he dreamed as he slept.[9] "Ho!" (the old dog) said to him. So he said, "I am about to leave."

b. Then he was at Sa'aiɫ-uphill. Now it was short, the ridge was only short, when he heard to the north,[10] where there was a young fir, he heard singing to the north. Now he saw them sitting, the ten.[11] He[12] said, "I am about to go away. I must give you my song. Hunt with it." He said, "Yes." Then he sang, that old dog. (The song is sung here.)

So he sang. Now the ten were all men. He[12] drew out his bow. Then he made a fire. Then he smoked his bow.[13] Then he sang again. He said: "I! Return and count ten swimming ones. But do not follow them. But when the eleventh comes, then follow it: go down (to the bank)." He[14] said, "Good."[15]

He fell asleep. They were gone, those who had sat there: the dogs he had seen were wolves (now). Then he cried. So he cried. The wolves cried. Then he descended, continuing to cry as he returned descending. He thought, "Let me stop," when he had descended. "I must wait for them."

c. Upstream he went. Now they[16] sat. They said, "Wait until ten swim by! You must count." He said, "Yes."[17] Now he sat on the bank. Then from

3. Probably not standing upright like a man, but on his feet, whereas he had only been able to lie before.

4. The young man.

5. Property is always kept in the living house. It would quickly become sooty in the sweathouse.

6. The town opposite Turip.

7. *U-kerertser.*

8. *Tsisi* and *megohkw* both occur in the original, whereas the rendering has only "dog." [Both words mean "dog," according to Robins, Yurok Language, p. 279.—Ed.]

9. Had dreamed?

10. *Hier, ok-hier-k.*

11. Dogs. The young man saw them as men now, as it is subsequently stated.

12. The old dog.

13. The Yurok hold bows over the fire before using them, probably to dry the wood and sinew, probably also so that the deer will not scent the human handling.

14. The young man.

15. *Tsu*, or *tsūl:* "very well," "yes," "let it be so," " it is finished," "good-bye."

16. The young man and the people of Turip.

17. *Ou* [?]

upstream he saw one coming. Then it[18] came. It swam past, downstream it swam, opposite below Turip,[19] to Sa'aiɬ, that is where it swam to. "You must look constantly! Look only there where they swim, upstream!" Now he saw another had come, swimming by, swimming downstream. They said to the young man, "You must count them!" He said,[20] "Yes." Then, where he sat, he saw, upstream, another one coming. Then it swam by downstream. "Look where they swim!" He was wiping away his tears, the young man, thinking of how they were about to leave (the world).[21] Then upstream another came. Then it swam past. Then upstream he saw another coming. "How many have swum?" "Four," those who sat there counted. He was bowing his head, that young man. They said, "But count!" He said, "Yes." Then upstream another came, (but) he continued. Others came, all swimming downstream. He said, "How many have swum by?" They said, "Eight have swum by." He said, "Yes?"[22] "But look up!" He said, "Yes." They said, "Ten have swum by!"

d. Then they looked upstream. They said, "Stand up and be ready! The one you wish is about to come!" They all put his arrows into his boat for him. Now he looked upstream: he saw it had come already. As if there were no river, so large were its antlers; appearing as if it were snow, (so white) was (its skin). "Come on!" It was abreast of them: downstream it went past. Then he followed it. Then a little downstream he killed[23] it. So now he saw that they were of woodpecker crest,[24] those antlers. Across the river he dragged it. It was the sky above where this deer[25] came from. He said, "I must go to see (the place)." As if they were piling (white deerskins), it seemed;[26] so he saw it, as if they were laying them one by one.

e. Now he cried, on the bank. Then all of those across the river cried: they cried, the wolves that had been dogs. Then he went above.[27] He gathered

18. The first of the deer of which the dogs have spoken, though without naming the word. What a dog teaches a man to hunt is obviously a deer, to the Yurok. The pronoun has been translated by "it" in order to make the English easier to follow.

19. Turip-hipurayo.

20. "He said" and "they said" are both *olem* in the original, and no nouns are used. The language is sufficiently compact to strain our comprehension.

21. The eternal refrain of Yurok mythology.

22. *Hes,* the ordinary interrogative particle, is used alone with the meaning of "yes?" "is it so?"

23. *Aɬaoi*: kill, take as game.

24. Perhaps covered with the precious substance; at any rate beautifully red and valuable. Deer whose skin is woodpecker crest are mentioned in other tales. The narrator subsequently explained that before going to the sky the hero distributed this treasure to his fellow townsmen.

25. *Puktik*: the first explicit mention.

26. Not clear. Possibly an anticipation of his experiences after he went to the sky; or his deerskin may have multiplied, or been divided up, at Turip.

27. *Wonek,* "up"; here: "to the sky."

his deer(skins), he took them along. That is how he did it. Then they left (this world). Now there is only that.[28]

12. Wohpekumeu Left Alone in the World

a. So it was with Wohpekumeu: he was going about, going about. All were gone, he could see no one. They had all gone off because they did not like him, this Wohpekumeu. So he was wandering, starting from Rekwoi, and went to Pulekuk, wanting to see someone. "Ee, I can see nobody, they have gone off." No one liked him: that is why they had left, because he was thus, this Wohpekumeu. If he saw them anywhere, even if he saw women far off, they had a child. That is how he did, this Wohpekumeu, and why all disliked him.

So he was going about, going about. "Ee," he said to the earth, this Wohpekumeu, "pity me.[1] I can find no one in the world." He went, and went, and he came to Petskuk,[2] having gone around (the world) to it.[3] And there was no growth: he could see no growth on the ground; it was all gone, because they did not want him to find anything growing. They had taken it all away because they thought he would make for himself a formula with that; for when he saw whatever kind of brush (or herb), he would talk to it as to a person (and achieve his desire by the medicine formula). But they had hidden them all.[4]

b. And he came on a hilltop prairie,[5] and said, "Ee, it is hot, it is hot." He looked all about but could see nothing. There he sat. "It is hot," he said. "Ee, I will whistle.[6] It is so hot I will try to make the wind blow." And now he was about to whistle. (A whistled song follows.)

c. When he finished whistling, he looked downriverward. "Ee, it seems I see something! I see someone coming; I see two women coming." So he was sitting there on the hilltop prairie, and now he saw them below[7] coming, the women coming. "It seems they do not see me. Yes, they have seen me." And now, "It is very hot," said those women. "Yes," he said, "yes indeed."

28. *Pis-tu-tspi-tomer,* indicating the end of the story. *Tspin* is "only"; *tmer,* "part."

1. *Äwok,* "alas."
2. Upriver end of the world. An English version mentions the "Scott's Valley" (Salmon) mountains.
3. *Kitsweyoh petsok.*
4. Some repetitions are omitted.
5. *Se'poleu ukegeihtso.*
6. *U-kweihkeryern.*
7. *Tsōleu.*

They said, "We are very thirsty." "Where do you think you will find water?" he said. "I don't know," they said. "It is hard to get water," he said. But the women said, "We must drink." Then he raised his feet,[8] and as he lifted them, he said, "You will find water here where I had my feet." And he raised his feet and they saw water welling up; and it sank back into that hollow (without disappearing), the water. And they drank that. Thus he did, Wohpekumeu. That is all.[9]

I3. Wohpekumeu's Flute-playing

This actionless bit of tale, as it were a setting or an excuse for a song, is in the Yurok lyric elegiac manner. In the pleasant sunny afternoon Wohpekumeu is sorry for the human beings who are to be—a sort of nostalgia in reverse, much as the Yurok think of and pity their older kinsmen who are gone. The finer the day, the more splendid the dance, the greater the sorrow. The Yurok text is published in Kroeber, Languages of the Coast of California North of San Francisco, UC-PAAE 9: (no. 3): 424, 1911.

•

At Kenek he[1] lived. Before the sweathouse exit[2] he always sat. When the sun was far toward downriver,[3] and he had had his fire inside, then he seated himself before the exit: that is where he always sat. And this is where he kept his flute:[4] under the ridge cover.[5] When the sun shone downriver, he always beat his hair dry.[6] It had begun to be warm, in the middle of summer;[7] it was at the height of summer when he did so. This is how he liked to do: he was always sorry[8] for those who would live, those human beings; so it was he was constantly sorry for them as it began to be evening. So he began to sing[9] on account of that: for that he played; he took out his flute[10] and proceeded to sing. (Song)

8. Or perhaps one foot.
9. *Tspīn,* "only." But the ending is abrupt if not incomplete.

---

1. Wohpekumeu is not named.
2. *Kwenomet,* the exit and ventilator.
3. *Puluk,* the flow at Kenek being westerly.
4. *We-tsyegwolo.*
5. *Leponoł,* often an old boat gunwale.
6. *Iyegererhserper',* with a stick kept for the purpose, *her'erhserp*; *-eg* is an iterative infix.
7. *Uki'sen,* summer.
8. "He pitied them because the weather was fine," the interpreter added in translating the record.
9. *Rurawo',* the ordinary word for sing, though flute-playing is meant.
10. *-tsigwolo,* "fluted."

I4. Buzzard's Medicine

a. This is what he[1] did when he was still a person—this is what he used to to: he ate everything. Far downstream, at the head (*sic*) of the river, he started, and came on from there. And everything he found, snakes, rattlesnakes, water dog salamanders,[2] frogs, every different kind he ate; all of them he ate. And the aborted foetuses he would see that were thrown in the river by those young girls who were pregnant, because they wanted no one to know that they were pregnant, and so they would throw their dead child into the water—then he would eat those too. So he ate everything as he went along, traveling upriver to here; and he arrived upstream, where the river comes from; and that is what he always did, eating things of all descriptions: anything living (reptilian)[3] he saw he would eat.

So now it was a year since he had done as he did, and he began to be thin and sickly. After a year, when he went to go uphill, his legs burned; he felt as if he had no bones in them; he was like dried up. Nothing made him feel better. Whatever he tried to make himself better, he felt bad.

b. Now once, while he was like this, he came to Ho'owen,[4] going southward (from the river), and he began to be very sick. Then he almost heard someone speaking to him and looked back. "Who spoke to me?" He saw a plant[5] moving, a plant growing there and moving; it was talking, that plant. It said, "Ii, you are very ill; you are about to die. You know, don't you, that you are about to die?" He said, "No! I do not know it." It said, "If you eat me, you will recover; because it is from this, from your eating everything, eating dead human beings, eating everything reptilian, and rattlesnakes, it is from this that you are sick." It said, "You will eat me. Prepare well, with a *keyom*-dipper, pound me up, put me into it. Then talk to me: 'You will get well from that, though you are weak now and have no flesh: look at yourself!' " He looked at his body. Alas,[6] he looked poorly! At his knees he had only bone. Only on bones he stood up on the ground. That is how he was, without flesh, because he had become sick from that.

It said, "I will do that. For that they will call me in the world, as long as

1. Buzzard. The name is not mentioned in the text. [K. has a notation to check UC-PAAE 9 (p. 425) cited at the end of the I3 headnote. The first paragraph of I4 is printed there in Yurok and in a literal English translation. But the Yurok name for buzzard does not appear to be given there.—Ed.]

2. [Actually newts.—Ed.]

3. *Sok.*

4. French Camp, a prairie on the Bald Hills ridge between the Klamath and Redwood Creek; on the old pack trail from Martin's Ferry to Bald Hills and Blue Lake; beyond Pine Creek, as one goes from Weitspus.

5. *Käpet* or *käpolit,* plant, herb, brush, grass. The species was not named. It may be an oxalis or trefoil; it grows "in creeks" (shady places); the leaves are round and "sweet."

6. *Nes.*

persons move about on it; for there will be another people. They are the ones who will eat me, the human beings.''

He said, ''*Tsa*, I will do that,'' and he ate it, chewed it, and drank it too. That is what he did with it. He said, ''That is how it will be, if human beings eat anything bad, if they eat anything that they should not eat: they will make this (medicine). Now it will be that way with human beings as I did. I am leaving it like that in the world: human beings will be as if I were about.''

That is how he thought, ''They will do thus if people are ill; they will eat and make the medicine;[7] because it did good to me.''

Well, that is all.

15. Coyote and the Pleiades

Coyote wished to dance with the women in the sky,[1] where the road (of the Milky Way) forks. ''You cannot do it,'' they said. ''I can,'' he said, and came. They sang,[2] and he danced with them. Then, what he was carrying fell off him, his body began to fall off. ''Stop, stop!'' he said, but they continued. Now all his flesh dropped down. Only his bones remained: they (fell and) became stone.

7. *Meskwo.*

---

1. Probably the Pleiades.
2. The song is sung here.

INFORMANTS J

JULIA WILSON AND KATE OF WAHSEK

This little collection represents my first contact with Yurok mythology. Inquiring in 1900 for an informant with a better command of English than most of the Yurok, I was referred to Julia Wilson, and looked her up at Martin's Ferry near Wahsek. I found her an amiable young woman who had been to school and spoke English fluently. With her in the house were her baby; her mother, Kate; and an aged kinsman who appeared hopelessly bedridden but was only spending his days in the recumbent stupor into which aged Indians often seem to let themselves fall until some necessity rouses their waning faculties. Julia told me several stories; and then, her stock running low, her mother narrated and she Englished a tale at a time. Once or twice, the mother's memory wavering, she appealed to the old man, who answered and then relapsed into his yogi-like unconcern among his tumbled bedclothes.

The stories are of a certain interest because they are recorded from the lips of women, and also because the family was living in fair comfort in an American-built house. Julia's schooling shows in the style and in the omission of indecencies, even to the suppression of one that is rather vital to the understanding of the plot. She was trained in the manner of the whites of 1900 and was speaking to a white man. At the same time, the great bulk of the stories are perfectly good Yurok substance.

They are, however, the mythology of persons little concerned with formulas and dentalia and the gathering of sweathouse wood and the things that are important and charged with significance for Yurok of the old school. The religious flavor is definitely wanting. However, Julia's mother, from whom most of the stories actually come, was middle-aged and a full-blooded Yurok living in an ancient Indian town under the same roof with a wholly uncorrupted old man.

All nine of the stories are either true folktales or detached episodes from a cycle. Each is a unit in itself. Each also centers almost wholly about one hero or agent. The action is rapid. Its significance to the world is sometimes touched on, but never at length, and usually at special points only. It is what happened, not how the world and its institutions came to be, that the narrator is really concerned with; although an ''explanation'' is felt to be appropriate and perhaps interesting, it is not in the foreground. The series is perhaps typical of the kind of stories that the Yurok tell their small children, or strangers. There is little development by dialogue, almost no poignant emotion, nor the localization which grounds what is old and important in the Yurok world. The nine tales possess a summarized quality of averageness of human appeal.

At the same time, the series is surprisingly representative of Yurok mythology. Nearly all the best-known characters are brought in: Wohpekumeu, Pulekukwerek, Kapuloyo, Kewomer, Coyote, Sun, Thunder, Grown-in-a-basket, Pa'aku, No'ots. Only Pelin-tsīk is omitted—that attempt to personify so impersonal a thing as money, whom the Yurok can endow with dignity and wisdom and power, but whom they cannot make do anything concrete other than speak and travel and foreordain. And each actor in the little collection has his proper characterization, though it is of the most rudimentary. There is even some background indication of Yurok philosophy: Wohpekumeu made things as they are in this world; the spirits of old still dance in the faraway land across the ocean or have assumed animal forms; blood money was instituted; the sun and sky were made or repaired. But all these phases are only incidental: what counts is the plot of fairy-tale order.

This is the family: Julia was the daughter of Billy Wilson of Weitspus and Kate of Wahsek. It was a full marriage, but Billy moved to Wahsek and got his allotment from the government there. Billy was from the house hiwo (Waterman, Geography, map 26, no. 22), which was of good standing; a former doctor called Hiwo'kege'i had high repute. Billy was the brother of Billy Werk (Informant D) and of Weitspus Doctor (Informant E); the three brothers were called Hiwo'pison and K'e-hiwo'h. Julia, as descended from this house, was known as Hiwo'psumä'i. Her mother, Kate, who is said also to have married a Chinese, was of the house rǟk (probably Waterman, map 24, no. 10) at Wahsek, and was a relative of Lucky of Wahsek (Informant L).[1] *Kate was one of three sisters. Kate's mother had come from Espeu on the coast, out of the same house as Fanny Flounder,*[2] *and was full-married from there to Wahsek.*

One of the women of Kate's mother's house in Espeu had married Oregon Charlie of Turip, and therefore Kate called the old man uncle.[3] *Old Oregon Charlie confided to his friends that he would leave his valuables to Kate because she had sense, but he did not trust her sisters to keep*

1. [Elsewhere in his typescript K. says that Kate Wilson was called Hiwo'pison.—Ed.]

2. [Fanny Flounder was a powerful doctor of Espeu, who lived from about 1870 to 1945, according to Kroeber and Gifford, World Renewal, p. 133. Traditionally, most Yurok doctors were women.—Ed.]

3. [Elsewhere in his typescript K. says that Oregon Charlie was born in Espeu in the same house as Kate's mother. Cf. also the biography of Informant X.—Ed.]

them, and his brother's son had gotten into trouble with the white man's law and would undoubtedly sell them right away. So Kate got what Oregon had, as well as his older brother's things, and something from her own house. She owned a white deerskin, five or six common deerskins, and a pair of red obsidians. Though old people say, "Bury me without my treasures," it is nevertheless customary to put in with them a woodpecker band or something of about that value; but most of the wealth is inherited by the next generation. When there was a dance at Weitspus, Kate used to come to the fireplace which Wahsek had there, and provide for one of the three tables which they set.

Her daughter, Julia Wilson, was still living in 1940 as Julia Jones.

J1. Wohpekumeu and Crow

a. At first people were going to eat pitch because they had no acorns. Wohpekumeu was the one who made everything along this river. He went to the sky and saw people eating acorns. He hid one in his mouth. The people saw and pursued him. Fleeing, he ran into a hollow tree and it closed on him. He could not come out.[1]

b. A bird came and pecked on the tree. Then Wohpekumeu told it to bring more birds and free him. It brought others and they all worked (at pecking a hole). Crow came too. At last Wohpekumeu got out.

c. Now he said that (in return) he would paint them pretty. Crow said, "I want to be red woodpecker crest all over my body. Wohpekumeu said, "I will make you so but you will then have to stay far back in the woods."[2] Crow said, "I do not want to be back in the woods. I want to be about the towns, and yet I want to be hard to catch." Then Wohpekumeu became angry, for he wanted to make the birds so that they could be used by people for woodpecker crest headbands. So he said to Crow, "I will make you." Now he told all the birds to close their eyes while he painted them and then to fly off to wherever they liked and there look at themselves. Then he painted Crow, but black all over. Crow flew off to a town. When he looked at himself and found himself wholly black, he was angry, for he had worked the hardest to free Wohpekumeu. He flew back to the place where they had been painted and found a few little birds still around. He shoved these into the ashes, and that is why they are dull and not so pretty as the others.

J2. Wohpekumeu and Kapuloyo

a. Wohpekumeu lived at Kenek. He made the road very short on the side of Kenek, and long on the other side of the river, so that people would come

1. The Yurok usually connect the flight into the hollow tree with less altruistic exploits. But they vary among themselves; and this version may be sound.

2. Being so resplendent and valuable, he would be hunted.

and he could see them. Now it was raining and snowing constantly, so that he could not go out. People did not want him about,[1] because he was too tricky.[2] Then once he saw a bird[3] eating a berry and knew that it was no longer winter. Then he started, went off, and found fine weather everywhere else.

b. He came to Ko'men.[4] There he married and had a son Kapuloyo. Then he came back downstream with Kapuloyo.[5]

c. Kapuloyo married and had a son, Kewomer. Then Wohpekumeu told Kapuloyo to catch a nestling as a pet for the little boy. Kapuloyo went, saw a chicken hawk in a tree, and climbed up. A great wind came and blew for ten days.[6] It blew off all the branches of the tree. Only those limbs on which Kapuloyo had his feet and his hands were not broken. He could not come down. Wohpekumeu was glad. He made his little grandson blind.[7] Kapuloyo had sugar-pine pitch to chew. He drew this out and let it down and descended by it to the ground.

d. Then he saw a blind boy wandering about, shooting in whatever direction he heard any bird, stretching out his hand, and having the bird fall into it. Kapuloyo held out his hand over the boy's and caught the bird. Then the boy cried, and said, "I do not like to be annoyed so. I am blind and have no father." Kapuloyo asked him, "What has become of your father?" The boy said, "I do not know. He went to get a pet for me and has never come back." Kapuloyo asked him, "Who made you blind?" The boy told him, "My grandfather." Then Kapuloyo was sorry for his son. He cried very much. His tears filled a hole in the rock. Then with the tears he washed his boy's eyes, and he could see again.

e. Then the two went off together. All the people of those days went off and left this world, or changed into animals and birds. Wohpekumeu was sorry to be alone. He went on after his son and grandson. Whenever he asked about them he was told, "They have just gone by." At last he saw them far ahead in a fog.

1. It was they who had made winter continue into summer about his house.
2. Amatory.
3. Usually the blue jay or other species is mentioned, and the berry is the elder.
4. Orleans.
5. A conventional episode is omitted. [Cf. F2*i-j*.—Ed.]
6. Wohpekumeu caused the storm. It is good enough Yurok style to omit saying so; but his motive, desire for his son's wife, would be brought out in a fuller version. Perhaps this seemed indecent before a strange American.
7. The manner of this act could also not well be told by a girl brought up in a government school. [See F2, n. 32.—Ed.]

f. He went on[8] and came to a woman, who took[9] him across the ocean to a land beyond the ocean. Her name was Wohpunika'a.[10]

g. There they are happy now, always dancing. Kewomer made the Deerskin and Jumping and other dances. But when Wohpekumeu arrived, Kapuloyo caused a fog which concealed their faces. He did not want Wohpekumeu to see them. Wohpekumeu saw only their feet as they danced. That is why Wohpekumeu wants a fire kept up at the dances, (to drive away the fog) so that their faces may be seen.

J3. PULEKUKWEREK

a. Pulekukwerek came to Kenek. Here[1] an old man split logs for canoes. He persuaded people to go into the crack, and then knocked out the wedges and killed them. When Pulekukwerek came, he also entered the crack but put a stick across between the two halves of the log and it did not close on him. He was not hurt. Then the old man no longer killed people with his log.

b. There were ten brothers at Kenek, whose tobacco was so strong that if people going by on the opposite side of the river smelled it they were killed. Human bones were lying all about. People would go high up on the mountain and climb down to the river again in order to avoid this place. Pulekukwerek came. First he slid down a rock and cut it up with his points:[2] the rock is still there. Then he went to the ten brothers and entered their sweathouse. He cut up the stone floor. They became angry. The youngest one gave him tobacco. Pulekukwerek smoked it. Then the others gave him tobacco which was successively stronger. The last that he smoked almost burned through his throat; but he had put a hollow stick[3] in his throat and survived. Then when the ten brothers could not injure him, they no longer gave tobacco to people to smoke.

8. His recovery of some of the world's dentalia with which Kapuloyo was fleeing is not mentioned; there is more import than action in the incident. "He went on" is more concise than accurate. Kapuloyo went north along the coast from the mouth of the river, Wohpekumeu south.

9. Another condensation to avoid indecency. [See H1*f*.—Ed.]

10. "Across-the-ocean blanket," a name for the Sea Otter. Usually it is the Skate.

---

1. The incident, sometimes repeated, is usually told as happening elsewhere, most often at Omen. [See F1, n. 7.—Ed.] The narrator may have meant to say, "On the way to Kenek, P came to. . . ." The log-closing episode is incomplete: nothing happens to the old man; he just loses his power.

2. With the horns on his buttocks.

3. Ten hollow elder sticks, in most versions, or elkhorn cylinders.

c. Pulekukwerek went downstream carrying a basket hat full of tobacco.[4] He came to Merip, where the jealous one[5] lived. He had two wives whose faces he painted when he went out to hunt. If the paint had faded when he came back, he knew that someone had passed by. Then he followed that man and killed him. Now Pulekukwerek entered the house. He had taken out his heart and put it on (in) his toe. The jealous one came home, saw him, and began to shoot. He had ten arrows. The last one was a burning one: it was the strongest.[6] He shot all his arrows into Pulekukwerek. He did not kill him, for his heart was not in his body. Pulekukwerek could not lie on the floor: the arrows stuck in him and held him off the ground. Then he rolled out of the door.[7] So he took away the burning and other arrows; and the jealous one of Merip no longer killed people.

d. Then Pulekukwerek found a small bird to work at the burning arrowhead. While he worked, Rattlesnake came underneath and caught pieces of the burning flint as they fell off. That is why the rattlesnake is poisonous. When he saw that he had eaten bits of the flint, Pulekukwerek struck him on the head and made it flat. Yellow Jacket also got some of the flint. But they took it away from him again, so his sting is not very bad. The bird got red eyes from working the flint.

e. Then, when his new arrow was made, Pulekukwerek went to Shelton Butte.[8] Here was sitting Hewonoł,[9] an immense bird. It had different kinds of feathers, which the people wanted. Pulekukwerek shot it;[10] and all took its feathers and thereby became birds and animals.

4. Tobacco is sometimes stored and sold in old basketry caps. The reason for the mention is not evident unless it is a reference to Pulekukwerek's constant smoking instead of eating food.

5. Merip o-kigemola.

6. Usually all ten have flaming flint heads, though the last is the most powerful.

7. In other versions, P persuades him to shoot only his last and strongest arrow. [See A15*x n* and F1*k*.—Ed.] However, the present version is consistent, in that P can only roll out the door like a pincushion. As the arrows, or their heads, are the original Uma'a sorcery mechanisms, it is evidently better for future human beings if P takes away all ten instead of only the strongest one.

8. Mekauhk. Some versions give other names.

9. Hegwono' is mentioned elsewhere as a species of bird of supernatural power, larger than a condor, but still existing.

10. Usually Grown-in-a-Basket (X1) or Screech Owl (A8) do the shooting, but I have one other version naming Pulekukwerek. [K.'s typescript indicated that he intended to supply a cross-reference.—Ed.] The episode is much condensed here, however; Coyote usually boasts that he will kill the bird, and then that he will get the best coat from the feathers, but oversleeps, etc. [See G2.—Ed.]

J4. Pulekukwerek, and Thunders, and Blood Money

a. There was a flood. Before this the world had been smooth and level; afterward it was rough. (This is how it happened.) A young Thunder went out and was killed. The Thunders did not know who had killed him: they had thought that no one was left. They were angry. It began to storm constantly. There was a great wind, the sky was torn, and rocks were flying about.

b. Then Pulekukwerek went south to Humboldt Bay.[1] Here the man lived who had killed the Thunder. Pulekukwerek wanted to make him pay (blood money). He found him with his house all blown away, lying with one board to cover him. Pulekukwerek told him that he should offer to settle for the Thunder.

Then he (Pulekukwerek) went up to the sky to tender the payment. The Thunders saw him coming, thought he was the murderer, and prepared to kill him. He said, "I know what you want to do. But if you try to hurt me, I will swallow the place where you are.[2] Take this pay for the dead one or you will all be killed." Then they accepted his settlement, and the storm stopped. That is why people pay when they have killed. If the Thunders had not accepted, there would be no settlement now. Then Pulekukwerek also repaired the rents in the sky.

J5. Coyote and Sun

a. Coyote lived at Kenek. It had been raining and snowing constantly. Then the sun came out. Coyote and his five children were starving. Then the children went out on the prairie to gather grass seeds. It began to storm again before the children could reach home, and they froze on the prairie.

b. Coyote was angry at Sun. He thought it was he who had come out to shine and then had made the snow. He took sharp stones and filled his net sack with them. Then he started for the ridge from which he had always seen Sun rise. But in the morning he found that the sun rose from another ridge. He went there and saw him rise beyond. So he went on for twenty days.

c. Then he came to a great water. There was an island in it, and from this he saw Sun rise. He found a sweathouse and entered it. He was very hungry.

1. In Wiyot territory. Pulekukwerek is rarely if ever carried south of the mouth of the Klamath on the coast in Yurok tales.

2. The sky. This sort of threatening does not fit Pulekukwerek's character. In Y1 it is Dentalium Shell that begins to swallow the sky.

The sweathouse pillows were of whale meat, and he ate them. Then he hid in the sweathouse firewood.

d. People came in. They talked of Sun and Moon living there. Then he was glad. Sun and Moon[1] were two of ten brothers. Now Sun came in. When he slept, Coyote took his stones and struck him in the face, on the body, arms, head, everywhere (and killed him). Then he went back to Kenek.

e. When Sun did not rise, people all over the world became afraid. They shouted and went about with kindlings and brands. Near Kenek is where Sun fell down. There there used to be a little pond shaped like a person, with two legs. That is where Sun fell. Then all the people gathered there, and the strong ones tried to throw Sun back into the sky. They could not do it. Raccoon came and everyone laughed at him because he was so little. He kicked Sun and moved him a little. He said, "If he who grew from sinew shreds in a *rumitsek* basket would help me, we could raise him up." Then that youth came. Raccoon painted himself white and black as he is now. Then together they threw Sun back into the sky.[2] As it became light once more, the people all shouted.

J6. Coyote Steals Dentalia

a. Coyote went to Setson.[1] A young man lived there. Coyote took California poppy petals and said that they were his dentalia. Setson young man said, "Your money is not good for anything." He showed him shell dentalia. Then Coyote wanted that kind. The young man told him that they were got from the people on the (farther) shore of the ocean. When Coyote was going to start, the young man said, "You will be killed."

b. But Coyote wanted to go. So he practiced running. The young man was an exceedingly swift runner. He would shoot an arrow and beat it to its mark. Then Coyote moistened a rock and ran down the mountain and back again before the water had dried. So the young man thought that he could run pretty fast, and accompanied him. This young man ate only deer marrow.

c. Now they came to (beyond) the ocean. Here they saw a fish dam. On this hung baskets in which were the dentalia. Setson young man took only two or three shells, but Coyote filled a large sack. The young man said, "Do not take so many, you will be caught." But Coyote filled his sack.

1. Kets-ainpega was given as Sun's name, and Ha'sew-ainpega as Moon's. [K. queries whether the first syllable of Moon's name should be Na'.—Ed.]
2. [In A14 Grown-in-a-Basket performs the feat alone.—Ed.]

---

1. This is part of the same story as A12, Kewet Omewa. Setson is unidentified, but might be Kewet (Rivet or Burrill Mountain), especially as Coyote runs "down the mountain and back again."

d. Then the people there at Dentalium Home[2] saw them and pursued. Setson young man urged Coyote to run faster, but Coyote kept going slowly. The people followed close. The harder Coyote ran, the heavier were his dentalia. Setson young man left him and got home. When Coyote knew that he would be caught, he put a few dentalia into his mouth. Then these people overtook him and killed him. They left him there and took his sack of dentalia back with them. But they did not see those in his mouth.

e. At daylight Coyote came to life again. He returned to Setson. His friend was astonished to see him. Because Coyote brought them back from Dentalium Home, people now have dentalia. If Coyote had not brought them, they would not use dentalia.

J7. Coyote's Thirst

[For another version of this tale, see E2.—Ed.]

•

a. Coyote was going to Ko'men.[1] He wanted to make himself a good (deerskin) blanket.[2] When it was wet, he stuffed it into a storage basket (instead of scraping it dry and soft). When he tried to take it out, it was so stiff that he could not draw it out of the basket.[3] Then he dragged the basket along after him.

b. When he came to Ko'men, he saw a sweathouse. Inside was a young man; outside stood baskets with something in them. Coyote did not know what it was. He tasted it and it was good. It was cracked[4] gooseberry juice. He drank it all and went off. When the young man came out of the sweathouse, he saw his food was gone. He was the one who drank no water,[5] and lived on nothing but this juice. Then he wished[6] that Coyote would find no water.

c. As Coyote traveled on, he became very thirsty. When he heard a creek running, it dried up before he came to it. Even though he ran hard, it dried up. Then, when he next heard water, he threw his moccasins[7] ahead of him, hoping they would be wetted. Then he threw his blanket, hoping it would

2. Tsīktsīko'ɬ, "Dentalium live," across the ocean or at the north end of the world.

---

1. "Orleans" in original.
2. Of one or two deerskins.
3. Wet buckskin, of course, dries stiff and hard.
4. [Crushed?—Ed.]
5. Sweated and fasted whil ritually gathering sweathouse fuel for ten days.
6. I.e., cursed.
7. Donned for travel.

become damp. Then he shot his arrow when he heard the next creek, that he might lick the moisture off it. But the creek dried before the arrow reached it. At last he came down to the river. There he drank so much that he drowned, drifted away, and stranded at the mouth of the river.

J8. No'ots

a. A girl and her grandmother were living at Ko'men.[1] Her grandmother told her, "When you dig for roots, do not dig *herłker*."[2] The girl wondered why. At last she thought she would try. She pulled up one of the roots. At the end was a little child. She ran back to the house and closed the door. But the little boy followed her and walked into the house. Her grandmother took care of him.[3]

b. He grew up and hunted and killed many deer. But his mother would have nothing to do with him: she would not call him her son. She said that only if he got the woodpecker crest-covered deer, in the sky, would she call him her son.[4] Then he killed that deer: now she went to the sky with him. There they saw many dances and festivals. Then they came back to Ko'men.

c. Now the young man was about to go away.[5] She did not want him to go, but could not stop him. So, when he had gone, she threw her pestle after him. The pestle struck the stern of his boat, broke in two,[6] and (one piece) became a rock off the coast south of the mouth of the Klamath.[7] But the young man went on and did not come back. His name was No'ots.

J9. Pa'aku

a. On Oka[1] there lived a man who had two daughters. His house was in the middle. There were ten houses on each side of his. He wanted a son-in-

1. Orleans.

2. *Herłker* are Brodiaeas, probably. In other versions, she is enjoined not to dig double-stalked ones, or late in the day. There was probably a confusion in the telling between mention of some such taboo and explaining what the bulbs were. [See A7, F6, and DD2 for other versions.—Ed.]

3. Because the girl, his "mother," would not.

4. Acknowledge him.

5. In other versions, he is angry because she would not accept him before his success. The whole telling lacks explicit motivation.

6. Some other versions mention the stern, more the feathers on his netted headdress. If a broken pestle is mentioned elsewhere, she breaks it, and her second cast is farther north. A stone pestle would hardly become broken against the fragile stern of a dugout. Perhaps the narrator said, "struck the stern of his boat and broke it" ("in two" misheard).

7. Redding Rock. Though it is not so stated, the girl probably threw her pestle from Orleans Summit. The localization has been whittled down to fit a stranger's understanding.

---

1. A long, high unforested ridge on the northeast side of the Klamath below Blue Creek.

law. Whoever killed the woodpecker-crest-covered deer in the sky, was to marry his daughters. Many tried but failed. Coyote tried.

b. Then one morning the one at Oka heard shouting. Someone was driving deer before him. He sent his two daughters to look. They found a little boy.[2] He was Pa'aku.[3] They brought him to the house. Next morning the people went out to hunt. They said to Pa'aku, "Come along!" He said, "I cannot; I am too little."

c. When they were gone, he started to go to the sky with the old man. They went up by a ladder. He told the old man, "Whatever happens, do not open your eyes." Then there was a high wind, but they climbed on. They went through hail, but the old man did not look. Then they came to the sky. They heard people driving deer. Then the deer came. Pa'aku shot an all-red deer. He told the old man, "You too shoot." Then the old man also killed a (woodpecker-covered) deer. Each of them began to pack his deer home, but it was too heavy for the old man, so Pa'aku carried both. Now they returned, and he married the two girls.

2. Reference to his size rather than tender years.
3. A small owl.

Informant K

SAINTS' REST JACK OF LO'OLEGO

I visited this old man at the remnant of the town of Lo'olego or Heyamu, or Saints' Rest, two miles upstream from Weitspus.[1] *I happened to inquire about the world rather than his home locality, probably with luck, for his tales, which he seemed to bring forth rather painfully, are not bad as native philosophy, but much below par as stories. His interests, in other words, approach those of Informant F, although they are not quite so one-sided and his communications maintain coherence. The manner in which he omits picturesque episodes in the life of Wohpekumeu, as pointed out in the footnotes to the second tale, in order to reach the consequences of his hero's acts, and the very bold handling in the third story of the "Married at Rumai" folktale, both evince his trends. His explanations are numerous, and generally of fairly important things: deer, childbirth, money, marriage by purchase, the forms of the animal kingdom, several rocks near Rumai, death, purification from it, rocks and landmarks in general, and their names, are all accounted for in a few paragraphs. This list embraces a fairly respectable proportion of all things in the Yurok world.*

Saints' Rest Jack was called Ki'nterk as his Indian name. He was also called K'e-heyamu, after his town of Heyamu. This is the real name of the settlement. It is sometimes also known as Lo'olego, but properly this is the spot on the bar, upstream from the farther houses, where the salmon dam was built. Heyamu was abandoned early. Robert Spott never saw any Indian houses there. Jack's wife was from tsekweł in Weitspus and was a doctor. She once was paid a small gray deerskin as a doctoring fee by a Karok. Jack was some kind of cousin of Bluff Creek Jim.[2]

1. [See Waterman, Geography, map 25, no. 30.—Ed.]
2. [According to Waterman, p. 259, Bluff Creek Jim was the leading man of Otsepor.—Ed.]

He owned two grey deerskins, two black obsidians, feathers, blankets, and arrows.

K1. Origin of Deer

a. At Kenek two girls were leaching acorns at the river. Then they heard something as if a child were crying. When they heard it again, one of them said, "Let us look." Then they went upstream along the river to (Kenek) creek. There they found a stranded lump of foam. Then they saw a baby sticking out from the foam and took it. They thought they would keep it and carried it home. They cared for it and made it a basket cradle of black-oak sticks.[1] After a time the boy grew. Then they made him a bow, and for a string they cut off one of the fringes of a buckskin dress.[2] They wanted him to hunt; that is why they made him the bow.

b. So he went to hunt. There were no deer then. He came to a prairie, looked and thought, "It is too bad that there are no deer. I should like to kill deer." Then he cut off a small piece of the soft flesh from the underpart of his thigh, rubbed it between his hands, blew it away, and said, "Let it become deer." Then when he looked on the prairie again he saw many deer and all kinds of game. So it was that deer came to be.[3]

K2. Wohpekumeu

a. Wohpekumeu came from Kenek.[1] He went far upstream and saw a woman. He desired her and married her[2] and had a son from her, Kapuloyo. But when the boy was to be born they were about to cut open the woman.[3] So Wohpekumeu made medicine for her. He used ashes, putting them into water; thus he made his medicine.[4] Then they found it was effective,[5] and did not cut open the woman.

1. Cradles are usually made of hazel shoots.
2. This might do for a very tiny boy's play bowstring.
3. The boy was Wohpekumeu, the narrator said when asked for his name, but I suspect a misunderstanding and have separated this fragment from the next tale. If it were Wohpekumeu, which the baby in the river suggests (cf. H1), the girls should have become pregnant from him, by the usual tenor of Yurok narrative. The second episode here is of the common type of instituting myth; and while these are sometimes associated with Wohpekumeu and Pulekukwerek, they are more often attributed to anonymous woge.

---

1. This might mean "came into being at" or "started on his travels from."
2. A tremendous abridgment. (Cf. F2 *a-e*.)
3. There was no birth in those days, and a child entailed the mother's death.
4. [Cf. F2*d*.—Ed.]
5. Delivery took place.

b. Wohpekumeu went downstream with his son to Kenek. All the woge were ready to go away and he saw no one: all of them had gone.[6] Then he thought, "It is too bad. Only I have been left."

c. And there was no dentalium money left; he was thinking about that. His son had gone:[7] it was he who had taken all the money. So Wohpekumeu followed him downstream. Then he saw fog on the hill opposite Sregon:[8] but when he came there he did not see it any more. Then he saw fog in another place farther downstream.[9] He went on, came to where he had seen it, and did not find it. He went on again and saw fog on the hill above Wełkwäu. He came there and did not see it any longer. Then he saw fog opposite on the hill above Rekwoi. So he called (?)[10] across. There at last he caught up with Kapuloyo, uphill from Rekwoi. He said, "I have followed you because I want some of the money left (in this world). If you leave none there will never be any along this river. Let people have some money, so that when a man wants a woman he may buy her." Then Kapuloyo said, "Yes, I shall leave some."[11] He blew out of his hand, scattering the money that would be everywhere. He left behind . . . .[12] Those are the names that Kapuloyo gave the (sizes of) money.

d. Now Wohpekumeu traveled southward. He stopped a little while at Tsuräu.[13] Then he went on again. Now at every little distance he would see a woman lying on the beach. As he came to each one, he tried not to look at her, for he thought that after all he was leaving.[14] Then at last he saw another woman, and he thought, "Well, anyway, I might take her." Then she began to move with him. She was Skate. She slid into the water and carried him across the ocean. That was the last time he was seen in the world.[15]

6. Another omission; his efforts to destroy his son are left out. [See F2*f-g* and *m*.—Ed.]

7. The same, with resulting lack of motivation. Kapuloyo goes because his father has attempted to kill him, seduced his wife, and blinded his son.

8. A small but wealthy town.

9. This is weak narration in Yurok, to fail to specify the places.

10. [K. has a notation to check this translation against his notebooks.—Ed.]

11. Rationalized and undramatic. The normal full version has something of a struggle between father and son, or one small dentalium is made to call out to Kapuloyo and delay him. [Cf. F2*o-q*.—Ed.]

12. [Omission in typescript. K. has a marginal notation referring to his original notebooks. See the table of money sizes in Kroeber, Handbook, p. 23.—Ed.]

13. Trinidad, near the southern limit of Coast Yurok territory. Beyond Little River were the sandy beaches of the Wiyot.

14. That is, his mind is intent on his final transformation or destiny, and he feels that he should not now be distracted by amorous considerations.

15. The interest is centered in the last two episodes, especially *c*; *a* and *b* are merely a briefly summarized introduction.

K3. Married at Rumai; Death; and Departure of the Woge

a. When the woge were about to move away from this world, they had no feathers (or fur) because they were human (in shape).[1] They said, "How can we go? We have no feathers." There was (a great bird) sitting on Shelton Butte[2] (who had feathers on). They thought, "It will be best if we kill him." Then they all came opposite the mountain, to Rumai.[3] There was a man from Kewet married at Rumai. Then, from Itperper[4] at Rumai, all began to shoot at that (bird). That is why that knoll is so fine there:[5] They all sat on it and shot. Coyote was shooting too. Whenever he drew he shouted, "Now I shall hit him!" But he always missed. Then they thought about the one married at Rumai. "Let him shoot," for they could not hit that (bird). "Shoot!" they told him. "Yes," he said.

Then he went to the place, brought two *permeryer*[6] rocks up from the river, put one under his foot, and the other under his knee.[7] Then he took his (miniature) bow of *permeryer*. He drew it out,[8] rubbed it, and everyone saw that the stone had become a (full) bow. Now he shot. He hit that one on the mountain. He fell down, rolling toward the river, and one can see now where he rolled. His name was Hegwono'.[9] He is in the sky now and very large. He stopped rolling just before he reached the river.

b. They wanted to go over to him but had no boat in which to cross the river. Then old Crane said, "I will tell you what to do. I will stretch my leg and you can walk across on it." The old woman at Rumai, the mother-in-law of the young man from Kewet, said, "I want his meat to cook." So they all

1. Although not human beings in kind, the Yurok invaribly declare, they are spirits and immortal.

2. For Shelton Butte, Rumai, and Kewet, see A8, A12, C5, G2, P5, Q2, and Z2.

3. Rumai is given on Waterman, Geography, map 25, no. 40, as Romoi, a flat in a bend of the river, opposite the small town of Otsepor, 1/2 mile below the mouth of Bluff Creek and 3-1/2 miles above Weitspus. It is not opposite Shelton Butte, though this peak, on the east side of the river, is probably visible from Rumai. [See map 4 in this volume.—Ed.]

4. [Given by Waterman as a small lake on a tributary of Bluff Creek (map 25, no. 1), 3-1/2 miles above Rumai. See map 4 in this volume.—Ed.]

5. They made it pretty for their convenience.

6. "Greasy-stone," very hard, smooth, and black, found in polished boulders and pebbles.

7. There are a number of references in their tales to the Yurok shooting from a kneeling position. The greasy-stone rests perhaps helped the strength of his greasy-stone bow.

8. This is a frequent incident.

9. Hegwono' (or Hewonoł) is mentioned also in J3, but the bird is also called Erł'erm, as in U2.

crossed. Each one took (a coat of) feathers (or fur). Every bird (and animal) in the world took feathers (or fur) from that one. Some took only one feather.[10]

c. Then they went down to the river and Crane stretched his leg across again, and they all returned. The old woman from Rumai came last, carrying the meat (in her carrying) basket.[11] When she came to the middle of the river Crane drew up his leg, and she fell into the water. She turned to stone. She is there now in the river and her basket is by her, a rock with a hole in it. When the river rises one can hear the water flowing into the basket and making a noise.

d. Now they all started to go off. He from Kewet said, "I shall go back to my place."[12] All the others named the places to which they would go, and so they scattered.

e. Now when they had been talking about where each would go, some of them said, "I think it will be best if when a person is old he becomes young again." But others said, "No. I think it will be best if when a person is old he dies and does not become young again." There were many who wanted people to die, very many; therefore those who did not wish it had to yield. So they let it be, though they did not like it. They were angry, but they said, "Very well."

f. But they said, "I think they must have medicine."[13] Then they made it that people would use medicine for purification after a death. They tried every kind of herb as medicine (to wash with) but none was good. Then they tried *hegwomes*.[14] When they made medicine with that, they felt better. Thus they found that this plant would be good for the medicine. So it is that we still use it.

g. Then of those who had said they did not wish people to die, some went down the river all along as far as the mouth and some at various spots along the ocean, and each one said where he would stay (in a rock) by the river, and named the place, and the next one beyond named his place and said, "I shall stay there. When people die, tell me." So he said to the one who was to stay upstream from him, and the one who would be the next downstream said the same to him.[15] So they did all the way down the river and then (northward)

10. Coyote's failure in anticipating the others is omitted. [See G2.—Ed.]

11. "Carrying the meat and baskets to cook it in," I wrote in abbreviation. But her cooking baskets she would have in her house at Rumai, whereas she would want a pack basket to transport the meat in, back from the east side.

12. Kewet, Rivet Mountain, where he was born.

13. Formula and herb.

14. Otherwise mentioned as used. [See H2.—Ed.]

15. The formula consists of an appeal by the mourner for help in his contamination. He addresses the spirit resident farthest upstream. This one professes to be unable to do anything, but refers the petitioner to his colleague next downstream. This happens ten or more times, until

along the coast. But those who had said that they wished people to die, they did not say that they wanted to be informed when a person died, nor that they would send them on. Now we do not know the places beyond the mouth of the river, but we do know the names (along the river) because then they told them. So they said, "Whenever a person dies, make the medicine in this way."

h. Now they were about to go off but stopped once more for a little while, and made the names of the hills and of the places across the river and along the river. They gave a name to every spot all the way to the mouth. That is how it is that every spot, even if they are only a short distance apart, has a name. Then they started to go away, not to be here any more. Some said, "I shall stay by the trail because I like girls, and if I stay by it I shall always see them." Some said, "I shall go to the river because when women bathe I shall see them."[16] So they moved off. Some went here and some there and some on top of the hills.[17]

K4. Man and Dog

a. He grew at Erłerger.[1] Then he thought he would like to have a dog. Then he got one: it was a bitch. So he wanted to hunt. And he went to Erger,[2] and only hunted a little and killed two deer, just with his dog, alone.

b. And it was ten days, and he had no more meat and he went out to hunt, he and his dog, and killed ten deer. And he had nothing but deer meat to feed her on.

c. Then he looked at the dog and thought he would take her as a woman. "It will be good if I take her; perhaps she will have children and I can raise people." So he took her; she just kept still.

d. Then he went to Erłerger and left her there at Erger. And at Erłerger he thought, "Well, I must return." So he went back, and it was nearly sundown, and near his camp he thought he saw a woman sitting. She had long hair. He looked at her long and thought, "Where is that woman from?" Then as he looked she turned into his dog again. And he thought, "That is my bitch. It must be that she is a woman." So he went and they stayed there.

e. After a while she began to speak to him, this bitch. "I want to know

---

the mouth of the river—or in other versions, Pulekuk—is reached. The lost spirit tells the mourner to wash with *hegwomes*. [Again, see H2.—Ed.]

16. These are probably rocks.

17. The woge became rocks or other landmarks, birds, and animals, or disembodied spirits that help men to riches or give them curative powers; still others went off across the ocean.

---

1. A town across from Weitspus on the southeast side of the Klamath.

2. Burnt Ranch, on Bald Hills ridge, 6 to 7 miles south of Weitspus.

what we will do,'' she said. ''About what?'' he asked. ''Well, about what we have done.'' And he said, ''I wanted to see people. I wanted to raise children to become people. That is why I did it.'' ''Well, then it is right,'' she said. And they lived there.

f. Then she said, ''If someone comes around here, I will turn into a dog again, because I do not want them to know that you are living with a woman.'' ''Yes,'' he said.

g. It was nearly a year and she gave birth to two, a boy and a girl. And they ate only deer. Whenever he wanted meat, the woman turned to a dog again and drove deer to him, and he killed them easily. And she had another child, a boy—three in all.

h. Then the man said, ''Well, let us go back to Erɫerger. There is going to be another kind (of beings) coming. So I think we had better return.'' And when they arrived, he said, ''Now they are about to begin to come into being.'' She said, ''Well, take the boys and I will take the girl. Whenever you want deer, I will drive them to you; that is how you will get them. When you hear a dog barking somewhere back in the timber, run up there, and it will be I driving deer, and you will shoot them.'' And he said, ''Yes.''

i. So he started, and went to Tsoikin.[3] And she went farther (south and west) to Ayê'go's[4] and said, ''Sometimes I will come around.''

His name was Tsaiɫkilwāwits, ''Sand-on-his-Back.''

3. A mile beyond Burnt Ranch toward Hupa, at Berryman Like's place.

4. This is 4 or 5 miles beyond. All three places in the hills seem to have been in Chilula territory.

INFORMANT L

LUCKY OF WAHSEK

I knew Lucky by sight as one of two old men at Wahsek, or Martin's Ferry, three miles downstream from Weitspus. I had no dealings with him until he came into Weitspus one day in June of 1907 and agreed to tell me a story. It proved to be well told but typical in treatment, and in no way notable except in content. He had offered to narrate a Wohpekumeu story, and I consented if it were something else than the conventional string of episodes about this hero. As the following shows, he kept his promise. And he told his tale well.

As to Lucky's family: I understood that he was originally from Weitspus. This may be true for his mother's side. However, he was raised at Wahsek, probably in the house rǟk: he was related to Informant J's mother Kate Wilson. Kate's father's brother bought his wife from Wohkel, and Wohkel Harry's wife called Lucky uncle, netsi'mos. *Lucky's Indian name was Tso'wo'rets, which means small driftwood or roots.*

Lucky's wife was of Weitspus, from a house which stood across the trail from oslok and was probably called tōleɬ. He lived in this house, and his wife, who was older than he, was called Lucky-wetsker, that is, married to Lucky after her sister's death. He and she called each other nǟts, ex-sibling-in-law. He appears to have had no children from either wife.

After his second wife's death, he lived on for a while in Weitspus, then returned to Wahsek, and was half-married there to a woman in the house tsōreu, who was called Tsōreu-me'lo. He was buried downriver in Ho'peu through his relationship to Wohkel Harry's wife, who called him uncle.

Lucky did not own much property. He had some sixteen or eighteen tandem eagle feathers of his own, and some dentalium beads which belonged to his wife.

L1. Wohpekumeu

a. Opposite Sa'ar[1] is where Wohpekumeu was. There are flat rocks there as from a sweathouse floor, and a headrest stone, where he used to lie and watch the girls going upriver along the trail.

b. Egor[2] is where he went when he removed from Sa'ar. There he made his fishing place of *permeryer* (greasy-stone): a floor, with a hole for a fireplace in the middle, and stones about like walls. Also he made his path (down to the fishing place) even and pretty. It is all there now, of stone. When he had made all this, he went uphill a little to the flat, to Egor, and thought, "I must make my house here."

Then he made his house. He made the floor of stone and the walls likewise. Then he began to make his sweathouse. Now he thought he had a place to live in. So he went back down to the river where he had built his fishing place. But it was not a real fishing place, for he had made it for himself only so that he might look across the river from it and watch persons going by on the trail. Then he set a rock of *permeryer* in the river to make the water eddy around it. He thought, "I wish it were deep here and shallow on the opposite shore, so that the salmon could not pass on that side and my fishing place would become very good." On the opposite side was a pretty flat—it has been nearly washed away by the river now—along which he could see for some distance if anyone came, and there were many people then. And right opposite him was a resting place in the shade.[3] He always sat where he had made it to be like his house, and looked across. Then he saw many sitting on the seats opposite. That is why he had wanted his fishing place as he made it, so that they could see him, for he wanted many to be looking at him when he began to catch salmon.

So he took up his round dipnet[4] and said (to it), "Catch many!"[5] because those in the shade were watching him. As soon as he dipped his net in the

1. The mouth of Hopkins Creek, on the south side of the Klamath, "about 3 miles" upstream from Weitspus; 2-1/2 m. according to Waterman, Geography, map 25, no. 33, Sä'är, acorn grounds. [Here and below, see map 4 in this volume.—Ed.]

2. On the same side of the river, "2 or 3 miles" farther up (about 1-1/2 by Waterman, map 25, no. 37, Aiqo'o), downstream from the mouth of Bluff Creek, perhaps half a mile below the town known as Otsepor or "Bluff Creek Jim's ranch." Waterman derives the name Aiqo'o from *egor*, a cylindrical basket used in the Jumping Dance and also a flat, folded carrying case of rawhide. He also gives the present episode about Wohpekumeu on p. 259.

3. All main trails had definite resting places, often marked by stones or seats, and selected either becuse of the attractiveness of the spot or on account of the completion of an ascent.

4. *Tromonał*, a dipnet on a round-ended frame (a frame looped back on itself), plunged, not set into the water. It can be used best at active rapids or falls, and is therefore perhaps more employed by the Karok than by the Yurok.

5. *Tsanikitenawok*.

water, it was as if someone were shaking him, so many salmon rushed in; and when he lifted the net it was entirely full.

c. He went upstream from Egor to Oteyo[6] and made himself a fishing place, but it was not so good as at Egor, because he could not see people across the river. Sometimes he caught a few salmon here; and he stayed only a little while.

d. Then he went upstream to Ko'men[7] and hung about because the people there were many. Wohpekumeu was not a bad man; yet no one liked him because he always disturbed women. Now he began a War Dance, but they did not come out to look on, the two who remained indoors.[8] So he began a Brush Dance, but they did not come to see.

e. Then he thought, "Let me see an elk swimming," Then as they looked toward the river from Ko'men, they saw an elk swim downstream, one with great horns;[9] but the two women never came out.

f. Now he thought, "What shall I do?" So he began to become a little boy, and made a tiny boat, such as small children have to play with, and entered it, and went out into the middle of the stream, and sailed down, singing. (Song. It is a good song to help one in dangerous water.) The people of Ko'men saw him, ran out, and shouted, "A baby is about to drown!" but the two women still remained indoors.

g. When he returned,[10] he thought, "Let me try to make a Brush Dance again." Their village mates said to the two women, "Let us go and see that: it is about to be a pretty dance." But the two women said, "No, I do not think I shall go. I am afraid that it may be Wohpekumeu." He who was speaking with them said, "Let me tell you what to do. His fishing place is upriver. I will run there and see if he is fishing." So he ran upriver, and came back, and said, "I saw him fishing on the opposite side, and he was singing." Wohpekumeu had set a stone at his fishing place upriver across from Ko'men. He made it look like a man fishing, and said "Sing like a man," for he knew that they would come to report on him.

h. So now the two women came out to watch the Brush Dance. Only one small boy was dancing, with a man on each side holding his arms. His hair was long and trimmed with something: it was dentalia. As soon as they arrived, the women said, "Look at the little boy! He is nice to dance with."

6. Near Otsepor, just below it; Waterman, map 25, no. 38, and p. 259.

7. Karok Panamenik, Orleans.

8. A Wohpekumeu episode at Orleans is normally understood to revolve about these two nameless girls. When Wohpekumeu puts on a dance, it is usually by young men he has made from his pubic hairs.

9. An elk in the river was probably a rare occurrence, and a fully antlered male would be especially prized on account of the value of its horns for wedges, spoons, and purses.

10. To Ko'men, past which he had floated.

They stood by him and danced along. They only danced a short time: then they found out that he was Wohpekumeu, that little boy.[11] As soon as he stepped out of the dance, he was the old man again.

i. He went back downriver to Kenek, where he had lived before. No one knows where he grew:[12] I did not learn it from the old people; he came of himself as the wind blows.

j. But his grandson,[13] anyone knows where he was born,[14] Tsoliłka;[15] that is he. Now he, that grandson, went upstream to Petskuk. At Oräuw, in the river in front of Erłerger,[16] that is where he lives now, that Tsoliłka. His lice are as large as grasshoppers. Sometimes one sees one of them and breaks off its horn[17] to put into one's purse. Then one has good luck, for the dentalia are like that.

k. (The episode of Wohpekumeu being snowed in at Kenek was referred to by the narrator as belonging here.)

l. After this, the ocean rose because they wished Wohpekumeu to drown: the woge did it. But he climbed a tree, and at last the water subsided. Many were killed at Kenek: but he was not drowned.

m. Now Wohpekumeu started upstream from Kenek. He did not know where he would go, but he went on, day after day. He went by Ko'men without stopping. He came far upstream.[18] Then he saw a single house. He entered and found two men and a woman. They only looked at him, not knowing where he was from. They had never heard of Wohpekumeu: they were a different people. Now he stayed there. In the evening, the two men said, "Let us go to the sweathouse for the night." He said, "Yes." Then they went in. Early in the morning Wohpekumeu arose and went after sweathouse firewood. When he returned, he began to put the wood in at the door. With the first stick he passed in, two large woodpecker crests fell on the floor. The two

11. He had probably accomplished his desire.

12. Kenek is sometimes mentioned, but many Wohpekumeu stories agree with this one in beginning with the hero adult and in action. Spott, in Spott and Kroeber, Narratives, no. 26, pp. 232-33, gives an aberrant version of his origin.

13. The interpreter said "boy," that is, son, throughout, but at the end of the myth, that Tsoliłka was the son of Kapuloyo and therefore grandson of Wohpekumeu. Kewomer is the name usually mentioned for Kapuloyo's son.

14. Presumably at Kenek; at least, that is where the episode of Kapuloyo and his blind son is usually placed, though it is omitted in this version.

15. Cf. Tsoleu, the site of Wohpekumeu's house at Kenek; Waterman, map 22, no. 7.

16. Waterman, map 25, no. 22, Orew, a fishing place before Erłerger, opposite Weitspus. Waterman, p. 258, calls him Tsooli-lqaa, son of Kapuloyo, and describes him as a titanic water monster with innumerable horns, including two extra-large striped ones.

17. The description suggests a longicorn beetle, but Waterman speaks of the wealth-attracting amulet as being a piece of Tsoliłka's own striped horn.

18. Inasmuch as on his return he passed by Segwu', he must have come into upper Karok or perhaps Shasta territory.

men picked them up. Then he passed in the remainder of the wood. Then he made fire. When they had sweated, the two said to each other, "I do not know where he is from. I have never before seen that sort of person. But it seems that he must be a good man."

In the middle of the day he again went up the hill,[19] and when he returned, the same thing happened when he put the first piece of wood into the sweathouse, but there were more woodpecker crests. Then the two men liked it, because they picked those up, although they did not know him. So they finished making a fire for sweating.

n. The woman there—she was only a girl—also used to go uphill after wood with her carrying basket. He who had come there thought, "I should like to see where she always gets wood." So he watched, saw the way she went up the hill, and began to follow. He followed her partway. Then he lost her. He looked all about but could not find her at all. Then he turned and went after his sweathouse wood. But the two men did not know that he wanted the girl that lived there. They only thought he was getting sweathouse wood.

Every day the woman went up for wood, and Wohpekumeu also got sweathouse wood every day, and when he returned with it, the woodpecker crests always fell off, more and more of them, until the two who lived there had many, and liked him for it. But he was constantly following that girl, although he never could see her (in the woods) and always lost her. Then he would return with sweathouse wood, and they did not know he was looking for her. And when he had returned and finished sweating, the girl always came home with her wood. So although he continued looking for her, he never saw her and heard nothing in the woods. But the girl always saw him and hid herself, for she did not want him to be near her.

o. Then one day he thought, "This time I will track her." So when the woman went up, he followed. When he got into the timber, he heard working. He turned there and saw the girl splitting wood with her wedge. He went to her and said, "Well, I have been wanting to see you. Let us sit down in the shade, for I want to talk to you." Then she said, "Yes," but did not yet know where he was from. He said, "I would like to marry you." She told him, "No." He said, "That is why I am living here." Again she said "No." He said to her, "Well, do you know where you are sitting now?" She said, "No." He said, "This is not the place where you always get wood. Look across to that hill, as far as you can see." She looked and saw the hill and something whitish, a stump. He said, "Now that is the stump at which you break your wood." The girl looked again and thought he was right:[20] she recognized the place. He

19. For sweathouse wood, *nunerergernis*.

20. He had changed the appearance of things; actually she was still on her familiar hillside near home. The stump may be what she broke dead limbs on to carry home for firewood; or possibly she wedged off pieces of the stump.

said, "You see you cannot escape and I shall take you." Then he sat close by her and she was afraid. "I want to cohabit," he said, and she did not wish to, but he said, "You cannot avoid me, for you are on another hill and I am going to have you." So she submitted.

p. Wohpekumeu said, "Well, let us go back to the house." Then he gathered sweathouse wood, and the woman carried her wood home. When she reached the house, her belly was big: she was about to have a child. The two men (her brothers) said, "How do you come to be like that?" She told them, "I am like this from him."[21] In the morning she gave birth. When it was two days old, it walked about.[22] It was a boy.

q. He wanted to return, Wohpekumeu did, to Kenek, where he belonged. He said, "I think I want to go back." The woman said "Well." The boy wished to go with him, but Wohpekumeu did not want him. The woman said, "Leave him here! Do not let him follow you!" Wohpekumeu assented, for as it was he did not want him. Then he started, Wohpekumeu. He said he would return.

r. Now he had gone far on his way. Then he heard someone calling. Nevertheless he went on. Then he heard it again. He looked back and saw his boy coming. He came on and reached Wohpekumeu. The old man thought, "I do not like to see him come, for I did not wish to take him, because I constantly want women. If I take him along he will always be in the way, for women will think I am old if they see I have a boy." He thought, "Well, I shall have to kill him, that is all." So he seized him, threw him down, and began to choke him. Thus he killed him. Then he went on.

s. He had gone a long way when he heard calling behind. He looked back and saw his boy coming again. He said to himself, "It is too bad! I don't want him." He stood there and thought, "Well, I shall have to take him with me." Then he remembered a place where he would pass many rattlesnakes. He thought he would send him there on an errand. So he let him come with him. Then they came near the place of the rattlesnakes. The old man pointed with his hand and said, "Go there and bring me what I want.[23] I shall wait for you downstream. And if you arrive first, wait for me." "Very well," said the boy and went. The old man also went. He came to the (appointed) place and did not see the boy. Then he waited a while, as it were. Still the boy did not come.

21. Presumably the reason why they accepted the seduction instead of considering it an injury calling for reparation was that he had more than paid for the girl with the woodpecker crests. In other versions (see F2, and Hupa and Karok parallels), the woodpecker crests are not mentioned, the woman is about to die, and Wohpekumeu escapes with his life only by causing her child to be born safely, that is, a childbirth formula.

22. Pregnancy and growth are both miraculously speedy.

23. As the sequel shows, this vague reference is probably intentional and not a lapse on the part of the narrator.

He said, "Well, he is surely dead, for no one has ever failed to be killed there." So he started once more. He had gone far, but was always looking back, as it were, to watch. Then as he looked around, it was as if he saw someone following in the distance. So the old man sat down right there and waited. Then he saw him come indeed. When he came near he saw that it was the same one, his own boy. He saw that he carried a case[24] under his arm which he had not had before. And he had a (woven) rabbit-skin blanket,[25] ornamented with woodpecker scalps. So he thought, "It is indeed my boy, for that is the sort I wear. Well, this time I will really accept him, and not try any more to kill him." He said to him, "Well, we are going home."[26]

t. They came to Segwu',[27] downstream from it, to Okwego.[28] There they rested. Then they saw many men and women across the river, woge. Wohpekumeu said, "You see them on the other side?" The boy said, "Yes." He told him, "Now I shall begin to sing. When you hear me, I want you to help me; but you must sing somewhat differently from me."[29] So the old man began to sing, and the boy did as he was told, singing differently. Then they started (downstream, singing).[30] They passed Ko'men, they stopped nowhere. So they came to Kenek, to his place. And so all learned that he had a boy: all the women knew it. Then they lived there, he and the boy.

u. One day the boy thought, "I will go to the sweathouse." It was the one of the Ke-kenomer[31] at Kenek. Thunder, Earthquake, and all of them used that sweathouse.[32] Wohpekumeu had his own,[33] he and his boy. But now the

24. *Egor*, a case made of a piece of folded-over elk rawhide, carried clamped under the arm.

25. *Tsapole*. The narrator said that such blankets were used on Mad River, that is, by the Whilkut or Nongatl. The Yurok do not seem to have used them. Inasmuch as this type of blanket has a practically universal distribution from the Southwest through California, the deficiency illustrates the specialization of Yurok culture. It is true that rabbits are not abundant along the lower Klamath; but some could no doubt have been killed and the skins of others might have been traded in. However, the fact of there being a Yurok name suggests that a certain supply of these warm blankets did trickle in.

26. To Kenek.

27. Karok Katimin.

28. Okwego is between Segwu' and Enek (Amaikiaram), on the same side as the latter. It is not a town.

29. He wants the boy to accompany him. The second singer monotonously chants or grunts one very low note carrying the rhythm. It is a very elementary form of part singing, without attempt at harmony.

30. In triumphal procession, as it were, and public acknowledgment of his son.

31. The Porpoises, as divulged later.

32. This sweathouse site is pointed out close behind the historic town of Kenek, but the depression is slight and seems a natural one. It may be the pit of sweathouse C in Waterman's map 22, near his houses no. 12, Thunder's, and no. 13, Porpoises'.

33. Wohpekumeu's sweathouse was by his house, Kenek-tsoleu, which stood at the edge of the bluff downstream from the town. See again Waterman, map 22, housepit 7.

boy went to the large sweathouse because he wished to show himself, being like a stranger there. So he entered, taking his case[34] with him. When he came in, he was as if about to sit down when someone said to him, "Go to *tepoleł*."[35] The boy went there and sat down quietly. They thought, "That is he that has come, his boy." Then the one at *kwenomet*[36] said, "I am very glad to see you. I have some pieces of flint for arrowheads. I want you to work them." The boy said, "Yes? Well, bring them." So the man rose and went to the house to get them.[37] Then he brought them back in an openwork plate basket: it was half full of chips, unworked ones. He set the basket down near where the boy was sitting. The boy merely sat and looked at the basket. Soon he took it, opened his case, poured in the contents of the plate, and closed the case. Then he sat down again and began to converse. They who belonged there conversed too. He sat quite a while. Then he opened his case, took up the plate, and poured out (the flints). No one had seen him work them, but they were all shaped and pretty.[38] Then he went out. All spoke after him: "Ah, this is an excellent person." All of them said that they thought well of him. And to those not in the sweathouse, they sent report to, that he was a good young man. They said, "I wish we would give him a woman because he is such an excellent man." Therefore they talked it about, to let all know how they thought, because they wanted that done.

v. Now Sumig[39] lived at Kenek: he had a sister. Then he sent her to the young man at Kenek-tsoleu, to Wohpekumeu's house, where he lived. So he had a wife, that young man:[40] he was married to Sumig's sister. And he too had a son. There they lived; they never traveled more.[41]

34. *Egor*, as in n. 24.

35. *Tepoleł* is the place in the sweathouse opposite the exit, and the place of honor. [See diagram in Kroeber, Handbook, p. 82.—Ed.]

36. *Kwenomet* is the place to the left of the exit, likely to be occupied by the "owner."

37. Property is kept in the house. The sweathouse is quite bare. It would not begin to accommodate half a dozen or more recumbent men if they commenced to keep furniture inside.

38. Quite in his father's manner, whose *egor* or quiver is a stock magician's box.

39. Sumig, Patrick's Point on the coast, is where the Porpoises are generally said to have gone from Kenek. The name has not been obtained otherwise for a person. K'e-sumig, "he of Sumig," would be a proper personal name of address.

40. Kapuloyo was the name of Wohpekumeu's son, the narrator said in answer to a question. He did not think it necessary to mention it in the story.

41. Not to be taken literally. They remained there until the departure from this world.

Informant M

SANDY OF KENEK

Sandy of Kenek was called We'leptīn. His wife was from the house hełkeu in Wahsek and had previously been married into Pekwtuł. They had two sons. He was probably not a tsäro, *or worker on the Kepel dam, because Kenek is too far from Kepel. He had a good many regalia for the Brush Dance, but probably did not own much else.*

M1. Origin of Night

This story is Englished phrase by phrase from five phonograph cylinders into which the informant spoke his Yurok.

It appears that Pulekukwerek has only one companion: Pelin-tsīk and Tego'o are the same.

In spite of a certain repetitiousness, the story moves, because of insistence on its single objective. It tells of institutionalization by achievement of will. There is no conflict, no theft or escape; "night" remains completely undescribed and is not a person: a "piece" of it is finally conceded by its owner. Concrete touches—awaking from fleas, feeling well after the morning sweat, the seriousness of sickness at night—do not appear in the action of the narrative but in the predictive dialogue.

•

a. This is how it was: it never became dark but was day constantly. And he thought, this Pulekukwerek, "It will not be well for people to live so, that it does not ever become night." Then he was about to accompany him, this Great Money[1] when they went upstream. He told him to have food, this Pulekukwerek: he only (smoked) tobacco; but Tego'o[2] ate food.

1. Pelin-tsīk.

2. The largest (or next to largest) size of dentalium money. It appears here that Tego'o and Pelin-tsīk are one person. Tego'o is the specific name of a size of shell; Pelin-tsīk, a generic term used in mythology for money personified. [Cf. A15, B14, and D5. See also the table of sizes and names of shells in Kroeber, Handbook, p. 23.—Ed.]

And he came again next day (and they went upriver), and where they were about to pass the night,[3] someone said "Come into the house,"[4] he said to Pulekukwerek. But he would not: he was thinking all the time of there being no darkness for the people on earth. And Tego'o (went in and) ate.

So they went upriver, went upriver. And that was all he thought of, this Pulekukwerek, and he said, "I am going upstream for that, because (otherwise) they will not be well off on earth, the people."

b. Then they came to Segwu'[5] to the old sweathouse;[6] that is where they arrived. And they were about to go to the sweathouse, those who lived there. So he said, "Well, this is why I have come: I do not like it as it is in the world." Those who lived there said, "Come into the house." But he said, "No, I shall go into the sweathouse. I never eat food. And I am not satisfied, for I am traveling to obtain this night which never comes." And he (went into the sweathouse and) smoked: he only smoked. And they said to him, "Come indoors," to Tego'o; and he went and ate indeed, this Tego'o; but he did not eat at all, the other one.

And they started and went upriver. And they said to them, "Come into the house," where they stopped for the night. And he said, "No, I shall not go. This Tego'o will go in, the Great Money; he will go with you; but as for me, I do not eat." He said, "I am only thinking how it will be in the world if night does not come. That is what I am going upriver for: I hear that there is night upriver opposite Petskuk.[7] That is where they have night: and I wish to try to get a piece of it. That is why I eat nothing, because I think of that." And whenever they came anywhere and they said to them, "Come indoors and eat," he said, "No, I eat only tobacco," and went to the sweathouse (to smoke), and only Tego'o ate.

Now they went on again, far upriver, and they said to them, "Come indoors," and he said, "No, I do not eat, but he will go into the house with you, this Tego'o. I never eat: I only use tobacco: I carry it with me, my tobacco." Whenever he came anywhere, he said, "I want only tobacco."[8]

3. "Camp." There was no darkness, but people are represented as going to eat supper and retiring into the sweathouse.

4. To eat.

5. Karok Katimin, some 20 miles beyond the upstream limit of Yurok habitation.

6. *Ki'molen ergerk*, "ugly," "old," or "useless" sweathouse. It is the ceremonial structure of Katimin, in which medicine is made for the New Year's rite. It is not used for ordinary sweating. In fact it is really not a sweathouse at all, but a squarish and dilapidated shack, not quite so completely sunk in the ground as a sweathouse, but presenting more of the appearance of one than of an ordinary dwelling. It is shown in Handbook, pl. 12. See also Gifford and Kroeber, World Renewal, figs. 1 and 2 and pl. 4b-d.

7. *Petskuk wohiko*, "across the water from Upstream End."

8. I omit one more repetition of the same talk about the foods they eat and how bad the absence of night will be.

c. Now they arrived at Petskuk, and went into the sweathouse after supper and talked in the night. Then (the man there) said, "Yaha'! No one has ever gone there[9] before. I have been there; but I do not think he will give you even a small piece."

d. And he said, "Very well," and went across,[10] and to the sweathouse (there). And he said, "No. This one will eat, but I do not eat. I am going to the sweathouse." And he went and was in the sweathouse.

And he[11] called, "Has First Moon come in?"[12] And he said, "Hou'u'-u'u'!"[13] And he asked if the next one had come in, and he said "Hou'u'u'u, I have come in." And he was outside the sweathouse, this Tego'o, he did not speak, this Pelin-tsīk; only he spoke, Pulekukwerek. He went on like this: he called, "Has Third Moon come in?" Then he said "Hou'u'u'u"; that is how he answered him. And he called Fourth Moon, and Fourth Moon said he had come in. He called Fifth Moon, whether he had come in, and he said "Hou'u-'u'u"; that is how he answered, that Moon. And he said, "Sixth Moon, has he come in?" And he said "Hou'u'u'u." And he said, "I have come here for this: I do not want it to be in the world as it is. It will not be well for people if they (do not) sleep and there is no night. But sleep, that is what I want. They will awake in the morning and go for sweathouse wood: then they will feel well after they have used this sweathouse wood (to sweat themselves with). They will feel well: that is how I want it," said Pulekukwerek.

Then he called, "Has Seventh Moon come in?" and he said, "Hou'u'-u'u." And he said, "That is what I like to hear. Has Eighth Moon come in?" And he said, "Hou'u'u'u." And it was thus. "Has Ninth Moon come in?" Then Tenth Moon came in. And he asked if he had come in, and he said, "Hou'u'u'u." And he said, "Has Kä'mo come in?" And he said "Hou'u'-u'u." And that was the last one to come in.[14]

e. Then he[15] said, "And this is how I want it: fleas[16] also will bite in the

9. To *Petskuk wohiko*, where they have night.

10. *Hiko*.

11. It is not wholly clear whether this refers to Pulekukwerek or to the owner of the sweathouse and night.

12. *Kohtsewets hes-kits-nok*. The same phrase is used each time with the names of the subsequent months replacing Kohtsewets: second (unnamed in the text), Nahksewets, Tsona'aiwets, Merayo, Kohtsewets, Tserwersik, Knewoletau, Kerermerk, (the tenth, eleventh, and twelfth are omitted), and Kä'mo (thirteenth, last of the three moons at the unnumbered, named end of the Yurok calendar). See the full list in Handbook, p. 75. [See also V2 below.—Ed.]

13. In affirmation.

14. Eleven only are mentioned. Kä'mo is the last moon of the year, in December, whether a total of twelve or thirteen are counted.

15. Apparently the owner of night.

16. *Tege'i*.

night and wake people. They will get up on account of them: so they will do. And in the morning they will go to get sweathouse wood and feel well: that is how it will be with them. But I shall not give you any night: I want it (all) for myself."

f. And he said, "Yaha'! Give me a little! Give me a small piece, because that is what I came after, and I want to see people be well off with it." Then he said, "Very well. I will give you a little of this night, and it will be well with people. If they are sick in the morning, they will become better. But if they become sick in the middle of the night, it will be bad with them." And he made it as it were not so good, in this way,[17] he who gave the night. He said, "Take it." And that is why there is night in the world, when they had not had it before. He is the one who made it to be night, this Pulekukwerek, he is the one that got it.

g. And so he started with Great Money, and returned, and came to Segwu'. He said, "I have it. He gave me a little." That is how night (after all) came to be in the world, when originally it was to be day constantly, and they would not have been well off if it had been so, these human beings.

M2. He Flew Alone and with Condor

[For a different setting for this tale, see DD7 below.—Ed.]

•

a. This is how it was at Wohtek. He wanted to do something because he thought he had been too poor. So he made himself wings, blankets of feathers. Under the roof of the sweathouse is where he kept these. He used to put them on and go flying because he was poor and wanted good luck.

Now he had a boy who grew up. So he made another pair of wings.[1] At the place *ertserger*[2] in the sweathouse is where the boy slept. And (the boy) thought, "I wonder where he is going, for he always leaves me when we sleep.

And when he went he always rose up across the river from Wohtek and circled ten times before he started. Then he would see everything. He would see it raining, or whatever was going on in the world. Then, because he was sorry that he owned so little property, he flew to Dentalium Home.[3] He thought to himself while going there, "I will see everything: snow and rain

17. In having night illness serious.

1. Not because he had a boy but so that he could change off, as appears below.
2. Or *atserger*, by the exit, on the side opposite the entrance.
3. Tsīktsīko'ɬ.

and frost and heat in summer."[4] Then he arrived at Dentalium Home and brought back dentalia. And when he returned he saw his boy in the sweathouse and went to sleep beside him, there in Wohtek.

b. Now his son was growing big and kept thinking, "I wonder where he always goes, for he never tells me." So he went to hide and see. Then at night he looked out from the sweathouse and he saw him take his wing blanket from *leponoɫ*[5] under the sweathouse roof. He saw that where there were two blankets one was gone; for his father had two because he used to change. And he also saw his father put away the one he had been using.

Now once the boy tried it on and that wing blanket fitted him. So when his father was away at Dentalium Home he tried it; ten times he circled around and knew that he could fly. He did not fall. Always his father was going away; sometimes he went oceanward.[6] So he thought, "I want to see too. I will follow him."

c. So once when the old man went flying the boy began to follow him. But he went elsewhere; he went to Dentalium Home. Then his father returned and did not find him. He wondered where he had gone. He felt sorry: at night he did not sleep. And then he started out again, and when he had gone partway to Dentalium Home, he heard someone crying, and he passed through where the sky continually comes down to the sea.[7] He went on to where the ocean is pitch behind the sky,[8] and there he heard him, heard his boy crying. He had got as far as the bad place.[9] There he had got stuck in the pitch and was crying. Now his father rose up ten times above where he was stuck, where his wings were all fastened with pitch. And he made his medicine[10] for him while the boy kept sinking in the pitch. Then he took him out and brought him along and they got home.

d. Now he always talked to his son, telling him what to do.[11] "Gather sweathouse wood: that is the way to try," he told him. So for ten nights he gathered sweathouse wood. Then downriver from Wohtek a little distance he lay down in the water. All night and all day he lay in the river, that boy, and no one saw him. For two days he lay in the water and nothing came. There were no birds. Now he had been lying there four days and a buzzard came.

4. The world is one of meteorological experiences and sensations.

5. The ridge of the roof, typically covered with a curving piece of old boat, often a gunwale.

6. *Tewolli* (Waterman, Geography, p. 194, *tegwoläw*).

7. *Wes'ona 'olego'*. [Given as *wes'ona oliken* in B5, n. 13.—Ed.]

8. *Kits-maegwoli*.

9. *Ola'po'-pa'a*, "pitch-water"? Waterman, p. 191, and fig. 1, has Kiolaapopa'a, a sea which is half-pitch, southwest across the ocean, south of Erkerger, where the woge dance. [This figure is reproduced here as map 3.—Ed.]

10. Spoke his formula.

11. Here begins the second half of this tale, which, like the first, has also been secured elsewhere (see T2 and B4).

e. And Raven[12] came too and said, "No, you must not. Alas!" (Raven) would not let the birds eat the boy's body. (A passage follows which is only partly audible, but it appears to contain a reference about ravens going to the sky.)

f. Now it was six days and the buzzards were gone and one Condor alit, just one. Now it was seven days, and eight days, and there were many condors. But that black one was there too, Raven, and said, "Do not eat him, for he is a person. No one must take out his eyes." And (Raven) began to talk to the boy. "He has ten of them, ten eye-gouging sticks.[13] You will feel it when he is close. When he uses his gouger the eye will almost come out of itself."

g. Then it was ten days (and the great Condor came with his gouging sticks, and Raven said to him), "Do not eat him right away, for he is a real man." And all the other birds had gone off (a little), and then Condor took out one of his gougers. But the boy never moved. Then he took out his second from his sack. It was a better one and covered with woodpecker crest,[14] but he laid it aside and took out a third, and a fourth. And Raven said to him, "Bring out another, a better one, for he is a real man." And he brought out his fifth, and his sixth, but Raven kept telling him to use a better one because it was a man lying there in the water, not a salmon.

And he took out his eighth, and his ninth; and at last he took out his tenth, and Raven (had) said, "When he takes that one out it will be as if your eyes were already being hurt before it touches you." So now the young man felt like that; as he was bringing it close, his eyes felt as if they were already starting out. Then he snatched the best gouger, the tenth one, and the birds, when they saw him get up, all flew up. But then there was a sound of something heavy falling on the ground: it was (the great) Condor lighting again, and walking on the ground alongside the river.

h. So the young man went back to the town, and Condor followed him. He went into the town and into the sweathouse and put the gouge under the floor at the place *mełku,*[15] and Condor came in after him and sat down on that place.

i. Then the young man went out after sweathouse wood and came back and made a fire. He made a large fire, but Condor kept sitting in the same place. That was one night.

12. Raven constitutes himself the youth's protector and adviser.

13. *Kyernerwern*. They must be conceived as short levers.

14. As so often, a precious substance. Among the Hupa, the *kihunai* (woge) have eyebrows of woodpecker crest.

15. *Mełku* is in the corner farthest from both entrance and exit. There is always a floor of smooth planks or stone slabs.

And it was two days, and still Condor sat at *mełku* and the boy made his fire, but Condor never went out and never spoke. Even though it was very hot, he did not speak. Then it was three days and four days, and he kept making his fire in the sweathouse and still Condor was sitting in the same spot. Every day he made his fire, and it was five days, and Condor was beginning to turn black. He was all of (scarlet) woodpecker crest before he came in, but he was turning black inside the sweathouse.[16]

Now it was six days and seven days and eight days, and still he sat there and it was hot.

And when it was eight days he began in the morning and had his fire, and then he thought, "I will have a fire at night too." And it was nine days, and he kept up his fire all night and all day.

j. Now it was ten days. Then Condor spoke, "It is too hot. I can do nothing. Give me back the stick you took from me, and come with me."

Then he gave him something to eat, but he took only a little. Now they were going. Condor said, "Get on my back." They were going to start from the entrance (*kwennet*);[17] there the young man got on his back; and he said to him, "You will feel everything as we go; you will feel rain and frost and cold and hot and snow and wind,[18] but do not open your eyes. Shut them and do not look around.

Then he started, that Condor. Ten times he circled downriver across from Wohtek, and then went across the ridge going oceanward.[19]

And the young man felt as if he were going through the air. He did not look but could feel it. He felt rain and snow. Then it felt as if he were going differently, as if he were coming down; all the way he felt it.

k. Then Condor lit on the ground. Then it was that he said, "Now you may look around." So the young man looked about and saw that it was a good place. Condor said to him, "Sit here, for I am going again. I am going to Pulukuk."[20] So he flew off to the other side of the sky, past where the sky comes down.[21] And the young man saw him going. He thought, "Perhaps he will leave me here and not come back." So he sat there waiting. Then he saw him coming back.

16. There is no smoke hole in the sweathouse. The exit, which is also a ventilator, is close to the floor. The entrance is 3 or 4 feet above the floor but is usually kept closed while the fire is burning. The soot hangs from the roof boards like a continuous beard. The inmates do not turn black because indoors they sweat, and when they emerge, they wash or bathe.

17. It is really the paved platform before the entrance, where men often sit and lounge, especially in the sun.

18. As before, n. 4.

19. *Tewolli*, as in n. 6.

20. The downstream end of the world across the ocean, more often heard as Pulekuk.

21. *Wes'ona 'olego'*, as in n. 7.

And when he reached him, Condor put into his hand just one woodpecker crest and one *wetskāk* small dentalium. And he said to him, "Now don't let it out of your hand; hold it fast. I am going to start again, and do not look around."

l. So the young man climbed on his back again and Condor rose, and he felt everything as before and then he felt him descending. And it rained and snowed and they went a long way.

m. And so they came back to Wohtek, and Condor said to him, "Now, put those things inside your *pahtekus* basket.[22] Do not look at them at once; look at them after five days." Now he had two of those baskets and he told them to make him ten all told.

Now it was five days and he looked at his baskets, and he saw that right up to the top they were full of what he had brought, woodpecker crests and dentalia too. And so he kept doing.

22. Or *pohtekus*. See Kroeber, Basket Designs of the Indians of Northwestern California, UC-PAAE 2: (no. 4), 107, 1905, which describes the *paaxtekwc* as a large acorn and food storage basket, up to three feet wide and high, constricting from base to opening; a similarly shaped basket, but much smaller, of size to be taken up in one hand, for tobacco or small objects, is there given as *perxtsekuc* (*perhtsekus*). Ten of these filled would make a man very wealthy, but the Yurok like to dwell on incalculable wealth. Indeed, the names may be the same, except for a diminutive *-ts-*, which might have been misheard.

INFORMANT N

AMITS OF KEPEL

This old man, who had been assistant to the lo' *or formulist for the Kepel fish dam, and who gave Waterman and me much information on that ceremony,*[1] *was born in Kepel, he told me, and had always lived there or in the adjoining town of Sa', where his house stood in 1906. His fishing place was at the foot of Sa'. I recorded his name as Umits, but Robert Spott gives it as A'mmīts, and confirms that he belonged in Kepel. He was brother of Hawley, Harry, and Charlie of that town; his wife was from Meta.*

He was of the same family as the old man of Kepel who was mīkisotok opyur, *which means that he owned enough treasures to provide his own dance and at the same time send an outfit to someone else. Originally, Amits's people lived in the same house as this old man, but later the family grew and an adjoining house was built at the end of the row. It was this house that Amits belonged to.*

Amits was a willing and rather clear informant, but only one myth was formally obtained from him, and he proved to be a mediocre narrator.

N1. STRONG FROM THE THUNDERS

This is probably one tale, but the last part (*h-i*) was obtained first, and then the first (*a-g*), as if it were a story about another man. It is one of the stock tales of the Yurok, with the hero usually attributed to one's home town, but the villain almost always to Ɫemekweɫ, which was either never inhabited or was abandoned before memory. The story is rendered undramatically, with several vivid or emotional incidents omitted: the throwing of gravel, the parents' shock at the youth's return, the discomfiture of the oppressor, the terms extracted from him. [See A13 and G6 for other versions.—Ed.]

•

1. Waterman and Kroeber, The Kepel Fish Dam, UC-PAAE, 35: (no. 6): 49-80, 1938; see esp. pp. 62-67.

a. He grew up at Kepel. They did not like him, and many abused him. Always he cried for that when he gathered sweathouse wood.

b. Now he was making fire in the sweathouse when he looked across-river to Tepola Creek[1] and saw a young deer there. He ran to the house, got his arrows and bow, and went to cross. On the other side, he saw it up the hill. He went up, shot, it fell. But when he came to it, it got up again and ran uphill. He followed. Nearly at the top, it fell again. Now he thought he would catch it, but when he came close, it again ran on up. Then he came to the top of the ridge, to the prairie Se'somen,[2] still following it. Here the deer turned upriver, but it was only a little way when the young man saw a lake. As soon as he saw it, it was as if he had lost his senses, he was so frightened.

c. The lake looked very white, and the deer entered it. The man followed, and inside the lake he saw a house. An old woman said, "Come in!" He entered. "My sons saw you," she said. "They have seen you when all the people were hurting you, and they pitied you. Stop and wait for them. I have ten of them. Each goes to visit a kind of fun. The oldest has gone to a settlement for killing; others to gambling and the Brush Dance. They will come home before dark."

A mountain lion lay on the house at one end, a grizzly bear at the other.

d. Now he heard a crash, and the house shook. "My sons are coming," the old woman said, and hid him, because he was scared. One entered. "Come in easily," she said, "because he has arrived whom you always speak of and want to see. He is here." Then that one felt him over. And another come in, and another.[3] When the oldest brother arrived, the house nearly tipped over, and the two lying on the roof roared so it could be heard far off. Peeping out of a small hole, he saw a person's legs stretching out of that one's quiver; and they had made the fire large. "Where is he?" shouted the oldest. "Here."

e. So he took him and threw him into the fire, though he cried out in fear: that is how they made him strong. Then they took their stone fighting clubs,[4] struck him with them, but could not injure him. They pulled his legs apart, and did not hurt him. He was right, and they were ready to tell him to go home. "When you see a large crotched black oak, jump between the forks." Then they sent him away.

f. He came out on Se'somen prairie. He saw the black oak, leaped between the limbs, and split it apart. Then he went back to Kepel, because his

1. [Waterman, Geography, map 17, no. 50, shows Tepolau weroi, or Kepel Creek. This map is reproduced here as map 5.—Ed.]

2. Not given by Waterman. He does give Łokoł-u-pa'a, Thunder's water (map 17, no. 62), for a small lake uphill and upstream from Kepel about 2 miles, but on the same side of the river, whereas Se'somen is opposite.

3. With repetition to nine.

4. *Kaweya* or *kawaya*.

mother and father lived there. He saw the old woman: her hair was cut short, and the old man's too, because he had been gone ten days, and they thought he had died somewhere.

g. The young men at once went to bullying him again: they did not know he had been in the lake. Then he became angry. He seized one and began to pull him apart. The rest ran off; that one cried, "Stop! I will not rough you again." Now all were afraid of him, when they discovered that he had been to the lake. He made many slaves;[5] all left him alone.

The lake is still there, but invisible. A man who has been gathering sweathouse wood (ceremonially) for ten days might see it, but he must think of the lake daily as he climbs the hill. If anyone tries to injure a person who has been in that lake, Thunder is heard running (rolling).

h. (He had grown up at Kepel.[6]) Now the vicious one of Ɫemekweɫ[7] came upstream to here and took away his wife and his slaves. Then he was angry and prepared himself.

i. When the vicious one came upriver again, with many boats, the one of Kepel was lying in the shade on the sandbar in front of the town. (As they poled by), the vicious one pushed his paddle against the old man's anus and said, "He used to be a fighter, this person." Then he of Kepel leaped up and on him, seized his legs, and pulled. "Stop!" that one cried, but he pulled more, began to tear him apart. Now that one said, "Do not hurt me! I will be your partner!" The old man said, "I can still do it; I am not yet too old." If he had continued pulling his legs apart, he would have split him to the neck. So he pulled all the boats ashore, took back his wife, and the wife of the vicious one of Ɫemekweɫ, and his own and the other's slaves.[8] The one of Ɫemekweɫ, went back downstream alone.

5. Generosity is scarcely a characteristic trait. Once he has the power, he treats others as they treated him.

6. This episode was obtained first, as if it were a story in itself; hence the conventional beginning.

7. Waterman, map 10, no. 13. [It is a small flat about 3 miles downstream from the mouth of Blue Creek. But in a marginal note, K. queries whether the location should be Kepel bar.—Ed.]

8. This is the third time slaves are mentioned in the tale. Slaves by war or violence are a stock part of this story (see Spott and Kroeber, Yurok Narratives, no. 25, pp. 227-32), although the Yurok say that they had only debt slaves.

INFORMANT O

LONG CHARLIE OF MŪREK

Charlie of Mūrek was a tall man, whence his nickname, Long Charlie. He wore his hair long, that is, trimmed at the shoulder. He died a very old man.

He was from the house răk in Mūrek, and hence he was called Răk-hiwoi. His father had only him and a daughter, who was called Rằks umä'. Her father would not let her go, and so she was half-married to Abe of Sregon. After that she was known as Rằks onohpuyo, and Abe as Rằk-es.

Charlie himself married a woman of Kepel and had a son and a daughter. Later he had a long illegitimate relation with a woman called Hi'n-olō from the house hi'nkelol in his home town of Mūrek. She had previously had a half-breed child. Finally Charlie got to living in her house. Inasmuch as both of them were of good family and wealthy, this arrangement caused considerable scandal. Once at least he was snubbed in public, but made no answer. His mistress' older sister was the wife of Kerner, head of the wealthiest family in Pekwon.

After Hi'n-olō began living openly with Charlie, this older sister—they had no brother—came and took the family heirlooms out of her house, saying, "You are nothing now. Anyone might take them away from you." When the older sister died, Kerner did not return the treasures, although they were no property of his. Charlie claimed them for his mistress, and a meeting or court was held over the matter. Kerner at once said, "She is not your wife, and you have nothing to say." Thereupon Charlie subsided, but the woman claimed them in her own name. Kerner answered that he was holding them as a pledge for gravedigging and burial which he had done for her relatives and for which he had never been paid. He proceeded to name the occasions; but she did not want to hear her dead kin mentioned in public, and said that Kerner could keep the objects. So the family wealth passed over into another family, because she had put herself into a shameful position and could not press her undoubted ownership.

Charlie was a skillful mounter and maker of woodpecker bands and therefore was often called Răk eskerwits, the expert at răk. He was probably a tsăro (a worker on the Kepel dam), but he was not a singer.

His wealth consisted of four engraved dentalium-bead necklaces and four plain ones; four woodpecker bands, one of which he had made for himself, the three others being inherited from his parents; many deerskin blankets; four dance aprons of marten fur; four of the tandem eagle-feather headdresses called telegei*; one red obsidian; one gray deerskin; eight or nine common deerskins of ordinary color; and fifteen or twenty elkhorn spoons.*

O1. Wohpekumeu

a. He was living at Kenek, Wohpekumeu was, that is where he was living. There it was that no one liked him.* Then they caused snow (to lie), because they disliked him:* they made it to be so. He desired women: because he desired them he was living there, and on that account they all disliked him. He went about (seducing) too much: that is why they caused snow (to lie) where he lived.[1] That was the only place in which there was snow: only to a short distance from where he lived, to Hegolok,[2] only to there was there snow. So he never went about. He only went just outdoors: only when he went to get sweathouse wood did he leave the sweathouse. And as he lay inside he did not know why it snowed so long: he thought it should be summer, but did not know what season it was.

b. And once he had got sweathouse wood and looked through the exit hole,[3] and he saw a *tso'tsis* bird sitting outside the exit, and saw that it carried berries. And he said, "Oh, it is becoming summer," for he saw those berries. And so he did that, Wohpekumeu: the next day he made himself snowshoes. That is why they know how to make snowshoes (now), because he made them. And he thought he would go to Wahsek;[4] he thought he would go there because it had become summer.

*The preceding clause is repeated in the original.

1. Wohpekumeu and the other inhabitants of Kenek are often represented as unfriendly to each other or at least holding aloof; his house was a little downstream from theirs. Cf. Waterman, Geography, map 22, no. 7.

2. "Upstream from Merip, 2 to 3 miles downstream from Kenek, on the north side of the river." Waterman, map 17, no. 99, Ego'olokw, "rock on the hillside." [This map is reproduced here as map 5.—Ed.]

3. *Lekwuso*.

4. Wahsek is a scant mile upstream from Kenek, on the opposite side. Why he should first go down to Hegolok on his way up to Wahsek is not clear, except that is as far as the snow lay.

So he crossed the river at Kenek, and put on his snowshoes and walked uphill over the top of the snow, even though it was deep. Then he came to Hegolok,* and saw that it seemed as if it would be a fine day: so it seemed. He went a little farther and saw that the day was fine. Then it was that he thought, "They all hate me: they have made it snow where I was." And he looked about and saw that the snow reached only a little way from Kenek: elsewhere it was only a little foggy. Then he came to Wahsek and wished to go on upstream. He did not want to stay long in one place; for no one liked him where he lived.

c. Then he had a child at Petskuk.[5] That is where he had his child, a boy; and he grew large.[6] That is why they make medicine for childbirth. They have medicine for that because he made it. They were going to cut open their bellies; that is how it was to be: the woman would be killed and only the child would live. So it was to be, at that time. And he is one who made it as it is, because he saw a woman then, and desired her, and stayed there long. There he stayed, for where he saw women he would stay.

Now she was pregnant (from him), this woman: he had gone to get sweathouse wood and the woman to get firewood, going out at the same time.[7] Now his fire had died down in the sweathouse. Then they said, "Come into the house." The woman was lying indoors, she who had gone to bring firewood: she was about to have a child. She had five brothers, this woman. And they were about to cut her open as the only way for the child in her to be born: so they were about to do.

d. And he sat there and said, "Well, I should like to do something: let me go out"; for whatever he thought of he got: that is how he was, what he thought of he got. So he said, "Let me go out to find my medicine herb." But they said, "No, you cannot go. You might run off." Then, from where he sat, he looked around. But the woman had begun to cry. Then he thought, "I wish I had medicine," and reached out, and felt that there was something in his hand: *sahsi'p*.[8] Then he made his medicine with sahsi'p: he merely turned himself around to speak (the formula) to the herb. And he finished speaking and making medicine with the herb sahsi'p, and gave it to the woman, this sahsi'p. He said, "Put it into her mouth and throat." And she gagged. Then he said, "Rub it on her, over all her body." And she lay there as before, very sick.

5. The upstream end of the world.

6. This paragraph is not so much narrative as anticipatory explanation of the results of the narrative which is to follow.

7. His device to seduce her, which is known from several other versions, is passed over here [See L1*n-o*, for example.—Ed.]

8. Probably Ceanothus sp., buck brush. The Yurok sometimes call it wild honeysuckle in English.

Then he got another medicine: madrone.[9] He got the sahsi'p and the madrone in the same manner, for whatever he wished he got thus. And the woman lay there. Then he said, "Where is your pack strap?[10] They said, "Right by the door." So he tied the strap halfway up the house: there he tied it. Ten times he drew his hand down it, ten times along the pack strap. Then he said, "She will be well," and she became well, and bore a boy: so she recovered because of the medicine. That is why they use such medicine now: human beings make it so because he made it then: that is how he did. Then he bathed the baby ten times in one night, because it would grow fast if it was bathed so often. And while it was still very little it walked.

e. And Wohpekumeu stayed there, and the boy was grown up. Then he wished to take him away with him. They said, "No, we shall not let you take him." But he insisted, and they let him take him. So he returned downstream with him, and arrived at Kenek. The son lived alone in the house, and he himself in the sweathouse. Now he did not like to see his son living alone: he wished him to be married. So he got him a wife, and his son lived with her in the house, and had a child. The old man stayed in the sweathouse constantly, but his son had a son now, the old man's grandson. That is how he lived at Kenek, (this) Wohpekumeu.

f. Then once he came into the house and said, "He should have birds for pets, the little boy. I have seen them on a tree, young chicken hawks:[11] you had better go and get them." And (his son) thought, "I will go after them." So he climbed up the tree. When he was far up, the wind began to blow: the old man made it so in his sweathouse. The wind blew ten days. All the limbs were blown away: the limbs on which his feet rested broke off, and those under his hands also. At last the wind stopped. And he cried and felt badly, because he had nearly been killed, and came down:[12] he had been ten days on the tree. He went toward his house.

g. Near the town he saw a boy going about. He saw he had bow and arrows and was shooting at birds. Whenever he shot he held out his hand. And he thought, "It looks as though he were blind": so he appeared to him. He went close and thought, "He looks like my son!" Now (the boy) had small woodpecker crests, many of them. When he heard a woodpecker cry on a tree, he shot, for he said he wanted it thus; and held out his hand, and (the bird) fell into it when he shot it. As it was with Wohpekumeu—what he thought of he

9. Ashes are substituted in some versions.

10. *Weskul*, the strap, usually of elkskin, by which a carrying basket or load of wood is slung from the head. His drawing his hand along it is imitative magic.

11. *Tspegi* or *spegis*.

12. Apparently unassisted or without special device, just climbing down the tree he had been hugging.

got—so it was with (that boy). Then he knew that it was his son, when he saw him there; but he was blind. And he sat down there where he saw him: he was feeling badly and sat down right where he saw him, and spoke to him, and said, "Let us go home." So it was. Then they sat at Kenek-woneu,[13] and he began to cry on account of his boy. Then he saw that a little spring had come into existence where they were sitting. So he washed his boy's face with it, and the boy became well and could see again.

h. Then he did not wish to go home with him, but said, "Let us go off." He did not wish to live in his house any longer. So they went uphill to Women.[14] There they spent the night. And next morning he took away everything from that place,[15] all that people used: he did not wish to see them have their property. It was in the morning, and they put *tserwerner*[16] and *rego'*[17] on their heads. And his name was Kewomer: he went to Petskuk,[18] that boy; and the man went to Pulekuk,[19] he whose name was Kapuloyo. That is how he went off, the boy; he went upstream, and took away all valuables:[20] he secured them all. And while he went upstream, (Kapuloyo) did the same (downstream); he took every valuable and all money.

i. And he carried all that he secured on the hill above Rekwoi: from there he was about to start out (again). Then he heard as if it were a great piece of money calling: that is how it sounded to him (as if it came) from upstream (south?) of Wełkwäu.[21] So he held out his hand behind him to take it. Then he found out that it was he.[22] It is thus on the hill above Rekwoi: they look pretty, the hillocks there, because they are his (Kapuloyo's) baskets for carrying away the money from the world. That is how he started to leave at that time. And he followed him (to here), and went on (wrongly), that old man Wohpekumeu, and went south along the coast.[23]

j. He (had been) living there:[24] there he was living, Wohpekumeu, at Sa'. Then he sang there:

13. "Uphill from Kenek," but perhaps the name of a specific spot.

14. Waterman, p. 260, describes Women as a "great open space on mountain back of Kewet," which would put it across the river. I recorded it elsewhere as a prairie on the ridge more or less behind Kenek. [Cf. notes for A12, A14, and T4.—Ed.]

15. Kenek, presumably.

16. A network headdress falling down the nape and back.

17. Long upright feathers—or woodpecker-covered sinew rods—worn at the occiput.

18. The upstream end of the world.

19. The downstream end.

20. *Kinumiłtu*.

21. Welkwäu-hipets, probably a specific spot.

22. Wohpekumeu. This and the next three sentences summarize sketchily the episode of Wohpekumeu's recovery of part of the world's treasures from his fugitive son.

23. *Tewilli werok*.

24. The narrator goes back in his story. A new phonograph record began here; perhaps he had been waiting for a clear blank that would take up his song unbroken.

Nikoneu kitholemo, I see people coming
kitkegoyawo, standing in a crowd
nis ayukwi, alas! I am sorry!
nikonuwok, I see
ketwolemeko, people coming
kisonini tyu'womaitl, as in a narrow place
tusonini kegoyawo, as if standing in a crowd*[25]
ketwolemeko, people coming
osa' hierki, to the rear of Sa'
kinumi megarhkwini mełnegokwomei, they come from
everywhere and bring here
we'ik'i horeu, their valuables*[26]
nis ayukwi, alas! I am sorry!
osa' hierki, to the rear of Sa'
nikonuwok, I see
ketwolemeko, people coming
osa' hierki, to the rear of Sa'
puleku osomiahłkepek, downstream I shall go*
ketnegunoyołkeik, not to return*
weławitsi kwermłeyer, ten times I look back
sonini sku' woksimek, as it is I like it*
nek negonenek, I who made it*
ha!*[27]

k. So it was with Wohpekumeu at the time he was about to go off from the world. His son had gone to Pulekuk, and the other to Petskuk. And the place called Erkerger was where his son always came. That was where they met: he who went to Petskuk and he also who went to Pulekuk came there. They called it thus; human beings do not know the place, but they named it so: Erkerger.[28] That is where dancing never stops. And Wohpekumeu arrives there too: that is where he always finds them, because he himself has gone there. But he cannot see his children well[29] and begins to cry, that old man,

25. This and the preceding two lines are repeated.

26. This and the preceding line are repeated; also the sixth and seventh lines beyond.

27. The final three lines are repeated. The song refers to the ceremonies connected with the fish weir at Kepel-Sa'. Although its connection with the plot is of the loosest, it led the narrator to name his tale as one about Wohpekumeu and the Kepel fish weir.

28. Erkerger is given as Wohpekumeu's country in Waterman, fig. 1. [This figure is reproduced here as map 3.—Ed.]

29. His son and grandson. He was half-blinded by the salt water when Skate carried him across the ocean—an episode omitted here.

sitting in the wood alcove:[30] that is where he always sits. Then the old man says to them to make the fire large so that he may see his children, for (otherwise) he sees them (only) in fog, so that he cannot distinguish them. Thus it is that Wohpekumeu lives there.

30. ***Re'roneu***, the alcove inside the front of the Yurok house, loosely partitioned off from the remainder of the structure and used as a woodshed. The old man dares not enter farther and probably peeps longingly through the chinks of the wall at his fog-wreathed progeny and their companions. As they are indoors, it would be the Jumping Dance they are performing.

INFORMANT P

JACK OF MŪREK

Mūrek Jack must have come from the house ple'ł in Mūrek,[1] *because he was known as K'e-ple'ł. His family was one of Indian women doctors. The famous doctor of Mūrek of a couple of generations ago was from the house erkeritser, which stands next to ple'ł and is related to it. Jack's wife was also a doctor. The status of his house is shown by the fact that at the Pekwon dance Mūrek had two cooking and feeding places, one for ple'ł and the other for Charlie's house, răk.*

Jack owned a white deerskin, a gray deerskin, a number of common deerskins, four silver-gray foxskins, about seven dance aprons of marten skin, four woodpecker bands of excellent quality and three not so good, two long red obsidians four fingers wide, and many deerskin blankets. When he came upriver, he contributed these objects to the dance which Pekwtuł made at Weitspus.

P1. WOHPEKUMEU'S EMERGENCE

The informant professed to know the story of Wohpekumeu's origin, who he declared was not born but grew from the ground. Inasmuch as the Yurok with all their talk about Wohpekumeu rarely tell much about his beginning, but the Hupa have him grow out of the ground at Kenek, I wished to record the tale. Opportunity was lacking at the time; Waterman was able to secure the story subsequently on phonograph cylinders. It proved to contain two episodes: Wohpekumeu's origin, and his producing the first childbirth, the latter a formula in substance if not in form.

The text was translated phrase by phrase by Mrs. Catherine Goodwin from seven phonograph records dictated for Waterman by the informant.

•

1. Waterman, Geography, map 18, no. 1.

a. This is what he did, (this) Wohpekumeu.[1] He heard them, heard them from underground, when they first began to exist, those that were not human beings; for they were not human beings that lived then. And Wohpekumeu wanted it so—for they were not human that lived then—"Why cannot we go out on the earth?" he said to Mole,[2] as Mole and he were talking together. For he was about and could hear everything that they said, those that were not human beings. So he said, "Let us go out on the earth: let others come into existence." And he said (again), "Go first, Mole!" And (Mole) said, "No, I am afraid. I have heard stones breaking, and have heard them say, 'I will cut his navel off.'" That is why he[3] did not want to go, (that) Mole. Then Wohpekumeu said to him, "I hope that if you ever go on earth you will die." And Wohpekumeu pulled off his own navel (string)[4] and went out on earth.[5] And they said, "See his head sticking out!" And they took hold of him and he was a person, a little boy. And so Wohpekumeu was on earth.

b. Every day he kept growing larger. "What shall I do?" thought Wohpekumeu, "What shall I do?" He had nothing to cover himself with when he slept. "I wish I had a blanket to put over me." Then at once they saw him have a blanket, (this) Wohpekumeu, and he slept with the blanket over him. So he got along thus: whatever he wished for he used to get.* So he was here, (was) Wohpekumeu, he was here. And he thought, "What shall I do?" Whatever he wished for he was getting.

Then he thought, "I want a place to live. I want a house." That is why it is called "house," because Wohpekumeu said, "I should like a house." Then he saw a house as he was there, and went indoors, into the house. So he had a house. Then suddenly he thought in himself, "I am hungry."* That is why it is called "I am hungry," because that is what Wohpekumeu thought in himself. Then he saw food there and took it, and so customarily it was with him like that: whatever he thought of he got: thus he existed and possessed whatever (he wanted).

He had his house. There were many about there, but he lived off by

*Asterisks denote that the preceding clause is repeated bodily in the text.

1. Almost every time the name Wohpekumeu is used in this tale, it comes not only at the end of the clause or sentence, but after a perceptible pause. There is a very strong impression given of the name being expletive, as if the speaker threw it in to fill the gap while he was thinking of what came next, but omitted it when his narration flowed smoothly. This is in line with the general style of Yurok storytelling: nouns are left out if the hearer's imagination might at all supply them, or are strewn in from time to time rather randomly; whereas the verb clusters, including conjunctions, adverbs, and the like, are often baldly repeated. See notes 16 and 17 as examples.

2. *Ɫkelikera*.

3. The Mole is Wohpekumeu's sister, according to F3. There is nothing in the Yurok to show whether the English pronoun here should be "he" or "she."

4. This obviously has reference to birth—"selfbirth," it might be styled.

5. This was at Kenek, to judge from other statements, and as implied by later passages in the present tale.

himself, did Wohpekumeu, he lived by himself in his house. He did not go into the houses of those that lived there (but) lived by himself, for he did not much like them and thought differently from them. He did not do as they did who lived there (but) did as he himself wished. Thus he did.* He thought, "I have made it all as I want to live." He had made (himself) everything. He had made a sweathouse: he had thought, "Well, I want a sweathouse," and then saw a sweathouse standing there. He would go into his house and look about and think of something more, and it would be there as he wanted it for (his way of) living. And he became so that he liked living there: he said, "Well, I have everything as I want it now."

c. Then he thought, "Now I wish human beings to live"· thus he did, (this) Wohpekumeu, (after) he had made everything that he wanted for his own existence. So he began to travel about to see how the others lived who lived then, (these who would be) animals. And he thought, "Let another kind live! Let human beings live!" He called them "persons":[6] "Let persons live!" He did not like those who were in existence then and thought, "Let another (kind of) people live." So then human beings began to be alive, and he provided everything for them and brought it about that the others would leave, those animals.[7] Thus he began to travel about because he wished persons to live.

d. Then at Merip there were two girls.* He used to travel to Merip and go about there, but he never could see the girls. He began to wonder, "How can I obtain those girls?"* Then, upstream from Merip, he made an elk, for he wished that, (did) Wohpekumeu. He thought, "I will have the elk swim downstream and pursue it in a boat." So he caused the elk to be in the river, and had ten dogs, and told them to follow the edge of the stream, he told the dogs. Now the elk had gone into the river,* and swam downstream, and he told the dogs to run downstrem along the edge, told them to howl and bark that people would hear them. And then he shouted. "There is an elk in the river!"*

And the people looked and saw the dogs running by the river—ten dogs. Then they (too) shouted, "There is an elk in the river!"* and pursued and caught it and dragged it on shore: and the dogs had arrived there.

e. And looking uphill, they[8] saw someone[9] come in sight.*[10] He stood above them (as) they skinned the elk. And Wohpekumeu looked across the river and saw the two girls opposite, both standing watching them skin the elk.

6. *Olekwoyoł*.

7. Three or four sentences of repetition occur in the text here, evidently because the narrator was talking against time while regathering his thread after a change of phonograph cylinder. Ordinarily he and other narrators have their continuity but little disturbed by such periodic interruptions.

8. For a number of sentences following, Mrs. Goodwin's translation has "he" more often than "they," but the person or persons who killed and skinned and butchered the elk seem to be referred to.

9. Wohpekumeu, whom they did not know.

10. "It (?) was running on the other side of him (?)" the translation adds here.

He was looking from across the river and they saw him looking on, standing above where they were skinning the elk. And they said, "Look, look at him standing over there! How nicely dressed he is! I wonder where he came from?"

Now they had skinned the elk and piled it up, and looked up and saw the one standing above them move, saw him move. And he came down to where the elk (meat) was piled, and took a shoulder, and began to cut it up and began to feed his dogs. He gave each dog a piece of meat.* Then he said to the people, "Just help yourselves to the meat"* and started upstream, calling to his dogs and whistling to them. And they saw him go up the hill, saw Wohpekumeu go up the hill, and watched him going and said "*O'ko!* I wonder who he is? How many dogs he has!" He left the girls standing on the opposite side and looked at them from up on the hill, looked at them standing there, the girls that he had not been able to encounter outdoors.[11] So he ran on up the hill, calling his dogs and whistling to them, and then ran on upstream and arrived at Kenek. He straightaway went into (his) sweathouse at Kenek.

f. So he was in the sweathouse, and the people at Merip went up to the house,* after they had finished skinning the elk. They saw the girls had disappeared from where they had been standing and had gone indoors. Then they saw the girls lying there: one was lying on one side of the house, the other on the other side. And they said, "*Yaha*, what is the matter? What has happened to you?" And they said, "Oh, we are feeling so badly! Look at us! See how we look! I think we shall die." Thus they spoke. "It must be he, the man we saw across the river. Let them go after him! We feel as if we were about to give birth."

So the people ran upstream and found him sitting right by his sweathouse, (this) Wohpekumeu. Then they said to him, "Come with us! Those girls are about to die, and we think you have brought it about." He said, "No." And they said, "You must come! If you do not come you too shall die." Then they took him along: they made him walk between them, (this) Wohpekumeu, after they had seized him at Kenek.

So Wohpekumeu came with them,* and they went downstream to Merip into the house at Merip.

g. He put his head in at the door, and saw one girl lying on one side of the house and the other on the other. Then he came inside, and they said, "What shall you do? How will the child be born? How will what is in them be born? For it is a child, for they are pregnant." They said, "You are the one who caused it." And they said they would cut them open, cut them open just where the baby was. "We shall cut them open and save the babies." And they

11. The original adds the repetition: "He watched them from up on the hill, Wohpekumeu (did), those girls standing on the opposite side of the river."

told him that they would kill him too. "We shall kill you too." But he said, "No." "No," said Wohpekumeu, "He'e'e'e![12] How will people live?[13] Go toward the door!"[14] And they said, "No, you cannot do anything. We shall have to kill the girls: we shall have to cut them open." And he said, "No! Go toward the door." And they took him toward the door.

And he began to speak[15] by the door. And he said, "Take it[16] into the house!" So they took it into the house and began to rub her belly;[17] and they rubbed the belly of the girl who was on the other side of the house. Then they said, "It is coming!" So Wohpekumeu caused his own child(ren) to be born.

After the baby was born, he said, "This is the way children shall be born. For I wish human beings to live." And they prepared two basket cradles. And he said (again), "This is how human beings shall live, because I wish human beings to live this way. For people will not live if you try to do as (you have been) doing, if you cut women open."

P2. Invention of Firemaking

a. In the beginning, when it was summer and the sun was hot, people carried what they wanted to cook out on the rocks; but it took a long time to cook in this way, and they found that when the sun was down, nothing would cook.

b. So they wanted something better. They thought, "We will try to make fire from young cedar roots." Then they made the woman (the fire drill hearth) of this. The man (the drill) they made of Xerophyllum stalk.[1] So they tried it with these; but it was a long time before they caught fire.

c. Then they tried willow roots, and found that these were good. The drill from the root taken in some spots had to be turned only three or four times, and fire started. Then they were satisfied.

12. The invocation of many formulas begins with this ejaculation.
13. If they kill women to have children.
14. Either that he might go with them to make his medicine, or that the girls might deliver in seclusion.
15. Recite the formula of his medicine.
16. The medicine proper, the material substance, usually a part of a plant, but in this case ashes, to judge from some other versions of the episode. Being confined indoors by his captors, he had nothing he could use but ashes from the hearth. This sentence is an illustration of the Yurok style of allowing the hearer to guess the thing talked about while satisfying him by a recital of the action.
17. With the medicine.

---

1. *X. tenax*, squawgrass, shiny-white overlay in basket weft.

P3. Origin of Blood-Money Settlement

Thunder's boy was killed. That is how it came about that those who are killed get paid for. When his son was killed, Thunder took settlement. He said, "I want you all, when your relative is killed, and they come to pay for him, to take those dentalia. That is why I am going to accept it now: I want it to be offered to all of you. When they have paid you, hide the money somewhere. Sometimes, when you want to see your dentalia, and go to look at them, you will feel sorry, because you will remember your poor kinsman who was killed."

P4. Makers of Treasure, Sky, and Death

a. Five brothers made the sky. They also made death, and they made dentalia and woodpecker crests and bows and arrows and everything that people would need. While they were making them they said, "We make all these, dentalia, woodpecker crests, and arrows, because if people have them they will think much of them and will feel satisfied. They will not want to be quarrelsome, for they have property. They will behave well if they have dentalia and arrows and things. They will not want to kill, for they will think so much of what they have, of their dentalia and other things, that they will not want to pay them out in settlement."

b. And they made the sky because men would feel good if they looked up into the air when it clears up. Some days it is fine, and people feel good on account of it. They did not want people to be quarrelsome, but good. They said, "Sometimes bad men will grow somewhere; perhaps one man in a town; but he will not be alive long; he will die soon. But if a man is wise and has his property and thinks of it and likes it, he will want to live."

c. Now these five brothers went off. The first went to Pulekuk, where he has his house at Dentalium Home.[1] The next went to Kewet, Rivet Mountain behind Weitspus. The third, to Otsepor, Bluff Creek. The fourth to Olege'l, Camp Creek near Orleans. The last went to Segwu', Katimin, just above the mouth of Salmon River.

d. There were many at Kenek. They were talking about death. Some wanted people to live always; but Wertspit[2] said, "No, there will be too many." Then they said, "Well, yes." Then he who had his house at Dentalium Home said, "Let them become old and then young once more and then die." And (it seemed) they agreed to make it thus: when a man was very old he was to be carried off into the woods, then come home young again. But

1. Tsīktsīko'ł, at the downriver end of the world in the north, Pulekuk.
2. The Jerusalem cricket.

Wertspit said, "No. I have lost my children. They are dead. Let them all die." So they said, "Well, let it be," angrily. The one who was the first to leave, and was angriest, was he who went to Dentalium Home. He said, "When people die, let them call my name."[3]

P5. Deer and Dog

a. Deer grew at the upriver end of the world.[1] There there was a house, and all came in. One[2] had made bows and set them up, against the walls all around. The best were in the middle (of the wall circuit, opposite the door). By each side of the door was a thick bow, not flattened; its string was made of a piece of fringe from a woman's deerskin dress.[3] All kinds of persons came in, Mountain Lion, Wolf, and others.

That night they slept there in the house,[4] with their feet toward the fire. Deer slept on the left side of the fire (as one enters), Dog opposite. Deer said, "It will be hard to catch and kill me." He who had made the bows said, "Well, they will kill you with these bows. That is why I made them." "That is well; but nevertheless it will be hard to catch me. I know that this Dog will not eat my flesh." Dog said, "Yes, I think sometimes I shall catch you."

b. Coyotes, two of them, were on each side of the house,[5] next the door. They took sharp sticks and set them up where they lay, the points under their heads, like pillows. They wanted the best bows and thought that thus they would (not sleep and would) get up first and take the best. That is why they set up the sharpened sticks, for they thought if they went to sleep the points would wake them.

c. Now they all slept, for he who wanted them to kill deer sang them to sleep. But Dog did not sleep. When he saw Deer asleep, with his feet on the fireplace stones, he put a stick into the fire, then laid it against Deer's feet and

3. To help them in the purification. Often the spirit called last in the formula is in the rock Oregos at the mouth of the Klamath, instead of the spirit at the downriver end of the world, as here.

---

1. Petskuk. When connected with the giant bird on Shelton Butte, this story, or parts of it, are usually located near the butte, on the Yurok–Karok border. Cf. A8, A12, C5, G2, Q2, and Z2.

2. Wohpekumeu, the narrator said afterwards when asked. It may have been a fall-back answer; the Yurok perhaps do not put the question, ordinarily.

3. The bow was unworked, the string such as a baby hero's magical toy might have.

4. Not usual for males, who customarily sleep in the sweathouse; but the occasion was unusual and a test.

5. Why two is not clear.

burned them. Deer in his sleep drew up his feet and shook them a little. Then Dog burned him more. After that he went to sleep.

d. Eagle got up first and selected the best bow; then Mountain Lion, then Wolf.[6] Then all the others awoke and took bows; but the first three took the three best. Coyotes had thought that they would take the best, but those who got up saw that the sticks has passed through their heads as they went on sleeping. Dog was lying there; Deer had already jumped outside. When Coyotes awoke, they thought, "Well, so let us take the bows with apron-fringe string." So they took those.

e. Dog came out of the house last of all. He saw the two Coyotes outside: they were the only ones still about. Then he scented until he found Deer's tracks. So he followed. That is why he had burned his feet: he thought he would smell the trail. Soon he came to a lake. Deer had jumped into the lake and swum across; nevertheless the dog found his trail. Then Deer knew that Dog was pursuing him. He ran around the world to the end, then upriver again, then up into the sky. He thought Dog would not follow him there. But then he saw Dog coming. He ran across the sky, Dog still following. Deer constantly ran fast, but Dog went slowly. Then at last Deer thought, "I cannot run any more. I do not think he will let up. I might as well wait for him." So he sat down.

f. Then as Dog come up, Deer was crying. He said, "I am sorry you will eat my flesh, for I know you will be careless. I think you will go to a menstruating woman's food and eat that too,[7] so I will not like to see you eat my flesh." Dog said, "I know it: that is why I followed you. I know that I shall not wash my hands after I have eaten your flesh, but people will wash their hands when they have eaten you. That is why I followed you, because I wanted to talk to you. People will make medicine to catch you, but I will not make medicine. I will just follow you."

g. Then Dog said, "Well, if one sets a snare, he will catch you with that." Then he set out a snare. He said, "Now run into that. Let us see how they will catch you." Deer started, jumped into the snare, and was caught. He said, "Whenever the snare is loose, it is because there is something the matter, perhaps (something ritually wrong) about the house. They must have medicine for that." Then he sang medicine. He said, "If the snare is loose on the throat, they will sing this song. Then they will kill me."

6. The good hunters.

7. Contaminating the deer's flesh. Venison was handled with care, being eaten off wooden platters that were to be washed only in basket water, never in a stream. The hands were carefully washed afterwards, scraps were kept off the floor, and women might not shift their feet while preparing and eating it (Kroeber, Handbook, p. 68). On the contrary, menstruant women had dried fish, etc., set aside for them, which defiled anything sacred or ritualistic.

h. Then he said, "If they catch me, they will not take me into the house by the door, but they will open the top of the house at one side."[8] So when deer are killed they are not taken in by the door because that is the door used by the woman.[9]

P6. Pulekukwerek and Tobacco

a. At first tobacco was not used. People took pepperwood leaves,[1] dried them, and smoked them as tobacco. Many were killed by that, it was so strong. Then Pulekukwerek came to smoke it, and did not like it. He is the one who threw it away. He used (true) tobacco: he was the only one who used it. So when he threw away the pepperwood tobacco, he said, "I will give you seeds so you can raise it for yourselves." Then they planted it, grew it, and smoked it after it was dry.

b. But some tobacco was still too strong. People smoking it fell over and died. Then Pulekukwerek, where he lived (at the) downriver (end of the world), heard that this tobacco was even worse than the other and killed more people. So he came upriver again. All along they were raising tobacco. He came to Rekwoi. There he began to smoke. He said, "No one will be killed by this," and he blew tobacco out from his hand. Then he went up along the river to other places.

c. At Kenek, he heard, the Earthquakes[2] lived, ten of them, and it was a bad place to smoke. That is why he went to Kenek, because the ten Earthquake brothers killed people there with their tobacco. When they saw anyone coming, one of them immediately gave him to smoke. When he had finished, another one came to give him smoke. Sometimes when six men had given him their pipes, he was dead; sometimes seven killed him. It was always (not more than) seven, but if a man was strong (it would take) seven to overcome him. When they had killed people, they always threw them into the brush without burying them.[3]

d. Pulekukwerek came into the sweathouse. He saw much tobacco

8. The side walls were low and supported nothing, so a somewhat loose board or two there did not matter; or the sense may be that lower roof planks were moved aside at the eaves to permit entry of the carcass.

9. Woman is the great defiler (besides corpses) because she menstruates.

---

1. California laurel, *Umbellularia californica*, also called bay or myrtle.

2. Yewoł. Some versions call the strong-tobacco brothers Kenomer or Ka-sumig-or, and connect them with Kewet Mountain or the porpoises at Sumig. [Cf. C5 and F1*h*.—Ed.]

3. This is insult added to injury. Even a killer, if he has a chance, arranges his victim's corpse, out of reach of river, tide, or further mutilation, under penalty of additional compensation.

hanging in baskets in the sweathouse, drying. He said, "That is what I want: I like to smoke." Then he smoked (with them). He smoked seven pipes. He was talking as if he did not feel anything: they saw him act like this. When he had smoked nine pipes, they saw that he was feeling it. When he had smoked ten, he fell over. They carried him out and threw him in the brush.

e. One day the children there said, "There is a little boy up here on the rocks. He is sliding down them." That was Pulekukwerek come to life again.[4] He was sliding on the rock upriver from Kenek.[5] He came back to the sweathouse. He did not enter by the door but by the (small) exit. The owners of the sweathouse did not like him inside because his rump was sharp.[6] They gave him a sweathouse pillow or something to sit on, because he was so sharp; but he would not use it. He sat on the stone floor, and whenever he got up they could see that he had cut it up.

He said, "This tobacco will kill no one any more. Anyone can smoke it." So it is that no one is killed by tobacco, because Pulekukwerek stopped them from killing people there. "Even," said Pulekukwerek, "though there is some tobacco which they will feel a little, nevertheless it will not kill them."[7]

P7. Coyote and Pleiades

a. Pleiades[1] lived upriver (at the end of the world). They were six women. Whenever they started at night, they began to dance. Then once, as they started, Coyote wanted to dance with them. So they took him along. But they told him, "Do not dance fast, for it is a long night, and we must dance all through." Coyote said, "I always dance this: it is not the first time: I know about it." "Well, then, you had better sing." So Coyote began to sing, and they danced. Now Coyote became exhausted. He could not dance through the night. He died, and the girls threw him away.[2]

b. After a time he came to life again. Then he did not know where to go.

4. In the temporary form of a playing boy.
5. Waterman, Geography, p. 252.
6. He had "horns" on his buttocks; *-kwerek* means pointed, sharp.
7. This version wholly omits the hollow elder or elkhorn lengths which Pulekukwerek swallows and then disgorges so that the tobacco does not burn him. [Cf. F1*h*.—Ed.] On the other hand, it connects the sliding episode with the smoking intrinsically instead of merely by locality.

---

1. Teinem, "many."
2. Along their road in the sky.

He looked down from the sky and thought, "Perhaps it is close (to earth)." Then he spat down. He saw his spittle like only a little way off; he could see it plainly. So he thought, "I will jump down," and jumped. But what he had seen were clouds. So he kept falling. Only his bones reached the earth.

After a time he came to life again.

Informant Q

OPN OF SREGON

Opn of Sregon had his name mispronounced as Obee by the Americans. From his birthplace he was called E-sräg or K'e-sräg. His mother was from Wahsek. He had a brother called Jim who later in life lived up the hill from the town of Sregon, but was called Nohtskus because his wife was from Nohtsku'm. This designation shows that he was half-married to her. This Jim was not the same person as Sregon Jim, the head man of Sregon, who was from another house, and older.

Opn's wife was from Weitspus of the house tsahpek, which is the one next to tsekweł. He was full married to her, but later lived for a time in Weitspus. The reason was that his wife's mother and her sister were left alone in the house. Other families got firewood and other necessities for them, but after a time grew tired, so Opn moved to Weitspus to take care of the old women. At this time he homesteaded a place between Weitspus and Martin's Ferry.[1] *Then his wife's aunt became ill with a lingering sickness. After her death, Opn took his family, including his mother, back to Sregon. His mother is buried there.*

He was regarded as quick-tempered and brave, but did not get into fights. He was an excellent hunter. This brought him in a good many deerskin blankets. He also made arrows for the Brush Dance. He knew the formula for curing the sickness called kwesoi. *He also was a* wegwolets wesomeges, *medicine maker for becoming alive; that is, he knew the formula for a woman unable to give birth,* tsahtseu wegwoletsik.

Like all families in Sregon, Opn's was wealthy, but he personally had little. The family wealth went to his older brother. He said that his relatives always passed him by for his brother. This was his explanation when he was taxed with having had property and sold it. After this brother's death, a good deal of treasure reverted to Opn: a pair of large flints, a gray deerskin, and more. Then his boys became sick, and he sold the deerskin and other things. At his own death he had left only the pair of obsidians.

1. [Martin's Ferry is at Wahsek, 3 miles downstream from Weitspus.—Ed.]

When I met Opn in 1900, on a homestead or allotment a mile or so downstream from Weitspus, he told these stories in his own broken English after some vaunting of his lore. He was probably poor at the time of our acquaintance, and seemed to me to show the traits that the Yurok ascribe to the poor: ingratiating, ready with a wide smile, and impulsive; forward with strangers, inclined to be eager and persuading, a man of schemes, unkempt of appearance. Later in life he returned to Sregon, and seems to have attained relative prosperity.

A man in his circumstance would be too occupied with planning advantages to leave many of his thoughts free for traditions. His tales reflect his personality. I asked for stories about Wohpekumeu, which he had professed to know. His one tale about this hero consists of two incidents, one of which perhaps does not appertain to him in general Yurok opinion. He brought Wohpekumeu also into the introduction to the tale Married at Rumai, by having him make the mountain Mekaukh, another incident that seems of doubtful Yurok authenticity. Of Wohpekumeu's son Kapuloyo he related an episode, but detached from its setting.

It appears that this informant had no system of mythology in his head because he was little interested in things remote from his personal affairs. What remained in his memory were stories of plot or adventure, of the folktale type, such as a child would be impressed by: Pa'aku, Married at Rumai, the Throwing of the Pestle. These he told tolerably well but without distinction. The characterization is of the kind that would impress an indifferent mind: Coyote is vainglorious, lying, and greedy, Wohpekumeu amatory.

Q1. Pa'aku

a. An old man and his wife lived in the sky.[1] They had ten sons and two daughters. Many people came from everywhere to marry the two girls. The ten sons always went hunting. Whenever they killed deer, Ƚmeiga[2] came as they were about to cut them up and took them away. The young men could not kill Ƚmeiga, and when they returned and told the old man, he was sorry. Sometimes they would find a little meat that Ƚmeiga had left and would bring it home.

Then the old man said that whoever killed Ƚmeiga could marry his two girls. Then they came from Kewet and from many places, but failed. Every day they went out, but did not kill him.

b. Now the old man was in the sweathouse. Someone came in slowly. The old man asked, "Did someone come in?"[3] He said, "Yes." Then the old

1. The tale is also localized on Oka, a ridge parallel to the Lower Klamath. Cf. J9.
2. *Ƚmei*- means violent, powerful, quarrelsome, vicious.
3. Perhaps a greeting; but the sweathouse is dark.

man said to him, "Let us go into the house.[4] Who are you?" "I am Coyote," he said. Then they ate supper. Coyote stayed there the night. In the morning he said, "I am returning." The old man told him, "Come again." Coyote said, "I know who will kill Ƚmeiga. It is my nephew who will kill him." The old man said, "I wish I could see him." Coyote knew that Pa'aku[5] was the one (who could do it). He (only) called him his nephew.

Now there were many people living with the old man, and every morning they went out to hunt. They did not eat until after they came back.

c. Next day Coyote returned. With him was a small young man who had a little bow and little arrows. They went into the sweathouse. "Let us go to eat," said the old man to them, but they would not go into the house. The people laughed at Pa'aku and said to each other, "Ah! He has come to marry the girls, this little one." Now all the men came into the sweathouse. Coyote and his nephew were in the middle, close together. They all sang deer songs. Then the old man said to Coyote and his nephew, "You had better sing too." But Coyote would not sing. He had no songs.

When it became day, the old man said, "It is time to go." Then as they were all about to leave, Pa'aku said, "Wait. I shall sing." Then he sang. Everyone said, "Well, he has a good song." Now they were ready. They had their hair tied in knots behind and their faces painted black.[6] They were still laughing at Coyote and Pa'aku. They thought about Coyote, "Poor fellow!"

d. Then Pa'aku said, "I forgot my deer mask! It is at the town (where I live)." Then he sat down and said, "*Pekw!*" and his deer mask sat on his head. Now they all began to say, "That is something of a man." Then Coyote also tried to call his deer mask and cried, "*Pekw!*" but could not bring it. Then he said, "Well, I will go get it." so he ran to his house[7] and got his mask. He was very swift and soon returned. "Well, I have my mask," he said. So they were ready to go. Now when they hunted, they ate no breakfast,[8] but only when they came home.

e. Now Rigome[9] drove the deer, and the others killed them until they had enough. But when they were ready to cut them up, Ƚmeiga came. Pa'aku was sitting looking aside. He did nothing while all the others shot (at the monster). But Ƚmeiga did not notice their shooting. He gathered the deer, put them all

4. To eat.

5. A small owl, probably Screech Owl.

6. As if for fighting.

7. On Kewet, Rivet Mountain? Or at Kenek?

8. As above, in *b*. Going without breakfast is a Yurok custom when anything important is on hand, and some men try to do all their heavy work before eating.

9. A small bird in the mountains.

on his back, and went off. Now the ten brothers found a little piece of meat that he had left, and carefully saved it for their father.

f. Soon they said, "Let us try again." Then they drove deer again. The herd came in a line toward Pa'aku. Raising an arrow, he shot them all. No one said a word now: they thought him a man. Then he went to the deer, made one cut the length of each, pulled at the skin twice, drew it off, and threw it aside.

g. Then the men began to say, "Now Ƚmeiga will come and take them away. You will see." But Coyote said, "No." He made a brush hut near the heap of carcasses, holding a knife that Pa'aku had given him. He also had sharp stones ready. Now he was in his shelter while Pa'aku was cutting up the deer. Coyote said, "Nephew, give me the hearts." Pa'aku threw him to him, and Coyote ate them.

h. Coyote had painted himself around the eyes. Some of the men had not thought his paint good.[10] Then he had gone off and painted himself over: he had made his eyes large and had painted his mouth across his cheeks. "Does he look like this?" he asked. "Almost," they said. "Well, I am not afraid of him," he said.

i. Now as Coyote was sitting behind the brush, he said, "Nephew, give me more." He ate many of the entrails. Then the men said, "Do not talk so much: he may be coming." Then Ƚmeiga came and began to take the meat. The men were all looking on. They saw the brush of the little shelter begin to shake: Coyote was trembling. When (the monster) had gone off with all the deer, Coyote pretended to have been asleep. He said, "Was he here? Did he really come? Is he gone already? You should have told me. I was asleep." But they all laughed at him.

j. Now it was beginning to be late and they wanted to go home, but Pa'aku said, "Wait! Let us try once more." So they drove deer again, and again he killed them with one shot, twenty of them, and cut them up. Again Coyote said, "Nephew, give me the livers," and ate the insides, sitting behind the brush shelter. "This time I shall kill him," he said. Now (the monster) came again. As he lifted the deer on his back, Pa'aku shot. The arrow passed through his body into the ground beyond. Then Coyote leaped on him and struck him with his sharp stones.

k. Now the old man was glad: that night they brought him as many deer as he wanted. When Pa'aku came in, he said, "My son-in-law!" he was so glad to get the deer.

l. After a time Pa'aku had a son. He told his wife to bring the boy to the

10. He was trying to make himself resemble the monster, and they did not consider his first attempt successful.

sweathouse every morning. Then as she went off to bring in firewood, she put the boy into the sweathouse. There Pa'aku danced, spat on the boy's hand, and rubbed it between his own, singing his deer song. He said, "I want you to be like me. I give you this song." He had three sons, all of them able to kill anything that they wished.[11]

Q2. Married at Rumai

a. Wohpekumeu made the mountain Mekaukh.[1] At first he made it so high that it touched the sky. All the people looked at it, and some of them did not like it. Then he said, "I will make it better." He broke off the top and threw it downstream, uphill from Weitspus. It became (the mountain) Kewet.

b. The little mountains were made by the people shooting at the large bird on Mekaukh.[2] They made them as places to stand on while they shot.

c. At Rumai there lived an old woman. Then a young man from Kewet married her daughter, but the old woman did not like him. He killed deer and squirrels and salmon for her, but she would eat none of them. He thought, "What can I do that she will like? I do not know what kind to kill for her." Then the old woman said, "I like to eat Sekoyeu." Then he did not know what that was. He caught all kinds of salmon and trout and other fish at Bluff Creek, but she would not eat them. He kept thinking what kind of fish she wanted.

Then he went again with his harpoon. He saw a small salmon moving in the water. It was very red at the gills. Then he harpooned it. The fish wriggled, kept on wriggling, grew, struggled, and soon was enormous. It drew the young man into the water to his waist, and then to his armpits. He tried to let go, but the spear stuck fast to his hands. He was pulled along through the water. He thought he would drown. He put the spear shaft under his chin to keep (afloat and) breathing.

Then he heard talking. It sounded pleasant, as if he were dreaming. He called, "Come help me! I am drowning!" Then he felt something fly on top of

11. This paragraph may not form part of the tale as such. It has the appearance of turning the myth into a formula, and yet does not give it the proper form of a formula. But the narrator had boasted of the song and the power it gave him to kill deer at any time. The story was the first he produced and evidently was his favorite. It has most detail. It certainly meant more to him than a mere tale.

---

1. Mekaukh (which this informant pronounced Mekau) is Shelton Butte, a steep peak on the south side of the Klamath, above Bluff Creek, below whose mouth lies Rumai. The making of mountains is not the sort of accomplishment usually attributed to Wohpekumeu.

2. This well-known incident—compare A8*c* and J3—is only alluded to here, either because the narrator did not know it in detail or because the events at Mekaukh are only introductory to the story of the young man at Rumai.

his head. "Help me," he said. It answered, "I will help you if you will give me *uwetspei*."[3] Then the bird struck Sekoyeu on the nape and killed it. So the young man was saved, and they pulled Sekoyeu ashore. Before the bird had struck it, he had sung his song. This song is good medicine: it keeps people from being drowned.

The old woman had known what Sekoyeu was and had wished that it would kill the young man. When he told her that he had its meat, she said, "Thanks, thanks. This is what I like." Then she carried it up to the house. Now she knew that she could not kill her son-in-law.

d. Next day she prepared to cook the Sekoyeu. She made a large fire, heated many stones, and got a cooking basket ready. Then Kewet young man said to his wife, "Let us go out." They went a little distance off. He said, "Louse me," and she loused him. Now much steam began to come from the house. A chicken hawk that Kewet young man kept tied there began to jump and flap his wings.[4] Then the young man climbed up on the roof and cut loose the bird. He looked and saw that the water had overflowed from the basket and filled the house. The old woman was dead. "Let her die," the girl had said. Then Kewet young man took the old woman's basket and threw it into the river. It is a rock there now.[5]

Q3. Wohpekumeu

a. Wohpekumeu went everywhere. People did not like him, for he made women pregnant without their knowledge. He came to Ko'men (Orleans). There were two young women there. He made them both pregnant. Their brothers tried to kill him, but he fled upstream.

When the women were about to give birth, he returned. "Wohpekumeu has come," they said. "He is the one: let us kill him." "Wait," he said. "Let me go into the house and see them." He had a quiver full of medicine herbs, arrows, his bow, and knives. He said, "Let me go into the house. I am sorry for the girls. Let me see them." One of the men said, "Well, go in. Let us see what you will do." So they consented.

3. An internal organ of the fish. In Spott and Kroeber, Yurok Narratives, no. 29, p. 238, the helper, who is Kingfisher, asks for the clotted blood along the backbone.

4. The narrator added a sentence which his imperfect English rendered obscure. Either the bird flapped his wings because it became so hot, or the young man left him at the smoke hole in order that he might fan the heat back into the house, as happens in other incidents in the sweathouse.

5. [In K3*c* Crane drowns the old woman of Rumai by drawing up his leg-bridge, and then both she and her basket turn into rocks.—Ed.]

The girls were lying and crying. People were there sharpening[1] knives to cut them open. They said, "Let it be[2] that when a child is born the woman is killed." Wohpekumeu said, "No. It is not well to cut open the woman. Wait! I will make medicine." He took medicine out of his quiver and sat down. All around him were the people, ready to kill him because the two girls were to die. He said, "If I do not cure them you can kill me. But let me try first." Then he rubbed his medicine on one woman's abdomen. Then they heard a child cry, and soon it was born. Then he did the same to the other woman. He said, "That is how people will live on earth. They will not cut women. They will live thus. Now I shall make everything good. Let me go about. I will finish the world."

b. At Tsa'etsk[3] he had another sweetheart. She was sterile. He did not want her to have a child and did not let it grow. That is why some women are sterile.

c. Then he left her. People said, "He has left his sweetheart and gone off." Then she was sorry.[4] She was pounding acorns. Then she pursued him with her pestle (in her hand). Wohpekumeu was painted and dressed in ornaments. He wore a long net headdress (from the back of his head). Then when she stood on the mountain she saw him far downstream on the ocean, paddling. Then she threw her pestle. She missed him, but struck his headdress and knocked off the feathers. They flew up and were seabirds. The pestle is standing: it is a pointed rock in the ocean.[5]

Q4. Kapuloyo

Kapuloyo took away all dentalia. Wohpekumeu ran after him and overtook him at the mouth of the river. He said, "Why do you want to take them all? How can people live without dentalia?" Kapuloyo said, "I was angry; that is why I took them." Wohpekumeu said, "That is not right." He sang and held out his hands and some of the dentalia came into them. That is why there are dentalia in this world now. Kapuloyo said, "Well, let it be." Wohpekumeu said, "I want some dentalia to be upriver and some along the coast. But there will not be many large ones, only a few." And he blew them out of his hand upstream and along the coast.

1. As if they were steel knives. To cut, the Yurok sometimes freshly break cobbles.
2. The custom of killing the mother is already practiced; they mean that it is to be perpetuated.
3. "Across the river from Orleans."
4. Or angry.
5. Redding Rock, no doubt. This incident is otherwise told of the woman's son, No'ots (see A7 and J8) or Megwomets (F6). It is more likely that the narrator (or his English) was confused than that his version represents an independent stream of Yurok tradition.

INFORMANT R

BARNEY OF SREGON

Sregon Barney was so-called by the Americans from his Indian name, Ponni. His house was sregon-hipur. There were doctors in his family. His mother may have been from Pekwon. He was not married, but a woman of the house opyuweg in Pekwon was his werres *or sweetheart. His daughter, presumably by this woman, is Redwood Henry's wife at Olōł opposite Wohkel.*

Barney was a tsāro *or worker on the Kepel dam. His wealth included the following: three woodpecker bands, two black obsidians reaching nearly to the elbow, four aprons of marten skins, which are worn like those of the ringtail cat but are more valuable, four headbands of sea lion tusks, nine dance baskets, ten deerkskin blankets for the Jumping Dance, and one complete outfit of twenty-four sets for the Brush Dance. He was buried without even one woodpecker band being put into the coffin: All his wealth went to his daughter.*

R1. INVENTION OF THE DRAGNET

a. White Duck, Murun, was living at murun ukepeli,[1] opposite Wohkero. Pigeon, Hemi', also lived there. Then they always fished with dragnets[2] in front of where they lived. Duck caught many salmon; but Pigeon caught none, because he used a carrying-net sack[3] for his net, having no other. Then he wanted to know how Duck caught so many salmon, but Duck never let him see his net. Then one night Pigeon thought, "I will watch." So he watched and saw Duck's net, and learned with what he caught salmon.

1. Waterman, Geography, map 11, no. 21 and p. 240: "murnū-kepe'ł, translated as 'merganser house pit.' A small flat with a depression. Murnū is described by the Indians as 'river-duck,' evidently the sawbill or merganser. In myth times he had his house at this point."
2. This may be the net referred to in S3.
3. As illustrated in Goddard, Life and Culture of the Hupa, pl. 6.

b. Now he had seen the net but he did not know how to make one. Then he heard that Duck was going to make a net. He said in his house, "I hear he is going to make nets." One of his housemates said, "Try somehow to get into his house." Pigeon said, "Yes." Now, when it was night, he crept into Duck's house: the door was open. He hid in the storage alcove ("woodshed"). Then they made a light in the house.

At the beginning, when they started to make the net, he heard them call it *wererpin* (the very beginning of the net, where it is fastened to the stick). Next they said *wohpekolis* (where six meshes are inserted). Then, *wo'ōlo'-oi* (where another six meshes are put in). Then, *winōmek'* (where the net widens and eight meshes are inserted). Then, *na'ainōlek'* ("second time," where eight meshes are again inserted). Then *ukōmek'* (where four meshes are added). Then they called it *ukūris* (the other end of the net). Then: *witsełpo* (the stick at the far end of the seine); and then they named *umūłpo* (the string passing the entire length of the net). Pigeon heard them mention every name, but did not know what they meant; nevertheless he tried to remember them.

c. So Pigeon sat in the entrance alcove while Duck made the net in the house. After a while Duck said, "I feel as if someone were looking at me from somewhere." Then one of them hastily put a stick in the fire and went outside with it as a torch. He saw no one. At last he went into the store room: there he found Pigeon, and shouted, "Someone is sitting here!" So Pigeon was caught. They pushed him down hard on the ground, repeatedly, while he shouted and cried. That is why Pigeon is so narrow in the chest now: because they pushed him against the ground and injured him. Thus it was found how that sort of net is made: before then, no one knew it.

R2. Wohpekumeu's Seat

a. Crane lived at merkwtek, at the downriver end of Wohkero.[1] He had daughters. Wohpekumeu was across the river constantly, watching those girls, looking over. He sat there all the time: every day he sat and looked for them, crying. Then after a time he saw that (the deposit of) his tears had made something like a stool.[2] He continued to cry: after a time it had become high enough for his seat. Still he cried constantly.

b. Then he said, "Whoever knows this seat of mine will have good luck. Let him come at night and cry here. He will not lack money. Whenever he goes anywhere, let him take moss from this seat and put it under the brush in

1. Waterman, Geography, map 12, nos. 1, 2, mocktek, "blue crane's house-pits." *Merkwteks* means crane.

2. Stools in the house were solid cylinders or cone frustums of redwood, sometimes with concave flare.

his boat. If he goes downriver to the mouth, when he arrives, let him leave the moss in the boat. When he comes back home, let him take the moss and throw it away where no one will find it. Then he will have good luck. Somehow he will get dentalia easily. Whoever thinks of me will always be lucky, and will never lack for women, because that is the kind I am. Whoever thinks of me, and knows this seat, will be well off. Let him come in the middle of the night, when no one sees him, and begin to cry while he thinks of me.[3] He will be lucky in everything if he knows my seat.''

c. The moss from this seat is as good for obtaining women as for money.[4]

3. The Yurok liked to think they would be cried for by their descendants, and attribute the sentiment also to their gods.

4. This is evidently a luck formula in substance, and perhaps also in form. There is an association of Wohpekumeu and his paraphernalia localized above Weitspus around Bluff Creek in L1 and Q2, and of Crane also, in tales A8, A9, and K3.

INFORMANT S

DOCTOR OF PEKWON

Pekwon Doctor was also called Doctor Jo. He was also called Wer-ergerk hego, Sweathouse-Maker, because of his reciting the formula and directing the rebuilding of the sacred sweathouse for the Pekwon Jumping Dance. Sometimes he was spoken of as Mä'äts-kus-egor after his mother, who was from Mä'äts on the coast. He was also known as Hipur-awa on account of his wife, who was from a house hipur in her home village, which is not remembered. Pekwon Doctor was himself from the house pekwon-pul in Pekwon. He had a brother who was nicknamed Tiraniwer, Long-Tooth; also a sister who was a werrum *or spinster, and died old and unmarried. He himself had no children, or they died young.*

He was a well-to-do man, owning four woodpecker bands of the best quality, one gray deerskin, a pair of black obsidians, and a single red obsidian, besides, no doubt, objects of lesser value.

S1. HE ATE HIS OWN BLOOD

a. Back[1] of Pekwon, that is where he lived, that young man. And he ate nothing. He constantly went to bring in sweathouse firewood, and he ate nothing. And the old woman gathered something like seeds[2] back on the prairie.[3] She prepared them like acorns: she pounded them with her pestle. Thus she prepared them, that old woman.

b. And he thought he would stop eating that, this young man. Constantly he went after sweathouse firewood. And he went on the hill, far up on the hill,

1. *Hierkik*, away from the stream, northeast.

2. An abstract, obtained at the time the story was spoken into the phonograph, says he lived on a red earth which his mother crushed and cooked for him. [K.'s note indicates that there were two translators of this story: Catherine Goodwin and Weitspus Frank.—Ed.]

3. *Hełkäus*.

after the firewood. And he arrived halfway and rested at Tsektseya.[4] He sat down. Then he wanted to cut himself.[5] Then he did that, cutting himself, there where he was sitting. And he saw much blood coming when he did that, and when he looked at it, he liked it. There was much, like water. Then he thought, "Let me try to eat this blood." And then he ate it.

Then after that when they gave him food he would not eat it. "No, I do not want it." And he thought, "I like the blood." And he ate his own blood. So he did, that young man. That is how it was with him. He was constantly going for sweathouse firewood. And they tried to give him the food that they ate in the house. And he would not have it. He would not eat it.

c. Then he did not know what to do. He said, "I would like to do something to have good luck." And of what he was doing he said, "I will do this because I shall have good luck," for it is thus with *tsektseyił*.[6] So it was with him, this young man.

At Wohpeku,[7] that is where he lay down. He was thinking of having good luck. That is why he lay at Wohpeku, because he wanted good luck.

d. And geese[8] were beginning to fly upstream. Then he continued to lie there while the geese were traveling. Then he was thinking very much that he wished good luck.[9] He thought, "I should like to see one of them alight and throw a woodpecker's crest where I am lying." Then it was thrown there where he was lying, a woodpecker crest was thrown. So one was left for him. Just when the geese were beginning to fly, because he wished for good luck, it happened so to him. Then was when he stopped doing so.[10] He thought, "I will stop doing this. I shall not do it any more as I have been doing."

Then he died. After he had done this, he died.[11]

S2. Crow, Grizzly Bear, and the Pekwon Tā̄ł

This tale refers to the *tā̄ł* who sing in the sacred or so-called "old sweathouse" which belongs to the Jumping Dance or world renewal ritual at Pekwon. The *tā̄ł* sing songs

4. *Tsektseya* or *tsekweł* is what the stone "seats" on mountains are called which prospective shamans frequent. They are semicircular walls of unmortared stones, a yard or two across, three or four feet high.

5. As was sometimes done, with jagged quartz, while sweathouse wood was being sought. The practice is called *ki-pehpego*. [Cf. D5.—Ed.]

6. *Sic*. Probably the same as *tsektseya*. The meaning may be that use of a *tsektseya* brings luck.

7. By the river in front of Pekwon, just below the mouth of Pekwon Creek. The word means "in the river" or "across river."

8. *Kelloku*.

9. *Koskololohkin*, to wish for luck, to seek to be wealthy.

10. Eating his own blood?

11. Not clear. Either the tale is incomplete or some explanation has been omitted. [See S5.—Ed.]

referring to Crow, Grizzly Bear, and Great Horned Owl, as told in Kroeber and Gifford, World Renewal, p. 95. The bit of tale given here simply reflects a piece of ritual, perhaps on account of its songs. It was recorded on three phonograph cylinders and later Englished by Weitspus Frank.

•

a. They were making[1] that sweathouse there. Then they finished it. And they began to go upriver by boat, to Petsawan.[2] There they made a fire,[3] and gathered their sweathouse firewood.[4] Then they went back down to the river, and down it in their boat, carrying their firewood, and singing. And one[5] was speaking outside the sweathouse. He said, "Listen! Tell me when you hear the boat returning." Then they arrived. They were at both sides of the sweathouse door with their ten bundles of firewood. So they went in; and they began to sing. (Song of the *tǟł*)

b. Then it was that Grizzly Bear came to the door. And they heard the sweathouse crack. He tried to enter (in order to listen), but only got halfway. Then he backed out and ran off to the creek. And that black one, Crow, was *tǟł* inside; and he said, "You will live in the creek;[6] that is where you will always stay."

And Great Horned Owl was *tǟł* too. And he said, "I have something I made myself: I have a song." And Crow had a song too. (Crow's song, without words) That is Crow's song. And this is Pleget's.[7] (Song, also without words) That is how he sang. Crow said to Grizzly, "You will be afraid in the woods when you hear my song; if people sing it, you will not attack them."

S3. He Brought Her Back from the Dead

The informant and his wife learned this tale from an old man of or near Turip; he was Harry Smoker's father-in-law, still alive in 1907. He knew the songs for *kemmeihtso*, those returned to life from coma, which were sung for such a person during the Brush Dance that was made for them.

•

1. The sacred "sweathouse" is remade or renovated for the rite.

2. Upriver from Pekwon. Petsawan is not mentioned by Waterman, and Spott did not remember its name, but it was opposite Yohter town on the hillside (Spott and Kroeber, World Renewal, p. 87). This would put it about 3/4 mile upstream of Pekwon, 3/8 mile below Sregon.

3. The formulist makes a fire, puts in angelica, and prays.

4. Of *sahsi'p*, probably Ceanothus, sometimes described as "wild honeysuckle."

5. Evidently Grizzly Bear.

6. That is, in thickets and woods.

7. Plegeł, the great horned or timber owl.

a. On the coast to the south[1] he had gone to summon a doctor[2] for his sweetheart.[3] And as he was returning, across a little lagoon, he thought he saw a woman approaching the shore. Then he thought, "It seems as if I knew her." And he knew it was the woman (his sweetheart) who was sick, the very one. So he tried to intercept her. And she was wearing a maple-bark skirt and a blanket of two deerskins; wearing that she was coming on. And he intended to intercept her, that woman, but he only felt something like wind against himself,[4] just a little of that did he feel. Now the woman was already dead.

b. So he came home to Turip. Then he saw that she had died while he had been procuring a doctor for her; that is how it was. So he thought, Hī, I liked her, I liked her. And he went to Tsorrek[5] (where the dead go). And he saw[6] Weasel[7] coming to him; and (Weasel) said, "I will go with you. Constantly I hear you crying because you liked her. So I will go down there with you, for I am accustomed to go there." Weasel said that. Then he thought, "Well, I will go with him." So he proceeded to go with him, and they started, and arrived there.

And (Weasel) said, "Sit down here. I will go to where she is and will tell her, 'He has come here'; I will tell her that." And he went to tell her that, did Weasel, he went to tell it to the woman. And they were dancing the Deerskin Dance right where this woman was; every kind of enjoyment they were having,[8] every kind of enjoyment in the world, they were doing that where the woman was, making Deerskin Dance[9] for that woman because she still lay there; so it was.

c. And (Weasel) thought, "Hī, let me come close." And he heard everything then. He heard, "Come, let us go net fishing."[10] So they went to the

1. *Tewolli*, "oceanward."
2. *Nonneuhpe'n.*
3. *Werres.* This means they were lovers, not married.
4. *Tse'muts meł roks.*
5. *Noł tsorreks kits-henes.* Tsorrek or Tsorrek-ik is the world of the dead below. Cf. Waterman, Geography, pp. 192 and 235.
6. *Inneu.*
7. Megesik. In other tales, such as D6x, the weasel that helps is a man's weasel-skin pipe case.
8. *Numitsyu serłer'pi'm*, "doing all kinds of fun."
9. *Upyewegił.*
10. *Tsuł kuweggeyome'm.* This is a method of seine fishing used on the lower river (as at Turip) in spring, because the spring salmon are "wild and shy." Two boats go out, each with a paddler and a net handler. The nets are long and joined at one end; at the other end of each is a long pole, *uwer'yermerł*, held from the boat. The boats move downstream, abreast, but headed somewhat apart, to keep the bag of the net, which drags far behind, from drawing them too close together. When a salmon is felt, both poles are lifted. The fish belongs to the owner of the net in which it is caught; but if luck is one-sided, the fortunate boat may divide. It is not clear whether it is the same net as described in R1.

boats; and one said, "Where shall we go first to fish?" And the other said, "To Mu'yau;[11] that is where we will go and then begin." That is how he heard it there. So he thought, "Hī, let me come closer up yet." And they were starting to dance again too, to dance for that woman. Then he thought, "What shall I do?" And Weasel said, "We will go nearer;[12] we will work in close and take the woman; I will get her for you." Then Weasel got her; he got her. And they took her back. They came to Turip, they brought her there.

d. Now she thought, "Well, I will stay, because I have come back. But I do not want to hear any bad word (about it)."[13] She said, "I do not want to hear them call me returned to life.[14] If they call me that, I will leave again, if they say that."

e. Then it was thus: they called her that; and she went off. She went and came to where she had been before. Then Weasel thought. "Hī, what shall I do?" He said, "We will go after her. Let us go again." And (the man) thought, "Yes." And they arrived there and got her. And he thought, "Hī, I will recover her if she leaves again," for he had him as if for a partner, this man, this Weasel (did). And they returned to Turip.

f. Then he had children by her. And someone outside the house was saying to the children, saying to them, "She has come back from the dead, has your mother."[15] That is how they spoke to the children.[16] So she left again. But she thought, "I will not go below again. Let me go to Pulekuk."[17] So she went downstream by boat,[18] and above the mouth[19] she landed. So it was. And the man followed, followed. On her head[20] she put a burden basket,[21] because she was going to Pulekuk, that is where[22] she was going. And she told the man (when he overtook her), "Go back, go back. I cannot return. I am going to Pulekuk and will never come back." Then he did that, the one who grew up at Turip: from there she went on to Pulekuk,[23] but he did not go on: so they did. And then he thought, "Well, let me go home."

11. Mu'yau is unplaced and unexplained.
12. Apparently the man has approached the crowd with Weasel.
13. *Kowitso ko'l nisonnoye'o.*
14. *Kemmeihtso.*
15. *Kemmeihtso k'etseko.*
16. Probably to taunt them.
17. The downstream edge of the world; also Pulukuk. [K. transcribed this informant's pronunciation as Pullekuk.—Ed.]
18. She is evidently conceived as more than wind now.
19. Rekwoi-hierk, at Hunter Creek.
20. Or, over her head?
21. *Terreks*—strictly, a close-woven conical basket for seed gathering, not the openwork *kewoi* for fuel gathering and load packing.
22. Or, how she was going?
23. *Sahunnoyołkä pulukuk kyekwto.*

S4. Gambling with Kapuloyo (fragment)

Informant S dictated a story, two phonograph cylinders long, of a young man from Tsotskwi, Dry Lagoon on the coast, who gambled with Kapuloyo. It includes a song which gives luck in gambling; but when it has been sung one must eat apart from other people. This snatch is evidently part of the same tale as BB2.[1]

S5. Man-Money and Woman-Money (fragment)

Informant S has a song, with brief story, about man-dentalium who went upriver and woman-dentalium who went downriver and north to the end of the world. The song has brought him wealth, he said, but one must eat apart after singing it. It is possible that this is the conclusion of tale S1, which now ends abruptly; at any rate, its phonograph cylinder followed immediately on those containing S1.

1. [See DD7 for mention of another tale known to Informant S.—Ed.]

Informant T

JIM OF PEKWON

Pekwon Jim was known as Toloł-awa because his wife was a Tolowa from Erger, Burnt Ranch. After her death this designation was of course changed to Toloł-umelo. Jim was also known as Lekwsa after his natal or family house. This was so called because it faced the entrance or exit of the sacred sweathouse.

The birthplace of Jim's mother is not known. He had a brother, Billy, who was also called Lekwsa. He had at least one daughter. The family was a good one. He was a täł *from boyhood on. Jim owned four or five woodpecker bands and various feather objects and arrows.*

According to another account, Pekwon Jim and Merip Lucky, and a third brother were themselves born at Kohpei, Crescent City, and were half-Tolowa.

Pekwon Jim in his life had gone south as far as Eureka; north to Tolowa Espeu, beyond Smith River, astride the California-Oregon boundary, a quarter-mile south of Winchuck River, not to be confused with the Espeu on the coast south of the Klamath; and upriver to Karok Kumawer, two day's travel above Enek-Amaikiaram, that is, nearly as far as Okonile'l at Clear Creek.

Merip Lucky (to be distinguished from Lucky of Wahsek, Informant L), the older brother of Informant T, dictated a deer formula on three phonograph cylinders. This starts from Sumig, or Patrick's Point, where there was only one house. The plant used is sahsi'p, *Ceanothus. Lucky also dictated four phonograph cylinders of sweathouse formula for acquiring wealth; the plant used is* kererpus egor.[1]

Pekwon Jim, the younger brother, dictated a similar formula, on four

1. [The deer and sweathouse formulas have been transcribed onto tape as Lowie Museum Audio Archive catalogue numbers 24-1004 and 24-1003, respectively. See Appendix I for further information.—Ed.]

cylinders.[2] *It differs in not mentioning setting four sticks of firewood at the corners of the firepit; at the end, the ashes are swept into the firepit, not outdoors as usual. After bathing, one sings the song whose words go:* Ayūkwegi netsīktsīk kiwo'o, *"Always alas, my money, I want it."*

Another money song on the cylinders tells of a Ko'otep man who sat at Wełkwäu and sang: Kwilek-neka wetine-rurawine ke-tsīk wetine-meł holem'o, *"That I singing for that money am fishing for it from the beach."*[3]

T1. Great Money Caught in the River

This is perhaps not an actual formula, but it is a story of formula type. The story is wholly concerned with the acquisition of the means of magical power; the interest in the human personalities is of the slightest. At the same time the narrative is evidently enjoyed, and rather well done. The struggle with the prey, though somewhat prolix, is not without skill in working up suspense.

•

a. At Pekwon, in the house wogi,[1] there was an old man; his wife was from meitser[2] in Ko'otep. He said to his son, "Bring sweathouse wood constantly!" Then the young man (at his father's orders), every day after he had carried firewood (and had sweated himself), fished for trout at Pekwutel[3] with pole, line, and hook.[4] He would begin at the downstream end of the rock and fish upstream to the end of the sand. His dog was always with him. It would lie behind him as he fished.

When he was through and came home, the old man always said, "Tell me if you have seen anything." "No, I saw nothing," he would say, and thought, "Perhaps I shall see something. Why does he always ask me?"

Now he had done that for five days, and the old man kept asking him the same. Then it was eight days, and the old man said, "Well, it is near now. You have almost finished: watch constantly." "Yes," the young man said. Again the old man said, "Tell me if you have seen anything," and he answered, "No, nothing." "Well, it will be for one night more; then you will be through." It was nine days then.

2. [This is Lowie catalogue number 24-1020.—Ed.]
3. [And this is Lowie catalogue number 24-1021.—Ed.]

---

1. Waterman, Geography, map 15, house 4; "in the middle."
2. Waterman, map 14, house 10, meitsero.
3. A rock in the river, downstream from Pekwon. Formerly a small sandbar stretched upstream from it. Waterman, map 11, no. 56, Pekwuteł, rock in river; no. 55, Erter, sandbar.
4. For hook and line fishing, see Goddard, Life and Culture of the Hupa, p. 25 and pl. 13, fig. 1.

b. In the morning the youth went down to fish again. "Now watch! If you feel anything, tell me." But the old man never said what he would see. Then he threw his line in close to the rock, and it floated, while he watched. Then he saw the line begin to go under: it went straight down by the rock. Then he could just feel something. He raised the stick and felt it twitching again a little. Whenever he felt it jerk, he lifted the pole a bit. He began to think, "That must be the one my father told me to watch for." He tried to raise it by the pole, but each time almost let it go. Then he laid down his pole and took the line in hand and pulled: then it drew away farther. He kept thinking as before, but did not know what was coming. He tried to pull once more: each time it jerked and went off with the line. Then he would draw harder and could see the surface of the water swishing to the sides. Meanwhile he kept thinking about the old man: "That is why he always spoke to me like that. Well, perhaps I shall see it, if I catch it." Then he pulled harder, and it too, and it seemed almost to come to the surface.

Now it was nearly sunset: he could no longer see the sun from where he stood: and it seemed easier to draw. So he pulled all he could. But when it started to run again, it almost dragged him underwater. Then he thought he should drown, because whenever he pulled, it almost drew him in. So he heaped up the sand with his feet and braced them and exerted himself. But it ran off again, so that he almost let go the line. But he pulled it back once more and saw it swimming on top now, with its mouth open, red inside. Again he thought he should drown,[5] but drew as hard as he could, and saw it coming nearer, and brought it up on the sand.

c. Then immediately he poured water on it which the old man had prepared for him in a little basket, with angelica root in it. He had said, "If you catch anything, pour that on it as soon as you land it, and do not club it." So he did. As soon as he poured, it was as if he had killed it: it no longer moved. So he carried it home.

When he came to the house, he saw that the old man had prepared something like a box out of a log[6] with water in it, and he put it in. Then he warmed water and poured it in until it was covered. Then it began to live again. And it became small also: it was as large as a sturgeon when he caught it, but now it was little.

d. The old man said: "That is Great Money.[7] It is a good rock, that Pekwuteɫ. If anyone brings in sweathouse wood and bathes[8] by that rock, it is very good (for becoming wealthy), because that is where this Great Money

5. Probably because he now realized that it was surely something supernatural or monstrous, and not a fish.

6. Like the Yurok "trunk," a cylinder hollowed out, with a convex cover.

7. Pelin-tsīk, Large Dentalium. It is conceived in this tale not as a person, but as a magnified, free-swimming, fishlike dentalium.

8. Or, washes on it.

lives. When one has caught it, money keeps coming as if thrown at one." He said, after they had it in the box, "This is what I was always telling you to watch for. It is a good thing to catch. Take care of it well." So he kept it, and property entered readily into that house; whatever they wished came to them. "Now if you see it moving too much in its box, sing thus," the old man said, and sang, and it quieted, and stirred but little and slowly. He said, "When it moves much and seems about to leap out, sing that and it will become quiet."

e. After a time he said, "Now we must take it back to where it was caught, for we do not want to kill it. We wished to catch it only to make money come easily." So they went down to the river and put it in. As soon as they set it in, it leaped, as if it wished to return.

Now it lives there, that Big Money, by that rock. When one who knows it passes in a boat, he watches, and when the boat is abreast of the rock, toward the middle of the stream, he claps his hands for luck and says, "I wish to be fortunate, to feel prosperous when I return."[9]

T2. He Flew to the Sea of Pitch

a. At Wohtek, the Asiksekweɬ sweathouse,[1] to that he always brought his sweathouse wood. Yet he was married. When he had finished sweating, he always looked across the river from before the sweathouse. Then he would see otters coming out of the water on the other shore, would run down and cross the river, and kill them. Many bought those otter skins, people from Wohtek (and elsewhere). So he had luck and acquired wealth.

b. Now he had a blanket.[2] No one knew it, for he kept it hidden under the boat gunwale on the ridge of the sweathouse. When everyone slept, he came out and flew (with his blanket). He flew upstream to Petskuk,[3] then around by the north.[4] When he reached Pulekuk,[5] he turned south.[6] This ocean, he saw, stretched only so far; but he went beyond it (past the sky). There he saw another one, like an ocean, the Kiolapopa'.[7] Then he turned

9. *Tsaskuin sanuheǥok kiahpelin mekwomɬitsok*.

---

1. This is the sweathouse belonging to the house in Wohtek (or Wohkero) to which tales U1-U3 refer.

2. Evidently conceived of as a sort of feather robe attached to the arms.

3. The eastern end of the world.

4. *Hierkik*.

5. The downstream end of the world, to the northwest.

6. *Hiwohpik*, across the ocean, here translated south. Perhaps it means at right angles to the upstream–downstream axis, hence southwest or west-southwest. Cf. *hierkik* as north.

7. "Half-pitch." [See Waterman, Geography, fig. 1, Kiolaaopaa. This is reproduced here as map 3.—Ed.]

back to the north, reached his sweathouse by daybreak, and put away his blanket.

c. Now he had a child. Then he told the boy, "I should like you to do what I always do. I will prepare you, and tell you what you must do." The boy said, "Very well." Then at night he led him out, put the blanket on him, and said, "Try to fly!" The boy flew up a little and came back. "Try again," his father said. He went higher. Then he said to him, "Now perhaps you can do as I do). First I fly upstream, then I return, then go south. But you must be careful, when you reach the strip of land,[8] to beware of the sea beyond it, for it is of pitch." "Very well." So the boy flew off—upstream, along the north, and southward. His father had said, "After you come to the land that divides (the two oceans), be sure to fly high." But when he reached it, he failed to do so. Then when he was over the (farther) sea, he touched it, (became stuck fast), tried to loosen himself, but could not.

d. The old man thought, "Surely he did get caught there," because by daybreak he did not see his boy return. "Let me wait a little and follow him," he thought. He had two such blankets.[9] Then he followed him, going around by the same way,[10] and when he came near the dividing land, heard him crying. When he arrived, he saw him in the water,[11] crying and trying to fly, but unable to. Then he caught him by the head to pull him out. Then he pulled him out and threw him on his back to carry him. So he brought him home, arriving just at daybreak.[12]

T3. Dripped on at Kohpei

a. That is how it was with him, the young man from Kohpei.[1] Always he was on the beach close to the salt water, catching *nohko*[2] fish. That is what he ate; therefore, he went on the beach. That was all he ate. He was the

8. *Sic*. Perhaps the sky's edge?

9. They were of condor feathers.

10. He might have shortened his route by going straight downstream to the edge of the sky at Pulekuk, but the Yurok love the idea of making the circuit of the world's edge. Also, he did not know with certainty where the boy had met mishap.

11. It was only half-pitch.

12. Evidently he did not start until night, since the round journey is described as taking a night, not a day and a night; or perhaps the daybreak motive has become so fastened in the narrator's mind that he works it in at the expense of inconsistency with the first sentence of the paragraph.

1. He was called Kohpe-s-otsin because he had grown at Kohpei, an important Tolowa town at Crescent City.

2. Unidentified salt water fish.

youngest one. The middle brother was constantly angry because he did not like to see him eat only that nohko. But it seemed the oldest did not mind. The middle one said, "Do not come into the house, because you will not eat the food we use, because that is all you will eat, that nohko." And on the beach he got sand all over himself (*tsäiłkil*) from off the fish. But one of them, the oldest one, felt sorry for his youngest brother.

b. And the old man (of the house) thought, "I will take him there." So he said to him, "I will take you where you can swim for yourself. There is a large rock with a hole in the side, and you can enter that.[3] Gather sweathouse wood for ten days. And I will make angelica root ready for you in the basket dipper;[4] wash with that and it will be your medicine when you are ready to enter that rock." So he took that.

Then his (oldest) brother (*u-pa'*) said, "I will go with him to that rock." Then he went with him in the boat to that rock and said, "This is the one you wanted to come to." So he swam to that rock and entered the hole. Then he saw that inside was where the one called Kämes[5] lived; he was one of the *łmeyur*.[6] So he went through the opening. When he got in a little distance, he saw that it was like dry. And there was no more water, and he saw a nice flat rock inside. That is what he sat down on. And the old man had said to him, "Come out at once when you feel one drop on your head; for if it drips on you twice you will not come out again, if it drips twice."

c. Then he felt a drop on his head but did not leave; he just continued sitting. He thought he wanted another drop, two drops on his head; so he sat. And it was only a little while and another drop fell on him. Then he began to stand up, but did not succeed, for the rock just came together as when a door is shut, and there was no way in which he could get out, and he was inside. Then he saw the water boiling up (*nikiwannawok*) and he saw like many little fishes; they were dentalia. And they fastened on his body (and ate his flesh).[7]

d. So he could not come out. But the boat was outside, his brother in the boat. Then he who was in the boat, this was when he thought, "He cannot come out; he has done what we told him not to do: we told him to beware. I will go home." That is what he thought, the one in the boat. So he went back to the town. He said, "My brother never came out; he is still inside the hole. It was you who told him to enter the hole in that rock."

3. In order to have a supernatural experience.

4. *Keyammo*, usually *keyem* or *keyom*, a small shallow basket used to dip boiled food out of a cooking basket.

5. A water monster; Kämes and Knewollek are the two kinds most often mentioned.

6. *Łmei*, to be evil, vicious, dangerous.

7. So in the abstract; not mentioned in the text, probably because it is taken for granted that dentalia live on human flesh.

But the old man said: "It will be all right. I did not tell him to do that; I wanted him to stay for only one drop. Nevertheless, I think he will be safe. You will see. I think I know what he will do; he will come out. I know that rock because I have been to it myself when I was young. I used it too. It is not hard to acquire wealth if you use that rock with the hole. That is why I told him to go there. He will have good luck from that, he will."

e. Then they both went along the beach to look for him, thinking he would float out of the hole and be thrown up on the beach. They looked for him at Ottegen and also at Knäwi[8] and could not find him. Then they searched as far as Nekeł[9] but did not find him.

f. Then his older brother who had gone with him in the boat went on a little hill near Kohpei and sat there all day crying for his brother. He thought, "Alas, we cannot find him, alas." And as he looked about, when he was sitting on that hillside, he saw where his brother had entered (*ayo'mulis*) the hole. Then he saw someone sitting on the rock: his head was white. Then he thought, "Perhaps that is he; perhaps he has climbed out on top of the rock." So he said, "Let us go out to see," when he had returned to the house; and the old man went with him. Then his brother climbed on top of the rock. There he was sitting: he had no flesh left on him, only bones; those dentalia had eaten his flesh off. That is where they found him. He had come out on top, not by the hole through which he went in below. So now they took him home, the old man and his brother. They laid him on a dressed buckskin[10] and brought him indoors and laid him at *mełku*.[11] And they went down to the stream and took sand to cover the place where he was lying. "That is where we will keep him," the old man said, "because we do not want anyone to see him; and we will restore his flesh with deer marrow."[12] Then they used that; every evening they rubbed it on him. In the morning he looked better. For five days they did that, and he began to look better. So they went on using that marrow, and it was ten days, and he was well. And he himself said, "I do not want to stay at *mełku* any longer. I am well again. I feel it." And his flesh was on him again.

g. Then someone came to tell that they were coming from the north (*pullu*) to gamble. When they played, it was just as if they gave him the property. Those who had come to gamble lost everything. For ten days they played, and he won as if they gave it to him.

h. Then he said to his mother, "Keep the house clean outside[13] and keep

8. Ottegen is said to be about 5 miles north of Kohpei, and Knäwi, Point St. George, is near it.

9. Some 4 miles south of Kohpei; now called Nickel Creek or Beach.

10. *Smetsoi*.

11. *Mełku* is the ground-level ledge or terrace between the house wall and the central pit. It is usually pretty well filled with large food-storage baskets. He lay hidden behind these.

12. *Sererperł*.

13. *Lekwusin*.

it clean in front of the sweathouse.[14] I am going away; I am going to *pulukuk*. From there I am going to *hierkik*[15] to gamble, and then I am going to the sky end of the world, Hostseyi-woni-wes'ona.[16] That is why I tell you to keep it clean outside the house, because dentalium money will be coming. It will be as if you saw money when I go gambling around the world to the upriver end. That is why you do not want any (refuse) lying about outside the house, because the money will be flying there and falling when I win it and send it home. That is where I will throw all the money I win.[17] In the morning, early in the morning, that is when you will see it outside, when I throw it there. You will think of me going upriver when you see the money flying down from there. So keep it clean, because I am going to Hostseyi-woni-wes'ona."

So he went. He went along the ocean on the north edge of the world[18] to the upriver end, and everywhere he won money and treasure. He was very powerful from having gone into that rock; because the money had eaten his flesh. That is how he had good luck with all kinds of wealth. So that is where he went to, to Petskuk-wostseya-won.[19]

T4. Origin of the Kepel Dam and the Deerskin Dances

This story was previously published in Kroeber and Gifford, World Renewal, Appendix II, no. 4. It is an institutional myth of the group-journey type. Hard to follow for one not knowing the rituals and their geography, it is nevertheless not bald in its manner but rather well told. It is interesting that the narrative has to do only with Deerskin Dance world renewals on the main line of the Klamath. The Jumping Dances of the lower Yurok, that of the Karok at Enek–Amaikiaram, and the Deerskin Dance in Hupa on the Trinity are all omitted. The informant's own town, Pekwon, is the seat of one of the omitted Jumping Dances.

•

Now he began to speak, he who lived at the downriver end of Kepel.[1] He said, "I do not like it that the salmon do not come up. It is too near the ocean, that fish dam at Turip, for the salmon do not run up, they go back,[2] and we

14. *Kwenometi*; in error for *kwennet*?

15. *Pulukuk* or pulekuk, literally downstream, means north along the coast; *hierkik* means to the right from downstream; here, eastward from the north end of the world. Continuing east he comes to the upper end of the world where the sky begins.

16. Edge of upper world, sky edge. [Given as Wes'ona hostseiwes in A14*f*.—Ed.]

17. *Noł-witu-käpriokore'm*.

18. *Hierkik werik'eu*.

19. Upriver-edge-up, a variant of Hostseyi-woni-wes'ona of n. 16.

---

1. Kepel-hipur; perhaps equivalent to Sa', where the sweathouse stood for the esoteric part of the Kepel dam ceremony.

2. *Tewolli*, into the ocean.

who live here get none. The little ones only come past. Those are the ones we catch, the little ones, only them. Now I think I will go there and take away their fish dam. They will get angry and perhaps we shall be killed, for I do not think they will allow it, they who own that dam."

Then they began to talk with each other about that. "We will try it. They are turning back, those salmon, for the dam is too near (the mouth)." So they said, "Well, yes." All of them said, "It is good; that is how it will be: we shall go from here."

Then they went, and they arrived where that fish dam was at Turip. Then they pulled up the dam on one side of the river and on the other too, and carried it away.

They there saw that their fish dam was gone. It was then that they learned that it had been taken away. And they were talking about getting it back; all of them living there talked about it. So they all started out. Then they arrived on the hill (opposite Kepel), above Mūrek,[3] having traveled upriver inland.[4] And he was ahead who is (now) standing at Umeggau.[5] For he was the chief one, the Redwood, he was the one that owned the dam at Turip, he who (now) stands at Umeggau. He was in advance, coming downhill, but others were behind him uphill.

And when he came near the river he said, "I am somewhat afraid; I do not think I will cross over. We had better give it up and let them keep it; I am afraid we shall get killed." There were many people there all over the (Kepel) flat, ready to (fight to) keep the fish dam. They had prepared everything and had put the dam into the water just as it stood at Turip. They were just putting in the pole *upekol*.[6] They had worked toward both shores from the middle, and now it was all finished.

Then he from Turip thought, "Well, we shall (help) take care of this dam also; we shall come up now and then to see it. They have to advise us when they are about to erect it. As long as they make the dam here they must inform us. Then we will take care of it as long as they continue to make it, and each time we shall see it." So they thought like this, that they could not take it back downriver with them, because they were afraid of the others.

Then he began to talk again, he who lived at Kepel. "I think we will leave the dam like this and begin a Deerskin Dance for it, because everything will come out well from that. But it will not be well if they omit it, even one

3. Mūrek-wonu.

4. *Hełkäi*.

5. Umeggau is partway up the hill opposite Kepel, where there was a clump of redwoods, the farthest upstream along the Klamath. Waterman, Geography, pl. 6, fig. 2; also map 17, no. 46, and p. 248. *Umegau o'tepon* means "standing at his payment place."

6. A split young fir. Most accounts tell of the dam being built from the shore ends to meet in the middle.

year only; for there will be much sickness if they do not make this dam as long as there are people in the world. For we (the woge) are about to leave: now we shall go."

One of them said, "Well, I am going; going downriver to Wohtek. That is where we shall make the Deerskin Dance,[7] where I am going to stay. But you can go wherever you wish, because we are leaving this dam and it will be a good thing."

Then he said, one of them, "I will go upriver." And they said to him, "Yes." And another one said, "I am going to Women,[8] that is where I am going, and I will have that place." And they said to him, "Yes, keep that. People will be well off on account of that when sickness spreads in the world, if they stamp on the ground there."

And one of them said, "Well, I am going to Opyegau[9] and I will watch for the people from that place." And another said he would stop at Po'toyo[10] and watch over the people from there. And another one said, "I am going to stay in Weitspus; that is where you can leave me and there is where all will have fun." And they said to him, "Very well, keep it well. Hold to it as long as they make the Deerskin Dance, because it will be good for the people." And he said, "Yes, I will do that; I will hold to it." So the others went on, leaving him there, and that is where he stayed, at Weitspus, the one who holds the Deerskin Dance there.

Then the others went on upriver,[11] and came to three places where one of them stayed, they who were going to watch over the world. And when they came to Olar[12] one of them said, "I will stay here; I will make that kind of good times too." And they said to him, "Yes, you take care of this place,

7. The dance place is a full mile downstream from Wohtek, on the same side as Wohtek. A creek comes in there called Helegäu. They begin to dance near the mouth and progress uphill perhaps a mile before the finale (Robert Spott thought 4 or 5 miles). See Waterman, map 11, nos. 12, 13, 14, dance places, and 15, the creek.

8. Women is a large prairie on the hill back of Kenek. [But see notes for A12 and A14, in which K. says that it is in back of Weitspus—and thus would be on the opposite side of the river.—Ed.] Waterman, p. 260, says: "Great open space on mountain back of Kewet" [behind Weitspus; see also O1, n. 14.—Ed.]

9. Opyegau is on top of the ridge opposite Martin's Ferry at Wahsek.

10. Po'toyo is Bloody Camp, on the same ridge, more or less opposite Weitspus; Waterman, map 23, no. 12. There is a tree here which is addressed in the formula for the Weitspus Jumping Dance.

11. *Petsik-weroi.*

12. Olar is opposite the mouth of Camp Creek. The relation of this to Olege'l-kes (n. 14) is not clear. The Orleans, or more exactly Camp Creek, ceremony for world renewing is usually said by the Yurok to be held at Camp Creek, Olege'l. This name and Olar may by etymologically related. Orleans proper is called Panamenik by the Karok and Ko'men by the Yurok.

because it will be well it they dance here. When it is bad in the world it will become well again when they dance here." "Do you know when they will do that? It will not be well if they begin again within one year. There will be a proper month for it."[13] And he said, "It is good; I will do it like that."

And another thought, "Well, I will stop here at Olege'l-kes."[14] And he stayed to take care of the Deerskin Dance there, and the others went on upriver.

So they came to Segwu',[15] and one of them said, "This is where I shall stay; there will be a dance here too and I will take care of it. And it will be a different dance from downriver." So now they dance there, and it is not so good a dance.[16] And he who was going to stay there said, "I do not know how they will dance here, but anyway I shall stay and take care of the place, and there will be a proper month for it; it will not be well if they do not dance in the month for it. But if they do, it will be well for the world." And they said to him, "Take care of it here; we are going on." And he said, "Goodbye;[17] but it will not be well if the downriver people come up to dance here at this place which I am taking care of at Segwu'.

And they went on up to Clear Creek, to where Okonile'l is,[18] and there they thought they would have a Deerskin Dance,[19] and they left one of them close by the river at Okonile'l where they now dance, and they said to him, "This is where you will stay." And he said, "Yes, I shall stay here." And they said, "This is as far as we will go. Here we shall go uphill onto the ridges."[20] There are ten little round hills[21] here; that is where the rest of them went to. From there they always look out when they make the dam downriver, when they begin to make it on the hill opposite Kepel.[22] When they begin to set the hillside opposite Kepel on fire, then in the evening they (upstream) always see much smoke coming up along the river.[23] Then they know that they have started their fire downriver there and have begun to make the dam. They said, "We shall leave it that way: that is how we shall always see it,

13. *Kiok-wonauslei*. This agrees with the actual Karok determination by the moon.

14. Olege'l-kes is at the river in front of Olege'l.

15. Segwu' is Karok Katimin.

16. By Yurok standards it is short—two to five days instead of from ten up; and some of the dancing is or may be with brush, etc., instead of with treasures.

17. Tsū.

18. Okonile'l is Karok Inam.

19. Usually so called by the Yurok, though many of them know that other skins are used, and that the dancing is more as in the War Dance.

20. *Wonnäu u-krerertser*.

21. *Uwogit*, knolls or hillocks.

22. Kepel wa-hi-won, where brush, etc., is gathered.

23. *Weroi*, "stream," evidently here meaning the Klamath.

smoke coming up in the river canyon, for we are leaving it to them to do like that, around the world.''

T5. The Water-Monster Helper

This story was recorded on six phonograph cylinders. The first one broke before it could be transcribed at the University. The beginning of the tale is therefore lacking, except that a brief abstract made at the time of recording says that the man whose child was stolen was helped—that is, given supernatural fighting strength—by a Sä'äł[1] at Wespen.

•

a. And he thought, this one who grew up at Wespen,[2] "I think I am strong; I think I shall be able to take care of myself and not be killed.'' So he prepared to go, and took a red obsidian, and went down to the river, and entered it. He went all about in the water to see if he could find someone to go with him. But he could see no one, because they had all gone off. So he went down along the river[3] (underwater), intending to try to enter the house, going along in the river.[4] All along the way he went into the houses (holes or caves under the water), but there was no one in them: they had all gone away.

b. And further downstream he arrived at Ho'peu-pul-hiko,[5] that is where he arrived. There he saw the shadow of the door of the house and began to enter it. And he came into a nest,[6] and felt it was warm, and he went on one side and entered farther, and he saw where the one was who lived in that house. So he said to him, "That is why I have come, in order to look about.'' And that one answered, "Yes? It is well that you have come. But they have all gone, these dangerous ones,[7] because they saw you coming and are afraid of you. They said, 'He is the one we want, the one that owns that child. We want to see if he is unafraid. So let us take away his child from him.' And that is why they took your child. They took it to where they live at Erwergerił;[8] but I have been wanting to

1. [Sä'äl are spirits in creeks, deep woods, or hills which bring sickness.—Ed.]

2. Wespen is a creek near the Gist hydraulic mine about 1/3 mile below Weitspus. It is evidently a prehistoric village site, to judge from the artifacts found there. The Yurok uniformly say that it was a woge but not a human town. Waterman, Geography, map 25, no. 16, places it 3/4 mile from Weitspus, below the mouth of the Otegeket Creek, a fair-sized stream. [This map is reproduced here as map 4.—Ed.] Wespen figures prominently in tales A2 and A16x*o*.

3. *Weroi*, any stream.

4. *Keski*, "below, downhill''; here, under water.

5. Opposite downstream from Ho'peu, a north-side town in the last bend of the river, about 3 miles above Rekwoi.

6. *Weres-ogus*.

7. *Łmeyukr*, here and below.

8. Erwergerił is a large seastack. Waterman, map 5, no. 12, puts it a scant mile offshore from the mouth of Wilson Creek (Omen) and due west out at sea. [This map is reproduced here as map 6.—Ed.] My informant said "not quite 3 miles north of Wilson Creek in the ocean.''

see you. I was waiting for you. I always go there myself, where all the dangerous ones are; but no one else goes there. There is a town there, and your child is there now. Lying behind the fire opposite the door, it is still well, in there. And you will give me tobacco. I want ten baskets of tobacco. That is what you will give me." And he said "Yes," he who had come from Wespen, "I will give you that. Let us go."

c. And when he came outdoors, that one said to him, "Sit on my neck. And when I enter salt water and the waves wash over you, come right up on top of my neck. We are going to Erwergeriɫ." So he climbed on his neck, right behind the horn(s), and sat there. Then that one began to swim, and it felt as if he were leaping, as he entered salt water. The breakers rolled over him, but nevertheless they went on through. He thought they had gone far on the ocean, but the tail of the one who was carrying him had not yet left the river, it was so long. And swimming on, they came to the house at Erwergeriɫ, and he said, "This is the place. When I open the door, I will tell you, and you must go right in. Straight across from the door, there he is who is keeping your child."

And when that one opened the door it was as if he could see nobody and hear nothing. But he leaped where he thought that one lay, and with his red obsidian he slashed his belly[9] open. Then he felt his child inside, and seized it and jumped outdoors again. And when the door shut again, everyone in the house stood up and said, "Someone has come in and has taken that little one."[10] But he was killed, he who had it, he was cut open. From inside the house they tried to shut the door,[11] but he was already outside. And the one who had carried him there said (to them), "You all thought that he would not come, but now he has been here." And they said, "No, we did not think so." But he said, "This is the one, he who grew up at Wespen. He is the one who took it."

d. Then he carried him upriver again. And he said, "In five days I will come to Weitspus. You will see that it is a little foggy across from Weitspus. Then it is you who will bring me the tobacco there." And he said, "Yes, I will do that."

And it was five days; and he saw there was a little fog there, at the place he said he would come to. So he carried the tobacco there, ten baskets, and put it on top of the rock. So he crawled up, that *K*ämes[12] to get his tobacco. It was his pay, that tobacco, for having helped him. And he said to the one who grew up at Wespen, "Take marrow[13] and rub it on him; that is how he will have his flesh again, that child. He will be well from that." And the child became wholly well.

9. *Weye*.

10. *Mätp'oɫ*, "not yet having sense." A common name for small children.

11. The door was of flint, according to the abstract.

12. Here, at last, the type of water monster which helped him is named. Kämes are very long and make the water rough. According to the abstract, the abductors were also Kämes.

13. *Sererperɫ*.

T6. Gambling at Dentalium Home

a. He grew up at Pekwon, and he had as his partner a young man from Wohtek.[1] So he said to him, "Let us go to get sweathouse wood." And his partner said, "Yes, let us do that. You go up the hill here, and I will go uphill from Wohtek. On top where the trails come together we will meet, at Kerrits-o-skegwo,[2] and there we will cut our wood." And the other said, "Yes, I will do that with you. We will get sweathouse wood only there."

And so that is how they did: they always met together up on the hill, and when they had finished taking their wood they would sit down and talk. So then when they said, "Well, let us go down," he would go *hipuris*, the one who lived at Wohtek, and the other would go *hipetsis*,[3] he that had come up from Pekwon. Each would hear the other crying as he went down and would be sorry;[4] and when they arrived and started fire in the sweathouse, smoke would come out from it. Then when they had finished sweating, he (from Wohtek) would go up to Pekwon and talk with his friend. That is all they did, to go up after wood; they did nothing else.

And toward evening he would say to him again, "Let us go up, and I will meet you at Kerrits-o-skegwo." And they counted their *werpk'erk*.[5] One of them used two daily and the other used two, so they counted them until they knew from the werpk'erk that they had been going ten days.[6]

b. Then he said, "What shall we do? Perhaps we shall have good luck from this wood; perhaps you will do well to make yourself guessing-game rods." And he said to him, "I will make those." So all one day he worked at that game and did not go up after sweathouse wood, and the other said, "I will come and help you." So they made their game, working on it all day.

Then he said, "Well tomorrow morning let us go up again to Kerrits-o-skegwo," and he said, "Yes, I will do that." So in the morning he arrived there just as the sun arose. He had eaten nothing; he only smoked. In coming to Kerrits-o-skegwo he met his partner. They gathered their wood, all they

1. The two towns are just about a mile apart.

2. The name suggests Werrets-o-tmäw, "where they break alder," a women's place for gathering firewood; Waterman, Geography, map 11, no. 41, which he puts about 1-1/4 miles from both Pekwon and Wohtek, up behind them.

3. Downriverward (toward Wohtek) and upriverward (toward Pekwon).

4. From affection for him.

5. The withe which serves as a frame or sling for carrying the load of ceremonial sweathouse wood is called *werpk'erk*. When the load is discharged, the withe is thrown on the sweathouse roof.

6. They knew how many days they had been going up by counting the werpk'erk withes which had accumulated. Each of them went up twice a day, so between them they counted four withes as a day.

needed, and loaded it into their werpk'erk. The one from Wohtek[7] said, "Go down first, and I will follow because I am turning off." So they threw their loads on their backs. Then he heard his partner crying; he heard him crying all the way to Wohtek, and he thought, "Alas!"[8] Then he himself began to cry, this one from Pekwon.[9]

c. He had made only one step, and when he tried to make another he could not. "The sweathouse wood has caught overhead somehow," he thought. Then he did not know how it had got caught, because there were no branches about. So he set his load on the ground, but he could see no brush which might have caught his wood. So he tried again: he threw the load on his back and took a step, but it was the same way; he was held fast. Then he commenced to cry about that and set his load down once more. He thought, "There are no branches overhead to catch it; I do not know what to do. Nothing holds the wood, but it is as if I were stuck fast." So it was this way ten times, and he cried; and it happened eleven times. Then he sat down again and thought, "Hi, what will I do?" and cried more. Then he saw two persons sitting on[10] his load, two women.[11] Both were wearing *wileppo'm*[12] headbands of woodpecker crest. He saw that they were good-looking women. It was they who were holding his load.

Then she said to him, "Sit down; do not go home. It is we who came after you. Perhaps you thought you did it of yourself, but we waited to see you coming after your wood, because we wanted you to go back with us. We have come after you because we always heard you when you were crying over your wood. It is only a little distance." Then the young man did not know those women and thought, "Where are they from?" And they said,[13] "Well, I will tell you where we come from. The place is called Dentalium Home;[14] that is where we are from. They told us there to come and bring you. They want you because always you gather sweathouse wood. So now we have come to get you." And he thought, "Hi, I have no clothes!" And the women said, "We

7. [Pekwon?—Ed.]

8. *Hi äwoku*—again from love of his friend.

9. It is the one from Pekwon—the narrator's town—who here becomes the principal hero.

10. *Wa-hi-woni*.

11. Wives, brides, and girls frequently appear in pairs in Yurok narrative, though in actual life dual marriage was not common. [K.'s typescript indicated that he intended to supply a cross-reference here. The Yurok did practice the levirate with the consent of the surviving brother's first wife, as discussed in Spott and Kroeber, Yurok Narratives, no. 3, pp. 148-149.—Ed.]

12. The *wileppo'm* is a headband worn by the woman formulist in the Brush Dance, but normally it is made of ordinary feathers, not of woodpecker scalps as here.

13. He thinks; they answer.

14. Tsīktsīko'ɬ.

have dressed buckskin.[15] You will wear that.'' So he thought, ''It is well I have it to wear.''[16]

And they carried him, between them in the middle.[17] They said, ''It is not very far to where we will take you; perhaps you will think it is far, but we always heard you cry. Where you always gathered, you will see that place from where you are going; it will look as if it were farther, but it is only a little way.'' And so they took him, and he felt that it was only a short distance, and then they went downhill and he looked about and saw that nothing was growing on the ground.[18] And that is all he knew, this young man who had gathered sweathouse wood, because the women said that the old man had sent them after him, the old man of Dentalium Home.

d. And they arrived there in the evening, and he sat down in the house, and they all came in and said, ''It is well you have come.'' And the young man thought, ''I had to come,'' but he said nothing; he just thought. And he thought he would not sleep that night, and they who lived there said, ''Let him go to the sweathouse,'' but the old man said, ''Let him sleep in the house; let my son-in-law[19] sleep in the house.''

And he told him he would come tomorrow, the one called Kapuloyo.[20] ''Always he comes to gamble and always he wins everything; that is why we wanted you and sent these two women to bring you.''

Then he was about to cry; he said, ''What shall I do?'' The old man said, ''He comes from Pulekuk. You will see him coming in his boat; it goes of itself, and its tie rope[21] is red.''

e. And in the morning someone called, ''He is coming.'' Then the young man saw it was like fog where the boat came, and it landed, and a tie rope was thrown ashore and its color was red like the backbone of a salmon.

And they said to him, ''Lie down at *atserger*[22] in the sweathouse.'' And they hid him, as it were. And he said, ''If you give me the rods to handle, then bet more.[23]

15. The loin covering seems to be called simply by the word for dehaired buckskin, *smetsoi*. Men gathering sweathouse wood were naked, except perhaps for a belt.

16. The Yurok were prudish about exposing genitals, except by old men; and there is some ribaldry about peeping at bathing women.

17. On their joined hands? Or on a limb? Or in a pack basket held by both of them?

18. The country where the dentalia live is usually described as bare of vegetation.

19. *Ne-tsne'u-kus*. The old man recognizes him as husband of the girls, by assigning him to the living house; the sweathouse of course is the men's club.

20. Recorded as Kepulloyo in this text.

21. *U-mene's, wa'äiket*. [K. has a notation to check his notebooks here.—Ed.]

22. *Atserger* is the corner diagonally opposite the entrance and next to the exit. [See diagram of sweathouse in Kroeber, Handbook, p. 82.—Ed.]

23. *Tsakersermikwerm*, add to the stakes.

Then from inside he saw him coming to *kwennet*.[24] But as far as he could see him was up to the knee; above, he was like fog. And with him came his two sisters—there were three of them. So he came inside the sweathouse, this Kapuloyo. All he could see of him was that he laid down dentalia in front of his foot. He could see nothing of him from the knee up. Where he sat down was at *hikes*;[25] that is where he went. And the two women came in and sat beside him.[26] He counted out so much as his bet, and the others matched it. Then they began to lose, they who lived at Dentalium Home. It was noon, and they had lost much in gambling.

f. Then that young man from Pekwon thought, "Hi, I wish my gambling rods would come; I wish they would come." Then he saw them come to himself, and he said, "Hi, I wish my basket dipper[27] were coming; I want it to put angelica in." Then he saw that dipper come also; and he thought, "Hi, my pipe; I wish it too would come." And he saw his pipe come. So he got everything that he wanted, when he thought he would like to have it come.

g. And it was early afternoon, and the old man wanted to stop playing, but the young man from Pekwon wanted to bet; so Kapuloyo said, "Well, I will match him." So, they bet more; they bet everything they had. And when they were ready, the old man said to him, "Well, you shuffle them." Then the young man stood up to take the gambler's seat, and the old man said to him, "Here are the rods." "No, I have my own. I want to go outdoors to wash them." So he went outside and put angelica into the basket and washed his game set with it.

Then he thought, "I will do so too, that he will not see me from the knees up; he will only see my legs." So he went to shuffle and divide the rods. Then he saw what Kapuloyo was (had been) doing. The marked rod[28] he threw over his head, and it hovered there. Whichever way one pointed, that marked ace went into the other hand. That is what it did, and five times they could not guess it.

Then when he began to shuffle, this one from Pekwon, he won three times before they guessed the ace. It was not three hours,[29] and he had won back everything the old man had lost. And then his opponent saw him the same way: he had the ace over his head. Then it was that Kapuloyo began to cry. He thought, "Always I thought I was the best, but now I am losing. Hi, where did he come from? He is the best."

24. *Kwennet* is the place outside the sweathouse door.

25. *Hikes* is the place just inside the sweathouse entrance, to the right if the exit is to the left.

26. Women in the sweathouse? Not, apparently, in real life, except in shaman training.

27. *Keyammo*. [For variants, see T3, n. 4.—Ed.]

28. The one marked rod or "ace" is called *we'kuser*. It is banded with black in the middle where the hand covers it. There are fifty to a hundred slender unmarked rods, and the guess is for the hand which holds the ace.

29. The informant said *pekw-a-nahksen-rook*, "not three sun places," meaning not yet three o'clock—a modern expression.

h. So he won back everything, and he also won Kapuloyo's dentalia, and he said he wanted to play for more, this Kapuloyo. He wanted to match everything he had lost, and he took his carrying case,[30] turned the dentalia out of it, and the money was alive[31] and moving about. So that Pekwon young man began to shuffle, and Kapuloyo's sisters were sitting on each side of him, and Pekwon young man thought, "Anyhow, I shall not lose even for that (if the money be alive), I shall not lose." So he won all the money that was alive.

And Kapuloyo wanted to play on. He wanted to bet more. He said, "I will match everything that I have lost; I will bet my two sisters against it." So they agreed. Then he shuffled and hid them again, this young man from Pekwon, and the other could not find the ace. The sun was nearly down. Then that young man from Pekwon won, and that young man Kapuloyo lost his two sisters.[32] And he said, "That is all; we will stop. I have nothing left to bet." So they ended. And he had lost his boat also.[33]

T7. Ritual Sweating

This text was obtained in 1907 on two phonograph cylinders as a myth, localized at Pekwon, of how sweathouse wood anciently said it should be gathered and burned to bring wealth. The account proved to be a description of ritual sweating. Perhaps it is also actually a formula for acquiring dentalia by sweathouse practices. For that reason I have left it in the past tense.

•

a. Now he was doing thus. He was lying in the sweathouse at *ertserger*[1] and thinking, "In the morning I will gather firewood." This is how he slept, thinking of getting wood in the morning, of breaking (the branches) off. And the (Douglas fir) wood itself spoke, "Whoever seeks me will have good luck. He will do well by thinking of me. That is how I leave it to be in the world."

b. And for ten days he did that. He went out from the sweathouse thinking about it and sat down at *kwennet*[2] and looked at the sky. He spoke to himself thus: "I will acquire dentalia." He was really going to get sweathouse wood, but he talked of dentalia. And he got up and went up the hill and saw where he

30. *Egor*.

31. *Nihegwollontsim*.

32. So now he has four wives? See n. 11.

33. The story resembles G7 in the "capture" by the women, and A2 or D6x in the deep friendship of the two young men.

---

1. Or *atserger*, at the back of the sweathouse near the exit. For a diagram of the places in the sweathouse, see Kroeber, Handbook, p. 82.

2. *Kwennet* is the stone-paved platform in front of the sweathous

was going to break his wood, having talked on the way up. Then he thought, "Hi, these are the ones that are going to descend on me, these fir leaves."[3] And he broke the limb and said, "They will stick on me, on my body; because I break it off, they will fall on me, all kinds of dentalia." Thus he talked when he broke off the first limb.

Then, taking his load on his back,[4] he started to go downhill, crying, "Hi, I have got them, I have dentalia. These are the sticks I will put into the fire, and when I throw them in they will all fasten on my body." That is how he talked when he was carrying his wood downhill.

c. Outside the sweathouse, there he put down his load of wood, and he threw it inside and began to make his fire. As he put it in he thought, "These are the ones I am putting into the fire, every kind of dentalia, and they will fasten to me; they are money, these sticks I am putting in the fire. You sticks, I am putting you in because you said it yourself, that you would help me get dentalia. Every one of you will remember what I said." That is how he talked to himself when he got wood for the sweathouse. He would have good luck from talking thus.

And the wood said, "You will put me in the fire, but it will be well: you will have good luck for that. And sometimes you will be sorry about it,[5] as long as people live in the world, because I spoke that way and said I would help them, and dentalia would come to them."

And then he brushed off[6] the floor, sweeping it into the fireplace. Then he thought, "This, that is burning, is dentalia. And it is smoking, and all the smoke is fastening on my body." And then he went outside, he who had been talking to himself, and sat down at *kwennet* and began to sing.

T8. Upriver-Coyote

a. He is the one who did it, thinking he would go downhill to this river, to its bed.[1] Then he thought, "Well, it will not be at all right if there is no water when they live and go about here. Then it will seem right if there is water about." Thereupon he said, "Well, I will go for that." So he went, he went everywhere, but he found no water. And he thought, "Hī, what will they do, those human beings? Because they will be well off only if they have water."

b. Then he circled its edge, the ocean;[2] its edge he traveled around. And

3. *U-käpoliɫ*, leaves or brush.
4. *Osroiktsegits*.
5. "Sorry for me," viz., for the firewood (?).
6. *Smertse'm*.

1. *Tetko-ɫ*, *tetkon-ek*, streambed, ditch, furrow. The Klamath is called simply *weroi*, stream.
2. *Tewoli*, prairie, plain. [Or oceanward? Elsewhere *tepolo* is translated as prairie.—Ed.]

he arrived far upstream, not finding water; back in the hills he traveled, and downstream, but found none, though he came far downstream and kept looking about there. That is why he went around, because it would not be well for them to live if they had no water when they arrived, when human beings arrived in this world. "That is why I go around: I want to find water."

c. So he went everywhere. Then he thought, "Well, to above I will go; up above let me look for that water." Then he arrived in the sky, and kept going about, and went around everywhere there in the sky, but he did not find it there. So he thought, "Well, upriver I will go, traveling in the sky to the upriver end and coming down there." So standing at the upriver end, by a ladder[3] he descended. Then he came there where this (river) water (now) issues; that is where he arrived. So he said, "I will look around; I have been all over the world above, but I have not found the water. And it appears to me it will not be as it should be if there is no water, but with that it will be well for human beings when they live around in the world, if they have that water."

d. Then he saw a woman there at Petskuk where it issues from, this water; that is where he saw a woman,[4] that is where she lived alone, this woman. He said, "There is no water where the river bed stretches; it goes for nothing where it is furrowed." She said, "Is it so?[5] There will be water. I will make it that there shall be water." He said, "Good,[6] I will go wherever the water issues from." (And he went.)[7] And she said, "From out of my body[8] it will issue,[9] that is how I will make water to be: from my body it will issue." He said, "Well, all right,[10] sit here." And he told her to go to the end (of the channel, riverbed). So she went.

Then it began to issue and made a lake. She said, "I will make water to be." Then she stirred it up, and said, "It is going to be all around everywhere on this earth.[11] Everywhere it is going to issue, everywhere they will have water, back in the hills[12] there will be deep ravines all around[13] which will carry water that issues (into them)."[14]

3. *Wiłke'ma* [?]
4. *Wei'ntsauks*.
5. *Hes*?
6. *Tsūł*.
7. Not clear.
8. *Neknewis*.
9. *Ki-mer'wermeri-k*.
10. *Tsūł*.
11. *Ki-we-łkel-ona*, earth, land.
12. *Tu-ka-hierkäu*.
13. *Ni-we-tegetko-ɫ*, the iterative form of tetko-ɫ.
14. A sentence follows that is obscure: *Moskiniyegole witukico' ki-o-kupa'a-na*, translated, "Others (?) said, 'You don't want to say that it will be like this, that there will be water.'"

Then she stirred it and blew out,[15] threw it[16] downstream and blew out. And she saw how it issued downstreamward and now was water.

e. And he said, "Hī," said Upriver-Coyote.[17] "Is it going to be that there will be salmon?[18] For it will not be good if there are no salmon in the streams."[19] Then she said, the one who had made this water, "Well, all right, for (if) it is like that it will not be right, if there are no salmon." So she thought like this, "I will make it indeed that there will be salmon." So she tore out the side from that lake that was there with the water in it, and made (another) lake below.

Then he began to sing, Upriver-Coyote, he began to sing his song, with this he sang it:[20] (Song) Come, trout![21] So she[22] made it that many of them came, those trout in the water; when he had finished (singing), they could see them like shadows beneath the water.[23] Then she[24] opened (the second lake), opened it, and (he) said, "*Tsūł,* turn them loose,[25] those that will be salmon," did Upriver-Coyote.

f. He began to go downstream, running; at the small creeks[26] was where he threw them in (the fish); he thought they would stay in those and there would be salmon everywhere that water flows into the river; because it would be right for human beings to have salmon. So he made it, and now they had salmon everywhere; wherever there were creeks[27] they went into them. So he himself made it, this Upriver-Coyote, that there would be salmon; but that one, that water, she made it to issue out from her,[28] the girl;[29] she is the one who made it issue from her own body to be water, this river. Now that is how it is.[30]

15. *Upegahksoyoli*, to blow off or out of the hand as in offering tobacco crumbs. The act is ritual; she was not blowing the water itself.

16. The words translated "stirred" and "threw" contain the same stem: *pis-wi'tu-olōloh* and *wi-ku-kem-olōloh-pini*.

17. Petskuk-o-segep. His first naming.

18. *We-nepuiy-ona*, from *ne'pui*, salmon.

19. *Ki-wi-kits-werōyoi*.

20. The stem *er-ner'meri* is used for "singing" throughout this passage instead of the ordinary *rurawo*.

21. *Wenos regokso*.

22. She or he?

23. *O-sa'äiwork awohpu*.

24. Or he?

25. The stem of "turn loose" is the same as of "open": *s'u'logeni*.

26. *Tu-kini-regāyoi*.

27. *We-'ki-tseni-merner-merner-ihkin*.

28. *Yekwine-mer'wermerih*.

29. *Umä'i*, a young but adult woman before birth of a child. In n. 4 she is called simply "woman." She is Mer'wermeri-s umä'i, Upriver-Ocean-Girl, of Spott and Kroeber, Yurok Narratives, no. 37, pp. 250-251. The ocean there, Mer'wermerei, seems to mean "that which issued out."

30. *Pīs wi'itu*.

Informant U

WETS'OWA OF PEKWON

His usual appellation was Wets'owa, from the fact that he married a woman of Weitspus. He bought her from the house tsekweł there, and his daughters were therefore known as Tsekweł-s-egor, after their mother. Asiksekweł, which he gave me as the name of his house in Wohkero,[1] *is not recognized as a house name, and evidently rests on a misunderstanding. The last two syllables evidently are tsekweł, his wife's house in Weitspus.*

Wets'owa's ancestry is not wholly certain. He was probably on his father's side from Wohkero. There, at any rate, he later lived, just upriver from the little Maston store. There there were an Indian house, a sweathouse, a cemetery, and the American house of one of his daughters. His mother appears to have been from Pekwon, and there it is thought that he brought his wife when he was first married. His daughters were named Lucy, Dolly, and Nora. Lucy, who was born in Pekwon, married a white man named Milton J. Thompson and, with his assistance, published in Eureka the book called To the American Indian, *in 1916. In the Preface she speaks of her father as being a* täł. *He was a* täł, *or singer, but he was not formulist for the Pekwon world renewal dance. This function was performed by Informant S.*[2]

Wets'owa owned dance regalia. These were kept in a cavelike place under a waterfall in the creek below Wohkero: Wohkero pulekuk weroi. Once there was to be a Deerskin Dance, and for this he had taken the regalia out of their hiding place and had them ready in the house. While his wife was leaching acorns outdoors and he was in the sweathouse, the house caught fire and the treasures were burned. They managed to pull some boards off the roof but could get no farther, and then fought to save the cemetery from catching fire. The family's Jumping Dance regalia, three woodpecker bands, remained safe under the waterfall. (This event may have happened to Wets'owa's mother and father rather than to himself and his wife.)

1. [Cf. U1, n. 1, below. Wohtek and Wohkero are adjoining towns.—Ed.]

2. [Kroeber and Gifford, World Renewal, pp. 88-89, reprinted Lucy Thompson's account of the Pekwon world renewal ritual.—Ed.]

Wets'owa professed to know four stories relating to the house Asiksekweł. One of these, concerned with deer, was not secured. The three others, which follow, proved to be formulas to treat illness. The relevance of the first one to curing is not clear; but the two others are explained sufficiently to corroborate the old man's statement.

The association of a place with the past as revealed by these tales is typically Yurok. In the very house in which this man lived he believed that there had lived predecessors who married a rattlesnake and had gigantic birds and serpent monsters as fanatically beloved pets. A strange undertone of feeling must accompany such a relation, probably intensified rather than muted by the Yurok measurelessness of time, which sets the events of myth at once in the beginning of the world and in a period just beyond the brief recollection of actual kinsmen. As against this temporal ambiguity, the fixation on the specific house site, perhaps on its very timbers, is in sharp contrast.

U1. The Rattlesnake Wife

a. He grew in Asiksekweł[1] in Wohtek. He brought in sweathouse wood and slept during the day.[2] Then as he slept he felt something on his belly. He continued getting sweathouse wood and staying in the sweathouse. Then once he head them come running, two of them. They looked into the sweathouse and called, "Father, come into the house!" He did not know them; he thought, "I have no children." They came again and looked into the sweathouse. "Come into the house," they said. "Our mother is there and wants you." Then they returned. They were two little girls. "Well, I think I shall go in and see her," he thought. He went over and saw her: she was a pretty woman. Then he entered. She said, "Those are your children. That which rested on you was I."

Now it began to be night and he started for the sweathouse: "Take these blankets to sleep on," he said. "No, I shall sleep outside," she said. Then he saw a large flat stone in the house.[3]

b. In the morning, he saw that there was much firewood. She had brought it during the night. She had carried only one load, but there was a great pile.

1. Or Asiksakweł, a house, still standing in 1907 in Wohtek, but not given by that name on Waterman, Geography, map 13. It is probably Waterman's house 7, 8, or 11. It was there, the informant said, when the woge lived along the river. This sort of statement means that the site was long inhabited, not that the original planks have survived. In fact, the informant stated that the two white-cedar plates and two ridgepoles—the longest timbers in a Yurok house—were brought from a place called Regerokets, uphill from Merip, ten miles or so from Wohtek (Waterman, map 17, no. 88). [This map is reproduced here as map 5. See also T2, n. 1, and Informant U's biography, n. 1, above.—Ed.]

2. This practice is called *atskei*.

3. She slept on this stone, the narrator said, and it was indoors, which does not clarify the situation.

Now the woman said, "Let us go up the hill.[4] That is where I grew. Come to where I live." Then he went up with her, to Nitepo.[5] Her house was in the middle (of the row): he saw many on the hillside. The platform in front was paved with permeryer (greasy-stone), and the inside of the houses was of obsidian.[6]

U2. Erł'erm Was His Pet

a. He grew in Asiksekweł at Wohtek, he who had the *erł'erm*.[1] Often it flew off. Once it went away and did not come back for three days. Then it returned, entered the house, and began to dance about. When it stopped, it vomited *toihkem* bulbs. It had been to Pulekuk: there it got them. Now it used to do that, and the man was glad that it brought the bulbs, and he put them into storage baskets. Soon the baskets were full.

b. Now he married. It was out of ketskeł[2] in Pekwon that he married a woman. Then the erł'erm did not like it and left him. When first it went off, he waited, for sometimes it had gone away and returned. But when it did not come back after three days (he knew that it would not).

c. Now they were eating the bulbs. Then they began to be sick. Because they used the bulbs after he had taken a wife, they became ill; but he did not know that. Now he had a little boy (left).[3] The boy vomited constantly. There was a doctor in Wohtek. They sent for her to cure the boy. The doctor said, "Tell (what you know)." He said, "All we did was to eat the bulbs." She told him, "That was bad. It is this that the child is sick from, the bulbs that the bird vomited." Then she cured the boy by speaking *u-pahsoi*.[4]

He had found the erł'erm when it was young, lying where the ground was soft. He did not know what it was, it was so small, but he carried it to his house and nourished it. When it grew up, he knew it was an erł'erm.

4. *Wonäus*.
5. Unidentified.
6. She was a rattlesnake.

---

1. A bird, perhaps mythical. It is described as of the size of a condor, whitish, with straight bill. The narrator had never seen one, but had heard them flying. This is a death omen. [Cf. Hewonol in J3 and Hegwono' in K3.—Ed.]
2. Waterman, Geography, map 15, no. 15.
3. His other children had already died.
4. *U-pahsoi* is curing by a recital, probably a formula. This and the preceding and following tales are *pahsoi*. [K. in a marginal note queries whether the formula is a confession for the breaking of a taboo.—Ed.]

U3. Long One Was His Pet

a. He who had had the *erlerm*[1] went to Noroyur.[2] There he saw a Long One[3] swimming. It was but a little thing, with horns, and he liked it. Then he thought he would catch it and bring it home. He put it on the roof of his house,[4] in a hollowed log with water, and kept it. He did not know what it was; only when it grew he knew. Nevertheless he kept it.

Now he constantly hunted. Sometimes he would kill two deer. Then he would throw one whole deer on the roof to feed his Long One; the other he took indoors to use. Then in the morning he always saw that the meat was gone which he had brought inside. But the women in the house did not see the one that lived on the roof; only the man knew it. Therefore they wanted to know what it was that took the meat, for they never saw anything enter. When he went hunting he always kept out one deer to feed to his pet; but nevertheless in the morning the women did not see the meat that he had taken indoors.

b. Then one of the women thought, "Let me stay awake to see what it is that comes in to eat our meat." She would only hear something crawling over the roof, and the house shook. It was large now, but only the man knew. So that night she did not sleep, but watched the smoke hole. Then, during the night, she saw something look in from above: she saw its tongue protruding into the house. So it consumed all the meat.[5] Then she knew, "That is what it is, a Long One."

c. Now when that man hunted he sometimes killed ten deer. Always he fed his pet, and the women sliced and smoked inside the house the meat he brought in. Then the woman, as she was out gathering firewood, thought, "I shall watch tonight and hit it with a stick if I see it eating the meat again." So she waited and saw it come and begin to lick up the meat, and she struck it. Then, that same night, it went off and never returned. The man did not know that the woman had struck it.[6]

1. See U2.

2. Noroyur or Oket'o-lomeɫ, a slough or backwater at the foot of Wohtek, between the terrace and the gravel bar. Neither name appears in Waterman; the second form seems to mean "lagoon-house."

3. Knewollek, the horned water serpent. [See A11, B2, and CC1 for other versions of this tale.—Ed.]

4. Namely, Asiksekweɫ.

5. It licked the meat up with its tongue from the frame or scaffold on which it was hung. It did not need to reach far down from the smoke hole.

6. When babies are sick with cramps and twitch their cradle basket, it is because a Knewollek has seized them and is holding on. Then this story seems to be spoken as cure. One doctor said that she had seen an adult seized by a Knewollek and become sick.

INFORMANT V

PETSUSLO OF PEKWON

This informant was usually known by his personal name, Petsuslo, which means "thrown upriver," rather than by any appellation referring to his house or marriage. I recall him as a wizened little man in his sixties, whom I met around Wohkero–Pekwon, and who told me two stories at Requa on July 21, 1906.[1] *His mother was of house wonnekw in Rekwoi and was married upriver to Pekwon; there Petsuslo was born. Her husband died, and she cut her hair. No one in the family married her, so she returned to Rekwoi, and later bore Billy Brooks. Billy and Petsuslo accordingly were half-brothers. Petsuslo was married in Wohtek and had one daughter, who was half-married to Enk'ewis from the house ketskeł of Pekwon.*

Petsuslo was not wealthy but owned something. He had at least one good woodpecker band. This he brought to his half-brother when the last Jumping Dance was made at Rekwoi. He also owned arrows for the Brush Dance.

There is a story that he was shot to death. A man near Wohkero heard a noise outside his house one night and came out with a gun. His dog was pointing at something. When he saw a crouching person, he concluded that it was someone trying to bewitch him with an Uma'a, and shot. The person leaped over a fence and ran away. In the morning, there was a trail of blood. At the same time word came that Petsuslo had died suddenly at home. He was buried in the old native way, except that his body was not unlashed and unwrapped from the plank on which it had been carried to the grave. The final washing there was omitted. People therefore concluded that it was he who had died from the gunshot wound inflicted the night before, and that his people did not want it to be known.

Petsuslo's two tales are bald, wholly undramatic, reasoned in the Yurok manner, and not completely consistent by our thinking. The first is a synoptic account of the origin of the world, containing a number of unique elements. The

1. [K. noted that more data had been dictated than appeared in the typescript.—Ed.]

second is an account of the origin of Night, and also shows special features. As narratives, both tales fall flat. Their significance is as specimens of Yurok philosophy.

V1. Origin of People, Ocean, and Food

This is a synthetic story: the origins of people, ocean and river, fish, deer, dogs, trees, and boats are strung into one sequence. The materials for creation are of the slightest; mainly the act consists of a willing or saying. The creator and his companion are nameless—just woge—except for identification with spots. This identification, however, is double: first rocks at the mouth of the river, then mountains inland from it. The consequence is a certain contraction of outlook: when a Yurok climbs on Oka to get himself gambling luck by crying and carrying sweathouse wood, he receives this little personal power from the spirit who made the whole world as it is.

I suspect the "sitting" companion to be the flat rock Erliker next to the great column Oregos, both at the very mouth of the river and at the foot of Rekwoi.

In accord with the institutional character of the myth, the usual dramatic incidents of the Deer–Dog episode, like the burning of sleeping Deer's hoof, are omitted.

•

a. There were no human beings yet. The ocean was all a prairie.[1] There was no water flowing. All the land was level, bare of trees, dry of water. One stood at the river mouth[2] and thought, "How will it be that there are human beings about like myself?[3] For they will have to be; I want people to live. Well, yes." Then he took up sand and threw[4] it north along the coast (*pulekuk*), south along the coast (*perwer*), and upstream (*petsik*); three ways he threw it. Then he saw human beings where he had thrown the sand.

b. Now he wanted to know, "How will there be water? For they must have it." Then he made urine in a stone dish and threw it westward (*hiwohp*). Then when he looked where the ocean is now, he no longer saw prairie, but only water. This urine was strong; therefore the ocean cannot be drunk. He urinated again and threw it upstream, and water began to run down the river. This was not so strong and could be drunk.

But when he looked north along the coast, there was no water there. The one who sat by him said, "No, it is not right. There must be water on all sides, all around." Then he threw water again, so that salt water extended all around the world.

1. *Sepolek*, a treeless area, usually more or less flat.
2. The pillar of rock, Oregos.
3. He was a woge, but humans were to be of his shape.
4. Later, the informant said that he blew sand or dust away as one blows tobacco for an offering.

c. "Well, there should be salmon in the river" (said his companion). "Yes," he said, and threw (blew, sprayed) more water upriver and into the ocean. Then he saw salmon leaping. So he named them all: young salmon,[5] *rohtun*, catfish, sturgeon, steelheads, suckers, lamprey eels, salmon,[6] every kind (of fish).

d. There were two of them: one who made these things, the other who asked him. Now he said, "Well, how about it? Are they going to use only salmon?" "Well, I will see." "They must have meat too." Then a madrone tree (suddenly) stood there; and the standing one stripped off some of the bark, held it in his outstretched hand, dropped it, and they saw a deer standing there, with its horns. "How will they catch the deer?" So he took earth, held it out, let it fall on the ground, and they saw a dog. The deer stood there, and the dog stood there.

e. Deer said, "If I speak like people, there will be no more human beings.[7] Well, you shall not eat my flesh," he said to Dog. "You will be worthless, and eat anything: therefore you shall not eat my body." As soon as he had said that, he gave a bound and ran. The one who was standing seized Dog, rubbed his nose around, said to him, "Follow him! If you overtake him, talk to him. If you do not, keep trying anyway." So Dog pursued, barking he, he, he, he. Deer ran around the world (to the north, east, south, west, and north again), Dog following without overtaking him. Deer leaped into the river to swim, for he did not want to be caught; but Dog swam after, and continued to pursue, until they came back to where they had started.[8]

Deer thought, "Well, I must go somewhere so he does not catch me." So he ran up into the sky:[9] there he found it all nice prairie. Dog went up too, and Deer ran around the sky twice, but Dog just followed and followed. "I shall catch you now," Dog said. "I said, 'I shall eat your flesh,' and you said, 'You cannot do it,' but now I shall overtake you and eat you."

f. So now they had Dog catch Deer, but it was the only way, for they had no arrow: there were no trees standing on the ground. The one who sat said, "Well, they must have wood, for fire." Then the standing one turned and faced upriver, and blew out water[10] (like blowing a tobacco-crumb offering). Now as they looked about, it seemed like night: there was no more prairie: trees stood

5. *Regok*, sometimes translated trout and sometimes minnows. [Cf. A20, n. 6.—Ed.]

6. *Ne'pui*, generic for all kinds of salmon; sometimes, as in the preceding sentences, for all fish. [Robins, Yurok Language, p. 243, translates *rohtun* as bullhead.—Ed.]

7. "If I talk like our language." Not clear. Possibly a belief analogous to the one that a dog's speaking would be fatal to human hearers.

8. At the Klamath river mouth.

9. This is usually at the upriver end of the world, unless one ascends by a ladder.

10. This repeated creating by blowing out "water" suggests that it may really have been his own saliva.

everywhere. Then he called all the names of the trees, a name for each kind.

g. And (the standing one) said, "They must have a boat; for wanting to cross the river they must have it. It must be of redwood, not of any wood. If they make it of other wood, it will be bad; there will be sickness about. Let them use only redwood.[11] They will use their boat on the ocean and on the river, but of that one kind only."

That is all.

h. They were woge; they had no (individual) names, as they stood (and sat) where Oregos is (now). Later, when they went off with the woge, one went to the mountain Oka, the other to Lohłko,[12] a mountain near it. That is why that mountain is so good. If a poor man goes there for sweathouse wood, he calls to it; after ten days, he can get what he calls for, wealth or gambling luck.

V2. Origin of Night

a. All over people were living, but it never became dark. They slept, but it looked as it looks here today: always the Sun stayed in one place only. It did not move, and was hot. He heard of it, the one who lived in Pulekuk, Pulekukwerek heard it, that the Sun always stood still, and he did not like it, because Night never came. So he thought he would come here, to see how it was; and he arrived at Rekwoi, and saw Sun staying in one place, and the people slept, though it was hot.

And he went on up the river. Wherever he came, someone would say to him, "Stay here, and eat, and do some fishing." But he answered, "No, I do not eat, I only smoke." So he would go on, and one would ask him, "Where are you going?" and he would say, "I travel because I do not want Sun to stay still." "Well, that is how we live: it is never dark, but when we are sleepy we go to sleep nevertheless."

(Similar conversations ensue at Wohtek, at Weitspus, and at Otsepor [Bluff Creek], with only these additions: If people sleep properly, "they will bathe in the morning and feel good, because they will have a sweathouse, and it will be better thus.")

b. Then he came to Segwu', where the river forks. There was an old

11. Typical psychology. Redwood is no doubt the easiest and best material, under Yurok technology. But, once customary, it must not be replaced by anything else, or health and life would be endangered, so great is the fear of change.

12. Oka is Red Mountain, toward the sea from the head of Blue Creek. It is frequently mentioned: B13, J9, and Spott and Kroeber, Yurok Narratives, nos. 23 and 24, pp. 219-227. Lohłko, near it, is mentioned (but not located) by Waterman, Geography, p. 233, perhaps on the basis of the present myth.

sweathouse there.[1] A young man standing outside asked him, "Where are you going? You had better stay the night here." "I am traveling to find Sun; I do not want it that Night does not come." "Well, I know where you are going. I go where he lives; and there Night comes." So he agreed to stay with him, and they went into the sweathouse, but he (the traveler) did not sleep. When they got up, the young man wanted first to eat, because he would show him the way. "There is a sweathouse there. The trail curves right to it, and the house is only just beyond. There is only the one trail." And that one led him partway and went back home.

c. Then he traveled faster, and soon he saw as if it were going to be sunset: he had never seen that before. When he came to the sweathouse,[2] the Sun did set. He thought, "That is how I like it to be in our world."

Now they spoke to him there. They were twelve brothers, and their names were Ketsos-hī,[3] Kohtsewets, Na'aiwets, Nahkse'aiwets, Tsona'aiwets, Meroyo, Kohtsä, Tserwerserk, Knewoletau, Krerermerk, Werłerwer, Kä'mo.[4]

d. "Let us go into the house and eat," they said. "No."[5] It began to be really dark. "That is how I like it. I think it will be like this," he said. They finished supper (without him), and all went into the sweathouse. They all smoked; he alone just sat there.[6] Then he began to talk. "This is why I came. I want Night to be about. I do not like it to be always light." They said, "No. It will not be well if Night comes where you live." Then he called the names of each of the moons. "I want to take one of them along." Now when it was nearly daybreak, one of them was missing from the sweathouse.[7] So they said, "Well, take the one that travels in the daytime, that Sun, and I think Night will come." He said, "I want it to be Night so that the birds will be glad of daybreak, and will sing because they are about to break their fast. And people will go to bathe and feel well."

1. Probably the "old" or sacred "sweathouse" (*wenaram*) of the world renewal rite at Karok Katimin, Yurok Segwu', just upriver from the mouth of the Salmon (hence "where the river forks").

2. The place was in the sky, the narrator said afterward. But it is described as only a little upriver from Segwu'.

3. "Goes in the day," that is, the Sun.

4. After Ketsos-hī, the other eleven are moons. The first ten are the numbered ones; the last is one of the two (or three) named moons in the twelve- or thirteen-month count of the Yurok; numbers 11 and 12 are omitted. [Cf. the list in M1.—Ed.]

5. Pulekukwerek never eats.

6. Usually he smokes, but now he is intent on persuading them.

7. This "missing" is not clear, unless it is the first, Sun, that has left to go on his day's journey. In some versions Pulekukwerek steals the boy Night; but here he finally wins consent for Sun to go with him. The "one was missing" is probably an anticipation of his being allowed to take him. The whole reasoning, with the Sun and eleven Moons making twelve brothers, seems confused to us. The Yurok logic probably is: Sun and Night are complementary. There-

e. Then the one who travels in the day went with him who wished for Night. When they came near Segwu', it began to darken. When they reached it, it was growing dark. "That is how I like it to be," he said. The one who travels in the day said, "This is as far as I will go with you. From here I return, because you have it now." So he stayed with him that night, the one who travels all day. In the morning they heard the birds sing. Then he who wanted Night thought, "That is how I like it to be."[8]

---

fore by getting Sun to come, Night also comes. That all the versions, however, should emphasize that it is Night which is desired, in distinction from the Sun-theft or Sun-securing of most Californian peoples, is a consistent Yurok quirk hard to understand.

8. The indirect formality, probably through formulistic phraseology, increases in this final paragraph: "the one who travels in the day," "he who wanted Night" instead of the names Sun and Pulekukwerek.

Informant W

DICK OF WOHKERO

The informant's Indian name was Re'mik. His American name was Dick, but he belonged to Wohkero, not to Wohtek. He was probably from the Pekwon house pekwon-pul. At any rate, he was related to Pekwon-pul Mi'lo', also known as Pekwon Dave. His wife was probably from Wohkero. This would mean that he was living in his wife's village.[1]

He owned some property. The last time the fish dam was made at Kepel, he contributed about nine ringtail-cat aprons to the Deerskin Dance which follows the dam below Wohkero. He also owned wolfskin headbands.

He was a good singer for the doctor-making dance, the Brush Dance, and the Deerskin Dance. Later in life he made medicine for the sickness which comes from deer, wer-neryermer. *He was twice called to Rekwoi to make this medicine. Kerner and Tekta Ben recommended him. Those who first called him had had several doctors for their boy, and all the doctors said that they saw deer heads in the corner of the house; therefore treatment by this formula was indicated. However, the boy died. With his other patient, Re'mik said that there was no hope, because he found his voice getting blocked as he tried to recite the formula.*

W1. Earthquake Drives Away the Sä'äi

What follows is a combination of an abstract written in a notebook in 1907, and a translation made in 1908 from two dictated cylinders. The two do not jibe very well; and the informant said later that he had not completed his story into the phonograph.

•

1. [K. made the accompanying handwritten notations: "Dick—from Wohkero, born at Yohter, opposite Sregon and Pekwon," and "At Wohkero, Dick lives in a house with carved round door. Dick married into it; it was owned by Johnnie George's parents."—Ed.]

a. Earthquake grew at Kenek. He heard they were all going to leave the world. Then he[1] went upriver from Rekwoi, and past Kenek, nearly to Weitspus at Wespen.[2] And he said to the Sä'äł[3] there, "Let us go away; for I want human beings to be about in the world." And the ones there went with him; all the evil ones[4] he gathered, those they call Sä'äł; he gathered them all, going to Pulekuk. And he came to Rekwoi, and then arrived at Pulekuk.

b. Then he[5] said, "No, I do not want humans to be about the world." And he went upstream and came to Kenek. And there one[6] of them was sitting a little apart, as if he were afraid, (the) one from Kenek. Then he[7] went up to him and pushed him, and said, "You have not fixed your hair;[8] you ought to have done that." Then no one could see where he[9] had gone. Then they saw him coming and heard him talking. And when he spoke, they all fell on the ground as if they had been pushed: not one could stand. And they tried to run off, they who did not want human beings to be in the world. Then he tore up the ground, and they all went down into it, those who did not want people to be here; he tore it up.[10]

The informant added: Now Earthquake is angry because the Americans have bought up Indian treasures and formulas and taken them away to San Francisco to keep. He knew that, so he tore the ground up there (referring to the earthquake of the year before, in 1906).

1. Earthquake, according to the abstract; but the phonograph text begins with a mention of Pulekuk and of "Rekwoi its Sä'äł" going upstream to Kenek and Wespen.
2. Wespen is a prehistoric townsite near the Gist hydraulic mine, downstream from Weitspus; it is called a woge, not a human, town by the Yurok. Waterman, Geography, map 25, no. 16, puts it 3/4 mile below Weitspus. [This map is reproduced here as map 4.—Ed.]
3. Spirits that live in creeks or deep woods and bring sickness.
4. *Kits-o-łmey-otkwi.*
5. Presumably one of the Sä'äł.
6. This seems to be Earthquake, by context.
7. Apparently a Sä'äł.
8. Sä'äł heads are sometimes elongated to great height, or a point.
9. Earthquake?
10. Surely Earthquake now. Possibly the confusion is to be resolved thus: Earthquake wanted people to occupy the earth, and therefore he took the Sä'äł, from Wespen down, away with him to Pulekuk, so that people could live in this world in safety. Then a Sä'äł (or other evil thing) changed his mind, came back, but was driven off again with his crew by Earthquake, who was again at Kenek, sitting as if afraid, but, when pushed, disappearing and tearing up the ground, which then swallowed the evil ones.

INFORMANT X

CAPTAIN SPOTT OF REKWOI

Spott's paternal ancestry has been given elsewhere.[1] *His mother, a doctor, was of the house wonnäu in Rekwoi. Her mother in turn was from the house oslok, so that she was some kind of a niece of Minot. Spott was a small boy when his father died. His first marriage was to a girl from the house wonnekw in Rekwoi, the half-sister of Billy Brooks. His mother and her male relatives were opposed to the marriage. For this reason Spott went to live with his mother-in-law. He had one daughter. His wife died, and the girl followed her when she was about five. This is how it is said to have happened. The mother-in-law in wonnekw saw her granddaughter playing with other children, among whom was one from a house with which she was at enmity. Then she prepared some pieces of* sloił, *dried lamprey eel, putting* ohpok *poison on one. She called in her granddaughter and gave her the food, telling her to distribute it among her playmates in a certain order. The child went back but forgot her instructions and ate the poisoned portion herself. Next year at the same season she sickened and died.*

Spott continued to live on with the old woman for a while, and then went to the Tolowa, gambling and visiting. While he was with friends at Ererł a man stepped in to announce that a woman wanted to see him. Spott finished breakfast with the family and went out and saw that it was Erł-pets-uwe, the sister of Erł-pets, so called because he was from the house petsku, as the Yurok named it, in Ererł. She told him that she had sold ohpok *poison to his mother-in-law (or to her mother?) but she would sell it only on condition that she was informed against whom it would be used, and the old woman had named him.*

When Spott returned to wonnekw, a basket of acorn soup with a plate of

1. [By his adopted son, Robert Spott, in Spott and Kroeber, Yurok Narratives, pp. 144-146. Captain Spott was Robert's father's sister's husband, according to Kroeber and Gifford, World Renewal, p. 133.—Ed.]

dried fish was waiting for him. He looked at it, but set it down again. "What is the matter?" the old woman asked him. "You are trying to poison me," he said. She denied it and protested and asked who had accused her. He did not reply, but went to the family box, took his personal belongings, consisting of four otter skins, five dentalium necklaces, and some feathers, and started to go out. She asked him to come back tomorrow to talk to her, but he still did not answer and went back to his mother's home in wonnäu.

The way the first part of the story came out was that the mother-in-law, who was called K'yūlert, which means silver-gray hair, and who was herself raised in wonnekw, had another daughter who was married to Oregon Charlie. They had a girl who became sick. They had two doctors, one of them from Mūrek, who both declared the child was sick from ohpok *poison, and that it was coast and not inland poison. Then the old woman said she would confess, and told the story of how she had mistakenly killed her first granddaughter. Thereupon the sick child recovered; but she died a few years later.*

Spott was a tā̄ł. *He was* nī'na'-ukergeri, *that is, one who tallies and distributes dance regalia. Such people cannot be occupied with ceremonial duties during a dance. The same was true of Sregon Jim. Spott, however, was* wernerper, *assistant to the formulist, for the First Salmon medicine.*

X1. Origins

This "story" was obtained from Spott in 1900, from one to seven years before the others he told. In the interval, I learned more of Yurok life, and both of us came to know each other better. The difference in the material is conspicuous. The present account is much inferior to the run of Spott's. He first insisted on attributing events to "God," whose Yurok name he finally translated as Wohpekumeu. The narrative is given chiefly as a sample of what a Yurok of the time was likely to tell a strange white man.

•

a. Wohpekumeu was at Kenek. Earthquake lived there and Thunder and many others. They played shinny, and when it was hot they swam and dived from the high rocks, and enjoyed themselves always. That is how (human) people learned to play. They did not know what would happen after they went off. They looked about to see how they would live (after their transformation). Sometimes they went up to the sky. It was Wohpekumeu who found what to do; and he did accordingly.

b. Some of them there were good. They wanted people to live, because when a person dies his relatives are sorry. Others were bad. They wanted people to die because the world would be too full if they lived. They said, "There will be too many. I want to see them die sometimes."

Thus they were always thinking of what they would do and how they would live. They could not go off because they had no wings (as yet). They were still thinking of a way to do.

c. Then one of them said, "Wait! Let us make the river first." Then they made it so that in places the river is rough and boats sometimes capsize. Then they also made it that some people choke to death when they are eating, and some burn up.

Those who arranged this were Wohpekumeu, Earthquake, Thunder, and Pulekukwerek. Pulekukwerek later came again and made things a little better. He did not come this (second) time to Rekwoi, and therefore that place is pretty bad.

d. Now Wohpekumeu had a large pile of all kinds of tails; a fisher tail, an otter tail, a rat tail, a fox tail, and others. They were going to be distributed. One of the people would say, "I want this rat tail"; another, "I want this raccoon tail"; and so on. Then, when it was nearly night, Wohpekumeu held up his hand and said, "Now go to sleep. When you wake in the morning, each of you get up and take one tail." Then in the morning each put on a tail and became hairy and an animal. The one who put on the otter tail became an otter; and so each one turned to an animal. Last of all to come was Coyote; and so he got the coyote tail.

e. Now these were all provided for, but the birds had no wings or feathers. Then those who made the world thought about it. "How shall we do for them?" they thought. There was a large bird, like a white eagle, but larger than a house, sitting on the top of Shelton Butte. It had on it all the wings, some white, some pretty, some not so beautiful. Now they went up to shoot him. They could not hit it. They shot every day for nearly a year.

Now there was a little man called He-Lives-at-Okego or Grew-in-a-Rumitsek-Basket. He also came there but sat quietly. At last they told him to shoot. "Here, take this bow," they said. "No, I have a bow," he said. He took something from the net sack at his side, moved it, and had a bow. Then he motioned once and the bow was strung. Then he rubbed a little piece of smooth black stone (*permeryer*) between his hands and had an arrow. Then, still sitting down, he shot. He struck the great bird in the throat. It fell and rolled to the river. Then Wohpekumeu told them all to go to Kenek and sleep there.[1] In the morning they were to come up again. Then they slept at Kenek. The white eagle was the first one to go up in the morning and got the best feathers. All the birds went up and got their feathers.[2]

f. Porpoise (Kegor) went to Sumig, Patrick Point. That was the place he wanted. He had a great fight for it and won the land.

g. Wohpekumeu said, "How shall we have human beings live? What shall we do for them?" No one knew what to say. Then he[3] said, "We will make it bad for them, so that they will be constantly dying. Otherwise there will be too many and the world will be too full. Some of them will live to be old before they

1. It is a dozen miles from the mouth of Bluff Creek (from which they are usually said to have shot at the bird on Shelton Butte) to Kenek; a long way to go for a night's sleep.

2. Most versions derive tails and feathers equally from the bird on Shelton Butte.

3. It is Wertspit, the Jerusalem cricket, that is usually mentioned as the one responsible for death.

die, but they will be very few. Every year some will die, children or women or men." Then they consented. Some of them wanted a better way: they wanted people to live; but the others prevailed.

h. At first Wohpekumeu said that people were to eat pitch for acorns. The people tried it but could not do it. Then he said, "How shall we make food for them?" Someone said, "Let them eat salmon and eels which they catch with nets and harpoons and gaffs, and let them eat acorns and other food." Then they made it like that.

i. At first the ocean was all land. Wohpekumeu made it water. Now people are sometimes drowned, but some, even though their boat founders, do not drown. They sing a song which saves them.

X2. Visit to the Dead

[In a marginal note K. describes this as half-myth, half-tale—Ed.]

•

a. Long ago, Turip young man lost his sweetheart. Then he was sorry. He began to die. He said, "Put a stone into my hand. I shall break his[1] boat." He was angry at him.

b. Next morning one took a sharp stick and began to dig his grave. They said, "He is long dead. Let us bury him." Then Turip young man took a long breath and sat up. He did not (yet) speak. All asked him, "Where have you been? What did you see? Tell us." He did not speak. They ran to the one who was digging and said, "Stop! He is alive!" All the people came to look. All day he did not speak. Next day he told them.

c. He said, "I broke his boat. I went down. I did not take the ghosts' trail.[2] If one follows it downward, he cannot come back. It is worn breast-deep from much traveling. I took another trail. I came to a river. I drew his boat out of the water and struck it and broke it. There were many houses on the other side. They were thick, and I saw many fires. There were very many people. They dance there."

d. Then he stood up, and began to walk about, and ate again. He was washed with the herb used after a burial. For ten years no one died in this world. There was no boat to ferry them across.

1. Illa'a, the ferryman of the dead.

2. The narrator added that on the ghosts' trail was a house in which lived Amaskawei, an old woman, and an old man. The latter took out the bones of the dead and substituted them. Illa'a would see the dead at this house and would cross the river to get them. Once they were ferried over, there was no return.

X3. Pulekukwerek at Rekwoi

This version is unusual in omitting, in favor of a mere song-spell, the swallowing of the boat with a load of hot stones; and in introducing a constellation of great gods: Sky-Owner,[1] Wohpekumeu, Great Money, and Pulekukwerek, much in the manner of Informant A. Spott quite likely knew a prayer and song for crossing rough water; hence the allusion to establishment by fiat. His religion was pragmatic rather than imaginative.

•

a. There was a place in the middle of the river at Rekwoi where the water boiled up and boats were always overturned and the men in them drowned. It was the Kimeyu who did this. Then Ki-wes'ona-megetoł, Sky-Owner, said, "Why is this? What shall we do? Who will make it (better)? I do not know who will remedy it." Then Wohpekumeu said, "I know the one who can do it," and went to get him. It was Pulekukwerek, who lived at the downstream end (of the world). Wohpekumeu went and brought him back. With him he brought Pelin-tsīk, Great Money. The three came back together.

b. Then they arranged that women were to be bought. Pelin-tsīk said, "Let it be that a man will buy a woman. He will pay much for a rich woman. A poor woman will be low-priced; and it will be well." Pulekukwerek and Wohpekumeu consented.

c. Then Pelin-tsīk also arranged that they would pay in settlement for killing. He said, "When they kill a man, let them pay. Then they can be friends again and it will be well. But if they do not pay, there will be fighting all the time." So they all were agreed that it was good that way.

d. Now they went down to the river to see about making the bad place good. The people told them, "Here is a large boat." Pulekukwerek said, "I do not want a large boat; I want a small one. I want to see whether they can turn us over." So they took a small boat. Pulekukwerek sat in the stern, Wohpekumeu paddled in the bow, and Pelin-tsīk sat in the middle doing nothing.[2] All watched from the shore. Then when they came to the middle, the water began to boil. Pulekukwerek sang and it became still. So they crossed. Then they crossed back and everything was quiet.

Then Pulekukwerek told some of the people, "Now you try." Some men went out. When they got to where the bad place had been, it began to boil up again. Then Pulekukwerek, who was on the shore, sang and talked to it. Then the water went down and the men crossed safely.

So they made that place good. Then they said, "Not many people will

1. [Throughout the collection, except in the tales told by this informant, K. has given this name as Sky-Possessor.—Ed.]

2. Like a really great and rich man.

drown. We do not want them all to drown. Perhaps once a year a man will drown, or one in two years. But it will not be often."[3]

X4. Origin of Birth

At first children were born only by the mother's being cut open and killed. Wohpekumeu made two women pregnant at Enek.[1] They had five brothers. These caught Wohpekumeu and dragged him into the house. They were about to kill him because their sisters were to die. He said, "Wait! Wait! You can kill me in a little while." Then they stopped. He said, "I will cure them. Let me go out and make medicine[2] for them." They would not let him go. So, with two of them staying at the door, he indoors in the corner, and the two women lying down, he took a basket and thought, "I wish I held tobacco in my hand." Then he was holding it. So he made medicine in the basket. He spoke and blew out the tobacco, and rubbed one of the women with the medicine. At once she gave birth. Then he rubbed the other, and she too gave birth. So women came to bear children.

X5. Wohpekumeu's War Dance

Wohpekumeu was at Ko'men. There were two women there who would not come out of their house. He desired them. He tried in many ways to make them come out but could not. Then he pulled out (pubic) hairs and laid them on the ground. They became thirty young men. Then he made them dance the war dance at Ko'men. At last the two girls came out to see the dance. Wohpekumeu looked at them, and they became pregnant.

X6. Wohpekumeu and Kapuloyo

This is a mangled account. How much of the aberration is due to my misunderstanding of Spott's broken English, and how much to his lack of interest in narrative per se, in myth as distinct from formula, is hard to say now. As the version was written down, Kapuloyo and his son Kewomer are telescoped into one personage. In the usual accounts it is Kapuloyo who is abandoned in the tree, Kewomer who is blinded by his grandfather but

3. In answer to an inquiry for further details, Spott added the following: After singing his song, Pulekukwerek blew three times and the water went down. When he was on shore and the water began to boil about the men, he sang, blew three times, and then said to the water, "Be still. Let people cross. I want them to live well. They will cross constantly from one town to the other. Do not boil up. I do not want people to be drowned."

---

1. Karok Amaikiaram, the town of the Karok First Salmon world renewal, a little below the mouth of the Salmon River.

2. Find an herb.

shoots the woodpecker and has his sight restored by his father.[1] The woman's name was here recorded as Kewomer umä'i, which would mean girl of a place Kewomer, which seems an impossible Yurok name for Kewomer's mother. However, even where the story is free from suspicion of error, it is condensed and bald. The manner of the blinding, the restoration of eyesight, Kapuloyo's taking all the world's money with him on his departure, Wohpekumeu's recovery of a little of it, Kapuloyo's dancing in the fog—all these sensory episodes are omitted.

•

a. Kapuloyo was living at Kenek. He had a beautiful wife. Her name was Kewomer umä'i (*sic*). Then Wohpekumeu came there. He desired the woman. He thought, "I want Kapuloyo to die." Then he said, "There is a young chicken hawk up in a tree. Get it (for a pet)." Then Kapuloyo went to take it. He left his wife in the house and climbed up the tree. Wohpekumeu thought, "Let a great wind blow. Let him be blind." A great wind came. The trees bent until they nearly touched the ground. Many blew over. Kapuloyo clung to his tree. For ten days the wind blew. Then Kapuloyo slowly came down.

b. He was blind. Then he heard a woodpecker. Shooting where the noise was, he held out his hand the bird fell into it. Wohpekumeu had gone to the house and lived with the woman. But she was sorry for her husband. She went out to look for him. Then she found him blind. She took him by the wrist and led him home. Then he washed his eyes and could see again.

c. Now he went downstream. He wanted to go away because he was ashamed. Wohpekumeu followed him. Kapuloyo came to Rekwoi. Wohpekumeu was following him. Kapuloyo, as he went over the hill northward along the coast, saw him. He said, "When he goes up this hill I want his legs to be heavy so that he cannot lift them and will not be able to come over the hill; but if he goes southward let him go easily." Then Wohpekumeu was following him and calling, "Stop! Do not go!" He came to the hill and could not raise his legs. He could not advance. He tried, and cried, but could not do it. Then he turned the other way and walked easily. So he went back. He went back to Ko'men (*sic*).

d. Sometimes Kapuloyo is seen. Fog moves as if it were a person: then Kapuloyo is there in the fog, but he himself is invisible. He lives to the south (*sic*) of the mouth of the river.

X7. Departure of the Woge

a. Wohpekumeu was living at Ko'men.[1] He constantly pursued women. Therefore the people disliked him and they decided to leave. Sky-Owner went

1. [Cf. F2 and J2.—Ed.]

---

1. Not quite accurate; all the Yurok have him have amatory adventure there, but his "residence" in this world is Kenek.

up to the sky. All the others went off and became animals. Many went from Kenek to (near) Trinidad and became porpoises.[2] Some turned to deer and other animals, and lamprey eels, and birds.

b. Now Elk had no horns; but Rabbit wanted horns. He said, "I want large antlers." Then Sky-Owner gave them to him. He said, "Run through this brush." Rabbit ran into the brush and stuck fast. There was not even a rustle: he could not move. Sky-Owner said, "This will not do." He put the antlers on Elk and told him to run through the brush. Then there was a noise as of boiling as Elk crashed through.

c. When they had all gone off, Wohpekumeu also wanted to leave. He took a bit of a boat—just so long—threw it into the river, jumped into it, and went downstream without paddling. He came to the mouth. Then he blew at his boat and it disappeared.

d. Gong along the coast southward, he cried (from loneliness) as he went along the beach toward Oketo, Big Lagoon. He did not know were to go to find anyone. Then, as he went, he saw a beautiful girl lying on the beach. But he went by her. Then the same girl was lying in front of him again. Four times he went by her. The fifth time he went to her. Then she began to move, gradually sliding toward the ocean. She would not let him go. They came to the surf and he cried out. But she went on through the salt water. Then he knew nothing more.

e. She came up out of the water on the other side of the ocean. She turned half over and he was freed. He awoke and saw land and a house. The girl was beautiful and beautifully dressed. Wohpekumeu said, "Let us go up to the house." It was a beautiful country, level and without timber. Wohpekumeu could see far over it. They went up to the house. Wohpekumeu sat and cried. Then he saw someone coming. He cried the more. He saw only his legs. The body was in fog. It was Kapuloyo. He came to him and said, "*Ayekwi!* I am glad that we have caught you. Now you will stay here. You will like to live here. You will have a beautiful house. You can live in the middle one, the best one. Pulekukwerek will come and you will see him." Soon they saw someone coming. It was Pulekukwerek. Now Wohpekumeu was no longer sorry. He no longer cried. They dance there constantly, and he goes about. Sometimes he is a little boy, sometimes a grown man. The place where they live and have dances is Kakerger, and the woman was Kakerger girl.[3]

X8. Death and Purification

a. There were ten who wanted people to live forever; but those through whom we die did not want people to live. The ten said, "Let people become old

2. Sumig, Patrick's Point, is near Trinidad, and the porpoises, Kegor, are mentioned in X1*f*.

3. The woman is Skate. The place is Akerger or Erkerger. She might be K'akerger, "person of Akerger."

and go to sleep for a little while and be young again.'' But the others would not have it so. Then they proposed, ''Let only the old die.'' But this also they made otherwise. Wohpekumeu[1] thought it best that people should die, for they would become too thick and crowded on the earth. So it is that people die.

b. Now the ten were sorry. They stayed[2] at Kaseguwaiu far upstream; at Oreu at Ikwanek below; at Kekohtau at Ko'orler;[3] at Ketsailkeu at Weitspus; at Okego near Kenek; at Tsekwa at Merip; at Merhkwi at Kepel; at Awiiger below Kepel; at Kemenai at Omenoku; and at Oregos at Rekwoi.

Three of them were most angry: those at Kenek, Merip, and Kepel. They said, ''Well, have your way. Let them die. But I do not want to see the dead pass by me. Take them around behind my back. If I see a dead person, all the people will quickly die and soon be gone.'' Therefore if a corpse is carried up or downstream, it is now taken on shore at these three rocks and carried over the land behind them and then put into the boat again.[4]

c. The one at Rekwoi thought, ''What shall I do? I want to find an herb to make people feel good again after a person has died.'' He went to look. The earth was entirely bare. There was no vegetation on it; so he went up to the sky. Then he heard someone coming behind him. It was the one from Weitspus. He also was looking for an herb. Then (Oregos) from Rekwoi found an herb and took its roots. He gave them to the nine others. Thus human beings received the herb to make them feel clean again after someone has died. So it is that these ten now are given tobacco when the formula is made. They ask the formulist for tobacco. Then he blows it out to them.

X9. Origin of Boats

Sky-Owner, Pulekukwerek, and Wohpekumeu did not know how the river would be crossed. Pulekukwerek said, ''What shall we do that persons may cross? How will they live? I do not know.'' Wohpekumeu did not know. They had no wood. Then suddenly someone grew up quickly there. He said, ''That is what I came for. I can be used for boats. They will make boats of me and cross the river.'' Pulekukwerek said, ''What is your name?'' He said, ''Do you not know my name?'' Pulekukwerek said, ''No, but I would like to know.'' He

1. As before, in X1*g*, Wohpekumeu is mentioned instead of the customary Wertspit.

2. Entered rocks along the river, in order downstream. Cf. Kroeber, Handbook, p. 70. [See also F4, H2, and T4, above.—Ed.]

3. Kaseguwaiu I cannot identify, except as a mishearing of Ka-segwu', he of Segwu', Katimin. Ikwanek is Ashanamkarak at Ike's Falls. Ko'orler may possibly be in error of Ko'men, Orleans (Karok Panamenik), or for Olege'l, Camp Creek (Karok Tishannik); or it may be Ka'olar, he of Olar, a variant of (or place near) Olege'l. [For Olar, see T4, n. 12.—Ed.]

4. Cf. Waterman, Geography, map 17, and notes on nos. 39, 54, 96, 103, 116, 140, and 142, pp. 248-253. [The map is reproduced here as map 5.—Ed.]

said, "I am called Redwood."[1] Pulekukwerek said, "It is good that you grew so quickly. Now persons will live (properly)." Redwood said, "I want them to put pitch on my head. I want them also to put pitch on my stern, and I want a withe around my neck.[2] That is the way I like it." Then Pulekukwerek told him, "Yes, that is good. That is how they will use you."[3]

X10. Sun

a. When people first grew, Sun said, "I shall live in the sky. I shall see some men having troubles, and good men living long. Those who are foolish I shall do nothing for. They will die soon. If women are chaste, they will live long. But if they are unchaste and run about, they will meet trouble. If a woman has had no child and is bought in marriage, it will be well. But if a woman has had a child without payment, or only a few dentalia have been paid, the child will die soon. I shall not like such people. I shall do nothing for them.

b. Sometimes I shall see war going on. Three or four persons will be killed on each side.[1] Then they will settle and pay each other and be friends again. Some men will be cut or pierced through the body. But when I look at them I shall feel sorry, and they will not die. For others I shall not feel sorry: they will die.

c. I have a path here. I shall go straight over it. I shall go along through the middle and see everything. In the evening I shall go down into the ocean and return under the earth and come up again in the morning. I shall see everything that human beings do. Sometimes I shall see women going about (on unchaste errands). Sometimes there will be black rings around me. That is persons' blood. Then there will be people killed."

Therefore men look at the sun, and when they see sundogs, they think that someone is about to be killed.

X11. Theft of Fire

a. Sky-Owner and others talked long. They planned how fire was to be obtained for human beings.[1] Fire-Owner kept it. He lived across the ocean. Then they spoke long how they could get it. Sky-Owner said, "I cannot do it.

1. *Kiɨ, Sequoia sempervirens*, the only material used for canoes.
2. This heavy withe, used to tie or draw the boat, is called "necklace" by the Yurok.
3. This institutional bit is in better style than many of the informant's stories in English. The dialogue is characteristic: "Do you not know my name?" So is the collaboration of the gods.

---

1. Most feuds did not result in more killings than this.

---

1. [For other versions of the myth, see D1x and y and Z1.—Ed.]

Perhaps you can." One of them said, "Let us take it away by gambling." So Sky-Owner said, "Yes, take it away from him that way if you can. I cannot."

b. At last Bald Eagle said, "I will get it. Who will go with me? Who is the swiftest runner?" Coyote said, "I am the best. I will run with it." Now they went. On every ridge they left one person. Bald Eagle said, "They will follow us. It is only in this way that we can escape. When one of us is tired, the next one will take the fire." Beyond Coyote he put Deer; beyond him, Fisher; and then Duck.

Bald Eagle said, "I will go and gamble. When it is nearly morning, I will sing this song." Then he sang. "After I have sung, I will hiccup ten times. Then I will stir the fire hard so the sparks fly. You must listen for that song."

c. Then he did as he had said. He gambled and sang and hiccuped and stirred the fire, and the sparks flew up. Coyote caught them and ran. All those there shouted and pursued. They did not overtake Coyote. When he was tired, Deer took the fire and ran in big jumps. Then Fisher ran with it, and then Duck. So they escaped with the fire.

d. But when they arrived, Duck had no more fire in his hands: it had gone out. Then he took sticks of willow and rubbed one in his hands (on the other) for a long time. He made a little smoke. He kept twirling. At last he got fire.

e. Now they were all glad. They made fire in the sweathouse and fire in the house. Now they all could swim. They learned to swim far and well and liked it. When they became cold in the water, they went to the fire. Women also were glad. Every morning they bathed in the creek. If they were cold they warmed themselves at the fire. So they do now. If they had got no fire, no one could bathe or get mussels in the ocean.

X12. Mankind Sprung from Dogs

People first grew from a dog. Ki-meł-olemonioł[1] lived with a bitch.[2] Then she bore him a girl. After that she bore him a boy. Then he wanted two dogs; and she bore him two bitch puppies. Then they grew up, and he lived with them, and they had children, until he had raised four girls and four boys.[3] Now people came[4] (to buy) the girls and married them. Every spring they had a child.[5] Some

1. One of "those through whom we live." Not an individual name but a ritual term for spirits. [Cf. D7, n. 12.—Ed.]

2. This incident is usually associated with the flood, but this narrator tells the two separately. See the next myth.

3. It is not clear in the original whether he procreated with his human or his dog children, or whether the two human children procreated.

4. Mythologic inconsistency.

5. Most Yurok children were born in spring. Husband and wife did not ordinarily sleep together in the house for fear of losing their wealth. In summer they made their bed together outdoors; other seasons were too cold in the willows; hence the expectancy of births in spring.

had four girls and four boys. This man became rich from selling his daughters.[6] The dogs were put out (of the house) after people began to come. On account of this growing of men, dogs now follow men; but men first came from them.

X13. The Flood

a. Once the ocean covered the earth. That is why there are redwood logs on the high ridges. The flood was caused by the surf.[1] Two men and two women were saved in a boat; all others drowned. Sky-Owner gave them a song. When they sang, the water receded. This song is used to prevent the ocean from again covering the land.[2]

b. The breakers are eleven brothers. The waves are made by the sky falling and striking the water so that it rises at the shore. It rises also on the land across the ocean, since the sky strikes the sea in the middle. In the summer it strikes the water gently and the swell is soft; but in winter the sky pounds the ocean hard. It was this striking of the sky on the water that made the flood. When a canoe is landed through the surf, a man who knows watches the breakers and counts. He lets ten go by. The eleventh, the youngest brother, is the one to ride in on. Then the boat will not be overturned.

X14x. The Mouth of the River

Narrator's English Version

This story of the Klamath once flowing into the ocean at Omen instead of Rekwoi should be of unusual interest to one whose parentage was of both places. Yet the tale was told scantily and baldly in English, more vividly but repetitiously in Yurok.

Wilson Creek, at whose mouth lay Omen, enters salt water in a considerable cove, whose appearance from the sea has earned it the name False Mouth of Klamath on charts. The tale has therefore an obvious geographic reason. What is more, it may be geologically well founded, though this no Yurok could know. Along the immediate coast, a considerable hill with steep bluffs toward the ocean separates the two mouths; but inland a mile or so, a sluggish stream from the north, Hunter Creek, which enters the tidal lagoon of the Klamath, leads by a branch close to a streamlet that drains into the lagoon near Omen, and their combined courses are level enough to have once been the river channel.

6. This would happen, but is not often mentioned.

---

1. The breakers rose higher and higher, a good Yurok notion.

2. Spott, who was an expert boatman in his prime, has a strong penchant for bringing in songs that ensure safety from water.

Two versions of this story are presented. The first was dictated in English in 1901, and contains the bald substance of the tale, minus the vivid picture of the sea lion. The second version was spoken in Yurok into the phonograph in 1907, and comprised some eight or ten minutes of utterance. Its literal rendering preserves the flavor of the Yurok, including the repetitions.

•

a. At first the mouth of the river was at Omen. There Ki-wes'ona-mege-toł[1] made an opening, and that was the mouth. Now the people stood on the bar at the mouth of the river with harpoons to spear salmon, and with gaffs to catch lamprey eels, but they could not see a fish. They said, "How can we live? What shall we eat?"

b. Then he changed the river and made it where it is now. So the mouth was farther upstream (south). He said of Omen (Wilson) Creek, "This will not do. The people have nothing to live by. Let there be only a small stream here." So it is. Then the people stood on the bar at Rekwoi and speared and got many salmon. So they were glad.

X14y. The Mouth of the River

SECOND VERSION: VERSION FROM PHONOGRAPH DICTATION IN YUROK

a. He[2] was speaking. He was speaking[3] of how the river would flow from the land into the ocean.[4] He spoke much. He wished to know what he would do, how it would be with the people on this world. This river that extends upstream, that is what he was speaking of. Then he said, "I will make it like a furrow."[5] So he said that. Then he thought that the river would flow out at Omen.

Then he began to think about fish. Then he made a harpoon,[6] and the gaff[7] for lamprey eels, that he made also. And the river flowed there, and they stood on both sides. They stood on both sides and saw no fish.

And he wanted to see the sea lion come. He called the sea lion, for he wanted him to be there where the water flowed out, to swim in the river as it flowed out. That is where the sea lion would live and there he would catch fish for himself and eat them. That is why he called him to come. But he never came.

1. "Sky-Keeper"; he who has or owns the sky.
2. Who he was, is not mentioned; but that is good Yurok form. He became the rock Oregos. He can hardly therefore have been Sky-Owner too, as the English version makes out.
3. Or "thinking."
4. *Tewolli werohsił.*
5. *Kileksin.*
6. *Uma'askił.*
7. *Lemoloł.*

They stood in a row on each side to watch,[8] trying to see the salmon. And they could not see the salmon. They could not see them.

b. Then he heard shouting. He heard shouting, and heard what they said back in the hills.[9] And they said, "No, I do not want the river to flow there. I think it will flow elsewhere. Let us make it elsewhere. At Rekwoi, that is where the river will flow." Then he wished to know if it would be well there, since they had been standing to look for the salmon and had not seen them come. That is why he ceased having the river flow at Omen, because the salmon did not come. He said, "Now it will be well if the sea lion comes, if he comes. And he will bark when he comes. And when he plunges under water, that sea lion, then he will hold a salmon when he emerges." And that is why the river does not flow at Omen, because the sea lion did not come.

So it was. Then it flowed at another place, at Rekwoi. There it flowed. And they stood on both sides, and the river flowed down the middle. They stood on both sides, the people, and all of them had a harpoon or a gaff. Then he said, "What shall we do? We must make how it shall be." And they thought, "Let it be so; (but) it will not be right." He said, "Because people will be well off in this world on account of this river, this is the best place for it to flow out, at Rekwoi." So he said, and that is why the river did not flow out elsewhere, (though) it had been about to be at Omen.

And he only called a little to the sea lion, and looked downstream, and he saw the sea lion coming, and he held a fish. And they were standing on both sides to look at that fish. Then the sea lion started from outside the bar. It came to the very mouth of the river, and it was barking. And they saw many salmon coming, and lamprey eels, and sometimes they caught salmon in three places at once, the people did, and eels too. On both sides they did thus. That is why he wanted them to have the river there, because it would be well for the people upstream on account of that. Then many fish came, of all kinds, lamprey eels and sturgeon. That is where they caught them.

c. Then he went to the rock Oregos.[10] And he said, "I shall watch this river where it enters the ocean, from that rock. I shall take care of it." And that is why it is so now. Whatever is near that rock he sees, the one who stands at Oregos. And that rock he brought there too, that Erliker, the one they fish from.[11] At the beginning it was so. A sea lion he heard barking, always barking, that sea lion. Then this river was good. And that is how he had been wanting the

8. *Kitsmikirayewuks*.

9. *Ni-hełkäu*.

10. The conspicuous pillar at the very mouth. Waterman, Geography, map 5, no. 43, and pl. 3, right. [The map is reproduced here as map 6.—Ed.] See also Kroeber, Handbook, pl. 5. "He went to the rock Oregos" presumably means that the woge spirit who had made the river mouth "went into Oregos," became the rock Oregos.

11. Erliker or Oliker, a rock near Oregos, projects into the water. Sea lions were speared from it. Through an oversight Waterman omits it.

river to flow. That is why it flowed there. That is how he made it then. And all were well off then: therefore all the people were well off.

And he is the one who watches this river, that Oregos. And if he does not like something, if he does not like it, that rock, he thinks, "Let me see him drown," and he makes it so. And that is the only way in which he is bad, because he is like that.[12] This is why the river flows there. Now they come every year from this place and that place to the mouth, because he made it so in the beginning.

X15. Dripped on at Erɫerger

[K.'s typescript also contained a slightly different version of this tale, made in 1917. The later version, given here, differs from the 1917 version mainly in the sentence breaks and in having parenthetical insertions that clarify certain obscurities.—Ed.]

•

a. Five brothers grew at Omen.[1] And the youngest one always fished with a line. He did not grow (bigger). They did not eat all together in the house. (The youngest) only brought his food to eat at the fireplace.[2] That is how he grew, and all his brothers did not like him on account of that.[3] That is why they did not eat together. And at Osyoi he fished with his line, and that is all he ate, that youngest one, what he caught with his line. And he (also) went to Erwergeriɫ[4] (to fish). That is what he did, this one that grew at Omen, that is what he did.

And now he was a man, but still he was doing so. He had a mother and father and a sister, and the sister always gave him food when there was no one in the house, that young woman of the same age as he.

b. Then he spoke to him; he said, "Hi, I wish it were well with you,"[5] said the old man.[6] He said, "I want you to see this place Erɫerger.[7] Come and

12. Sometimes making people drown, when they have done wrong.

---

1. Omen-s-otsin.
2. *Wərurkoɫ*.
3. On account of the one kind of fish which was his sole food. It is not clear whether he confined himself to this voluntarily or whether he had to subsist on it because the others gave him nothing.
4. Erwergeriɫ is a seastack "two miles north of Omen." [Cf. T5, n. 8.—Ed.] Waterman does not mention Osyoi of the preceding sentence.
5. In regard to fortune and riches.
6. The literal translation has an answer here: "He said, 'I have heard nothing.'" It is not clear whether the youngest or one of the other brothers makes this answer, nor to what it refers.
7. Erɫerger is False Klamath Rock, a third of a mile offshore. Waterman, Geography, map 5, no. 28, with outline of this myth on p. 230. [The map is reproduced here as map 6.—Ed.] The U.S. Coast Pilot (1924) p. 127, says: "False Klamath Rock, 195 feet high and round-topped, is the most prominent rock on this part of the coast. It lies 650 yards westward of the south point" of Wilson Creek or False Klamath Cove.

look at this Erlerger.[8] Take your pipe case. Take that when you go there. And when you look about do not think this: do not think you will let it drip twice. Only once let it drip. And you will die and remain in that rock if it drips twice. And the rope that you descend by, shake it like this when you feel the first drop, and we shall know and draw you up at once."[9]

c. Then they let down the rope, and when he felt a drop then he was to seize the rope and shake it. So he descended. Then it happened so: a drop fell. Then he thought, "I will wait for two drops, because I have always been without luck.[10] Let me take two." He felt the first drop and did not shake the rope. And the rock began to close. He was inside, and it began to close above. So it happened when he went into that rock Erlerger, this one that grew up at Omen.

d. And the rock closed above, and they went about the top of it all day. They thought, "Perhaps we shall see him." And it was nearly sunset, but they did not see him. And then they left him so. They did not sleep that night. And in the morning they went again to look about. And they looked all day but did not find him. That is how it happened to the one who grew up at Omen, the smallest one. It is not everybody knows that he is very good,[11] this one who grew at Omen.

e. And he thought, "Whoever thinks of this rock where I live, he will be well. He will never have bad luck, but will always have good fortune. So it will be well with him. And if someone comes to this rock to visit me, I will think of him thus, for I shall pity him if he comes to me." That is how he said, this one who went into Erlerger, who grew at Omen. And brush grew on this rock.[12] Above his head is where he wished to see it growing, brush of all kinds.

f. And he said, "It looks as if they were sorry,[13] the way they are going about, the people. It is a small town, that town where I grew. If there is a young man growing up who does not want to be poor, I will watch him, myself. He will have good luck. It will be well with him. Even if he is the only one[14] of that town, it will be so with him if he comes to see me at this rock, for I live in this rock. And it will be well with him. I shall hear it when he speaks. And there will

8. Again an obscure reply follows: "And he said, 'Do not let him go. You had better do it.'" Possibly one of the older brothers is urging the father to desist from sending the youngest on his dangerous errand. Each time the narrator repeats something, he omits something else.

9. The rock was hollow, and he was to be let down into it for a supernatural experience. The purpose of the undertaking would no doubt be obvious to a Yurok.

10. Viz., I have always been poor and need a change. If one drop is good, let me risk that two may bring an even better future.

11. Probably: Not everyone knows that communication with him brings wealth.

12. The rock rises high enough above the spray of the breakers to support some scanty vegetation.

13. *Ayekwī*.

14. The only one to think of me, is perhaps the meaning.

be men like that. I have seen it so. They[15] will seem not to hear if (one) speaks. But when a rich person speaks, everyone will listen to him in the houses; and he will speak in the sweathouse also. So it is when a rich man says something. And so it will be with me watching whether anyone is thinking of me. I am not dead. I am living. I shall watch as long as the world lasts. That is how it will be with me: I shall watch. *Ayekwi!* I go.[16] If one comes over the water[17] to where I live, it will be well and he will have good luck.[18] Whenever he speaks, they will listen all about, for he will grow up well. That is how I shall help him, from being in this rock. Then I shall watch how it is with him. And if it is a woman, it shall be the same. Ayekwi! I go. Ayekwi! I want them to think of me. He shall not be poor, he who thinks of me.

g. "And it will not hurt him, my pipe case, if he sees my pipe case. It will be just as if I were coming home, if he sees my pipe case coming into the house.[19] If it eats something, and goes to one side, do not hurt it. For that is how I shall come into the house. Ayekwi! I go. I shall be in this rock and watch over people. He will be well who thinks of me. And if there is only one, it will be the same. He will be well if he comes to see me in this rock. And sometimes he will see that the top of this rock is burned. Then I have done that."[20]

X16. The Obsidian Cliff at Rekwoi

a. That is where they were about to make obsidian: at Ostsegep[1] it was to

15. People in general.
16. He is not leaving, but the utterance is a formal salutation of departure. *Ayekwī* is often clearly the equivalent of "Alas!" And the Yurok frequently translate it "I am sorry"—compare n. 13 above—but it is also the greeting when friends meet. Yurok life is rarely free of a tinge of regret.
17. The rock must be reached by boat or swimming.
18. Wealth.
19. Perhaps in the form of a weasel. [Cf. D6x and S3.—Ed.]
20. [For another version of this myth in a different setting, see T3.—Ed.]

---

1. "Where they disembark," "boat landing." Ostsegep is a reddish cliff north (northwest) of the mouth of the Klamath. The color evidently suggested prized red obsidian to the Yurok. Hence the wish-fulfillment myth of shooting flaking tools against it from the seastacks in order to chip off blades of treasure.

Waterman alludes to this fantasy, including its "spoiling" by Wohpekumeu (Geography, p. 231, no. 47), but his mapping is in error. He has two Ostsegeps, no. 36 and 47 of map 5. The latter was inside the bar, in the harbor, and was the regular boat landing for Rekwoi from the river; it is to this he attaches the story, but erroneously. The actual red cliff stands near the ocean beach landing, no. 36, which he puts 3/4 mile outside the mouth. This distance may be right, but his no. 36 is attached to a seastack, which is evidently one of the four off the beach and cliff. (Other corrections: 35, Ekor-otep, 1/2 mile nearer Rekwoi than shown, a little above 44; 51, stand.* All over he[2] had been going with it. "Where shall I make it stand?" He was carrying it around, this rock, close to the ocean, standing there at Ostsegep. Like a cliff he tried to have it stand there. But it did not look right as he saw it standing there. He was thinking of the obsidian. "Let me make it stand close to where people live, so it will be easy for them to work it." That is why he carried it about, this rock; but it did sit right where he put it at Ostsegep. It seemed reddish; he was going to make it red, as he carried it about, planning to set it up. Then he thought, "Well, it will stand here, at this Ostsegep; that is where it will sit." And (from) those rocks out in the ocean, four of them lying there, some of them farther out, off Ostsegep on the shore which he was going to make of red obsidian, from (?) those, shooting with an arrow-flaker, they were going to chip off (obsidian) from that rock (cliff);* that is how they were to make their obsidian blades.

b. Hī, he is the one who was there then, Wohpekumeu. It was he, Wohpekumeu, who spoiled that: no one liked him, that is why he spoiled it, this Wohpekumeu. He is the one, the old man, because of whom they do not make obsidians there,* when they thought they would be able to chip them off with an arrow-flaker. Thus they were going to chip them off, when Wohpekumeu spoiled it.[3]

Rekwoi town, just above 47; 48, Nu'u ("double"), not Ro'o, and not near middle of harbor but close to shore outside of 43, Oregos, and mouth; 38, Su'u, "fishing place," shown on map as a seastack well out in the open ocean, should be on shore toward the mouth near 40, Mega, a cliff: 49, Pikets-o-pegemu, is a second name for the large low rock more often called Erliker (as in X14y, n. 11), immediately next to 43, Oregos; 52, Weitspekw, not W'tspūs.) [The map is reproduced here as map 6.—Ed.]

*The clause preceding * is repeated in Yurok.

2. An unnamed woge.

3. That is, I infer, he changed the cliff of precious red obsidian into base or common rock, though it is still reddish. [K. queries whether there is a free version of this myth.—Ed.]

INFORMANT Y

WILLIAM JOHNSON OF REKWOI

William Johnson was known as K'e-meitser, because his father was from the house meitser in Ko'otep.[1] *This was a house of good family. His mother was from ple'ł, also called opyuweg, in Rekwoi. The story of her divorce is told elsewhere:*[2] *she was sent on a wood-gathering errand by the old woman of her husband's house and happened to be bitten by a rattlesnake. This injury was considered to cancel the bride price paid for her. Accordingly, she returned home to Rekwoi. The family in Ko'otep, however, kept the boy. He did not follow his mother back to Rekwoi to live until he was grown.*

He became crippled from sickness caused by kāhseläu. *Both his legs were competely useless. He could not even attend to necessities unaided. However, he was skillful with his hands and specialized in making woodpecker bands, whence he was called Rekwoi eskerwits.* Skerwits *means craftsman, or fine work. It is used also of a woman who makes fine designs on her baskets. William used to be paid $25 for each woodpecker band which he assembled. He inherited some dance wealth and bought other things from his earnings. He remained unmarried, and lost his life in a runaway wagon accident when returning from Crescent City.*

This lone little tale may or may not be typical of its narrator, but it illuminates the spirit of Yurok civilization. There are few nations that would set up Money as one of the most powerful of their gods.

•

1. Waterman, Geography, map 14, house 10.
2. Spott and Kroeber, Yurok Narratives, no. 18, p. 206.

Y1. Money Eats the Sky

a. Once all things were alive. Baskets were people, dentalia were people, and all other were people. Now the woge knew that they must all leave: they were already in the sweathouse talking about it. Some said they were going to the sky. Others said that they would go off on the mountains.

b. But Dentalium said, "I will not go. I wish to live where I am. I shall stay." Now he who had said they must go asked, "What shall you be able to do? You are very small." Dentalium said, "I know it. I am small, but it would be a bad thing if I went off. People would not live well. They would kill one another, and they would have no way of settling the feud. So I shall remain here." Then he began to (suck in and) swallow the sky (to show his power) and ate most of it. Then that one said, "Stop!" So Dentalium remained, and is kept in purses by human beings.

INFORMANT Z

JOHNNY SHORTMAN OF WEŁKWÄU

Johnny Shortman was born about 1840, or somewhat earlier. His personal name was Ha'nīr', and he was of the house tǟł-wo'oł in Rekwoi, the house in which the tǟł *singers eat while they are under restrictions for the Jumping Dance. His mother was of the house oslok.*[1] *Spott, whose mother's mother was also from oslok, therefore recognized Shortman as* pä, *literally, brother, but in this case meaning cousin.*

Shortman married into pegwoläu, across the river in Wełkwäu. He was probably half-married, because he lived and died there. His wife died before him, of mussel poisoning.

He was tǟł *for the Rekwoi Jumping Dance. He was also the formulist the last time it was performed, about 1904. There was some question of his authentic knowledge of this formula, because the previous formulist, Old Tom of the house wonek, had refused to impart it, and Johnny had only "picked up" his acquaintance with it. However, the rite went off without mishap, there was no unusual amount of sickness during the winter, and the community concluded Johnny must have spoken it about right.*

Like Spott, Johnny was assistant in the First Salmon medicine, but never spoke the formula himself, although it belonged to the house of his wife's people. The last formulist for this ritual was his wife's uncle or great-uncle, and the wife herself, before her marriage, had served as girl assistant in the ceremony. Johnny had acted as the man assistant, and after the old

1. [K. supplied conflicting names for the houses of Johnny's mother and wife (pegwoläu for the mother and täl-wo'oł for the wife), but queried their accuracy. Those I have given here are from Captain Spott's biography, above, and from Kroeber and Gifford, World Renewal, Appendix V, p. 133.—Ed.]

formulist's death, he became, as head of the house, at least de facto curator of the pair of sacred pipes to which the First Salmon rite each spring related. The pipes were too sacred to tell a stranger like me much about, and Johnny kept evading the subject.

He had some wealth by inheritance, including a very old woodpecker band from tǟł-wo'oł. He owned more things which he had earned or bought himself. The Indians of his generation used to work for wages for white people and spend very little of their earnings. When they had enough, they would buy dance treasures from other Indians or the materials for them. In this way Johnny acquired six otter skins, four fisher skins, many eagle feathers for the Jumping and Brush Dance, six dentalium necklaces, four deerskin blankets, sixteen of the head rings with woodpecker on them which are called ma'äk, *four short obsidians, called* mełkweł, *mounted on sticks for the Brush Dance (one pair of these was black, the other white), and perhaps 150 to 200 arrows. Although this was a considerable quantity of goods, it was not extraordinarily valuable. Most of the objects were for the Brush Dance, and the others were accessories for the Jumping Dance.*

Johnny poured out his knowledge readily enough, if it did not impinge too closely on the subject of his sacred pipes; but it was a series of scraps. His mind leaped from one subject to another. The little tale about the obsidian cliff (Z6) is an example. A few sentences really suffice to tell what he has to say. But the cliff recalls to him a rock in the ocean six miles away; he explains that, then returns to conclude his story. The account of the origin of death and purification (Z3) was recited in half a dozen pieces, which partly overlap. Parts of the series are myth, parts descriptive of customs. In general the informant showed the same unsystematic turn of mind.

His literary interest is feeble, his skill deficient. His concerns are crudely philosophical, not aesthetic. He gives an intelligible enough account of the woge race, their functions and relation to mankind. This is the distinct merit of his utterances. Other Yurok tend to assume the woge; they draw upon their existence as a background from which stories spring. For Johnny the background is the thing of interest. When he proceeds to incident, his memory is meager, his portrayal colorless. The story of the taking of tails, that is, of the origin of animal forms (Z2), is in point. There is no verve, no dialogue, no picturing; the story is a summary. The result of the events overshadows the happenings. Compare what other narrators have done with the same tale in myths G2 and K3.

Johnny's fullest myth is the Theft of Fire (Z1); but this is bald by the side of what average narrators make of the theme (D1 and X11). Everything is reasoned. When fire is found, an offer is made to buy it! Plans for the escape are carefully issued. When the fire is at last securely deposited in the willows, there is discussion and manufacture and trial until it is got out again. Artistically, the depositing of the fire in the willow roots is the termination of the story; but Johnny is a reasoner, and cares little about plot. Tskerkr charges his departing woge with a poignant regret, and Lame Billy would have made the episode of Thunder and Wetskāk (Z5) a living drama; but Wełkwäu Johnny explains.

He also knew the myth of the origin of the legendary White Deerskin Dance at Wełkwäu. This he told to his friend Captain Spott of Rekwoi, Informant X, and the latter's adopted son Robert Spott, who in turn told it to me as it is published in Spott and Kroeber, Yurok Narratives.[2]

Johnny was therefore well informed; but he proved a poor narrator. That this generalizer is one of the least coherent of the narrators represented in this volume is due to the nature of his predilection rather than to any inherent logical deficiency. A tale once heard spins itself. Everyone feels what belongs in it and what does not, and when it has come to an end. But an abstraction or explanation can go on forever, and ramify randomly. It has no compelling form. The Yurok are frequently inconsistent, as much so as Johnny is disjointed in his summaries. But their discrepancies are in fact or in sequence or in logic; the plot mostly maintains its consistency as plot. Johnny's account lacks both plot interest and emotional tone; hence the deficiencies of Yurok intellectualization stand out the more starkly in his versions.

Z1. Theft of Fire

a. At first they had no fire. They had food but had to cook it on their bodies, each one for himself, not as now the women cook it on the fire. Each one cooked it under his armpit. Thus they all prepared whatever they ate. They had no (true) acorns, but made them of pitch.

b. Then one of them told that he had seen fire. They said, "We want that. Where did you see it?" He said, "I saw fire in the sky." So they gathered and planned and went to the sky, to buy the fire. But he who had it, Sun, would not sell it. They continued trying to buy it, but he would not sell, he said.

c. When they found that they could not buy it from him, they began to confer again. They said, "We must have it. Let us begin to gamble. We will play at the house where it is, and one of us will sit at every short distance along the path." This path was the one by which Fire-Owner[1] (Sun) went to his house when he traveled during the day. At one place there was a large hill; at the end of the path was water. The last one who was to receive the fire, Turtle,[2] lay in the water, with his hands on shore. The one who was to do the gambling, Raven, said: "When you hear me singing, tell the one next to you, and he to the next one, to be ready, because it will be as if I were telling them

2. No. 35, pp. 244-49.

---

1. Kuwis-umets.
2. Esko.

that I am about to snatch fire.'' On the drying frame in the house two Fishers seated themselves; two others sat on the roof. Raven saw Bald Eagle,[3] the fire-owner,[4] stir the fire. As sparks flew up, the Fishers tried to catch them with wood shavings, but he that stirred the fire[5] always caught the sparks himself.

d. When Raven began to sing, all knew that he was about to seize fire, and they became ready. Then he snatched it and passed it to the Fishers. Fire-Owner followed. The fire kept traveling, one handing it to the next, Fire-Owner close behind. When Round Rock got it, he rolled down the long hill and gained. At the foot of the hill another one took it and passed it on to Turtle, who clutched it in his hand and dived, just as Fire-Owner came up. Under the water, turtle rubbed fire on willow roots until it had all gone out. Thus they obtained fire.

e. Now when they had the fire, the woge came together and began to question how they would extract it. One said, ''I think we shall get it out of the willow roots. Let us make one of them flat, the other round and long.'' So they made the fire drill like that. Then they tried it. Many went to try it; but no fire came. There was tinder ready, but nearly all had tried and got nothing. Then when another set to work, they saw the drill begin to smoke, and cried, ''It looks as if it were about to come.'' So they continued until at last they got a spark. Now all of them stood about, wishing to have for themselves a bit of the fire. Every woge got some. Only Tsegił[6] said, ''I want no fire. I have a good blanket.'' So now you see him lying somewhere frozen dead. Thus they obtained fire.

Z2. The Furs of Animals

a. After the woge had fire, they came to one house to get tails. Some said, ''I wish a tail.'' Some said, ''I should like feathers.'' Of all the tails and feathers, only one was not good: no one wanted that. They agreed, ''Whoever gets up earliest will take the best one for himself.'' In the morning Fisher woke first and took the best tail (i.e., fur). One by one they all got up, or sometimes two would rise together. But none would wake any other. As they got their tails they (put them on and) went off (as animals). Old man Coyote was the

3. Pergis.
4. *Sic*; it was Sun before. Evidently I misunderstood the narrator. Probably Bald Eagle was one of the fire-stealers whose task it was to make the sparks rise, as in X11*b*.
5. Correct to: Fire-Owner, viz., Sun.
6. A bird; perhaps Meadowlark?

very last. He still slept (when they had all left). So he got the worst tail, the one that was half-singed.

b. Dog was in the house too. When Deer slept, Dog touched a (glowing) stick against his foot and burned it so that when he followed him he might smell (his tracks).

Z3. Death and Purification

a. They thought there would be too many people. At first they thought that they would make it that people did not die. Then they thought that they would be too many, and that there would not be room for them. So they began to think, "Perhaps it will be best if they die." Then, as they were talking, Wertspit[1] lost his child. So he went to bury it. Many of them did not like it, but they could do nothing: he had buried the child already. Then they thought, "Well, let it be so." Thus it began that people died.

b. Thereupon they said: "It will be best if when people die they use a formula." So they made it that way. Then they began to arrange it how they would speak that formula; how many words they would say, and at what places. Now sometimes one hears of old men living somewhere, very old people. Sometimes there is only one in a place. They have lived for a whole lifetime. That comes from the first planning that people should not die but live on forever. That is how these few people come to be so old.

c. After that, all the woge went off into the hills, after they had made that death-purification formula. They provided for everything. Human beings would have formulas to kill deer, and when a child was about to be born, and a formula for every purpose. The person that knows the formula has to know what plant to use with it. Not everyone knows the right plant.

d. The woge said, "We shall live on the hills but will help you people with this (purification) formula." In using this death formula, it is not only one who is called upon, for there were many planning how it was to be. When a man speaks this formula, he calls the name of the first one. Then the one called upon says, "You will have to go on to the next one." Thus he goes the whole way through the world. Each one tells him to see another.

Now the woge are always glad when one calls upon them in formula. They hear what one tells them. In all formulas a name has to be called upon. Then they are glad that they are talked to. They always pity the people because they are only few. If they had done as they wanted to, if Wertspit had not done wrong, there would be many people now. That is why the woge are sorry.

1. [The Jerusalem cricket.—Ed.]

In the death-purification formula there are ten woge who are addressed. The first one is named and asked for the plant. He is the one farthest upstream. He answers that he does not have it, and tells the human being to ask the next one. The next one is asked and refers to the next one, and so on until the tenth is reached. He is at the downstream end of the world, at Pulekuk. He at last says that he has the plant. It is he who declared that he did not wish people to die; but when most of them said, "There will be too many if they all live," he said, "Well, let it be so," and went off to Pulekuk because he did not like to see human beings die. When someone dies, this one, from where he is at Pulekuk, hears the relatives crying, and knows that a person has died. Then he listens because he knows that he will be called upon in the formula.[2]

e. In the making of this purification the two Thunders in the sky start the fire in the sweathouse. The man who is making the purification does not blow the fire, but he drops crushed sticks and fine-rubbed splinters on the coals. After a time these blaze up and the new wood for the fire catches. It is the two Thunders who blow the shavings into flame.

f. The woge said, "When people die, where will they go?" Then they agreed: "They will go under the earth. They will not leave them above the ground but will bury them. So it will be done to them."

Z4. Payment for Wives and Killings

a. Then they made women to be, too. For people would not live a whole lifetime; only one, or a few in some towns, would live so long; but with a woman a man has children, and so there are more persons again, and in that way human beings would continue. But they did not want one to take the woman for nothing. They made it so that one would have to pay before he called her his wife. If he has children without buying her, they will be just like dogs; it will be like a bitch breeding pups.

b. They also made it that when a man becomes angry and kills a person, he pays for him: they settle. And if the one that killed him has a sister, he gives her in payment also. Then if he who was killed has relatives, one of them will marry that woman; and he will have children, and it will be just as if he were alive again, he who was killed. That is why people do so, because the woge left their instructions, that everything might go well. For if they did not pay, many would think, "I will commit murder again," or "I too will kill." But since they have to pay, they are afraid. Therefore few kill.

2. This is a valid synopsis of the average death-purification recital, but no two formulas are alike. Different men call on 3, 10, 12, 15, 18, 20, or 22 spirits. The last spirit, who finally brings relief, is as often in the rock Oregos at the river mouth in front of Rekwoi as at mythical Pulekuk. The geographical order, however, seems invariably to be downstream. [Cf. H2, K3*g*, and X8.—Ed.]

Z5. Thunder and Small Money

Thunder had a son. The boy went about on the hills. The Sä'äł[1] in the hills had never seen him: therefore they killed him.[2] Then Thunder went over the world looking for his boy. That is why we see, in places on the tops of hills, prairies in the woods: that is where he looked for his son.[3] But he could not find him. Now he was about to destroy everything in this world.[4] Then Small Money, Wetskāk, said, "I know who killed him." He tried to talk to him; but Thunder would not listen. Then Wetskāk too became angry: he began to swallow this world.[5] He swallowed half of it. Now Thunder said, "Stop! Let it be! I will let it be." Then Wetskāk stopped.[6]

Z6. The Obsidian Cliff at Rekwoi

a. A woge said that he would make red obsidian.[1] That is why the cliff beyond the mouth of the river is red.[2] One can see that it is striped, as some obsidian is. He who said this was one of those who later went off into the hills. When the woge went off into the hills, they stopped turning the cliff into obsidian. If these human beings had not arrived, the woge would have made obsidian there. Because they withdrew, back from the river, they no longer wanted to see that place be obsidian and stopped making it so.[3]

b. All the large rocks along the coast have vegetation on top because there is soil on them. So it is also with the large rock off Omen[4] on which they dig bulbs. At first the soil was continuous from the mainland over to these rocks, but the sea has since washed them out, leaving the earth and growth on top.

Z7. Departure of the Woge

a. The woge lived along the river and all about, just as human beings do now. They would go to see their friends and return, traveling the same ways as

1. Spirits in the hills which can cause sickness.
2. The motivation is typical. Strangers are disliked.
3. Destroying the forest in his search.
4. More Yurok sentiment.
5. Or: sky? *Wes'ona* denotes both. Cf. Waterman, Geography, p. 191: "This sky . . . together with its flooring of landscape, constitutes 'our world.'"
6. The first part of this bit is paralleled by J4 and P3, the last by Y1.

---

1. Red obsidian is rarer and more valuable than black. A cliff of obsidian would be rated by the Yurok much as a ledge of ruby by us.
2. Ostsegep, just north of the mouth. The color easily suggests red obsidian. Waterman's location and error are discussed in X16, n. 1.
3. X16*b* says that Wohpekumeu spoiled their plan.
4. Erłerger is False Klamath Rock; see X15, n. 7.

we do. Then they heard that there was a human being toward *wohpeu*.[1] Thereupon they wanted to leave. They said they did not want to mix with human beings. They thought, "We shall have to go somewhere."

b. So they prepared everything for this world. They made it that if one had done wrong and was killed for it, a settlement had to be made. If people wanted women, they had to buy them, and then they called them their wives. So they instituted everything before they went away from all these towns in which they lived. When these human beings came, all the woge went off to the hills.

1. Across the ocean, sometimes in a direction more or less south of west. The interpreter had translated "south," which perhaps meant far off along the coast rather than overseas.

INFORMANT AA

GEORGE MÄHÄTS OF REKWOI (AND MÄ'ÄTS)

George Mähäts was from the coast town of Mä'äts on Big Lagoon. His parents must have been full-married because George was called K'e-mä'äts, which the whites changed to Mähäts. His mother was from Rekwoi of the house ketskeɬ, which was early abandoned. His mother and father lived mostly in Rekwoi in the house knäu. Later George had a house in the American town of Requa.

His wife was from Wohkel, so that he was also called Wohkel-awa and his wife was called Mä'äts-ison after his paternal home. She was a doctor. George was not tä̱ɬ, *but he knew a medicine formula for* kwegesoyek *sickness.*

He specialized in regalia for the Brush Dance. When his son killed a white man, he sold all these things in order to pay the lawyer, but the son died in prison. Two grandchildren of this son survived.

George and his wife, old and rather decrepit, lived in a shack in the center of Requa, the American portion of Rekwoi. He had spent most of his life about the mouth of the river. The couple were very poor, friendly, gentle, and grateful. The one story obtained from George is rather well told, a little in the manner of Tskerkr, but without the latter's elliptical intensity. The circumstances by which George was surrounded did not make it seem likely that he would prove a good religious informant, and the acquaintance was therefore not followed up—perhaps unwisely.

AA1. THE SKY BLANKETS

The story is the familiar North American one of the scabby younger brother or grandson who triumphs and marries in the end. Characteristically Yurok is the greater concern over the wealth-blankets than over the girls. Also, the oppressors are not punished, but are only humiliated at being surpassed. And finally, the hero simply withdraws to his more splendid new environment, but, being a good Yurok in his attachment to his natal house, he takes it with him.

•

a. At Tsotskwi[1] there grew four brothers. They were married, and their father and mother were still alive. The smallest one was covered with sores. They did not like their youngest brother because he was so scabby, and his dog was like him. Even the old man hated him, though he was his own son. The old woman was the only one that liked him. They lived outside the house in the menstrual hut, he and his mother.[2] They did not give him much food because they hated him so. When his three brothers married, he was the one that got no wife. Then the old woman thought she would move her house a little way up the hill. So she removed it.

b. All day always the boy remained lying down. He told his mother, "Wash yourself every morning." Then whenever the old woman went to the creek to bathe, she would find two headless geese. Sometimes she found three. Now sometimes one of his brothers' wives came into the hut where he lay. There she worked at her buckskin dress. Sometimes she would cut off a piece of the fringe and give it to him. "I give it to you to tie your hair with,"[3] she said. Then her husband told her, "I do not want you to go in there to see him." The three older brothers used to go to the sky to dance; sometimes one of them went hunting on the ocean.

c. Then once the scabby boy said to his mother, "My feet are sore." The old woman thought, "I have never seen you go anywhere. You lie in bed all day." But the boy said to her, "I want you to look at them. My feet hurt me." So the old woman looked at his feet and saw they were cut. She asked, "How did your feet come to be so? You never went anywhere." He said, "I will tell you where I cut them. It was at Weskunet-oteneu."[4] Every night he went there and caught geese, left them where his mother bathed, and let her find them in the morning.

d. Now his brother's wife always continued to come in. She brought her dress to work at, and sometimes gave him a piece of fringe. The three men,

1. Tsotskwi is Dry Lagoon, where there was a former Coast Yurok town; Waterman, Geography, map 31, no. 14. [This map is reproduced here as map 7. K. had a marginal notation indicating he intended to revise the notes for this myth.—Ed.]

2. A lean-to or penthouse at the rear of the living house. Menstrual blood is exceedingly defiling and dangerous, and a man would scarcely enter the hut. To be condemned to it expresses utter opprobrium.

3. Good hair ties are of otter or mink skin, with a few woodpecker scalps attached; but the boy appears to have had nothing at all.

4. In Wiyot territory. This is Waterman's map 2, no. 49, Weskwenet-o-tnäu, at the NE corner of Humboldt Bay.

when they went off to the sky, said to her, "You who are always going in to him there; perhaps you think you shall get the blanket from him." (They spoke of) blankets covered with woodpecker crest which they saw in the sky and which they hoped to get when they went there. Nevertheless the woman went to him. Then she said, "Tomorrow my husband is going on the ocean to kill sea lions. The others are going to the sky." Then they went up to the sky, and one on the ocean.

e. Now scabby young man thought, "I also will go to the sky." He took his dog along. He made it that his dog was free from sores. His two brothers saw the dog in the sky. Then they did not go on to the dance, but turned back.[5] When the scabby one returned, his brother's wife was in the house. When she looked at him she did not know him, he was dressed so finely. After she had closed her eyes, she saw him covered with sores again.

f. Then he went to the sky once more. He found two girls there. On account of them, all the young men came to dance. Then he spoke with his dog. The dog said, "There are two blankets where those two girls are. They have made them of woodpecker crest. All who come there go to one place to put on their finery. Now I shall not go into that house in the sky, but stay at a distance. I shall make medicine[6] because you will want those girls." Then he made medicine. He was talking with the young man as if he were a person. When they came to the sky, the young man saw many men outside the house. Then he was ashamed a little. Nevertheless he went on to the house. Then one of the sky girls said, "I hear someone outside. Go to see." Then her sister went to look and saw him standing. She told him, "Come into the house." She said, "I never saw him before; nevertheless I told him to enter." When he came in, he saw a stool between the two girls. He sat on it, and all the others went off.

g. There was a large sweathouse there. It belonged to ten brothers that lived in the sky: the two girls were their sisters. In the evening the ten men came into the house to eat, and spoke to the young man.[7] When they went to go into the sweathouse, they said to him, "You may sleep in the house if you like."[8] The two girls slept on the house terrace;[9] there they lay down, and called the young man, "Come, sleep here."

h. When he lay down with them and looked about, he saw two blankets

5. Perhaps they were ashamed.

6. The making of medicine comprises both the recital of a formula and one or more acts performed with an herb, plant, or other substance.

7. In a friendly manner, as prospective brother-in-law.

8. Yurok men and women do not sleep together in the living house—never in theory and apparently rarely and shamefacedly in fact. Either the brothers kept elsewhere their money, which would be endangered by such procedure, or custom is wrenched to make the story more effective.

9. Or platform: the ground level, indoors, but 3 or 4 feet above the excavated pit.

covered with woodpecker crest. The girls told him, "Many would like to get these two blankets. Many have tried to take them away. They steal them, but whenever they go a little distance, before they have gone far, they find that there are many rocks in the way, that it is rough ground, or that there are many logs. Then they are always caught up with. Sometimes they stick fast, as in mud, although there is only prairie." That was why they all came there to the dancing, because they wanted those blankets. But none escaped with them because when they took them the ground began to be impassable. The young man did not sleep that night; he thought much of those blankets, for he too had gone in order to take them.

i. In the morning, just as it began to be day, he went and took them. The girls thought, "I do not want to tell my brothers; not at once. Let him go a little way before I tell them." Then the young man heard shouting behind him. Still he did not run. After a time he heard louder shouting. They called, "Leave those blankets." Then, when he heard the shouting still nearer, he began to run. Then the ground was bad, full of logs and rocks and brush, and there were steep hills around. He ran on to where he had hidden his dog. When he reached him, he gave him the blankets and the dog carried them. Then they came to a large lake, and he thought, "How shall I cross it?" He was carrying a folding case.[10] He looked in it and found the dress fringes that his sister-in-law had given him. These he threw across the lake. Then the thong lay over the water, and he and his dog crossed on it. When they had crossed, he drew the thong to him and put it back in his case. Then those blanket owners shouted across the lake, "You will see us again."[11]

j. Then he returned and saw his brother's wife in his hut, and thought, "She is the one who gave me those fringes." When she started to go to her house he thought, "Alas! I ought to give her something because she always gave me the fringe. I think I had better cut one of the blankets in the middle." So he gave it to her. She told him, "You had better come to the house with me." He said, "When you enter, use the half blanket for your seat." When he came in, his three brothers said, "What do you want here?" When his sister-in-law entered and began to sit on the woodpecker-crest blanket, one of them cried, "Stop! Stop!" and leaped and snatched it up (to preserve it from damage). That day his brothers did not eat anything. They went into the sweat-house and fasted.[12] One of them went to bring sweathouse wood ceremonially. Then they sweated. When they came back into the house, they brought their skin purses. They wanted to buy their younger brother a wife; but he would not take their money.[13]

10. *Egor*, of rawhide folded once over.
11. Meaning that the two girls would follow him.
12. [K. has a marginal notation: "shame."—Ed.]
13. So recorded; possibly they wanted to help him pay for the sky wives he already had?

The old woman had said to him, "Do not go into the house; your brothers will not like you." But he had not listened to her and had gone in.

After the young man had come home, the two sky girls also came: they followed the blankets.

k. Next morning the brothers did not see their house. He had taken it into the sky. They looked for him, but did not know where he had gone. He too was in the sky now. He took with him his mother and his sister-in-law and his two wives. He had one blanket and a half, his sister-in-law the other half.[14]

14. This wish-fulfillment daydream story is contrary to Yurok custom and attitude at several points: the boy in the menstrual hut; the honeymoon in the sky family's house; the robbed brothers in the sky desisting from pursuit and sending their sisters after him; and the nonmention of payment for his brides.

Informant BB

ANN OF ESPEU

Ann was sister to Informant B, Tskerkr. On their father's side they were from Espeu. The mother's town is not remembered. Fanny Flounder, who was also from Espeu, called Tskerkr uncle, and she gave one of her doctor power-pains to his daughter Laura, Ann's niece.[1]

Ann's first husband died. Then she was *kerer'*, a widow who did not cut her hair.[2] She had had a daughter by this marriage. After this she had a halfbreed son, James Maston, who kept a little store at Wohkero for many years. Then she married a man from Nä'ägeɫ, by whom she had another daughter. After this she was *werres*[3] with an old Coast Yurok named Ɫenok.

Ann was recommended to me as being as well stored with tales as her brother. One circumstance and another prevented my ever seeing her. Once I was to meet her at Tskerkr's house at Orekw; but she failed to come. She lived some miles away, on top of a hill. Once I went to her cabin, only to find her out. T. T. Waterman, on a visit to the Yurok country subsequent to mine, made a point of connecting with her, and brought back a couple of dozen phonograph cylinders of her dictation. These contained three, or rather two and a half, stories, and were translated into literal but idiomatic English by Mrs. Catherine Goodwin.

Ann's narrative faculties are very similar to her brother's, and scarcely inferior. I should not hesitate to regard her as his equal were it not that her tales stand in the superior medium of Mrs. Goodwin's Englishing, against which Frank's vocabulary fails. The family resemblance in literary quality is strong. Ann and Tskerkr evince the same emotional suffusion, the lyrical tone, the rapid passing over of action as such, the lack of characterization, the dwelling instead on the sentiments of their personages, the feeling for nature. The same emotions are dealt with: regret, longing, affection, home-

1. [For an account of how Fanny Flounder became a doctor, see Spott and Kroeber, Yurok Narratives, no. 8, pp. 158-64.—Ed.]

2. [Evidently she did not observe the customary year of mourning; see Informant CC's biography, n. 2.—Ed.]

3. [K. has earlier translated this as "sweetheart."—Ed.]

sickness, at once tender and poignant and diffuse. And there is the same inordinate repetition.[4]

The first of the three tales, incomplete though it is, displays these qualities at their height. All that happens is that a man is overcome with a nameless and irresistible drawing to play the flute to the exclusion of everything else, and finally to enter the ocean and swim westward until he passes under the sky and reaches the land beyond. Yet so insistently pathetic is the handling of this slender theme that I at least am left in unsatisfied suspense when the tale is snapped off by external accident of recording. And there is poetry in the exclamation that the swimmer utters far out at sea as he turns and sees the beauty of the mountains he has left. The second story, or formula, is as lachrymose as its title; but the bond between brother and sister is touchingly portrayed, and the final touch of her yearning remembrance of their old home is elegiac. The third tale deals with an origin, as the first two do not, and is thus less in the manner of the narrator. Its handling is suggestive of the one by Tskerkr which deals with the same characters, Earthquake and Thunder (B5), although the theme is quite different. All three stories have the same setting of coast and ocean and the shadowy beyond, and the same fond dwelling on this setting, as the majority of Tskerkr's.

BB1. He Swam Across the Ocean

a. That is where he lived, he that played the flute: at Espeu, that is where he lived, he that played the flute. All at once he thought, "Now I shall learn to play," and he used to make music all day. Then he would go for sweathouse wood, after he had finished playing, and then play at night. He did not sleep; he played the flute constantly. (It was) all at once (that) he thought, "I shall do that." In the day he used to go to Plek'en and to Neges[1] and cry.

He was the father of a child, of one child. And he had a wife, but suddenly he paid no more attention to her, for he had decided to play, and had made a flute—not the sort of flute they have now, but the flute of long ago, the kind the people[2] used to play. And he used to play on this until far in the night: some nights he did not sleep at all, he played so long, and from the house she would hear him, his wife.[3] The playing seemed so near and she could hear him so plainly,* that she thought, "What makes him like that?" his wife (thought).[4]

4. [K. queries in the margin of his manuscript: "and ellipsis?"—Ed.]

1. Plek'en is Waterman, Geography, map 29, no. 10, a high cliff, one of the Gold Bluffs, 1 to 1-1/2 miles north of Espeu. Neges I cannot place. [K. has a marginal note indicating that the footnotes for this group of tales need revising.—Ed.]

2. The Indians, as opposed to the Americans.

3. This word order evinces the supplementary and incidental function of nouns in the Yurok sentence, and helps to explain why proper names are mentioned or omitted so randomly.

*Asterisked clauses or sentences are repeated in the Yurok.

4. The text then again repeats "the playing seemed so near and she could hear him so plainly."

Their child was a little girl. And so he paid no attention to his wife; and began to play, and as soon as day broke started to get sweathouse wood, and would go to Neges and to Plek'en, crying.

b. So he did that, playing flute: every night he played.* He used not to sleep, but played continually: he would play and then cry. He thought, "I will do thus." He longed for he did not know what, and used to think, "What am I longing for?" All day and all night until morning he would cry and play the flute.[5] In the morning he would lay down his flute and go for sweathouse wood: he would (always) do the same: he would go from crag to crag at Espeu, and to Neges, and sit and think of many things. He did not at all want to see his wife. Their child was a little girl: (but) he no longer noticed her: all he did was to play. He played until morning and cried, longing for he did not know what. He would say, "I do not know what I am longing for." And he did not want to eat. All he would eat was angelica:[6] that is all he ate, in the sweathouse: he did not even go to the house, (and) did not wish to see his wife.

c. It had gone on like this for a month, (that) he would not see his wife. His child used to come and look into the sweathouse and call him "Father," but he would not answer her; for he thought, "I do not want to see them;* I do not want to see my child." So he was; and would go to Kegesonaik[7] crying; and bring more sweathouse wood than he needed for the sweathouse.[8]

d. Then once he saw something running about and thought, "How pretty it is: I should like to have it for a pipe case.*[9] Let me try to kill what is running about here and have it for a pipe case." It was running very near him, and he caught and killed it. He put it with his flute: (where) he used to lie by the small exit of the sweathouse, there he kept his belongings: (the fur of) which he was going to make his pipe case was there, and his flute too. When he went for sweathouse wood he used to hide them both,* and when he returned he found them as he left them. He cried incessantly: he did not know what made him cry, did not know what made him so. He would not go into the house. All he ate was angelica, and he smoked tobacco: he drank no water. For he thought, "I am becoming like this. I do not know what is happening to me." He thought perhaps he would become invisible. So a month passed.

e. Then he went to Plek'en. He went downhill after he had been to

5. The narrator repeated, "Such as they used to have, not the kind they have now, but the flute that the Indians used to play on (before the Americans came), on that he played."

6. *Wołpei*, the woody root of which is scraped for incense and medicine.

7. Kegesonaik I cannot place.

8. That is, he carried out the ritual or ascetic act of gathering faster than he could burn the wood.

9. The Yurok tobacco pouch is a case just large enough to contain the tubular pipe and a small quantity of tobacco. It is made either of deer fur or of the skin of a small mammal such as a weasel.

Plek'en and jumped down on the beach and thought, "Now I will swim! I will swim out into the ocean." He went into the water (but) was thrown back on the sand (by a breaker). Then he thought, "Let me dive," and he dived under a wave, and dived again, and came up beyond the second wave after he had dived. Then he swam and swam. And he thought, "What matter where I come to! For I do not believe I shall ever return." So he swam and cried at the same time, just cried as he swam. He cried, thinking, "For I do not know where I am going."

f. Then he came to Sekwona,[10] and looked at the rock, and thought, "I will go up on it! I wonder how I shall feel?" And he climbed on the rock, on Sekwona; he started to step on it with one of his feet and said,[11] "He'e'i'i! This must be the place where I shall die, on this rock! This is where I shall die." And he climbed altogether upon the rock Sekwona, and walked around on top looking all about, and looked back into the mountains. And he thought, "It looks beautiful back in the mountains. The knolls and hills look like caps, far in the mountains." Wherefore he cried all the more, thinking, "I wonder what is about to happen to me?" But he did not once think of his home.

And he leaped into the water again, leaped in on the ocean side, thinking, "I will swim out farther." He kept swimming, thinking, "It makes no difference where I go. This is the only rock that I see,* this rock I climbed out on: there is only the one." He swam far out into the ocean, not knowing where he was going.

g. And now he heard a noise coming from the direction in which he was swimming. And he thought, "He'e'i'i! I have heard that the (edge of the) sky falls (incessantly) in the ocean somewhere, (that) the ocean is raised where the sky falls on it." Now he swam on and came near: then the ocean began to become very rough. He looked and saw that the sky would go far up, and then would drop. He stayed some distance away, continuing to swim around, and thought, "I will watch and count how many times the sky falls[12] and then pass underneath." And he swam and swam around and counted on his fingers how often the sky had fallen, (until) he thought, "Now it has fallen ten times, and I will pass under." Then he swam toward it and dived and came (out) on the other side.

h. And he swam and looked about and thought, "Indeed this is very beautiful." He was swimming as they used to swim, only partly in the water,[13] and looked over the ocean before him and thought, "It does not seem as if I had much farther to go; let me (swim) on." And he swam and

10. "Pestle," Redding Rock, about 5 miles offshore.
11. "Did that," the interpreter said.
12. Most of the sentence up to this point is repeated here.
13. With a paddle stroke, keeping the head above water, not with a crawl stroke.

swam and swam, a considerable distance, and thought, "It looks good there!" He could see the (drift) logs on the beach (now), so far could he see:[14] the waves were becoming smaller. It looked as if (there were) dentalia along the shore. Then he swam faster: the sun was almost down, so long had he swum. And now he came close indeed to the shore and swam about and thought, "He'e'i'i! I wonder where I am?"

i. And he reached the shore, and went on it, and thought, "I will stand up," And he tried to stand and fell. Then he thought, "I believe I am about to die." And he cried. And he thought (again), "He'e'i'i! I ought to know better than to believe I should live after reaching here when I did not know where I was going." And he crawled up the beach, using his hands and his knees to crawl on the sand. (As) he crawled he dragged a large trail in the sand where he had crawled, going up over it.

(Unfinished)

BB2. The Crying Baby

This was said to be a formula, presumably to still a crying child. It might also be a gambling medicine. While it has all the elements of a formula, it is hardly so organized: there is no invocation, in fact no application to the situation of the petitioner. It is therefore probably best regarded as formulaic substance in myth form.

•

a. At Tsotskwi[1] he lived, he that used to cry and go to Pulekuk. He had a sister, he who used to cry at Tsotskwi. Now he cried continually and annoyed the people that lived near him[2] by his incessant crying. He was in a basket cradle, he that constantly cried. They wondered what made him cry so much. So once he told,[3] "I do not want you to think that I am crying! I am not crying," said he that cried. "I am where Kapuloyo[4] lives: there I gamble[5] and you think I am crying," he said to his sister. "(But) I am not crying: I am gambling and singing my gambling songs: that is what I am doing and you think

14. "So near was he," we would say.

---

1. Tsotskwi, Dry Lagoon on the coast, between Stone and Big Lagoons.

2. Neighbors. He and his sister seem to have had their house to themselves, though how he came into being the story does not tell.

3. *Sic.*

4. The son of Wohpekumeu, and a dancer and gambler across the ocean at the downstream end of the world, as his name indicates: Pul-ekuk, Ka-pul-oyo.

5. Guessing which hand holds the marked one of fifty or more slender rods that are shuffled and divided into two lots with only their undifferentiated ends showing. The rod-holder sings: that is the baby's crying.

that I cry; but I am not crying. That is where[6] I gamble with Kapuloyo. My poor sister, I do not want you to rock me always, for I am gambling with Kapuloyo. So do not rock me (but) set me down and go off and leave me. I become so sorry for you as you constantly rock me. Therefore do not rock me,[7] since I am not crying, for I am with Kapuloyo, when you think I cry,* for I sing the gambling songs and play with Kapuloyo."

b. So his sister would set him down, and he would cry and cry and cry. Then she would take her pestle and grind acorns and he would cry, for he had told her that he was gambling at Dentalium Home:[8] "That is what makes me so: I am not crying, for I am singing gambling songs at Dentalium Home. This is what I tell you, sister: In five days I shall go where Kapuloyo lives. For I have won his sister from him and shall go to bring her, her whom I have won.[9] So do not rock me but let me cry, for I am not really crying.* I am singing a gambling song. So I shall leave during the night. Therefore do not rock me, and the fifth day from this I want you to come and wait for me, on the fifth day counting from last night. I want you to look in that direction."[10]

c. Then she went to Okegei.[11] The sun was almost down, and she had been weeping. She had left her brother crying in the house, left him in the cradle in the house, and had started out, for he had told her to grind acorns for him. "I shall want them to take with me, for I shall bring her whom I have won. And I want you to come and meet me at Osegen.[12] The day will be fair when you come to meet me, five days from now, and see me there." And (so) she was sitting there weeping. She tried to stop weeping but could not. She thought, "He'e'e'e! Why is he like that? I wonder what is about to happen to him?"

She stopped weeping—the sun was almost down—and she looked from Osegen and saw him descending to the Osegen beach,[13] her brother. He had descended to the sand and she saw him coming, saw him coming at Osegen.

6. Characteristic Yurok reference: he has implied but not yet specified the place.

7. Swaying the cradle in the arms. The "cradle" is a basketry container, without mechanical appliance for rocking.

*Asterisked clauses or phrases are repeated in the Yurok.

8. Tsīktsīko'ɬ, "Money-Live," across the ocean.

9. As the story eventuates, he does not bring her but her brother Kapuloyo, and on a visit only.

10. Cf. n. 6. "The direction in which I shall be coming as I return from Dentalium Home" is implied, namely from the north along the coast.

11. Okegei I cannot place. The word might mean "its doctor-shaman." [K. has identified it as a sharp ridge south of Tsahpekw in B11. See map 7, no. 13, above.—Ed.]

12. Osegen is a town about halfway between Espeu and Rekwoi on the coast.

13. I suspect that Osegen beach is the Gold Bluffs beach of the Americans, and that he came down to it a couple of miles south of the Klamath mouth.

And she saw someone else was with him: a wisp of fog traveled with him, but her own brother she could see (plainly): it seemed as if he carried something bright: it was an *egor*,[14] an egor belonging to Kapuloyo: although she had left him (as a baby) crying at the house, him whom she (now) saw coming.

d. Next she saw him at Otłau.[15] She could see the wisp of fog very plainly (now) and could see what he carried that shone, her brother—shone as he walked.

Then she did not see him again until he reached Oknäu[16] and (she) saw him walking there: the wisp of fog was still with him, and she could very plainly see him who cried so incessantly. He had told her, before he left, to return home, when he reached Osig:[17] "Then go home and prepare for us," he had told his sister. And she sat there and looked.

And she saw him again at Pegwololeg,[18] saw him go down to the beach. She could see the wisp of fog with him still and thought, "That must be the one who was to come with him," So she stopped weeping: "I will go home and get food ready for them."

e. Then she returned and entered the house. And she saw her brother still there (in the cradle), still crying as before. It sounded like an animal crying, which made her weep all the more, for she thought, "H'e'e'e! I wonder what makes him so?[19] For I saw him coming along the beach and now he is here crying." So she cooked[20] acorns. She laid the wood ready, thinking, "I will put the wood in the fire when they come into the house, so that I shall not have to get up after they come in."[21]

f. Then she heard a noise at the door. She had got everything ready for them to eat, set in one place for them. Now (as) she heard the noise at the door

14. An *egor* is either a carrying case of ordinary folded deerskin, such as Wohpekumeu used to travel with, or an ornamental cylindrical basket held in the hand in the Jumping Dance. Both are sheets folded to meet in a slit along the top.

15. Otłau is perhaps a trickle of water, shown on Waterman, Geography, map 29, no. 2, 2 miles from Osegen, but south of it, whereas she was supposed to be looking for him northward from there.

16. Oknäu is Waterman, map 29, no. 20, "landslide high on mountain," 1/2 miles southeast of Espeu. As this is 7 miles south of Osegen, there is evidently a confusion in the geography and she is looking north from some spot well south of Osegen.

17. Osig I do not place. (Waterman's nearest is Oskiig, map 29, no. 29, on "edge of bluff" near Redwood Creek mouth. This would fit if she were watching from near their home at Tsotskwi instead of from Osegen. However, Waterman's Oskiig is several miles north of the next place mentioned.) On p. 263 Waterman does mention Osig, but says its location is uncertain except for being south of Espeu.

18. Pegwololeg is Waterman's Pegwo-o-leg, map 29, no. 9, north of Espeu.

19. There is an inaudible word on the record here.

20. Probably: made them ready to cook.

21. Bustle would be incompatible with genteel dignity, and women sit still in the house.

and was still weeping, she thought, "He'e'e'e! Why does he wish to deceive me like this?" And she looked up[22] toward the door. Then she saw him coming, and looked and saw that he was magnificently dressed. Far down over his forehead came a woodpecker headband. And she thought, "He'e'e'e! That is what made him look so to me: he had this egor!"

He passed straight to the other side of the house[23] and said, "He'e'e'e, sister! See, I have my brother-in-law with me. Do you see my brother-in-law? He is with me." And she said, "No, I do not see him. I do not see all of him: I only see a wisp of fog," said the girl. Then her brother blew a breath twice, and she saw a fine-looking person sitting there on the stool. He was so beautifully dressed that it dazzled her.

Then he said, "Now sister, give us to eat." And she gave them food and said, "Now eat!" And her brother said, "Give him food who sits there." Then she set food in front of him who had come along, and he ate what they were eating.

g. It was a long time that her brother talked of (in)different matters, he that used to live there, (while) the baby still cried in the cradle. Then he said, "Hurry, sister! I have not come to stay long. Hurry and get ready what you have to: I want you to hurry, (for) I have come to get you, sister. I shall take you along. I am so sorry for you, sister, you have taken care of me so long, that I want you to come with me, sister." And she said, "Very well." "Put these away that we have been eating!" So she put them away. The baby still cried.

h. Then he said, "Lie down!" to his sister. "Get your mat![24] I do not wish you to see what I am about to do, sister." And she got her mat, his sister, and he said, "Lie down, sister, lie down!" And she lay down. "Cover your head!" She covered her head, the girl. She was still weeping. She thought, "I wonder what will happen to me? What is about to happen to me?" thought the girl.

i. She had covered her head, she had been lying for some time, when her brother said, "Sister! What shall I do with my house, sister? What shall I do with my house? I want to take my house with me, sister; I want to take the ground with me; I shall take it to where I am married." And she who was lying there said, "Very well," she said. "What shall I do with my house, sister? How shall I paint it? I shall paint my house, that I shall do." And she said, "Very well," she who was lying there. He said, "How shall I cause it to be,

22. She was in the pit of the house, on the floor.

23. Across the fireplace, on the far side of the pit.

24. Sleeping mat of cattail rushes twined or sewn together. [K. queried whether "twined" or "sewn" was accurate.—Ed.]

sister?'' And she said, ''Have a stripe of black[25] in the middle; have red on both sides; that is the way for you to do it; that is the way for you to paint your house: have red on both sides and put the stripe of black in the middle.[26] That is how to cause your house to be, that is how to take it away.''

j. And he said, ''I have finished, sister. I have made it like that; I have made my house so: I have black in the middle, I have red on both sides. He'e'e, sister! Where shall I put my cradle?'' He was still crying in the cradle. ''Where shall I put my cradle, sister?'' And she said, ''Very well, put it above the rock Pergis-otsya.[27] The cradle will be full of person:[28] he will own much who finds it. Hurry and take your cradle there.'' Then he stopped crying as soon as he carried the cradle out.[29] And his brother-in-law still sat there.

k. He was gone only a little and returned. Then he said when he came back in, ''Sleep, sister! We shall leave. Sleep! You will not know how we go. Sleep! You will not awake until we arrive.'' And truly she did not awake until she arrived where Kapuloyo lived. And then she awoke, his sister.

And then she thought, ''Well, I am here. This is a pleasant place to live,'' although she used to cry, his sister. She would become homesick for where she had used to live, for she liked to live where they had used to live.

BB3. How the Prairie Became Ocean

a. That is where it happened, where they wanted it to become, there is where it was that it happened, near Oketo[1]—I forget the name of the place—at Sumig.[2] He lived at Sumig, Thunder[3] lived at Sumig. He was the one who said, ''Where shall we make water to be? How will they live if we leave prairie[4] there?[5] Let us have it so.[6] What do you think? (We shall do) whatever you think,'' said Thunder. He said to Earthquake,[7] ''What do you think? Do

25. *Wisa'w*.
26. There is no record known to me of any Yurok ever painting his house.
27. Pergis-otsya is ''Eagle-perch-rock,'' which I cannot place.
28. Said to mean: ''He who finds it will be extremely wealthy.''
29. The baby stopped crying as soon as the young man who was the baby carried it out!

---

1. Oketo is a town on Big Lagoon.
2. Sumig is Patrick's Point.
3. Łohkoł.
4. *Tepolo*, ''prairie,'' open and generally level grassland.
5. Where the ocean is now. The Yurok are always making such ellipses.
6. Viz., replace the prairie by ocean.
7. Yewoł.

you think it would be right to have it so? I want water to be there, so that people may live. (Otherwise) they will have nothing to subsist on.'' Then Earthquake thought, ''That is what I believe.'' He said, ''That is true. Far off I always see it, see water there, and there are salmon there, at Opis,[8] (and) water.'' So he said ''Go,'' said Thunder; ''(and) you go with him who sit there; go with him, Pi'pi'r,[9] go along and get water at Opis, the water that is to come here.''

b. Then they went, went far. He went with him, Pi'pi'r (did), and Earthquake too went with him,[10] to see the water, to go to get water at Opis. They took two abalone shells with them: they had two abalone shells. And he said,[11] ''Take them! Get water in them at Opis which will spread.'' And they said, ''It will be best to go to Pulekuk. We shall stop and see what they do there. I believe I shall do so that the ground sinks,'' said Earthquake. ''So we shall go there to Pulekuk. We shall stop and see and then we shall come back by Perwerhkuk[12] when we have the water, and it will spread here, the water that is in front of us.''[13] And Thunder said, ''Good: then take those abalone shells.'' And they took the abalone shells to bring the water in. And he said, ''I shall do this: I shall stay here at Sumig,'' said Thunder. ''I shall stay here at Sumig. For I shall do this: I shall bend the trees over, since in the gulches there grow big trees. I shall have it as it is back in the mountains: for there are knolls,[14] that is how it is in the prairie.''

c. Then he (Earthquake) started and arrived there, at Pulekuk, he and his companion. And they arrived and he thought, ''I will try. Look at this. Here it is easy''—speaking to his companion—''it will be easy for me to do that, to sink this prairie. So I shall do that first,'' said Earthquake. And he said, ''Very well.'' So he ran about a little and the ground sank, there at Pulekuk.

d. And then they started for Opis, which is at the end of the water. That is where he did it, making the ground sink as a means of letting the water out: at the end of the water, there he did that, making the ground sink. And so they arrived at Opis, and saw all kinds there: seals all about, at Opis; salmon and what there is to be eaten were there—all kinds were there in the water at Opis. So they took water there. ''Now let us go, let us go to Perwerhkuk and stop and look at the water there,'' said Earthquake, ''for he is there (at Sumig) who

8. Opis is unidentified.

9. Pi'pi'r (or Pipir), a ''water panther''; in other tales a small bird with a long bill. [See F2*k*.—Ed.]

10. This seems to be an involved way of saying that Earthquake and Pi'pi'r went together.

11. Probably Thunder.

12. Perwerhkuk is the south end of the world, corresponding to Pulekuk at the north. [See map 3 in this volume.—Ed.]

13. *Hi-wohpi*, ''out in the water.''

14. *Wogeɫ*.

will aid us by breaking down the trees.[15] As far as the water extends to Pulekuk there will be salmon and hake.[16] There will be salmon and hake and perch—all kinds will come there at Opis.''[17]

e. And then they arrived[18] with their shells full: they had got water at the end of the water. And he said, ''See! See! It is easy. I shall do it a little so that it will be easy for the water to flow out, the water that we shall cause to spread.'' Then Pi'pi'r said, ''Very well,'' and he sank the ground there, too. So they came to Perwerhkuk. He had partly done that, had partly sunk the ground, Earthquake had; and the other had the water in the abalone shells, Pi'pi'r; he had the water in the abalone shells. So they (had) come to Perwerhkuk: they had gone around.[19]

f. And they returned to Sumig, and saw that the trees were down: that is what he had done, Thunder. And then he[20] thought, ''Good! We will consider how we shall have the water, the water that we shall have. We have sunk the ground far off at Pulekuk. How shall it be?'' He said, ''Wait! Wait!'' said Thunder, ''Wait! What shall we do with the knolls that the crags grow out of? Shall we leave them like the hills back in the mountains? These crags, growing out of the hills there, are knolls. That is how, that is how, the knolls grow: they grow in(to) crags. They would not show if they grew in gulches: but it was the knolls that made the crags grow.'' And he said, ''You see that is how it is in the mountains.'' ''I see it like that there,'' said Earthquake. On the knolls grew what grows in the mountains: acorns. ''And now we shall do thus: we shall sink the crags just a little, for we shall put the water there which we got.'' And he said, ''Yes, we shall have it like that; that is so.''[21]

g. And then they went out in front,[22] they went out in front of Sumig, Thunder with them. Pi'pi'r had the water which he was about to spread here in front. They went in front of Sumig and he poured the water out of one shell: it went only halfway toward Pulekuk, the water that had been in one shell. Then this is what Thunder said: ''Yaha![23] I do not believe there will be enough water: pour some more!''

15. The text here has: ''You will do that.''
16. *Mege'ek*.
17. From Opis?
18. At Perwerhkuk or on the way to it?
19. Around the world or future ocean: first north to Pulekuk and Opis, then southward (presumably west of what is now ocean) to Perwerhkuk; and now they are on the way north along the coast to the starting point at Sumig.
20. Earthquake.
21. [In his footnotes K. had the Yurok *keukhwen* relating to an English word in this paragraph but did not indicate which word it referred to.—Ed.]
22. *Hi-wohp*: on the ocean side, as in n. 13.
23. ''Well now! This won't do!''

h. And so they went all the way to Espeu:[24] they poured out the water in front of Espeu, the water that was in the other shell. They poured it there and it ran down(stream) toward Pulekuk. "Ya, the tops of the trees are sticking out! The brush is not covered! No, the brush is sticking out! What shall we do?" said Thunder. "The brush is (still) in sight)," they said. "You will know after a time. I shall make it," said Earthquake. "I shall run about: that is what I shall do." For they had poured out the water in front of Espeu without its being sufficient, since the brush still stuck out.

i. And he said, "Yaha! See, the brush sticks out. What do you think?" he said to Pi'pi'r, "what do you think? Can't you help me?" And he said, "What shall I do? I can do nothing," said Pi'pi'r, "I can do nothing by myself." And he said, "Yaha! You must not say you are good for nothing. Now do this: urinate and increase the water." Then he did that. "You will do that to the ground." And he did that, he helped him. Then they saw that the brush had disappeared, some time after he had urinated. That is why they used to see . . .[25] when the weather was good: it is because he did that.

j. And then from there they went south. They said, "We shall have to go there: we two shall go together." They went south first and sank the ground. They were still together, those that (later) went back into the mountains.[26] So they (two) went south with one another. And then he did that: he repeatedly caused the ground to sink in the south. He kept sinking it: every little while there would be an earthquake, then another earthquake, and another earthquake: that is what he was doing. And then the water would fill those (depressed) places, the water coming from the mountains, at Osig.[27] And then they would look again (at what was being accomplished).

k. Then they stopped and saw Thunder, who lived at Sumig. He said, "Look at the water running down! It is as I wanted it to be." "That is what human beings will thrive on," said Earthquake. "For they would have no subsistence if there were nothing for the creatures (of the sea) to live in. For that is where they will obtain what they will subsist on, when this prairie has become water, this stretch that was prairie: there will be ocean there." He said, "Yes, that is true. That is true. That is how they will subsist," said Thunder. "Now go north."

Then they went north together and did the same: they kept sinking the ground. The earth would quake and quake again and quake again. And the water was flowing all over.

24. [Espeu is about 16 miles north of Sumig, on the coast.—Ed.]

25. Word lost.

26. Unless the reference is to Earthquake and Pi'pi'r, the meaning must be, "The woge who later scattered into the mountains were still living where men live now."

27. For Osig, see BB2, n. 17.

l. And they saw that the creatures that were to serve as food really swarmed in this water. They saw seals: they looked as if thrown in by handfuls swimming toward shore. And then they went south, where they had sunk the ground before. They saw salmon running through the water. Where they had made gullies whales were coming, because the water was deep enough for them to travel through. All (game) had gone—deer: they had disappeared into this land:[28] that is where they had gone—all kinds, deer, elk, foxes, minks, all creatures of the land, otters, all that had lived there, had lived on the prairie where the ocean was now. For now water was there, and salmon, . . .,[29] hake, and all that were good (to eat) lived in that water. And they said, "Now that is enough: enough for human beings to subsist on when they shall live. You see that everything (needed) is in the water." And they thought that it was so.

m. "Now I shall do this," said Thunder. "I shall cut off the tops of the brush," said Thunder. And he did so: he would leap only once into the top of a great tree and it would snap off entire. He did this merely by running about (and leaping).

That is why it is thus, that all kinds of creatures are in this ocean in front of us, because Thunder wanted it so, Earthquake wanted it so. He wished human beings to subsist thus, wished them to eat what was in the water, all kinds that are in the water, seals (and others).

n. And then he wished it to be thus: "People will see the wind at a distance. It will be a help for it to be so, when they can see the wind. They can know then in which direction the waves are traveling.[30] The waves will travel whichever way the wind blows," said Thunder. "Whichever way the wind blows the waves will travel. That is how I want it to be." Now one can see that it is like that. If the wind blows from the south the waves travel north; if the wind blows from the north the waves travel south.

o. "That is how people will live; and what they subsist on will be in the water: salmon, perch, hake, all kinds, whales, seals will live in this water." And so it is thus: one sees how the water is now. That is why (people) used sometimes to hear (in a myth) that it was he who made it so: that is how it was: one can see now how it was: the knolls that sit on the mountains once grew, before they got water, where the water is now. That is where they got the water: at Kerwerł,[31] far off, that is where they got it.

And that is why it is thus, that everything is in this ocean that (lies) in front of us. The land sank where they had run about, (where) Earthquake had run about, Thunder had run about. One can see now that the water is deep—of

28. As it is now.
29. Word lost.
30. "Water is running."
31. Kerwerł is unidentified.

course we do not know how deep it is—because once it was a prairie. Every kind of (land creature) lived on that prairie. (For instance,) one can see now the rocks in front of Sumig: one can see there now where the deer once were: their tracks on the rocks: it seems as if they had been there only this morning. Everything must have been good indeed in those times.

p. On those rocks in front of Sumig is (a spot called) Tsaliwał:[32] for he lives there now, (does) Thunder. He was the one who made things so. He wished people to live like this; and indeed it is so.

And he (too) is alive, (this) Earthquake: That is why it is called "Earthquake's house pit"; he lives at Espeu:[33] that is where he grew.[34]

And their companion grew at the place they call Pektsu: that is where he grew, (this) Pi'pi'r.[35]

That is how the ocean comes to be as it is: they are the ones who made it. There was a prairie there: on it all (land creatures) lived. He is the one who made it as it is: Thunder. (For) he said, "How will human beings subsist? They have nothing to subsist on! Let us try to make it so (that they may live)."

•

Had the order "salmon, perch, hake, all kinds, whales, seals," as it stands in part *o*, with the "all kinds" in the middle, occurred only once, one might conclude that the Yurok thought as we do, and that "whales, seals" was an afterthought. That the narrator speaks this way repeatedly, using the "all kinds" as coordinate with the specific kinds mentioned, as it were, rather than as a recapitulation or final guard against omissions, is evidence not only of a lack of logical neatness but of the habit of even the best Yurok narrators to use stopgaps, to talk continuously at all costs. If three species have been enumerated and the speaker cannot at once think of the fourth, he tides over with his "et cetera" until he remembers what his mind is seeking, and then calmly resumes his list as if he had not logically brought it to an end with the blanket phrase.

I am confident that the eternal repetitions to which this narrator, her brother, and several others are so inclined, but of which all representative Yurok are more or less guilty, are due to the same impulse of maintaining the auditory continuity of the story. Against this obsession their fluency of memory or imagination is unable to cope. Therefore they fall back on a repetition while thinking of what comes next. I am inclined to believe that, given equal facility of telling, it is the earnest or emotionally

32. Tsaliwał: the description "rocks in front of Sumig" might fit Turtle Rocks, 3/4 mile offshore (Waterman, Geography, map 32, nos. 12, 13), but Waterman gives them other Yurok names.

33. Earthquake and Thunder have house pits at Kenek also. [See Waterman, Geography, map 22.—Ed.]

34. The text follows with the word "Thunder," which I take to be a slip of the tongue.

35. The homes seem to be: Thunder at Sumig, Earthquake at Espeu, Pi'pi'r at Pektsu. [Waterman, map 2, no. 7, shows Pektsu as north along the coast in Tolowa country. This map is reproduced here as map 1.—Ed.]

tense narrator that is most prone to this fault because he is most intent on omitting nothing. Of course, a poor speaker will repeat through mere awkwardness, and a specially gifted one, like Lame Billy, will succeed in relatively freeing himself from the defect through sheer suppleness of mind.

The Yurok, and with them the majority of Californian nationalities, are evidently more given to repetition—which we find so difficult to pardon stylistically—than the Indians of either the Northwest or Southwest, and certainly far more than the Plains and Eastern tribes. There seem to be at least two reasons for this deficiency. The first is the close association of myth and formula. A formula of any length is not committed literally to memory, like a Pueblo prayer. The idea and the names are held in mind, many phrases are conventional, and more or less frequent recital has usually established an approximately uniform habit of expression. But all recorded texts of formulas that repeat an episode, with intended change only of name or place or number, show variations of wording sufficient to prove that there is no complete and letter-perfect memorization. From some cause, however, a formula must be recited rapidly and fluently. At least such is the usage; and no doubt adherence to usage is deemed essential. Then, a formula is always mumbled, in order that an auditor may not overhear and learn it, presumably because it is valuable private property. So strong are these habits that it has proved impossible with a number of elderly Yurok to secure either texts—because they could not restrain their fluency—or usable phonograph dictations—because they could not break their crystallized impulse to let their voice die away toward the end of sentences. Tskerkr (Informant B), who was willing enough, was among this number.

Now a myth, it is true, is generally distinguished from a formula,[36] although a sharp line of demarcation cannot be effected; but it can hardly be doubted that speech and thought habits developed around the formula have tended to be transferred to the myth. It is for this reason, I think, that traditions dictated in English, or passing through an interpreter, are much less marred by blank and disorderly repetition than are written texts,[37] and these rank above phonograph dictations, where the informant could speak most nearly as he was accustomed to speak in telling a tale.

But this cause alone is insufficient as an explanation, since considerable tendency to narrative prolixity and chaotic repetition prevails in parts of native California which do not possess the formula of Yurok type. The supplementary cause I believe to be the comparative lack of mental and physical tenseness in the life of the Californian tribes, a slackness which is manifest in many phases of their civilization and was commented on even by their earliest observers, although on the side of behavior rather than as expressed in cultural forms. There is nothing like oratory among the Yurok; no formal or even public assemblies devoted to discussion and serving as an opportunity for development of compact and controlled speech; no herald or public crier.[38]

36. [For the distinction between the two, see the headnote to tale A1.—Ed.]

37. [By "written texts" is presumably meant those in which the informant spoke in Yurok and the speech was transcribed verbatim.—Ed.]

38. The central Californians possess such a functionary, but his addresses, while couched in a certain degree of external style, mainly acoustic, are as barrenly repetitive as anything in Yurok mythology.

Yurok mythology is never taught in anything like an organized ritualistic initiation, but learned in the easy relaxation of the family, where substance rather than manner is stressed. His property sense and inculcated jealousy probably would prevent a Yurok from narrating myths, even those relatively divorced from formulaic ritual, in the presence of any but relatives or intimates. Then, a sense of form, both on the side of conception and of finish or definiteness, is conspicuously rudimentary in all concretely visible phases of Californian civilization: the arts, the utensils, boats and houses, dress and personal decoration. Plastic or depictive art in fact is practically wanting, and the decorative and industrial arts are rather weak. Even basketry, which at best offers but limited opportunities for aesthetic achievement, is generally overrated as we encounter it in native California, because our own basketry has become devoid of expression—a thing made by the blind or the uneducated or by machines. It is true that the Yurok and their northwestern neighbors evince greater neatness and ingenuity in their manufactures than do other Indians of California, but the best of their handiwork, ornamental or purely utilitarian, is aesthetically insignificant alongside the products of all other American tribes saving a few of the poorest.[39]

With all these evidences of a relative absence of what may be called style in the civilization of the Yurok, it is rather to be expected that this quality should have remained slight in their traditions, and that these literary efforts should be devoid of any great striving after order, compact definiteness, or aversion to prolixity and monotony. One phase of a culture may of course develop in comparative independence of the other phases of the same culture; but normally it will be sufficiently linked with them to be influenced, not to mention the indirect effect of the habits of mind engendered in each individual by living in the culture. Such an oblique or psychological means of transmission is evidently provided, for the Yurok and other Californians, by the modes of daily speech, which, from all we know on the subject, were sprawling, unfigurative, bald, often querulous, and heavily given to repetition. A Californian might be brief because he was too awkward to express himself at length; he would rarely seem pithy and never be laconic. It would therefore require a cultural stimulus of a very special sort to drive such a people into a concentrated form of expression in their narrative endeavors; and such a stimulus was evidently absent.

39. The art of the Southwestern ethnographic province might be characterized as imbued with a fair amount of imaginative conception but half-hearted in execution and slovenly in finish; that of the Plains as narrow on the conceptual side but with tolerable attention to execution; that of the Northwest as strong in both imagination and finish; and that of the East, and still more that of the Mackenzie and Great Basin regions, as approaching the art of California in weakness in both directions. This formulation takes no account of other aesthetic aspects, such as the symbolism of much of Indian art, especially in the Southwest, and the unimaginative but felicitous and realistic faculties of the Eskimo.

Informant CC

JIM OF TSURÄU (AND WEITSPUS)

Trinidad Jim was called K'-erkīr, because he was of the house erkīgeri in Weitspus. He was married twice among the Coast Yurok. He second wife was a relative of the first, perhaps a sister. She was born at Herwer or Hergweris, also called Plepei, on Stone Lagoon,[1] *which the Chilula destroyed soon after 1860. Her natal house there was ple'loi. She was called* kerräp, *widow with hair growing out again.*[2] *She was also called Erki-son, which denotes that Jim had full-married her. From her home people she had learned to pray people to death, so that she was feared by those whom she did not like. She used to go to the refuse dump or ash heap,* oslega, *and say her prayer or curse there, whereas the Coast Yurok in such a case usually go to a rock.*

Jim owned chiefly Brush Dance ornaments. The last dance held in Trinidad was a Brush Dance, meagerly equipped, mostly with arrows and with but few feathers. Most of what was displayed belonged to Jim.

The couple were living in the house wonäu[3] *at the northwest end of Tsuräu, at Trinidad, when I visited them in June, 1907. They gave me considerable geographical information on the southern coast, some of which Waterman used in his Yurok Geography. Jim dictated the first story that follows onto eight phonograph cylinders, which in 1908 were Englished phrase by phrase by Frank of Weitspus. The localization suggests that Jim learned the tale from his wife or her Coast relatives. It is a well-told account, especially*

1. Waterman, map 31, no. 8. [This map is reproduced here as map 7.—Ed.]

2. [A widow during her customary year of mourning kept her hair cut very short, according to Kroeber, Handbook, p. 31.—Ed.]

3. Waterman, map 34, no. 2.

for a first attempt with the phonograph. Jim's second story is also local, a fragment about Wohpekumeu.

CC1. He Fished Across the Ocean

a. He was of Hewo'li.[1] He was fishing[2] with a line[3] at Poik.[4] He was fishing with it, but he never caught anything. He thought he wanted to be wealthy, that is why he was fishing all day. Next day he went to fish again, and every day.

b. Then once he thought he was going to catch something. Then he threw his line across the ocean.[5] Now he felt something on it. Then he tried to pull his line in; nearly all day he pulled but could not haul it in. Now it was nearly sunset and he was still pulling at his line. Then all at once the line came easily, and it was a little minnow[6] that was on the hook. And the reason that rock[7] stands the way it does is because it was from that rock that he fished, and it was nearly pulled into the ocean. Now he kept what he had caught on his line; so he took it off the hook and thought, "I will go home." He went back[8] in his boat, and came to shore, and pulled his boat up on the beach, and went up to the town.

c. And he went into the house, to the rear across from the door,[9] and said to the old man, "Go down and see what I have caught." And the old man said "Yes?" And he went down to look and came back and said, "That is good; that is what I have been wanting you to do. I wanted you to have luck. That is why I always talked to you and told you what to do."

1. Hewo'li is a creek (Waterman, Geography, map 33, no. 44) that comes into the ocean a quarter- to a half-mile southeast of Tsuräu, the Yurok town at Trinidad. It is just beyond Trinidad beach. The word means "large" in Coast Yurok; Waterman says the same. The informant and his wife, who was coast-born, said there had been a town there, consisting, in their experience, of one house at a site called amiɫkä, but formerly of three houses. Hewo'li may be considered an outlier or suburb of Tsuräu.

2. He declined to go fishing with others, but continued to roll (spin) string so as to have a long line, with which he hoped to catch something that would bring him luck.

3. *Werekewits.*

4. Poik is a very large seastack, offshore between Luffenholtz Creek and Honda Landing, about 2 miles south of Trinidad; Waterman, map 33, no. 64. The top of the rock is uneven. The word *poik* means nighthawk, *pookw* (or *kweyuts*, Waterman) in River Yurok.

5. *Wohpäuks legoit.*

6. *Mīs.*

7. Poik, from which he cast. At the spot where he stood, the seastack overhangs the base of the rock.

8. To his home at Hewo'li.

9. *Pa'sau.*

And the old man took care of it. He made something like a trunk,[10] and that is where he kept what he had caught. It was very small, and he did not know what kind it was. And he saw it in the trunk and it looked like a snake: that was the one he had caught on his line. And he saw it swim in the trunk.

d. Then the young man went after sweathouse wood while the old man took care of what he had caught. He had only gone a little way on the hill when he saw two large woodpeckers, and with stones he killed them.[11] That is how he always did. And it began to grow, the one he had caught. Sometimes he would kill elk, two or sometimes three. And in the morning when he looked for the elk they were gone. That is how it happened to this young man: he got money easily. So he learned that it was a good thing which he had caught on his line.

e. Then he looked at it again and saw that it was going to have a horn. It swam about in the trunk and swam about. But when he caught elk, he never saw them in the morning. It was the one he caught that always ate them. So he took care of it well because he learned that it was good for all kinds of wealth coming to him easily, and he had only to go a little way from town and he would kill a deer or other game; and dentalia came to him of themselves.

f. Now he had a baby, and the boy was growing; and he did not think that the thing he had caught would do any harm; but when he fed it, it would not eat; his pet[12] would not eat. It ate only when the old man fed it; that is how it was. And all the elk he killed they hung to dry in the house, and it always ate them all, all the elk; even if there were two, there was nothing left. It ate them from where they were kept at *meɫku.*[13]

g. Sometimes the young man went to gamble. Then he would be lucky in that too. Always he won money because of the pet he had.

h. Now his boy was growing, and once the woman[14] went to get water, leaving his boy in his cradle in the house. And the old woman who lived in the house went to *keskiɫ*[15] to get wood. And when (his wife) got back she did not see the boy in his cradle, and she said to her husband, "Did you take him?" He was in the house." And he said, "No." And she asked the old woman, and she said, "No."

Then the young man went to the rear of the house where his pet's trunk was among the baskets, and it was gone and the trunk too.

10. *Tekwanuks.*

11. His luck was already coming on him: they are wary birds, hard to kill even with a bow.

12. *Ka'er.*

13. The ground-level ledge around the pit of the house, viz., among the storage at the rear or sides.

14. His wife.

15. *Keskiɫ* is the woodshed anteroom.

i. Now he looked out over the ocean[16] and saw it swimming. On its horn it had the baby. Then he knew it was a Knewollek[17] which he had caught on his line. And their baby was crying. And the man followed, but he could not catch up. He was riding on his horn, that baby, but he did not get him back; and he returned.

j. That night he heard the child crying on the salt water, and he went after him, but could not find him. That is how they heard him about, crying at night over the ocean, that child which it had taken away on its horn. Ten nights they heard him. Then they no longer heard him: he was far off by then. And the woman cried for her child. And the man cried too. He thought, "I should not have brought it back when I caught it. But the old man told me to do it."

k. Then he went hunting, thinking he would easily kill elk; but now he caught nothing. All the time he had had that Knewollek he had good luck, but now he got nothing. Then the old man said, "Well, that Knewollek was eating the elk; that is why it was so easy to kill them. It was he that was doing the hunting, and you thought he was staying in the house."

And with money it was the same way: he could never get dentalia, and when he gambled he could not win. And he thought, "I do not want that kind any more. If I see one I will not bring it into the house; I am afraid of it. For I thought it was good because it made me get everything easily."[18]

CC2. Wohpekumeu's End (fragment)

a. (Wohpekumeu at Kenek abandons his son on a tree whose limbs blow away. Returning, the son leaves. Wohpekumeu follows, but at the mouth of the river turns south along the coast.)

b. He went on southward past Nekel,[1] to Trinidad, and on to Poyura.[2] There it was he saw Skate on the beach, went to her, and she carried him across the ocean. Now he was blind, and cried. A woman asked him why.

c. He[3] rubbed spittle on his eyes and could see again. He went on up to a town, was received by the headman, and was given two wives.

16. *Hiwo'pis*.

17. [A giant horned water serpent.—Ed.]

18. [For other versions of this tale, but with different endings, see A11, B2, B6, and U3.—Ed.]

1. Nekel, where the rocks begin, south of Big Lagoon and north of Patrick's and Rocky Point; Waterman, Geography, map 32, no. 17, nekeɬ, a creek there.

2. Poyura is just beyond Little River mouth, and therefore on Wiyot beach; it is a place, not a settlement. The name is said to mean "first creek (beyond)," or *hewan weroi* in River Yurok.

3. Or she?

d. They fished for whales there, from two sides of the water.[4] The other side always pulled them away; sometimes they let them have a very little one. The headman gave him the women because he thought he would help them.

(Unfinished)

4. Two sides of a river or of the ocean?

DD-13. Various Informants

FRAGMENTS AND OUTLINES

DD1. Pulekukwerek Grows from Tobacco

An old doctor, widow of Bluff Creek Jim,[1] had a story of how Pulekukwerek grew from a tobacco plant at Pulekuk.

DD2. No'ots

She also knew the tale of the birth of No'ots from a twin root that was dug up, but as happening in Hupa, not at Karok Ko'men. [Cf. tales A7 and J8.—Ed.]

DD3. The Klamath and Trinity Join at Weitspus

Martha, of Informant C's household, was said to know a story of where the two rivers, Klamath and Trinity, came from, and why they joined at Weitspus.

DD4. Kämes Steals a Child

Informant D knew this tale: A man was working by the river, his child sleeping nearby on the sand. Suddenly it was gone. He found that a Kämes had drawn it

1. [According to Waterman, Geography, p. 259, Bluff Creek Jim was the leading man of Otsepor.—Ed.]

into the river. The man took fire, entered the river, found the house of the Kämes, and burned it. (Cf. T5.)

DD5. Wohpekumeu Makes Childbirth Medicine

The wife of Informant D possessed a formula for childbirth, derived from Wohpekumeu when he had made a girl pregnant, was kept in the house in expectation of her death, and had no medicine available but the hearth ashes. [Cf. F2 and X4.—Ed.]

DD6. Sä'äł Formula Against Sterility

Another formula known to her was for a childless woman: A Weitspus woman got a child from a Sä'äł spirit living in the creek there. While she went out into the brush (to give birth), her husband ornamented the cradle basket with dentalium beads, and she came back carrying her baby.

DD7. He Flew to the Sea of Pitch

The story of the man who flew was known to Informant S (Pekwon Doctor), much as told in tale M2 by Sandy of Kenek, except that the hero was of Pekwon instead of Wohtek.

DD8. Meikili Was Their Pet

From the wife of Informant B, of Orekw: In Siwitsu[2] three brothers lived, with their women. The old woman always said to them: "Do you know where you have been today?" "Yes, we know where we went," they said, for they constantly traveled to a place and did not tell her of it. Then she said: "Have you seen that which is where you go? That Meikili?"[3] Then they went out again, wanting to find it, because they constantly hunted but never caught

2. The natal place of the narrator, at the northern end of Orekw, on the sand spit toward the mouth of Redwood Creek. Waterman, map 30, *x*, puts the spot nearly a quarter-mile north of the settlement, and indicates no recent house.

3. Described as an actual, not supernatural, animal, with a head at each end, with horns like those of a snail. It contracts and lengthens and burrows but cannot travel. Its power over deer appears to rest on similarity to the young of the mythical Knewollek monster.

deer, and they had been told that it was good luck as regards deer to have that thing. Then once they returned and said, "We have it. Now we shall take deer and what we wish." So they made ready a storage box, filled it with water, and put the Meikili in. In the morning they looked at it, and it was longer. In the morning, it was longer again. Then they went to hunt. They had only gone a little way when they killed a deer. As many as they wished they killed easily. Then one morning they went to look at it again, and it was gone. Its box was gone too. They searched but could not find it; and so they had to desist, and got no more deer. [Cf. A11, B2, B6, U3, and CC1.—Ed.]

DD9. The Uma'a's Arrows and His Abandonment

Mrs. Frey of Orick, of a house in Espeu famous for its doctors, a sister of Fanny Flounder[4] and married to a white man, once told the following to Informant G, my chief interpreter: At Orekw all the people had gone to Olege'l to gather seeds[5] Only one young man was at home, in the upper part of the house.[6] Then an Uma'a[7] came in. He took out his (poison flint) arrows and counted them. The tenth he named as best (for killing human beings). "Let me eat here," he said. "No, I will go out and drink first." Five times he went out thus. Then the young man seized the best arrow and fled. Soon he heard a shout. The Uma'a was pursuing. He was calling him to stop, but the youth ran on. At last he was overtaken. Then he returned with the Uma'a, but refused to give up the arrow, so they remained together. Then once they went to Redding Rock to take mussels. The boat was full and they started to leave. Then the young man said it would hold more mussels, and steered back. When the Uma'a climbed on the rock, the young man pushed off, and though the Uma'a called to him, left him and returned. After (five?) days the Uma'a appeared. He had crossed without a boat.[8]

DD10. Married Across the Ocean

The wife of Informant CC, who was born at Herwer on Stone Lagoon, said that she knew Tskerkr's tale B9, about the young man whose sister followed

4. [For Fanny Flounder, see Spott and Kroeber, Yurok Narratives, nos. 8, 9, and 10, and Theodora Kroeber's Foreword to this volume.—Ed.]

5. The second-hand narrator was not certain of this localization.

6. Probably behind the storage baskets and invisible.

7. A class of spirits living mostly in thickets along small streams, who kill human beings through sickness, especially by shooting them with magical burning flint arrows.

8. It is over 4 miles to shore.

him across the ocean, with minor variations, one of them being that the siblings grew up at Metsko, a Yurok town of four houses and one sweathouse on the north side of the mouth of Little River.[9]

I asked an old woman at Tsuräu, Trinidad, whether the Coast Yurok knew Wohpekumeu, Pulekukwerek, Pelin-tsīk, and the other characters of River Yurok mythology. The following three fragments are her attempt to summarize.

DD11. Wohpekumeu at Tsuräu

Wohpekumeu came to Tsuräu from the north. He was going to make acorns grow there, and iris for string; but he wanted girls in payment. Then, when they were not given him, he became angry, and tore up what he was making and threw it away. (Hence no oaks or string iris on the immediate coast.) He went off southward. He did not go very far when he was carried across the ocean. He left the fire drill of willow root, and that is how people have fire.

Pulekukwerek did not come to Tsuräu but went upriver. Coyote, however, was at Tsuräu.

DD12. Big and Little Dentalium

Pelin-tsīk had a younger brother, Tseihkeni-tsīk.[10] This one came to Tsuräu, but Pelin-tsīk stayed in the north. He blew southward (along the coast) and said, ''If I see a man bending over his (basketry) plate (and eating fast), he shall not be rich. But if a man leans back and eats slowly, I shall like him. When food is set before him, if he folds his arms and sits straight and thinks of something else, he will be a rich man.''[11]

9. All the Yurok give Metsko as the southern limit of their territory, but most of them speak of it as a place, not a town.

10. ''Great Money'' and ''Small Money.'' It is significant of the economic status of the two divisions that the Coast Yurok themselves make the large money travel only up the Klamath. Cf. B14.

11. Self-restrain brings success and wealth, indulgence dissipates it: an often-repeated Yurok dictum.

DD13. Raccoons Lift Sun to the Sky

Once Sun fell near Tsuräu, to the south.[12] Then it became dark in this world. All the people tried to lift him back into place, but could not. Finally the two Raccoons came. They began to sing, stamping their feet. When they stamped first, Sun rose a little. When they stamped again, it rose higher. They went on singing and stamping, until they raised Sun into the sky and it was light again.

12. Waterman, Geography, map 33, no. 74, and p. 272, gives the spot of Sun's raising by the Raccoons as O-ksolig, on the spit opposite the mouth of Little River.

BIBLIOGRAPHY

[The works listed here are of two types: those cited directly in the text, and other studies of the Yurok by Kroeber and his colleagues, especially those published in the University of California Publications in American Archaeology and Ethnology and the University of California Anthropological Record series. Complete volumes only of UC-PAAE may be ordered from Kraus Reprint Corporation, 16 E. 46th Street, New York 10017. At press time, the UC-AR volumes listed here were out of print, but current information may be obtained from the Sales Office of the University of California Press.
For the completeness of this list we are indebted to Robert F. Heizer of the Department of Anthropology, University of California, Berkeley.—Ed.]

Cook, S. F.
1955. The Aboriginal Population of the North Coast of California. UC-AR 16:(no. 3): 81-130, esp. 81-92.

Driver, H. E.
1939. Culture Element Distributions: X. Northwest California. UC-AR 1:(no. 6): 297-433.

Drucker, P.
1937. The Tolowa and Their Southwest Oregon Kin. UC-PAAE 36:(no. 4): 221-300.

Erikson, E. H.
1943. Observations on the Yurok: Childhood and World Image. UC-PAAE 35:(no. 10): 257-302.

Gibbs, G.
1853. Journal of the Expedition of Colonel Redick McKee, United States Indian Agent, Through North-Western California. Performed in the Summer and Fall of 1851. *In* H. R. Schoolcraft, Historical and Statistical Information Respecting the History, Condition and Prospects of the Indian Tribes of the United States. Philadelphia. Vol. 3:99-177. Photoreproduction, with annotations

by R. F. Heizer, published 1972 by Archaeological Research Facility, Department of Anthropology, University of California, Berkeley.

1973. Observations on the Indians of the Klamath River and Humboldt Bay [in 1852]. Archaeological Research Facility, Department of Anthropology, University of California, Berkeley.

Goddard, P. E.

1903. Life and Culture of the Hupa. UC-PAAE 1:(no. 1): 1-88.

1904. Hupa Texts. UC-PAAE 1:(no. 2): 89-368.

Goldschmidt, W. R.

1951. Ethics and the Structure of Society. American Anthropologist 53:(no. 4): 506-524.

Heizer, R. F., and J. E. Mills.

1952. The Four Ages of Tsurai: A Documentary History of the Indian Village on Trinidad Bay. Berkeley and Los Angeles: University of California Press. 218 pp.

Kelly, I. T.

1930. The Carver's Art of the Indians of Northwestern California. UC-PAAE 24:(no. 7): 343-360.

Klimek, S.

1935. Culture Element Distributions: I. The Structure of California Indian Culture. UC-PAAE 37:(no. 1): 1-70.

Kroeber, A. L.

1904. Types of Indian Culture in California. UC-PAAE 2:(no. 3): 81-103.

1905. Basket Designs of the Indians of Northwestern California. UC-PAAE 2:(no. 4): 105-164.

1907. The Religion of the Indians of California. UC-PAAE 4:(no. 6): 319-356.

1911. The Languages of the Coast of California North of San Francisco. UC-PAAE 9:(no. 3): 273-435, esp. 414-426.

1920. California Culture Provinces. UC-PAAE 17:(no. 2): 151-169.

1923. The History of Native Culture in California. UC-PAAE 20: 125-142.

1925. Handbook of the Indians of California. Bureau of American Ethnology, Smithsonian Institution, Bull. 78:1-995, esp. 1-97. Reprinted 1972 by Scholarly Press, St. Clair Shores, Mich.

1926. Law of the Yurok Indians. Proceedings of the 22nd International Congress of Americanists, Rome. Vol. 2: 511-516.

1934. Yurok and Neighboring Kin Term Systems. UC-PAAE 35:(no. 2): 15-22.

1937. Culture Element Distributions: III. Area and Climax. UC-PAAE 37:(no. 3): 101-116.

1939. Cultural and Natural Areas of Native North America. UC-PAAE 38: 1-242.

1945. A Yurok War Reminiscence: The Use of Autobiographical Evidence. Southwestern Journal of Anthropology 1:(no. 3): 318-332.

1957. Ethnographic Interpretations, 1-6. UC-PAAE 47:(no. 2): 191-234, esp. 205-206.

1959. Ethnographic Interpretations, 7-11. UC-PAAE 47:(no. 3): 235-310, esp. 235-240.

1960. Yurok Speech Usages. *In* Culture in History: Essays in Honor of Paul Radin, ed. S. Diamond. New York: Columbia University Press, pp. 993-999.

Kroeber, A. L., and S. A. Barrett.
1960. Fishing Among the Indians of Northwestern California. UC-AR 21:(no. 1): 1-210.

Kroeber, A. L., and E. W. Gifford.
1949. World Renewal: A Cult System of Native Northwest California. UC-AR 13:(no. 1): 1-155.

O'Neale, L. M.
1932. Yurok-Karok Basket Weavers. UC-PAAE 32:(no. 1): 1-184.

Posinsky, S. H.
1956. Yurok Shell Money and "Pains": A Freudian Interpretation. Psychiatric Quarterly 30: 598-632.

1957. The Problem of Yurok Anality. American Imago 14: 3-31.

Powers, S.
1877. Tribes of California. Contributions to North American Ethnology 3: 44-64, 460-473.

Robins, R. H.
1958. The Yurok Language: Grammer, Texts, Lexicon. UC-PL 15: 1-300.

Sapir, E.
1928. Yurok Tales. Journal of American Folklore 41: 253-261.

Schenck, M., and E. W. Gifford.
1952. Karok Ethnobotany. UC-AR 13:(no. 6): 377-392.

Spott, Robert, and A. L. Kroeber.
1942. Yurok Narratives. UC-PAAE 35:(no. 9): 143-256.

Thompson, L.
1916. To the American Indian. Eureka, Calif.

Waterman, T. T.
1920. Yurok Geography. UC-PAAE 16:(no. 5): 177-314.
1923. Yurok Affixes. UC-PAAE 20: 369-386.

Waterman, T. T., and A. L. Kroeber.
1934. Yurok Marriages. UC-PAAE 35:(no. 1): 1-14.
1938. The Kepel Fish Dam. UC-PAAE 35:(no. 6): 49-80.

Appendix

RECORDINGS OF YUROK MYTHS

[The phonograph cylinders recorded by A. L. Kroeber are part of the Audio Archive of the R. H. Lowie Museum of Anthropology, University of California, Berkeley 94720. At the time this Appendix was compiled, the entire collection was being transcribed onto tape and recatalogued, and it is available for bona-fide research and educational use. The table below lists the Kroeber recordings of Yurok myths by informant, myth title, and Lowie Museum catalogue number.—Ed.]

	Informant	Myth*	Lowie Catalogue Number
B	Tskerkr of Espeu	B16, "Great Money in the South"	24-1882
C	Stone of Weitspus	C2*y*, "The Salmon and Kowetsek" (section *d*)	24-994
D	Billy Werk of Weitspus	D1*y*, "Theft of Fire"	24-979
		D2*x*, "Crane, Quail, and Pigeon"	24-976
		D3*y*, "Moon and Frog Formula for Curing Wounds"	24-981
		D4, "A Formula for Salmon"†	24-980
		D5*y*, "The Dentalia Leave from Pekwtuł"	24-977

*Titles shown are those from the printed collection; the Lowie Museum titles, taken from Kroeber's cylinders, differ somewhat in wording.

†Translation of phonograph version is not included in the text above.

		D6y, "Origin of the Weitspus Jumping Dance"	24-978
		D7, "Origin of the Several Deerskin Dances"	24-974, -975
H	Dave Durban of Weitspus	H2, "Death and Purification"	24-1001
I	Domingo of Weitspus	I2, "Wopekumeu Left Alone in the World"	24-986
		I4, "Buzzard's Medicine"	24-985
M	Sandy of Kenek	M1, "Origin of Night"	24-988
		M2, "He Flew Alone and with Condor"	24-1002
O	Long Charlie of Mūrek	O1, "Wohpekumeu"	24-1005
P	Jack of Mūrek‡	P1, "Wohpekumeu's Emergence"	24-1884
S	Doctor of Pekwon	S1, "He Ate His Own Blood"	24-1011
		S2, "Crow, Grizzly Bear, and the Pekwon Täł"	24-1008
		S3, "He Brought Her Back from the Dead"	24-1013
		S4, "Gambling with Kapuloyo"	24-1007
		S5, "Man-Money and Woman-Money"	24-1012
T	Jim of Pekwon	T4, "Origin of the Kepel Dam and the Deerskin Dances"	24-1018
		T5, "The Water-Monster Helper"	24-1019
		T7, "Ritual Sweating"	24-1016
		T8, "Upriver-Coyote"	
W	Dick of Wohkero	W1, "Earthquake Drives Away the Sä'äl"	24-1014
X	Captain Spott of Rekwoi	X14y, "Mouth of the River"	24-1030
		X15, "Dripped on at Erlerger"	24-1029
		X16, "The Obsidian Cliff at Rekwoi"	24-1031
BB	Ann of Espeu‡	BB1, "He Swam Across the Ocean"	24-1874
		BB2, "The Crying Baby"	24-1876
		BB3, "How the Prairie Became Ocean"	24-1875
CC	Jim of Tsuräu (and Weitspus)	CC1, "He Fished Across the Ocean"	24-1033

‡Recorded by T. T. Waterman.

INDEX

[The index of Major Personages and the list of Characteristic Stories and Themes were based on drafts prepared by Kroeber. The index of Minor Personages was compiled by the editor. In addition to these, the Bancroft Library has in its files some two hundred typescript pages of Kroeber's detailed summaries of the myths, which will be of interest to the specialist. The summaries were omitted from this volume because of space limitations.

The abbreviation YN in the index below indicates that a version of the myth was printed in Spott and Kroeber, Yurok Narratives.—Ed.]

MAJOR PERSONAGES

Varying from whole tales to incidents, themes, or mentions

MINOR ANIMAL AND OTHER PERSONAGES

(See also under Characteristic Stories and Themes: Monsters and harmful spirits, and Personifications.)

CHARACTERISTIC STORIES AND THEMES